The Jewish Trinity

The Jewish Trinity

When Rabbis Believed in the Father, Son and Holy Spirit

By

Yoel Natan

Aventine Press LLC

Look for other books by
Yoel Natan coming soon!

Web site: www.yoel.info

Published by Aventine Press, LLC
2208 Cabo Bahia
Chula Vista, CA 91914, USA

www.aventinepress.com

ISBN: 1-59330-068-9
Printed in the United States of America

Table of Contents

Foreword

Tradition says that Moses and the rest of the OT writers seldom hinted at the existence of the Trinity. This book, however, shows that the NT writers knew that Moses and the other OT writers wrote strikingly and often about the Trinity and about the deity of Christ. The OT and NT writers both wrote about the Trinity and the glory and grace of the Messiah so that their readers could be saved.

The aim of this book is to disperse the smog of those who would obfuscate the witness of the OT and NT to the Trinity and to the deity of Christ, so that the OT and NT will continue to save as many as possible through their witness to the truth. This book ought to accomplish this aim, God willing, because even if someone were to arbitrarily reject the majority of the Trinitarian proofs mentioned in this book, the minority of OT and NT proofs that remained would still total more than the number of proofs known before the publication of this book.

By God's grace, many readers of this book will conclude that:

- Many of the cults and world religions from which people need to escape are based on the mistaken idea that Moses was unitarian rather than Trinitarian, and
- If Moses, *Yeshua*, and all the OT and NT writers were through and through Trinitarian, then the reader should forsake all anti-Trinitarian religions, cults, and churches, as well as their leaders, teachers, theologians and philosophers, and quickly join a Trinitarian church.

Yoel Natan
May 2003

Glossary and Abbreviations

Note: Words and abbreviations can be looked up on Web sites such as: *Britannica.com*™, *Infoplease.com*™ and *GuruNet.com*™. Internet search engines such as *Google.com*™ are also helpful. Most of the Bible texts and reference works listed below can be found in scholarly Bible software products such as *BibleWorks*™ or *Logos*™. Some books, such as the *Koran*, can be found in the public domain on the Web.

Transliterated Aramaic: Translation and Interpretation

Ilayah: Most High. *Strong's Concordance* has '*illay* with a pronunciation of *il-lah'-ee*.

Ilyonin: Most High. *Strong's Concordance* has '*elyown* with a pronunciation of *el-yone'*.

Transliterated Greek: Translation and Interpretation

egw eimi: "I am" or "I AM"
ho wn: "who is" or "WHO IS"
kurios: "lord" or "Lord"

Transliterated Hebrew: Translation and Interpretation

Note 1: Capitalization convention: There is no capitalization in Hebrew. This makes it a matter of interpretation whether the English translations and transliterations read, for instance, "lord" or "Lord" (*adon* or *Adon*), "god" or "God" (*elohim* or *Elohim*), "face" or "Face" (*panim* or *Panim*), or spirit or Spirit (*ruach* or *Ruach*).

The lack of capitalization, or any convention, for differentiating the Hebrew for "god" from "God" (*elohim* from *Elohim*) can be confusing. For instance, it has led to two translations of Exo 22:28: "Do not revile the gods" (*KJV*, *LXE*), and "Do not blaspheme God" (*NIV*, *RSV*, *YLT*).

Note 2: Italicization convention: Book titles and words that have not yet become a part of the English language below are italicized. MT, LXX, DSS, TR and similar works are not italicized since, though they seem to be titles, they are used as proper nouns to denote families of manuscripts.

Note 3: Many of the following nouns are discussed in the collective plurals chapter.

adon: "master"
Adon: "Lord." Capitalized when used to refer to *Yahveh*.
adonai: "my master(s)." *adonai*, like *adonim*, is a plural form of *adonee*.

adonai is a plural of delegation, a type of collective noun, when used to refer to a single master who has delegated authority to another master or slave driver.

Adonai: "my Lord(s)." *Adonai* is capitalized when used to refer to *Yahveh*. *Adonai* is a plural of delegation, a type of collective noun, when used to refer to a single member of the Trinity, but a quantitative plural or a plural collective noun when used to refer to two or the three persons of the Trinity.

adonee: "my master"

Adonee: "my Master." Capitalized when used to refer to the Son or Spirit. No instances of *Adonee* happen to refer to the Father.

Atah-hu: "You-he" are paired pronouns.

echad: "one," or "united one" when referring to a group.

echadim: "united ones" or "a few."

ehyeh asher ehyeh: "I AM who I AM"

el: "god"

El: "God." Capitalized when referring to *Yahveh*. The Hebrew root means "mighty one." The plural is *elohim*.

El Shaddai: "God of Mighty Ones." *Shaddai* is a "masculine plural" according to the Westminster Morphology and Lemma Database (WTM), Release 3.5, Westminster Theological Seminary, 2001.

elohim: "god(s)." "*elohim*" is a plural of delegation, a type of collective noun, when referring to a single false god among his cohorts. "*elohim*" is a plural collective noun or a quantitative plural when referring to angels or human judges.

Elohim: "God(s)." "*Elohim*" is capitalized when used to refer to *Yahveh*. "*Elohim*" is a plural of delegation, a type of collective noun, when used to refer to a single member of the Trinity. "*Elohim*" is a quantitative plural or a plural collective noun when used to refer to two or three persons of the Trinity.

Elyon: "*Elyon*" literally means "high," but is commonly interpreted to mean "Most High" or "Highest."

haElohim: "[All] the Gods"

khayyim: Adjective meaning, "living."

malek: "messenger," often interpreted to mean "angel."

Malek Yahveh: "Angel of *Yahveh*." Capitalized when used to refer to the Son.

panim: "face(s)," "person(s)," or "presence(s)." "*panim*" is a Hebrew dual form that can be singular or plural, depending on the context.

Panim: "Face(s)," "Person(s)" or "Presence(s)" (of *Yahveh*). *Panim* is capitalized when used to refer to the Son or Spirit (Exo 33:14-15). *Panim* is a plural of delegation, a type of collective noun, when used to refer to a single member of the Trinity. *Panim* is a quantitative plural or a plural collective noun when used to refer to two or three persons of the Trinity.

ruach: "spirit," "mind," or "wind"

Ruach: "Spirit." *Ruach* is capitalized when used to refer to the Spirit.

Shekinah, The: The Son or Spirit who are the *Panim*. In rabbinic theology, however, the *Shekinah* is a visible, impersonal manifestation of the divine presence.

***Shema*, The**: *Shema* means, "Hear!" in Hebrew. The *Shema* refers to Moses' statement, "Hear, O Israel: *Yahveh* [the Father] [and] our *Elohim* [the Son], *Yahveh* [the Spirit] [are] a united one [*echad*]" (Deu 06:04).

yachid: "sole," "alone," "unique"

Yahveh: "*Yahveh*" is the personal name of the Hebrew God. *Yahveh* is commonly translated as "LORD" in English Bibles, and as *Kurios*, meaning, "Lord," in the Greek LXX (the Septuagint).

Yeshua: "Jesus" in English, or *Iesous* in Koine Greek. *Yeshua* is the Aramaic derivation of the Hebrew name Joshua. Aramaic and other languages were spoken in Palestine in *Yeshua*'s day.

Bible Book Name Abbreviations

Conventions

All Bible book name abbreviations are three-lettered. This citation method has advantages over other abbreviation systems. The three-letter abbreviations are the same as the first three letters of the English Bible book name, except in a few cases:
• Judges (Jdg) and Philemon (Phm) are differentiated from Jude (Jud) and Philippians (Phi), and
• Song of Solomon is abbreviated "Sol" to avoid confusion with the word "Son."

For the most part, all three-lettered book name abbreviations sort just as their corresponding book names would in search engines and indexes. The exceptions are Judges (Jdg) and Jude (Jud). Jude, however, is only one chapter in length, so this is not a major concern.

Old Testament

1. **Gen**: Genesis; 2. **Exo**: Exodus; 3. **Lev**: Leviticus; 4. **Num**: Numbers; 5. **Deu**: Deuteronomy; 6. **Jos**: Joshua; 7. **Jdg**: Judges; 8. **Rut**: Ruth; 9. **1Sa**: 1 Samuel; 10. **2Sa**: 2 Samuel; 11. **1Ki**: 1 Kings; 12. **2Ki**: 2 Kings; 13. **1Ch**: 1 Chronicles; 14. **2Ch**: 2 Chronicles; 15. **Ezr**: Ezra; 16. **Neh**: Nehemiah; 17. **Est**: Esther; 18. **Job**: Job; 19. **Psa**: Psalm; 20. **Pro**: Proverbs; 21. **Ecc**: Ecclesiastes; 22. **Sol**: Song of Solomon; 23. **Isa**: Isaiah; 24. **Jer**: Jeremiah; 25. **Lam**: Lamentations; 26. **Eze**: Ezekiel; 27. **Dan**: Daniel; 28. **Hos**: Hosea; 29. **Joe**: Joel; 30. **Amo**: Amos; 31. **Oba**: Obadiah; 32. **Jon**: Jonah; 33. **Mic**: Micah; 34. **Nah**: Nahum; 35. **Hab**: Habakkuk; 36. **Zep**: Zephaniah; 37. **Hag**: Haggai; 38. **Zec**: Zechariah; 39. **Mal**: Malachi.

New Testament

40. **Mat**: Matthew; 41. **Mar**: Mark; 42. **Luk**: Luke; 43. **Joh**: John; 44. **Act**: Acts; 45. **Rom**: Romans; 46. **1Co**: 1 Corinthians; 47. **2Co**: 2 Corinthians; 48.

Gal: Galatians; 49. **Eph:** Ephesians; 50. **Phi:** Philippians; 51. **Col:** Colossians; 52.
1Th: 1 Thessalonians; 53. **2Th:** 2 Thessalonians; 54. **1Ti:** 1 Timothy; 55. **2Ti:** 2
Timothy; 56. **Tit:** Titus; 57. **Phm:** Philemon; 58. **Heb:** Hebrews; 59. **Jam:** James;
60. **1Pe:** 1 Peter; 61. **2Pe:** 2 Peter; 62. **1Jo:** 1 John; 63. **2Jo:** 2 John; 64. **3Jo:** 3
John; 65. **Jud:** Jude; 66. **Rev:** Revelation.

Citation Convention for the Bible and *Koran*

All the chapter and verse Bible citations are two-digit, for example, Mat 01:
01, except for Psalms, which has three-digit chapter references. Leading zeroes
are used when necessary, for example, Psa 001:01. This method of citation means
that the chapter and verse citations sort numerically in search engines and indexes.
All the chapter and verse citations for the *Koran* are three-digit (*Koran* 009:005).
"*Sura(h)*" is Arabic and refers to the 114 chapters of the *Koran*.

Other Books, References and Abbreviations

1Ma: First Maccabees (Intertestamental apocryphal book)
2Ma: Second Maccabees (Intertestamental apocryphal book)
a.k.a.: Abbreviation for "also known as"
BDB: *Brown, Driver, Briggs: Hebrew-Aramaic and English Lexicon of the OT*
BHS: *Biblia Hebraica Stuttgartensia* (an annotated MT recension)
DSS: The Dead Sea Scrolls and fragments found in the twentieth century at
Qumran and its environs near the Dead Sea. Most of the scrolls that survived were
stored in clay jars in caves.
Hadith: A report of the sayings or actions of Muhammad or his companions,
together with the tradition of its chain of transmission (isnad). The plural is Hadith
or Hadiths.
ISBE: *International Standard Bible Encyclopedia*, 1934 (Public Domain)
Jdt: Judith (Intertestamental apocryphal book)
KJV: King James Version of the Bible (English)
Koran: The sacred text of Islam, considered by Muslims to contain the
revelations of Allah to Muhammad. *Koran* is also spelled *Qur'an*, *Quran* and
Alcoran.
LXE: The English Translation of *The Septuagint Version of the Old Testament*
(*LXE*), by Sir Lancelot C. L. Brenton, 1844, 1851, published by Samuel Bagster
and Sons, London.
LXX: The Septuagint is a second and third century B.C. Greek translation of
the OT and some apocryphal books.
MT: The Masoretic Text (OT Hebrew and Aramaic) is a recension. A
definition of a recension is:
A critical revision of a text incorporating the elements deemed most plausible
from varying sources.

The MT recension was compiled from various Hebrew manuscripts by Talmudic academies in Babylonia and Palestine during the 6th to 10th centuries AD. The name of the text comes from Talmudic academy of the Masoretes, meaning, "Traditionalists," that flourished in Tiberias on the Sea of Galilee between the 7th and 9th centuries AD.

The oldest surviving MT recension manuscript is the "Cairo Prophets" (895 AD), which was produced by Moses ben Asher in Tiberias, Galilee. The second oldest MT recension manuscript is the Leningrad Codex of the Latter Prophets (916 AD), which has Babylonian vowel pointing.

This book sometimes uses the term MT as an inclusive term for the MT recension and the family of manuscripts that served as the basis for the MT recension. This family of manuscripts no longer exists except for scrolls found among the Dead Sea Scrolls.

NIV: *New International Version*, 1984 (US English Bible)

NT: New Testament (the original was written in *Koine* Greek)

OT: Old Testament (Jewish *Tanakh*) (the original is in Hebrew, but parts are in Aramaic).

RSV: *Revised Standard Version* (1952) (English Bible)

Sir: Wisdom of Sirach (an Intertestamental apocryphal book, a.k.a., Ecclesiasticus)

Sunna: The way of life prescribed as normative in Islam, based both on the teachings and practices of Muhammad, and on exegesis of the *Koran*.

TR: Textus Receptus, from the Latin meaning, "Received Text." This is the Greek text of the New Testament that was standard in printed editions from the 16th to the end of the 19th century.

TWOT: *The Theological Wordbook of the OT*

YLT: *The English Young's Literal Translation of the Holy Bible* 1862/1887/ 1898 (*YLT*) by J. N. Young

WEB: *The World English Bible* is one of the public domain versions of the OT and NT in modern English that is downloadable from ebible.org. The *WEB* NT consistently follows the Greek Majority Text, but provides footnotes noting any significant variant readings listed in these Greek NT recensions: Textus Receptus (TR), *Nestle-Aland* (*NA*), and *United Bible Society* (*UBS*).

Synopsis of the Jewish Trinity

Augustine said that Christology is latent in the OT, and patent in the NT.[1] Christians have applied Augustine's analysis to other distinctively Christian doctrines. For instance, conventional wisdom says that while the doctrine of the Trinity was implicit in the OT, it is explicit in the NT.[2][3]

This book shows that if one reads the OT without wearing unitarian blinders, the OT is as explicit about the Trinity as the NT. The reader of this book will come to know the OT as ancient Trinitarian Yahvists knew the OT—a book replete with Trinitarian proofs.

Synopsis of Chapter 01: The Syntax War Between Trinitarians and Unitarians

This chapter deals with the main difference between the ancient reading and the modern reading of the OT. The ancients read the several thousand plurals that refer to *Yahveh* as collective nouns with different nuances. Collective nouns that refer to *Yahveh* are potent Trinitarian proofs, especially considering the sheer number of instances.

During Intertestamental times, unitarian readers argued that all plurals referring to *Yahveh* were majestic plurals. The majestic plural proponents said that plurals referring to *Yahveh* indicate majesty, but do not hint at the existence of persons called *Yahveh*. This chapter shows that the majestic plural usage is an incorrect reading of thousands of plurals referring to *Yahveh*, and that these plurals, in fact, constitute Trinitarian proofs.

Synopsis of Chapter 02: Proto-Sinaitic Trinitarianism

At Mount Sinai, the Son revealed that his name was *Yahveh*. Previously, only the Father was known as *Yahveh*. So Genesis contains both the Proto-Gospel (Gen 03:15) and Proto-Sinaitic Trinitarianism.

In Genesis, the Father was known as *Yahveh* and the Most High (*Elyon*), the Son was known both as God of Mighty Ones (*El Shaddai*) and as the *Malek Yahveh*, and the Spirit was known as the Spirit (*Ruach*). The Trinity was known as *haElohim*, literally, "[All] the Gods."

This analysis of Genesis is confirmed by examining the Genesis narrative, as well as other sections of the OT that refer back to Genesis. The Trinitarian interpretation of Genesis debunks the JEDP theory. Also, the theories that say the *Malek Yahveh* was a mere creature, or was impersonal, are refuted.

Synopsis of Chapter 03: The Presences of *Elyon*

This chapter discusses the Presences of *Elyon*. Important passages include how the Israelites saw the "Living Gods" (*khayyim Elohim*) (Deu 05:26) during

the giving of the law. Moses said that at the giving of the law, "[All] the Gods"
(*haElohim*) stood on three mountains:

> This is the blessing that Moses the man of [All] the Gods [*haElohim*]
> pronounced on the Israelites before his death. *Yahveh* [the Father] came
> from Sinai, and [the Son] dawned over them from Seir; he [the Spirit] shone
> forth from Mount Paran. He [the Father] came with myriads of holy ones
> from the south, from his [the Father's] mountain slopes (Deu 33:01-02).

Later, the Father sent his Presences, the Son and Spirit, to Canaan. The Father
said:

> 'My Presences [plural noun], they will go [plural verb] with you, and I will
> give you rest.' Then Moses said to him, 'Your Presences [plural noun], if they
> do not go [plural verb] with us, do not send us up from here' (Exo 33:14-15).

The Presences' other appearances in the OT are also discussed.

Synopsis of Chapter 04: The *Shema*

The *Shema* is a simple Trinitarian formula:

Hear, O Israel: *Yahveh* [the Father] [and] our *Elohim* [the Son], *Yahveh* [the
Spirit] [are] a united one [*echad*] (Deu 06:04).

The correct interpretation and import of the *Shema* can be inferred from OT
Shema-like statements (Hos 12:06; Zec 14:09).

Yeshua's short version of the *Shema* is, "I and the Father are one" (Joh 10:30).
Whenever *Yeshua* discussed the *Shema*, he always mentions two or three of the
divine persons of the Trinity, for instance:

- After quoting the *Shema* (Mat 22:36-40), *Yeshua* said that David was inspired
  by the Spirit when David said that the Father and Son were his Lord (Psa 110:
  01, 05; Mat 22:43-45; Mar 12:36-37; Luk 20:42, 44), and
- After speaking a *Shema*-like statement, "I and the Father are one" (Joh 10:30),
  Yeshua said that the judges to whom the word of God came were called "gods"
  (Psa 082:06; Joh 10:35). *Yeshua* added:

What about the one whom the Father set apart as his very own and sent into the
world? (Psa 082:08; Joh 10:36a).

Yeshua here alluded to *Yahveh* the Father's statement to the Son in the same
Psalm:

Rise up, O God [the Son] and judge the earth, for all the nations are your [the
Son's] inheritance (Psa 082:08; Joh 10:36a)!

Synopsis of Chapter 05: The Trinity in Daniel 01-05

Daniel informed Nebuchadnezzar that the golden head of his dreamscape statue
represented Nebuchadnezzar's kingdom, the Babylonian Empire. The statue's
other body parts represent succeeding kingdoms down to the end of time as we
know it.

The gold head showed that a distinguishing characteristic of Nebuchadnezzar's kingdom was wealth. The other body parts were made of inferior metals and clay to show that the distinguishing characteristics of subsequent kingdoms would not be wealth.

The gold head also revealed that a distinguishing characteristic of Nebuchadnezzar's kingdom was homogeneity. His was a unified kingdom. The Medo-Persian that followed was bifurcated as shown in the arms united to the torso. Alexander's kingdom bifurcated into the Seleucid and Ptolemaic dynasties, as was shown by the bronze thighs. Rome was divided into the Western Latin–speaking and Eastern Greek–speaking parts, as was shown by the two iron calves. The Roman Empire dissolved leaving nations of iron to exist in the midst of nations of clay.

In the end the Son would establish a kingdom not built on the foundations of the old kingdoms represented in the statue. The Son's kingdom would last forever. Nebuchadnezzar saw the Son in Dan 03:25, and Daniel saw the Son in the Dan 07 Son of Man vision.

There is a relationship between the statue of Nebuchadnezzar's dream (Dan 02) and the golden statue that Nebuchadnezzar built (Dan 03). Nebuchadnezzar's landscape statue of Dan 03 was like the dreamscape statue of Dan 02, but was golden from head to toe (Dan 03).

Nebuchadnezzar's statue represented Nebuchadnezzar's prayer to his gods. Nebuchadnezzar wanted his gods to veto *Yahveh*'s plan to cut Nebuchadnezzar's golden kingdom off at the neck—hence, the gold from head to toe. Nebuchadnezzar wanted the Babylonian Empire to be the sole empire until the end of the world, and not just until the Medo-Persian Empire was formed.

Daniel instructed Nebuchadnezzar about *Yahveh*, the "Most High," just as Joseph had instructed Egyptian royalty (Gen 45:08; Psa 105:17-22). Nebuchadnezzar used OT Trinitarian terminology that Moses, Joshua, and others had used. Nebuchadnezzar's Trinitarian speech is recorded in Dan 02—03. By Dan 04, it seems Nebuchadnezzar matured into a full-fledged Trinitarian, as his letter to his subjects shows (Dan 04).

Synopsis of Chapter 06: The Prophet Behind the Prophets

The OT prophetic books should be read as the words of the preincarnate Son rather than as the words of the prophets. The few phrases and sections that are obvious words of the prophets should be considered mere inspired interjections. That the OT prophetic books can, for the most part, be understood as the words of the Son implies Trinitarianism.

In OT prophetic books, first person speech (for example, "I," "me," "my") should generally be read as the words of the Son. Quotations are most often the words of the Father as quoted by the Son. Third person speech (for example, "he," "him," "his") referring to *Yahveh* generally is the Son speaking about the Father or the Spirit.

Synopsis of Chapter 07: Various OT Presentations of the Trinity

Ezekiel, Jonah and Zechariah give interesting presentations of the Trinity.
Jonah distinguished between *Yahveh* the Father and the Presences of *Yahveh*, who
are the Son and Spirit. Jonah's Trinitarian language includes mention of "[All] the
Gods" (*haElohim*) and "*Yahveh Elohim*."

In Ezekiel and Zechariah, both the Spirit and Son take on various roles, call
each other *Yahveh*, and refer to the Father and quote the Father.

Synopsis of Chapter 08: The NT Use of OT *Yahveh* Texts

The first part of this chapter concerns NT quotations and allusions to OT *Yahveh*
texts. Many examples are given in the appendix that complements this chapter.
The list of NT allusions and quotations to OT *Yahveh* text is meant to be representative rather than exhaustive.

The second part of this chapter concerns whether *Yeshua* primarily spoke Greek
or Aramaic. This has some bearing on whether *Yeshua* identified himself as:
- *Yahveh* the Son by his applying OT *Yahveh* texts to himself,
- The divine Son of Man described in the Dan 07 vision (as is discussed in the
  Song of Moses chapter),
- The "I AM" (as is discussed in the "I AM" and the Song of Moses chapters), and
- The subject of the *Shema* along with the Father and the Spirit (as is discussed in
  the *Shema* chapter).

The evidence will show that *Yeshua* spoke both Aramaic and Greek. Galilee,
where *Yeshua* grew, was home to many gentiles who tended to speak Greek. While
Aramaic was more prevalent in Judea, inscriptions and literary evidence show that
Greek was common there, too.

Given *Yeshua*'s language abilities, it is implausible that he inadvertently gave
the impression that he was, for instance, the "I AM." His audiences were astute
enough to know what *Yeshua* was saying, and they even tried to stone *Yeshua* more
than once for blasphemy. Not once did *Yeshua* say he was misunderstood.

The NT writers knew both Aramaic and Greek, and they were familiar with
the OT Hebrew. This means that the NT writers consciously applied OT "I
AM" statements and *Yahveh* texts to *Yeshua*. Given their language abilities, they
faithfully recorded *Yeshua*'s statements, and no meaning was inadvertently added
or lost during translation or transcription.

Synopsis of Chapter 09: The "I AM" Statements

Yahveh the Son was the divine speaker of Exo 03—06, as was discussed in the
chapter on Proto-Sinaitic Trinitarianism. *Yahveh* the Son said in Hebrew:

I AM who I AM [Hebrew: "*ehyeh asher ehyeh*"]. This is what you are
to say to the Israelites: 'I AM [*ehyeh*] has sent me to you' (Exo 03:14).

The Greek LXX version reads:

I AM [Greek: *egw eimi*] WHO IS [*ho wn*]…WHO IS [*ho wn*]…(LXX Exo 03:14).

Note that the Hebrew word *ehyeh* mentioned three times in Exo 03:14 is translated as "*egw eimi*" and "*ho wn*." This chapter discusses the occurrences where *Yeshua* and the NT writers applied "*egw eimi*" and "*ho wn*" to *Yeshua*. In this way, the NT writers show that *Yeshua* is *Yahveh* the Son—the divine speaker in Exo 03.

Synopsis of Chapter 10: The Song of Moses (Deu 32)

The Song of Moses shows God's strategy for saving Jews and gentiles. The Father's strategy is to try to save errant Israel by every means possible, lastly by sending his Son. The Son is far superior to Moses. After being rejected by the Jewish leaders, the Son turns to save the gentiles. This has the effect of making Israel jealous enough to come back into the Trinity's fold.

One section in this chapter presents a Son of Man theology where the Dan 07 Son of Man is linked to the Proto-Gospel (Gen 03:15). The chapter ends with a discussion on how the Son is far superior to Moses in that the Son is:
- The "I AM,"
- The Son of Man (Dan 07), and
- God the Son.

Synopsis of Appendix A: MT Plurals Referring to *Yahveh*

This appendix discusses plurals referring to *Yahveh* that are found in 38 chapters of 18 MT books. These are plural verbs, adjectives and nouns other than the common plural noun *Elohim* (literally, "Gods"). All plurals referring to *Yahveh* should be considered Trinitarian proofs.

Synopsis of Appendix B: OT Texts That Suggest or Speak of the Deity of the Messiah

This appendix lists the texts, provides a short summary statement of each text, and directs the reader to where there is further discussion of each text.

Synopsis of Appendix C: Trinitarian Proofs

This appendix first summarizes four categories of Trinitarian proofs. Four categories of Trinitarian proofs are:
1. Many passages that are *prima facie* evidence for the doctrine of Trinity contain MT or LXX plurals referring to *Yahveh*. Examples include the "us" in Gen 01: 26; 03:22; 11:07 and Isa 06:08. More examples are found in the MT plurals appendix,

2. OT *Yahveh* texts applied to individual persons of the Trinity in the OT and NT are *prima facie* evidence for the doctrine of Trinity. These are discussed in the "I AM" and Song of Moses chapters, as well as in the NT use of OT *Yahveh* texts chapter and its complementary appendix that goes by the same name,
3. Texts that suggest or speak to the deity of the Messiah should be considered indirect proofs of the Trinity. These proofs are summarized in a table in a separate appendix, and
4. General Trinitarian proofs are listed with an explanation in this Trinitarian proofs appendix.

Synopsis of Appendix D: A Sampling of the NT Use of OT *Yahveh* Texts

A list of OT *Yahveh* texts quoted or alluded to in the NT is provided with an explanation of their significance. The passages are grouped according to the person or persons of the Trinity to whom the OT *Yahveh* text is applied.

Chapter 1

The Syntax War Between Trinitarians and Unitarians

The OT Battleground

The task of a translator and interpreter is to express the author's intended meaning in another language. The quandary is that the intended meaning of the OT authors is in dispute. Were the OT authors unitarian as is supposed by the rabbinic unitarians, Protestant Unitarians, Jehovah's Witnesses, Oneness Pentecostals and others? Did the authors of the OT just hint of the Trinity as mainstream Christian scholars contend? Or were the authors of the OT full-fledged Trinitarians?

One might ask, "Just how did such divergent views of the OT develop?" This is surprisingly simple to explain. Many laymen will be surprised to know that, with just a few exceptions, thousands of OT Hebrew plurals referring to *Yahveh* are translated as singulars. These plurals are translated as singulars because rabbinic and Christian scholars are taught that all plurals referring to *Yahveh* are majestic plurals. The majestic plural syntax is counterintuitive in that the plural form supposedly does not indicate any sort of plurality in the godhead. A majestic plural, as the name indicates, supposedly speaks only of *Yahveh*'s majesty.

Most Christian scholars grudgingly accept the existence of majestic plurals. They quickly point out, however, that majestic plurals accommodate the doctrine of the Trinity, and even hint that *Yahveh* is the Trinity. Christian scholars bolster these assertions by referring to the OT and NT Trinitarian proofs.

By contrast, this book contends that the OT writers would find the majestic plural rationalization to be a foreign concept. Likewise, the OT prophets would assert that the unitarian misinterpretation of the OT was adopted first during Intertestamental times. They would assert that the real reason why people do not believe in the Trinity is they do not want to listen to Moses (Joh 05:47; Luk 16:31).

A casual reading of the NT reveals that *Yeshua* and the NT writers would not agree with the assertion that the OT merely hints at the Trinity. The NT writers speak of the Father, Son and Spirit without an introduction, without apology, and without any sense of novelty. The NT writers knew the Trinity to be readily apparent in the OT. That many Jews readily became Christians shows that they too had a Trinitarian outlook on the OT. The apostles said that the NT merely made the words of the prophets about the deity of the Messiah more certain (2Pe 01:16, 19).

So to summarize, this chapter deals with a principle difference between the ancient reading and the modern reading of the OT. The ancients read the several thousand plural nouns referring to *Yahveh* as collective nouns with different nuances. These collective nouns are potent Trinitarian proofs, especially considering how often they occur in the OT. Moderns, however, read these same plural nouns as majestic plurals. Supposed majestic plurals indicate majesty, but in no way hint that there are persons called *Yahveh*.

Hebrew Collective Nouns

Before the discussion of Hebrew collective nouns begins in earnest, it is worthwhile to note that Hebrew is like other languages in that it has its own distinctive syntax. For instance, an American English speaker might think it odd that in Hebrew:
- Collective nouns, whether singular or plural, can take plural verbs and predicates, and
- Plural collective nouns can refer to a single group, and can take singular verbs and modifiers.

Hebrew collective noun usage is not entirely different from that of other languages. A case in point is that British English uses collective nouns much like ancient Hebrew, but American English does less so. *The American Heritage Dictionary of the English Language* states:

> In American usage, a collective noun takes a singular verb when it refers to the collection considered as a whole, as in *The family was united on this question. The enemy is suing for peace.* It takes a plural verb when it refers to the members of the group considered as individuals, as in *My family are always fighting among themselves. The enemy were showing up in groups of three or four to turn in their weapons.* In British usage, however, collective nouns are more often treated as plurals: *The government have not announced a new policy. The team are playing in the test matches next week.* A collective noun should not be treated as both singular and plural in the same construction; thus *The family is determined to press its* (not *their*) *claim...*[4]

Singular Collective Nouns with Plural Predicates

The famous Hebraist, H. W. F. Gesenius (1786-1842 AD) wrote that Hebrew singular collective nouns "readily" have plural predicates.[5] Here are a few examples:
- Joseph said, "The whole earth [singular] came [plural verb]" (Gen 41:57), so persons are indicated by the singular "earth,"

- "Each man [Hebrew singular is *eesh*] threw down [plural verb] his staff" (Exo 07:12),
- "Each man [singular *eesh*] gather [plural imperative] as much as he needs" (Exo 16:16),
- "So man [singular *eesh*] lies down [singular verb] and rises [singular verb] not again; till the heavens are no more they will not awake [plural verb], or be roused [plural verb] out of their sleep" (Job 14:12),
- "Surely man [singular *eesh*] walks about [singular verb] as a shadow! Surely, for nothing they strive [plural verb]; man accumulates [singular verb] and does not know [singular verb]" (Psa 039:06 [*BHS* 039:07]),
- "They open [plural verb] their mouth [singular noun]" (Job 16:10), and
- "The evil man [singular *eesh*]" (Pro 02:12) is the subject of the plural verbs "leaves," "exults" and "are devious" (Pro 02:13-15).

Plural Collective Nouns with Singular Predicates

Hebrew collective nouns that refer to a group may be plural, yet can take singular predicates. Here are some examples:
- "Luminaries" takes a singular verb ("let be") in Gen 01:14a, but plural verbs in Gen 01:14b-16,
- "Nations and a group of nations" take a singular verb (Gen 35:11),
- "Children" takes a singular verb (Exo 10:24),
- "People" takes singular verbs (Exo 20:18; Jos 24:16, 21), but can also take plural verbs (Jos 24:16, 21, 24),
- "Animals" takes a singular verb (Job 12:07), and
- "Worthless idols" takes the singular verb "pass away" (Isa 02:18).

The Hebrew Plural Collective Noun *Elohim*, literally "Gods"

The Athanasian Creed speaks against the heresy of Tritheism, and warns against speaking of the Trinity as "Gods" or "Lords." The Athanasian Creed was written in the western church in the sixth century by an unknown author who may have had no familiarity with the Bible in the original languages.[6]

The Athanasian Creed concerns doctrine, and should not necessarily be interpreted as an exegetical gag rule. Exegetes can discuss the fact that the literal translations of plural forms referring to *Yahveh* are plural. What to make of that fact, and how to express it doctrinally, is where the Athanasian Creed becomes helpful.

The Hebrew plural collective noun *Elohim/elohim* (literally, "Gods" or "gods") occurs 2,600 times in 2,247 MT verses. Most instances refer to *Yahveh*, but *elohim* is also used to refer to angels (Psa 008:005 [*BHS* 008:006]), judges (Exo 21:06; 22: 08-09 [*BHS* 22:07-08]; Jos 24:01), rulers (Psa 082:01, 06), as well as false gods and idols.

The ancient Hebrews considered *Elohim* to be a plural collective noun, or a nuanced collective noun, denoting the persons of the Trinity. *Elohim* was not used to refer to *Yahveh* in any polytheistic sense. Like other Hebrew plural collective nouns, *Elohim/elohim* could take singular or plural verbs and modifiers. For example, *Elohim/elohim* could take:

- Singular modifiers, for example, "Their gods [*elohim*] will be [plural verb] a snare [singular noun]" (Exo 23:33; Jdg 02:03),
- Singular verbs, for instance, "The God/gods [*Elohim/elohim*] who answers [singular verb] by fire—he is *Elohim*" (1Ki 18:24). Note that either the *haBaalim* ("the *Baals*") (1Ki 18:18), who are *Baal* and *Asherah* (1Ki 18:19), or "the Word" (the Son) (1Ki 18:01, 31) and the Spirit (1Ki 18:12), are the collective subject of the conditional sentence (1Ki 18:24),
- Plural verbs and modifiers such as:
  - "...gods [*elohim*] are near [plural modifier]..." (Deu 04:07),
  - "...make us gods [*elohim*] who will go [plural verb] before us..." (Exo 32:01, 23),
  - "...gods [*elohim*] neither see...hear...eat...smell..." [plural verbs] (Deu 04:28), and
  - The plural verbs and modifier referring to *Yahveh* (Gen 20:13; 35:07; Exo 32:04, 08; Jos 24:19 and the like) that are mentioned in the MT plurals appendix.

Sometimes Hebrew speakers used singular and plural verbs with *Elohim* in the same conversation. This tends to prove that *Elohim* was indeed considered a collective noun. For instance, Sennacherib's officers asked in Hebrew (2Ki 18:28):

> How can your *Elohim* [Gods] deliver [singular verb] you out of mine hand (2Ch 32:14)?...How much less shall your *Elohim* [plural noun] deliver [plural verb] you out of my hand (2Ch 32:15)!

The chronicler wrote, "Sennacherib's officers spoke further against *Yahveh Elohim*" (2Ch 32:16). Other passages with singular and plural verbs referring to *Elohim* can be found in the MT plurals appendix.

Plural collective nouns used with singular verbs suggest that there are the plural members of "a united" (*echad*) group. So the plural *Elohim* (literally, "Gods") used with a singular verb is meant to emphasize that there are three persons of the Trinity. Likewise, the plural form "gods" (*elohim*) is used with singular verbs to refer to a false god and his goddess consort or progeny. Other plural collective nouns that are similar to *Elohim* are *haElohim* ("[All] the Gods"), *Adonai* ("my Lords") and *adonai* ("my masters"). These words are discussed in depth later in this chapter.

A form similar to the collective noun *Elohim* is the plural collective noun *Mitsrayim*. *Mitsrayim* can be translated as a singular collective noun "Egypt" (Gen 13:10; 15:18), or as a plural collective noun "Egyptians," according to contextual clues. For example:

- In Exo 14:25 *Mitsrayim* is used with two singular verbs ("he said" and "let me get away"), but both times *Mitsrayim* should be translated in the plural as "The Egyptians said, 'Let us get away,'" and
- In Exo 14:18 a plural verb is used with *Mitsrayim*, so Moses must have meant the plural *Mitsrayim* to be translated in the plural as "the Egyptians will know," rather than in the singular as "Egypt will know."

So the plural form *Mitsrayim* can be translated as a singular collective noun, "Egypt," or as a plural collective noun, "Egyptians." This suggests that the plural form *Elohim* should, depending on the context, be treated as a singular collective noun (God), or as a plural collective noun referring to the persons of *Yahveh*. For example, *Yahveh* is a "God [*Elohim*] of Gods [*Elohim*], and Lord [*Adonai*] of Lords [*Adonai*]" (compare Jos 22:22; Psa 050:01; Isa 26:13; Dan 02:47; 11:36; 1Ti 06:15; Rev 17:14; 19:16).

Elohim, a plural form, can be translated as "God" or "Gods." The plural form *Adonai* can be translated as "Lord" or "Lords." In the above-listed passages, the first *Elohim* and *Adonai* of each phrase should be translated as a singular collective noun, while the second *Elohim* and *Adonai* of each phrase should be considered a plural collective noun: "God of Gods" and "Lord of Lords."

The singular collective noun emphasizes *Yahveh*'s unity, while the plural collective noun emphasizes that there are persons called *Yahveh*. That one phrase has both singular and plural collective nouns referring to *Yahveh* indicates that *Yahveh* is the Trinity: one God, yet three persons.

The "God of Gods and Lord of Lords" passages are similar to the *Shema* in that they are Trinitarian expressions. The *Shema* is mentioned later in this chapter, and in the chapter on the *Shema*.

Weaknesses of the Majestic Plural Hypothesis

Grammar issues can rest for a moment as other issues with broad implications are here discussed. A bird's eye view of the debate reveals that there are some obvious weaknesses in the majestic plural hypothesis.

Exceptions Become the Rule Rather Than Just "Proving [in the sense of "Testing"] the Rule"

A weakness of the majestic plural hypothesis is that the proofs consist of exceptional examples where plural nouns seemingly refer to single persons or objects. In the majestic plural schema, the lessons drawn from exceptional examples determine the translation and interpretation of thousands of words. Rather than letting "the exceptions prove [in other words, "test"] the rule"—as the proverb says,[7] majestic plural proponents say, "The exceptions are the rule."

There are at least two pitfalls involved when using exceptions to explain the majority of instances. First, exceptions by definition are always few, and thus are easier to misconstrue. The misinterpretation is then used to distort the meaning of many words. Second, even if exceptional data were interpreted correctly, the connection between the exceptions and the mass of data that the exceptions supposedly explain may be tenuous.

What this means is that even if a few exceptions are proven to be majestic plurals, this does not necessarily mean there are thousands of majestic plurals in the OT.

Analogous situations where erroneous extrapolations could be drawn from scant data include:

- If one determined what English grammar rules are by analyzing the exceptional forms "its" and "it's," one would mistake contractions for possessives, and abbreviations for possessives. "Its" looks plural, but is really a possessive pronoun, and "it's" looks like a possessive pronoun, but is really the abbreviated form of "it is,"
- A planet might be mistaken for a star, or vice versa, but this does not mean all luminaries are planets, and
- A Tom Clancy fiction novel might be mistaken for history, but this does not mean that Tom Clancy is a historian rather than a novelist.

Statistically speaking, it is unwise to suppose that thousands of OT majestic plurals exist based on the analysis of a few examples. Perhaps the majestic plural rationalization exists merely because no one has bothered to offer viable alternative explanations. I use the word "viable" because theological liberals have offered alternative explanations.

Liberals commonly believe that the majestic plural rationalization was unknown in the patriarchal and Mosaic periods. Many liberals believe that the Hebrew plurals referring to *Yahveh* actually are vestiges of monolatry (henotheism), binitarianism, or polytheism.[8]

Monolatry is the belief that there are many gods worthy of worship, but that each person ought to choose one god to worship and ignore the others. Binitarianism is the worship of two divine persons who are worshipped as one god. Of course, these theories are flawed in that they do not satisfactorily explain all the data. The evidence calls out for a Trinitarian explanation, but the call has fallen on deaf ears until now.

Someone might ask, "Why must anyone think up explanations for plural forms?" The answer is that there is no surviving ancient Hebrew grammar book that states how the Hebrew Scripture should be translated. So a Hebrew grammar must be based on the study of the language itself. This is problematical because languages tend to become regular and less complicated over time. Inscriptions and archaic word forms may be the only evidence that certain words, usages, cases and conjugations ever existed.

Unfortunately, there are few undisputed samples of extra-Biblical, ancient Hebrew. These are mainly found on walls and potshards. Unlike some ancient languages, ancient Hebrew seems to have been written almost entirely on perishable materials. Whole libraries went up in smoke or disintegrated to dust in a process that began already in OT times (2Ki 22:08).

There are only a few samples of extra-Biblical, OT-era Hebrew. This means that OT Hebrew grammars and lexicons cannot be crosschecked and verified against non-Biblical sources from the same period. By contrast, the NT Greek grammars and lexicons can be crosschecked against NT-era, extra-Biblical Greek sources to expose built-in bias.

Certain ways to read the OT can be taught through Hebrew grammars and lexicons. The danger of Hebrew grammars doubling as *de facto* doctrinal books is that any reading besides the "official" rendering is considered a grammar mistake.

The reader who is nonchalant about the power of grammars to change perception and influence doctrine should consider how some grammar issues are not just academic issues. Indeed, over the centuries, a student who wished to read Trinitarian texts as they were intended to be read ran the risk of being charged with false doctrine or blasphemy. These charges entailed various consequences depending on the century and cultural setting.

Examples could be multiplied about how far dogma and rules can remove the pious interpretation of a text from its literal reading, but here are two examples that may give pause. One example is from Judaism and other from Islam:

- In Hebrew grammars it was taught that in order to avoid the charge of blasphemy, it was best to read out loud "Lord" (*Adonai*), or another word, instead of saying the name *Yahveh*. The grammar books referred to "what is read" as *qere,* and "what is written" as *kethib.* Just how effective this *qere-kethib* system was is shown by the fact that after awhile, the exact pronunciation of the name *Yahveh* became a matter for debate. This is the case even though *Yahveh* occurs about 6,828 times in 5,790 OT verses, and
- In early Islamic times, in order to show the supposed superiority of Islam, Muslims devised the dogma that the *Koran* was both eternal, and the very words of Allah.[9] So, to transform Muhammad's discourse into words that Allah commanded Muhammad to repeat, compilers inserted the imperative form "say" 350 times into the *Koran*ic text.[10][11] Many scholars, unlike most Muslims, sense the many absurdities that the "say!" interpolations create.[12]

The *qere-kethib* and "Say!" rules affected hundreds or thousands of passages, and thus changed how an entire book was read. Similarly, the majestic plural rule affected the interpretation of thousands of passages with the result that many read the Trinitarian Bible as though it taught unitarianism. The majestic plural rule is nothing but a veil (2Co 03:13-16; 2Co 04:03).

So it behooves the reader to suspect any *qere* interpretative translation that is unitarian when the *kethib* literal reading of the text is Trinitarian. For instance, the many plural and dual forms that are translated as majestic plurals ought to be translated as collective plurals. Examples include *Elohim* (God) and *Panim* (meaning, "face(s)," or "presence," or "Presences").

The Majestic Plural Rationalization Has Not Been Seriously Cross Examined Due to a Sanitized History

Another weakness of the majestic plural rationalization is that this grammatical construction has not been seriously analyzed in the past. The majestic plural usage has been accepted uncritically based on its long rabbinical tradition. However, the majestic plural tradition may not be very ancient.

The success of the early Trinitarian church among Jews suggests that the Intertestamental Jews interpreted OT majestic plurals as being Trinitarian. Cultures, however, are notorious for presenting idealized, sanitized pictures of the past. Cultural memory selectively preserves cherished ideas while suppressing and forgetting dissent. As the saying goes, "The victors write history."

It is a matter of history that unitarians managed to ostracize Trinitarians from Jewish society. The Jewish Trinitarian tradition was deemed heretical and was forgotten. Records not deemed canonical were burned or allowed to disintegrate into oblivion, unless, of course, they were fortunate enough to be left in pots in caves.

The idea that classical Judaism had unanimous agreement on unitarianism and the majestic plural syntax may soon fall on hard times. Other cherished ideas about classical Judaism have been discarded in the twentieth century due to archeology finds, namely, that:

- The language of Palestine was wholly Aramaic and Hebrew. This issue will be discussed in the chapter on the NT Use of OT *Yahveh* Texts, and
- Classical Judaism was untainted by astrology and human figural art.

Jewish tradition had presented classical Judaism as being untainted by astrology and human figural art. Some rabbis wrote that astrology applied to gentiles, but not to Jews.[13] Astrology, however, appears in Jewish apocalyptic writings,[14] and astrology even made an incursion into the Herodian temple itself![15][16] Lester Ness wrote:

> [Flavius] Josephus [37 AD-?][17] and Philo [Judaeus (c. 20 BC–c. AD 40)][18]…do not hesitate to identify the twelve signs with the twelve loaves of [show]bread offered each day in the temple or the seven planets with the seven branches of the menorah.[19]

The Arch of Titus in Rome that commemorates the 70 AD conquest of Jerusalem confirms Josephus and Philo's assertion that the temple menorah had astral connotations. Erwin Goodenough wrote:

> From these independent sources, then, we have evidence that Jews actually made their temple cultus, made Judaism itself, into an astral religion.[20]

Figure 1. What remains of the Jerusalem temple menorah relief on the Arch of Titus.

Additional examples of astral art infiltration could be cited to show that astrology made major inroads into Judaism from the Maccabean through the Byzantine period. Bernard Goldman notes that in the Maccabean period "the star of the Maccabees" was placed over the temple façade."[21] Popular Maccabean and Herodian coins look suspiciously like a crescent and Venus orb couplet on a pole or finial. The coin purported to portray a double cornucopia with a pomegranate orb on a stem between the horns of plenty. Ya'akov Meshorer wrote:

> It is logical to assume that the symbol filtered into Judaism as an object related to fertility, and then acquired additional Jewish connotations.[22]

Figure 2. Popular Maccabean and Herodian coin.

Classical Judaism absorbed astrological art and concepts, and this caused friction with the Christian church. Stephen's speech refers to the astral worship of the forefathers, the implication being that the NT Jewish leaders whom Stephen addressed had erred in the same way (Act 07:43).

It was not the astrology so much as the creeping homegrown heresy called unitarianism that did the most to squeeze OT Trinitarianism entirely out of Judaism. Astrology in the temple, of course, was one of the factors that led to the rejection of Trinitarianism, to the destruction of the temple, and to the further dispersal of the Jews.

The Majestic Plural Has Been Accepted Uncritically on an *Ad Hominem* Basis

There are other reasons the majestic plural has not undergone serious cross-examination. Many hold to the *ad hominem* assumption that unitarians are especially qualified to read Hebrew. This is not right since *Yeshua*, the apostles, and many early Trinitarians were fluent in Hebrew and Aramaic.

The NT shows that *Yeshua*, the apostles and early Christians considered the OT to be thoroughly Trinitarian. Since the NT was not as yet written, they surely did not derive their Trinitarian beliefs from the NT. The NT shows that the people were not beholden to every official dogma (Mat 07:29; Mar 01:22). So the majestic plural rationalization may have caused friction between the people and the religious authorities. Whatever the case, the fact that so many Intertestamental Jews held Trinitarian beliefs suggests they did not believe the OT was awash in majestic plurals referring to *Yahveh* as though he were a single majestic person.

Despite conventional wisdom, unitarians are not especially qualified to rule on OT Hebrew. First of all, the Bible is not like other documents that are doctrinally neutral, so the translation and interpretation is not purely academic. Humans, being what they are, find it all too easy to give in to sectarian bias.

Contrary to what some might believe, no one speaks Biblical Hebrew. The first language of grammarians like Gesenius and other Ashkenazi Jews of Central and Eastern Europe was Yiddish. Yiddish is a blend of medieval German, Slavic, Old French, Old Italian, Aramaic and Hebrew.

Sephardic Jews, who lived in the Iberian Peninsula, wrote mainly in Arabic. For instance, Moses ben Maimon, a.k.a. Maimonides (1135-1204 AD), wrote in Arabic, but did incorporate some non-Biblical Hebrew. S. D. Goitein wrote about the Arabic influence on medieval Hebrew:

> The Jews took their full share in this great Middle-Eastern mercantile civilization, in particular from the tenth to the thirteenth centuries, and it was at that time and in that part of the world that Judaism itself received its final shape. There, under Arab-Muslim influence, Jewish thought and philosophy and even Jewish law and religious practice were systematized and finally formulated. Even the Hebrew language developed its grammar and vocabulary on the model of the Arab language. The revival of Hebrew in our own times would be entirely unthinkable without the services rendered to it by Arabic in various ways a thousand years ago. Arabic itself became a Jewish language and, unlike Latin in Europe, was employed by Jews for all secular and religious purposes, with the sole exception of the synagogue service.[23]

The Hebrew that Jews speak today is Modern Hebrew. The syntax of Modern Hebrew is quite removed from that of the OT. In fact, the Hebrew language is usually divided into four developmental stages: Biblical, Mishnaic (also called "Rabbinic"), Medieval and Modern Hebrew. The syntax of Modern Hebrew is Mishnaic, and Mishnaic has different rules from Biblical syntax![24]

The vocabulary of Modern Hebrew also is very different from Biblical Hebrew. Eliezer Ben-Yehuda (1858-1922 AD), the father of Modern Hebrew, spearheaded the revival of Hebrew as a living, spoken language. Ben-Yehuda began with the 7,704 Hebrew words of the Torah, but proceeded to coin and borrow other words. Modern Hebrew acquired 100,000 words by 1978 AD.[25] By some estimates, in 2000 AD Hebrew had 120,000 words.

Speakers of non-Hebrew languages perhaps could take a fresh approach to Biblical Hebrew. Modern Hebrew speakers, however, are burdened by more than two millennia's worth of linguistic baggage. So it may be easier to reach a level of objectivity concerning Hebrew when one has no preconceived notions, and no habits that need to be unlearned.

All these facts taken together suggest that disagreements about majestic plurals may be driven by sectarian bias rather than a lack of relevant OT data. There is no hint that *Yeshua* and the apostles or any early Christians deferred to the establishment for authoritative grammatical rulings (Mat 07:29; Mar 01:22). Likewise, Christians should learn from the data rather than accept *ad hominem* argumentation, even if the authorities scoff (Joh 07:49).

OT Data Inconsistent With the Existence of the Majestic Plural Syntax

Joshua and the Israelites

In a speech against polytheism, Joshua referred to *Yahveh* as the "holy [plural adjective] Gods [*Elohim*]" (Jos 24:19). Unless Joshua was teaching Trinitarianism, it would have been counterproductive to refer to God using a plural in a speech against polytheism. So the phrase "holy [plural adjective] Gods [*Elohim*]" is a plural collective noun rather than a majestic plural.

Jehoiakim as Adon

Yahveh said that when Jehoiakim died, no one would lament his death as though he were a brother, nor would anyone say:

Alas, [what a] master [*adon*]! Alas, [what] majesty! (Jer 22:18).

The Hebrew translated "master" is the singular form *adon*.

If there were such a thing as an OT majestic plural, one would think that the plural form *adonai* would have been used before the phrase, "Alas, [what] majesty." If the plural *adonai* meant "majestic master" just by itself, then the second phrase "Alas, [what] majesty!" would have been redundant.

The Majestic Plural Construction is at Odds with the *Shema*

Trinitarianism is based on the Biblical version of the *Shema* that reads *Elohim* (Gods) is "a united one" (*echad*). Unitarianism, however, currently is based on an altered version of the *Shema* introduced by Maimonides.

Maimonides changed the *Shema* from *Elohim* (Gods) is "a united one" (*echad*) to *Elohim* (Gods) is "a unique one" (*yachid*). Though the OT never used *yachid* to refer to *Yahveh*, Maimonides' altered *yachid* version of the *Shema* has become a pivotal article of the modern Jewish faith.

The Majestic Plural Concept is at Odds with Unitarianism

The majestic plural concept suggests that the quality of majesty is somehow related to the concept of plurality. This association between majesty and plurality seems artificial and contrived. For the sake of argument, however, it is worthwhile to think the association is hypothetically valid. For instance, if the association between plurality and majesty were valid, the persons of the Trinity would necessarily be more majestic than the lone divine figure touted by majestic plural proponents.

The Majestic Plural is at Odds with the OT Use of the Plural for God

If the OT taught unitarianism, one would expect that the singular Hebrew forms for God, *El* (Gen 14:18) and *Elo(w)ah* (Deu 32:15, 17; Hab 03:03) would have been used throughout the OT. Furthermore, the singular form *El* would have been useful to counter the prevailing polytheistic notions.

Overall, the OT looks very Trinitarian. The singular forms *El* and *Elo(w)ah* are used mainly in poetic sections. As was noted above, there are 2,600 occurrences of the plural form *Elohim* in 2,247 OT verses. The singular form *El*, however, occurs 219 times in 212 verses, while the singular form *Elo(w)ah* occurs 58 times in 57 verses.

The prevalence of the plural *Elohim* suggests that the plural form *Elohim* would have been used in poetry, too, except that the forms *El* and *Elo(w)ah* were easier to work with given the constraints of Hebrew poetry.

The Form *HaElohim* is Not Consistent With the Existence of the Majestic Plural Syntax

The Hebrew definite article *ha* (the) prefix implies "all the...," but does not explicitly state "all the..." Massey gives the example that *hayam* [*ha + yam*] literally means "the people," but "all the people" is implied.[26] The definite article "the" (*ha*) prefixed to *Elohim* (*haElohim*) suggests the Trinity: "[All] the Gods."

So when the article *ha* is prefixed to *Elohim* (or *elohim*), the form should be taken to mean:

- "[All] the Gods" when referring to the Trinity,
- "[All] the gods" when referring to false gods (Exo 18:11; Jdg 10:14; 2Ch 02:04; Jer 11:12), and
- "[All] the judges" when referring to humans (Exo 21:06; 22:08-09 (*BHS* 22:07-08); Jos 24:01).

The reader of modern translations, of course, will not find *haElohim* translated as a plural collective noun when referring to *Yahveh*, except in 1Sa 04:08 (as is noted in the MT plurals appendix). Like thousands of other plurals that refer to *Yahveh*, translators consider the form *haElohim* to be a majestic plural. Accordingly, when referring to *Yahveh*, *haElohim* is translated in the singular as

"God" (Gen 05:22, 24; 06:02, 04, 09, 11; 17:18; 20:06, 17; 22:03, 09; 27:28; 31:11; 35:07, etc.)

Only when the translators figured, wrongly or rightly, that *haelohim* referred to false gods was *haelohim* translated in the plural as "gods" (Exo 18:11; Deu 10:17; Jdg 10:14; 1Sa 04:08; 2Ch 02:04; Psa 136:02; Jer 11:12). It goes without saying that translating a plural form as a singular sometimes and as a plural other times is inconsistent. This treatment of *haElohim* is also inconsistent with the translation of other plurals prefixed by the definite article. Examples include: "...the *Baals* [*haBaalim*] and the *Asherahs* [*haAsherot*]" (*NIV* Jdg 03:07).

If *Yahveh* were a singular person, it is curious that God is called *haElohim* ("[All] the Gods"). *HaElohim* occurs 366 times in 337 OT verses, and nearly always refers to *Yahveh* (Gen 05:22, 24; 06:02, 04, 09, 11, etc., but not in Exo 21: 06; 22:08, 09). However, when "all" [Hebrew is *cowl*] is explicitly prefixed to "the gods" (*cowl elohim*), the phrase refers to:

- Angels (Psa 097:07, 09), or
- Pagan gods (for instance, Gen 35:04; Exo 12:12; 18:11; 2Ki 18:35; 1Ch 16:25-26; 2Ch 02:05 (*BHS* 2Ch 02:04); 32:14; Psa 095:03; 096:04-05; 135:05; Isa 36: 20; Zep 02:11).

At least three incidents show that the form *haElohim* ("[All] the Gods") refers to persons called *Yahveh*, and so implicitly speaks of the Trinity:

- In Deu 33:01 Moses is called "the man of [All] the Gods," and then in the next verse *Yahveh* was said to have appeared on three mountains during the giving of the law (Exo 20). Deu 33:01-02 is discussed in the chapter on the Presences of *Elyon*,
- In a section where *Yahveh* is twice called "[All] the Gods" (Jos 22:34; 24:01), the Transjordan tribes called upon *Yahveh* to be the Mosaic minimum of two concurring witnesses, saying:

God of Gods, *Yahveh* [the Father]! God of Gods, *Yahveh* [the Son]! He knows (Jos 22:22), and

- Similarly, Elijah called *Yahveh* "[All] the Gods" (1Ki 18:21, 24, 37). Later, the people twice said:

Yahveh, he is [All] the Gods; *Yahveh*, he is [All] the Gods (1Ki 18:39).

The extensive use of the form *haElohim* suggests that "[All] the Gods" implicitly speaks of the Trinity:

- These people saw or talked to *haElohim*: Enoch (Gen 05:22, 24), Noah (Gen 06:09), Abraham (Gen 17:18; 20:17; 22:03, 09), Abimelech (Gen 20:06), Jacob (Gen 27:28; 35:07; 48:15), Moses (Exo 03:06, 11, 12, 13; 19:03), the Israelites (Exo 18:12; 19:17; 20:20, 21; 24:11), Balaam (Num 22:10; 23:27) and Gideon (Jdg 06:36, 39),
- Moses is called "the man of [All] the Gods" (Deu 33:01; Jos 14:06; 2Ch 30:16; Ezr 03:02; Psa 090:01), Moses is called the "servant of [All] the Gods" (1Ch 06:34; 2Ch 24:09; Neh 10:29 (*BHS* 10:30); Dan 09:11), and Moses received the "Law of [All] the Gods (Exo 18:16; Neh 08:08; 10:29 [*BHS* 10:30]) on the "Mount of [All] the Gods" (Exo 03:01; 04:27; 18:05; 24:13; 1Ki 19:08; 2Ki 04:25),

- The Ark of the Covenant was later called the "Ark of [All] the Gods" 35 times in 31 verses (Jdg 20:27; 1Sa 04:04, 13, 18, 19, 21, 22; 05:01, 02, 10 (twice); 14: 18 (twice); 2Sa 06:02, 03, 04, 06, 07, 12 (twice); 15:24 (twice), 25, 29; 1Ch 13: 05, 06, 07, 12, 14; 15:02, 15, 24; 16:01, 06; and 2Ch 01:04), and
- The ark resided in the "House of [All] the Gods." The "House of [All] the Gods" is mentioned 55 times in 54 verses (Jdg 18:31; 1Ch 06:33; 09:11, 13, 26, 27; 22:02; 23:28; 25:06; 26:20; 28:12, 21; 29:07; 2Ch 03:03; 04:11, 19; 05:01, 14; 07:05; 15:18; 22:12; 23:03, 09; 24:07, 13, 27; 25:24; 28:24 (twice), 31:13, 21; 33:07; 35:08; 36:18, 19; Ezr 01:04; 02:68; 03:08, 09; 06:22; 08:36; 10:01, 06, 09; Neh 06:10; 08:16; 11:11, 16, 22; 12:40; 13:07, 09, 11; Ecc 04:17; and Dan 01:02).

The Affinity Between Hebrew Plurals That Refer to *Yahveh*

Massey wrote:
> The only way to explicitly exclude the implicit 'all' from 'the people' is to mark it with a qualification, e.g., 'some of the people.'[27]

So in the case of *haElohim*, the only way to remove the implicit "all" is to use a qualifier like "some." No qualifier is ever used when *haElohim* refers to the Trinity. Besides, a "some" qualifier would still refer to more than one person, not just a singular majestic person. So when *haElohim* refers to *Yahveh*, the plural form suggests that there are persons who are called *Yahveh* both individually and collectively.

Far from using qualifiers to exclude the implicit "all" understanding of *haElohim* ("[All] the Gods"), *haElohim* is used in conjunction with other MT elements that refer to the persons of *Yahveh*. Of course, the plural form *Elohim* (literally, "Gods") occurs so often that its proximity to other Trinitarian proofs is statistically insignificant. However, there are other Trinitarian proofs besides *Elohim* scattered throughout the OT. For example, the affinity between *haElohim* ("[All] the Gods") and these other Trinitarian proofs is statistically significant.

To appreciate the statistical significance of *haElohim*'s proximity to OT Trinitarian proofs, note that there are only 336 verses with an instance or two of *haElohim* out of 23,213 verses in the Hebrew OT. Furthermore, the distribution of *haElohim* throughout the OT is not even. Most instances of *haElohim* (91.5 percent or 335 instances of 366 total instances) occur in just twelve OT books.[28] Also, most instances of *haElohim* (80.6 percent or 295 instances of 366 total instances) are clustered in just 83 chapters.[29]

So chance would only account for a few instances of proximity between *haElohim* and Trinitarian proofs. Furthermore, the fact that *haElohim* is clustered seems significant—as though these chapters were meant to teach the Trinity. The affinity between *haElohim* and plurals referring to *Yahveh* is demonstrated in the following table:

The Affinity Between Elements (Besides the Common Plural Form *Elohim*) That Indicate *Yahveh* is Plural Persons

The elements concerned are:

- **"[All] the Gods"** (*haElohim*) occurs 366 times in 337 OT verses. *haElohim* is discussed above,
- **"You-he"** (*atah-hu*) **paired pronouns** occur nine times in nine OT verses. *Atah-hu* is discussed later in the chapter,
- **"Yahveh Elohim"** (*Yahveh* **Gods**) occur 37 times in 35 OT verses. *"Yahveh Elohim"* is discussed later in the chapter, and
- **MT plural verbs and modifiers referring to *Yahveh*** occur once or more in 38 MT Chapters. MT plurals referring to *Yahveh* are discussed in Collective Plurals chapter and in the MT plurals appendix.

Groupings of Trinitarian elements (besides the common plural form *Elohim*) are found at:

- **The Creation Account:**
  - o *Yahveh Elohim*: Gen 02:04b—03:23
  - o MT Plurals: Gen 01:26; 03:22; and LXX Gen 02:18; LXX Gen 03:05b
- **Gen 20 and Neh 9:**
  - o *haElohim*: Gen 20:06, 17; Neh 09:07
  - o *Atah-hu*: Neh 09:06a, 07
  - o MT Plurals: Gen 20:13; LXX Neh 09:18
- **Gen 35:**
  - o *haElohim*: Gen 35:07
  - o MT Plural: Gen 35:07
- **Deu 04 and Jer 23:**
  - o *haElohim*: Deu 04:35, 39; Jer 23:23
  - o MT Plurals: Deu 04:07; Jer 23:36
- **Jos 22, 24:**
  - o *haElohim*: Jos 22:34; 24:01
  - o MT Plural: Jos 24:19
- **1Sa 04:**
  - o *haElohim*: 1Sa 04:04, 08 (twice), 13, 17, 18, 19, 21, 22; 05:01, 02, 10 (twice), 11
  - o MT Plurals: 1Sa 04:07-08
- **2Sa 07:**
  - o *haElohim*: 2Sa 07:02, 28
  - o *Atah-hu*: 2Sa 07:28
  - o *Yahveh Elohim*: 2Sa 07:25
  - o MT Plural: 2Sa 07:23
- **2Ki 19:**
  - o *haElohim*: 2Ki 19:15
  - o *Atah-hu*: 2Ki 19:15
  - o *Yahveh Elohim*: 2Ki 19:19

- **1Ch 17 and 2Sa 07**:
  - o *haElohim*: 1Ch 17:02, 21, 26
  - o *Atah-hu*: 1Ch 17:26
  - o *Yahveh Elohim*: 1Ch 17:16-17
  - o MT Plural: 2Sa 07:23
- **1Ch 28**:
  - o *haElohim*: 1Ch 28:12, 21
  - o *Yahveh Elohim*: 1Ch 28:20
- **2Ch 01**:
  - o *haElohim*: 2Ch 01:03-04
  - o *Yahveh Elohim*: 2Ch 01:09
- **2Ch 07**:
  - o *haElohim*: 2Ch 07:05
  - o *Yahveh Elohim*: 2Ch 06:41-42
- **2Ch 19**:
  - o *haElohim*: 2Ch 19:03
  - o *Atah-hu*: 2Ch 20:06
- **2Ch 32**:
  - o *haElohim*: 2Ch 32:16, 31
  - o MT Plurals: 2Ch 32:14, 15
- **Isa 37**:
  - o *haElohim*: Isa 37:16
  - o *Atah-hu*: Isa 37:16
- **Isa 41**:
  - o MT Plurals: Isa 41:04, 21-23, 26
- **Dan 04**:
  - o MT Plurals: Dan 04:08, 09, 17, 18, 25, 26, 31, 32; 05:11, 20, 21; 07:18, 22, 25b, 26, 27
- **Jon 04**:
  - o *haElohim*: Jon 04:07
  - o *Yahveh Elohim*: Jon 04:06
- **Ecc 12**:
  - o *haElohim*: Ecc 12:07, 13-14
  - o MT Plural: Ecc 12:01
- **Hos 11-12**:
  - o MT Plurals: Hos 11:02, 12 (*BHS* 12:01); Hos 12:04 (*BHS* 12:05)

The Paired Words *Yahveh Elohim*

Yahveh Elohim are the Father (*Yahveh*) and the Son (*Elohim*). *Yahveh Elohim* are the "us" mentioned several times in Genesis (Gen 01:26, 03:22; 11:07 and LXX Gen 02:18). *Yahveh Elohim* are mentioned twenty times in Gen 02—03. The nouns *Yahveh Elohim* are discussed in the MT plurals appendix, as are all the plural elements mentioned in the "Affinity" table, above.

The Paired Pronouns "You-he" (*Atah-hu*)

The paired pronouns *atah-hu* ("you-he") occur nine times in the MT (2Sa 07: 28; 2Ki 19:15; 1Ch 17:26; 2Ch 20:06; Neh 09:06a, 07; Psa 044:05a; Isa 37:16; Jer 14:22). Five times *atah-hu* is associated with the form *haElohim* ([All] the Gods). This suggests *atah-hu* refers to the persons called *Yahveh*. Here are literal trans- lations of all nine occurrences of paired pronouns "you-he":

- *Yahveh*, you-he [are] [All] the Gods [*haElohim*] (2Sa 07:28),
- *Yahveh*, Gods [*Elohim*] of Israel who dwell [between] the cherubim, you-he [are] [All] the Gods [*haElohim*] (2Ki 19:15),
- Now *Yahveh*, you-he [are] [All] the Gods [*haElohim*] (1Ch 17:26),
- *Yahveh* Gods [*Elohim*] of our fathers, [are] you-he not Gods [*Elohim*] in heaven? (2Ch 20:06),
- You-he [are] *Yahveh* alone...you-he [are] *Yahveh*, [All] the Gods [*haElohim*] (Neh 09:06-07),
- You-he [are] my king, O Gods [*Elohim*] (Psa 044:04),
- *Yahveh* of hosts, Gods [*Elohim*] of Israel who dwell [between] the cherubim, you-he [are] [All] the Gods [*haElohim*] (Isa 37:16), and
- [Are] not you-he, *Yahveh*, our Gods [*Elohenu*]? (Jer 14:22).

The Presences of *Elyon* chapter discusses how the Father dwelt in heaven, while the Son and Spirit as Presences of *Yahveh* dwelt first in the tabernacle and then the temple. The "you" of the paired "you-he" pronouns may have been meant as a collective pronoun referring to the Presences in the temple. The members of the Trinity were often addressed with singular collective nouns.

The "he" of the paired "you-he" pronouns may have been meant as a singular pronoun referring to the Father in heaven. "You" naturally refers to a person or persons who are near—such as the Presences in the temple. "He" naturally refers to a person more distant such as the Father in heaven. "You" is a singular col- lective noun referring to the Son and Spirit.

The Lack of Evidence for the Majestic Plural Syntax in Any Language

Since Biblical Hebrew is a Semitic language, one would expect to find copious examples of majestic plurals in other contemporary Semitic languages. Though large ancient Near East libraries have been unearthed, only a few dubious examples have been offered as proof that other Semitic languages used majestic plurals. Instead, what one finds is, as the *Encyclopaedia Britannica* states:

> Some rulers speak of their own dynastic deity. A king who owes his po- sition to the Assyrian emperor refers to the latter and the dynastic deity equally as 'my master.'[30]

Notice the king and god are referred to by the singular "my master," not by a majestic plural "my masters."

Case Studies on Supposed Majestic Plurals

Supposed Arabic Majestic Plurals
Majestic plural proponents say that the *Koran* contains many majestic plurals. Muhammad has *Allah* saying, "we," "us" and "our" often. Many plural pronouns that are best understood as referring to angels are instead interpreted as referring to *Allah*.[31] The *Koran*, however, is not of any great antiquity, but is merely medieval-era literature written between 610 and 632 AD. Furthermore, pre-Islamic documents yield scant evidence for the existence of majestic plurals in Arabia. James Hastings wrote:

> Curiously enough, the two oldest documents which mention her [the goddess *Manat*], a Nabataean and a Latin inscription, use the plural form *Manawat* (spelt *Manavat* in Latin), just as the plural *Manaya* is used for *Maniya* [meaning, "doom to death" or "destruction"],[32] and
> It may be added that the divine name *Iyal*, which occurs once in an ancient verse, is possibly a plural of majesty formed from *El*.[33]

Latin had no majestic plural rationalization, so the above Latin transliterations cited by Hastings may have reflected a plural in either Aramaic or Arabic. These few pre-Islamic plurals could be explained without resorting to the majestic plural rationalization. Later in this chapter, for example, the plurals referring to *Baal* and *Ashtorah* are explained without referring to the majestic plural rationalization.

These Arabian documents were probably based on Arabic language sources. The Arabic language was first written down with a crude alphabet a few centuries before the Islamic era. It would seem, therefore, that none of the examples from Arabia are of great antiquity. Thus, it cannot be proven that the majestic plural concept was found in Arabia before Jewish influences infiltrated the peninsula.

If the pre-Islamic writers meant these plurals to be understood as majestic plurals, they probably were just copying Jewish custom. There is, however, no doubt that *Koran*ic majestic plurals reflect Jewish teaching. Ibn Warraq wrote about the Jewish influence:

> Cook points out the similarity of certain Muslim beliefs and practices to those of the Samaritans...He also points out that the fundamental idea of Muhammad developed of the religion of Abraham was already present in the Jewish apocryphal work (dated to circa 140-100 BC) called the Book of Jubilees and may well have influenced the formation of Islamic ideas.... Sozomenus [a fifth century AD historian] goes on to describe how certain Arab tribes that learned of their Ishmaelite origins from Jews adopted Jewish observances [circumcision, abstaining from eating pork, etc.][34]

J. Wansbrough wrote about the Jewish influence on the *Koran*'s development:

> Quranic allusion presupposes familiarity with the narrative material of Judaeo-Christian scripture, which was not so much reformulated as merely referred to....Taken together, the quantity of reference, the mechanically repetitive employment of rhetorical convention, and the stridently polemical style, all suggest a strongly sectarian atmosphere in which a

corpus of familiar scripture was being pressed into the service of as yet unfamiliar doctrine.[35]

The *Koran* repeatedly notes how critics accused Muhammad of having no new stories (*Koran* 006:025; 008:031; 016:024; 023:083; 025:005; 027:068; 046:017; 068:015; 083:013). The detractors said the old information was pieced together with the help of others (*Koran* 016:103; 044:014). *Koran* 025:004-005 reads:

> Those who disbelieve say: This is nothing but a lie that he [Muhammad] has forged, and other people have helped him at it; so indeed they have done injustice and (uttered) a falsehood. And they [critics] say: The stories of the ancients—he [Muhammad] has got them written, and these are read out to him morning and evening.

One heckler vexed the apostle by saying:

> Muhammad is only an ear. If anyone tells him a thing he believes it.[36]

The *Koran* even records that a non-indigenous Arabic speaker helped Muhammad formulate Islam:

> We [Allah] know indeed that they say, 'It is a man that teaches him [Muhammad].' The tongue of him [Muhammad's tutor] they [the Mekkans] wickedly point to is outlandish, while this [the *Koran*] is Arabic, pure and clear (*Koran* 016:103; compare 026:195).

The language and cultural identity of Muhammad's tutor is suggested elsewhere in the *Koran*. Allah told Muhammad to go to the People of the Book, meaning the Jews, to verify that the *Koran* was consistent with Hebrew scripture (*Koran* 010:094).

> Muhammad's biographer, Ibn Ishaq, mentions there being many rabbis at Medina. Medina is Arabic meaning, "The City [of the Prophet Muhammad]." Several rabbis converted to Islam, including Mukhayriq[37] and Husayn ibn Sallam.[38] One of the most learned rabbis in the area lived at Medina. Ibn Ishaq wrote: 'Abdullah b. Suriya the one-eyed who was the most learned man of his time in the Hijaz in Torah studies…[39]

History records that the Jews in Arabia did not speak pure Arabic, at least to express their religion. S. D. Goitein wrote that even during medieval times, the Jews around the Mediterranean did not use Arabic during synagogue services.[40] In Arabia up to Muhammad's time, the Jews had a specialized vocabulary that was unfamiliar to the Arabs. The difference between the Judeo-Arabic dialect and Arabic was much less than the difference between German and Yiddish. Gordon Newby wrote:

> Muhammad's amanuensis, Zayd b. Thabit, is said to have learned *al-yahudiyyah* in seventeen days in order to be able to understand what the Jews were writing, an indication that the difference between Arabic and *al-yahudiyyah* were matters of vocabulary and script; they were not different languages.[41]

So in the *Koran* Muhammad contrasted the Judeo-Arabic dialect with Arabic. This explains why Muhammad had to emphasize that the *Koran* was written in "pure" Arabic rather than just saying the *Koran* was written in Arabic (*Koran* 12:

002; 013:037; 016:103; 020:113; 026:195; 039:028; 041:003; 042:007; 043:003; 046:012). Muhammad argued that the different dialect proved that his material was not just a rehash of rabbinic material, but was original revelation.

History also points to the Jews being Muhammad's source of inspiration, as Gordon Newby wrote:

> The circulation of non-Islamic materials for use as the basis for Qur'an commentary was present during Muhammad's lifetime and saw a considerable increase in the two generations after his death. The Companion, Abu Hurayrah, although illiterate, had extensive knowledge of the Torah, as did 'Ali, Salman al-Farisi, and, of course, the 'Ocean of Tafsir,' Ibn 'Abbas, who is often called the *'hibr al-'umma,'* or 'Rabbi of the [Muslim] Community,' on account of his extensive knowledge of Judeo-Christian as well as Muslim Scripture and commentary acquired in Arabia. Muhammad, Abu Bakr, and 'Umar are reported to have made several trips to the Bet Midrash ["House of Study"] in Medina, and Muhammad's amanuensis, Zayd b. Thabit, who was so central in matters Qur'anic, is reported to have gone so far as to learn *al-yahudiyyah* [Judeo-Arabic] in a Bet Midrash at Muhammad's behest in order to read Jewish material.[42]

So it seems that the only plausible explanation, given all the data, is:
- Muhammad's tutor mentioned in *Koran* 016:103 was a Jewish Arab, and
- Muhammad learned the majestic plural rationalization from the Jews.

Logic also suggests that Muhammad learned the majestic plural rationalization from the Jewish sources rather than Arabic sources. If Allah was ever made to say "we" or "our" or "us" in pre-Islamic times, the Mekkans surely would have meant the plural pronouns to refer to *Allah* and his goddess daughters *Allat, Manat* and *Uzza* (*Koran* 053:019-020). In fact, the *Koran* may record the Mekkan objection to Muhammad's merging *Allah* and his daughters into one god by interpreting plurals as majestic plurals:

> So they [Mekkan critics] wonder that a Warner [Muhammad] has come to them from among themselves! and the unbelievers say, 'This is a sorcerer telling lies! Has he made the gods into a single *Allah*? Truly this is a strange thing!' And the leader among them goes away (impatiently), (saying), 'Walk ye away, and remain constant to your gods! This is most surely a thing sought after' (*Koran* 038:004-006).

It seems evident that the source of majestic plurals in the *Koran* traces back partly to rabbinic pseudo-scholarship and partly to OT Trinitarianism. Muhammad purposely made *Allah* speak often like *Yahveh* occasionally spoke—using plural pronouns like "we" and "us" (Gen 01:26; 03:22; 11:07; Isa 06:08). So it would seem that majestic plurals both in the *Koran* and in extra-biblical Jewish literature are an unwitting or a grudging imitation of OT Trinitarianism.

Supposed Majestic Plurals in First Maccabees

Some majestic plural proponents say that the OT apocryphal book of First Maccabees contains majestic plurals. Of course, this is Intertestamental literature, so it probably reflects newfangled rabbinic teaching on the majestic plural.

Intertestamental times, of course, were more than a thousand years after Moses penned the Pentateuch (Exo 34:27; Deu 31:19). Grammar rules are introduced and are discarded all the time. A thousand years is more than enough time for the majestic plural innovation to be conceptualized, be introduced, and become kosher grammar. Then majestic plural proponents monopolized Jewish scholarship by forcing out traditional Trinitarian scholars.

In First Maccabees various kings wrote messages using the pronouns "we" and "us" (1Ma 10:19-20, 26-28, 53-54, 56, 70-72; 11:31, 33-35). The "we" and the "us" of the letters refer not to a single king, but to two petty kings, or the king and his court. For instance:

> Demetrius sent Jonathan a letter in peaceable words to honor him; for he said, 'Let us [Demetrius and his court] act first to make peace with him [Jonathan] before he makes peace with Alexander against us, for [otherwise] he will remember all the wrongs which we did to him and to his brothers and his nation' (1Ma 10:03-05),

> So he said, 'Shall we [Alexander and his court] find another such man? Come now, we will make him our friend and ally.' And he wrote a letter and sent it to him…in the following words: 'King Alexander to his brother Jonathan, greeting. We [Alexander and his court] have heard about you, that you are a mighty warrior and worthy to be our friend' (1Ma 10:16-19), and

> When Demetrius heard of these things he was grieved and said, 'What is this that we [Demetrius and his court] have done? Alexander has gotten ahead of us in forming a friendship with the Jews to strengthen himself' (1Ma 10:22-23).

It seems inconceivable that the above statements would be the king's self-deliberative thoughts. It would be unnatural for a king to think to himself using majestic plural pronouns such "us" and "we."

Besides, a king using majestic plurals publicly would surely have caused endless confusion. When the king used a plural pronoun, everyone would wonder whether the king was referring just to his majestic self. Perhaps he meant himself and his court, or queen, or allies, or whatnot. That kings ever used majestic plurals sounds as fictitious as Hans Christian Andersen's tale "The Emperor's New Clothes" (1837 AD).

Supposed Majestic Plurals in the Apocryphal and Pseudepigraphal Books

Many pseudepigraphal books and apocryphal books like First Maccabees survive only in Greek or Coptic versions. Many such books may have been written originally in Greek. Since there is no majestic plural construction in Greek grammar, one can assume there are no majestic plurals in any apocryphal and pseudepigraphal book that originally was written in Greek.

Supposed Majestic Plurals in the Septuagint (LXX)

There is no majestic plural construction in Greek grammar. So no one can automatically assume there are no majestic plurals in the Septuagint, the Greek Translation of the Hebrew OT. Someone might ask:

Did the LXX translators recognize many Hebrew nouns to be majestic plurals, and then translate them as singulars?

It is possible that the LXX translators mistook Hebrew plurals to be majestic plurals. It seems more plausible that the LXX translators understood many Hebrew plurals were plural collective nouns. The Greek may have used singular collective nouns more frequently than plural collective nouns, so Hebrew plural collective nouns were translated as singular collective nouns.

The situation is analogous to a British English book being translated into American English. The plural collective nouns would be changed to singular collective nouns to conform to the sensibilities of American English readers.[43]

Supposed Majestic Plurals in Ezra

Majestic plural proponents offer an example from the Aramaic book of Ezra:

The letter you sent us has been read and translated in my presence" (Ezr 04:18).

King Artaxerxes' use of a singular pronoun (my) would be inconsistent with his having used a majestic plural (us) earlier in the verse.

Artaxerxes' letter mentions a translator and a reader being in his presence, and that the letter was written out of loyalty to "the palace" and king (Ezr 04:14). So Artaxerxes' use of "us" is best interpreted as the king speaking for himself and his court, or perhaps the translator, the reader and himself.

King Artaxerxes' response must have been translated from the king's Persian language, an Indo-European language similar to Vedic Sanskrit (Ezr 04:18).[44] Surely, the king and translator did not use majestic plurals since, apparently, neither the Aramaic nor Indo-European languages had a majestic plural usage.

Nicodemus' Supposed Majestic Plural

Nicodemus came stealthily to *Yeshua* at night and said, "Rabbi, we know..." (Joh 03:02). Some have supposed that since Nicodemus was a Pharisee and a "ruler of the Jews" (Joh 03:01), he was entitled to use majestic plurals when referring to himself. That Nicodemus was referring to himself and his colleagues seems apparent when *Yeshua* addressed Nicodemus and said, "you people" (Joh 03:11).

Supposed Majestic Plurals in the Apostle Paul's Writings

Paul said "us" and "we" often in Colossians, in First and Second Thessalonians, and in other epistles. Since Greek has no majestic plural syntax, it is unlikely that Paul would write using majestic plurals. Historically, Paul's plural pronouns have been understood to refer to himself and his coworker(s), friend(s) or congregation(s).

Supposed Majestic Plural Usage in Victorian England

Alexandrina Victoria, Queen of England from 1837–1901 AD, reportedly said, "We are not amused." This has been offered as support for the majestic plural rationalization. Everyone in court, however, surely understood the queen to be speaking for herself and the royal family, or herself and the court.

If Queen Victoria really had used a majestic plural, there ought to be thousands of other examples of majestic plurals in the English royal archives. Apparently, none are to be found since only this one example has been offered.

Because this isolated example is of late date, it says nothing about whether the majestic plural can be traced back to antiquity in any language. The example proves, if anything, that English royalty had read a rabbinic grammar book about majestic plurals. In reality, however, this example proves absolutely nothing about the majestic plural since it represents a typical use of the plural pronoun "we."

Supposed Majestic Plural Referring to Kemosh

The Ammonites had not integrated into Israelite society as had other ethnic groups like the Kenites (Jdg 05:24; 1Sa 15:06) and the Hittites (1Sa 26:06; 2Sa 11:11). The lack of integration was due to Ammonite reliance on sorcery and their false god, *Kemosh* (Deu 23:03-06). The segregation also was a result of the Ammonites and Moabites, the descendants of Lot, living on buffer state "reservations" (Gen 19:38; Deu 02:09-11, 19-21). They shared this status with the Edomites, the descendants of Esau (Deu 02:04-06; Jos 24:04).

The marginalized Ammonites waited three centuries until the Israelites were weak, and then they demanded land back that was not theirs in the first place. The Ammonite rationale was not that they were the majority occupants or "the powers that be" over the disputed land (Jdg 11:26; Rom 13:01). Instead, a corrupted oral history, or a misreading of Israelite history, informed the Ammonites that the Israelites had taken their land (Jdg 11:13). Nevertheless, the Ammonites wanted to undo three hundred years of history (Jdg 11:26).

The Israelites operated on the manifest destiny principle that *Yahveh* had given certain lands to the Israelites and certain lands to the gentiles (Deu 02:05-24; Act 17:26). Jephthah noted that *Yahveh* himself had driven out the previous occupants, and that *Yahveh* had given Israel three hundred years of uncontested occupancy in the contested land (Jdg 11:23).

Jephthah set the record straight by pointing out that Israel had taken the contested land from the Amorites (Num 21:21-24; Jdg 11:19-23), not from the Ammonites (Deu 02:19-21, 37). So in reality, the Ammonites were attempting a naked land grab of territory that belonged first to the Amorites and then to the Israelites.

Jephthah argued that if the Ammonites had been given an opportunity, they would have confiscated land given to them by "your *elohim* [literally, "gods"), *Kemosh*" (Jdg 11:24). Jephthah's argument was not so hypothetical, for the Ammonites had driven out tribes to take their land (Deu 02:19-23). Moreover, the Ammonites were about to do so again by dislodging Israel.

The situation between the Ammonites and Israel occurred because the Ammonites relied on their sanitized and corrupted oral history. This history left them feeling both self-righteous and wronged. Their history was as effective as a myth since it provided the pretext for group action and cohesion.

The Ammonites could selectively misread Israel's written history to make land claims and construct moral superiority arguments. Jephthah, however, could not "fight fire with fire" by reading the Ammonite's disinfected history. Jephthah could only counter with the correct reading of Israelite history. The correct reading probably sounded like only so much propaganda to the Ammonites (Jdg 11:28).

So why did Jephthah call *Kemosh* "*elohim*," literally, "gods"? Using a majestic plural to honor an enemy's god does not motivate one's troops, nor does it make for effective psychological warfare. Furthermore, it would be inconsistent for Jephthah first to honor *Kemosh* by using a majestic plural (Jdg 11:24), and then belittle the Ammonite king, saying:

> Are you better than Balak son of Zippor, king of Moab? Did he ever
> quarrel with Israel or fight with them? (Jdg 11:25).

Archaeology seems to provide an answer for why Jephthah called *Kemosh* plural "gods." Centuries after the Jephthah incident in Judges, Mesha had the Moabite Stone made to boast about his rebellion against Israel. Mesha happens to be mentioned in the Bible (2Ki 03:04).

Though Jephthah fought an Ammonite king, and Mesha was Moabite, both kings referred to the same god(s) *Kemosh*. The Ammonites and Moabites and their gods are mentioned together in the OT often, for instance, in Deu 23:03-04. The Ammonites and Moabites were related (Gen 19:37-38). Their gods *Molech* and *Kemosh* are noted for having territorial ambitions (Jer 49:01-03). William Foxwell Albright wrote:

> As a male, *Athtart* was known as *Athtar* and corresponded to the
> Moabite god *Kemosh*, as well as the Ammonite god *Milcom*, or *Molech*
> (1Ki 11:33).[45]

Mesha then built a temple to *Kemosh* and *Ashtar* that showcased the Moabite Stone. The 34-line inscription chiseled around 850 BC is called the Mesha inscription.[46] The stone was rediscovered in 1868 AD. The stele (also spelled "stela") boasted of Mesha's dastardly deeds and mundane acts. In lines 14-18 of the inscription, Mesha calls his gods by the compound name *Ashtar-Kemosh*:

> ...Now *Kemosh* said to me, 'Go seize Nebo from Israel.' So I went at
> night and fought against it from the break of dawn until noon. I seized
> it and killed everyone of [it]—seven thousand native men, foreign men,
> native women, for[eign] women, and concubines—for I devoted it to
> *Ashtar-Kemosh*. I took from there th[e ves]sels of *Yahveh* and dragged
> them before *Kemosh*. Now the king of Israel had built...[47]

Another Moabite stone, the Balua Stele, shows a king flanked by two figures. Archaeologists suspect that the figures are *Kemosh* with a sun disk, and the goddess *Ashtar* with a crescent moon.[48] The Mesha inscription mentions *Kemosh* often (lines 03, 05, 09, 13, 14, 18, 19, 33), but there is one mention of *Ashtar-Kemosh* (see quote above).

The mention of *Ashtar-Kemosh* on the Moabite Stone and the figures on the Balua Stele suggest that *Kemosh* was an inclusive term meaning *Ashtar-Kemosh*. That *Kemosh* is a collective noun explains why Jephthah spoke of *Kemosh* using a singular verb "causes to possess" with the plural "gods" (*elohim*):

> That which *Kemosh* your gods causes you to possess—will you not possess it? (Jdg 11:24).

Though the Moabite language was closely related to Hebrew,[49] no Moabite stele sports a majestic plural. Apparently, the Moabites did not assimilate the majestic plural rationalization from the Israelites, though there is evidence that Moabites and Israelites intermingled:

- The Moabites were descendants of Lot (Gen 19:37). Lot undoubtedly knew and spoke the same Hebrew that his uncle Abraham spoke (Gen 12:05; 14:12),
- The Jewish Transjordan tribes mingled with the Moabites. Mesha's inscription even mentions a sanctuary of *Yahveh* at Nebo at the edge of Moabite territory (see lines 14 and 18 quoted above),
- A man of Judean descent was once a Moabite king (1Ch 04:22),[50]
- The book of Ruth reveals that the tribes west of the Jordan River also mixed with the Moabites, and
- The Moabite god *Kemosh* was worshipped in Jerusalem for two centuries between the reigns of Solomon and Josiah (1Ki 11:07, 33; 2Ki 23:13).

This data suggests that the majestic plural usage was unknown in ancient times, and was devised only in Intertestamental times.

The Supposed Majestic Plural Baalim (Lords)

In many ancient Near East languages, the word *baalim* (lords) was a near synonym for *elohim* (gods). If *elohim* were used as a majestic plural, one would expect that *baalim* and other *elohim* synonyms would have been used as majestic plurals, too. However, ancient Near East libraries reveals that *baalim* referred to persons or things rather than to single, majestic persons. A study of the Biblical data also shows that *baalim* always refers to persons or things.

Here is a study of how the word *baal* was used in the OT. When referring to the god *Baal*, the Hebrew word *baal* is made definite by:

- Prefixing the definite article "the" (*ha*) as in *haBaal* (the *Baal*) and *haBaalim* ("the *Baals*"),
- Putting *baal* in a Hebrew construct makes *baal* a possessive ("*Baal*'s," or "of *Baal*"), or
- Prefixing a preposition to *baal* such as "by" (*beth*) (Jer 02:08; 12:16; 23:13) or the preposition "to" (*lamadh*) (Jdg 02:13; 06:31; 1Ki 16:32; 19:18).

Otherwise, the Hebrew form *baal* is used as:

- A title meaning, "masters" or "husbands" (Gen 20:03),
- A personal name (1Ch 05:05; 08:30; 09:36), or as
- A syllable in compound:

o Place names (Exo 14:02), and

o Personal names (Gen 36:38-39).

The account of Elijah on Mount Carmel shows that the word *haBaalim* ("the *Baals*") refers to both *Baal* and *Ashtorah*. Elijah uses the singular term *haBaal* (1Ki 18:19, 21, 22, 25, 26, 40) and the plural *haBaalim* (1Ki 18:18) interchangeably in the account of Elijah and the Prophets of *Baal*. Elijah revealed who the *haBaalim* were by saying:

...bring the four hundred and fifty prophets of *Baal* and the four hundred prophets of *Ashtorah* (1Ki 18:19).

So Elijah used the plural form *haBaalim* ("the *Baals*") as a plural collective noun referring to the god *Baal* and his goddess consort *Ashtorah*.

In the account of the Prophets of *Baal*, both the singular form *haBaal* and the plural *haBaalim* likely were collective nouns referring to *Baal* and *Ashtorah*. It is easy to understand how in patriarchal societies the singular term *haBaal* came to be an inclusive, collective noun referring to the god *Baal* and his goddess consort.

Many gods were assumed to have goddess consorts, though the names of the goddesses may have never been invoked in literature. The names of the goddesses were often the feminine form of a god's name, for example, *Baal*'s goddess consort in Byblos was *Baalat* of Byblos.[51] Similarly, *Allah*'s goddess consort or daughter, depending on the location and period, was *Allat* (*Koran* 053:019).

Sometimes the goddess consort was a goddess with an entirely different name than the god, but their spheres of influence were related. For example, *Baal*'s goddess consort *Ashtorah* has a name with no etymological connection to *Baal*, but *Baal-Shamash* was "Lord of Heaven" and *Ashtorah* happened to be the "Queen of Heaven" (Jer 07:18; 44:17, 19).

Baal's symbol sometimes was the sun. *Ashtorah*'s astral association was Venus. The sun and Venus often rise and set together. That *Baal* and *Ashtorah*'s spheres of influence are related help to account for their being known as *haBaalim* (1Ki 18: 18). Calling *Baal* and *Ashtorah Baalim* is similar to calling a husband and wife by the plural "the Joneses."

The word *haBaalim* also was used as a collective noun referring to a pantheon. Hosea, evidently speaking of a pantheon, said the *haBaalim* have a "their name [singular]" (Hos 02:17). That *haBaalim* ("the *Baals*") became synonymous with "pantheon" is because the god *Baal* was a rain god, among other things. In the parched environment of the ancient Near East, his rain and fertility roles meant *Baal* was the *de facto* top god in most Canaanite pantheons.

So the term *habaalim* was used as a collective plural to refer to many gods (Jdg 02:11; 03:07; 08:33; 10:06, 10; 1Sa 07:04; 12:10; 1Ki 18:18; 2Ch 17:03; 24:07; 28: 02; 33:03; 34:04; Jer 02:23; 09:14; 11:13; Hos 02:13). Certain verses provide especially strong evidence that *haBaalim* referred to several deities (Jdg 02:11-12; 03:07; 08:33; 10:06). The *Encyclopaedia Britannica* states that there were many *Baals*:

It is clear that several different deities are referred to by the form *Baal*-X ("Lord of X"). *Hadad* is probably represented by *Baal-Shamen* ("Lord of the Heavens"). *El* appeared under the title *Baal-Hammon*.[52]

Supposed Majestic Plurals Referring to Goddess Consorts
Asherah (*haAsherah*) was the Canaanite goddess of fortune and happiness. *Asherah* is only referred to as a personal goddess a few times (1Ki 18:19; 2Ki 23: 04, 07). Most translations only have the plural form of *Asherah*'s name once in the phrase: "the *Baals* and the *Asherahs*" (*NIV* Jdg 03:07, but *RSV* transliterates the plural as *Asheroth*). Otherwise, "groves" or "*Asherah* poles" is the standard translation of the Hebrew plural forms *haAsheroth* (Jdg 03:07; 2Ch 19:03; 33:03) and *haAsherim* (2Ki 23:14; 2Ch 14:02; 17:06; 24:18; 31:01, 19; 34:07; Isa 27:09; Eze 27:06). This leaves only one plural form of *Asherah* in the whole OT that might be classified as a plural of majesty—"the *Asherahs*" in Jdg 03:07.

There are a few alternative explanations for the plural form "*Asherahs*" or "*Asheroth*" in Jdg 03:07, other than that *Asherahs* is a majestic plural. Perhaps the plural form *haAsheroth* should be translated as "groves" (*KJV, LXE* Jdg 03: 07) or "shrines" (*YLT* Jdg 03:07). If "the *Baals*" are understood to mean the male population of the pantheon, than "the *Asherahs*" may stand for the goddesses of the pantheon.

The plural *Asherahs* may also stand for *Baal*'s three goddess consorts who, according to certain Ugaritic myths, were jealous rivals: *Ashtorah, Astarte*, and *Anath*. The jealous, love-hate relationship of *Baal* and *Ashtorah* was the explanation provided for the cold and hot seasons experienced each year in many Mediterranean regions.

Israel's Neighbors Knew No Majestic Plural Syntax

The following examples show that in Palestine collective nouns, but not majestic plurals, were used to refer to gods and even to *Yahveh*.

Abraham and the Three Men
Three heavenly men came to visit Abraham. These men did not pose as Israelites since Israel did not exist at the time. Abraham must have assumed at first that they were Arameans, perhaps from Haran. Abraham addressed the three men as "my Lords" (*Adonai*). The plural form *Adonai* literally means "my Lords," but modern translations read "Lord."

That "they answered Abraham" (Gen 18:05) shows that the Father was Lord, the Son was Lord, and the Spirit was Lord, as the Athanasian Creed teaches. Abraham said, "If now I have found favor in your [singular] sight..." (Gen 18:03). That Abraham used a singular "sight" shows that Abraham meant "Lords" as a plural collective noun.

If the three visitors had understood *Adonai* as a majestic plural, then they would have understood Abraham to say "majestic lord [singular]" rather than "lords [plural]." If the three men were familiar with majestic plurals, they would have thought that Abraham had addressed only one majestic lord of the three.

That all three visitors replied (Gen 18:05) shows that the three visitors thought Abraham had addressed them collectively as a group of lords. This shows that the

majestic plural was not known in the Near East (Palestine or Mesopotamia). Since
the three visitors were from heaven, evidently the majestic plural was unknown
even in heaven during Abraham's day.

Lot and the Two Men
Similar to the situation with Abraham and the three visitors (Gen 18), Lot addressed the two visitors as "my Lords" (*Adonai*). They both answered (Gen 19:
02). If the two visitors were familiar with the majestic plural, they would have
thought Lot addressed only one majestic lord, but not both. That the Son and Spirit
answered Lot suggests that the two visitors knew of no majestic plural syntax (Gen
19:02).

Abraham and Abimelech the Philistine Ruler
The Philistines called Dagon *elohim* (gods) (Jdg 16:23-24; 1Sa 05:07). The
Philistines also used singular verbs with the plural form *elohim* (Jdg 16:23-24).
The plural *elohim* used with a singular verb indicates that when the Philistines re-
ferred to Dagon as "gods," they used *elohim* as a plural collective noun.
The Philistines could have used the plural collective noun *elohim* to refer to
both Dagon and his goddess consort(s).[53] The plural form *elohim* may have been
used to indicate that Dagon was a pluriform god. Dagon may have been pluriform
meaning that Dagon had a:
- Dual nature, since Dagon was supposedly part fish and part man, or an
- Androgynous nature. Dagon would have been like *Astarte, who* originally was
  thought to be androgynous.[54]
Abraham told Abimelech:
   Gods [*Elohim*], they caused [plural verb] me to wander...(Gen 20:13).
Abimelech must have understood Abraham to be using a plural collective noun
with a plural verb to speak of persons comprising one god. If Abimelech had not
been familiar with plural collective nouns, then Abimelech would have assumed
Abraham was using quantitative plurals. If Abimelech only knew of quantitative
plurals, than Abimelech would have understood Abraham to be speaking as a polytheist—as though Abraham had several gods.
Abraham could speak to Abimelech using plurals nouns and verbs referring to
the persons of *Yahveh*. Other pagans, however, would have understood such talk to
be polytheistic. The difference between Abimelech and other pagans is that "[All]
the Gods [*haElohim*]" (the Trinity) had appeared to Abimelech (Gen 20:06).
Because Abimelech had seen the three persons known as *Yahveh*, Abimelech
knew that Abraham was speaking as a Trinitarian rather than as a polytheist. Later
in the account, Abraham prayed to "[All] the Gods [*haElohim*]" (the Trinity) to
heal Abimelech (Gen 20:17).
The Philistines came to know the Trinity from ancient Yahvists who were
Abraham's contemporaries, Yahvists such as Melchizedek (Gen 14:18-20).
Yahvists subsequently kept the Philistines informed of *Yahveh*—Yahvists such as

Jacob (Gen 26:28), Balaam (Num 22−24) and the Israelites during the Exodus (Exo 13:17; Num 14:14; Deu 32:31; Jos 05:01).

During the time of the Judges, the Philistines seem to have known that *Yahveh* was the Trinity. The Philistines used singular verbs to refer to Dagon (Jdg 16: 23), but sometimes spoke of *Yahveh* using plural nouns and plural verbs. The Philistines said:

> Gods [plural noun] have come [singular verb]...Who can deliver us from the hand [singular noun] of the mighty [plural adjective] Gods [plural noun]? They [plural pronoun] are the same [plural pronoun] Gods [plural noun] who struck [plural verb] the Egyptians with all kinds of plagues (1Sa 04:07-08).

Jacob and His Family

Since Laban of Haran was considered an Aramean (Gen 28:05; 31:20; 31:24), and Jacob was considered a "wandering Aramean" (Deu 26:05), one could say that Jacob's family was as much Aramean as Israelite (Gen 32:28; 35:10). The language of Arameans was Aramaic or a sister language. As was discussed before, the Aramaic language apparently did not use majestic plurals.

Jacob told his family to bury all their foreign gods (Gen 35:02). It is interesting that just after Jacob and his clan made a clean break with polytheism, the narrator used a plural noun and verb to refer to *Yahveh*: "Gods [*Elohim*], they had revealed [plural verb] himself to him" (Gen 35:07). If the narrator were not Trinitarian, it would have made better sense to use singulars in this situation.

Sennacherib's Officials

Sennacherib's officers asked in Hebrew (2Ki 18:28):

> How can your *Elohim* [Gods] deliver [singular verb] you out of mine hand (2Ch 32:14)?...How much less shall your *Elohim* [plural noun] deliver [plural verb] you out of my hand (2Ch 32:15)!

The Chronicler wrote, "Sennacherib's officers spoke further against *Yahveh Elohim*" (2Ch 32:16). The Chronicler also wrote:

> They spoke about the *Elohim* of Jerusalem as they did about the *Elohim* of the other peoples of the world (2Ch 32:19).

The officers referred to *Yahveh* using the plural form *Elohim* with both singular and plural verbs. Since the other nations did not use a majestic plural syntax, and since the officers spoke of *Yahveh* as they did of other gods, Sennacherib's officials must not have used majestic plurals to refer to *Yahveh*.

Another indication that majestic plurals were not used is that the officer was waging psychological warfare. He would want to diminish the glory of *Yahveh* (2Ch 32:15). All this suggests that Sennacherib's officers knew of no majestic plural syntax, but they did know there were persons called *Yahveh*—the Trinity.

David's Psalm

David complained about foreign rulers, and prayed that God would judge the earth so the nations would say:

Most assuredly, Gods [plural noun], they judge [plural participle] the earth (Psa 058:11).

Surely, the gentiles did not use majestic plurals, so David's phrase would sound awfully polytheistic on gentile lips. The plurals suggest that David hoped the gentiles would one day come to know the Trinity *en masse*.

Indeclinable Nouns as Collective Nouns

As was mentioned at the start of this chapter, Hebrew speakers sometimes paired singular collective nouns with plural predicates. One example is that the seemingly singular form *Yahveh* is sometimes paired with plural verbs, plural modifiers, and plural nouns such as *Elohim* (Gods). Apparently, *Yahveh* is an indeclinable noun.

Indeclinable nouns are not all that uncommon, perhaps in any language. English has indeclinable nouns (sometimes called "invariant nouns") where the singular and plural forms are identical. The pluralized form of any of these nouns seems forced and unnatural, for instance, "progenies." Examples include:

aircraft, apparatus, bison, darkness, deer, fish, grouse, hardware, hiatus, homework, information, logistics, might, offspring, progeny, prospectus, scissors, series, sheep, silverware, software, species, status, thunder and wool.

Hebrew also has indeclinable nouns such as *owph* ("bird" or "birds"). For example, in Job 12:07, *owph* should be translated "birds" rather than "bird," since in the preceding parallel construction in Job 12:07, the noun "animals" is plural, yet takes a singular verb.

Hebrew singulars may be used to denote singular persons or things, or a collection of persons or things, even when there is a perfectly valid plural form that could have been employed. For instance:

- *adam* can mean Adam (Gen 05:01), both Adam and Eve together (Gen 01:26-28), a man, or humanity,
- *eytz* can mean a tree, grove or forest, or a stick or sticks (Eze 37:17 is discussed later in the chapter). Note that the plural *eytsim* is also used,
- *bahemah* can mean an ox or cattle (Gen 01:24),
- *dimah* can mean a tear or tears (Psa 006:07; 042:04). The plural form of *dimah* is found once in the OT (Lam 02:11),
- *goy* can mean a gentile or a nation (Gen 18:18). The plural form *goyim* is also used,
- *yahd* can mean a hand or hands (Gen 19:10, 16). The Hebrew singular "hand" (Psa 031:05; *BHS* Psa 031:06) is translated into the Greek as "hands" (LXX Psa 031:06; Luk 23:46), and
- *zerah* can mean a seed or seeds (compare Gal 03:16).

The context and the subject-verb agreement indicate whether indeclinable nouns are to be understood as singulars or as collective nouns. Sometimes singular nouns are used, seemingly to emphasize that persons or things are a collective entity. For instance:

- The people [singular noun] journeyed [plural verb] from Hazeroth (Num 12: 16),
- The Amalekite [in other words, "the Amalekites"] and Canaanite [in other words, "the Canaanites"] that lived on that mountain came [singular verb] down (Num 14:45), and
- Let Israel [singular noun] rejoice [singular verb] in his Makers [plural noun], let the people [plural noun] of Zion be glad [plural verb] in their King (Psa 149:02).

Case Studies on Hebrew Collective Nouns

Yahveh as an Indeclinable Collective Noun
Most OT translations never mention the Hebrew word *Yahveh*, though some mention the pseudonym Jehovah. To indicate that *Yahveh* is the underlying Hebrew word, translators capitalize the entire word as "LORD" or as "GOD."

Yahveh occurs 6,828 times in 5,790 OT verses. Though *Yahveh* occurs so often, *Yahveh* is not declined once,[55] even when paired with plural verbs and modifiers (as is noted in the MT plurals appendix). *Yahveh* is not declined even when used as a possessive Hebrew "construct." In English translations, however, the possessive *Yahveh* is translated as LORD's.

That *Yahveh* is an indeclinable noun is made conspicuous by:
- The sheer number of occurrences of the Name, *Yahveh*, in the OT, and
- The fact that Hebrew is an inflected language.

How did *Yahveh* become an indeclinable noun? Eve knew the Father by the Name, *Yahveh* (Gen 04:01). People spoke or heard the Name, *Yahveh*, in 52 Genesis verses.[56] That Moses knew of the Name, *Yahveh*, is evidenced by the fact that the shortened form of *Yahveh* (*Ya*) is embedded in the names of persons born before the events of Exo 03 and 06, for instance:
- Jochebed (meaning, "*Yahveh* is glory") was the mother of Moses, Aaron and Miriam (Exo 06:20; Num 26:59), and
- Joshua (meaning, "*Yahveh* saves") was born before the Exodus from Egypt (Num 32:11-12), and was a leader as early as Exo 17:09.

The Name, *Yahveh*, was likely derived from a form (*Qal* imperfect, 1st person singular) of the verb "I am" that was current at the Creation (Gen 02:04b; 04:26). The Name, *Yahveh*, ossified while the conjugation for "I am" gradually changed. This is not unlike how many archaic forms come into existence. A certain form ossifies while the rest of the conjugation or declension morphs around it, or the form fossilizes while the rest of the conjugation or declension becomes extinct.

Language students know that entire languages flux over time. Heavily used conjugations like the "I am" conjugation often acquire so many irregular forms that separate conjugation tables are necessitated. The breakdown of irregular conjugations sometimes defies explanation, so rote memorization is necessitated.

The above was a general explanation of the Name, *Yahveh*, however, here is a more detailed analysis. At the burning bush, the Son told Moses that his name was *Yahveh* (Exo 03:15-16, 18).[57] The Son pointed out that the Name, *Yahveh*, had been derived from *ehyeh*. *Ehyeh* is the *Qal* imperfect first person form of the verb "I am." The *BHS* Hebrew of Exo 03:14 has the form *ehyeh* three times:

> God said to Moses, 'I AM [*ehyeh*] who I AM [*ehyeh*].' And he said, 'Say this to the people of Israel, 'I AM [*ehyeh*] has sent me to you" (Exo 03:14).

The grammatical and etymological specifics on the form *Yahveh* are disputed, but the meaning, "I AM," is what is most important. In NT times, for instance, the Son pointed out to Septuagint (LXX) readers that he was the "I AM" ("*egw eimi*"). This is the same Greek phrase used to translate the Hebrew for "I AM" phrases in LXX Exo 03:14 and elsewhere.

The form *Yahveh* is not a form in any conjugation table, and there is no consensus on the exact etymology of *Yahveh*. These facts give the author license to propose an explanation. In the Garden of Eden, the Father said his name was "I AM." This existential-sounding name was told Adam and Eve (Gen 04: 01,26). Revealing this name was appropriate since Adam and Eve surely were thinking cosmological and existential thoughts.

In the proto-Hebrew that Adam and Eve spoke, the *Qal* imperfect of the verb "I am" likely was *yahveh*. There was the danger that Adam and Eve might think the Name, *Yahveh*, was just a homonym of the "I am" verb form *yahveh*. So the Father likely indicated this name actually meant, "I AM."

Moses met the Son at Mount Sinai many centuries after the Creation. Moses knew that the Father's name was *Yahveh*, but did not know the *Malek Yahveh*'s name. The Son said his name was *Yahveh*, too. The Son referred to the Hebrew verb form *ehyeh* ("I am") to explain the name *Yahveh*'s meaning of "I AM." Of course, the forms *ehyeh* and *Yahveh* no longer were identical because the ancient proto-Hebrew form *yahveh* had softened to *ehyeh* in Hebrew.

The process of softening hard words occurred with greater frequency before the advent of dictionaries. Dictionaries have the affect of standardizing spelling and pronunciation. For instance, the harder sounding "annoy" and softer sounding "ennui" are derived from the same French word. The reason for the different pronunciation is that "annoy" was borrowed in the 1275 AD from Old French, while "ennui" was borrowed in 1732 AD from Middle French. This example of a word softening occurred before dictionaries became ubiquitous in Europe.

Etymological studies show that soft letters go silent, especially soft letters that begin words. Deep, harsh gutturals have all but disappeared from most languages, and hard phonemes tend to soften. This would explain why in Moses' day the Name, *Yahveh*, no longer matched the *Qal* imperfect first person of the verb "I am" (*ehyeh*). Apparently, the initial soft sounding "y" of *Yahveh* had dropped, and the hard "v" sound had changed to the soft "y" sound, leaving the form *ehyeh*.

Factors that led to the ossification of the Name, *Yahveh*, include:

- Respect for the divine name, and
- There was no need for a plural form of *Yahveh* from the time of Eve until the time of Moses. Only on Mount Sinai did Moses find out that the Son as well as the Father was named *Yahveh*.

This book's chapter on Proto-Sinaitic Trinitarianism explains that the patriarchs knew only the Father as *Yahveh*. Of course, the post-Sinaitic narrator of Genesis knew that the Father, Son and Spirit were all named *Yahveh*, but the patriarchs did not know the Spirit as *Yahveh*. The patriarchs knew the Son only as *El Shaddai* and as the *Malek Yahveh* (the Angel of *Yahveh*).

After meeting *Yahveh* on Mount Sinai, Moses continued to use the form *Yahveh* as an indeclinable noun. Moses did not update the Name, *Yahveh*, to *ehyeh* since Moses knew that the underlying meaning was what was really important. Moreover, the ancient Name, *Yahveh*, surely was dear to many Near East Yahvists.

Moses did not also contrive a plural for *Yahveh*. Moses knew that *Yahveh* could be understood as a singular or as a collective noun, thereby obviating the need for a plural. Furthermore, to say that there were three *Yahveh*s might lead to polytheistic notions about *Yahveh*, but God is one (Deu 06:04).

Using the context as a guide, Hebrew speakers used other indeclinable nouns without confusion, for instance, *owph* ("bird" or "birds"). Hebrew speakers could differentiate when *Yahveh* was used as a singular to refer to one person, or as a collective noun to refer to the Trinity. That is, of course, as long as there were no ingrained, preconceived notions to obfuscate matters.

The fact that *Yahveh* is an indeclinable noun has never been the real problem. From Intertestamental times to the present, however, the failure or refusal to recognize that *Yahveh* is an indeclinable noun has led many down the rocky road from Trinitarianism to unitarianism. Many exegetes have failed to see that *Yahveh* can be used as a singular or as a collective noun even though *Yahveh* is associated with:

- Singular as well as plural verbs, pronouns and modifiers (as is noted in the MT plurals appendix),
- The plural form *haElohim*, meaning, "[All] the Gods."[58] *HaElohim*, of course, was discussed previously in this chapter, and
- Most of the 2,600 instances of the plural form *Elohim* (literally, "Gods") found in 2,247 verses.

Translators always treat *Yahveh* and *Elohim* as singulars, but never as collective nouns referring to *Yahveh*. The upshot of this practice is that readers of translations mistakenly assume that thousands of occurrences of *Yahveh* and God are *prima facie* evidence that God is a single person. Most translation readers would be surprised to learn that plural forms for God such as *Elohim* vastly outnumber singular forms such as *El* and *Elo(w)ah*.

That translations never treat *Yahveh* and *Elohim* as collective nouns is especially insidious when coupled with Maimonides' non-biblical *yachid* version of the *Shema*. The *yachid* version says *Yahveh* is "a unique one" while the Biblical *echad* version says *Yahveh* is "a united one."

While the majestic plural may have been introduced to combat polytheistic notions prevalent during Intertestamental times, Maimonides' non-biblical *yachid* version of the *Shema* was introduced to combat Trinitarianism. Maimonides (1138–1204) lived in southern Spain during the Islamic occupation where no polytheism existed. Thus, Maimonides' *Shema*, along the majestic plural usage and other arguments, are taught to ensure that students read the Trinitarian Bible as though it were a unitarian book.

The Bible in the original languages contains overwhelming evidence of the Trinity, and translations would too if the Hebrew and Aramaic plural collective nouns, plural verbs and plural modifiers were translated as plurals. This would constitute overwhelming evidence that *Yahveh* is the Trinity. However, due to the policy of translating nearly all plurals referring to *Yahveh* as singulars, many Trinitarian proofs are lost in translation. Trinitarians are left talking about how the OT "hints" of the Trinity. This, of course, underwhelms opponents and skeptics. As translations now read:

- Proving monotheism to be biblical is an overly easy, downhill battle against would-be polytheists, but
- Proving Trinitarianism to be biblical is an unnecessarily hard, uphill battle against would-be unitarians.

Echad and Echadim Used as Collective Nouns

Studying the use of *echad(im)* ("united one(s)") is informative for the study of other collective nouns such *Yahveh, El* and *Elohim*. Furthermore, the words *Yahveh, Elohim* and *echad* all happen to be found in the *Shema* (Deu 06:04):

Hear, O Israel: *Yahveh* [the Father] [and] our *Elohim* [the Son], *Yahveh* [the Spirit] [are] a united one [*echad*] (Deu 06:04).

Yahveh, Elohim and *echad*'s use as collective nouns indicates that the *Shema* speaks of *Yahveh* as being persons who are "a united one" (*echad*). For instance, the narrator of Judges uses *echad* as a collective noun to refer to persons:

All the men of Israel were gathered [singular verb] to the city as one [*echad*] man [singular noun], companions (Jdg 20:11).[59]

Note that plural "companions" are called "one [*echad*] man," and a singular verb is used. There are many more passages where *echad* is used similarly, for instance:

- Evening and morning were one day (Gen 01:05),
- Man and woman become one flesh (Gen 02:24; Mal 02:15; compare 1Co 06:16),
- Assemblies, soldiers and nations were considered one (Gen 11:06; Num 14:15; Jos 09:02; 10:42; Jdg 06:16; 20:01, 08, 11; 2Sa 02:25; 07:23; 19:14; Ezr 02:64; 03:01; Neh 08:01),
- Two groups planning to intermarry would have been one people (Gen 34:16),
- The two dreams that the pharaoh dreamt (Gen 41:32) had one interpretation (Gen 41:25-26),
- The people answered with one voice (Exo 24:03),
- Curtains were strung together so the tabernacle became one (Exo 26:06, 11; 36:13),
- A quantity of grapes was considered one cluster though the cluster was so large that two men had to carry it on a pole (Num 13:23), and
- Trumpeters and singers made one voice (2Ch 05:13).

Two OT verses have the singular form *echad* and the plural form *echadim* in the same verse. The narrator, Moses, wrote:

The whole earth had one [*echad*] language of a few [*echadim*] dialects [literally, "words"] (Gen 11:01).

The plural form *echadim* can mean "one" (Eze 37:17), but *echadim* likely should be translated as "a few" when modifying plural nouns.[60] For example, *echadim* paired with the plural word "days" should be translated as "a few days" (Gen 27:44; 29:20; Dan 11:20).[61]

The plural form *echadim* ("united ones") is meant to emphasize—even more than the singular form *echad* ("a united one"), that a whole is comprised of parts. In other words, several days equals a few (*echadim*) days, a few (*echadim*) dialects comprise a language, and the like. The author labels this use of the plural a plural of distribution—a type of plural collective noun. A plural of distribution is meant to show that a whole is distributed over parts.

The other instance of *echad* and *echadim* being used in the same verse occurs when *Yahveh* told Ezekiel:

Join them one to the other, so that to you the stick will be one, and they will become a united one in your hand (Eze 37:17).

Eze 37:17 differentiates three uses of *echad* ("a united one") and *echadim* ("united ones"):

Join them [two sticks] one [*echad* (singular noun)] to the other [*echad* (singular noun)], so that to you the stick [*eytz* (collective noun)] will be one [*echad* (collective noun)], and they will become a united one [*echadim* (plural of distribution)] in your hand (Eze 37:17).

Here is a more detailed look at the three uses of *echad* and *echadim* found in Eze 37:17:

1. Ezekiel used *echad* as a regular singular form to refer to the individual sticks before they were assembled. Ezekiel called the parts "one" (*echad*) and the "other" (*echad*),
2. Ezekiel used the singular form *echad* ("a united one") as a collective noun to underscore the aspect of union. Similarly, another prophet, Zechariah, called his shepherd's staff "Union" (*echad*) to emphasize the union of brotherhood between Judah and Israel (Zec 11:07, 14). Zechariah then broke the stick into two to stress how there once had been a union (Zec 11:14), and
3. Ezekiel used the plural *echadim* ("united ones") to call attention to how the stick was assembled from component parts called:
- "Them" and "they," as well as
- "One (*echad*) and the other (*echad*)."

So in Eze 37:17 *echadim* is a plural of distribution—a type of plural collective noun.

In Eze 37:17, *echad* is paired with the singular form *eytz* meaning, "stick":

Join them one [*echad* (singular noun)] to the other [*echad* (singular noun)], so that to you the stick [*eytz* (collective noun)] will be one [*echad* (collective noun)].

Note that two united sticks were considered one (*echad*) stick (Eze 37:17). The singular form *eytz* (Gen 02:17) is used often as a collective noun meaning, "sticks" and "trees" (Gen 01:11), though the plural form *eytsim* (trees) is used often elsewhere (Lev 01:07).

Eytz in Eze 37:17 and *Yahveh* in the *Shema* (Deu 06:04) are comparable in that they are both paired with the word *echad*. *Yahveh*, as we have seen, can be a collective noun just as *eytz* is commonly used as a collective noun. So just as Eze 37:17 says that sticks (*eytz*) are a united one (*echad*), the *Shema* could very well indicate that *Yahveh* are persons who are a united one (*echad*).

Echadim is Not a Plural of Intensity

Some majestic plural proponents might venture that *echadim* is a plural of intensity, a variation on the so-called majestic plural rationalization. They would say a plural of intensity is like a majestic plural in that the plural form fails to indicate any sort of plurality. The plural supposedly gives a superlative meaning to the singular—like "highest" rather than just "high."

Majestic plural proponents think that the existence of the plural of intensity tends to prove the existence of the plural of majesty, since both usages are similar. Moreover, proving that both grammatical constructions exist would buttress the unitarian interpretation of the OT.

If *echadim* (literally, "ones") were translated as a plural of intensity, the superlative meaning would be "very one" or "absolute one" or "alone." If, however, *echadim* is a type of plural collective noun, than *echadim* would mean "a few." Notice that the different definitions the plural of intensity and the collective noun produce are nearly antonyms: "absolutely one" versus "a few."

We've already seen that *echadim* is usually translated "a few" (Gen 11:01; 27:44; 29:20; Dan 11:20). Moreover, the "alone" (*yachid*) interpretation of the *Shema* is not helped by an "alone" translation of *echadim*. The reason is that the *Shema* has the singular form *echad* and not the plural form *echadim*. So it would seem that *echadim* is a plural collective noun ("united one") rather than a plural of intensity (uniquely one).

There are other examples of the supposed plural of intensity. For instance, it is said that the singular form *olam* means "old," so the plural form *olamim* in Ecc 01:10 must mean "ancient." This definition might be correct, however, the proponents for the plural of intensity arrived at the correct definition through the wrong methodology. After all, a broken clock is still accurate twice each day!

The English equivalent of what the Hebrew author had in mind by the plural *olamim* perhaps was not so much "oldest" or "ancient," but rather "old, old, old." The plural form *olamim*, therefore, stood for multiple uses of the singular *olam*. This is similar to how:

- The plural *echadim* ("united ones") stood for two uses of the singular in Eze 37:17: *echad* (one) and *echad* (the other). *Echad* and *echadim* were discussed above.

- *Elohim* ("Gods") may be a plural standing for "God, God, God" (*El, El, El*) —
three persons who are one God, or in other words, the Trinity.

Perhaps consideration of Hebrew dual forms would be instructive. Whether
dual forms are translated as singulars or plurals is dependent on the context. Either
way, dual forms are not translated as plurals of intensity. However, even when dual
forms are translated as singulars, there is some sense of plurality:

- "Heaven(s)" (*shamayim*) refers to the several "spheres." The clouds were
known to be closer since they covered the moon. Occultation and the varying
swiftness of the heavenly bodies suggested that certain regions were farther than
others,
- "Face(s)" (*panim*) may refer to how the face has bilateral symmetry: two ears,
two eyes, two nostrils, and so forth, and
- "Water(s)" (*mayim*) may refer to how many dewdrops form a droplet, how
many drops form a unit of water, and how a unit of water can form rivulets
(Gen 02:10).

Majestic plural proponents offer more examples in their attempt to prove plurals
of intensity exist. These examples, however, indicate plurality rather than intensity.
The plural form may be used to indicate repeated behavior, or abstractness.

Abstract ideas are plural in the sense that they are abstracted from the study of
many examples or lessons, and then the abstract idea is in turn applied to many situations or dimensions. Here are some examples supposed to be plurals of intensity
that perhaps are better interpreted in a plural sense:

- "Wisdoms" does not necessarily mean "great wisdom," but merely that a person
is wise about a number of subjects (Psa 049:04),
- "Darknesses" does not necessarily mean "great darkness," but rather "dark
places" (*KJV, YLT* Lam 03:06). Another interpretation is that a deep shadow is
usually comprised of both a partial (penumbra) and full (umbra) shadow,
- "Compassions" does not necessarily mean one has "great compassion," but
merely indicates many acts of compassion (Lam 03:22),
- "Harlotries" does not necessarily mean "great harlotries," but merely that many
acts of fornication is tantamount to harlotry (Hos 01:02),
- "Bitternesses" does not necessarily mean "great bitterness," but merely indicates that there are multiple bitter situations (Hos 12:14 (*BHS* 12:15), and
- "Bloods" does not mean "very bloody," but merely indicates multiple stab
wounds (Exo 22:02-03; Hos 04:02).

Summary Findings on Echadim

Moses showed that things called *echad* ("a united one") could be comprised of
echadim ("united ones"), for example:

- One (*echad*) language could be comprised of "a few" (*echadim*) dialects (Gen
11:01), and
- One (*echadim*) period of time is "a few" days (Gen 27:44; 29:20; see also Dan
11:20).

The writer of Judges wrote that people can be considered in a singular or plural sense—both *echad* ("a united one") and "companions" (Jdg 20:11). Ezekiel referred to an unassembled part (a stick) as *echad* (one). Ezekiel showed that the assembled parts (two sticks put end to end) could be referred to both as *echad* ("a united one") and *echadim* ("united ones").

That Moses and Ezekiel used both the singular (*echad*) and plural (*echadim*) as collective nouns to describe the same things is no wonder. *Echad* comes from a Hebrew root that means "to unify" or "to collect together." So *echad* was used to emphasize unity, while *echadim* highlighted the individual parts of the collection.

The Hebrew use of singular and plural collective nouns is similar to the collective noun usage in many languages. A singular collective noun and predicate emphasize the collection as a whole, while a plural collective noun and plural predicate emphasize the components of the collection. Then, of course, there is the hybrid version where a singular collective noun is paired with a plural predicate, or a plural collective noun is paired with a singular predicate.

Zechariah called his shepherd's staff "Union" (*echad*) to indicate the brotherhood between Judah and Israel (Zec 11:07, 14). The *echad* surely did not emphasize any assembly of Zechariah's stick since the stick was still in one piece until Zechariah broke it in two (Zec 11:14).

Because *echad* and *echadim* can both serve as collective nouns, the *echad* that ends the *Shema* could be a collective noun. We've already seen that *Yahveh* can be a collective noun, and *Elohim*, of course, is a plural form. So grammatically speaking, the *Shema* is decidedly Trinitarian:

> Hear, O Israel: *Yahveh* [the Father] [and] our *Elohim* [the Son], *Yahveh* [the Spirit] [are] a united one [*echad*] (Deu 06:04).

The Plural of Distribution In Languages Other Than Hebrew

The Arameans apparently used plural collective nouns as plurals of distribution just as the Hebrews did. In Dan 05:25 the handwriting on the wall included the Aramaic plural word *parsin* (divided). When Daniel spoke of the writing on the wall, however, he used the singular form of *parsin* (*pares*) (Dan 05:28). This seems to indicate that Daniel considered Belshazzar's kingdom to be a whole composed of parts. Two reasons for this might be:

- The Babylonian kingdom was already split administratively. Belshazzar was the coregent who ruled from Babylon, while the coregent Nabonidus ruled from the north Arabian oasis city of Tema, and
- That very night Belshazzar's kingdom was about to be divided between the Medes and Persians (Dan 05:28), yet the divided kingdom was ruled by one top leader (Dan 05:30).

Repetition of *Elohim* as the Subject of a Singular Verb Indicates *Elohim* is Persons

Sometimes *Elohim* is repeated as the subject of a singular verb. Sometimes a few different names for God, such as *Yahveh, Elohim, haElohim* and *Shaddai*, are given as the collective subject of a singular verb. Jacob provides content for the study of seemingly redundant subjects. Jacob used multiple names for God as the subject of the same singular verb on at least five occasions (Gen 28:20-22, 31:42, 32:09, 48:15-16; 49:24-25). The narrator of Genesis wrote:

> He [Jacob]...said, '[All] the Gods (*haElohim*)...[All] the Gods (*haElohim*)...the *Malek*...bless [singular verb] the lads [two of Joseph's sons]' (Gen 48:15-16).

Here Jacob used two instances of "[All] the Gods" (*haElohim*) and the *Malek* as subjects of the same singular verb "to bless." This shows that Jacob knew the *Malek* to be one of "[All] the Gods" (*haElohim*). Otherwise, if Jacob had not considered the *Malek* to be God, Jacob would have used a plural verb to say that both God and an angel, "...they bless."[62]

That the *Malek Yahveh* is one of *haElohim* ("[All] the Gods") is verified by the fact that Jacob elsewhere used a plural verb with *haElohim* ("[All] the Gods"). Jacob said, "Gods [*Elohim*], they had revealed [plural verb] himself to him" at Bethel in Gen 28 (Gen 35:07). Note that Jacob spoke of God as "they" (Gen 35:07) right after the Father spoke of the Son in the third person:

> Then God [the Father] said to Jacob, 'Go up to Bethel and settle there, and build an altar there to God [the Son], who appeared to you when you were fleeing from your brother Esau' (Gen 35:01).

The *Malek* of [All] the Gods (*haElohim*) (Gen 31:11) said that he was God (*El*) who appeared to Jacob at Bethel (Gen 31:13). So Gen 31:11, 13 show that the *Malek Yahveh* was one of the *Elohim* who appeared at Bethel in Gen 28 (Gen 35:07).

That the *Malek* mentioned in Gen 48:16 is one of [All] the Gods (*haElohim*) can also be ascertained from Moses' words:

> ...and with the best gifts of the earth and its fullness, and the favor of him [the *Malek Yahveh*] who dwelt in the burning bush [Exo 03:02]. Let all these rest on the head of Joseph [Joseph's sons' descendants], on the brow of the prince among his brothers (Deu 33:16).

In Deu 33:16 Moses connected Jacob's blessing and the burning bush accounts where the *Malek* is mentioned each time:

- Jacob's blessing asked that God and the *Malek* bless Ephraim and Manasseh's descendants (Gen 48:15-16), and
- The *Malek Yahveh* was at the burning bush (Exo 03:02; Act 07:30, 35). Note that the narrator of Exodus places the *Malek Yahveh* (Exo 03:02) right in the same bush as God and *Yahveh* (Exo 03:04), meaning that the *Malek Yahveh* was *Yahveh* the Son.

There is plenty of proof that the *Malek Yahveh* was one of *haElohim* ("[All] the Gods") mentioned in the account of the burning bush (Exo 03:01, 06, 11, 12, 13). The *Malek Yahveh* (Exo 03:02) said:

'I am the *Elohim* of your father—the *Elohim* of Abraham, the *Elohim* of Isaac and the *Elohim* of Jacob.' At this, Moses hid his face, because he was afraid to look at '[All] the Gods' (*haElohim*) (Exo 03:06).

That the *Malek Yahveh* was one of *haElohim* ("[All] the Gods") can also be inferred from how, in connection with the burning bush account, the *Malek Yahveh* is called:

* *Yahveh* (Exo 03:04, 07, 15, 16, 18 (twice)), and
* God (Exo 03:04, 05, 06 (five times), 11, 12 (twice), 13 (twice), 14, 15 (five times), 16 (twice), 18 (twice)).

Another passage similar to Gen 48:15-16 is Gen 31:42 where Jacob used a singular verb with the collective subjects: God, God, and the Fear of Isaac. The parallel structure between Gen 48:15-16 (*haElohim, haElohim, Malek*) and Gen 31:42 (*Elohim, Elohim*, Fear) suggests that "the Fear" is the *Malek*.

That Jacob considered the *Malek* to be God (Gen 31:42) and one of "[All] the Gods" (*haElohim*) (Gen 48:15-16) is consistent with how elsewhere:

* The *Malek Yahveh* referred to himself as *Elohim* (Gen 31:11, 13; Exo 03:02, 06), and
* The *Malek Yahveh* was called *Elohim* often (Gen 16; 21−22; 31−32; Exo 03; 14; 23; Num 22−24; Jdg 02; Jdg 06; 13; 1Ki 19; 2Ki 19; and Zec 02−03).

The Plural of Delegation—a Plural Collective Noun Variant

The proofs usually offered for the majestic plural construction are OT texts where a creature is called *elohim* (gods) and *adonai* (masters). Majestic plural proponents create a false dilemma by saying that the speaker must have used the plural to indicate the person is majestic. They say, "Surely the plural form cannot mean a single person is plural persons!"

Passages referring to a single person using a plural are offered as proof that plurals referring to *Yahveh* are mere majestic plurals. The case for majestic plurals unravels, however, when other grammatical possibilities are explored. The plural in question may have been intended as a quantitative plural, a plural collective noun, a plural of delegation, a plural of distribution, or another type of plural.

The plural of delegation by itself explains most of the examples offered as majestic plural proofs. For instance, a servant would normally refer to his master using the singular *adonee*, meaning, "my master." Sometimes, however, the servant would refer to his master using the plural *adonai*, meaning, "my masters." The servant used the plural form to acknowledge that a master had delegated managerial responsibilities to:

* Another master,
* A slave driver, or even to
* The servant himself.

So plurals were sometimes meant to acknowledge the multitier command structure.

Discussion of Majestic Plural Proof Texts

The study of majestic plural proof texts shows that supposed majestic plurals are really plurals of delegation, or another construction that expresses plurality.

Masters as Adonai[63]

The Genesis narrator said that Abraham was masters (*adonai*) to his servant Eliezer (Gen 24:09-10). Laban also said that Abraham was masters (*adonai*) to Eliezer (Gen 24:51). Plurals of delegation are applied to Abraham because he had delegated authority to his servant Eliezer (Gen 24:02). Abraham also had delegated authority to Isaac, whom Eliezer considered his master (*adonee*) (Gen 24:65).

Eliezer referred to Isaac using the singular *adonee* ("my master") rather than using a plural of delegation (*adonai*). This was likely because Isaac had not yet delegated authority to any person whom Eliezer recognized as an equal or superior.

Potiphar is called *adonai* (masters) (Gen 39:02, 03, 07, 08, 16, 19, 20) because Potiphar had delegated much authority to Joseph (Gen 39:04-06, 08-09, 11).

Joseph's warden is called *adonai* (masters) (Gen 39:20; 40:07) because he had delegated authority to Joseph (Gen 39:21-23).

Joseph was called Egypt's *adonai* (masters) (Gen 42:30, 33), and Joseph was *adonai* (masters) to his servants (Gen 44:08). Joseph was called *adonai* because Pharaoh had delegated authority to Joseph (Gen 41:40, 44, 55; 44:08, 18; 45:08).

Those who were not Joseph's servants seemed to not have used plurals of delegation referring to Joseph. For instance, Jacob and Joseph's brothers referred to Joseph as *adon* (master) (Gen 45:08-09) and as *adonee* (my master) (Gen 44:16, 18 (twice), 19). Another example is the Egyptian populace calling Joseph *adonee* (my master) (Gen 47:18 (twice), 25).

Joseph was called *adonee* for the same reason that Eliezer referred to Isaac as *adonee* (Gen 24:65). Isaac was *adonee* to Eliezer since Isaac had not delegated authority to anyone that Eliezer recognized as an equal or superior. Joseph was *adonee* because Joseph had not delegated authority to any subordinate that Jacob, Joseph's brothers, or the Egyptian populace recognized as their superior.

That the Egyptians populace dealt directly with Joseph rather than his delegate can be inferred from:

- The detail of Joseph's commissioning (Gen 41:40-45).
- From the Egyptians' statement:

    You have saved our lives. May we find favor in the eyes of my lord (*adonee*) [Joseph]. Our land and we will be in bondage to Pharaoh (Gen 47:19, 25).

In Mosaic Law, a master was simply an *adonee* (master) (Exo 21:05). If, however, a servant had declined his chance to be a freeman in order to serve a master for life, then the master (*adonee*) became masters (*adonai*) (Exo 21:06).

The switch from *adonee* to *adonai* occurred because the master delegated authority. The servant may have become a manager or supervisor, or even an inheritor (Gen 15:02) and adopted son-in-law (Gen 29:18; 31:31; Exo 21:04-05).

An alternative explanation of the use of the plural (*adonai*) takes into account the ceremony that made the servant into a servant for life. The ceremony involved piercing the servant's ear with an awl before the elders (Exo 21:06). So the *adonai* (masters) may indicate that the servant was now beholden to the elders and his master who together were called "masters" (*adonai*).

David was called *adonai* (1Ki 01:11, 43) because he had delegated kingship to Solomon on oath. The agreed upon delegation of kingship went into effect when David ruled with Solomon. This co-regency began at the time Adonijah failed to usurp the throne and lasted until the time of David's death (1Ki 01:13, 30; 02:01; 1Ch 22:17).

Job said:

> Captives also enjoy their ease [in Sheol where the souls of the damned await Judgment Day]; they no longer hear the slave driver's shout. The small and the great are there, and the slave is freed from his masters [*adonai*]" (Job 03:18-19).

Here "masters" is plural because the servant's master had delegated authority to a slave driver. So the slave had two masters (*adonai*): the master and the slave driver.

Isaiah prophesied that an Assyrian king would rule Egypt (Isa 20:04). Elsewhere, this king is called "a cruel [singular] *adonim* [masters] and a fierce [singular] king [singular]" (Isa 19:04). The "king" was Esarhaddon who conquered Egypt in 670 BC. "Masters" (*adonim*) is a plural of delegation that refers to the king and his commanders. This is consistent with how an Assyrian king once boasted, "Are not my commanders all kings?" (1Ki 20:24; Isa 10:08).

Isaiah called a donkey's owner "masters" (Isa 01:03). One might wonder, "Why would a donkey's owner necessarily be majestic?" Majestic plural proponents provide no overriding reason why the plural form "masters" must be translated as a singular, especially considering how:
- The colt that *Yeshua* rode into Jerusalem had "owners" (Luk 19:33), and
- Eliezer had two masters, Abraham (*adonai*) (Gen 15:02) and Isaac (*adonee*) (Gen 24:12, 65).

The Trinitarian interpretation of Isa 01:03 is revealed when one considers how:
- Elsewhere *Yahveh* said they (meaning the Trinity) are "masters" (*Adonim*) (Mal 01:06), and that
- Isa 01:03 is a parallel construction.

The parallel construction shows that there are two ellipses in the train of thought. Isa 01:03 should be understood as:

> The ox knows its owner [*qanah* (masculine singular)], the donkey its masters' manger, but Israel does not know... [...its owner, in other words, God (Exo 06:07; 19:05-06)], my people do not perceive... [...its masters, in other words, the Trinity (Mal 01:06)] (Isa 01:03).

Moses and Aaron as Elohim

Yahveh said to Moses, "Behold, I have made you gods [*elohim*] to pharaoh…" (Exo 07:01a). The plural form *elohim* is a plural of delegation that denotes how Moses delegated authority to Aaron. Pharaoh obviously knew that Aaron was speaking on behalf of Moses. A plural of delegation is a collective noun variant, so one could say that pharaoh knew Moses and Aaron collectively as "gods."

The delegation of authority from Moses to Aaron can be seen when the whole verse is considered:

Behold, I have made you gods [*elohim*] to pharaoh, and your brother
Aaron will be your [Moses'] prophet (Exo 07:01b).

God had delegated authority to Moses (Exo 03:10; 04:12), and then from Moses to Aaron saying:

He [Aaron] will speak to the people for you [Moses], and it will be as
if he [Aaron] were your [Moses'] mouth, and as if you [Moses] were like
[*lamedh* preposition] God to him [Aaron] (Exo 04:16).

Angels and Judges as Elohim

As was just discussed, Moses and Aaron were called "gods" (*elohim*). Angels also were called "gods" (*elohim*) (Psa 097:07). Judges were also called:
- "gods" (*elohim*) (Psa 082:01, 06), and
- "[all] the gods" (*haelohim*) (Exo 21:06; 22:08-09 (*BHS* 22:07-08); Jos 24:01).

Humans and angels were only called *elohim* collectively. There is no occurrence in the OT of a mere angel or human working alone being called "god" (*el*) or "gods" (*elohim*). Thus, *elohim* should be considered a plural collective noun when referring to mere angels or humans.

God had delegated authority from himself to angels and humans to rule and to judge. This delegation explains the plural since the plural recognizes that two or more persons are, by definition, involved in any delegation of authority. God's delegation of authority also explains why the judges or angels were called "gods" (*elohim*). They were God's delegates who represented God.

The Golden Calf as Elohim

Some say that the golden calf that Aaron made (Exo 32:20, 24; Deu 09:21) was called "gods" (*elohim*), so this *elohim* must be a majestic plural. One might wonder, "Why would a calf image be so majestic?" Why the plural form *elohim* was used in connection with a lone calf is discussed under Exo 32 in the Trinitarian proofs appendix.

Samuel as Elohim

Saul asked a spiritist what she saw:

The woman answered Saul, 'I see *elohim* [gods] coming up [plural
participle] out of the earth' (1Sa 28:13).

Majestic plural proponents argue that because the necromancer referred to Samuel as *elohim* (gods), *elohim* must denote majesty rather than plurality.

Majestic plural proponents, however, have not accounted for all the participants at the spiritist's dwelling, whether real or impersonated. The plural participle "coming up" means that the spiritist saw two spirits whom she called *elohim* (gods). The Septuagint translators retained the plural participle: "I see gods, they are coming up..." (LXX 1Sa 28:13).

The plural participle in 1Sa 28:13, mentioned above, is perhaps why the *KJV* and *RSV* chose to use the phrase "by the familiar spirit" in 1Sa 28:07-08. The Hebrew word translated "familiar spirit" is *owb*. "Having a familiar spirit" is a definition given for *owb* in the *Thayer/BDB* lexicon and the *TWOT*.[64] *Owb* is mentioned five times in the spiritist of Endor account (1Sa 28:03, 07 (twice), 08, 09).[65]

When Saul heard the spiritist say that she saw *elohim*, Saul asked what "he," meaning Samuel, looked like. After all, Saul had requested that the spiritist bring up Samuel (1Sa 28:11). The spiritist used singulars to say that an old man rose from the earth (1Sa 28:14).

It would seem the plurals in 1Sa 28:13 referred to both Samuel and the familiar spirit, while the singulars in 1Sa 28:14 refer to Samuel only. So the spiritist called Samuel and the familiar spirit "gods" (1Sa 28:13), but did not refer to Samuel alone as "gods."

So the "gods" (*elohim*) (1Sa 28:13) is a plural collective noun referring to Samuel and the familiar spirit. This is similar to how the angels and judges were only called *elohim* (gods) collectively, but not individually. This fact was mentioned above in this section.

Two Demons as Elohim

Whether the demons were real or impersonated by the spiritist is inconsequential to our study of grammar. Whether real or not, the spiritist would have used the same grammar either way so as not to give herself away. It is well known that spiritists impersonate demons, for instance, Samuel Zwemer wrote:

> The expectant mother, in fear of the *qarina* [an "evil twin" spirit] visits the *sheikha* (learned woman) three months before the birth of the child, and does whatever she indicates as a remedy. These *sheikhas* exercise great influence over the women, and batten on their superstitious beliefs, often impersonating the *qarina* and frightening the ignorant.[66]

The case can be made that Samuel's spirit was not present at the spiritist of Endor's dwelling. This would mean that two demons were called *elohim*, or at least two impersonated demons. The demons were called *elohim* because demons liked to pose as pagan gods (*elohim*). This is what Moses said on the subject:

> They sacrificed to demons, which are not God—gods (*elohim*) they had not known, gods (*elohim*) that recently appeared, gods (*elohim*) your fathers did not fear (Deu 32:17; see also Psa 106:37).

Saul said, "Please divine by the familiar spirit" (1Sa 28:08), so one spirit was a demon for sure. The other entity likely was a second demon posing as Samuel. Everything the demon told Saul seemed to have been part of a calculated plan to extinguish Saul's hope and destroy Saul spiritually and physically. This would lead one to conclude that a demon had indeed posed as Samuel.

The demon perhaps had a plan of attack since there was forewarning of Saul's visit to the spiritist of Endor (1Sa 28:07). Saul's occult experience began with the clairvoyant saying that Samuel came up out of the ground rather than from heaven (1Sa 28:13, 15). This was calculated to destroy any hope that Saul may have had about the afterlife. Now the best that Saul could hope for would be to dwell in nether regions with Samuel.

That Samuel's spirit came out of the ground suggests a demon was posing as Samuel. Samuel's body but not spirit would be residing underground awaiting judgment (Deu 32:22; Job 03:18-19; Psa 009:17; 016:10; 055:15; 086:13). Samuel's spirit would instead be residing in heaven with Enoch, and later with Elijah (2Ki 02:11; Luk 08:55; 16:26; 20:37-38; 24:05; Rev 07:09).

If the real Samuel had talked to Saul the day before Saul was about to die, Samuel would have given Saul an uplifting law and gospel sermon. Samuel would have presented the way of salvation through faith in the promised Messiah (Gen 03:15; 49:10-11; Num 24:17).

The demon posing as Samuel, however, only spoke of law and wrath. In this way, the demon presented a mere caricature of Samuel and, indirectly, of *Yahveh.* Samuel's impostor gruffly asked Saul, "Why have you disturbed me by bringing me up?" (1Sa 28:15). The true Samuel, who grieved for Saul until Samuel's dying day (1Sa 15:35), would not have been so gruff. The only reason Samuel did not minister to Saul more when Samuel was alive was Samuel feared for his life, as did David (1Sa 02:34; 16:02; 19:15; Psa 059:01).

Samuel's satanic impostor said that *Yahveh* had turned away from Saul because Saul had not destroyed the Amalekites (1Sa 28:16-18). Saul, however, was the prodigal son who had turned away from *Yahveh.* *Yahveh* had not turned away from Saul (1Sa 15:11). That *Yahveh* had not hardened Saul in his sin is evident from how, after Saul admitted that he had sinned, Samuel went to worship *Yahveh* with Saul (1Sa 15:31).

Samuel's demonic impostor said that *Yahveh* had become Saul's enemy (1Sa 28:16). It is true that the special measure of the Spirit had left Saul and rested on David (1Sa 16:13-14). It is also true that *Yahveh* allowed a "spirit of sadness" (*YLT*) or an "evil spirit" (*NIV, LXE, KJV*) to torment Saul (1Sa 16:14, 23; 18:10; 19:09). However, the last spirit mentioned as possessing Saul was the "Spirit of God" (1Sa 19:23-24).

Interestingly, Saul prophesied (1Sa 10:11-13; 18:10; 19:21, 23-24; 28:15) even while being tormented (1Sa 18:10). So if the "evil spirit" was more than just a bad mood, it may have been a "lying spirit" uttering false prophesies (1Ki 22:22-23; 2Ch 18:21-22).

If the spirit that afflicted Saul was a demon, then David's songs and harp playing were a form of exorcism (1Sa 16:23; 18:10; 19:09). David was a prophet (Act 02:30) who spoke by the Spirit (1Sa 16:13; Act 04:25). David sang inspired psalms that had the power to drive out evil spirits. The demon, however, would return after each exorcism because Saul did not repent (Luk 11:24-26).

That Samuel grieved for Saul until Samuel's dying day suggests that *Yahveh* did not end Saul's time of grace before Saul died (1Sa 15:35; Heb 09:27). The only reason Samuel did not preach to Saul was Samuel feared for his life (1Sa 16:02). So evidently the evil spirit was sent not to harden Saul's heart (Rom 09:18). Rather, it seems, the spirit was sent to destroy Saul's sinful nature so his soul might be saved (1Co 05:04-05).

It seems unlikely that the name Saul would have remained a popular name among the Jews if God had hardened Saul's heart (1Sa 06:06; Act 07:58). A demon, however, wanted Saul to think that *Yahveh* was his permanent enemy. Then the prodigal son would never think of returning home (Luk 15:24, 32; Col 01:21-22).

Given Israel's military situation and Saul's loss of heart (1Sa 28:04-05), the prophecy that Samuel's impostor gave was a prophecy any prescient demon could proffer (1Sa 28:19). The demon knew that self-fulfilling prophecies have the best chance of success, so the demon graphically predicated that Saul and his sons would be in hell the next day. The fear the prophecy instilled in Saul (1Sa 28:15-20) became a contributing factor in Saul's battlefield defeat (1Sa 31:02-06).

The prophecy the demon gave about Saul and his sons being with Samuel the next day probably contributed to Saul's choice to commit suicide (1Sa 31:04-05). The sense of fatalism the prophecy introduced meant that Saul did not explore any options to avoid death. Options could have included tactical retreat, mustering additional forces against the Philistines (1Sa 11:07), paying tribute, or abdicating in favor of Jonathan or David.

The false prophecy that Saul and his sons would be with Samuel underground (1Sa 28:19) likely helped Saul resign to his fate and commit suicide (Job 03:17-19). After all, could Saul hope for anything better in the afterlife than to be where Samuel was?

A good law and gospel sermon, however, would have produced different results in Saul. The real Samuel would have told Saul of God's grace and the gift of paradise (Luk 23:43), while at the same time warning of hell for rejecting God's gracious offers.

The fatal error that caused Saul's demise was his attendance at a "synagogue of Satan" (Rev 02:09; 03:09). Saul heard a sermonette from a demon (2Co 11:14). Saul was beat up spiritually and emotionally by the demon posing as Samuel. Saul's experience is somewhat analogous to how a demon beat up the seven sons of Sceva (Act 17:14-16).

Perhaps God allowed this demon to further destroy Saul's sinful nature so his soul might be saved (1Ch 10:13-14; 1Co 05:04-05). Scripture, however, does not hold out much hope that Saul ever repented and went to heaven (1Ch 10:13-14).

So the case has here been made that two demons were called *elohim*, and that the real Samuel was never called *elohim*. So demons are called *elohim* collectively, just as earlier we learned that humans and angels were only called *elohim* collectively and not individually.

A Grave as "Graves"

The prophetess Huldah referred to King Josiah's "graves" (2Ki 22:20; 2Ch 34:28). Later, however, Josiah was buried in a singular "grave" (2Ki 23:30). Majestic plural proponents believe the plural indicates a royal grave as opposed to a common grave.

If there were an occasion to refer to a grave using a majestic plural, it would have been when Abraham, the "prince of God," was offered any of the Hittites' "choicest graves" (Gen 23:06). Notice that "grave" is in the singular as would be expected. The Hittites said:

You are a mighty prince among us. Bury your dead in the choicest
[singular] of our graves. None of us will refuse you his grave [singular]
for burying your dead (Gen 23:06).

Here is an alternative interpretation of Josiah's plural "graves." Huldah began the prophecy by saying Josiah would be gathered to his "fathers." So the plural "graves" may refer to a grave complex such as a mausoleum, family plot, or catacomb where his "fathers" are buried. So the mention of "graves" may be similar to how English speakers often use the plural "catacombs" even when referring to a single catacomb.

Another interpretation of the plural "graves" is that the prophetess Huldah knew Josiah would first be laid in one tomb, and then in another. Joseph, for example, was placed in one tomb and then another (Gen 50:24-25; Exo 13:19; Jos 24:32).

There was another way that bodies came to be laid in two tombs. Between 20 BC and 70 AD[67] a Jewish practice involved burying a person in a cave or a tomb. Then after the soft tissues had turned to dust, the bones were collected and put in an ossuary in a family tomb. The person whose body was so handled could be said to have "graves."

The most likely interpretation of "graves," however, can be found in Ezekiel. In Ezekiel's "Dirge for Egypt" (Eze 32:17-32), Ezekiel intersperses the singular word "grave" (*qeber*) (Eze 32:23, 24) with the plural "graves" (Eze 32:22, 23, 25, 26). In the same chapter, Ezekiel mentions the singular "Sheol" (Eze 32:21, 27).

The *NIV* most often translates "Sheol" as "grave." Once, however, the *NIV* translates Sheol as "realm of death" (Deu 32:22). Twice the *NIV* translates Sheol as "death" in the phrase "gates of death" (Job 17:16; Isa 38:10). So it seems that the plural "graves" refers to first the physical grave, and then secondly to the metaphysical place called Sheol.

Based on the information from Ezekiel, one can say the prophecy about Josiah going to his "graves" in peace (2Ki 22:20; 2Ch 34:28) deals with more than just temporal death. The prophecy must also mean that Josiah would find peace with God in the afterlife. Huldah's prophecy meant Josiah could look forward to a bodily resurrection just as Job had (Job 19:27). Huldah's prophecy assured Josiah of heaven just as the thief on the cross was assured of heaven (Luk 23:43).

Josiah was buried in his own singular grave (2Ki 23:30). Perhaps Josiah's body was left undisturbed until the body turned totally to dust. Surely, Josiah's grave was not desecrated along with the graves of the other kings who had worshiped

false gods (Jer 08:01-02). Perhaps Josiah's grave lasted as long as David's grave
(Act 02:29).

Sennacherib as "Kings"

Hezekiah's men said, "Why should the kings of Assyria come and find plenty
of water?" (2Ch 32:04). Majestic plural proponents say that "kings" is a majestic
plural that refers to Sennacherib, since other occurrences of "king" are singular in
the same chapter (2Ch 32:01, 07). Majestic plural proponents say that early translators must have thought "kings" was a majestic plural, since the LXX, Syriac, and
Arabic translations of 2Co 32:04 have "king" rather than "kings."

One explanation of the plural "kings" is that the Assyrians boasted about
their armies being so large that each commander was like a king (Isa 10:08).
Interestingly, in the NT the Corinthians were so proud that Paul said they thought
of themselves as being kings (1Co 04:08). The early Muslims had similar
thoughts:

> We were kings of men before Muhammad,
> And when Islam came we had the superiority.[68]

So the "kings" in 2Ch 32:04 may be a plural collective noun referring to the
Assyrian king and his commanders.

The *Encyclopaedia Britannica* provides information that supports the idea that
there were in fact more than one Assyrian king:

> Some rulers speak of their own dynastic deity. A king who owes his
> position to the Assyrian emperor refers to the latter and the dynastic deity
> equally as 'my master.'[69]

If the Assyrian king is considered an "emperor," then his regional administrators
could be considered "kings." After all, by definition an emperor is a king of kings.
The commanders of the Assyrian armies may have already been regional kings, or
soon would be. After each successful campaign, the newly conquered land likely
was divided into fiefdoms for commanders to rule.

The singular instances of "king" may refer to the Assyrian emperor, or the
singular "king" may be a collective noun referring to the king and his king-like
commanders. Translations such as the LXX, Syriac and Arabic translate "kings"
in the singular. The translators likely thought it more sensible that collective nouns
be singular in form rather than plural.

There is another explanation of the plural "kings" in 2Ch 32:04. Stopping
up all the wells throughout Israel was a large public works project. This may
have required more justification than the threat of invasion by one Assyrian king.
Stopping up wells was a draconian policy that inconvenienced the population
by interfering with the water supply. Stopping up all the wells may have been
implemented only when there was a threat of repeated invasion by two or more
kings—hence the plural "kings."

At an earlier time the Philistines had implemented a policy of stopping up wells
(Gen 26:15, 18). Archaeology shows that Palestine was rife with invasions during
patriarchal times, and that all of Palestine was an armed camp. Genesis mentions

how even Abraham had 318 servants who could bear arms (Gen 14:14), and Esau had 400 servant soldiers (Gen 32:06). Genesis even notes how Abraham's clan (Gen 14:02) and Jacob's clan (Gen 34:26; 48:22) were involved in armed conflicts.

So Hezekiah's men were saying that stopping up the wells was important because of the long-term threat of invasion by Assyrian kings. Indeed, Hezekiah's men were prescient. In the fourth year of Hezekiah's reign, Shalmaneser came threateningly close to Judea (2Ki 18:09). In the fourteenth year of Hezekiah's reign, Sennacherib threatened to invade (2Ki 18:13). That plural kings were involved can be seen from Hezekiah's prayer:

O *Yahveh*, the kings of Assyria have laid waste [plural verb] the nations and their lands (2Ki 19:17).

A Possessor as "Possessors"

For the protection of wisdom is like the protection of money; the advantage of knowledge is that wisdom preserves the life of its possessors (Ecc 07:12).

Majestic plural proponents sometimes offer Ecc 07:12 as proof of the majestic plural, since the word "possessors" is plural. Since more than one person can possess wisdom, the plural "possessors" should be understood as a plural collective noun.

The Malek Yahveh as Elohim

Majestic plural proponents say that the *Malek Yahveh* being called *Elohim* is proof of the majestic plural, for the *Malek Yahveh* is one person but *Elohim* is a plural noun:

- The *Malek Yahveh* referred to himself as *Elohim* (Gen 31:11, 13; Exo 03:02, 06), and
- The *Malek Yahveh* was called *Elohim* often (Gen 16; 21−22; 31−32; Exo 03; 14; 23; Num 22−24; Jdg 02; 06; 13; 1Ki 19; 2Ki 19; and Zec 02−03).

Elohim is used as a plural collective noun when referring to the Trinity, but as a plural of delegation when referring to individual members of the Trinity. The plural of delegation, *Elohim,* is used to note that the *Malek Yahveh*'s is a member of the Trinity. Since *malek* means "messenger" in Hebrew, the *Malek Yahveh* definitely is both a member of the Trinity, and a delegate of the Trinity.

The context and other clues help the reader to determine whether *Elohim* is being used as a plural collective noun, or as a plural of delegation. Sometimes, the plain sense of the verse tells the reader that first one and then another person is called *Elohim.* For instance, in Psa 045:06-07 and Psa 082:01, 08, *Elohim* is used as a plural of delegation twice. Each time *Elohim* refers to a different individual of the Trinity, the Father and then the Son. These verses are discussed in the Trinitarian proofs appendix.

How the NT Writers Understood MT Hebrew Plurals

There are many quotations of the OT in the NT. Many of these quotations in-cluded the plural form *Elohim* in original Hebrew. The NT application of these quotations shows that NT writers:
- Knew whom the OT passage applied to, and
- Distinguished whether the plural was a plural collective noun or a plural of del-egation.

For instance:
- The writer of Hebrews knows that the Father called the Son *Elohim* in Psa 045: 06-07 (Heb 01:08),
- John knows that the Father called human judges *elohim* in *Psa* 082:01 (Joh 10: 34-35), and
- John knows that the Father called the Son, who would be the Messiah, *Elohim* in Psa 082:08 (Joh 10:36).

Psa 045 and 082 are discussed in the Trinitarian proofs appendix. Many NT quotations of the OT are discussed further in the chapter and appendix on the NT use of OT *Yahveh* texts.

The NT was written in a way consistent with the grammar and meaning of the OT. For instance, take the Hebrew form *Elohim,* meaning, "God." *Elohim* was applied to the Trinity as a collective noun, and *Elohim* was applied to individual persons of the Trinity as a plural of delegation. Greek words for God like *theos* were also applied to individual persons of the Trinity, and sometimes to the Trinity collectively.

The NT writers knew that the OT sometimes applied *Elohim* to the Trinity, and sometimes to the individual members of the Trinity. This is evidenced not only in quotations of the OT, but also in doctrine. For instance, the NT writers knew they could ascribe NT activity to the Trinity (God), or they could distribute the credit to one or two members. For example, the Trinity (God) was credited with all the fol-lowing activities, but individual members of the Trinity were also given separate credit:
- The Father (Act 02:32; 13:30; Rom 06:04; Gal 01:01; Eph 01:19-20), the Son (Joh 02:19-22; 10:17-18), and the Spirit (Rom 01:04; 08:09-11) raised *Yeshua* from the dead,
- The Father (Joh 05:21), the Son (Joh 06:39-40, 44, 54), and the Spirit (Rom 08: 09-11) will raise the dead,
- The Father (Joh 15:16; 16:23), the Son (Joh 14:13-14), and the Spirit (Rom 08: 26) answer prayer,
- The Father (Gen 02:07; Psa 102:25; Heb 01:02), the Son (Joh 01:03; Col 01: 16; Heb 01:02), and the Spirit (Gen 01:02; Job 33:04; Psa 104:30) created the world, and
- The Father ("Most High") and the Spirit (Luk 01:35), and the Son (Heb 02:14) were involved in the incarnation.

The NT writers not only saw the Trinity in the OT, but also occasionally expressed the Trinity using the same grammar. For instance, there are solecisms in the Greek that could be thought of as Hebraisms in 1Th 03:11 and Rev 21:22-23; 22:01,03-04. These verses are discussed in the Trinitarian proofs appendix.

Concluding Remark

As was stated in the introductory remarks to this chapter, one can see that the OT is thoroughly Trinitarian when one has a correct understanding of OT Hebrew grammar.

Chapter 2

Proto-Sinaitic Trinitarianism

Who the *Malek Yahveh* Was

The title *Malek Yahveh* literally means "Messenger of *Yahveh*," but is often translated as "Angel of the Lord." Unlike other messengers (*maleks*), the *Malek Yahveh* was the preincarnate Son of God. Proofs of the *Malek Yahveh*'s divinity are many, and are discussed in the Trinitarian proofs appendix. Corroborating passages include those where the *Malek Yahveh*;

- Spoke as only *Yahveh* can speak (for instance, Gen 16:11; 21:17; 22:15-18, Num 22:35; Jdg 02:01, 06:14, 16),
- Called himself God (*El*) (Gen 31:11, 13; Exo 03:06),
- Was called God (*Elohim*) or *Yahveh* in most *Malek Yahveh* accounts (Gen 16; 21—22; 31—32; Exo 03; 14; 23; Num 22—24; Jdg 02; 06; 13; 1Ki 19; 2Ki 19; and Zec 02—03),
- Was located in the same bush as God (*Elohim*) and *Yahveh* (Exo 03:02, 04), and
- Instructed Moses to say that *Yahveh* had appeared and met him (Exo 03:16, 18). Note that in the Burning Bush account, Moses was "afraid to look at God [*Elohim*]" (Exo 03:06).

The *Malek Yahveh* directly quoted the Father once (Gen 22:15-18). Most often, the *Malek Yahveh* spoke of the Father in the third person as "God" (Gen 21:17) or as *Yahveh* (Gen 22:16). The *Malek Yahveh* often spoke in his capacity as God, and even called himself God, for instance, Jacob said:

> The Angel (*Malek*) of [All] the Gods [*haElohim*] said to me [Jacob] in the dream, '...I am the God (*El*) of Bethel' (Gen 31:11, 13).

The *Malek Yahveh* accounts mention the Trinity, *haElohim*, literally, "[All] the Gods" (Gen 22:03, 09; Num 22:10; 23:27). The accounts also refer to the Son as the *Malek* of *haElohim* ([All] the Gods)" (Gen 31:11; Exo 14:19; Jdg 06:20; 13: 06, 09). As was noted above, during many of the *Malek Yahveh* appearances, the *Malek Yahveh* was called *Yahveh* and God. This indicates that the *Malek Yahveh* was both God and *Yahveh*, and a member of the Trinity, the *haElohim* ([All] the Gods).

A parallel exists between the *Malek Yahveh* and the Messiah, *Yeshua*. The OT presents the *Malek Yahveh* both as a messenger and as *Yahveh* the Son. Likewise, the NT presents *Yeshua* as both messenger (Joh 08:28; 12:49) and God (Joh 20:28; Heb 01:08). This led OT readers to conclude that *Yeshua* was the *Malek Yahveh* in the flesh, and that *Yeshua* was both God and *Yahveh* the Son.

Acting as a messenger, the *Malek Yahveh* demonstrated the preincarnate Son's love for fallen humanity. The preincarnate Son was not too proud to become a messenger. Likewise, the Son was not too proud to become the Messiah (Mat 20: 28; Mar 10:45; Rom 15:08-09; 2Co 08:09; Heb 12:02).

Interestingly, the *Malek Yahveh* demonstrated the preincarnate Son's love for fallen humanity when he took on the form of a man. He temporarily appeared in the form of a man when he made preincarnate appearances as the:

- *Malek Yahveh* (Gen 18—19, 32; Jos 05; Jdg 06, 13),
- Son of Man (Eze 01:26; Dan 07:13), and as the
- Son of God (Dan 03:25).

These texts led Intertestamental readers like Simeon (Luk 02:25-34) to expect the Son's appearance as the God-man Messiah (Isa 07:14; 09:06; Mic 05:02; Mat 01:23; Joh 01:14; Rom 09:05; Phi 02:06-07; Heb 02:09-18).

Jacob and *El Shaddai* (Gen 32 and 35)

We can know with certainty that the "man" with whom Jacob wrestled was *El Shaddai* and not a mere creature. The wrestler called himself "God" (Gen 32:28), Jacob called the wrestler *Elohim* (Gen 32:30), and Jacob called the place where they wrestled *Peniel* ("Face of God") (Gen 32:30-31). The wrestler gave Jacob the eponym Israel, and the narrator of Kings said it was *Yahveh* who gave Jacob the name Israel (1Ki 18:31; 2Ki 17:34).

The divine wrestler (Gen 32) appeared again to Jacob as *El Shaddai* at Bethel (Gen 35). This appearance occurred after the Father spoke of the Son in the third person:

Then God [the Father] said to Jacob, 'Go up to Bethel and settle there, and build an altar there to God [the Son], who appeared to you when you were fleeing from your brother Esau' (Gen 35:01),

The wrestler (Gen 32) appeared again to Jacob after the narrator, Moses, spoke of God using plurals:

[All] the Gods [*haElohim*], they appeared [plural verb] to him [Jacob] [at Bethel in Gen 28] (Gen 35:07).

Then, by way of introduction, the narrator, Moses, recalled how the wrestler (Gen 32:28) had given Jacob the name Israel (Gen 35:09-10). This was Moses' way of telling the reader that *El Shaddai*, who was about to appear to Jacob again (Gen 35:11-13), had previously wrestled with Jacob (Gen 32).

So, based entirely on evidence internal to Genesis, the wrestler can be identified both as *El Shaddai* and as God the Son. We can also know, based on the *Malek Yahveh*'s directions concerning Genesis (Exo 06:03), that God the Son was both the *Malek Yahveh* and *El Shaddai*.

El Shaddai means "God of Mighty Ones." The _El_ is singular and refers to the Son. _Shaddai_ is a plural collective noun referring to the Trinity. So _El Shaddai_ could be translated as "God of Mighty Ones," and _El Shaddai_ could be interpreted as "Divine member of the Trinity."

Since _Elohim_ and _El Shaddai_ are titles and not names, Jacob requested to know the name of the _Malek Yahveh_. The _Malek Yahveh_ denied Jacob's request saying that Jacob did not have a sufficient need to know (Gen 32:29). This is not unexpected since God has many secrets (Deu 29:29; Mat 07:06; 13:17, 35; Joh 15:15).

Moses and _El Shaddai_ (Exo 03 and 06)

Moses learned from Genesis that the Father was _Yahveh_. As was mentioned in the chapter on collective plurals, Eve knew the Father was _Yahveh_ (Gen 04:01). The Name, _Yahveh_, is found 124 times in Genesis. Furthermore, the shortened form of _Yahveh_ (_Ya_) is embedded in the names of persons born before Exo 03 and 06, for instance: Jochebed (Exo 06:20; Num 26:59) and Joshua (Exo 17:09).

Jacob's experience with the divine wrestler informed Moses that he needed to present a need to know the _Malek Yahveh_'s name. Moses said that the Israelites would not believe the _Malek Yahveh_ had sent him if Moses did not know the _Malek Yahveh_'s name (Exo 13:02, 13).

Jacob, Moses and the Hebrew elders did not know the _Malek Yahveh_'s name. Throughout the book of Genesis and to Exodus 03:13, only the post-Sinaitic Yahvist narrator, Moses, knew the _Malek Yahveh_ as _Yahveh_ (Gen 16:13; Exo 03:04, 07). The patriarchs only knew the Son as:

- _Elohim_ (Gen 16:13; 22:12; 31:13; Exo 03:06, 13, 15, 16; 04:05), and as
- _El Shaddai_ (Gen 17:01; 35:11; Exo 06:03).

Moses undoubtedly knew from studying Genesis and extra-biblical sources that the man with whom Jacob wrestled was the _Malek Yahveh_. The Hebrews knew the details of Jacob's encounter with the divine wrestler so well that it affected their eating habits (Gen 32:32). This same _Malek Yahveh_ now met Moses on Mount Sinai (Exo 03:02). The _Malek Yahveh_ thought Moses and the Israelites had been in a state of suspense long enough, and had sufficient reason to know his Name, _Yahveh_ (Exo 03:14-16).

The _Malek Yahveh_'s (Exo 03:02) revealing that he was _Yahveh_ allowed Hosea to write that the wrestler was both the _Malek Yahveh_ (Hos 12:04 [_BHS_ 12:05]) and _Yahveh_ (Hos 12:05 [_BHS_ 12:06]):

> In the womb he [Jacob] took his brother [Esau] by the heel; and in his manhood he [Jacob] had power with God [i.e., with the _Peniel_, literally "The Face(s) of God" (Gen 32:30-31)]. 04 Indeed, he [Jacob] had power over the _Malek_ [the Son] and prevailed [Gen 32:24-32]; He [Jacob] wept, and made supplication to him [the Son]. He [Jacob] found him [the Son] at Bethel [Gen 35:09-15], and there he [Jacob] spoke with us [the Trinity],

05 even *Yahveh* [the Father], God [the Son] of hosts; *Yahveh* is his [the Trinity's] name of renown (Hos 12:03-05 [*BHS* 12:04-06]).

Since Jacob encountered God twice at Bethel (Gen 28 and 35), someone might ask, "Which appearance of God at Bethel was Hosea referring to?" Hosea said that after God wrestled with Jacob at the Jabbok ford (Heb 12:04; Gen 32), God talked to Jacob at Bethel (Hos 12:04; Gen 35). This means that Hosea had the Gen 35 Bethel meeting in mind—the encounter between Jacob and *El Shaddai* (Gen 35: 11).

Moses Received the Trinitarian Interpretation of Genesis on Mount Sinai

The *Malek Yahveh* revealed to Moses that he was "I AM" and *Yahveh* (Exo 03: 14-15; 06:03). After Moses returned to Mount Sinai from Egypt, the *Malek Yahveh* further clarified the proper interpretation of Genesis. The *Malek Yahveh* said the patriarchs had known him as *El Shaddai*, but not as *Yahveh* (Exo 06:03). True to the *Malek Yahveh*'s words, only the Genesis post-Sinaitic Yahvist narrator, Moses, knew that *El Shaddai* was also *Yahveh*. There is only one mention in Genesis of *El Shaddai* being *Yahveh*, and that is by the narrator, Moses:

> When Abram was ninety-nine years old, *Yahveh* appeared to him and said, 'I am God Almighty [*El Shaddai*]; walk before me and be blameless' (Gen 17:01).

The *Malek Yahveh* thought it was important to reaffirm that in the book of Genesis, the *Malek Yahveh* was the same person as *El Shaddai*. *El Shaddai* had appeared to the patriarchs and made promises concerning Israel (Gen 17:01; 35:11). The patriarchs also mentioned *El Shaddai* in blessings and prayers (Gen 28:03; 43: 14; 48:03; 49:25). Furthermore, the *Malek Yahveh* did not want Moses to think that *El Shaddai* was a fourth person of the Godhead.

Knowing that *El Shaddai* was the *Malek Yahveh* would help Moses convince the Hebrew elders that Genesis was Trinitarian. Already at that time the Hebrew elders may have leaned toward a unitarian interpretation of Genesis. The Hebrew elders may have entertained the thought that:

- *El Shaddai* was *Yahveh* (the Father),
- The Spirit was an impersonal force, and
- The *Malek Yahveh* was a created angel or an impersonal *Shekinah* apparition of *Yahveh*.

That the *Malek Yahveh* was *Yahveh* means that Exo 03—06 is very similar to the Jos 05:13—06:05 account. Joshua does not specifically mention the *Malek Yahveh*, but calls the Son *Yahveh* (Jos 06:02, 06). The same *Malek Yahveh* told both Moses and Joshua to take off their sandals because his presence made places holy (Exo 03:05; Jos 05:15). Note that, though the *Malek Yahveh* was *Yahveh* (Exo 03:04, 07, 14-16, 18; Jos 06:02, 08), the *Malek Yahveh* distinguished himself from *Yahveh* the Father (Exo 06:03; Jos 05:14-15).

Clearly, Jos 06:01-05 is a continuation of the conversation between Joshua and the *Malek Yahveh* (Jos 05:13-15). The chapter division between Jos 05—06 is clearly misplaced. Otherwise, the commander of *Yahveh*'s armies appeared in Jos 05 without having any substantive message for Joshua. So it would seem the Jos 05:13—06:05 account buttresses the Trinitarian interpretation of both Exo 03—06 and Genesis.

Distinguishing the Trinity in Genesis

Specific persons of the Trinity can be distinguished easily in some verses of Genesis:
- *Yahveh*'s saying, "us" (Gen 01:26; 03:22; 11:07),
- *HaElohim* is a Hebrew form meaning, "[All] the Gods." When referring to *Yahveh*, *haElohim* denotes the persons of the Trinity. The OT mentions that these people saw or talked to *haElohim* (the Trinity): Enoch (Gen 05:22, 24), Noah (Gen 06:09), Abraham (Gen 17:18; 20:17; 22:03, 09), Abimelech (Gen 20:06), Jacob (Gen 27:28; 35:07; 48:15), Moses (Exo 03:06, 11, 12, 13; 19:03), the Israelites (Exo 18:12; 19:17; 20:20, 21; 24:11), Balaam (Num 22:10; 23:27) and Gideon (Jdg 06:36, 39),
- Abraham said, "Gods [*Elohim*], they caused me to wander [plural verb] from my father's house..." (Gen 20:13). Based on Gen 20:13, we should expect to find at least two persons of the Trinity in Gen 12:01-07. Indeed, God did appear to Abraham twice to tell Abraham to leave his father's household (Gen 12:01, 07). One person appearing twice to promise essentially the same thing makes less sense than an alternative explanation. A plausible interpretation is that two persons of the Trinity appeared consecutively to tell Abraham to leave Haran. This allowed two persons of the Trinity to extend promises of reward for Abraham acting on his faith by journeying to the Promised Land,
- The narrator, Moses, recounted how "[All] the Gods [*haElohim*], they had appeared [plural verb] to him [Jacob] when he was fleeing from his brother [Esau] [at Bethel in Gen 28]" (Gen 35:07). The *Malek* of [All] the Gods (*haElohim*) (Gen 31:11) said that he was God (*El*) who appeared to Jacob at Bethel (Gen 31:13). So Gen 31:11, 13 show that the *Malek Yahveh* was one of the persons of *haElohim* ("[All] the Gods") who appeared at Bethel in Gen 28 (Gen 35:07), and
- The *Malek Yahveh* (Exo 03:02) said he was the *El Shaddai* (Exo 06:03) who appeared to the patriarchs (Gen 17:01; 35:11).

One need not distinguish the persons of the Trinity throughout Genesis to see that the *Malek Yahveh*'s Exo 06:03 interpretation of Genesis is a major Trinitarian proof text. People are free, however, to attempt to distinguish the persons of the Trinity throughout Genesis. Deductions and inferences can be made from the data in Genesis as well as from other books of the Bible that touch on subjects in Genesis. We have seen, for instance, that the books Exodus, Kings and Hosea refer to Genesis.

According to the *Malek Yahveh*'s directions, noting whom the patriarchs knew as *Yahveh* helps to identify the Father in Genesis. Only the post-Sinaitic Yahvist narrator, Moses, knew that the Son and Spirit were *Yahveh*. The Name, *Yahveh*, occurs 165 times in 143 Genesis verses. The people spoke or heard the Name, *Yahveh*, in only 52 verses,[70] so most occurrences of *Yahveh* in Genesis occur in the narration.

The NT writers mention "God" and "Lord" often. These likely refer to the Father or to the Trinity—provided there is no mention of the Son or the Spirit nearby. Likewise, in Genesis, *Elohim* and *Adonai* likely refer to the Father or the Trinity when there is no nearby mention of the *Malek Yahveh*, *El Shaddai* or the Spirit. When the context mentions a specific person of the Trinity, then *Elohim* and *Adonai* likely are plurals of delegation. A plural of delegation is a type of collective noun that refers to the Father, the Son or the Spirit's membership in the Trinity.

Identifying the divine persons in Genesis by the *Malek Yahveh*'s criterion in Exo 06:03 yields doctrinal dividends. It becomes clear that the patriarchs referred to the Trinity by the form *haElohim* ("[All] the Gods"). *HaElohim* is found 23 times in 21 verses of Genesis,[71] and, in total, 337 OT verses. The patriarchs referred to the individual persons of the Trinity by additional names and titles:

- In patriarchal times the Father was known as:
  o *Yahveh*,
  o *Elohim* ("God"),
  o *El Elyon* ("God Most High" (Gen 14:18, 19, 20, 22)),
  o *El Olam* ("God Eternal" (Gen 21:33)), and
  o *Adonai Yahveh* ("Lord *Yahveh*" (Gen 15:02, 08)),
- In patriarchal times the Son was known as:
  o *El Shaddai* ("God of Mighty Ones" (Gen 17:01; 28:03; 35:11; 43:14; 48:03; 49:25)),
  o *Elohim* ("God" (Gen 16:13; 22:12; 31:13; Exo 03:06)),
  o The *Malek Elohim* ("the Messenger of God" (Gen 21:17; 31:11)), and
  o The *Malek Yahveh* (Gen 16:07, 09, 11; 22:11, 15), and
- The Spirit was known to the patriarchs as the:
  o The "*Ruach* of *Elohim*" ("Spirit of God" (Gen 01:02)), and
  o The "*Ruach* of *Yahveh*" (Gen 06:03).

Three "Controls" that Verify the Trinitarian Interpretation of Genesis: Num 22—24, Job, and Books I and II of the Psalms

The Trinity in Num 22—24

Balaam provided sorcery services to anyone willing to pay the fee, whether that person happened to be idolatrous or not. Balaam, however, considered himself a Yahvist since he said that *Yahveh* was his God (Num 22:18, 38). Balaam was from the "old" Yahvist school, as was Melchizedek (Gen 14:18).

The proto-patriarchal Yahvists would have considered Balaam an erring soul. Not only was sorcery wrong, but also Balaam hired himself out to anyone regardless of his religious persuasion. Balaam would have been to the ancient Yahvists what these men were to early Christians:

- Simon of Samaria (Act 08:09),
- Bar-Jesus Elymas, the Jewish sorcerer (Act 13:06-11), and
- The seven sons of Sceva, a Jewish chief priest, who likely syncretized pagan and Jewish beliefs (Act 19:14).

Eventually, the Israelites killed Balaam for practicing sorcery against Israel (Num 31:08).

Since Balaam lived near the river in "Aram" (Num 23:05, 07; Deu 23:04), he was unaware of doctrinal developments involving the patriarchs or Moses. Balaam's Yahvism, therefore, was proto-Sinaitic and even proto-patriarchal. The name "Jacob" is found on Balaam's lips (Num 23:10, 21, etc.), but only because Balak and his princes informed Balaam about Jacob (Num 23:07). Sorcerers always needed details supplied to them to develop a:

- Relevant curse or interpretation,
- Plausible communication from the "other" side, or a
- Self-fulfilling prophecy (Dan 02:07-09).

Since Balaam's Yahvism was proto-patriarchal and proto-Sinaitic, Num 22−24 is a benchmark for the Trinitarian interpretation of Genesis. We can expect that Balaam would not know facts first revealed to the patriarchs or to Moses on Mount Sinai. For instance, Balaam would not have known that the *Malek Yahveh* was "I AM" and *Yahveh* the Son (Exo 03:13-15; 06:03).

The several Creation, Fall and Flood stories of the ancient Near East suggest that the Yahvists possessed at least Gen 01−11 as Scripture. Gilgamesh, for instance, is just a spin off from the Genesis Flood account. Liberal theologians, of course, assert just the opposite. They maintain that the Genesis Flood account stems from the Gilgamesh account, but without evidence and justification.

Balaam would have known all the names of God found in the first part of Genesis. In Gen 01−11 the Trinity is called *haElohim* ("[All] the Gods"). As was the case with Jacob (Gen 32:29), the patriarchs had no need to know additional names for God. Thus, even a proto-patriarchal Yahvist such as Balaam would have known all the names of *Yahveh* that Melchizedek and the patriarchs knew. Balaam would have known, for instance, that:

- The Trinity was called *haElohim* ("[All] the Gods") (Gen 05:22, 24; 06:02, 04, 09, 11...),
- The title *Elyon*, "the Most High," was uniquely the Father's (Gen 14:18, 19, 20, 22),
- The title *(El) Shaddai*, "God of Mighty Ones" was uniquely the Son's (Gen 17: 01; 28:03; 35:11; 43:14; 48:03; 49:25),
- The Spirit was called the *Ruach*, meaning, "Spirit" (Gen 01:02; 06:03; 41:38), and
- The Son was called the *Malek Yahveh* (Gen 16:07, 09, 10, 11; 22:11, 15; Exo 03:02) and *El Shaddai* (Exo 06:03).

Indeed, we find that Balaam referred to the persons of the Trinity just as the patriarchs had (Num 22−24). As was the case in Genesis, only the proto-Sinaitic narrator of Num 22−24 knew that the *Malek Yahveh*'s name was *Yahveh* (Num 22:

28, 31). Balaam often spoke of the Father as *Yahveh*, and Balaam knew the Trinity as *haElohim* ("[All] the Gods") (Num 22:10, 23:27). Balaam referred to the Father as *Elyon* ("Most High") (Num 24:16). Balaam referred to the Spirit both as "God" (Num 24:04, 16) and as "the Spirit of God" (Num 24:02).

Balaam referred to the *Malek Yahveh* as *Shaddai* (Num 24:04, 16). *Shaddai* is short for *El Shaddai*, meaning, "God of Mighty Ones." The Son was called *El Shaddai* often during the patriarchal period (Gen 17:01; 28:03; 35:11; 43:14; 48: 03; 49:25). *Shaddai* by itself could be understood as a plural of delegation, a type of collective noun. *Shaddai* would then indicate that the *Malek Yahveh* is one of the "Mights" (*Shaddai*), or in other words, a member of the Trinity.

Since Balaam said he saw a vision of *Shaddai* and fell down prostrate (Num 24: 16), Balaam must have been referring to the *Malek Yahveh* by the title *Shaddai*. The *Malek Yahveh* is the only heavenly person who appeared to Balaam (Num 22:22-35).

The Son is often called (*El*) *Shaddai* (Gen 17:01; 28:03; 35:11; 43:14; 48:03; 49:25; Exo 06:03; Num 24:04, 16, and the like). That Balaam knew the *Malek Yahveh* to be *El Shaddai* explains why Balaam fell down prostrate before the *Malek Yahveh* (Num 22:31). That Balaam bowed to the *Malek Yahveh* may itself suggest that the *Malek Yahveh* was divine (Num 22:31). Bowing to angels was not necessary (Luk 01:11-12; Rev 22:08-09).

Balaam said he saw a vision of "him" (Num 24:17), meaning *Shaddai* (Num 24: 16), as the future Messiah (Num 24:07b-08, 17):

- His [Israel's] King [The Son as Messiah] shall be higher than Agag, His [the Messiah's] kingdom shall be exalted (Num 24:07b). *El* [the Father] brings him [The Son as Messiah] forth out of Egypt (Num 24:08),
- He [Balaam] said, who hears the words of *El* [the Spirit mentioned earlier in Num 24:02, 04.], who knows the knowledge of the Most High [the Father], who sees the vision of *Shaddai* [the Son as *Malek Yahveh* and *Shaddai*], falling down, and having his eyes open [see Num 22:31] (Num 24:16), and
- I see him [The Son as Messiah], but not now; I see him [The Son as Messiah], but not near: There shall come forth a Star [The Son as Messiah] out of Jacob, a scepter [The Son as Messiah] shall rise out of Israel [The scepter or "branch" is associated with the Messiah in Gen 49:10-11, Num 24:17; Isa 04:02, 11:01; 53: 02; Jer 23:05; 33:15; Zec 03:08; 06:12, and elsewhere] (Num 24:17).

Shaddai in Num 24:16 is the only plausible referent for the pronoun "him" found in Num 24:17. So Balaam saw the *Malek Yahveh* who was *Shaddai*, and then Balaam saw "him," meaning *Shaddai*, as the future Messiah. This agrees with how Balaam later called the Messiah "God":

> He took up his parable, and said, 'Alas, who shall live when *El* [meaning *Shaddai* as Messiah] does this?' (Num 24:23).

Balaam's passage:

> *El* [the Father] brings him [The Son as Messiah] forth out of Egypt (Num 24:08),

allowed Matthew to apply a similar passage from Hosea to *Yeshua*'s childhood round trip to Egypt and back (Mat 02:15):

When Israel was a child, I [the Father] loved him [the Son], and out of Egypt I called my son (Hos 11:01).

Balaam's messianic prophecy is similar to other messianic prophecies in that Balaam spoke of the Messiah as king (Gen 49:10; Eze 21:26-27; Mic 05:02 [*BHS* 05:01]). Balaam's prophecy in Numbers is similar to Psa 091 in that both speak of the Messiah being *El Shaddai*. The Psalmist wrote that the Messiah would be *Shaddai*, and the Messiah would take refuge in *Elyon* (the Most High), meaning the Father (Psa 091:01, 09).

The Trinity in Job

Job lived between 2,000 and 1,500 BC. Job's Yahvism would have been proto-patriarchal since Job most likely did not know of the patriarchs. Though Job mentions *malek*s (angels), Job makes no mention of the *Malek Yahveh*. Job does, however, mention *Shaddai* twenty-three times.

The book of Job can serve as another benchmark that verifies the Trinitarian interpretation of Genesis. As a proto-patriarchal Yahvist, Job would have known the Son as *Shaddai* and as *Elohim*, but not as *Yahveh* (Exo 03:13-15; 06:03). Therefore, it is not surprising that the Name, *Yahveh*, does not appear in the same chapter as the name *Shaddai*—except in Job 40.[72] *Yahveh* and *Shaddai* were both known as God since Job's friend Elihu said:

> But no one says, 'Where is Gods [plural noun], my Makers [plural noun]...?' (Job 35:10).

In Job 40, the informed, post-Sinaitic Yahvist narrator mentions *Yahveh* three times (Job 40:01, 03, 06), while God mentions the name *Shaddai* (Job 40:02). So Job had a proto-patriarchal theology, while a later narrator or redactor had a post-Sinaitic theology. Job knew the Father as *Yahveh* and Job knew the Son as *Shaddai*, but Job did not know the Son as *Yahveh*.

The Trinity in Books I and II of the Psalms

The usage of divine names in Books I and II of the Psalms is somewhat akin to Job's alternating use of *Yahveh* and *Shaddai* in different chapters. In the Psalms:

- To honor the Father and the Trinity, *Yahveh* is the predominant name for God in Book I (Psa 001 — 041), and
- To honor the Son, *Elohim* is the predominant name for God in Book II (Psa 042 — 072). Also, to honor the Son, the first mention in the Psalms of the name *Shaddai* occurs in Book II (Psa 068:14 [*BHS* 068:15]).

The arrangement of Book I and II was intended to honor the Father and the Son individually. It was appropriate for the Psalms to honor the Son since the Son would one day become the God-man offspring of David (2Sa 07:12). David was responsible for writing many psalms. Appropriately, in 2Sa 07 and in the Psalms there are many proofs both of the divinity of the Messiah, and of the Trinity. These proofs are discussed in the MT plurals appendix.

What better way was there to honor the Father and the Son individually than to recall Proto-Sinaitic theology in poetic verse? Book I recalls how only the Father was known as *Yahveh* during Genesis. Book II recalls how the Son was known as *El Shaddai* and *Elohim*, but not as *Yahveh* (Exo 06:03). Thus, Books I and II of the Psalms help to verify the Trinitarian interpretation of Genesis.

The Impact of the Trinitarian Interpretation of Genesis on Exegesis

The JEDP theory is buttressed mainly on the assumption that different writers and redactors preferred the title *Elohim* over the Name, *Yahveh,* or vice versa. The *Malek Yahveh*'s instruction about Genesis (Exo 06:03), however, shows that the different names tend to indicate different persons of the Trinity. This means that the JEDP theory is merely eisegesis passed off as exegesis.[73]

It is interesting to note that if the same JEDP assumptions were applied to other texts known to have only one author, the process would result in many wild conclusions. For instance, Norman Geisler makes this interest note about the *Koran*:

...the same anti-supernaturalism that led liberal critics of the Bible to deny that Moses wrote the Pentateuch, noting the different words for God used in different passages, would likewise argue that the *Qur'an* did not come from Muhammad. For the *Qur'an* also uses different names for God in different places. *Allah* is used for God in suras 4, 9, 24, 33, but *Rab* is used in suras 18, 23 and 25.[74]

The Impact of the Trinitarian Interpretation of Genesis on Angel of the Lord Theories

The *Malek Yahveh* (Exo 03:02) said that the patriarchs knew him as *El Shaddai*, but not as *Yahveh* (Exo 06:03). This means the *Malek Yahveh* was known to be a divine person separate and distinct from *Yahveh* the Father.

The evidence simply does not support any theory that says the *Malek Yahveh* was a mere spirit creature, much less an impersonal *Shekinah* or apparition of *Yahveh*. These theories postulate that the *Malek Yahveh* was "God" and "*Yahveh*" only by association with the Father, out of deference to the Father, or by derivation from the Father. If the *Malek Yahveh* were impersonal, this would tend to make God into a puppeteer or ventriloquist.

Oneness theology is popular in many Pentecostal circles. Oneness is just a warmed-over, repackaged version of the ancient heresy called Modalism. Oneness adherents believe that there is only one person called *Yahveh*. He play-acted the part of Father, Son and Spirit—as the occasion required. Oneness enthusiasts believe that, among other things, the Son:

- Quoted himself (Gen 22:15-16; Joh 14:10, 24),
- Spoke of himself as being the Father often,
- Play-acted two (Joh 12:28-30) or three (Mat 03:16-17) divine persons at a time, and
- Prayed to the Father often (Joh 17:01-26).

Only the *Malek Yahveh*'s being a divine person distinct from the Father would allow the *Malek Yahveh* to state that:

- He was *El Shaddai*, and
- The patriarchs did not know him by the Name, *Yahveh* (Exo 06:03).

Both the Predeluvians and patriarchs knew at least one person to be *Yahveh* (Gen 04:01, 26). If the Father, the *Malek Yahveh* and the Spirit were all the same person, as Modalists assert, there is no sidestepping the fact that that person definitely was known as *Yahveh*. Only distinct persons of the Trinity could, without contrivance, claim that the Patriarchs did not know him as *Yahveh* (Exo 06: 03).

Besides Exo 06:03, there are many indications that the Father and Son are two distinct persons in both testaments. Examples include:

- The *Malek Yahveh* quoting the Father (Gen 22:15-18), and
- The prophecy that the kings of the earth would speak against *Yahveh* and his Messiah (Psa 002:02) saying:

> Let us break their [plural] chains...and throw off their [plural] fetters (Psa 002:03).

NT examples that show the Father and Son are distinct persons include *Yeshua*'s baptism. At *Yeshua*'s baptism, the Father spoke from heaven while the Spirit alighted on *Yeshua* in the form of a dove (Mat 03:16-17). Another NT example occurred when *Yeshua* was in the temple and the Father spoke from heaven (Joh 12:28-30).

It would seem that either the Trinity is three distinct persons, or else we must believe that God is a ventriloquist or a puppeteer. That God is a ventriloquist or puppeteer is a doctrine unworthy of belief (1Co 15:19).

Chapter 3

The Presences of Elyon

Background

The Hebrew word *Elyon* is often translated as "Most High." *Elyon* is the Father. The Hebrew word *panim* is translated as "presence(s)," "face(s)," or "person(s)." *Panim* looks like a Hebrew plural, but is in fact a dual form. The singular form *paneh* went unused in Hebrew Scripture. Whether dual forms are translated as singulars or plurals depends on the context. Dual forms such as *panim* are discussed in the chapter on Hebrew collective nouns.

Since most translations are not literal, the phrase "before my face [*panim*]" becomes "before me" (Gen 17:01; 33:14). Sometimes the word *panim* is ignored altogether. For instance, Jonah ran away "from the Presences [*Panim*] of *Yahveh*" is sometimes translated as "from the LORD" (*NIV* Jon 01:03 (twice), 10).

The phrase *Panim Yahveh*:
- Preceded by the preposition "before" ("*l*" = *lamedh*) literally means "before *Yahveh*'s presence," or "before *Yahveh*," or words to that effect,
- Preceded by the preposition "from" (*min*) literally means "from *Yahveh*'s presence," and
- Without a prepositional phrase literally means "Presences of *Yahveh*."[75] There are two exceptions discussed later in this chapter (Psa 034:15-16; Lam 04:16).

As was stated before, whether *Panim* is translated as a singular or plural depends on the context. This means the dual form *Panim* can refer to the Son or Spirit, or both. For instance, here the plural verbs indicate that *Panim* refers to the Son and Spirit, and therefore should be translated in the plural as "Presences":

> *Yahveh* [*Elyon* the Father] replied, 'My Presences [Hebrew plural *Panim*], they will go [plural verb] with you, and I will give you rest.' Then Moses said to him [*Elyon* the Father], 'Your Presences, if they [the Son and Spirit] do not go [plural verb] with us [to the Promised Land], do not send us up from here [Mount Sinai]' (Exo 33:14-15).

Who Are *Elyon*'s Presences?

The Son as Elyon's Presence

The existence of God's omnipresence can be inferred by observing the world and universe (Act 17:27-28; Rom 01:19-20). Just as no mere spirit creature can convey God's omnipresence, neither can a mere creature convey God's especial, personal presence. It is therefore no surprise that Scripture associates *Yahveh*'s Presence only with the Son and Spirit.[76] The Son is called a Presence of *Yahveh* in these instances:

- The *Malek Yahveh* (Exo 03:02; 23:20, 23; 33:02) is called the Presence of *Yahveh* (Exo 06:12, 30; 23:17; 34:14, 15, 23, 24, 34, 35; Deu 16:16; 31:11). Note that these passages are found in, or refer back to, sections where the Son is said to have divine names:
  o *Yahveh* and the "I AM" (Exo 03:14-15),
  o *El Shaddai* (Exo 06:03), and
  o The *Malek* with *Yahveh*'s Name in Him (Exo 23:21; 33:02),
- The *Malek Yahveh*'s presence made the surroundings so holy that Moses and Joshua were obliged to take off their sandals (Exo 03:05; Jos 05:15), and
- The narrator of the book of Joshua wrote:

  Seven priests carried seven trumpets before the Presence [*Panim*] of *Yahveh* (Jos 06:08).

  The "Presence of *Yahveh*" refers back to the commander of *Yahveh*'s armies—the *Malek Yahveh* (Jos 05:14-15). Evidently, the *Malek Yahveh* marched ahead of the Israelites around Jericho just as the *Malek Yahveh* had marched ahead of the Israelites during the Exodus (Exo 14:19).

Isaiah said that the Messiah would be "Immanuel," meaning, "God [present] with us" (Isa 07:14; Mat 01:23). The word "Immanuel" was Isaiah's way of saying that the coming Messiah would be a Presence of *Yahveh*. Luke wrote about *Yeshua* as a Presence…

  …when times of spiritual refreshment may come from the Presence [the Son] of the Lord [the Father], and that he [the Father] may send him [the Son as a Presence] who has been appointed for you—even Christ *Yeshua* (Act 03:19-20 (Greek 03:20)).

Isaiah also wrote about the Messiah being the Father's Presence on the Last Day:

  Enter into the rock, and hide in the dust, from before the Presence of the Fear [the Son] of *Yahveh* [the Father], and from the glory [the Son] of his [the Father's] majesty (Isa 02:10).

Speaking about the Son's return on the Last Day (2Th 01:07), Paul alluded to Isa 02:10 to say that the Messiah was the Presence and the glory of the Father:

  Who shall be punished with everlasting destruction from the Presence [the Son] of the Lord [the Father], and from the glory [the Son] of his [the Father's] power (2Th 01:09).

Speaking of the New Heaven and New Earth, the Apostle John wrote in Revelation of the Son's presence with the Father. John wrote that the Lord God and the Lamb "is" a temple (Rev 21:22). John also wrote of the Son's presence with the Father as though the Son were a lamp and as though the Father were the emitted light (Rev 21:23):

I saw no temple in it, for the Lord God, the Almighty, and the Lamb, is [singular verb] its temple. The city has no need for the sun or moon to shine, for the very glory of God illuminated it, and its lamp is the Lamb (Rev 21:22-23).

The Apostle John wrote that the Father and Son had one throne, one face, and one name. That the Father and Son have a singular throne agrees with *Yahveh*'s OT statement:

A glorious throne, exalted from the beginning, is the place of our sanctuary (Jer 17:12).

Note that there was one throne in "our sanctuary." Jer 17:12 is mentioned in the MT plurals appendix. John even addressed both the Father and Son together using the singular pronouns "his" and "him" (Rev 22:01, 03-04):

He showed me a river of water of life, clear as crystal, proceeding out of the throne [singular] of God [the Father] and of the Lamb [the Son]...The throne [singular] of God and of the Lamb will be in it, and his [singular pronoun] servants serve him [singular pronoun]. They will see his [singular pronoun] face, and his [singular pronoun] name will be on their foreheads (Rev 22:01, 03-04).

The Son is said to be present at the Eucharist. Surely, only a Presence of *Yahveh* could accomplish such a divine feat! The Eucharist is a meal commemorating *Yeshua*'s sacrifice for sins (Rom 08:03; Eph 05:02; Heb 09:14; 10:12). The wine is called the blood of the covenant (Mat 26:26-29; Mar 14:22-25; Luk 22:17-20; 1Co 11:23-29).

To avoid misunderstandings, it would be beneficial to set out the Lutheran position on the Lord's Supper here. Koehler wrote:

'...we hereby utterly condemn the Capernaitic eating of the body of Christ, as though His body were rent with the teeth, and digested like other food' (F. C. Epit., Art. VIII, 42, *Triglot*, p. 817). We do not 'hold that the body and blood of Christ are included in the bread locally, or are otherwise permanently united therewith apart from the use of the Sacrament' (F. C. Th. D., Art. VII, 14, *Triglot*, p. 977). The Lutheran Church does not teach 'consubstantiation,' which means that bread and body form one substance, or that the body is present, like the bread, in a *natural manner*; nor does it teach 'impanation,' which means that the body is locally enclosed in the bread...The body and blood of Christ are *really*, but *supernaturally* present in the Sacrament, and all communicants receive them orally, with their mouths, together with the bread and wine.[77]

The Son's supernatural, metaphysical presence in the bread and wine is expressed by:

- The Son saying, "This is my body" (Mat 26:26; Mar 14:22; Luk 22:19),
- The Son saying, "This is my blood" (Mat 26:28; Mar 14:24; Luk 22:20), and by
- Paul saying that the celebrants and communicants must recognize the body of the Lord (1Co 10:16; 11:27).

Yeshua's supernatural, metaphysical presence with the bread and wine is prefigured by:

- The supernatural benefits that accompanied the eating of manna (Deu 08:03-04; 29:05-06; Neh 09:20-21; Joh 06:41, 51). Moses said that *Yahveh* walked through the midst of Israelite camp, so the camp had to remain holy so *Yahveh* would not turn away (Deu 23:14),
- Melchizedek, an ancient Yahvist priest-king of Jerusalem, came out to meet Abraham with bread and wine (Gen 14:18). Melchizedek was greater than Abraham (Heb 07:07). The Son became a kingly priest in the order of Melchizedek after his death and resurrection (Psa 110:04; Heb 05:06). That the Son is a priest-king in the order of Melchizedek explains why *Yeshua* said that he would not drink wine until "it finds fulfillment in the kingdom of God" (Isa 25:06-07; Mat 26:29; Mar 14:25; Luk 22:16, 18). *Yeshua* then appeared on the first day of the week (Mat 28:01, 09-10; Luk 24:21, 33-35; Joh 20:19, 26) and broke bread and drank wine with the disciples (Act 10:41). Thus, wine "found its fulfillment" (its highest use) when it became customary to meet and have the Lord's Supper on the first day of the week (Act 20:07; 1Co 16:02; Rev 01:10). True communion, of course, occurs only in the kingdom of the priest-king *Yeshua*,
- When the Trinity appeared to Abraham, he told Sarah to make bread from three *seahs* of flour (Gen 18:06). Then Abraham ate with the Trinity,
- Moses, his father-in-law, and the Israelite elders ate in the presence of *Yahveh* (Exo 18:12; 24:11),
- Moses instructed the Israelites to build an altar and eat and rejoice in the presence of *Yahveh* once they had entered the Promised Land (Deu 12:07, 18; 14:23, 26; 15:20; 27:07; Eze 44:03),
- During the time of the Judges, Samuel told Saul about three men making what seems to be a Trinitarian offering to [All] the Gods (*haElohim*) at Bethel (1Sa 10:03-04): three loaves of bread and three goats, yet one skin of wine. The Trinity may have posed as three men in 1Sa 10 as they did in Gen 18. Instead of bread made with three *seahs* of flour (Gen 18:06), the three men had three loaves (1Sa 10:03). One of the men, perhaps the Son, shared two loaves of offering bread with Saul. This seems to prefigure the Lord's Supper,
- The 1Sa 10 incident with Saul has similarities to David and his men eating the Bread of the Presences (Exo 25:30) at the tabernacle (1Sa 21:04-06; Mat 12:03-04). Paul said a person partaking of the Lord's Supper should examine himself before eating and drinking (1Co 11:28). Before giving David the Bread of the Presences, the priests asked David whether his men had kept themselves from women. To men on the march, this is likely a euphemistic way of saying "forni-

cation" (1Sa 21:04-06; compare Rev 14:04). Considered together, the incidents concerning Saul and David certainly seem to foreshadow the Lord's Supper,

- The Son's disappearances during Manoah and Gideon's blood and grain offerings (Jdg 06:19-21; 13:15-20), and
- The Son's continuing the conversation with Gideon even after he disappeared in the smoke of Gideon's grain offering (Jdg 06:23). The narrator said that after the *Malek Yahveh* disappeared,

> *Yahveh* said to him: 'Peace be to you; do not fear, you shall not die' (Jdg 06:23).

Yeshua's supernatural, metaphysical presence with the bread and wine is underscored by:

- The Son's saying his flesh was bread (Joh 06:50-58), and "I AM the bread of life" (Joh 06:35 is discussed in the "I AM" chapter),
- The Son's reappearance in Jerusalem during the disciples' discussion of the Son's previous disappearance during the breaking of bread with the Emmaus disciples (Luk 24:31, 35-36). The Son said upon his reappearance to the disciples, "Peace be to you" (Luk 24:36). This brings to mind how, after the *Malek Yahveh* had disappeared:

> *Yahveh* said to him [Gideon], 'Peace be to you; do not fear, you shall not die' (Jdg 06:23 is noted just above),

- The Son saying:

For where two or three come together in my name, there am I with them (Mat 18:20), and

- The supernatural benefits that accompany the celebration of the Lord's Supper (1Co 10:16-17; 11:29-30).

The Spirit as Elyon's Presence

Scripture associates *Yahveh*'s Presence with the Spirit. The narrator wrote that the Spirit of *Yahveh* stirred within Samson (Jdg 13:24), but that *Yahveh* eventually left Samson (Jdg 16:20). This shows that the Spirit is more than an impersonal force, for *Yahveh* would need to be personally present in order to leave. Ezekiel wrote about the Spirit being *Yahveh*'s Presence:

> 'Neither will I hide my Presence [*Panim*] any more from them; for I have poured out my Spirit on the house of Israel,' says the Lord *Yahveh* [the Father] (Eze 39:29).

Both the Son and Spirit as Elyon's Presences

Several passages show that both the Son and the Spirit are *Elyon*'s Presences:
- David wrote:
  o Where could I go from your [the Father's] Spirit? Or where could I flee from your [the Father's] Presence [*Panim*] [the Son]? (Psa 139:07), and
  o Hide your [the Father's] face from my sins...but do not banish me from your [the Father's] Presence [the Son], nor take your Holy Spirit from me (Psa 051:09-11).

- Isaiah wrote:

      In their entire affliction he [the Father] was afflicted, and the *Malek*
      [the Son], his [the Father's] Presence [*Panim* (the Son)], saved them...But
      they rebelled, and grieved his Holy Spirit...his Holy Spirit in the midst of
      them ["in the midst" is tantamount to saying the Spirit is a Presence] (Isa
      63:09-11).

- The Son said that the Father would send the Messiah and the Spirit to be present
  with believers. The Son said:

      Now the Lord *Yahveh* [the Father] has sent me [the Son] and his [the
      Father's] Spirit (Isa 48:16).

- During his earthly ministry, *Yeshua* said that he (Mat 28:20) and the Spirit (Joh
  16:07) would be present for believers. John recorded how *Yeshua* said the Spirit
  is "another Counselor," meaning that both the Spirit and Son were Counselors.
  Yeshua then said that the Spirit and *Yeshua* would be present with Christians:

      I will pray to the Father, and he will give you another Counselor, that
      he may be with you forever—the Spirit of truth, whom the world cannot
      receive; for the world does not see him or know him. You know him, for
      he lives with you, and will be in you. I will not leave you orphans. I will
      come to you (Joh 14:16-18).

- Luke wrote that parents brought infants to *Yeshua* for his blessing (Luk 18:15-
  17). This incident correlates well with what Jeremiah wrote about the Presences
  of *Yahveh*:

      Pour out your heart before the Presences [the Son and Spirit] of the
      Lord [the Father]. Lift up your hands to him [the Trinity] for the lives of
      your infants (Lam 02:19).

- Isaiah records *Yahveh*'s words about the Presences after the Last Day:

      As the new heavens and new earth that I make will endure before my
      Presences [the Son and Spirit]...From one New Moon to another and from
      one Sabbath to another, all mankind will come and bow down before my
      Presences [the Son and Spirit] (Isa 66:22-23).

The next section discusses more events where the Son and Spirit appear as the
Presences of *Elyon*.

Some Encounters with *Elyon*'s Presences

Abraham and the Trinity

Gen 18—19 comprise the longest Trinitarian proof text in the Bible. Gen 19
mentions *Yahveh*'s Presences (Gen 19:13, 27). *Yahveh* appeared as three men to
Abraham (Gen 18:01-02). Moses, the narrator of Genesis, wrote:

      Yahveh [the Son] said...'I will go down now, and see if what they have
      done is as bad as the outcry about it that has come to me [the Son]. If
      not, I will know.' The men [the Son and Spirit] turned and went toward
      Sodom, but Abraham remained standing before *Yahveh* [the Father] (Gen
      18:20-22).

Yahveh the Father remained behind to talk to Abraham, but then returned to heaven without going to Sodom (Gen 18:33). The Son and Spirit went to Sodom and Gomorrah because the inhabitants had been sinning against *Yahveh* for some time (Gen 13:13). Still, they were presumed innocent until proven guilty. After duly investigating the situation, *Yahveh* the Son and Spirit called down sulfur upon Sodom from *Yahveh* the Father in heaven:

Then *Yahveh* [the Son and Spirit] rained on Sodom and on Gomorrah sulfur and fire from *Yahveh* [the Father] out of the sky (Gen 19:24).

The Son may have called down sulfur specifically on Sodom, while the Spirit may have called down sulfur specifically on Gomorrah.

Lot and the Two "Presences" (Gen 19:13, 27)

The narrator wrote:

Then *Yahveh* [the Son] said, 'The outcry against Sodom and Gomorrah is so great and their sin so grievous that I [the Son] will go down and see if what they have done is as bad as the outcry that has reached me [the Son]. If not, I will know.' The men [the Son and Spirit] turned away and went toward Sodom, but Abraham remained standing before *Yahveh* [the Father] (Gen 18:20-22).

The above Trinitarian interpretation of Gen 18:20-22 fits well with what the two men told Lot in Sodom:

We [the Son and Spirit] will destroy this place [Sodom], because the cry about them has grown great before the Presences [the Son and Spirit] of *Yahveh* [the Father]. *Yahveh* [the Father] has sent us [the Son and Spirit] to destroy it (Gen 19:13).

The Son had told Abraham that the outcry had reached him (Gen 18:21). The Father sent the Son and Spirit to Sodom (Gen 18:22). Once in Sodom the Son and Spirit identified themselves to Lot as the Presences of *Yahveh* who had heard the outcry against Sodom (Gen 19:13). Later the narrator wrote:

Abraham got up early in the morning to the place where he had stood before the Presences [the Son and Spirit] of *Yahveh* [the Father]. He [Abraham] looked down toward Sodom and Gomorrah, toward all the land of the plain, and he saw dense smoke rising from the land, like smoke from a furnace (Gen 19:27-28).

The place with an overlook of Sodom (Gen 19:27-28) where Abraham saw Sodom with the men is mentioned in Gen 18:16:

The men [the Son and Spirit] rose up from there, and looked toward Sodom. Abraham went with them to see them on their [the Son and Spirit's] way.

The "men" mentioned in Gen 18:16 are the Son and Spirit since they were the only two persons headed toward Sodom (Gen 18:22). The Father remained behind to talk to Abraham, and then the Father returned to heaven to rain down sulfur on Sodom (Gen 18:22, 33; 19:24). So analysis of Gen 18—19 reveals:

- The chapter is thoroughly Trinitarian,
  and

- The Presences of *Yahveh* who are mentioned in Gen 19:13, 27 are the Son and Spirit.

Jacob at the Jabbok
Jacob wrestled with a Presence at the ford of the Jabbok River (Gen 32:28). Jacob named the ford *Peniel* (*Panim + El*), meaning, "Face of God" or "Presence of God." Jacob said he saw God "Face to face" (*Panim* to *panim*) (Gen 32:30). *Yahveh* and the *Malek Yahveh* often met people "Face to face" (Exo 33:11; Num 12:08; 14:14; Deu 05:04; 34:10; Jdg 06:22). The Gen 32:28 incident is discussed in the Proto-Sinaitic Trinitarianism chapter.

The Israelites and the Presences
The Presences of *Yahveh* were present at the giving of the law (Exo 20). Moses recounted the event:
> This is the blessing that Moses the man of [All] the Gods [*haElohim*] pronounced on the Israelites before his death. *Yahveh* [the Father] came from Sinai, and [the Son] dawned over them from Seir; he [the Spirit] shone forth from Mount Paran. He [the Father] came with myriads of holy ones from the south, from his [the Father's] mountain slopes (Deu 33:01-02).

The *NIV Study Bible* says Sinai, Seir and Mount Paran (Deu 33:02) are three mountains associated with the giving of the law. G. R. Hawting wrote:
> In Jewish and Christian elaborations the biblical story of Hagar's expulsion by Abraham (Genesis 21:14-21) had developed strong Arabian associations. Paran, the place where Ishmael grew up and lived (Genesis 21:21), was identified as a region of northwest Arabia, and in Paul's allegorical development of the story Hagar was identified with Mount Sinai 'which is a mountain in Arabia.'[78]

Mark Cohen wrote about medieval Jews:
> Ibn Ezra knew the old rabbinic *midrash* on the Sinai-Seir-Paran verse. For Deuteronomy 33:2-3, he quoted Saadya's apparently apologetic treatment of the passage. 'The Gaon of blessed memory stated that Mount Sinai, Seir, and Paran in the biblical verse are near one another and that this verse tells about the revelation at Mount Sinai.'[79]

Mark Cohen adds an explanatory note that the Hebrew form translated...
> ...'from Sinai' is exactly like 'at Sinai,' as is [the case with the form commonly translated] 'from Seir.'[80]

So Deu 33:02 could be translated either "from Sinai...from Seir...from Paran," or "at Sinai...at Seir...at Paran."

The Muslim misinterpretation of Deu 33:02-03 should be noted. Samuel M. Zwemer wrote:
> Muslims have always been eager to find further proof of the coming of Muhammad in the Old and New Testament Scriptures in addition to their misinterpretation of John 16:7, regarding the Paraclete [Helper]. They therefore not only quote the words of the *Koran* but also refer to

Deuteronomy 33:2....The passage in Deuteronomy states that Jehovah [*Yahveh*] came from Sinai and rose from Seir unto them; he shined forth from Mount Paran. Sinai is a Jewish mountain; Seir, they say, is a mountain in Galilee where Christ died. Paran, however, is a mountain near Mecca and signifies the Muslim religion.[81]

Obviously, the Muslim interpretation is contradicted not only by geography, but also by the OT and NT narratives.

That *Yahveh* appeared on three mountains in the same region during the giving of the law is confirmed by Moses' later quotation of a statement the Israelites made during the giving of the law:

For what mortal man has ever heard the voice of the living Gods [plurals: *khayyim Elohim*] speaking out of fire, as we have, and survived? (Deu 05:26).[82]

That the Israelites were speaking about the giving of the law (Exo 20) is evident from the context of Deu 05:26. That God spoke out of fire (Deu 05:26) at the giving of the law is well attested (Exo 19:18; 20:19; Deu 05:24-28; 09:10; 18:16-17). The Israelites' mention of the "living Gods" (Deu 05:26) is another indicator that the persons of the Trinity appeared simultaneously: a person on Mount Seir, a person on Mount Paran, and the Father on Mount Sinai (Deu 33:02).

There is another indication that Deu 33:02 speaks of the Trinity appearing on three mountains: the previous verse says Moses was "the man of [All] the Gods" (*haElohim*) (Deu 33:01). During the giving of the law (Exo 20) as well as at other times, Moses (Exo 03:06, 11, 12, 13; 19:03) and the Israelites (Exo 18:12; 19:17; 20:20, 21; 24:11) saw [All] the Gods (*haElohim*). Related points discussed in the chapter on Hebrew collective nouns include how:

- *haElohim* refers to the Trinity, and
- Moses is elsewhere called "the man of [All] the Gods" and the "servant of [All] the Gods."

That chapters Deu 32—33 contain other Trinitarian proof passages further supports the Trinitarian interpretation of Deu 33:01-02. See the Trinitarian proofs appendix for a discussion of these texts: Deu 32:08-09; LXX Deu 32:43; and Deu 33:27. Furthermore, Deu 33:16 refers to a divine person in the "burning bush" of Exo 03:02 (see also Act 07:30). This would seem to indicate that the *Malek Yahveh* was one of the persons of the Trinity who appeared on one of the three mountains (Sinai, Seir, or Paran) during the giving of the law (Deu 33:02).

Moses and the Presences

Awhile after the giving of the law, Moses spoke to the Father at Mount Sinai:

Yahveh [*Elyon* the Father] replied, 'My Presences [Hebrew plural *Panim*], they will go [plural verb] with you, and I will give you rest.' Then Moses said to him [*Elyon* the Father], 'Your Presences, if they [the Son and Spirit] do not go [plural verb] with us [to the Promised Land], do not send us up from here [Mount Sinai]' (Exo 33:14-15).

Many passages discussed in this chapter note how the Son and Spirit were sent as Presences to carry out some divine purpose.[83] Moses wanted the three members of the Trinity to go to Canaan for a variety of reasons, the foremost reason being defense (Psa 048:01-03; 132:13-14, 18; Isa 31:09; Jer 49:01-02; Eze 35:10; 36:05; Zec 02:05).

Moses knew that the Son and Spirit, the Presences of *Yahveh* (Gen 19:13, 27), had been sent to Sodom. Moses knew that they had rained down sulfur from *Yahveh* the Father in heaven (Gen 19:24 is discussed above). Moses also saw firsthand how *Yahveh* had brought Israel "out of Egypt by his Presences and his great strength" (Deu 04:37; Num 20:16). Moses spoke of how the Presences would accompany Israel into the Promised Land:

> The eternal God [the Father] is [Israel's] dwelling-place, underneath are the everlasting arms [the Son and Spirit]. He [the Father] will drive out the enemy from before you, saying [to the Son and Spirit], 'Destroy! [the enemy]' (Deu 33:27).

The Judges Deborah and Barak celebrated how, earlier during the Exodus, the Father had directed the Son and Spirit to go with Israel toward the Promised Land:

> O *Yahveh* [the Trinity], when you [the Son] went out from Seir, when you [the Spirit] marched from the land of Edom, the earth shook, the heavens poured, the clouds poured down water. The mountains quaked before *Yahveh*, the One of Sinai [the Father], before *Yahveh*, the *Elohim* of Israel [the Trinity] (Jdg 05:04-05).

David also wrote about how the Son and Spirit helped conquer the Promised Land:

> It was not by their sword that they won the land, nor did their arm bring them victory; it was your right hand [the Son], your [the Father's] arm [the Spirit], and the light of your [the Father's] Presences [the Son and Spirit], for you [the Father] loved them. You-He [*atah-hu*] [the Trinity] are my King, O God, who decrees victories for Jacob (Psa 044:03-04 [*BHS* 044: 04-05]).

Moses wanted the Son and Spirit to travel to the Promised Land (Exo 33:14-15). Moses knew that *Yahveh* was God of both the Jews and gentiles, but Moses wanted *Yahveh* the Son and Spirit to function as Israel's national God for the time being. Moses knew that most of Israel would eventually fall into unbelief (Deu 31:16-18).

If *Yahveh* the Son and Spirit took up residence in Canaan, the Promised Land would become *Yahveh*'s land (Jos 22:19; Isa 14:02; Hos 09:03). It is not hard to figure out how Moses got this idea since Moses was at Mount Sinai in the Wilderness of Sin. The names Sin and Sinai likely refer to Sin the moon god—as judged from the etymology and archeological evidence.

Moses knew that if *Yahveh*'s Presences were in Canaan, it would be harder for *Yahveh* to abandon *Yahveh*'s land and *Yahveh*'s temple (Eze 08:06). Then all three persons rather than just one person of the Trinity would need to reject Israel if the occasion called for it, as Jeremiah wrote:

The Word [the Son] of *Yahveh* [the Father] came to Jeremiah, saying, 'Have you [Jeremiah] not noticed what this people have spoken? Specifically: 'The two kingdoms that *Yahveh* chose [Israel & Judah], he [*Yahveh*] has rejected them, and they [*Yahveh*] spurn my people [Judah] so that they are no longer a nation before them [*Yahveh*]"(Jer 33:24).

Hosea wrote similarly:

As they [the Trinity] called [plural verb] them [Israel], so they [the Trinity] went [plural verb] from them [Israel] (Hos 11:02).

With *Yahveh* in the Promised Land, the separation of *Yahveh* from Israel would be like:

- A divorce (Jer 03:08),
- Disowning a son (Hos 11:01), or
- Traveling companions parting ways (Amo 03:02-03).

With *Yahveh* in residence in Canaan, it would be surreal if *Yahveh* were to become a stranger in his own land (Jer 14:08-09). It would be noticeable if *Yahveh* retreated back to the Mount of [All] the Gods (*haElohim*) (Exo 03:01; 1Ki 19:08).

Yahveh's last resort was abandoning the temple where his Name and Presences resided (Exo 25:30; 28:30; 1Ki 08:29; 09:03; 2Ki 23:27; Eze 08:06). *Yahveh* preferred to eliminate (Eze 33:24-29) or banish idolaters and career sinners from his Presences,[84] often by exiling them to other countries.[85] In this regard, the prophets taught nothing new. The prophets merely reminded Israel of *Yahveh*'s methods of dealing with flagrant sinners, a policy known to Moses (Deu 30:02-06) and to Solomon (2Ch 06:24-39).

At first the Father was just planning to send the *Malek* with *Yahveh*'s Name in him to Canaan with the Israelites (Exo 23:20-23). The Father called the *Malek*, "*Yahveh*, your God" (Exo 23:19). The Father said, "Three times a year all your males shall appear before the Presence [the Son] of the Lord *Yahveh* [the Father]" (Exo 23:17; repeated in Deu 16:16; 31:11).

The Father said that the *Malek* was "my [the Father's] Presence" (*YLT* Exo 23:15). The Father also said:

Be watchful because of his [the Son's] Presence [*panim*] (*YLT* Exo 23:21).

The *Malek* sent to the Promised Land is "the *Malek*, His [the Father's] Presence [*Panim*]" (Isa 63:09). So the *Malek* was the Father's Presence, yet the *Malek* had "his [own] presence." That the *Malek* had his own presence means the *Malek* was no mere *Shekinah*—the impersonal apparition posited by rabbinic theologians.

The early NT Church understood *Yeshua* to be *Yahveh* the Son and the *Malek Yahveh* with *Yahveh*'s Name "in him" (Exo 23:21). Many mentions are made in the NT of "the Name of *Yeshua*."[86] In Act 05:40-41 the Name of *Yeshua* is called "the Name" (see also 3Jo 01:07). *Yeshua* means, "*Yahveh* saves" (Mat 01:21; 1Ti 01:15), so the name *Yahveh* is "in" the name *Yeshua* as well as "in" *Yeshua*.

A parallel to the *Malek*'s being sent with the authority to retain sins (Exo 23:21) occurred when *Yeshua* commissioned the ten disciples in fulfillment of his promise: "I will give you the keys of the kingdom of heaven" (Mat 16:19). *Yeshua* breathed the Spirit on the disciples, and then said that they could forgive or retain sins (Joh 20:21-23).

Notice that the disciples were only able to forgive or retain sins after they received the Spirit that proceeded from the Father through the Son. Note that it was the OT *Malek Yahveh* who became the Messiah and then breathed out the Spirit on the disciples (Joh 20:21-23). Ultimately only God can forgive or retain sins (Mar 02:07; Luk 05:21). These facts lead to the conclusion that the *Malek Yahveh* was a person of the Trinity.

Immediately after the golden calf incident, the Father said that he was still planning to send "my *Malek*" to the Promised Land ahead of the Israelites (compare Exo 32:34 to Exo 23:23). A little later, however, the Father decided to send a creature spirit—"an angel" (Exo 33:02). The golden calf incident caused the Father to reconsider sending the *Malek* with his name "in him"—as had been planned (Exo 23:20-23).

The Father concluded that if he traveled in the midst of the Israelites, he might destroy the Israelites (Exo 33:03). That the Father did not want to "go in the midst" of Israel also explains why the Father did not want to send his Presence, the *Malek Yahveh* (*YLT* Exo 23:15; Isa 63:09). The proximity to open rebellion would cause the *Malek Yahveh* to refuse forgiveness (Exo 23:21; Heb 12:17).

The Israelites mourned over the news that the Father was planning to send a mere angel (Exo 33:04). That the Israelites mourned confirms that the Father decided to send a mere spirit creature (Exo 33:02) rather than the divine "my *Malek*," the *Malek Yahveh* (Exo 23:20-23; 32:34).

Another confirmation that the Father was planning to send "an angel" rather than the *Malek Yahveh* is Moses said:

You have not let me know whom you will send with me (Exo 33:12).

Apparently, the Father had not mentioned whether the spirit creature now tasked with going to Canaan would be Michael, Gabriel, or another angel.

There were developments that changed the unfortunate situation in which the Israelites found themselves. The plagues (Exo 32:35) that resulted from the golden calf incident were not indiscriminate, but affected those who had engaged in "pagan revelry" (Exo 32:06; 1Co 10:07). Pagan worship often involved orgies and other behaviors that sociologists term "high risk behaviors." The danger, of course, is the spread of STDs (Sexually Transmitted Diseases).

That plagues mainly affected gross sinners can be seen from Num 25:05-18 and other passages.[87] After the plagues took their toll on the hardened sinners, *Yahveh*'s Presence could again go with the survivors without inflicting further judgment on the nation as a whole (Exo 33:03-05; Jer 31:02; Eze 20:18). The Israelites who were spared either did not participate in the sin, or had mourned over the golden calf incident and were forgiven (Exo 33:04).

After the hardhearted were gone and the survivors were forgiven, the Father said, "My Presences, they will go" to Canaan (Exo 33:14). The plural verb "they will go" indicates that *Panim* should be translated in the plural as "Presences," meaning the Son and Spirit. Before the golden calf incident, the Father was just planning to send the Son, but now the Father was planning to send both the Son and Spirit. This is definitely an instance of grace abounding more than sin:

> The law was added so that the offense might increase. But where sin
> abounded, grace increased all the more. (Rom 05:20).

Moses liked the Father's idea of sending both the Son and Spirit so much that Moses asked the Father not to reconsider this decision (Exo 33:15). Moses then asked the Father to go to Canaan with the Israelites even though the Father earlier had said:

> I will not go with you, because you are a stiff-necked people and I
> might destroy you on the way (Exo 34:03).

Later in the conversation, Moses said:

> Yet, how would anyone know that I have found favor in your sight,
> I and your people, unless you [the Father] go with us, so that we are
> distinguished, I and your people, from all the people who are on the
> surface of the earth? (Exo 33:16).

Moses here argued that the Father's not traveling to the Promised Land would leave the wrong impression—that the Father was still too angry to be among the Israelites (Exo 33:05).

Moses and Aaron had a hard enough time holding sway over the Israelites. Moses did not want the Israelites to think Israel or its leaders were out of favor with *Yahveh* the Father. They had already rebelled once when they doubted *Yahveh* was with them:

> And he [Moses] called the place Massah and Meribah because the
> Israelites quarreled and because they tested *Yahveh* saying, 'Is *Yahveh*
> among us or not?' (Exo 17:07).

The Father's sending the Son and the Spirit would parallel how the Father sent the Son and the Spirit during NT times (Isa 11:02; 42:01; 48:16; Luk 04:18-19; Joh 03:34). The NT Jews did not recognize that the Messiah had the Father's favor (Psa 022:08; Mat 27:43), though the Father voiced from heaven that he was pleased with the Son (Mat 03:17; 17:05; Mar 01:11; Luk 03:22; Joh 12:28; 2Pe 01:17). So Moses was wise in asking that the Father come to Palestine, too (Exo 33:16).

Moses was not only concerned about the Father going to the Promised Land because of how the Israelites might act, but also on account of the gentiles. The Israelites had become a laughingstock to their enemies on account of the golden calf incident (Exo 32:25).

The gentiles could sense a people's weakness when that people did not have a good relationship with their god(s) (Num 21:29; Deu 32:27; 2Ch 28:23; 32:15-16; Psa 042:10; 079:10; 115:02; Joe 02:17b). Without the Father going to Canaan, Israel's enemies would not be able to discern (Isa 10:09-11; 36:18-20; Jer 50:07; Eze 25:08) that Israel was the apple (pupil) of the Father's eye (Deu 32:10; Zec 02:08).

One of the words for pupil in the OT is *'iyshown*, meaning, "the little man" (Deu 32:10; Psa 017:08). If one looks real close at the pupil, one sees a reflection of one's self. That Israel was the "little man" reflected in *Yahveh*'s eyes meant the Father was looking at Israel, blessing and being gracious toward and giving

Israel peace (Num 06:25-26). Any believer who has the Aaronic Blessing named over them similarly becomes the apple of the Father's eye. Moreover, a close relationship between *Yahveh* and Israel is implied. One only gets so close so as to see the reflection in another's eye when there is an intimate, personal, affectionate relationship.

Based on his experience in Egypt, Moses knew that God helped nations in ordinary ways (Psa 145:09; Amo 09:07; Mat 05:45; Act 14:17; 17:27). Moses therefore wanted the Father to help Israel in an extraordinary way. Moses convinced the Father to go to the Promised Land so that the nations would see that the Father favored Israel enough to dwell with Israel (Exo 19:05-06; Deu 10:15; 23:14; 26:19; 28:01; Hos 11:08; Mal 03:14-18). The Father told Moses:

> I will do also this thing that you have spoken [accompany Israel to the Promised Land (Exo 33:16)]; for you have found favor in my sight, and I know you by name (Exo 33:17).

That the Father went to the Promised Land was how Jeremiah could say that Israel lived under the shadow of *Yahveh* (Lam 04:20).

Because of the golden calf incident, the covenants between *Yahveh* and Israel had to be formally reinstated. The covenants had been annulled when *Yahveh* was about to destroy Israel. *Yahveh* considered fulfilling his promises to the patriarchs through a nation populated by Moses' own descendants:

> Leave me alone now so my anger may burn against them to destroy them. Then I will make you into a great nation (Exo 32:10; Deu 09:25-26).

Moses, however, convinced *Yahveh* to reconsider this course of action, and then to renew the covenants. Israel had a covenantal relationship with the Father that was first established in Gen 15, and a covenantal relationship with the Son that was first established in Gen 17. *Yahveh* the Son referred to his Gen 17 covenant when he said:

> I also established my covenant with the patriarchs (Exo 06:04).

Yahveh invited Moses back up the mountain the next day to see *Yahveh*'s glory (Exo 34:01-03). Previously, *Yahveh* was invisible and his presence was known only from a voice, sometimes accompanied by fire or some other phenomenon (Deu 04:12, 15). After Moses saw *Yahveh*'s glory, Israel would see Moses' face glowing with *Yahveh*'s glory. Then they would know with certainty that Israel was once again in God's good graces. They would also know the covenants had been renewed, and *Yahveh* would again be going to Palestine with Israel.

The next day the Father stood near to Moses in a nimbus cloud (Exo 34:05). The Father proclaimed his Name, *Yahveh*—just as he said he would (Exo 33:19; 34:05). The cloud was the Spirit who served as a covering "hand" that shielded Moses from seeing the Father's own face (Exo 33:22-23).

The Spirit sometimes appeared as a cloud. For instance, as was noted above, Barak and Deborah described the Spirit sent in Exo 33:14-15 as a cloud (Jdg 05:04-05). Also, the Trinitarian proofs appendix discusses how the Spirit was the pillar of cloud in Exo 14:19-24.

According to Paul, the nimbus cloud at Sinai in Exo 34 emitted the Spirit's glory. Paul wrote that the Spirit is the glory of the Lord that shines on our faces just as the Spirit's light shone on Moses:

> But we all, with unveiled face behold the glory of the Lord, and are transformed into the same image with ever-increasing glory that comes from the Lord, the Spirit (2Co 03:18).

Paul mentions Moses and the veil that covered his glowing face starting in 2Co 03:13, so 2Co 03:18 surely alludes to Moses' Mount Sinai experience (Exo 34:33-35).

After the Father descended in the nimbus cloud of the Spirit and proclaimed his name (Exo 34:05), *Yahveh* the Son passed by and proclaimed the Name, *Yahveh* (Exo 34:06). The actions of the Father and Son distinguish the Father and Son—the Father stood and proclaimed while the Son passed by Moses.

The wording also reveals that the subject of Exo 34:05 is the Father, while the subject of Exo 34:06 is the Son. The previous day the Father said that he would say:

> I will be gracious to whom I will be gracious, and will show mercy to whom I will show mercy (Exo 33:19).

The Father's statement is in the first person ("I"), while the Son talked of the Father in the third person ("he"):

> *Yahveh* [the Son] passed in front of Moses, proclaiming, '*Yahveh* [the Father], *Yahveh*, the compassionate and gracious God...Yet he...he...' (Exo 34:06-07).

The Father spoke from within a bright nimbus cloud, but the Son showed his face. How the Son appeared in Exo 34 can be ascertained from Ezekiel's Son of Man vision and the Transfiguration accounts. During the Transfiguration, the Messiah appeared to be as bright as the sun (Mat 17:02) and his clothes were as bright as lightning (Luk 09:29). Ezekiel described the Son of Man:

> ...on the likeness of the throne was a likeness as the appearance of a man. I saw that from what appeared to be his waist up he looked like glowing metal, as if full of fire, and that from there down he looked like fire, and there was brightness round about him. As the appearance of the bow that is in the cloud in the day of rain, so was the appearance of the brightness round about. This was the appearance of the likeness [the Son] of the glory of *Yahveh* [the Father] (Eze 01:26-28).

Even though *Yeshua* is now incarnate, Paul wrote that he still shows the "glory of God":

> Even if our gospel is veiled, it is veiled in those who perish; in whom the god of this world has blinded the minds of the unbelieving, that the light of the gospel of the glory of Christ, who is the image of God, should not dawn on them. For we do not preach ourselves, but Christ *Yeshua* as Lord, and ourselves as your servants for *Yeshua*'s sake; seeing it is God who said, 'Light will shine out of darkness,' who has shone in our hearts, to give the light of the knowledge of the glory of God in the face of Christ (2Co 04:03-06).

Scriptural parallels to Moses' experience on the mount (Exo 33—34) include how the Father spoke to Elijah in a "whisper of a gentle breeze" (LXX 1Ki 19:12; compare Gen 03:08, 10; Joh 03:08). Just as the nimbus cloud was the Spirit (Exo 34:05), the breeze was the Spirit (LXX 1Ki 19:12). Just as Moses was protected in the cleft of a rock on Mount Sinai, Elijah was protected in a cave entrance on Mount Sinai.

Another parallel to Exo 33—34 occurred at the Transfiguration. There the Father spoke to the disciples from within a bright nimbus cloud that was the Spirit (Mat 17:05). The Transfiguration and 1Ki 19 are discussed later in this chapter.

After *Yahveh* the Son appeared to Moses on Mount Sinai (Exo 34:06), Moses made this request of the Son:

> If now I have found favor in your sight, Lord, please let the Lord [the Son] go in the midst of us [as a Presence], although it is a stiff-necked people; and pardon our iniquity and our sin, and take us for thy inheritance (Exo 34:09).

That the Promised Land was *Yahveh*'s "inheritance" is another indication that Moses here talked to *Yahveh* the Son. Moses said elsewhere that *Yahveh* the Son had received Israel as an inheritance from *Elyon,* the Father (Deu 32:08-09). The Father can receive an inheritance from neither himself nor his Son, but the Son can receive an inheritance from the Father.

Other indicators that the divine person to whom Moses spoke in Exo 34 was the Son are:

- Moses already had the Father's favor, and
- The Father had already agreed to go to Canaan (Exo 33:12, 16-17).

Moses was not asking the Father a second time for something the Father had already granted. Rather, Moses requested the Son's favor, and that the Son renew his Gen 17 covenant. Out of courtesy Moses asked the Son to agree to go to the Promised Land as a Presence (Exo 34:09). The Son would naturally agree to do this last favor, since the Father had already agreed to send the Son and Spirit (Exo 34:14-15).

In response to Moses' request, *Yahveh* the Son made a covenant to go to Canaan. Previously, the Father had stated what his intermediary, the *Malek* with *Yahveh*'s Name, would do (Exo 23:20-33). Now, however, the intermediary himself, the *Malek* with *Yahveh*'s Name, stated what he would do in Canaan (Exo 34:10-26). That the *Malek Yahveh* roughly restated in Exo 34:10-16 what the Father had promised the *Malek* would do in Exo 23:20-33 can be seen from the similar elements in each section:

- A command to appear before *Yahveh* the Son three times a year (Exo 23:14, 17; 34:23-24),
- A prohibition against cooking a goat in its mother's milk (Exo 23:19; 34:26),
- A command to smash sacred stones (idols and betyls) (Exo 23:24; 34:13), and
- A promise that *Yahveh* the Son would drive out Canaanite tribes such as the Perizzites (Exo 23:23; 34:11).

That both Exo 23 and 34 were all about what the *Malek Yahveh* would do is confirmed by several facts. The promises in Exo 23 and 34 coincide with the covenant that the Son, *El Shaddai*, made in Gen 17. *El Shaddai*, who was the *Malek Yahveh* (Exo 03:02; 06:03), referred to his Gen 17 covenant when he said:

I also established my covenant with the patriarchs (Exo 06:04).

The *Malek Yahveh* was involved with the conquest of the Promised Land (Jos 05:13—06:08). Conquering Palestine was conducted in fulfillment of what the Son said he would do (Gen 17; Exo 34) and what the Father said the *Malek Yahveh* would do (Exo 23). The *Malek Yahveh* even mentioned his Gen 17 covenant with the patriarchs, the covenant that was renewed in Exo 23 and 34:

The Malek Yahveh went up from Gilgal to Bokim and said, 'I brought you up out of Egypt and led you into the land that I swore to give to your forefathers [Gen 17].' I said, 'I will never break my [Exo 34] covenant with you, and you shall not make a covenant with the people of this land, but you shall break down their altars [Exo 34:13].' Yet you have disobeyed me. Why have you done this?' (Jdg 02:01-02).

The *Malek Yahveh* said that Israel failed to break down the pagan altars (Jdg 02:02). The only covenant in which this was a provision was the Exo 34 covenant between the Son and Israel (Exo 34:13). Therefore, the *Malek Yahveh* claimed the Exo 34 covenant was his (Jdg 02:02), and this means the *Malek Yahveh* is the *Yahveh* of Exo 34:06-29.

Moses' Encounters with the Presences at the Rocks That Brought Forth Water

Overview

Moses' other encounters with the Presences include the times Moses struck rocks that then produced a flow of water. One rock was at a place near Sinai called Massah and Meribah (Exo 17:07). The other rock was at a place called Meribah Kadesh in the Desert of Zin (Num 27:14).

Yahveh stood by the rock at Mount Sinai to show Israel that *Yahveh* was present in Israel despite their previous doubts:

Yahveh answered Moses, 'Walk on ahead of the people. Take with you some of the elders of Israel and take in your hand the staff with which you struck the Nile, and go. I will stand there before you by the rock at Horeb. Strike the rock, and water will come out of it for the people to drink.' So Moses did this in the sight of the elders of Israel. And he called the place Massah and Meribah because the Israelites quarreled and because they tested *Yahveh* saying, 'Is *Yahveh* among us or not?' (Exo 17:05-07).

At Mount Sinai Moses struck the watering rock once (Exo 17:06), perhaps to indicate that there was one spiritual Presence at the rock:

...our forefathers were all under the cloud and they all passed through the sea. They were all baptized into Moses in the cloud and in the sea. They all ate the same spiritual food and drank the same spiritual drink;

for they drank from the supernatural rock that accompanied them, and that
rock was Christ (1Co 10:01-04).

That the "supernatural rock...accompanied them" suggests that Christ was
Present both at the rock at Sinai (Exo 17) and at the rock at Kadesh (Num 20).
David associated the Spirit with the rock at Kadesh incident:

By the waters of Meribah they angered Yahveh, and trouble came to
Moses because of them; for they rebelled against the Spirit of God, and
rash words came from Moses' lips (Psa 106:32-33).

David also wrote:

Tremble, you earth, at the Presence [the Spirit] of the Lord [the Father],
at the Presence [the Son] of the God [the Father] of Jacob, who turned the
rock into a pool of water, the flint into a spring of waters (Psa 114:07-08).

Comparing what David and Paul wrote, there seems to have been two Presences
at the rock at Kadesh. Previously, Moses struck the rock at Sinai once—perhaps to
indicate that one Presence stood by the rock, namely, Christ (Exo 17:06; 1Co 10:
04).

At the rock of Kadesh, however, Moses left the Presences (*Panim*) of *Yahveh*,
and then returned and struck "that rock" twice (Num 20:07-09). Also, it is interesting that the rock at Kadesh is called "the rock" and Paul refers to Christ as "the
rock" (Num 20:08, 10-11; 1Co 10:04). The two knocks seems to indicate that the
two Presences mentioned in Exo 33:14-15, the Son and Spirit, were both at the
rock at Kadesh.

At the rock of Kadesh, *Yahveh* said that Moses failed to keep *Yahveh* holy
before the people (Num 20:12; Deu 32:51). The basic meaning of "holy" is "to
separate" or to "set apart." So it seems Moses failed to keep *Yahveh* "holy" by allowing the Israelites to make an unauthorized near approach to the Presences of
Yahveh. Bringing the elders of Israel close to *Yahveh* was not a concern, but the
rebels were:

Moses and Aaron gathered the assembly together in front of the rock
and Moses said to them, 'Listen, you rebels, must we bring you water out
of this rock?' (Num 20:10).

So Moses' "rash words" (Psa 106:32-33) were his announcing before *Yahveh*
that some of the Israelites were rebels. It is one thing to bring people before
Yahveh, but it is another thing to declare them rebels even if it were true. This
declaration unnecessarily raised matters of conscience (1Co 10:25-29). Moreover,
calling people "rebels" while they are standing right in front of *Yahveh* is
tantamount to calling down judgment before the rebels' time of grace had expired
(Exo 33:03).

Moses' rash words were similar to the rash words *Yeshua* warned against—even
if the words could be construed as being true:

Anyone who says, 'You fool!' will be in danger of the fire of hell (Mat 05:22).

Yeshua's words are especially poignant considering how God called the rich
man who entertained Epicurean thoughts a "fool":

Fool! This night your soul is required of you; the things you have prepared, whose will they be? (Luk 12:20).

A More Detailed Look

Let us, however, take a closer look at the accounts of the rocks at Massah-Meribah (Exo 17:07), and Meribah-Kadesh (Num 20). When Israel was in Kadesh, the "glory of *Yahveh*" appeared (Num 20:06). The "glory" is likely a reference to the Son (1Co 10:04). *Yahveh* told Moses to gather the people together and then bring water out of "that rock" "before their eyes" (*NIV* Num 20:07-09). Moses then took a staff from *Yahveh*'s Presences (Num 20:09), and gathered Israel to the face (*panim*) of "that" certain rock (Num 20:10).

Yahveh, however, did not tell Moses to bring the people up to the rock face (*panim*). *Yahveh* just told Moses to bring Israel "within sight" of the rock, literally "before their eyes" (Num 20:08). "Within sight" could have meant a hundred meters or more, not right up to the rock face. Previously, the people viewed events from "the foot of the mountain" (Exo 19:17), and "the people stood at a distance" (Exo 20:21). Since the people were at the rock face (*panim*), this meant the people were in the presence (*panim*) of *Yahveh* standing there (Num 20:10; Deu 32:51).

No one was supposed to come near *Yahveh* unless *Yahveh* authorized an approach (Exo 19:12-13, 21-25; 24:01-02; Lev 10:01-03). *Yahveh* then told Moses that he had failed to keep *Yahveh* holy before the people (Num 20:12; Deu 32:51). The basic meaning of "holy" is "to separate" or to "set apart." So Moses failed to keep *Yahveh* "holy" by allowing the Israelites, especially the "rebels," to make an unauthorized near approach to *Yahveh*. Also, there is no mention of anyone removing his or her sandals in recognition of the holy presence of *Yahveh* (Exo 03:05; Jos 05:15).

Previously, the people were always kept separate, and only Moses, Aaron, the priests and sometimes elders were allowed to approach *Yahveh* (Exo 19:12-13, 21-25; 34:03). Those few who did approach *Yahveh* removed their sandals (Exo 03:05; Jos 05:15). For instance, the first time water gushed from a rock at Sinai, only Moses and the elders were in *Yahveh*'s presence (*panim*) (Exo 17:06). The people were not in *Yahveh*'s presence, since Moses and some elders had walked ahead of the people to the rock (Exo 17:05). At Kadesh, however, even the assembly came to the face (*panim*) of the rock were *Yahveh* was standing (Num 20:10).

It is true that Moses also failed to honor *Yahveh* by speaking rash words to the rebellious Israelites in *Yahveh*'s presence (Psa 106:32-33). Deu 32:51 does seem to mention that Moses did two things wrong at the Kadesh rock:

This is because [1] both of you broke faith with me in the presence of the Israelites at the waters of Meribah Kadesh in the Wilderness of Zin, and because [2] you did not uphold my holiness [separateness] among the Israelites (Deu 32:51).

Moses, however, later said it was the Israelites' fault that he was not able to enter the Promised Land (Deu 01:37; 03:26). Some have said this was because, instead of speaking to the rock, Moses struck the rock with his staff. *Yahveh* said that both Moses and Aaron committed that same sin (Num 27:12-14; Deu 32:50-52). It would seem hard to believe that Aaron or any of the people caused Moses to strike the rock twice rather than speak to it.

The only single sin that Moses, Aaron and the people committed was not keeping the people separate from *Yahveh*. It seems that allowing the people to approach *Yahveh* without authorization was the only sin that Moses and Aaron committed that was serious enough to:

- Otherwise be a stoning offense (Exo 19:12-13, 22; 24:02; Num 16:17), and
- Keep Moses and Aaron out of the Promised Land (Num 20:12, 24; Deu 32:51-52).

Exegetes may posit or deduce many things about Scripture, but this does not change Scripture. Scripture does not explicitly state that Moses was in trouble with *Yahveh* over striking the rock twice rather than speaking to it. The same could be said for Moses' rash words. In fact, *Yahveh*'s giving Moses a staff at Kadesh suggests that Moses was supposed to strike the rock at Kadesh.

Striking the rock at Kadesh would be consistent with *Yahveh*'s command to strike the rock at Mount Sinai (Num 20:08; compare Exo 17:06). So it would seem that the sin that kept Moses and Aaron out of the Promised Land was the failure to keep the Israelites separate from *Yahveh*'s Presences.

Elijah and the Presences on the Mount of [All] the Gods

The account of Elijah confronting the prophets of Baal and Ashtorah at Mount Carmel contains several Trinitarian elements. The Word of *Yahveh* (1Ki 18:01, 31) and the Spirit (1Ki 18:12) are mentioned. The Israelites seem to have alluded to the Word and Spirit when they said:

    Yahveh—he [the Son] is God! *Yahveh*—he [the Spirit] is God (1Ki 18:39)!

In the next chapter, Elijah went to Mount Horeb, otherwise called Mount Sinai and the "Mount of [All] the Gods" (*haElohim*) (1Ki 19:08; also Exo 03:01; 04:27; 18:05; 24:13; 2Ki 04:25). The form *HaElohim* refers to the Trinity, as was discussed in the chapter on Hebrew collective nouns.

Elijah went to the Mount of [All] the Gods at the invitation of the *Malek Yahveh* (1Ki 19:05-08). Previously, the Trinity issued invitations for visits on hills and mountains. *Yahveh* even had a reputation among the pagans for being a god of the hills (1Ki 20:28). Example of *Yahveh*'s Trinitarian invitations to mountains include:

- "[All] the Gods" invited Abraham to Mount Moriah by (Gen 22:03, 09) where he met the *Malek Yahveh* (Gen 22:02-03, 09, 11-12). The *Malek Yahveh* also quoted the Father (Gen 22:16),
- Jacob met "[All] the Gods" at Bethel (Gen 31:11, 13; 35:07). Jacob went back to Bethel at the invitation of the Father (Gen 35:01) where he met *El Shaddai*, the Son (Gen 35:11). Bethel was known as hill country (Gen 12:08; Jos 16:01; 1Sa 13:02),

- Moses was drawn to the "Mount of [All] the Gods" (Exo 03:01) by the spectacle of the burning bush. Moses returned to the "Mount of [All] the Gods" at the invitation (Exo 03:12) of the *Malek Yahveh* (Exo 03:02; Act 07:30, 35). During the Exodus, Moses was invited up the mountain often, for instance, Exo 34:02. There Moses met "[All] the Gods" (Exo 03:06, 11, 12, 13; 18:12; 19:03, 17; 20: 20, 21; 24:11), and
- Aaron was invited to meet Moses at the "Mount of [All] the Gods" (Exo 04:27).

The *Malek Yahveh* invited Elijah to Mount Sinai, and aided Elijah's trip there (1Ki 19:05, 07). The narrator referred to this *Malek Yahveh* as the Word of *Yahveh* (1Ki 19:09) and as *Yahveh* (1Ki 19:11). The Word of *Yahveh* told Elijah to stand before the Presence of *Yahveh* (the Son) at the mouth of the cave, because *Yahveh* the Father was about to "pass by" (1Ki 19:11).

A wind, an earthquake and a fire passed "before the Presence [the Son] of *Yahveh* [the Father]" (1Ki 19:11). *Yahveh* the Father, however, was not in the wind, the earthquake nor the fire (1Ki 19:11-12). Then *Yahveh* the Father spoke in a whisper (1Ki 19:12-13). The LXX has "the voice of a gentle breeze" (*LXE* 1Ki 19: 12). The whisper was the Father, while the breeze was the Spirit. This is similar to how earlier in Exo 34 the Father was in the cloud of the Spirit.

The Hebrew word *Ruach* means "Spirit," "breeze" or "wind." The Spirit is elsewhere compared to the wind (Joh 03:08). The statement that "the Spirit of God moved over the water" (Gen 01:02) suggests a breeze. "The voice of a gentle breeze" would explain how the Father's whisper could "pass by" (1Ki 19:11).

That the whisper was in a breeze explains why Elijah proceeded to the mouth of the cave upon hearing the whisper (1Ki 19:13). Elijah had retreated into the safety of the cave to avoid the wind, the fire, and the tumbling rocks dislodged by the earthquake (1Ki 19:11-12). That the Father would speak from within a breeze is not unusual since:

- *Yahveh* spoke from within a bush (Exo 03:02, 04),
- *Yahveh* spoke from within clouds (Exo 16:10; 24:16; 34:05; 40:38; Lev 16:2; Num 11:25; Deu 01:33; Mat 17:05),
- The Father's voice once even sounded like thunder (Joh 12:28-30), and
- *Yahveh* apparently also appeared in a gentle breeze in the Garden of Eden. "In the cool of the day" likely refers to the cooling breezes that occur around sunset:

  They [Adam and Eve] heard the sound of *Yahveh* God walking in the garden in the cool of the day, and the man and his wife hid themselves from the presences of *Yahveh* [Father] God [Son] among the trees of the garden (Gen 03:08).

  Note that Adam and Eve hid among the trees upon hearing God in the breeze. Likewise, Elijah pulled his cloak over his face (1Ki 19:13) upon hearing "the voice of a gentle breeze" (*LXE* 1Ki 19:12).

So it would seem that the LXX translation of "the voice of a gentle breeze" likely reflects the original Hebrew text. The Son being the Word, and the Father being the whisper in the breeze of the Spirit, makes 1Ki 19 a thoroughly Trinitarian chapter. 1Ki 19 will be discussed again later in this chapter.

That the Father met Elijah last fits the storyline. Elijah left Israel to meet the Trinity on the Mount of [All] the Gods, Sinai. Israel's problems could only be solved by foreign intervention. The Son was the national God of Israel, while the Father ruled all the nations, as is discussed in chapter on the Song of Moses. The Father told Elijah to anoint Hazael king over Aram, and Jehu son of Nimshi king over Israel. They were to deal with God's enemies in Israel (1Ki 19:15-17).

The Presences in the Temple

Scripture often mentions the Presences in the temple (1Sa 01:22; 02:17, 18; 26:20; 2Sa 21:01; 1Ki 13:06; 2Ki 13:04; 2Ch 33:12; Job 01:12; 02:07; Jer 26:19; Zec 07:02; 08:21, 22). Ezekiel mentioned the two Presences in the temple extensively. Ezekiel referred to the Son as "the Glory," and to the Spirit as "the man."

The narrator referred to "the man" as *Yahveh* (Eze 44:02, 05), and "the man" refers to the Glory (Eze 43:01) as *Yahveh* (Eze 44:02). So one can deduce that the two Presences in the temple are the Son and Spirit. Ezekiel is discussed further in the chapter on the Various Presentations of the Trinity.

The Name, *Yahveh*, was borne by his Presences (*Panim*) in the temple (2Ch 20:09; see also Deu 14:23; 18:07; 1Ki 08:29; 09:03; 2Ki 23:27; Jer 07:10; 34:15). The *Malek* with *Yahveh*'s Name in him was one of God's Presences who bore the Name, *Yahveh*, in the temple (Exo 23:21; Exo 34:20; Luk 13:35). The Father said:

Put the bread of the Presences on the table to be before my Presences [*Panim*] at all times (Exo 25:30).

So it seems the Son and Spirit were associated with the Bread of the Presences.

Yahveh sat between the wings of the cherubim (Exo 25:22; Lev 16:02; Num 07:89; 1Sa 04:04; 2Sa 06:02; 2Ki 19:15; 1Ch 13:06; Psa 080:01; 099:01; Isa 37:16) of the "Ark of [All] the Gods" that was placed in the "House of [All] the Gods." The name "[All] the Gods" (*haElohim*) implies that members of the Trinity were associated with the Ark and the Temple. The Hebrew collective nouns chapter discusses the:

- Thirty-five mentions of the "Ark of [All] the Gods," and
- Fifty-five mentions of the "House of [All] the Gods."

Even before the temple was built, David went before the Presences of *Yahveh* (2Sa 07:18; 1Ch 16:01; 17:16) in the tabernacle that contained the Ark of [All] the Gods (2Sa 06:16-17). The Spirit in the form of a cloud of glory was associated with the:

- Ark (Lev 16:02),
- Tabernacle (Exo 40:34-38; Num 09:15-22; 10:11), and
- Solomon's temple (1Ki 8:10-12; 2Ch 5:13-14).

Luke wrote concerning Isa 06 that Isaiah talked to the Spirit in the temple (Act 28:25-26; Isa 06:08-13). The Spirit was sometimes associated with a cloud, as was discussed above concerning Exo 34:05.

The Son was also present in the temple. The Apostle John wrote concerning the Isa 06 temple vision that Isaiah saw and spoke "about" the glory of *Yeshua* (Joh 12: 41). The Apostle Paul also knew the Son was an OT Presence or Face of *Yahveh*. Paul wrote that *Yeshua* is the "image of God," and that the light of the knowledge of the glory of God shows in the face of *Yeshua* (2Co 04:04-06; compare 2 Co 03: 14-18 and Rev 01:16).

The Presences of *Elyon* in the temple were the Son and Spirit, and they allowed the Father to speak as though he were especially present in the temple (1Ki 09:03; 11:36; Jer 07:10; 34:15; Eze 44:15 and Hag 02:14). That the Presences dwelt in the temple is how the Father:

- Could be present in heaven (Dan 07:13; Psa 011:04), and
- Hear from heaven (2Ch 07:14b), while his Faces (2Ch 07:14a) and his eyes, ears and heart were present at the temple (1Ki 09:03; 2Ch 07:15-16). Stephen taught that the Father dwelt in heaven rather than the temple:

> The Most High [*Elyon*] does not live in houses made by men. As the prophet says: 'Heaven is my throne, and the earth is my footstool. What kind of house will you build for me?' says the Lord [the Father]. 'Or where will my resting place be?' (Act 07:48-49).

The Father sent his Presences, the Son and Spirit, to be especially present in the temple. The Most High (*Elyon*), however, determined that he would dwell in the heavens and not be especially present elsewhere (1Ki 08:27; 2Ch 02:06; 06:18; Act 07:48-50; Isa 66:01-02; Joh 14:02). This arrangement was meant to emphasize how there were individual persons of the Trinity, yet they were a united one—as the *Shema* pointed out.

This Trinitarian explanation solves the apparent contradiction of how *Yahveh* was said to dwell in the tabernacle and temple (2Sa 07:05-07), yet not in the temple (Isa 66:01-02). This Trinitarian explanation also explains why the Psalmists could speak of *Yahveh* having "tabernacles"—one being in heaven and the other on earth (Psa 043:03; 046:04; 084:01; 132:07; Heb 08:05; 09:24). That the Father dwelt in heaven over the Promised Land is how Jeremiah could say that Israel lived under the shadow of *Yahveh* (Lam 04:20).

That Israel lived under the shadow of *Elyon*, and the Presences of *Yahveh* were in the temple, explains why Jonah thought he could run from the Presences (*Panim*) of *Yahveh* in the temple (Jon 01:03, 10). The account of Jonah is discussed in the chapter on The Various Presentations of the Trinity.

That the Father dwelt in heaven and the Presences dwelt in the temple is why Hezekiah could use the paired pronouns "you-he" (*atah-hu*) to pray:

> O *Yahveh*, God of Israel, enthroned between the cherubim, you-he are God over all the kingdoms of the earth (2Ki 19:15; Isa 37:16).

The other seven occurrences of the "you-he" (*atah-hu*) paired pronouns also were likely spoken in the vicinity of the first and second temples (2Sa 07:28; 1Ch 17:26; 2Ch 20:06; Neh 09:06a, 07; Psa 044:05a; Jer 14:22).

It was noted in the chapter on Hebrew collective nouns that the "you-he" paired pronouns occur with other plural elements indicating plural persons. The members of the Trinity were often addressed with singular collective nouns and pronouns as well as plural collective nouns and pronouns.

The "you" of the paired "you-he" pronouns may have been meant as a collective pronoun referring to the Presences in the temple. The "he" of the paired "you-he" pronouns may have been meant as a singular pronoun referring to the Father in heaven. "You" naturally refers to a person or persons who are near—such as the Presences in the temple. "He" naturally refers to a more distant person such as the Father in heaven.

The Presences Did Not Always Inhabit the Temple

The Presences who bore the Name of *Yahveh* did not always dwell in the temple. The Presences did not dwell in the first temple until it was dedicated (1Ki 08:10-11; 2Ch 05:13-14). Likewise, the Presences did not dwell in the ruins of Solomon's temple (2Ki 23:27; Lam 05:18; Dan 09:17; Zec 08:03).

Apparently, the Presences who bore the Name, *Yahveh,* never inhabited Herod's temple, apart from the time that *Yeshua* was there. *Yeshua* considered the temple a den of thieves due to the presence of crooked moneychangers. Also, the high priestly positions routinely went to the shrewdest schemers. The highest bidders usually were the Hellenistic Sadducees who did not even believe in the resurrection or spirits (Act 23:08).

Herod the Great initiated the construction of the temple in 19 BC. This is the same Herod who tried to kill *Yeshua* in Bethlehem when *Yeshua* was about two years old (Mat 02:07, 16). When *Yeshua* came to the temple during his ministry, it had been under construction for forty-six years (Joh 02:20). People picked up stones, perhaps from the temple construction project, and twice tried to stone *Yeshua* in the temple courts (Joh 08:59; 10:31-32; 11:08).

Herod's temple likely would not have been inhabited by the Presences only after its completion and dedication, if at all. This was the case with Solomon's temple (1Ki 08:06-13; 2Ch 05:13-14). Herod the Great had the temple that Zerubbabel built destroyed. Herod's temple was not completed until 62 or 64 AD—long after *Yeshua* declared it desolate (Mat 23:38; Luk 13:35). Then in 70 AD the Romans destroyed Herod's temple.

That God's Presences no longer dwelt in the temple left open the possibility that a Presence might visit the temple. The Jewish leadership, however, "did not recognize the time of God's coming to you" (*NIV* Luk 19:44), even though John the Baptist had cried out:

> Prepare in the wilderness the way of *Yahveh* [the Son]; make level in
> the desert a highway for our God [the Son] (Isa 40:03; compare Mat 03:
> 03; Mar 01:02-03; Luk 03:04-06; Joh 01:23).

The Father also said:

> 'Behold, I send my messenger [John the Baptist] to prepare the way
> before my Presence [*Yahveh* the Son], and the Lord [*Yeshua*] whom you
> seek will suddenly come to his temple; the *Malek* of the covenant in whom

you delight, behold, he is coming,' says *Yahveh* of angelic armies [the Father] (Mal 03:01).

Yeshua confirmed that the Father spoke of sending a messenger ahead of his Presence, *Yahveh* the Son. *Yeshua* quoted what the Father had told him:

I [the Father] will send my messenger ahead of you [the Son], who will prepare your [the Son's] way before you [the Son] (Mat 11:10; Mar 01:02; Luk 07:27).

What the Father said to the Son is reflected in Isa 40:03 and Mal 03:01. Isa 40:03 predicted the message of John the Baptist, so naturally, Isa 40:03 reads as though John the Baptist were speaking. Mal 03:01, however, reads as though the Father were speaking to the Judeans. So either the Father spoke three times on the subject, or the Son adapted the Father's conversation for Isaiah and Malachi's message.

Yeshua's version of Mal 03:01 shows how to translate and interpret Mal 03:01. The phrase commonly translated as "...before me" should be translated as "...send my messenger before my [the Father's] Presence [the Son]." The rest of Mal 03:01 confirms the "my Presence" translation of *Panim*.

The Presence is described as "the *Malek* of the covenant" who would come to his temple (Mal 03:01b). The word *Malek* describes the Son, who is elsewhere called the "*Malek*, his Presence" (Isa 63:09). The Presences were members of the Trinity, and they dwelt in the OT temples. So it is natural that the temple would be called "his temple" (Mal 03:01).

Yahveh the Son also prophesied about his [the Messiah's] ministry, "Now the Lord *Yahveh* has sent me and his Spirit" (Isa 48:16). Of course, if the Son and Spirit were already in the temple during NT times, they would not need to be "sent" to the Promised Land. So Herod's temple was not inhabited by the Presences—the Son and Spirit. The Son was sent back to the Promised Land when *Yeshua* was conceived, and the Spirit was sent at *Yeshua*'s baptism in the form of a dove.

Mal 03:01 says that the *Malek* of his Presence would "come" to the temple, but there is no mention of the Presence dwelling in the temple. The Pharisees made sure *Yeshua*'s coming would remain a short visit. Since *Yeshua* was rebuffed at the temple, he said:

Look, your house is left to you [as] desolate [as it was already]. I tell you, you will not see me again until you say, 'Blessed is he who comes in the Name of the Lord' (Mat 23:38-39; Luk 13:35).

Yahveh said that he watched his temple being turned into a den of thieves (Jer 07:11). *Yahveh* said that he would thrust the evildoers from the temple and from his Presences (Jer 07:15). Interestingly, the evening before *Yeshua* cleansed the temple, Mark recorded:

Yeshua entered Jerusalem and went to the temple. He looked around at everything (Mar 11:11).

Yeshua took note of the evil occurring at the temple just as *Yahveh* had (Jer 07:11). Then, the next day, *Yeshua* thrust the evildoers from temple and from his presence (Mar 11:15; see also Mat 21:12 and Joh 02:15) just as *Yahveh* had (Jer 07:

15). This suggests that *Yeshua* was the Presence who was prophesied to return to the temple (Isa 40:03; Mal 03:01). Later, *Yeshua* told the parable of the vineyard to say that he was *Yahveh* the Son, showing that he was authorized to cleanse the temple (Luk 19:47—20:20).

Interestingly, only when he was present in the temple did *Yeshua* call the temple "his Father's house" (Luk 02:49; Joh 02:16). The temple that concerned *Yeshua* was his own body (Joh 02:21) and the body of the Church (1Co 06:19). These bodies were mystically linked (Joh 02:19-21; 06:51-58; 1Co 06:19; Eph 03:06; 05: 30-32; Col 01:24).

Yeshua and his disciples only paid temple tax so as not to cause unnecessary offense. The tax was paid from money found in a fish rather than from earned money (Mat 17:24-27). This seems as though *Yeshua* thought the temple was a mere building left unoccupied by *Yahveh*.

When *Yeshua* was in Samaria, he did not affirm the assertion of the Jews that *Yahveh* had to be worshipped in Jerusalem. *Yeshua* in fact said that the "time...has now come" that the temple was irrelevant (Joh 04:20-24). *Yeshua* also said that heaven is his Father's house and omitted any reference to the temple (Joh 14:02).

Toward the end of his ministry, *Yeshua* consigned the temple to desolation and destruction (Mat 24:02; Mar 13:02; Luk 21:06). *Yeshua* also said that the temple was "your house" rather than "my Father's house" (Mat 23:38-39; Luk 13:35). So *Yeshua* was unconcerned about the temple except when his life and ministry unavoidably brought him to the temple. This seems to show that *Yeshua* had been *Yahveh*'s Presence in the temple, and that the temple was desolate whenever *Yeshua* was not there.

Yeshua's example of following certain token Jewish customs, as well as paying the temple tax so as not to offend, evidently influenced the early Church (Mat 17: 24-27). That is why Paul and the Jewish disciples followed a modicum of Mosaic customs concerning the temple (Act 21:20-29). The early Church otherwise taught that the temple was irrelevant.

The early Church did not openly teach against the temple, despite what their detractors claimed (Act 06:13-14; 21:28). There was no point in pressing the issue that the temple was desolate since the early Church knew that the temple would be destroyed shortly (Mat 24:02; Mar 13:02; Luk 21:06). With the temple gone, they could stop practicing certain Mosaic customs without causing unnecessary offense (Mat 17:27).

The Connection Between Exo 33—34 and the Aaronic Blessing (Benediction)

Yahveh told Moses:

> This is how you should bless the children of Israel: you shall tell them:
> '*Yahveh* bless you, and keep you;
> *Yahveh* make his Face [*Panim*] shine on you, and be gracious to you;
> *Yahveh* turn his Face [*Panim*] toward you, and give you peace.'

So shall they [the priests] put my Name [singular] on the children of Israel; and I will bless them (Num 06:22-27).

In the Aaronic Blessing, the Name, *Yahveh,* is mentioned three times. Only after the second and third mention of *Yahveh* is there a mention of "Presences" or "Faces." The Faces refer to the Spirit and Son. The reason the face of *Yahveh* the Father is not mentioned in the Aaronic blessing is found in Exo 33—34.

Moses asked to see *Yahveh* the Father's glory (Exo 33:18). The Father said that seeing the Father's own face would prove fatal for Moses (Exo 33:20; compare Rev 06:16). The reason was Moses was a sinful mortal, since sinless angels continually see the Father's own face and survive (Mat 18:10).

The Father invited Moses up the mount the next day so that Moses could see the Son and the Spirit's glory. Moses would also see the Father's glory, albeit partially shielded from view. The glory of the Son and Spirit is not necessarily lethal to sinners. This is due both to the concept of grace and the principle that the Son is the "form" (Num 12:08; Phi 02:06), "image" (Gen 01:26-27; 09:06; 2Co 04:04; Col 01:15), and "likeness" (Eze 01:26-28; Heb 01:03) of *Yahveh* the Father. Likewise, the Spirit's glory is not necessarily lethal due to grace and to the fact that the Spirit proceeds from the Father and through the Son.

Instead of showing his full glory, the Father said that he would merely proclaim his presence. The Father would proclaim his presence by saying his Name, *Yahveh,* and by proclaiming his goodness, grace and mercy (Exo 33:19). The Father said that when his glory was about to pass by, he would cover Moses with his hand. Upon passing by, the Father said he would remove his hand so Moses could see the Father's back (Exo 33:22-23).

Placing Moses in the cleft of a rock and covering Moses with his hand was the Father's way of "blessing and keeping" Moses alive. This parallels the first part of the Aaronic Blessing (Num 06:24). The Father's hand, meaning the bright cloud, was the Spirit (Exo 34:05; Mat 17:05). In this way the Father "made his Face [*Panim*] shine upon...and be gracious" to Moses (Num 06:25).

Moses also saw the Son both as he passed by (Exo 34:06), and during the face-to-face, forty-day discussion that followed (Exo 34:07-28). This was part of the Father "turning his Face [*Panim*] toward" Moses and giving Moses peace" (Num 06:26). The preincarnate Son turned his face toward Moses as he passed by Moses, and talked to Moses face to face during the forty days (Exo 34:06).

So Moses saw the back of the Father and the faces of the Son and Spirit, who are called the "Presences" or "Faces" of the Father in Exo 33:14-15. Just as the Aaronic Blessing articulates, Moses was kept safe and was blessed by the Father (Num 06:24), and he saw the Faces of the Son and Spirit. Otherwise, Moses would have been one of the disfavored, for according to Jeremiah, the disfavored see the back of *Yahveh* but not *Yahveh*'s Faces:

I [the Father] will show them the back, but not the Faces [the Son and Spirit] in the day of their calamity (Jer 18:17).

So it becomes apparent why in the Aaronic Blessing, the Name, *Yahveh,* is mentioned three times, but only after the second and third mentions of *Yahveh* are the "Faces" mentioned. In the Aaronic Blessing the Father is mentioned as blessing and keeping, but not as looking at the Israelites. Seeing the Father's own face would prove lethal for the sinners (Exo 33:20).

In the Aaronic Blessing, the Father is mentioned first since the Father was the first to appear before Moses (Exo 34:05). The Spirit is mentioned second since he, in the form of a cloud, shielded Moses from seeing the Father's own face (Exo 34:05). The Son is mentioned third since he appeared last (Exo 34:06). "Turn...Face" applies to the Son since the phrase is anthropomorphic and is most characteristic of the preincarnate Son (Eze 01:26; Dan 07:13).

So the Aaronic Blessing should be understood as being thoroughly Trinitarian:

This is how you should bless the children of Israel: you shall tell them:
'Yahveh [the Father] bless you, and keep you;
Yahveh [the Father] make his [the Father's] Face [*Panim*, meaning the Spirit] shine on you, and be gracious to you;
Yahveh [the Father] turn his [the Father's] Face [*Panim*, meaning the Son] toward you, and give you peace.'
So shall they [the priests] put my [the Father's] Name [*Yahveh*] on the children of Israel; and I [the Father] will bless them (Num 06:22-27).

Passages with Similarities to Exo 34 and the Aaronic Blessing (Num 06:23-27)

There are several passages that speak of *Yahveh* looking on the favored, but not on the disfavored. If the OT were unitarian, however, the situation ought to be reversed. For, if *Yahveh* were only one person and no one can see *Yahveh*'s face and live (Exo 33:20), then *Yahveh* should look on the disfavored and look away from the favored!

The above-mentioned seeming contradiction can be reconciled implementing a Trinitarian interpretation of the passages concerned:

- Examples of the Son and Spirit looking on the favored include:
  o When you [the Father] said, 'Seek my Faces' [(1Ch 16:11; Psa 105:04)], my heart said to you [the Father], 'I will seek your [the Father's] Faces [the Son and Spirit], *Yahveh* [the Father]. Do not hide your [the Father's] Faces [the Son and Spirit] from me' (Psa 027:08-09),
  o Let your [the Father's] Faces [the Son and Spirit] shine on your servant; save me in your unfailing love (Psa 031:16 [*BHS* 031:17]),
  o May God [the Father] be merciful to us, bless us, and cause his Faces [the Son and Spirit] to shine on us (Psa 067:01),
  o Restore us, O God [the Father]; make your Faces [Son and Spirit] shine upon us, that we may be saved (Psa 080:03 [*BHS* 080:04]); also Psa 080:07 [*BHS* 080:08]), and
  o 'In a surge of anger I [the Father] hid my Faces [Son and Spirit] from you for a moment, but with everlasting kindness I will have compassion on you,' says *Yahveh* [the Father] your Redeemer (Isa 54:08).

- Examples of the Father looking on the disfavored include:
  o *Yahveh's* [the Father's own] face has divided them (Lam 04:16a).
- Examples of the Father looking on the disfavored while the Son and Spirit look on the favored include:
  o *Yahveh's* eyes [the Son and Spirit] are toward the righteous. His ears [the Son and Spirit] listen to their cry. *Yahveh's* [the Father's] face is against those who do evil, to cut off the memory of them from the earth (Psa 034: 15-16 [*BHS* 034:16-17]).
- Examples of the Father not looking on the favored, but the Son and Spirit looking on the favored include:
  o Hide your [the Father's] face from my sins…[but] do not cast me away from your Face [the Son], or take your Holy Spirit from me (Psa 051:09-11 [*BHS* 051:11-13]).

Peter quotes the above passage and said God's face is on (Greek: *epi*), meaning, "toward," both the favored and the evil:

> The eyes [the Son and Spirit] of the Lord [the Father] are on [Greek: *epi*] the righteous, and His [the Father's] ears [the Son and Spirit's] hear their supplication, but the face of the Lord [the Father] is upon [Greek: *epi*] those doing evil (1Pe 03:12).

Incidents with Similarities to Exo 34 and the Aaronic Blessing (Num 06:23-27)

Elijah at Mount Sinai

1Ki 18—19 was discussed earlier in this chapter. This section discusses the connection between 1Ki 19 and the Aaronic Blessing. Elijah went to Mount Horeb, otherwise known as Mount Sinai and the "Mount of [All] the Gods" (1Ki 19:08; also Exo 03:01; 04:27; 18:05; 24:13; 2Ki 04:25).

The Word of *Yahveh* (1Ki 19:09), who was previously called the *Malek Yahveh* (1Ki 19:05-07), told Elijah to stand before the Face of *Yahveh* the Son at the mouth of the cave. From this vantage point Elijah would see the procession of the Father and the Spirit (1Ki 19:11, 13).

Notice that Elijah did not cover his face before standing beside the Presence of *Yahveh* the Son at the mouth of the cave. Elijah only retreated into the safety of the cave to avoid the wind, the fire, and the rockslides from the earthquake. Only when Elijah heard the Father whisper in a gentle breeze did Elijah cover his face with his cloak. Elijah then proceeded to the mouth of the cave a second time (1Ki 19:13).

Elijah knew that *Elyon's* Presences, the Son and the Spirit, would have a gracious disposition due to Exo 33—34, the Aaronic Blessing and other Scriptures. These passages were discussed above. Elijah, however, knew from the same Scriptures that for a sinful person to see the Father's own face would prove lethal. This is why Elijah covered his face with his cloak only upon hearing *Yahveh* the Father, but not when speaking with the *Malek* and Word of *Yahveh*.

Elijah's covering his face with his cloak (1Ki 19:13) is similar to how at a later time the prophet Isaiah saw the face of *Yahveh* in the temple (Isa 06:01). Isaiah thought that because of his sinfulness, he might die on account of seeing *Yahveh* (Isa 06:05). Isaiah only saw the gracious face of the Son, perhaps on account of the train that filled the temple (Isa 06:01). *Yahveh* the Son was gracious and had Isaiah's sin blotted out (Isa 06:07).

The Transfiguration

At the Transfiguration, the Trinity bestowed the same honor and favor on the three disciples that was previously bestowed on Moses and Elijah. That honor was hearing the Father and seeing his Faces, the Son and Spirit. The Transfiguration was a literal acting out of the Aaronic Blessing and a reenactment of Exo 33—34.

The Father passed by Moses in a cloud that shielded Moses from the Father's glory (Exo 34:05). So too, a bright cloud enveloped the disciples and shielded them from the glory of the Father. The bright cloud in Exo 34 and at the Transfiguration was the Spirit. The bright cloud was the Spirit shining his face on the disciples, as the Aaronic Blessing describes (Num 06:25).

The voice within the cloud in Exo 34:05 and at the Transfiguration was the Father keeping the disciples safe (Num 06:24). The Father kept them safe by advising them to listen to the Son (Mat 17:05; Mar 09:07; Luk 09:35) rather than listen to Peter's ramblings (Mat 17:04-05; Mar 09:05-06; Luk 09:32-34).

At the Transfiguration, *Yeshua*'s face and clothes shone brightly (Mat 17:02). *Yeshua* turned from talking to Moses and Elijah to tell the disciples, "Do not be afraid" (Mat 17:07). This was a real life example of the Aaronic Blessings:

Yahveh [the Father] turn his [the Father's] Face [the Son] toward you and give you peace (Num 06:26).

That *Yeshua*'s face shone on the disciples on the Mount of the Transfiguration is similar to Moses' forty-day and night stay on Mount Sinai:

Moses did not know that the skin of his face shone because of his speaking with him [*Yahveh* the Son] (Exo 34:29).

Yeshua's Baptism

Another incident with similarities to the Transfiguration and the Aaronic Blessing is *Yeshua*'s baptism (Mat 03:13-17). A dove alighted on *Yeshua*'s shoulder after *Yeshua* was baptized. Then, Matthew said, "the heaven was opened," and a voice said:

This is my beloved Son with whom I am well pleased (Mat 03:17).

It seems clouds hid the Father's own face during *Yeshua*'s baptism. Ezekiel, Matthew and Luke even use the same Greek words *"anoigw ouranos"* for "heaven opened" (LXX Eze 01:01; Mat 03:16; Luk 03:21). Ezekiel mentions clouds (Eze 01:04, 28) after saying the heavens opened (Eze 01:01).

An interesting parallel is when *Yeshua* was in the temple courts, the Father's voice spoke from heaven saying:

I have glorified it [his Name], and will glorify it again.

John wrote that some people thought the voice was thunder. This may indicate that there were clouds obscuring the Father's own face (Joh 12:29). So in respect to the Father's voice coming from within or behind clouds, *Yeshua*'s baptism was similar to Exo 34 and the Transfiguration.

Now returning to *Yeshua*'s baptism, the Father "kept" John the Baptist (Num 06:24). The Father told John that the one on whom he saw the Spirit alight would be the one who would baptize with the Spirit (Joh 01:33). The Father also "kept" John by saying from heaven that *Yeshua* was his beloved son (Mat 03:17).

John did not think it was right for him to baptize *Yeshua*, but *Yeshua* graciously assured John that it was the right thing to do (Mat 03:15). This was *Yahveh* the Son turning his face toward John and giving him peace (Num 06:26).

After *Yeshua*'s baptism the Spirit came down in the form of a dove and alighted on *Yeshua*'s shoulder (Mat 03:16). The clouds that opened and shown light, and the dove that alighted are both examples of the Father having the Spirit shine his face on John the Baptist and *Yeshua* (Num 06:25). Since the Aaronic Blessing was acted out during *Yeshua*'s baptism, one could say that the Name of *Yahveh* was put on *Yeshua* during his baptism (Num 06:27; Mat 28:19).

Stephen's Stoning
Another incident with similarities to the Transfiguration and to the Aaronic Blessing occurred at Stephen's stoning. Stephen's face shone like an angel's (Act 06:15) because Stephen was full of the Spirit (Act 06:05; 07:55). Then Stephen looked to heaven and saw the glory of God the Spirit.

The glory may have looked like a halo or sunburst in the clouds. Stephen also saw the face of *Yeshua* as he stood at the right hand of the Father (Act 07:55-56). Notice, however, that Stephen did not say he saw the Father's own face, which was likely obscured by the clouds and the sunburst of glory.

The First Commandment

The first commandment is often translated as: "You shall have no other gods before me" (Exo 20:03). The first commandment literally reads:
> Let there be [singular verb] to you no others [plural adjective *acherim*] gods [plural noun *elohim*] before my Presences [plural noun *Panim*] (Exo 20:03; Deu 05:07).

Understanding the First Commandment in Terms of Space
One must think in spatial and Trinitarian terms to understand the first commandment properly. As was noted previously concerning Deu 05:26 and Deu 33:01-02, during the giving of the Ten Commandments, the "living Gods" appeared on three mountains: the Father on Mount Sinai, the Son on Mount Seir, and the Spirit on Mount Paran.

During the Exodus, the clouds generally were positioned between Israel and Israel's enemies for tactical reasons (Exo 14:20; Num 10:12). Later, when the Father sent the Son and Spirit to the Promised Land (Exo 33:14-15), the Father happened to be on Mount Sinai, the Son was on Mount Seir, and the Spirit happened to be in Edom (Jdg 05:04-05). This may have been meant to deter enemies and to give Israel a measure of comfort, if Israel was positioned between the three mountains.

Comparing Deu 33 and Jdg 05 reveals that at the giving of the Ten Commandments, the Son was on Mount Seir and Spirit was on Mount Paran. They were "before" the Father who was on Mount Sinai (Exo 20:03; Deu 05:07). Concerning the preposition "before," note that the Father elsewhere spoke of the Spirit being "before" him. The Father said, "…the Spirit from before me will grow faint" (Isa 57:16).[88]

The First Commandment Legislates Against Pseudo-Trinities

The Father used the word "other," literally, "others" (*acherim*), in the first commandment to make both a distinction and an allowance:

- The distinction is between the divine Son and Spirit who were "before" the Father, and the so-called gods that the Israelites would be tempted to put before the Father, and
- The allowance is that while the so-called gods put before the Father are not worthy of worship, the Son and Spirit who happen to be before the Father are divine persons worthy of worship.

By saying, "You shall have no other gods before my Presences," the Father was warning against a type of syncretism where the Israelites would swap the Son or Spirit with false gods to create a pseudo-trinity. Genesis provides an example of such a pseudo-trinity.

As was seen in the chapter on Hebrew collective plurals, the Hebrews liked to address the members of the Trinity as, for instance, the God of Abraham, the God of Isaac, and the God of Jacob. Laban, however, swore by a pseudo-trinity when he said:

> May the God of Abraham, the god of Nahor, and the god of their father [Terah], judge [plural verb] between us (Gen 31:53).

The plural verb "judge" shows that Laban may have been referring to three deities merged into a pseudo-trinity. Scripture does not say whether Abraham's brother, Nahor, worshipped false gods, but Scripture does reveal that Laban (Gen 31:19) and Terah (Jos 24:02) were both pagans. Interestingly, Laban was from Haran (Gen 27:43; 29:04), and Sinasi Gunduz wrote:

> The children of Sin, Ishtar, his daughter, and Shamash, his son, are mentioned with him in one of the Nabonidus inscriptions from Harran [Arabic spelling of Haran]. It seems there was a trinity of gods, but this may be due to the custom of mentioning gods in threes.[89]

J. Spencer Trimingham wrote similarly:

> Mesopotamian cults in particular were based on the triad, 'Our Lord, our Lady, and the Son of our two Lords, with *Be'el-Shamim*,' which correspond to the great Syrian deities, Hadad, Atagatis, Simios, and the Sky-god, *Ba'al Shamim*.[90]

The commandment against pseudo-trinities was necessary because syncretism was rampant in the ancient world. Several ancient religions even had pseudo-trinities or triads.

Pseudo-trinities and triads may have resulted from corrupted memories of Yahvism's Trinity. This situation is parallel to how many ancient cultures have worldwide flood stories that are distant echoes of the Genesis flood account (Gen 06—09). Many cultures knew of the Genesis flood upon being dispersed from the Tower of Babel (Gen 11:08-09).

Similarly, many post-Babel cultures remembered that *Yahveh* was the Trinity. They especially remembered that *Yahveh* referred to himself as "us" (Gen 01:26; 03:22; 11:07). Perhaps, if it were not for the fragmented memories of the true Trinity, many cultures might have lapsed into different brands of unitarianism rather than variegated polytheism.

Another factor that gave rise to pagan pseudo-trinities is the Devil humors himself by creating religions that mimic the true faith. In fact, the Apostle John prophesied how the Devil would create a pseudo-trinity. John wrote that a second beast that spoke like a dragon appeared (Rev 13:11). The dragon controlled the first beast whose fatal wound has healed (Rev 13:12). The dragon had an image of the first beast created and caused the deceived people to worship the first and second beast, and the image of the first beast (Rev 13:15). So in essence John described Satan creating a pseudo-trinity.

The First Commandment Legislates Against Unitarianism

If the Father had just said, "You shall have no gods before me," there would have been serious theological consequences. Without the word "others" (*acherim*), hearers might assume that the first commandment taught unitarianism.

An omission of the word "others" from the First Commandment would be taken to mean that the Son on Mount Seir and the Spirit on Mount Paran were not divine persons of *Yahveh*. With the word "others," however, the Israelites knew the Father meant "others" besides the Son and Spirit.

It should be noted that the Father elsewhere referred to the Son as God. For instance, the Father called the *Malek* with his Name "God" (Exo 23:19, 25). The Father twice called the Son "God" in the Psalms (Psa 045:06-07; 082:08). Furthermore, the Father said his Presences always existed with him and were un-created:

> Before my Presences [*Panim*] there was no God created, and after me
> there is none [created] (Isa 43:10).

That the Father, Son and Spirit are to be considered divine can be ascertained even from the Trinitarian title of Mount Horeb (*haElohim*). Horeb is the mountain where the first commandment was given. Mount Horeb is sometimes called Mount Sinai or the "Mount of [All] the Gods" (*haElohim*) (Exo 03:01; 04:27; 18:05; 24:13; 1Ki 19:08; 2Ki 04:25).

The name Sinai has pagan origins and refers to the moon god Sin. The name *haElohim*, however, refers to the Trinity, since *haElohim* is repeatedly associated with the Trinity, Moses, the Ark of the Covenant and the temple. *HaElohim* was discussed in the chapter on Hebrew collective nouns. Further proof that "the Mount of [All] the Gods" refers to the Trinity comes from Samuel's time.

A musical group of *Yahveh*'s prophets manned a high place on a hill called "Gibeah of [All] the Gods" (1Sa 10:05). "Gibeah" means "hill" in Hebrew. The hill had different names just as Mount Sinai was known by different names. The hill was known as Gibeah of Benjamin (1 Sam 13:2, 15; 14:16), Gibeah of the children of Benjamin (2 Sam 23:29), and Gibeah of Saul (1 Sam 11:04; Isa 10:29). That the hill had different names does not detract from the fact that the hill was also known as "[All] the Gods [*haElohim*]" because the hill was associated with *Yahveh*, the Trinity.

In Deu 13:02, Moses showed that in the first commandment (Exo 20:03) the plural word "others" (*acherim*) distinguishes between the persons of the Trinity and so-called gods. Moses wrote that false prophets would say:

Let us follow others [*acherim*] gods, gods you have not known, and let us worship them (Deu 13:02).

Notice that Moses defined "others [*acherim*] gods" as gods "that you have not known." Moses, however, knew that the Israelites already knew "the living Gods," since they had appeared on three mountains during the giving of the law (Deu 05:26; 33:02).

By defining "others [*acherim*] gods" as being "gods you have not known," Moses meant to ensure that the Israelites would never come to think of *Yahveh* the Son and *Yahveh* the Spirit as being "other" gods. Likewise, Moses spoke the *Shema* to ensure that Israel would never come to think of Trinitarianism as a form of polytheism.

The *Shema*'s message is that the Father, Son and Spirit are "a united one" (*echad*), in other words, that they are the Trinity (Deu 06:04). As was discussed in the chapter on Hebrew collective nouns, theologians actually had to change Moses' wording from *echad* to *yachid* to interpret the *Shema* in a non-Trinitarian way.

The First Commandment Legislates Against Binitarianism

The Father's use of the plural, literally, "others" (*acherim*), instead of the singular "other" (*acher*), is important. If the Father were Binitarian and not Trinitarian, he would think that the Son was a divine person, but that the Spirit was an impersonal force. Then, in the first commandment, the Father would have used the singular word "other" and not "others" (*acher* instead of the plural *acherim*). The singular word "other" would indicate that Israel should worship none other than the Father and Son.

To recap—if the Father were a Binitarian, *Yahveh* could have said:

You shall have no other [singular adjective *acher*] God [singular noun *El*] before my Face.

The singular "other" would signal to the Israelites that they were to have no other god before the Father besides the Son. The same could be said if the Binitarianism were reversed—if the Father considered the Spirit, but not the Son, to be God.

Chapter 4

The *Shema*

Introduction

During the Exodus, Moses made many statements that, when considered together, form a doctrine of God. For instance, Moses' doctrine of God was bounded
at the top by statements that *Yahveh* the Father was the Most High (*Elyon*) (Gen 14:
18, 19, 20, 22; Num 24:16; Deu 32:08). This meant there was no god greater than
Yahveh.

During the giving of the Ten Commandments, the Israelites saw the persons of
Yahveh on three mountains. This was discussed in the chapter on the Presences
concerning Deu 05:26 and 33:02. During the giving of the first commandment, the
Father told the Israelites not to have any other gods before him. So the doctrine
of God was bounded on the bottom. The Israelites knew there were only three
persons called *Yahveh*.

Still, there was one polytheistic notion that had to be nipped in the bud—
tritheism. Tritheism is the idea that Israel had three gods rather than one God. So
Moses spoke the *Shema* to express the unity of the three persons called *Yahveh*:

Hear, O Israel: *Yahveh* [the Father] [and] our *Elohim* [the Son], *Yahveh*
[the Spirit] [are] a united one [*echad*] (Deu 06:04).

The concept of unity expressed by the *Shema* was necessary to counterbalance
the many elements in the Pentateuch that speak about the persons of the Trinity.
These include:

- The Trinitarian proofs such as Deu 33:02 that are mentioned in the previous
  chapters, as well as the Trinitarian proofs mentioned in the Trinitarian proofs
  appendix,

- Most of the 812 instances of the plural form *Elohim* (Gods) found in 683 verses
  of the Pentateuch. Some instances of *elohim*, of course, refer to false gods, and

- 56 of the 57 instances of the form "[All] the Gods" (*haElohim*) found in 54
  verses of the Pentateuch. In Exo 18:11, however, *haelohim* refers to false gods.

So the *Shema* stresses that the three persons called *Yahveh* were the Trinity (also
called the Triunity). One can bypass the Trinitarian message of the *Shema* only by

changing the wording, such as by changing *echad* to *yachid*. So one could say that the *Shema* is a Trinitarian creed.

All subsequent data about the Trinity merely adds precision to the *Shema*. An analogy would be how the value of *pi* (3.14) has become increasing clear-cut over time (3.14159265358979323846...). Precision was added to *pi* and accepted as factual by the scientific community only when such precision became meaningful, useful or necessary.

The *Shema* had been an adequate creed throughout OT times as is evidenced by the fact that the OT reads Trinitarian throughout. By the time the Son came as the Messiah, the Trinitarian *Shema* had, since Intertestamental times, been reinterpreted as being unitarian. Because their hearts were hardened to what the OT actually said, the motley crew of Pharisees, Sadducees, Essenes and other could all claim to be true OT believers along with Trinitarian Yahvists.

So *Yeshua* made the Trinitarianism message more explicit by talking often about the Father, Son and Spirit. At the end of his earthly career, *Yeshua* gave a *Shema*-like formula just as Moses had given *Shema* at the end of his career. *Yeshua* gave the command to baptize in the name of the Father, Son and Spirit. This Trinitarian formula was meant to drive a wedge between true believers and unitarian heretics.

The NT along with explicit doctrinal statements are the sword that *Yeshua* said would divide families along orthodox and heretical fault lines (Mat 10:34-36; Luk 12:51-53). Paul said true believers would work toward doctrinal unity by a more detailed study of God's word (Rom 16:17; 1Co 01:10; 2Ti 02:15-16). Paul said divisions caused by statements of faith help to distinguish those whom God approves (1Co 11:18-19).

After awhile, "hypocritical liars, whose consciences have been seared as with a hot iron" (1Ti 04:02) were able to reinterpret the NT to accommodate their unbelief. John had to remind believers who were confronted with seductive teachings that both the Father and Son were indispensable to the faith (2Jo 01:08-11). In fact, the NT is full of reminders about correct doctrine (Joh 14:26; Rom 15:15; 1Co 04:17; 15:01; 2Ti 01:06; 2Pe 01:12; Jud 01:05).

After awhile more mnemonics such as the Apostles, the Nicene and Athanasian Creeds were necessitated. Christians have found out that other doctrinal statements have been and will continue to be necessary so that the Church does not degenerate into unending donnybrook brawl until the Last Day.

Maimonides (1135-1204 AD)

Maimonides is the most famous medieval rabbinic scholar. Maimonides' nickname, Rambam, is an acronym derived from his title and name: Rabbi Moses Ben Maimon. Rambam codified the Talmud. He also wrote the *Guide for the Perplexed* (1190 AD), an attempt to reconcile Aristotelian philosophy with rabbinic theology. Rambam formulated the *Thirteen Articles of Faith* that still serve as a fundamental creed of Orthodox Judaism.

Moses used the word *echad* in the *Shema* to describe *Yahveh* as a "united one." Rambam, however, substituted *yachid* for *echad* to describe God as "alone," "an absolute one," or "an only one." The OT never refers to *Yahveh* as being *yachid* (alone). By substituting the word *yachid*, Rambam thought he could sidestep the Trinitarian implications of the *Shema*.

Rambam's substitution, however, does not make the entire *Shema* read unitarian. Rambam's version of the *Shema* is here translated: "*Yahveh*, our God [*Elohenu*] [are] *Yahveh* alone [*yachid*]." Notice that one Trinitarian element is still left intact, literally, "our Gods" (*Elohenu*). *Elohenu* is the plural construct form of *Elohim*. So even Rambam's modified *Shema* still teaches that there are divine persons named *Yahveh*!

Moses had expressed the uniqueness of *Yahveh*, yet without compromising his Trinitarian beliefs. Moses' *Shema*-like statement uses the plural form *Elohim* (Gods) to say that the plural persons of *Yahveh* are God alone:

Yahveh, he is [All] the Gods [*haElohim*], there is none beside (Deu 04: 35, 39).

Note that these passages in Deu 04 are found only two chapters away from the *Shema* (Deu 06:04). Solomon (1Ki 08:60) and Isaiah (Isa 45:05) also echo Moses' statement that there is no God besides the Trinity.

Jeremiah provided a fifth "alone," *Shema*-like passage when he said there was none like *Yahveh* who could send rain. Jeremiah wrote:

[Are] not you-he [*atah-hu*] *Yahveh*, *Elohenu* [literally, "our Gods"]? (Jer 14:22).

The reader will recognize that Jeremiah used the same phrase, *Yahveh Elohenu*, that is found in the *Shema*. The plural form *Elohenu* and the "you-he" paired pronouns indicate that Jeremiah knew persons named *Yahveh*. So Jeremiah expressed *Yahveh*'s uniqueness without compromising his Trinitarian beliefs.

Would God be honored by Rambam's attempt to transform the *Shema* into a unitarian statement of faith? Perhaps looking at the theological implications of unitarianism will help decide. A recurring rabbinic theological theme is that since God is a single person, he became lonely. Loneliness is supposedly why God decided to create angels and humans. Christians, however, do not posit that God was lonely, but say that God created angels and humans for his glory.

In rabbinic theology, God was like the lone (*echad*) man of whom Solomon spoke (Ecc 04:08). Solomon said two persons together were better than one forlorn person (Ecc 04:09-12a), but a cord of three strands was best of all (Ecc 04: 12b)! Surely, Solomon's had the Trinity in mind when he said this.

In Pro 09:10 and 30:03, Solomon spoke of *Yahveh* the Father and *Yahveh* the Son. In Ecc 12:01 and Sol 01:11, Solomon spoke of the Trinity as plural persons. These passages are discussed in the MT plurals appendix. Solomon would likely say that Rambam's *yachid* version of the *Shema* promotes a "dejected loner" interpretation of God.

United in Essence

The *Shema* should be understood to mean foremost that the three persons are a united in their name—*Yahveh*. The Trinity's union in name arises from the fact that three persons are united in essence. In fact, all expressions of the Trinity's unity such as being united in action and purpose arise from the Trinity's underlying union in essence. Since a single person cannot have the quality of being united, the Trinity is the most powerful example of the Gestalt theory: "the whole is greater than the sum of its parts."

The chapter on Hebrew collective nouns gives many examples of things said to be a "united one" (*echad*), such as grapes, days, sticks, and soldiers. Not once was there any differentiation as to the size or the importance of the objects comprising the united one (*echad*). The consecutive days said to be *echadim* ("united ones" or "a few") were equal, since days measured by the sundial are always twelve hours long (Joh 11:09).

The *Shema*'s insistence that persons of *Yahveh* are one (*echad*) therefore seems to suggest that the persons comprising the whole should be viewed as equals—at least according to essence. Being united in essence means that the Trinity can be addressed as:

- God of Gods (*Elohim*) and Lord of Lords (*Adonai*) (Jos 22:22; Psa 050:01; Isa 26:13; Dan 02:47; 11:36; 1Ti 06:15; Rev 17:14; 19:16),
- Lord of [All] the Lords (*haAdonim*) (Deu 10:17; Psa 136:03),
- God of [All] the Gods (*haElohim*) (Psa 136:02),
- Lords (*Adonai*), since Abraham addressed three persons as "Lords" (*Adonai*), and all three replied (Gen 18:03-05). Also, Lot addressed two persons as "Lords" (*Adonai*), and they both answered (Gen 19:02). Further, *Yahveh* called himself "Lords" (*Adonim*) in Mal 01:06,
- *Yahveh*, since the narrator, Moses, indicates that there was a *Yahveh* in heaven and a *Yahveh* on earth (Gen 19:24). Also, *Yahveh* often spoke in the third person of another person named *Yahveh*, as is discussed in the Trinitarian proofs appendix,
- God (*El* or *Elohim*), since the author of Hebrews said that the Father addressed the Son as "God" in Psa 045:06-07 (Heb 01:08), and *Yeshua* said that the Father addressed him as "God" (Psa 082:08; Joh 10:36a), and
- Most High (Aramaic is *Ilyonin*), since a heavenly dweller called both the Father and the Son the Most Highs (Dan 07:18, 22, 25b, 27).

United in Name

Zechariah interpreted and expanded on the *Shema* saying that the members of the Trinity are united both in essence and in name to rule Israel. Zechariah said:

> *Yahveh* [the Trinity] has become king over all the land, in that day there shall be a united one [echad], *Yahveh* [the Trinity], and his [the Trinity's] name is a united one [echad] (Zec 14:09).

The three members of the Trinity each have the Name, *Yahveh,* and this meant they are united in the pursuit of making themselves a name (Exo 09:16; 2Sa 07:23; 1Ch 17:21; Isa 63:12, 14; Eze 20:09).

A passage similar to Zec 14:09 shows that *Yahveh* are persons united to make themselves a name (Hos 12:04-05). The Son referred to the Father and himself as "us" (Hos 12:04),[91] and then made the *Shema*-like statement:

> *Yahveh* [the Father], God [the Son] of hosts, *Yahveh* is his [the Trinity]
> name of renown (Hos 12:05 [*BHS* 12:06]).

The Hebrew word that the *NIV* translates as "name of renown" is *zeker* (Hos 12: 05). *Zeker* usually means "memory" or "memorial," but here it makes better sense to say that *Yahveh* is the Trinity's "name of renown." Elsewhere, *zeker* is associated with the Hebrew word for "name" (*sheim*) (Exo 03:15; Job 18:17; Psa 009: 05-06; 135:13; Pro 10:07; Isa 26:08, 13-14). So Hos 12:04 is Trinitarian ("us") and is paired with a passage (Hos 12:05) that is similar to the *Shema*-like statement in Zec 14:09.

The concept of being a united one (*echad*) to make oneself a name was not novel. Perhaps the Tower of Babel builders were inspired by the concept of the Trinity when they united to make themselves a name. They said:

> Let us build a city and a tower...let us make a name for ourselves (Gen
> 11:04).

God said that the people had become a "united one" (*echad*) who spoke a "united one" (*echad*) language (Gen 11:06).

The reason the builders' language was a "united one" (*echad*) was that the language as a whole consisted of a "few dialects" (*echadim davarim*) (Gen 11:01). *Yahveh* said:

> If as a united one [echad] people speaking a united one [echad]
> language—if they have begun to do this, then nothing they plan to do will
> be impossible for them (Gen 11:06).

So God, united in resolve, said, "Let us..." (Gen 11:07), and then proceeded to disrupt the plans of the united one people who set out to do the impossible.

The Tower of Babel account gave comfort to the Israelites who were facing many enemies. Though the Tower of Babel builders were united as one, they were scattered to the four winds by the united one *Yahveh.*

So it seems Moses meant the *Shema* to communicate that the united persons of *Yahveh* could choose to scatter all Israel's enemies—no matter how united they appeared (Gen 34:30; Exo 01:10; Psa 083:04; Est 03:09). In this way, *Yahveh* would make a name for himself just as he defeated the Egyptians to make a name for himself (1Ch 17:21; Dan 09:15; Jer 32:20-21).

United in Action

Notice that the narrator of Judges referred to people as *echad* (a united one) and used singular verbs with *echad:*

- The assembly is gathered [singular verb] as one [echad] man [singular noun] (Jdg 20:01),
- All the people rose [singular verb] as one [echad] man (Jdg 20:08), and
- All the men of Israel were gathered [singular verb] to the city as one [echad] man, companions (Jdg 20:11).

In the last verse, Jdg 20:11, notice that the plural noun "companions" is used as an appositive modifying the singular forms *echad* and "man." This shows that in the *Shema*, the form *echad* could refer to united persons:

> Hear, O Israel: *Yahveh* [the Father] [and] our *Elohim* [the Son], *Yahveh* [the Spirit] [are] a united one [*echad*] (Deu 06:04).

The plural form *Elohim* (Gods) is used over 2,000 times in the OT with singular verbs and other modifiers. Occasionally, plural verbs and other modifiers are used with *Elohim*. These show that three persons united in essence are also united in action, as is discussed in the chapter on Hebrew collective nouns. Similarly, singular verbs are used with over 300 instances of the plural form *haElohim* ([All] the Gods) referring to *Yahveh*.

The many occurrences of the collective nouns *Elohim* and *haElohim* used with singular verbs are helpful in understanding the *Shema*. Indeed, any collective noun referring to *Yahveh* used with a singular verb can be considered an informal version of the *Shema*. The collective noun refers to persons called *Yahveh*, and the singular verb shows that *Yahveh* is, and acts as, a united one.

United in Determination and Purpose

Echad is often used to show the united determination of a group of persons. For example, the Chronicler wrote, "The hand of God gave them one [echad] mind" (2Ch 30:12). Joseph told Pharaoh that his two dreams (Gen 41:32) had one (*echad*) interpretation (Gen 41:25-26). Joseph explained that two dreams with one (*echad*) interpretation meant that "the matter has been firmly decided by God, and God will do it soon" (Gen 41:32).

The *Shema* shows that the persons of the Trinity are united [echad]. The *Shema* was spoken in circumstances when Israel needed to know that the Trinity was united in their determination to:
- Relocate Israel out of the desert and into Palestine, and
- Establish a theocracy.

The Scriptures show that the persons of the Trinity are united in their determination to make persons and peoples. The "us" made Adam and Eve (Gen 01:26; LXX Gen 02:18). People have "creators" (Ecc 12:01) and "makers" (Job 35:10), and the nation Israel has "makers" (Psa 149:02; Isa 54:05). These MT plurals are discussed in the MT plurals appendix.

Similarly, persons of the Trinity are united in their determination as to where people and nations live (Jos 24:18; Act 17:26):
- God said, "Let us" when God determined that Adam and Eve would live in Eden (Gen 01:26),

- The "us" determined that it was best that Adam and Eve live outside the Garden of Eden (Gen 03:22),
- When God determined that the population should be distributed across the earth, God said, "Let us" (Gen 11:07),
- Abraham literally said, "Gods [*Elohim*], they caused me to wander" (Gen 20: 13) to the Promised Land (Gen 12:01),
- Jacob literally said, "Gods [*Elohim*], they revealed himself" (Gen 35:07) when they promised to bring Jacob back to the Promised Land (Gen 28:12-15),
- Aaron said that *Yahveh* (Exo 32:05), "they brought" Israel out of Egypt (Exo 32: 04, 08),
- *Yahveh* said, "My Presences, they will go with you" to conquer the Promised Land (Exo 33:14-15),
- Moses, shortly before saying the *Shema*, said that the gods are not as near the nations as *Yahveh* our God [are near]" (Deu 04:07),
- Joshua recalled how "the Holy Ones" had brought Israel out of Egypt to the Promised Land (Jos 24:19),
- The Philistines, who were fighting to keep land taken from Israel, said about *Yahveh*:

  These are the Gods, they who struck the Egyptians with all kinds of plagues (1Sa 04:07-08), and
- David said, "Gods, they went to redeem to himself a people...from Egypt" (2Sa 07:23).

The MT plurals mentioned above are discussed further in the MT plurals appendix.

The *Shema* as Ancient Israel's National Motto

The "united one" interpretation of the *Shema* is appropriate to the context of the *Shema*. Moses was giving a motivational speech to the Israelites to conquer the Promised Land and set up a theocratic state. The Israelites needed to know that the Trinity was united for Israel against Israel's foes. For this reason, the *Shema* became a national motto for ancient Israel.

To show that the *Shema* is an entirely appropriate motto for national Israel, one can compare the *Shema* to a very similar national motto of the United States: *e pluribus unum*. This is a Latin phrase meaning, "out of many, one." Since Moses was the founder of a Trinitarian theocracy, he would naturally speak of the Father, Son and the Spirit as being united for the nation. Likewise, the founders of a republic naturally would speak of themselves and their colonies being united as one nation against the nation's foe.

That *Yahveh* were one and the United States were one would not rule out the use of plural verbs and modifiers with either *Yahveh* or the United States. For example, Moses used both singular and plural verbs to refer to *Yahveh*. Likewise, the founders of the United States could say:

The United States is [singular verb] no longer at war with Britain, and more than two-thirds of the United States have ratified the Constitution.

To prove that the unifying motivation and logic was the same in the case of Israel and the United States, consider this: Benjamin Franklin aptly said at the signing of the Declaration of Independence, "We must all hang together, or assuredly we shall all hang separately" (July 4, 1776). That same day the Continental Congress appointed the Great Seal committee: Benjamin Franklin, John Adams, and Thomas Jefferson. Interestingly, it was this trio who chose the motto: *"e pluribus unum."*

During the United States Civil War (1861-1865 AD), the words and actions of the Confederacy belied the motto *"e pluribus unum."* So a second motto was needed to express unity during civil war. The argument for the second motto ran thus: in a nation with Judeo-Christian values, "There is but one God." So "In God We Trust" was chosen. This sentiment is the same unifying sentiment expressed by the *yachid* version of the *Shema*.

From 1864 AD onward, the United States retained both the *echad* and *yachid*-type mottos. In the heat of the Cold War that pitted nations with Judeo-Christian values against atheistic communism, President Eisenhower signed Public Law 140. This law stated that all United States coinage and paper currency must display the motto "In God We Trust." This is how the "In God We Trust" motto became the prominent motto of the United States.

The history of United States mottos parallels the history of the *Shema*. The *echad* motto of the founding fathers, *"e pluribus unum,"* expresses the unity of many, while the *yachid* motto introduced later, "In God We Trust," expresses the generic belief in one God. The *echad* version of the *Shema* was a motto of Israel's founding father, Moses.

The *echad* version of the *Shema* expresses the unity of the Trinity, while the *yachid* version of the *Shema*, introduced long after, merely expresses the belief that there is only one God. Both *yachid* mottos were introduced because some people rejected the earlier *echad* mottos, so a compromised *yachid* motto was adopted instead.

The NT and the *Shema*[92]

Zechariah alluded to the *Shema* and then expanded on the *Shema*:
    In that day *Yahveh* [the Trinity] will be one [Hebrew masculine *echad*], and
    His [the Trinity] name will be one [Hebrew masculine *echad*] (Zec 14:09).
The LXX translators translated the Hebrew masculine *echad* in Deu 06:04 and Zec 14:09a with the Greek masculine *heis*. In Zech 14:09b, however, the same Hebrew masculine word *echad* is translated with the Greek neuter *hen*.

The reason for the discrepancy is that in Deu 06:04 and Zec 14:09a, *echad* stands by itself and is usually translated as "one." The reader must complete the thought by supplying a word such as "united one...in name." So in Deu 06:04 and

Zec 14:09a, the LXX translators used the Greek equivalent of *echad* with the same masculine gender: *heis*.

In Zec 14:09b, however, Zechariah expanded and interpreted the *Shema* and supplied the implied noun: "name." Zechariah therefore understood the *Shema* to mean:

> Hear, O Israel: *Yahveh* [the Father] [and] our *Elohim* [the Son], *Yahveh* [the Spirit] [are] a united one [*echad*] [in name (*Yahveh*)] (Deu 06:04).

Because "united one" must now agree in gender with the neuter Greek word for "name" (*onoma*), the LXX translators used the Greek neuter word *hen* to translate the masculine *echad*. Evidently, the LXX translators did not realize that Zechariah expanded and interpreted the *Shema* and supplied the implied word "united one... in name."

If the translators were not Trinitarian, there would be no sense or purpose in declaring that a single divine person is "one in name." However, if the LXX translators had been Trinitarian, they would have consistently used the Greek neuter word *hen* rather than *heis* (Deu 06:04, Zec 14:09a and 14:09b) when translating *Shema*-like statements.

The Greek NT sometimes follows the Greek LXX translation of the Hebrew *Shema*:

> ...the Lord is one [masculine *heis*]" (Deu 06:04; Zec 14:09a; Mar 02: 07; 10:18; 12:29; Luk 18:19; Rom 03:30; 1Co 08:04, 06; Gal 03:20; Jam 02:19).

At other times the NT follows the LXX translation of Zechariah's expanded version of the *Shema*: "the Lord...is one [neuter hen]" (Zec 14:09b; Joh 11:52; 17: 11, 23). Another *Shema*-like statement that uses both *heis* and *hen* is discussed in the Trinitarian proofs appendix at 1Jo 05:07-08.

The NT use of *hen* and *heis* in *Shema*-like statements is easily justified. The NT writers were correct in following either the LXX of the *Shema* (Deu 06:04), or the LXX of Zechariah's expanded version of the *Shema* (Zec 14:09). Also, the Hebrew word for "name" (*sheim*) is masculine, while the Greek word for "name" (*onoma*) is neuter. So whether the NT writers quoted or alluded to the *Shema* using the masculine *heis* or neuter *hen*, they likely understood the *Shema* to mean: "united one in name." So *heis* is correct, while *hen* is technically correct.

When the NT writers used the masculine *heis* in their quotations and allusions to the *Shema*, this was probably to accommodate readers and listeners familiar with the LXX. For example, *Yeshua* likely was accommodating the teacher of the law when he quoted the LXX of the *Shema* using *heis* (Mar 12:29, 32).

That *Yeshua* actually understood the *Shema* as:

> *Yahveh* [the Father], our God [the Son], *Yahveh* [the Spirit] [are] one [*hen*] [in name] (Deu 06:04),

can be inferred from *Yeshua*'s *Shema*-like statement, "I and the Father are one [hen]" (Joh 10:30). Here, *Yeshua*'s use of *hen* agrees with the LXX of Zechariah's expanded version of the *Shema* (Zec 14:09). The neuter *hen* agrees with the neuter word *onoma* meaning, "name."

Yeshua's High Priestly Prayer also has a statement very similar to Zechariah's expanded version of the *Shema* (Zec 14:09). *Yeshua* said:

Father, keep in your name [onoma is neuter] those you have given me,
that they may be one [hen is neuter suggesting onoma (name) is meant] as
we are [one] [in name] (Joh 17:11, see also Joh 11:52; 17:23).

Yeshua's prayer was fulfilled because Christians are kept by the Name. Christians become "one" by virtue how the Name is named over Christians in baptism. Also, the Name is named over Christians during blessings such as the Aaronic Blessing (Num 06:27).

That *Yeshua* understood the *Shema* and the Aaronic Blessing to be Trinitarian can be surmised from *Yeshua*'s command that the disciples baptize "in the name [neuter singular onoma] of the Father and the Son and the Holy Spirit" (Mat 28: 19). This baptismal command is similar to the Aaronic Blessing in that the Name is put on the Israelites by mentioning the Name, *Yahveh*, three times (Num 06:22-27).

In both the Aaronic Blessing (Num 06:27; LXX 06:23) and in Zechariah's expanded version of the *Shema* (Zec 14:09), the Hebrew word "name" (*sheim*) is translated into Greek as *onoma* (singular, neuter). *Onoma* is the Greek word translated as "name" in the Great Commission (Mat 28:19). So in baptism the Name of the Trinity is put on the baptized just as the Name of the Trinity was put on the Israelites during the Aaronic Benediction.

What *Yeshua* Said About the *Shema*

Yeshua was in the temple area in December during the Feast of Dedication—Hanukkah. When *Yeshua* walked along Solomon's Colonnade, the Jews demanded, "If you are the Christ, tell us plainly" (Joh 10:24). *Yeshua* answered, "I did tell you, but you do not believe" (Joh 10:25).

Then *Yeshua* spoke of how he was the Son to the Father, and he said, "I and the Father are one" (Joh 10:30). The Jews then picked up stones, likely from the temple construction site. The Jews wanted to stone *Yeshua*, because they understood that *Yeshua* was claiming to be God (Joh 10:34).

Yeshua purposely foiled their "Kangaroo Court" conviction of blasphemy by referring to two verses from Psa 082. *Yeshua* said that the judges to whom the Word of God (the Son) came were called "gods" (Psa 082:06; Joh 10:35), so "what about the one [the Son] whom the Father set apart as his very own and sent into the world?" (Psa 082:08; Joh 10:36a). This last statement is *Yeshua*'s allusion to *Yahveh* the Father's statement:

Rise up, O God [the Son] and judge the earth, for all the nations are
your [the Son's] inheritance (Psa 082:08; Joh 10:36a)!

That Psa 082:08 is the Father speaking to the Son can be ascertained by the fact that the Father cannot have the earth as an inheritance, but only as a possession. The Father, however, can give the earth to the Son as an inheritance. Also, it should be noted that the Father's calling the Son "God" (Psa 082:08; Joh 10:36a) is not a unique occurrence, since the writer of Hebrews said that the Father calls the Son "God" (Psa 045:06-07 [*BHS* 045:07-08]; Heb 01:08).

After defeating this would-be lynch mob, *Yeshua* reiterated the challenge that if the Jews could not rightly convict him of sin, then they should believe his words (Joh 08:46-47; 10:37-38; 18:21-23). Perhaps the words that *Yeshua* had in mind that the Jews should believe were:

- The Father and he were one (Joh 10:30), and
- The Father is in me, and I am in the Father" (Joh 10:38).

When *Yeshua* mentioned that he was the Son of the Father, and that he and the Father were one (Joh 10:30), the Jews understood *Yeshua* to be making an allusion to the *Shema* (Deu 06:04; Zec 14:09). The fact that:

- *Yeshua* was walking along Solomon's Colonnade at the temple when *Yeshua* said, "Do not believe me unless I do what my Father does" (Joh 10:37), and that
- *Yeshua* said he was God's Son who was sent into the world (Joh 10: 36),seems to indicate that *Yeshua* was alluding to Solomon's book of Proverbs (Pro 30:03-04).

Agur mentioned that *Yahveh*, who came to earth and ascended to heaven, also had a Son (Pro 30:04). The implication of *Yeshua*'s allusion was that the Son does what the Father does (Joh 06:62; 10:36-37), namely, descend to earth from heaven and ascend back to heaven (Pro 30:04). Indeed, *Yeshua* said earlier that the disciples would believe once they saw "the Son of Man ascend to where he was before" (Joh 06:62).

Agur called the Father and Son the "Holy Ones" (Pro 30:03), and the "Holy Ones" (plural) are previously called *Yahveh* (Pro 09:10). That the Holy Ones are *Yahveh* shows that the Father and Son are one in the Name, *Yahveh*. That persons are one in name means that an informal version of the *Shema* is found in Proverbs.

The above interpretation and other OT Trinitarianism is behind *Yeshua*'s statement, "I and the Father are one" (Joh 10:30). The anti-Trinitarian Jews knew this was the case, and were sure enough of *Yeshua*'s intended meaning to pick up stones to stone him.

Several months after the incident recorded in Joh 10, *Yeshua* was again at the temple during the Passover Week. *Yeshua* reminded the audience that Moses had called the *Malek Yahveh* at the burning bush both:

- "God" (Mat 22:31-32; Mar 12:26-27; Luk 20:37-38), and
- "Lord" (Luk 20:37).

These statements disturbed one scribe. The scribe may have also heard *Yeshua*'s Trinitarian statements spoken during Hanukkah (Joh 10). The scribe wanted *Yeshua* to affirm unitarianism and back off his Trinitarian-sounding statements.

The scribe asked *Yeshua* what was the greatest commandment, knowing that *Yeshua* would say the *Shema* (Mat 22:35-36; Mar 12:28). *Yeshua* accommodated the scribe (Deu 06:04-05; Mar 12:29-30; Mat 22:36-38). The scribe then tried to put words into *Yeshua*'s mouth and said:

Well said, teacher. You are right in saying that God is one [*heis*] and
there is no other but him (Mar 12:32).

The teacher of the law's statement shows that the unitarian misinterpretation of
the *Shema*, which would later culminate in Rambam's *yachid* version of the *Shema*,
was already current in *Yeshua*'s day.

Yeshua took exception to the teacher of the law's unitarian misinterpretation of
the *Shema*. *Yeshua* told the scribe that he was only near, but not in, the kingdom
of God (Mar 12:34). *Yeshua*'s statement was calculated to pique the interest of
the scribe in the Jewish Trinity. The Jewish Trinity was a belief that those "in"
the kingdom knew. Those only "near" the kingdom did not know the Trinity, or
refused to believe in the Trinity (Deu 29:29; Mat 13:11; 1Co 02:07).

Yeshua then proceeded to teach the scribe about the Trinity, and he countered
the scribe's unitarian *yachid* interpretation of the *Shema*. *Yeshua* said that David
spoke by the Spirit when David spoke of the Father and Son as Lord (Psa 110:
01, 05; Mat 22:43-45; Mar 12:36-37; Luk 20:42, 44). Note the mention of three
persons: the Spirit was the witness to a conversation between David's Lord, the
Father and Son.

In this way *Yeshua* hinted at the intended Trinitarian interpretation of the
Shema. *Yeshua*'s statements, of course, were guarded and subtle since he was
teaching in the temple (Mat 22:31-45; Mar 12:26-37; Luk 20:37-47). Only a few
months earlier *Yeshua* was nearly stoned at the temple (Joh 07:06-08, 30; 08:20).
Paul was beaten in the temple area (Act 21:27-32). James, the brother of *Yeshua*,
was thrown off the temple mount into the rocky Kidron Valley, and then pelted
with stones.[93] So Trinitarian Yahvist "rabbis" such as John the Baptist and *Yeshua*
resorted to hinting about the Trinity in public (Mat 26:25, 49; Mar 09:05; 10:51;
11:21; 14:45; Joh 01:38, 49; 03:02, 26; 04:31; 06:25; 09:02; 11:08).

Though *Yeshua* was forced to speak—and the disciples write, in guarded
terms about the deity of Christ and the doctrine of the Trinity, this is a blessing
in disguise. If *Yeshua* had stated that he was divine, or if he had coined the word
"Trinity," he would have been branded a doctrinal innovator as surely as he was
falsely branded a glutton and a drunkard (Mat 11:19; Luk 07:34). Besides, there
is no lack of proof for the Trinity in the OT. Anyone who denies that the deity of
Christ or the Trinity is biblical merely exposes his or her willful ignorance of the
OT Trinitarianism.

Yeshua's Other Comments on the *Yachid* Interpretation of the *Shema*

Healing the Paralytic
Yeshua forgave a man his sins. Some teachers of the law were thinking along
the lines of the *yachid* (alone) interpretation of the *Shema* when they thought:

Why does this fellow talk like that? He's blaspheming! Who can
forgive sins but God alone [*heis ho theos*])?" (Mar 02:07; Luk 05:21).

The thought that there might be a second or third divine person who could
forgive sins was anathema to these teachers of the law. *Yeshua* challenged their

yachid interpretation of the *Shema* by alluding to the Dan 07 Son of Man vision with these words:

'But so that you may know that the Son of Man has authority on earth to forgive sins'....Then he said to the paralytic, 'Get up, take your mat and go home.' And the man got up and went home (Mar 09:06-07; Mar 02:10-12; Luk 05:24-25).

The Man Who Called Yeshua "Good"

Yeshua also challenged the *yachid* interpretation of the *Shema* when he said:

Why do you call me good?...No one is good—except God alone [the Greek is *heis*] (Mat 19:17; Mar 10:18; Luk 18:19).

Yeshua was alluding to Psa 014:03; 053:03 where it says no mere man is good, but *Yahveh* is good. Nearby is penned: "God is present in the company of the righteous" (Psa 014:05). So *Yeshua* meant that he is Immanuel (meaning, "God with us") who imputes righteousness to sinners (Isa 07:14; Mat 01:23). The bottom line is that *Yeshua* said the man's calling him "good" was tantamount to calling *Yeshua* God—because who could plausibly and convincingly deny that *Yeshua* was good?

Yeshua said that the rich man lacked perfection only because he had not yet given away his earthly possessions to follow *Yeshua* (Mat 19:21; Mar 10:21; Luk 18:22). Thus, *Yeshua* implied that the man did not perfectly keep the commandment attached to the *Shema* (Deu 06:04):

You shall love *Yahveh* [the Father] [and] our *Elohim* [the Son] with all your heart, with all your soul, and with all your might (Deu 06:05).

The rich man did not honor and love God the Son with all his heart, soul and mind (Joh 05:23, 36-37). In this way, *Yeshua* pointed out the Trinitarian interpretation of the *Shema*. *Yeshua* also showed that one cannot keep the *Shema*, the Greatest Commandment, without honoring God the Son.

Parenthetically, the command to give away riches was not given to everyone for all time, but was meant for this particular rich man. The command was meant to:

* Reveal the condition of the rich man's heart, and
* Show that *Yeshua* was *Yahveh* the Son, who was within his rights to make such demands.

In Psalm 014, two verses after the verse that *Yeshua* alluded to (Psa 014:03), is the statement "for God is present in the company of the righteous" (Psa 014:05). The answer to the conundrum that there is no one good (Psa 014:03), yet "God is present in the company of the righteous," is that God imputes righteousness to his followers just as God credited Abraham with righteousness (Gen 15:06).

Righteousness was credited to Abraham even before the rite of circumcision was given (Gen 17), and centuries before the Mosaic Law was handed down. So *Yeshua* inferred that he is Immanuel ("God with us") (Isa 07:14; Mat 01:23), and that he imputes righteousness to sinners.

On the Last Day, those who think that *Yeshua* is a mere angel or a human, but not God, will come before the throne. *Yeshua* will then ask, "Why do you call me good?" (Mat 19:17; Mar 10:18; Luk 18:19). The correct answer is, "Because *Yeshua* is God." Many, however, will respond that *Yeshua* is good because he is a great teacher. *Yeshua* will ask them:

> If you believe that I am good, then why did you not believe that I am
> God the Son as I claim to be?

Yeshua will respond to those who think him a mere man or an angel that they are accusing him of not being good. Only God is good, and God even charges angels with error (Job 04:18; 15:15-16). Furthermore, as C. S. Lewis pointed out concerning *Yeshua*'s claimed of deity, either *Yeshua* was a lunatic, a liar, or Lord. Only God can claim to be God and still be called sane, truthful, and good.

Yeshua's opinion of those who say he is a mere angel is that they are bold and daring. They dare to demote *Yeshua* down to the level of an archangel like Michael, who is called "one of the chief princes" (Dan 10:13). If the archangel Michael hesitated to rebuke Satan (2Pe 02:11; Jud 01:09), they should definitely not accuse a person greater than Michael of having erred (Job 04:18; 15:15-16).

Peter's words apply to those who think *Yeshua* is an erring angel:

> Daring, self-willed, they are not afraid to speak evil of dignitaries;
> whereas angels, though greater in might and power, do not bring a
> railing judgment against them before the Lord. But these, as unreasoning
> creatures, born natural animals to be taken and destroyed, speaking evil in
> matters about which they are ignorant, will in their destroying surely be
> destroyed, receiving the wages of unrighteousness (2Pe 02:10-13).

For the impertinence of calling *Yeshua* "good" as though he were just another human, *Yeshua* could respond:

> You [mistakenly] thought the 'I AM' was like you, but I will rebuke
> you and accuse you to your face (Psa 050:21).

Chapter 5

The Trinity in Daniel 01—05

Introduction

Many Christians have a general bias against the spiritual aptitude of pagans. The bias is especially strong against Nebuchadnezzar II (reigned 605 to 561 BC) because he set up a giant idol (Dan 03). However, Daniel, Shadrach, Meshach and Abednego informed Nebuchadnezzar about *Yahveh* over a period of time. So there is no reason for Bible readers to automatically give Nebuchadnezzar's Trinitarian-sounding letter about *Yahveh* (Dan 04) short shrift.

This chapter will show that Nebuchadnezzar progressed in his understanding of *Yahveh*, and that Dan 04 has a Trinitarian rather than a pagan message. Of course, it would be anachronistic to think that Nebuchadnezzar's understanding of the Trinity was as refined as the Athanasian Creed. One can hold to a simple Trinitarian creed like the *Shema* and still be considered a Trinitarian.

The False Bias Against the Religious Aptitude of Pagans

Many people think that pagans had reams of gods with a high god at the top of the heap. Many pagans, however, had sophisticated pantheons and even pseudo-trinities. The reason pagan cultures have pseudo-trinities is the same reason pagan cultures have flood myths, as well as other semblances and imitations of Yahvism or Christianity.

The awareness of the Trinity was passed down from the age between Noah's Flood and the Tower of Babel debacle. Also, just as syncretism occurred between pagan cultures, syncretism occurred between Yahvists and pagans. Pagan cultures also gleaned some knowledge about God directly from nature (Rom 01:20).

The bias against the religious aptitude of pagans is not borne out by history or Scripture (Eze 03:05-07; Mat 11:23). For instance, when the Philistine Abimelech (Gen 20:06) and the Aramean Balaam (Num 22:10; 23:27) saw the Trinity (*haElohim*), they were not baffled that three persons were one God. In fact, the high gods of the Mesopotamia, the heartland of Nebuchadnezzar's kingdom, were pseudo-trinities. J. Spencer Trimingham wrote:

Mesopotamian cults in particular were based on the triad, 'Our Lord, our Lady, and the Son of our two Lords, with *Be'el-Shamim*,' which correspond to the great Syrian deities, Hadad, Atagatis, Simios, and the Sky-god, *Ba'al Shamim*.[94]

Sinasi Gunduz wrote:

The children of Sin [moon], Ishtar [Venus], his daughter, and Shamash [sun], his son, are mentioned with him in one of the Nabonidus inscriptions from Harran [Arabic spelling of Haran]. It seems there was a trinity of gods, but this may be due to the custom of mentioning gods in threes.[95]

The Dreamscape Statue

Nebuchadnezzar dreamt of a statue representing the kingdoms of the world down to the end of time (Dan 02):

- The head of gold represented Nebuchadnezzar's rule over the Babylonian Empire (605-562 BC),
- The chest and arms of silver were the two branches of the Medo-Persian Empire (546-331 BC),
- The bronze abdomen was the Macedonian Empire (331-323 BC),
- The bronze thighs were the Ptolemaic (323-030 BC) and Seleucid (312-064 BC) branches,
- The legs of iron were the Roman (27 BC-476 AD) and Byzantine (395-1453 AD) Empires, and
- The feet and toes of clay and iron are nations that have arisen since the fall of the Roman Empire (476 AD).

The nations comprising the iron of the feet are those that model themselves on the Roman Empire (the iron calves). The copied features tend to perpetuate and strengthen government institutions. These features include an official language, a legal tradition, a senate (legislative branch), a strong executive, a massive public works infrastructure, and the like.

Clay nations are those that do not model themselves on the Roman model. What keeps iron and clay nations apart are the different cultures and religion, and the realization that trading makes better economic sense than conquest and occupation (Dan 02:43).

The rock that Nebuchadnezzar saw smash the statue was cut out of a mountain, but not by human hands (Dan 02:34, 45). The mountain refers to the mass of humanity, and the rock cut out from the mountain is Christ, the living stone (1Co 10:04; 1Pe 02:04-08) and Christians (1Co 03:16-17; 06:19; 2Co 06:16; Eph 02:20-22; Heb 03:06).

The spread of Christianity (the rock tumbling down the mountain) sends seismic shockwaves through the pagan kingdoms represented by the statue. The tumbling rock represents *Yeshua* ruling the Christian Church in the midst of his enemies (Psa 110:02; compare Psa 106:47; Rom 08:37; 2Co 02:14-16). The last day will come when the rock finally collides with and smashes the statue representing earthly kingdoms.

After the Last Day, *Yeshua* will rule on the mountain that grew from the rock that finally smashed the statue. The mountain growing from the rock represents the resurrected believers from all ages joining the believers who happened to be living when the Last Day occurred. Then there will be a New Heaven, New Earth and New Jerusalem that will last forever (Isa 65:17; 66:22; Joh 18:36; Jam 02:05; 2Pe 03:13; Rev 03:12; 11:15; 21:01-02).

Nebuchadnezzar's Reaction to the Statue

Daniel told Nebuchadnezzar that he was the golden head. There is no mention, however, that the dream statue even had a golden neck. So Nebuchadnezzar knew that if *Yahveh* had his way, Nebuchadnezzar would not have a dynastic successor worthy of a prophetic mention (Dan 02:38).

Nebuchadnezzar was not satisfied being just the golden head, the first of several kingdoms. He either wanted his dynasty to last forever, or he wanted to be the eternal king that Daniel mentioned in interpretation. Perhaps Nebuchadnezzar started to believe the flattering salute given to him everywhere: "O king, live forever!" (Dan 02:04; 03:09).

That the statue relates to Nebuchadnezzar or his dynasty suggests that the statue may have been made to look either like Nebuchadnezzar, or a stereotypical Babylon monarch.

Nebuchadnezzar was not a person to sit around and just hope for favorable change (Dan 02:09). Nebuchadnezzar mused about how *Yahveh* had communicated his intention about the kingdoms of history through a dreamscape statue. So Nebuchadnezzar decided to signal what he wanted the kingdoms of history to look like using a 27-meter high, 2.7-meter wide gold leaf statue.[96]

The statue was placed in the plain of Dura in the province of Babylon (Dan 03:01). That the statue was covered entirely with gold, rather than being partly gold, silver, bronze, iron and clay, had meaning. Nebuchadnezzar wanted to communicate that he wanted his golden kingdom to last to the end of the world. He did not want his kingdom cut off at the neck.

The astrologers must have reasoned that Nebuchadnezzar's gods of the plain would be more accommodating than *Yahveh*, especially since Nebuchadnezzar had conquered "*Yahveh*'s land" (Jos 22:19; Isa 14:02; Hos 09:03). Since Babylon was in the heart of the relatively flat river valley of Mesopotamia, foreign gods were likely often viewed to be mountain gods. The astrologers perhaps considered *Yahveh* a "god of hills" (1Ki 20:23-28), and reasoned that is why:

- The statue was destroyed by a rock cut out of a mountain (Dan 02:34, 45), and
- The rock subsequently grew into a mountain that filled the earth (Dan 02:35).

That *Yahveh* was considered a mountain god is likely the reason why Nebuchadnezzar situated his statue on the plain of Dura in the province of Babylon (Dan 03:01). There the gods of the plain could view the statue, and none of the favorite astral deities would be hidden behind hills and mountains. Moreover, the statue would be out of the view of mountain gods. The statue would be well away from any mountain where the "god of hills" might smash the statue with a tumbling stone.

That Nebuchadnezzar was appealing to the gods of the plain is why the astrologers and Nebuchadnezzar demanded everyone pay homage to the statue. The gods of the plain would then look favorably on Nebuchadnezzar's proposed version of the future as communicated by the statue.

Certain Jews continued to worship *Yahveh* despite Nebuchadnezzar's orders. Nebuchadnezzar became infuriated because worshipping *Yahveh* was tantamount to asking that his golden dynasty be cut off at the neck. After all, it was *Yahveh* who had sent Nebuchadnezzar the statue dream saying that his kingdom would pretty much end with him (Dan 03:08-18; also again in 06:07-13).

A Misinterpretation Leads to Mistranslation That in Turn Reinforces the Misinterpretation

Every Bible reader is familiar with Dan 06 account of Daniel in the lions' den. Daniel was sent to the lions' den because he petitioned *Yahveh* during a certain thirty-day period. Daniel broke a law that said during a certain month, everyone was to petition King Darius instead of their gods.

It is not clear whether the people were to petition the king as though he were a god, or just petition by courier or through a personal audience. The rationale for the command may have been that Darius wanted to magnify himself by granting petitions directly. Perhaps Darius wanted to act as high priest and petition the gods for his people. Perhaps Darius just wanted the undivided attention of the gods for his own petitions.

The Dan 06 interpretation may have influenced the interpretation and translation of Dan 02—03. Dan 06 may have led translators to think that Nebuchadnezzar ordered people to worship a statue representing either a god or King Nebuchadnezzar himself. The interpreters figured that if the people were to pray to a King Darius in Dan 06, Dan 02—03 must involve praying to King Nebuchadnezzar or an idol.

So interpreters apparently made Dan 02—03 conform to their preconceived notions. That is why a few Aramaic words are not translated consistently throughout Daniel 02 and 03. If the words were translated consistently, one would read that the people were to "pay homage" to the statue rather than "worship" the statue. Furthermore, the statue would be called a "statue" or an "icon" rather than an "idol." Here are the details:

- In Dan 02:46, the Aramaic word *cegid* is usually translated as "pay homage," but in Dan 03 the ten occurrences of *cegid* are all translated as "worship" (Dan 03:05, 06, 07, 10, 11, 12, 14, 15, 18, 28), and

- In Dan 02, the Aramaic word *tselem* is translated "statue" four times (Dan 02: 31, 32, 34, 35). However, in Dan 03, the same word *tselem* is translated "idol" eleven times (Dan 03:01, 02, 03; 05, 07, 10, 12, 14, 15, 18, 19).

Faulty translations cause readers to miss the intended meaning of the golden statue. Also lost in translation is the transition between the dreamscape statue in Dan 02 and the golden statue of Dan 03. A consistent translation, however, reveals that just as Nebuchadnezzar had fallen down and paid homage to Daniel, the people were to fall down and pay homage to the statue. The statue was not meant as an idol to be worshipped since it merely represented Nebuchadnezzar's ambitious hopes for the future of his kingdom.

The statue that Nebuchadnezzar set up was no more an idol than Daniel was an idol to Nebuchadnezzar. The Dan 03 landscape statue that Nebuchadnezzar made was no more an idol than the Dan 02 dreamscape statue that Nebuchadnezzar mimicked. Note that the astrologers and Shadrach, Meshach and Abednego all made a distinction between:

- Nebuchadnezzar's gods [Aramaic is *elahh*] and the golden image [Aramaic is *tselem*], and
- Worship [Aramaic is *pelach*] and paying homage [Aramaic is *cedig*].

The pertinent texts read:

> They neither worship [Aramaic is *pelach*] your gods [Aramaic is *elahh*] nor pay homage to [Aramaic is *cedig*] the image [Aramaic is *tselem*] of gold you have set up...we will not worship [Aramaic is *pelach*] your gods [Aramaic is *elahh*] or pay homage to [Aramaic is *cedig*] the image [Aramaic is *tselem*] of gold you have set up (Dan 03:12, 18).

So all the principle characters in the account knew exactly why Nebuchadnezzar had set up the golden statue (Dan 02:49). They knew Nebuchadnezzar built the statue not as an idol *per se*, but to indicate the alternative future he wanted the gods to bring about.

It should also be noted that Nebuchadnezzar was not practicing sympathetic magic because he was not trying to manipulate nature or impersonal metaphysical forces. The gods he was trying to communicate with were persons, just as the God who sent Nebuchadnezzar the statue dream was a person (Deu 04:07).

Pagans usually barter with the gods, and sometimes vowed that if a god fulfilled a prayer request, he or she would worship that god forever. Nebuchadnezzar may have reasoned that the gods would grant his wish because, unlike *Yahveh*, his gods of gold (Dan 05:04, 23) would be happiest with his golden kingdom.

Nebuchadnezzar perhaps reasoned:

> Why would my gods want kingdoms made of inferior metals, clay and stone (Dan 02:39)?

Nebuchadnezzar, of course, unwittingly set himself up against the Son of God and his eternal kingdom as predicted in the Dan 02 statue dream (Dan 04:03, 34; compare also Dan 06:26).

Nebuchadnezzar apparently did not learn from the fiery furnace incident that pagan gods cannot overrule what *Yahveh* has determined. Only after another dream followed by a seven-year bout of mental illness would Nebuchadnezzar accept that *Yahveh* was the Most High God who doled out the kingdoms to anyone he pleased (Dan 04:17, 25, 32, 34; see also Dan 02:21; 05:18-23).

So the reader can see that the dreamscape statue and the landscape statue are not two isolated and disconnected events. They are individual lessons in Nebuchadnezzar's spiritual schooling leading up to Nebuchadnezzar becoming a Trinitarian Yahvist.

Trinitarian Proof Texts in Dan 01—05

Kings thought it wise to know about the gods of their kingdoms (2Ki 17: 26). Knowing the enemy's gods helped when conducting psychological warfare (2Ki 18:25). Some kings even adopted the gods of their enemies (2Ch 28:23). Nebuchadnezzar paid homage to Daniel because he told Nebuchadnezzar both the dream and the interpretation (Dan 02:46). Surely, this incident must have made Nebuchadnezzar curious about *Yahveh*.

[All] the Gods (*haElohim*)

Daniel undoubtedly told Nebuchadnezzar about "[All] the Gods" (*haElohim*) (Dan 01:02, 09, 17), especially since Nebuchadnezzar had robbed the temple of "[All] the Gods" (*haElohim*) in Jerusalem (Dan 01: 02). In 604 BC, Nebuchadnezzar may have even stolen or destroyed the Ark of the Covenant. The Ark was often called the "Ark of [All] the Gods" (*haElohim*). The last mention of the existence of the Ark (Jer 03:16) precedes the first mention of Nebuchadnezzar by only eighteen chapters (Jer 21: 02). The temple was destroyed after 586 BC, the ark's *terminus ad quem*.

If Daniel told Nebuchadnezzar anything about the OT, it would have been hard not to mention the Trinity. There are so many Trinitarian proofs in the OT. Moreover, a former polytheist like Nebuchadnezzar would naturally interpret the thousands of plural nouns, verbs and modifiers referring to *Yahveh* as references to plural persons. Dan 04, the chapter that Nebuchadnezzar wrote, seems to indicate that Nebuchadnezzar knew a lot about *Yahveh*.[97]

Remember that Nebuchadnezzar lived in an age that predated translations such as the LXX. Translations transformed nearly all the Hebrew plurals referring to *Yahveh* into singulars. In fact, it seems it was not until the advent of Trinity-adverse translations that people came to think of *Yahveh* in unitarian terms.

Initially, when Nebuchadnezzar was still a pagan, he told Daniel:

Truly, your god is a god of gods [a triad], and the lord of kings [three divine persons], and a revealer of secrets, seeing that you have been able to reveal this secret (Dan 02:47).

The pagan triads were thought to be the more powerful gods. Pagans may have addressed their pseudo-trinities as "a god of gods." The phrase "God of Gods" is used elsewhere in the OT to describe the Trinity (Deu 10:17; Jos 22:22; Psa 050:

01; Dan 11:36). Nebuchadnezzar's phrase "lord of kings" (Dan 02:47) is similar to the phrase "Lord of Lords" that is elsewhere used to describe the Trinity (Deu 10: 17; Jos 22:22; Psa 050:01; 136:03; Isa 26:13; Dan 02:47; 11:36; 1Ti 06:15; Rev 17: 14; 19:16).   Nebuchadnezzar told Daniel that *Yahveh* was "your god" (Dan 02: 47). Nebuchadnezzar said of Shadrach, Meshach and Abednego that *Yahveh* was "their own God" (Dan 03:28). Note that Nebuchadnezzar did not say "my God" or "our God." This meant that when Nebuchadnezzar said *Yahveh* was a "god of gods," he had a standard Semitic triad of gods in mind.

Nebuchadnezzar did not mean the phrase "god of gods" to be understood as though *Yahveh* were the head of his pantheon. Otherwise, Nebuchadnezzar would have said that *Yahveh* was "his God" and "our God." So initially, it seems, Nebuchadnezzar merely repeated Trinitarian phrases that Daniel spoke about *Yahveh*. Nebuchadnezzar initially understood these phrases in terms of his Semitic pagan religion, not in terms of Trinitarian Yahvism.

The fact that Nebuchadnezzar used Trinitarian language about *Yahveh* reveals that Daniel taught that *Yahveh* was the Trinity. Evidently, Daniel instructed Nebuchadnezzar about *Yahveh* just as Joseph instructed Egyptian royalty about *Yahveh* (Gen 45:08; Psa 105:17-22). Later, Nebuchadnezzar said that Daniel had "the Spirit of the Holy [plural] Gods [plural] in him" (Dan 04:08, 09, 18). This is similar to Pharaoh's statement about Joseph:

Can we find such a one as this, a man in whom is the Spirit of God?
(Gen 41:38).

It was only after Nebuchadnezzar witnessed Shadrach, Meshach and Abednego being saved from the fiery furnace that Nebuchadnezzar started to take *Yahveh* seriously. Only then did Nebuchadnezzar call *Yahveh* the Most High God (Dan 03: 26). Yet, Nebuchadnezzar later had to write that he learned *Yahveh* was his God the hard way—after another dream and a seven-year bout of mental illness. Only then did Nebuchadnezzar accept that *Yahveh* was the Most High God who doled out the kingdoms to anyone he pleased (Dan 04:17, 25, 32, 34; see also Dan 02:21; 05:18-23).

One Like the Son of the Gods is Also Called *Malek*

After Nebuchadnezzar had the statue dream (Dan 02) explained to him, Nebuchadnezzar undoubtedly wanted to know more about *Yahveh* and the last kingdom's eternal ruler. Daniel told Nebuchadnezzar that the eternal ruler would be the Son of *Yahveh* (Pro 30:03-04).

Daniel must have told Nebuchadnezzar that the Son had appeared many times as the *Malek Yahveh*. Daniel probably mentioned that the Son made some preincarnate appearances (Gen 18—19; 32; Jos 05; Jdg 06, 13).[98] That Nebuchadnezzar knew the Son appeared sometimes as a man and sometimes as the Angel of *Yahveh* explains why Nebuchadnezzar said the fourth person in the furnace was a "Son of God" (LXX Dan 03:25) and a *malek* ("messenger") sent by God (Dan 03:28).

According to the MT recension reading for Dan 03:25, however,

Nebuchadnezzar said the *Malek* (Dan 03:28) was "like a son of God." This is similar to how Job called the angels "sons of God" (Job 01:06; 02:01; 38:07). This does not contradict the LXX rendering, as though the LXX spoke of the divine Son while the MT recension spoke of a mere angel.

The versions are easily reconciled if one understands that the Son appeared in the fiery furnace as a man (Dan 03:25), and then Nebuchadnezzar was told he was the divine *Malek Yahveh* (Dan 03:28). In fact, twice during the time of the Judges, the Son appeared as a man and then as the *Malek Yahveh* in fire to Manoah and Gideon (Jdg 06:21; 13:20). The *Malek Yahveh*'s appearance in the fiery furnace must have been like "a man of [All] the Gods" (Jdg 13:06, 08) and "like the *Malek* of [All] the Gods" (Jdg 13:06). Manoah knew the *Malek Yahveh* to be God (Jdg 13:22), and Manoah's wife knew the *Malek Yahveh* to be *Yahveh* (Jdg 13:23). Nebuchadnezzar's spiritual instincts perhaps taught him that the "one like the Son of God" was God and *Yahveh*. With his interest piqued, Nebuchadnezzar surely searched the Scriptures with Daniel and found out more about the Son of God and the Trinity.

The Spirit of the Holy [Plural] Gods [Plural]

Nebuchadnezzar said that Daniel had "the Spirit of the Holy [plural] Gods [plural] in him" (Dan 04:08, 09, 18). This is similar to Pharaoh's statement about Joseph:

Can we find such a one as this, a man in whom is the Spirit of God? (Gen 41:38).

Moreover, Nebuchadnezzar's phrasing is similar to Joshua's statement about *Yahveh* being "the Holy [plural] Gods [plural]" (Jos 24:19).

"Holy" means "separate." The phrase "Holy Gods" means that *Yahveh* was in a separate category from other gods. The characteristics of that category would be that:

- *Yahveh* is the Trinity whereas no pagan gods are true trinities. Some gods and their consorts might be considered triads or pseudo-trinities, and
- The Trinity is really God while pagan gods are merely demons in disguise. The demons composing pagan pseudo-trinities, of course, are not three persons united in nature.

That Nebuchadnezzar spoke of "the Spirit of the Holy Gods" who dwelt in Daniel means that Nebuchadnezzar was really referring to the Trinity. Otherwise, Daniel would have protested and said that he was not possessed by demons (Deu 32:17; see also Psa 106:37).

Belshazzar's Impertinence

Belshazzar, the son of Nebuchadnezzar, succeeded Nebuchadnezzar to the throne. Belshazzar threw a party during which the Hand of *Yahveh* wrote on a wall. The partygoers happened to be imbibing from vessels from *Yahveh*'s temple.

Perhaps the queen noticed that the script on the wall was like the Hebrew script inscribed on the vessels. This in turn reminded the queen of how Daniel was a Hebrew and worshipped the Hebrew's Trinity. Of course, the queen knew all about Nebuchadnezzar's letter promulgated throughout the kingdom (Dan 04). The queen also remembered that Daniel had succeeded at rendering an interpretation after the other wise men had failed. The queen then told Belshazzar that Daniel...

...has the Spirit of the Holy [plural] Gods [plural] in him. In the time
of your father he was found to have insight and intelligence and wisdom
like that of the gods (Dan 05:11).

When Daniel arrived, Belshazzar told Daniel that he had "the spirit of the gods in him" (Dan 05:14). This contrasts with how Nebuchadnezzar had written that Daniel had the "Spirit of the Holy [plural] Gods" in him (Dan 04:08, 09, 18). Belshazzar's wife had used the same wording that Nebuchadnezzar used (Dan 05:11).

Note that Belshazzar omitted the plural adjective "holy" before the word "Gods." Because Belshazzar did not honor God as "holy," a similar fate befell Belshazzar as befell Moses. *Yahveh* took away leadership from Belshazzar just as *Yahveh* had taken away leadership from Moses when Moses did not honor *Yahveh* as being "holy" (Num 20:12).

Before Belshazzar received his punishment, he received a good tongue-lashing from Daniel. Belshazzar's statement, mentioned above, was ambiguous as to whether the Spirit of the Trinity indwelt Daniel, or whether a spirit of a pagan god indwelt Daniel. Daniel, of course, knew that pagan gods were really demons (Deu 32:17; see also Psa 106:37). Therefore, Daniel told Belshazzar that he had failed to honor the "God who holds in his hand your life and all your ways" (Dan 05:23).

Daniel's mention of God's "hand" was apt, not only because God's finger had just written on the wall, but because the Spirit of *Yahveh* is called the hand and finger of God several times in the Bible. Belshazzar's failure to call God "holy" meant he failed to specify whether Daniel was indwelt by the Spirit or by a demon. This indeed was a sin against the Spirit (Mar 03:29-30).

The Writing on the Wall

Daniel then interpreted the writing on the wall which read:
Mene [numbered], *mene* [numbered], *tekel* [weighed], *parsin* [divided]
(Dan 05:25).
Daniel said:
This is what these words mean: *Mene*: God has numbered the days of
your reign and brought it to an end. *Tekel*: You have been weighed on the
scales and found wanting. *Peres* [singular form of *parsin*]: Your kingdom
is divided and given to the Medes and Persians (Dan 05:27-28).

Daniel's readership no doubt knew this passage alluded to how ancient transactions were conducted. Exactly how this passage related to ancient commerce takes a lot of explaining to uninitiated moderns.

Understanding the handwriting on the wall is of some importance, since it was meant to make unfavorable comparisons between the polytheistic Belshazzar and the Trinitarian Nebuchadnezzar.

The dreamscape statue and the golden statue also deserve a lengthy treatment since they concern the history of the world, and the future kingdom of *Yahveh* the Son.

How the Writing on the Wall and Nebuchadnezzar's Statue Are Related

Ancients often weighed and counted coins, while moderns just count coins. One might be surprised to learn that many museums have large collections of coin weights.[99] Weighing coins was important since each coin's value was, to some extent, based on its metal content. Treasuries and mints did not back the face value of coins, whether they were authentic or not.

Often, ancient coinage systems were not well standardized, so silver and gold coins had to be weighed. Coins meant to be weighed were called *al marco* in Arabic.[100] One benefit of empires was a standardized coinage so merchants and taxmen could forego weighing coins during each transaction—at their own risk. Coins standardized for counting were called *al pezzo* in Arabic. However, even *al pezzo* coins sometimes were not worth their face value:

- Many mints had little quality control,
- There were many imitation and counterfeit coins,
- People would crop (meaning, "clip" or "trim") coins, since ancient coins did not have raised margins or reeded edges where grooved lines run vertically around the coin's perimeter,
- Often coins were holed to make jewelry, and
- Alloy coins would lose precious metal due to wear and corrosion. Corrosion wears off quickly.

To complicate matters, coins were made of alloys because alloys resist wear better than pure gold, silver and copper. Alloys do not corrode as quickly as pure silver and copper. Mints and even counterfeiters knew that the face value of coins was greater than the bullion from which the coins were made.[101]

So an ancient mint only issued a coin with a high gold or silver content until that mint's coin became accepted. "The coin of the realm" often was debased due to greed, or the kingdom experienced financial distress. Ya'akov Meshorer wrote:

> Of course, it was impossible in those days to gauge the silver content of coins...when, in the course of time, it became an accepted currency, the Nabateans could permit themselves to reduce the weight of the coins.[102]

Interestingly, during Belshazzar's feast, the Medes and Persians were about to take over Babylon. So perhaps Babylonian coinage was already debased at the time of the handwriting on the wall incident. Perhaps the debasing used one of the following methods, or a combination of the following:

- Inflating the face value,
- Using less precious and more base metal in the alloy, and
- Shrinking the size or thickness of the coin flan.

Collectors have many names for the materials in debased coins including billon, electrum, pale-gold, gold-washed, gold-plated, gold-coated, clad, and copper core. Color alone cannot be used to accurately peg a coin's gold or silver content because:

- Many ancient coins consisted of base metals coated in gold or silver,
- Different colored metals could be alloyed with gold and silver, and
- Gold-silver alloys have subtle tones of yellow. The gold-silver alloy only turns white when the silver content approaches seventy percent.[103]

Gold, however, has a specific gravity (denseness) of 19.3, which makes gold nearly twice as heavy by volume as lead (11.34), silver (10.5), copper (8.92) and iron (7.86). This sizeable difference in density meant ancient balance scales could readily ferret out coins with a lower than expected gold content.

The reason *mene* (counted) is repeated twice in Dan 05:25 is that coins representing the days of Belshazzar's reign were counted. Then an equal number of known good coins or coin weights were counted and added to the other side of the balance scale.

In order for Belshazzar's "coins" to be acceptable, they would need to be gold, since in Nebuchadnezzar's dream the statue's golden head represented the Babylonian kingdom (Dan 02:32, 38). In fact, the mention of gold, silver and bronze describing Belshazzar's feast (Dan 05:02, 04, 23) seems to be an allusion to Nebuchadnezzar's statue of Dan 02.

The gold coins or coin weights against which Belshazzar's "coins" were weighed perhaps represented the days of Nebuchadnezzar's reign. Consider how Daniel made comparisons between Belshazzar and Belshazzar's father Nebuchadnezzar (Dan 05:18-22). The scale tipped in favor of the coin weights (or Nebuchadnezzar's gold coins) which meant Belshazzar's reign was found wanting (*tekel*).

Belshazzar's reign was supposed to be more gold than silver, but weighing proved his reign was more silver than gold. The reader will recall that the chest and arms of the statue were silver (Dan 02:32), which characterized the next kingdom of the Medes and Persians. So appropriately, Belshazzar's coins, which were more silver than gold, were divided (*peres*) among the Medes and Persians (Dan 05:28).

Silver was the element that comprised the statue's chest and arms. Silver was commonly alloyed with gold to make billon and electrum coins. Gold comprised the statue's head. Copper was commonly alloyed with silver to make silver coins. Copper and tin make the alloy bronze. The statue's belly and thighs happen to be made of bronze. Besides bronze's use in weapons and tools, bronze was widely used in coinage. Most "copper" coins are, in fact, bronze, since copper in its pure form is soft. Copper is also susceptible to tarnishing and wear.

So one can see that from top to bottom, the baser metal in the alloy of one kingdom becomes the dominant metal of the next. The statue went from a gold-silver alloy for the head, to a silver-copper for the chest and arms, to copper-tin (bronze) alloy for the belly and thighs.

Just as adding too much silver debased gold coins, adding too much copper readily debased silver coins. Silver has nearly the same density as copper and other base metals, while gold is nearly twice as dense silver and other base metals. Therefore, debased silver coins are harder to ferret out by use of scales than are debased gold coins. This fact meant ancient mints could debase silver coins with near impunity.

Using modern, non-destructive techniques, numismatists commonly find that many ancient silver coins contain twenty-five percent or less silver! Some ancient coins even have copper cores and are called "clad," "silver-washed," "silver-coated" or "silver-plated." Such coins are "commonly encountered and are known collectively as *subaerata*."[104] The Romans provide an example of how ingenious debasing techniques became:

> In the later Roman Empire (3rd century AD) silver issues were heavily
> debased with copper; prior to striking, the blanks were immersed in an
> acid bath that leached out the surface copper to expose more silver, giving
> a much more acceptable appearance to the coins when they were first
> issued."[105]

That a kingdom or counterfeiter could profit immensely by debasing silver reveals why medieval alchemists tried hard to produce a secret alloy of base metals that had the same properties as gold.

There also is a connection between the bronze belly, the bronze thighs and the iron calves:

> Bronze is harder than copper as a result of alloying that metal with tin
> or other metals. Bronze is also more fusible (i.e., more readily melted)
> and is hence easier to cast. It is also harder than pure iron and far more
> resistant to corrosion. The substitution of iron for bronze in tools and
> weapons from about 1000 BC was the result of iron's abundance compared
> to copper and tin rather than any inherent advantages of [pure] iron.[106]

What made bronze more expensive than iron was the scarcity of tin. Though copper was plentiful, in ancient times the known deposits of tin were small, and these were found in remote locations such as Britain and Afghanistan.

The scarcity of tin would have led to the extensive use of iron at an earlier time if it were not for the fact that iron's high melting point (1,535 degrees Celsius) required the development of techniques not necessary for copper and tin production. Copper and tin, when smelted together, have a low melting point of 950 degrees Celsius.

Since bronze is an alloy, different proportions of copper and tin have different properties:

> A low proportion of from 2-9% tin to circa 90-98% copper produces a
> 'soft' bronze. This is the alloy usually used for casting coin flans and most
> other decorative, votive or practical artifacts...[coin] dies [for example]...
> contain variously from 18-22% tin resulting in a very hard cast object.[107]

If enough tin is used, bronze is even harder than pure iron. Weaponry, however, was one application where "carburized" iron ("iron carbide" or "steel") was better than bronze. Iron became impregnated with carbon by repeatedly being heated in charcoal fires during the smelting, forging and quenching (tempering) processes. The hammering process drove slag out of the iron, and the quenching process involved plunging red-hot iron into water to turn the iron brittle. Upon reheating the brittle iron forms a crystalline matrix that makes the iron durable and springy.

So Nebuchadnezzar's statue's legs of steel are a prophecy of the militaristic character of the Roman Empire.[108] That the statue's legs were made of steel and its feet partly of iron shows that the real centers of power would move out of the iron-poor Middle East to iron-rich Europe:

> Indian steel blades were still sought after, though by the ninth century they seem to have taken a back place to those from the Rhineland... Bronze was used to a much greater extent [in the Mideast] than in Europe presumably because of the shortage of iron in the Islamic world.[109]

Interestingly, bronze was in short supply and expensive in Medieval Europe with the result that ancient Roman bronze statuary was melted down while marble statuary was left intact. Only one Roman bronze statue has remained above ground in Italy since it was made—the equestrian Marcus Aurelius in Rome. This fact once led archeologists to assume that Roman statuary was made mostly of marble rather than bronze, "which is not necessarily true."[110]

That Europe had iron, and enough wood and coal to fire the iron, helped propel Christian Europe and the Bible into the world. Thus, at the very time the gospel and the Bible lost influence in the Middle East, Europe was transformed from a backwater into an expansionist power with global reach. The newly found lands also tended to have iron, timber and coal.

This meant Noah's prophesy about Japheth was fulfilled (Gen 09:27). Japheth's territory was enlarged, especially when Europeans settled everywhere land was sparsely populated—relatively speaking. Christianity and the Bible spread globally. Truly, God did determine when and where nations migrate and settle "so that men would seek him and perhaps reach out for him and find him" (Act 17:26-27).

There also was a connection between the statue's feet that are a mixture of iron and clay, and the statue's iron calves. Molten iron and other metals were commonly poured into clay molds. The molds were formed using the "lost beeswax" method. The clay mold was not used again, but was broken up to uncover the cast iron.

Clay was used as a mold for iron for the very reason cited in Dan 02:43—clay and iron do not mix. Since the statue's feet were constituted of iron still in the clay mold, this meant the iron was not formed into weapons. The iron in the clay was weaker, too, since it was not "carburized" into steel by going through the forging and quenching (tempering) processes.

Iron, not steel, describes how the western and eastern Roman Empires disintegrated into smaller countries that copied the Roman Republic and Empires in many respects. The copycat states, however, are not tempered by century after century of warfare. They are not as militaristic as the Roman Empire, at least on a long-term basis on the order of centuries. Weak countries of clay often surround the Roman copycat states and shape the iron as though they were a mold or cast.

Interestingly, during this last period of the world, coinage of iron-like metals such as low-grade steel and nickel have nearly replaced gold, silver, bronze and copper coinage. This is especially the case during times of war. Furthermore, coins made of aluminum circulate side by side with iron-like coinage.

Because aluminum is reactive chemically, it never naturally occurs as nuggets or in veins. Aluminum, however, is abundant in rocks, vegetation, and animals. Nonferrous metals like aluminum should be considered part of the clay of the statue's feet along with the other components of clay: silicon (sand and quartz), potassium oxide, calcium oxide, nitrogen and whatnot.[111] So it seems that iron and clay feet foreshadow the coinage of modern nation states.

More on the Trinity in Daniel

The chapter on Hebrew collective nouns and the MT plurals appendix discuss the Trinitarian proof texts in Dan 04—05 and 07 that involve plurals nouns and plural verbs. The Trinitarian proofs appendix discusses Dan 09:19. The Song of Moses chapter discusses the implications of the Trinitarian texts in Dan 07.

Chapter 6

The Prophet Behind the Prophets

Introduction

The purpose of this chapter is to show that the OT prophetic books should be read as the words of the preincarnate Son. That the OT prophetic books can, for the most part, be understood as the words of the Son implies Trinitarianism.

The first person speech (for example, "I," "me," "my") that are not quotations should generally be considered the words of the Son. The Son often refers to the Father and Spirit in the third person (for example, "he," "him," "his"). Quotations most often are the words of the Father as quoted by the Son. The few phrases and sections that are obvious words of the prophets should be considered mere interjections interspersed in what is otherwise the Son's narrative.

Isaiah Was a Proxy for the Prophetic Role of *Yahveh* the Son

Some have taught that *Yahveh* did not verbally inspire the OT prophets. Some say the OT prophets only had a "feel" for what *Yahveh* might have said in a given situation. The prophets then gave verbal messages, some of which were collected and written down in anthologies. These anthologies survived only if readers of subsequent generations thought the material was applicable to their times.

This low view of the canon and inspiration invites criticism. Critics might say the prophet and his listeners mistook a prophet's sanctified sentiments for the words of *Yahveh* (Eze 13:02-07, 17; 22:28; see also Jer 05:13; 18:18; Hos 09:07). *Yahveh*, however, warned the Israelites that they must discern between sanctified sentiments and the inspired word of God:

> You must not mention 'the oracle of *Yahveh*' again, because every
> man's own word becomes his oracle (Jer 23:36a).

Yahveh did not ask the prophets to be his ghostwriters or his editorial columnists. God's idea of a prophet is expressed already in Exodus. God said:

- 'He will speak to the people for you, and it will be as if he were your mouth and as if you were God to him' (Exo 04:16), and

- Then *Yahveh* said to Moses, 'See, I have made you like God to Pharaoh, and your brother Aaron will be your prophet' (Exo 07:01).

Yahveh said that he spoke "by the hands" of the prophets. The phrase "by the hand" points to "verbal inspiration" rather than any wishy-washy, touchy-feely type of inspiration. Unfortunately, most translations do not let Scripture claim verbal inspiration for itself. For instance, the phrase "by the hand" is commonly mistranslated as "by." The MT recension, however, literally says "by the hand of" in dozens of passages.[112]

One of the "by the hand of" passages reads:

By your Spirit you admonished them by the hand of your prophets
(Neh 09:30).

Another reads:

I spoke to the prophets, gave them many visions and told parables by
the hand of the prophets (Hos 12:10).

The prophet's hand was a hand once removed from the anthropomorphic hand of the Spirit, who is sometimes called the "hand of *Yahveh*." For instance, the chronicler wrote:

He [David] gave him [Solomon] the plans of all that the Spirit had put
in his mind for the courts of the temple of *Yahveh* (1Ch 28:12).

Then David told Solomon:

I have in writing from the hand of *Yahveh* upon me, and he gave me
understanding in all the details of the plan (1Ch 28:19).

So David identified the 'hand of *Yahveh*' (1Ch 28:19) as the Spirit (1Ch 28:12). Ezekiel also identified the "hand of *Yahveh*" that was upon him (Eze 01:03; 03:22) as the Spirit (Eze 03:14).

So it seems the phrase "by the hand" indicates that the prophets' main contribution to the Bible was taking dictation through the Spirit from the preincarnate Son (Eze 43:10). The prophetic books are not just the product of a committee on which God is a member. In fact, the prophets often say that God is the real author, for instance:

- **David**: The Spirit of *Yahveh* spoke through me; his word was on my tongue (2Sa 23:02),
- **Elijah**: This is the Word of *Yahveh* that he [the Word] spoke through his servant Elijah (2Ki 09:36),
- **Isaiah**: The vision concerning Judah and Jerusalem that Isaiah son of Amoz saw (Isa 01:01). At that time *Yahveh* spoke through Isaiah (Isa 20:02),
- **Jeremiah**: The Word of *Yahveh* came to him [Jeremiah]…The Word of *Yahveh* came to me [Jeremiah] saying (Jer 01:02, 04). You [*Yahveh*] know I [Jeremiah] have not desired the day of despair. What passes my lips is on behalf of your Presences (Jer 17:16). The word that *Yahveh* spoke concerning Babylon…by Jeremiah the prophet (Jer 50:01),
- **Ezekiel**: The heavens were opened and I saw visions of God… the Word of *Yahveh* came expressly to Ezekiel the priest (Eze 01:01, 03). *Yahveh* told

Ezekiel, 'Son of man, go to the house of Israel and speak my words to them' (Eze 03:04),

- **Hosea**: The Word of *Yahveh* who came to Hosea…When *Yahveh* began to speak through Hosea, *Yahveh* said to him… (Hos 01:01-02),
- **Joel**: The Word of *Yahveh* who came to Joel (Joe 01:01),
- **Amos**: The words of Amos…[concerning] what he saw concerning Israel (Amo 01:01),
- **Obadiah**: The vision of Obadiah. This is what the Lord *Yahveh* says about Edom—we have heard news from *Yahveh* (Oba 01:01),
- **Jonah**: The Word of *Yahveh* came to Jonah (Jon 01:01),
- **Micah**: The Word of *Yahveh* who came to Micah…the vision he saw (Mic 01:01),
- **Nahum**: The book of the vision of Nahum (Nah 01:01),
- **Habakkuk**: The oracle that Habakkuk the prophet saw (Hab 01:01),
- **Zephaniah**: The Word of *Yahveh* who came to Zephaniah (Zep 01:01),
- **Haggai**: The Word of *Yahveh* came through the prophet Haggai…saying (Hag 01:01). Then the Word of *Yahveh* came through Haggai, the prophet, saying (Hag 01:03),
- **Zechariah**: The Word of *Yahveh* came to the prophet Zechariah (Zec 01:01),
- **Malachi**: An oracle of the Word of *Yahveh* to Israel through the hand of my angel [*malachi*] (Mal 01:01), and
- **Elsewhere**: Dozens of other passages say that *Yahveh* spoke through the prophets.[113]

Someone might ask, "If *Yahveh* is speaking through the prophets, who is the specific person of the Trinity doing the speaking?" Some Christians might say, "The Father," since they remember *Yeshua* saying that the Father taught Peter certain truths (Mat 16:16-17). *Yeshua* also said the Father gave him the words that he spoke (Joh 14:10, 24). Most Christians, however, would automatically think, "the Spirit," because:

- The Spirit and the prophets are often associated (Num 11:29; 1Sa 10:10; 19:20; Neh 09:30; Zec 07:12; Act 28:25; Eph 03:05),
- Passages associate David's words, especially his Psalms, with the Spirit (1Sa 16:13; Mat 22:43; Mar 12:36; Act 01:16; 04:25-26),
- Paul's statement, 'This is what we speak, not in words taught us by human wisdom, but in words taught by the Spirit, expressing spiritual truths in spiritual words' (1Co 02:13), and
- The writer of Hebrews quotes Jer 31:33-34 and said that the Spirit was quoting the Father):

> The Holy Spirit also testifies to us, for after saying, 'This is the covenant that I [the Father] will make with them: 'After those days,' says the Lord [the Father], 'I will put my laws on their heart, I will also write them on their mind;" then he says [the Spirit quotes the Father], 'I will remember their sins and their iniquities no more' (Heb 10:15-17).

Peter, however, wrote that the spirit of Christ spoke through the OT prophets, especially of the Son being the future Messiah:

> Concerning this salvation, the prophets sought and searched diligently, who prophesied of the grace that would come to you, searching for who or what kind of time the spirit of Christ, which was in them, pointed to, when he predicted the sufferings of Christ, and the glories that would follow them. To them it was revealed that they were serving you and not themselves when they revealed the things now announced to you through those who preached the gospel to you by the Holy Spirit sent out from heaven; which things angels desire to look into (1Pe 01:10-11).

Revelation is the only NT book that resembles the OT prophetic books. The Apostle John wrote concerning Revelation that the Father delivered the revelation to *Yeshua*, and *Yeshua* delivered the revelation to John though the agency of an angel:

> The apocalypse of *Yeshua* Christ that God [the Father] gave him [*Yeshua*] to show his [*Yeshua*'s] servants what must soon take place. He [*Yeshua*] made it known by sending his [*Yeshua*'s] angel to his [*Yeshua*'s] servant, John (Rev 01:01).

In Revelation, *Yeshua* is identified as "the spirit of the prophets." *Yeshua* said, "I, *Yeshua*, have sent my angel" (Rev 22:16). This meant *Yeshua* was the "Lord, the God of the spirits of the prophets" who had "sent his angel" (Rev 22:06). Besides delivering a message through an angel, *Yeshua* also delivered his message through the Spirit. *Yeshua* said:

> 'I have yet many things to tell you, but you cannot bear them now. However when he, the Spirit of truth, has come, he will guide you into all truth, for he will not speak from himself; but whatever he hears, he will speak. He will declare to you things that are coming. He will glorify me, for he will take from what is mine, and will declare it to you. All things whatever the Father has are mine; therefore I said that he takes of mine, and will declare it to you (Joh 16:12-15).

Rev 01 and 22 and Joh 16 adequately explain how the writer of Hebrews could say the Spirit rather than the Son quoted the Father in Jer 31:33-34 (Heb 10:15-17, quoted above). The chain of transmission for inspired messages went thus:

> Throughout the OT prophetic books, generally the preincarnate Son spoke, or he quoted the Father. The Son then gave his compiled message to the prophets directly, or through the agency of the Spirit or an angel.

Interestingly, sometimes a prophet even spoke as though he were himself *Yahveh* the Son, and not just as a prophet inspired by the Son. The Son could have the prophet speak for him and as him because the prophet had the "mind of Christ" (1Co 02:16 alludes to Isa 40:13). The prophets also had the spirit of Christ and the Holy Spirit dwelling in them (Rom 08:09-11). An example of a prophet speaking as the Son is when Jeremiah told his assistant to say over the Euphrates:

> Thus shall Babylon sink, and shall not rise again because of the evil that I will bring on her (Jer 51:64).

Though there is no quotation formula, this is an obvious quote of *Yahveh*.

A prophet's spiritual makeup was the same as other believers through whom God chose to speak (Mat 10:20; Rom 08:15, 26; Gal 04:06; Eph 06:18). Paul helps elucidate the prophetic phenomenon when he delved into what makes genuine tongues-speakers tick. Paul said that tongues-speakers were no different from other Christians, except in one point. They had the gift of being able to verbalize, but not necessarily understand, some of what the Spirit teaches human spirits to pray and prophesy.

A tongues-speaker can never verbalize or understand the totality of what the Spirit himself says while pleading a believer's cause. Words can only express so much (Rom 08:26). Paul said a person who spoke in tongues utters mysteries with his spirit (1Co 14:02, 14-16, 32).

Paul said that unless a tongues-speaker can interpret what his spirit says, his mind is uninvolved in the tongue speaking process (1Co 14:14, 20). Glossolalia without interpretation is similar to mindlessly reciting a song with lyrics in a foreign language. Of course, if someone is mistaken about having the gift of tongues in the first place, he or she just mindlessly babbles.

The human spirit can pray, sing and speak in a meaningful foreign language independent of the mind. The mind can simultaneously carry out independent mental processes such as praying, singing and speaking in a meaningful language (1Co 14: 10, 14, 15). Most believers are oblivious to both the communications of the Spirit within them, and the prayers of their own human spirit. Moreover, believers can blurt out divinely inspired speech without knowing it (Luk 21:13-15)—just as the unbeliever Caiaphas did (Joh 11:50-52).

The prophets were conscious of, and wrote down, what the Spirit and the spirit of Christ taught their human spirit and mind to say. The prophets were like tongues-speakers in that the words they jotted down came from the Son. They did not ruminate on a subject and then write an essay in their own words. As *Yahveh* said, the prophets spoke visions "from the mouth of *Yahveh*" (Jer 23:16). They did not "follow their own spirit" (Eze 13:03) and the "the delusions of their own minds" (Jer 14:14).

The NT speakers and writers knew that some of the prophets' writings that do not look prophetic at first glance are indeed prophetic. The Psalms, for example, do not look prophetic, however, some events described in the Psalms did not literally happen to the Psalmists. Many of the events described in the Psalms did, however, happen to the Messiah. For instance:

- The disciples (Joh 02:17) and Paul (Rom 15:02-03) applied Psa 069:09 to *Yeshua*,
- Peter also applied a verse from the same Psalm (Psa 069:25) and a verse from another Psalm (Psa 109:08) to events in *Yeshua*'s life, and
- *Yeshua* applied Psa 035:19 to himself (Joh 15:25).

The Psalms often read in the first person (I, me, my), and some Psalms are messianic. These facts tend to show that *Yeshua* was the real Psalmist (Act 01:20).

Early on in *Yeshua*'s ministry, the disciples thought of the Psalms in messianic terms (Joh 02:17). *Yeshua* may have reminded the Emmaus disciples (Luk 24: 27) and the twelve disciples (Luk 24:45-47) that the Psalms were messianic. Perhaps this is why Peter applied Psa 016:10 to *Yeshua* at Pentecost (Act 02:29-31). Matthew said *Yeshua* fulfilled a Psalm's prophecy by his activity of telling parables:

> I will open my mouth in parables; I will utter things hidden since the creation of the world (Psa 078:02; Mat 13:33).

That the Psalms were part of the Messiah's script is consistent with *Yeshua*'s assertion that he did not speak or act extemporaneously, but according to:

- Scripture (Luk 04:21; Joh 13:18; 17:12; 19:24, 28; 19:36; Act 01:16), and
- What the Father wanted (Joh 14:10).

In the Psalms, David often spoke in the first person (for example, "I," "me," "my"). David did not often use quotation formulas. Usually this would indicate that the author is speaking his own words of himself. Peter, however, said that what David described in the Psalms did not happen to David. For instance, there was no OT application of David's words:

> You will not abandon me to the grave, nor will you let your Holy One see decay (Psa 016:10).

The OT writers, *Yeshua*, Peter and the NT Church, believed that the Spirit spoke through David (1Sa 16:13; Mat 22:43; Mar 12:36; Act 01:16; 04:25). Peter even called David a prophet:

> Brothers, I can tell you confidently that the patriarch David died and was buried, and his tomb is here to this day. But he was a prophet [2Sa 23: 02] and knew that God had promised him on oath that he would place one of his descendants on his throne [2Sa 07:11-16]. Seeing what was ahead, he spoke of the resurrection of the Christ, that he was not abandoned to the grave, nor did his body see decay (Act 02:29-30).

So David served as a proxy and as a type for the Messiah who is the antitype.

Isaiah also served as a prophetic proxy just as David had. In the same chapter where Paul said that Psa 016:10 was messianic (Act 13:35-38), Paul said that *Yeshua* is the Suffering Servant (Act 13:34 quotes Isa 55:03 [compare 2Sa 07:15]). Paul was merely agreeing with Peter who said the same thing earlier—that Psa 016:10 was messianic (Act 02:27-31).

Another example of where the NT writers read Isaiah as though the Son were speaking and quoting the Father is where Matthew quotes Isa 07:14:

> All this took place to fulfill what the Lord had said through the prophet: 'The virgin will be with child and will give birth to a son, and they will call him Immanuel,' which means, 'God with us" (Mat 01:22-23).

Another example where Matthew knew *Yahveh* was speaking is his quote of Hosea 11:01:

> And so was fulfilled what the Lord had said through the prophet: 'Out of Egypt I called my son' (Mat 02:15).

Another instance is Paul's allusion to Isa 26:19. Isaiah said on behalf of the future Messiah:

Your dead shall live [just as] my dead body, they shall arise.

Paul wrote:

Christ has indeed been raised from the dead, the first fruits of those who have fallen asleep. For since death came through a man, the resurrection of the dead comes also through a man. For as in Adam all die, so in Christ all will be made alive (1Co 15:20-22).

Another instance of an Isaiah excerpt being read as though Christ were the speaker is provided by John (Joh 12:38) and Paul (Rom 10:16-17).[114] The event described by Isaiah occurred during the life of Christ:

Who has believed our message? And to whom has the arm of *Yahveh* been revealed? (Isa 53:01).

Paul wrote:

And Isaiah boldly says, 'I was found by those who did not seek me; I revealed myself to those who did not ask for me.' But concerning Israel he says, 'All day long I have held out my hands to a disobedient and obstinate people' (Rom 10:20-21).

Paul surely understood that Isaiah was quoting *Yahveh*'s words, since Isaiah would not talk as though he were God. Also, *Yeshua* said that Isa 06:09-10 was fulfilled in Mat 13:14-15:

In them the prophecy of Isaiah is fulfilled, which says, 'By hearing you will hear, and will in no way understand; seeing you will see, and will in no way perceive; for this people's heart has grown callous, their ears are dull of hearing, they have closed their eyes; or else perhaps they might perceive with their eyes, hear with their ears, understand with their heart, and should turn again; and I would heal them' (Mat 13:14-15).

The writer of Hebrews also read Isaiah as though the Messiah were the speaker. The author of Hebrews said that Isa 08:17-18 applied to *Yeshua*:

Again, 'I [the Messiah] will put my trust in him.' Again, 'Behold, here am I and the children [believers (Joh 17:12)] whom God [the Father] has given me' (Heb 02:13).

The writer of Hebrews knew it was not unusual for God to say that he had children (Isa 45:11: Jer 10:20; Lam 01:16; Eze 16:21), so Christ could say he had children, too. Another instance of Isaiah being read as though Christ were the speaker is *Yeshua*'s saying he was the speaker of Isa 29:13 (Mat 15:07-08):

You hypocrites! Well did Isaiah prophesy of you, saying, 'These people draw near to me with their mouth, and honor me with their lips; but their heart is far from me' (Mat 15:07-08).

Yeshua also said that Isa 61:01-02a was fulfilled in Luk 04:17-19 (compare Heb 10:07, 09):

The book of the prophet Isaiah was handed to him. He opened the book, and found the place where it was written: 'The Spirit of the Lord is on me, because he has anointed me to preach good news to the poor. He has sent me to heal the brokenhearted, to proclaim release to the captives, recovering of sight to the blind, to deliver those who are crushed, and to proclaim the acceptable year of the Lord' (Luk 04:17-19).

Other sections in the prophetic books that should be considered messianic include Jer 11:18—12:17, 15:10-21 and 17:14-18. Also messianic are those sections that discuss the Shepherd in Zechariah, since *Yeshua* said he was the Shepherd of Zec 13:07 (Mar 14:27).

Even the early Church fathers knew that the prophets were prophets once removed from the real prophet. That is why the early Church fathers interpreted some phrases and sections as prophecies that a quick perusal might not reveal to be prophecies, for instance, Psa 022:16.

Sometimes the assessment that the Son is speaking directly through the OT prophets is not borne out by the punctuation marks. This is because the original Hebrew text did not have punctuation marks. The Masoretes first added diacritical marks and punctuation to the Hebrew text in the sixth through ninth centuries AD. The result was the Masoretic Text (MT) recension.

Unfortunately, the intended sense of the original may not have been as important as what appealed to the Masoretes' unitarian sensibilities. That the MT is a recension means the compilers were free to choose what reading to follow and what reading to discard or footnote. The exact criteria that the Masoretes used to determine the correct reading are sketchy.

Translators also feel they have a license to force passages to read as though the prophet were the one speaking or quoting. Texts that do not conform to translator expectations regularly have their pronouns and punctuation adjusted. In this way, the Son is excised out of Scripture, and most of the Trinitarian Scripture is made into unitarian literature.

Many examples of textual changes will be given later. Here, however, is an example of a Trinitarian passage being changed to conform to the unitarian sensibilities of the translators. The Son quoted the Father who said:

I [the Father] overthrew some of you as God [the Son] overthrew Sodom and Gomorrah (Amo 04:11a).

Though the MT and LXX both have "God," the *NIV* translators thought that changing "God" to the pronoun "I" would make better sense.

Whenever third person speech—where God speaks of God, is changed to first person speech, another Trinitarian proof text is lost in translation. A similar change is made in Hos 12:04 where the last word in the Hebrew, "us," is rendered as "him" in the *NIV*.

Still, even in translation some passages are best understood as though the Son were speaking or quoting the Father. For instance, when Isaiah talked to King Ahaz, the narrator wrote the very telling phrase, "Again *Yahveh* spoke to Ahaz" (Isa 07:10). Elsewhere, the narrator said:

At that time *Yahveh* spoke by Isaiah the son of Amoz, saying…(Isa 20:02).

Yahveh even told Isaiah to take out a "large" scroll and a pen to take down dictation (Isa 08:01)! Isaiah sometimes mentioned *Yahveh* speaking words to him directly (Isa 01:02; 08:05, 11; 20:02; 29:11-12, 18; 30:08; 34:16).

Examples where the prophetic experience involved minimal input by the prophets include Ezekiel's saying that he saw "God's visions" (Eze 01:01; 08: 08-04; 11:24; 40:02). Ezekiel said that the "vision I had seen went up from me" (Eze 11:24). That Ezekiel wrote down what God was seeing and saying about the vision becomes evident when Ezekiel wrote, "I destroyed the city" (Eze 43: 03). Unfortunately, the "I" in the MT recension is often translated as "he." This masks the fact that Ezekiel is recording *Yahveh*'s words directly. It was God who envisioned destroying the city, as Ezekiel wrote:

> It was according to the appearance of the vision that I saw, even according
> to the vision that I saw when I came to destroy the city (Eze 43:03).

Another example where the prophetic experience involved minimal input by the prophets comes from the NT. Paul said that everyone present could hear what the Son had said to him, but only Paul actually saw the Son (Act 09:07). So sometimes being a prophet required no special prophetic insight or prescience, but merely the ability to take dictation. Malachi is the best example of a prophet who is a mouthpiece. In fact, it is not known whether there really was an actual prophet named "Malachi." Malachi is discussed further at the end of this chapter.

When a prophet spoke in the first person (I, me, my) without any quotation formulas, such as "thus says *Yahveh*," this is likely the words of *Yahveh* the Son. When the Son spoke of, but does not quote, the Father or the Spirit, he uses third person speech (for example, "he," "him," "his"). For instance, in the following section, *Yahveh* the Son refers to the Father, the Most High, using the pronoun "he":

> My [the Son's] people are determined to turn from me [the Son].
> Though they call to the Most High [the Father], He [the Father] certainly
> will not exalt them.
>
> How can I [the Son] give you up, Ephraim? How can I [the Son]
> hand you over, Israel? How can I [the Son] make you like Admah?
> How can I [the Son] make you like Zeboiim?
>
> My [the Son's] heart is turned within me [the Son], My [the Son's]
> compassion is aroused.
>
> I [the Son] will not execute the fierceness of my [the
> Son's] anger. I [the Son] will not return to destroy Ephraim:
> For I [the Son] am God [the Son], and not man [this is the preincarnate
> Son speaking]; the Holy One [the Son] in the midst of you;
> And I [the Son] will not come in wrath (Hos 11:07-09).

Peter indicated that the person of *Yahveh* speaking using first person speech throughout Isaiah is specifically the Son (1Pe 01:10-11). This assertion is consistent with the pronoun usage in Isaiah. There are even passages where God uses direct speech and mentions both the Father and Spirit in the third person, for instance, see Isa 34:16 and 48:12-16 in the Trinitarian proofs appendix. By the process of elimination, one can determine that the person of *Yahveh* who is speaking in Isa 34:16 and 48:12-16 is the Son.

Double Quotation Formulas

When there is a double quotation formula such as:
Hear you the Word [the Son] of *Yahveh* [the Father], 'Thus says the Lord *Yahveh* [the Father]' (Eze 13:02b-03a),
the prophet is telling his listeners to hear the words of the Son who then quotes the Father. So the first phrase is spoken by the prophet, and the second phrase is spoken by the Son. Double quotation formulas are found often in the OT.[115]
Furthermore, the phrase "the Word came" followed by the words "Thus says..." should also be considered a double quotation formula. This formula is used to indicate that the prophet quoted the Son's quotation of the Father's direct speech (Jer 21:01, 04; 25:01-05; 26:01-02; 27:01-02; 34:01-02; 34:08, 12-13; 44:01-02.

The Prophets were Sometimes a Proxy for the Priestly Role of *Yahveh* the Son

When Isaiah pleaded with God concerning the sinfulness of his people and even of himself, this is the Spirit and the Son in action working through Isaiah.[116] As Paul said:
The Spirit helps us in our weakness. We do not know what we ought to pray for, but the Spirit himself intercedes for us with groans that words cannot express.   And he [the Father] who searches our hearts knows the mind of the Spirit, because the Spirit intercedes for the saints in accordance with God's [the Father's] will (Rom 08:26-27; see also Joh 03:06; Rom 08:16).
Here Paul is saying that since the Father knows every thought of the Spirit, the Spirit's intercession need not be audible. Paul also said the spirit of the Son intercedes for believers:
God sent out the spirit of his Son into your hearts, crying, 'Abba, Father!' (Gal 04:06; see also Rom 08:15-16).
So when Isaiah seems to confess the sins of himself and of the nation Israel (for instance, Isa 06:05), that really is *Yahveh* the Son acting as the ultimate priest through his proxies—the prophets. Isaiah wrote:
Thus says your Lord *Yahveh* [the Father], and your God [the Son], who pleads the cause of his [the Son's] people (Isa 51:22; see also Jdg 10:16; Psa 043:01; Mic 07:09; Heb 02:18; 04:15).
There are instances, however, where the MT recension has the Son confessing sin where the LXX does not, for example, Jer 04:08:
▪ LXX: For these things gird yourselves with sack clothes, and lament, and howl: for the anger of the Lord is not turned away from you.
▪ MT: For this, gird on sackcloth, lament and howl, for the fierce anger of *Yahveh* hath not turned back from us [Son and Israel].

Someone might think it unseemly for the Son to be confessing the sins of the people as though they were his own sins—as he does in Psa 069:05. The alternative, however, is that the prophet confessed the sins of others as though they were his own. The OT prophets were not the ones committing gross sin and idolatry, however. So the issue is a non-issue, a nonstarter. Besides, the Son is not only a prophet, but also a priest and king and even a sacrifice for sin. So who better than the Son could confess the sins of others as though they were his own?

The Priest in Isaiah Was Also the Sacrifice

The Son is not only the ultimate priest, but also the sacrifice (Heb 07:27; 09:14, 28; Act 08:32-33). That Isa 53 spoke of the Son as a sacrifice was confirmed when the eunuch asked Philip about Isa 53:07-08:

> Tell me, please, who is the prophet talking about, himself or someone else? (Act 08:34).

Luke wrote:

> Philip then began with that very passage of Scripture [Isa 53:07-08] and told him the good news about *Yeshua* (Act 08:35).

The Son confessed the sins of the people. This is similar to how the OT priests confessed the sins of the people over the sacrificial lamb and over the scapegoat (Lev 16:21; Isa 53:10; 1Pe 03:18). Since the Spirit and the Son dwell in Christians, and the Son takes humanity's sins on himself, God himself becomes afflicted when his people are afflicted (Isa 63:09; Act 09:04). In this way, God thoroughly identifies himself with his people (Mat 10:40; 18:05; 25:40, 45, and the like).

Since the Son became the scapegoat, he was afflicted for the sins of his people (Isa 53:04; Jer 15:10-21; Mat 08:17; 2Co 05:21; Heb 09:26, 28; 10:10; 1Pe 02:24). So he can associate with sinners (Mat 27:43; Luk 07:39; 19:07), and allow himself to be thought of as a sinner (Psa 069:04; Joh 09:24), and even as a criminal (Isa 53: 12; Mar 15:28; Luk 22:37). When we read Isaiah saying that he is sinful (Isa 06: 05), it really was *Yahveh* the Son talking through Isaiah—talking as a scapegoat would. The Son should be seen as the ultimate speaker behind the statement:

> We [the Son and believers] all, like sheep, have gone astray, each of us has turned to his own way; and *Yahveh* [the Father] has laid on him [the Messiah] the iniquity of us all [the Son and believers] (Isa 53:06; see also Heb 10:10-12).

Interestingly, there are instances, such as Jer 10:18-20, where the MT recension has the Son suffering punishment for sin where the LXX does not. The LXX translators merely translated the first person pronouns in the MT as third person pronouns to keep the prophet from suffering punishment for sin. The translators evidently did not realize that the Son would suffer as a scapegoat.

Yahveh the Son Can Properly Call _Yahveh_ the Father "My God" and "Our God"

Though the Servant of _Yahveh_ called himself _Yahveh_ (Isa 61:08), the Servant of _Yahveh_ also calls the Father "my God" (Isa 07:13; 25:01; 49:04; 61:10) and "our God" (Isa 01:10; 40:08; 57:07; 61:06). A critic might say that this disproves the Trinity, or at least it disproves that all three members are equal. This criticism, however, can be countered just like any other straw argument.

Trinitarians do not try to prove that the three persons of the Trinity are the same—just equal. There are not three Fathers, but rather the Father, Son and Spirit! Moreover, Scripture explicitly states that the Son humbled himself and took on the form of a man (Phi 02:08). So a passage showing that the Son submits to the Father does not prove the Son's substance is inferior to that of the Father's. Subordinate does not necessarily mean inferior—as any prince studying with a tutor realizes sooner or later.

A critic might also say that the phrase "my God" shows the speaker must have been the prophet, or anyone other than the Son. There are several possible responses to this criticism. To start, the issue is not as important as it might seem statistically. The LXX often does not has the "my God" and "our" God" reading when the MT recension does. This is significant because, though the NT writers has:

- _Yeshua_ saying, "my God," a few times (for instance, Mat 27:46; Joh 20:17; Rev 03:12), and
- The Father being "his [_Yeshua_'s] God" (Rev 01:06), the number of these occurrences is not so great that it suggests _Yeshua_ was only a man and not the God-man. So the book of Isaiah can still be viewed as though the Son were the author, just as some Psalms are viewed as messianic, though David used words such as "my God" (for example, Psa 022:01 [LXX 021:01]).

Apparently, the scribes, especially the _Soferim_, "emended" the MT recension to make the prophets sound more human, humble and polite. However, they did not give due consideration to the divine origin of the prophets' words (Jer 08:08-09; Hos 08:12; Mat 15:06). The _Soferim_ were like the Israelites who did not want to hear the direct speech of _Yahveh_, but only wanted to hear Moses' rendition of what _Yahveh_ told him:

> Speak to us yourself and we will listen. But do not have God speak to us or we will die (Exo 20:19; see also Deu 04:33; 05:24-28; 18:16-17; Jer 20:09; 36:32; Heb 12:19).

The scribes would not be the last people to mistake the humanness of God's servants as evidence for the human origin of their:

- Words (Joh 14:10, 24),
- Deeds (Mar 11:27, 29-33; Joh 05:19), or
- Person (Luk 03:23).

For instance, though many would think that _Yahveh_ is talking to Jeremiah in Jer 25:15-16, a careful reading suggests that the Father is talking to the Son.

The LXX (second or third century BC) is much older than the MT recension (tenth century AD), and the LXX predates the Trinitarianism versus unitarianism debates on record. So one can assume that at least in areas affecting the doctrine of God, the LXX would more often reflect the original text. What one finds is that in one area where the LXX hints of the Trinity, the MT was changed so the author of prophetic books became merely human. For instance:

- The prophet said "our God" in the MT recension, but not in the LXX (Isa 01:10; 35:02; 55:07; 61:02, 06; Jer 08:14; 14:22; 23:36; 31:06; 37:03; 42:20; 43:02; Hos 08:02; Joe 01:16; Zec 13:09),
- The prophet said "my God" in the MT recension, but not in the LXX (Isa 07:13; 25:01; 57:21; 61:10; Hos 09:08, 17; Joe 01:13; Hab 01:12; Zec 11:04), and
- The prophet said "my Lord" in the MT recension, but not in the LXX (Isa 21:08).

A search shows that the LXX has:

- Fewer instances of the prophet saying, "my God," than in the MT recension (Isa 12:02; 33:22; Mic 06:06; Hab 01:11),
- Fewer instances of the prophet saying, "our God," than in the MT recension (Isa 26:12; 35:04; Jer 23:38; 42:04; 46:10), and
- No instances of "my Lord," or "our Lord" when the MT recension does not say the same.

Here are some examples of how the changes in the MT recension tend to demote the author from being the creator to being a creature:

- Isa 01:10:
  - LXX: Listen to the law of God
  - MT: Listen to the law of our God
- Isa 07:10, 13:
  - LXX: The Lord again spoke to Ahaz...will you also contend against the Lord?
  - MT: Again *Yahveh* spoke to Ahaz...will you also weary my God?
- Isa 25:01:
  - LXX: O Lord God, I will glorify you
  - MT: *Yahveh*, you are my God
- Isa 32:15
  - LXX: ...until the Spirit shall come upon you
  - MT: ...until the Spirit is poured out on us
- Isa 33:14
  - LXX: Who will tell you that a fire is kindled? Who will tell you of the eternal place?
  - MT: Who of us can dwell with the consuming fire? Who of us can dwell with everlasting burning?
- Isa 35:02:
  - LXX: ... the majesty of God
  - MT: ...the excellency of our God

- Isa 47:04:
  - o LXX: Your deliverer is *Yahveh*
  - o MT: Our Redeemer, *Yahveh*
- Isa 52:10:
  - o LXX: ...salvation of God
  - o MT: ...salvation of our God
- Isa 55:07:
  - o LXX: Let him return to the Lord, and he shall find mercy; for he shall abundantly pardon your sins.
  - o MT: Let him turn to *Yahveh*...and to our God, for he will freely pardon.
- Isa 57:21:
  - o LXX: 'There is no joy to the ungodly,' said God
  - o MT: 'There is no peace,' says my God, 'for the wicked.'
- Isa 61:02:
  - o LXX: ...the day of recompense, to comfort all that mourn
  - o MT: ...the day of vengeance of our God, to comfort all who mourn
- Isa 61:06:
  - o LXX: You shall be called...ministers of God
  - o MT: You will be named ministers of our God
- Isa 61:10:
  - o LXX: Let my soul rejoice in the Lord
  - o MT: My soul rejoices in my God
- Joe 01:13
  - o LXX: ...you who minister to God
  - o MT: ...you who minister before my God
- Joe 01:16
  - o LXX: Your meat has been destroyed before your eyes, joy and gladness from out of the house of your God.
  - o MT: Is not the food cut off before our eyes, joy and gladness from the house of our God?
- Mic 05:05-06 [*BHS* 05:04-05]:
  - o LXX: When Ashur shall come into your land, and when he shall come up upon your country....and there shall be raised up against him seven shepherds...and He [the Messiah] shall deliver you from the Assyrian, when he shall come upon your land, and when he shall invade your coasts.
  - o MT: When the Assyrian invades our land and marches through our fortresses, we will raise against him seven shepherds...He [the Messiah] will deliver us from the Assyrian when he invades our land and marches into our borders.
- Hab 01:12:
  - o LXX: O Lord God, my Holy One
  - o MT: My God, my Holy One
- Zec 11:04
  - o LXX: Thus says the Lord Almighty

- o MT: This is what *Yahveh*, my God, says
- ▪ Mal 02:10
  - o LXX: Did not one God create you?
  - o MT: Did not one God create us?

Many manuscripts, even among the Dead Sea Scrolls, establish how the LXX read a century or more before Christ's time. The LXX, generally speaking, was translated from one family of Hebrew manuscripts while the MT recension was compiled from another family.

A comparison of the MT recension with the family of Hebrew manuscripts that led to the LXX helps to show where the copyists and scribes (especially the *Soferim*) made inadvertent or intentional changes in the MT recension. Here are two more examples of where the MT and LXX differ, and where the *Soferim* may have made the changes:

- ▪ Gen 02:18:
  - o LXX: "And the Lord God said, 'It is not good that the man should be alone, let us make [plural verb] for him a help suitable to him,'"
  - o MT: "I will make..." rather than "Let us make...,"
- ▪ Neh 09:18:
  - o LXX: Nehemiah recounted the golden calf incident using plural nouns and plural verbs:

  ...they even made to themselves a molten calf, and said, 'These are the Gods that brought [plural] us up out of Egypt' (LXX Neh 09:18), and
  - o MT: The *BHS* has the singular form "brought," but the *BHS* critical apparatus says that the LXX and many Hebrew manuscripts have the plural form "brought."

Comparison of sections of the OT shows how changes were made from time to time. For instance, the poetry sections were harder to edit, and so they tend to have more archaic Hebrew. By contrast, prose sections have less archaic Hebrew. That changes were made explains why:

...few traces of dialects exist in Biblical Hebrew...scholars believe this to be the result of Masoretic editing of the text.[117]

Systematic editing resulted in the bifurcation of the Hebrew into families that led to the MT recension and the family on which the LXX was based. If edits were rarely made, there would only be one family with variant readings. Comprehensive changes are only possible when a family of manuscripts is in the hands of a few people. Then all copies not marked "official" can eventually be discarded or destroyed.

While comprehensive changes in the LXX were not possible after the third century BC due to the popularity of the LXX, portions of the MT may have been changed up to the time of the Masoretes (6th to 10th centuries AD). It was then that the Masoretes standardized the text to create the MT recension (Job 05:12). During the recension process, the MT family likely underwent the most radical changes. The reason is that a unitarian bias rather than statistical analysis determined what readings became the standard.

Humanizing the prophets, as was discussed above, could not undo all the Trinitarianism inherent in the MT. The Greek LXX and MT recension still agree concerning most Trinitarian proof texts. For instance, the "us" referring to *Yahveh* still survives in both the MT recension and the LXX in several places (Gen 01: 26; 03:22; 11:07; Isa 06:08). However, only the LXX retains the "us" referring to *Yahveh* in Gen 02:18.

For centuries the LXX was held in high regard. The Jewish establishment did not consider the LXX translators suspect until after Christianity adopted the LXX as its *de facto* official translation. Even then, the LXX remained in use in the synagogues until at least 130 AD when Aquila's Greek translation was first introduced. Aquila's translation was produced under rabbinic supervision.

The history of the LXX shows that we can be sure the LXX translators did not insert Trinitarian language based on a whim or heretical notions. Trinitarian proofs that survived in the MT recension are not necessarily more legitimate than those found in the LXX. They were just so well known that MT editors could not ax them.

MT edits tended to make the MT more unitarian and less Trinitarian. Trinitarian proofs had to survive the anti-Trinitarian bias of unitarian *Soferim* scribes, and the unitarian bias of the Masoretes who compiled the MT recension. The provenance[118] of surviving Trinitarian texts must have been sound, or else they would not have escaped the eraser and scissors century after century.

Less known Trinitarian proofs such as the "us" in Gen 02:18 were not safe from tampering hands. These passages tended to accumulate variant readings, because unitarian copyists would assume a plural referring to *Yahveh* was a mistake. Then when it came time to compile a recension, the manuscripts with the unitarian reading would outnumber manuscripts with the original Trinitarian reading.

So one can be sure that any Trinitarianism remaining in either the MT recension or the Greek LXX was a part of the inspired original. This would be in accordance with the exegetical principle: *durior lectio praeferatur*, meaning, "the harsher reading is to be preferred."[119] In this case, the "harsher" reading would be the Trinitarian reading, and the more palatable reading would be the unitarian reading.

Another response concerning the Son saying, "my God," and "our God" is that critics read more into the "my God" and "our God" statements than is warranted. The Son can still be divine and refer to the Father as "his God," just as:

- The writer of Hebrews says that the Father addressed the Son as "God" in Psa 045:06-07 (Heb 01:08),
- *Yeshua* said that the Father addressed him as "God" (Psa 082:08; Joh 10:36a),
- The Father called the Son "my King" (Psa 002:07), and
- The Messiah is the Father's ("your") "Holy One" (Psa 016:10).

So the Son's calling the Father "my God" does not necessarily prove an involuntary subordination on the part of the Son. Besides, Paul explained why the Son called the Father his God. Paul said that though the Son is equal to the Father, when the Son became the God-man, he voluntarily subordinated himself so that the Father's wish became his command (Mat 06:10; 26:42; Heb 10:07, 09).

In Paul's words, *Yeshua* is "in very nature God, [but] did not consider equality with God something to be held dearly" (Phi 02:06). After the resurrection, however, *Yeshua* was exalted to be Most High along with the Father (Phi 02:09-11). *Yeshua*'s exaltation is discussed further in the Song of Moses chapter.

Who is the Author Behind the Author in Malachi?

The Title Malachi
"Malachi" means "my messenger" in Hebrew. Nothing is known about a man named Malachi who might be the author of Malachi. The title may refer to the Son, who was often called the *Malek Yahveh* in the OT. The Son was also the *Malek* with the Father's Name, *Yahveh*, "in him" (Exo 23:21). The Father even referred to the Son as "Malachi" (Exo 23:23; 32:34).

The name Malachi could refer to an angel that *Yahveh* the Son had sent. For instance, *Yeshua* referred to a creature angel (Rev 22:08-09) whom he had sent as "my angel" (Rev 22:16). Malachi could refer to a prophet or priest since prophets (Hag 01:13) and priests (Mal 02:07) were called *maleks*. However, even if there were a person named Malachi, the name ultimately refers to the Son in the antitype-typal sense. This would be similar to how a priest-king was named Melchizedek, but the name is a theophoric name referring to Melchizedek's God, *Yahveh*. "Melchizedek" means "My King is Righteousness" (Gen 14:18).

The Greek LXX lists the book's title as "His *Malek*," rather than "My *Malek*." This is significant because it indicates the LXX translators thought "Malachi" was not a proper name. Otherwise, they might have transliterated the Hebrew name directly into Greek. This may indicate that the LXX translators thought "Malachi" referred to the *Malek Yahveh*, who is called "his *Malek*" (Dan 03:28; Gen 24:07, 40; Dan 06:22). Of course, "his angel" may refer to an angel sent by the Son (Act 12:11, 15; Rev 01:01; 22:06). In any event, as with the name Melchizedek, the LXX name "His *Malek*" ultimately points to the *Malek Yahveh* who inspired the whole OT (1Pe 01:10-11 was discussed above).

The Book of Malachi Itself Provides an Insight
Whether an angel or a prophet named Malachi delivered the words of the Son, ultimately the Malachi behind the Malachi is the Son. This is consistent with the opening line of the book:

> The oracle of the Word [the Son] of *Yahveh* [the Father] to Israel by the
> hand of my [the Son's] angel [*malachi*] (Mal 01:01).

If the "my *malek*" (*malachi*) in the opening line refers to a prophet, this shows the prophet's contribution to the book was merely taking dictation. If the Son were the Malachi, this would be especially appropriate. Then the Son would begin the OT by creating the universe (Gen 01:01-03; Joh 01:01-03), and end the OT as the last prophet, Malachi. Similarly, *Yeshua* began the NT as the subject of four biographies called the Gospels, and ended the NT as the main divine speaker of

Revelation (Rev 22:16, 20). By bookending both the Old and New Testaments, the Son truly is the Alpha and Omega, the Beginning and the End (Rev 21:06; 22:13).

An Issue

One passage in Malachi that may have been changed in the MT recension reads in the LXX as:

Have you not all one father? Did not one God create you? Why have you forsaken every man his brother, to profane the covenant of your fathers? (LXX Mal 02:10).

The MT reads:

Do we [the LXX reads "you"] not all have one Father? Has not one God created us [the LXX reads "you"]? Why do we [the LXX reads "you"] deal treacherously every man against his brother, profaning the covenant of our [the LXX reads "your"] fathers? (Mal 02:10).

That the LXX has Malachi saying "you" Israelites were created, but apparently does not include himself as being created, shows that the ultimate author of the book Malachi is the Son.

The LXX was translated from the Hebrew sometime between the second or third century BC and 70 BC. Apparently, sometime after the LXX was translated but before the tenth century AD, a copyist changed a verse in the MT recension. The change demoted Malachi from being God to being a creature (Mal 02:10).

That "your God" was changed to "my God" and "our God" in many prophetic books apparently was an attempt to demote the author from creator to creature. This reflected the general trend in Judaic thought. As Judaism became increasingly unitarian, it was thought that no *malek*, not even the *Malek Yahveh*, could be divine.

Chapter 7

Various OT Presentations of the Trinity

The Trinity in Ezekiel

The Son
The Word (Eze 01:03), who is also called the Glory (Eze 01:28), is *Yahveh* the Son. The Glory has the appearance of a man (Eze 01:26-28). The NT refers to the Son as the Glory and as the Word (Joh 01:14; Heb 01:03). Ezekiel said the Glory by the river (Eze 01:03, 28) was the same Glory mentioned throughout Ezekiel (Eze 03:22-23; 10:18-20; 43:03).

The Spirit
"The man" is first mentioned in Eze 08:01-03 and is again introduced in Eze 40:03. "The man" is an anthropomorphic representation of the Spirit (Eze 08:02-03; 43:05-06). The "Hand of *Yahveh*" is also the Spirit (Eze 03:14; 08:03; 37:01).

Both "the man" and the Glory are associated with *Yahveh* often. In one instance, "the man" brought Ezekiel "back" to the east gate (Eze 44:01). Ezekiel had been by the east gate with "the man" in the previous chapter (Eze 43:01). The reason they had to go "back" to the gate is, apparently, the man and Ezekiel had followed the Glory (the Son) from the east gate to the temple where the Son had talked to Ezekiel (Eze 43:06-27).

Since the Glory (the Son) was in the temple and only Ezekiel and the man were back at the east gate, the narrator must have been referring to "the man" (Eze 44:01) as *Yahveh* the Spirit (Eze 44:02, 05).

The Trinity
The Spirit and the Glory are sometimes mentioned together, but at the same time they are distinguished from each other (Eze 01:28—02:02; 03:12-14, 23-24; 08:03-04; 10:18—11:01, 22-23; 43:01-05). Neither the Glory nor "the man" is *Yahveh* the Father, since:
- "The man" quoted the Father (Eze 44:06; 45:09, 18; 46:01, 16; 47:13), and
- The Glory quoted the Father (Eze 03:11-12; 11:05; 43:18, 19, 27).

The man (Eze 44:01) referred to the Glory who went through the east gate into the temple (Eze 43:02-05) as *Yahveh* (Eze 44:02). Therefore, the Glory (also called "the Word") is *Yahveh* the Son, "the man" (also called "the hand of *Yahveh*") is *Yahveh* the Spirit, and the *Yahveh* that is often quoted in Ezekiel is *Yahveh* the Father.

The Trinity in Jonah

The Presences of Yahveh
In the book of Jonah, the Presences of *Yahveh* are mentioned four times (Jon 01: 02, 03 (twice), 10). The sailors knew that Jonah was running from the Presences (the Son and Spirit) of *Yahveh* (Jon 01:10). Jonah was not necessarily running from the Father, since it was the Word (the Son) who gave Jonah the assignment to go to Nineveh (Jon 01:01; 03:01, 03).

That Jonah was running from the Presences in the temple rather than from *Yahveh* the Father in heaven makes sense. Otherwise, the sailors would have thought Jonah was making a mistake. The sailors likely were well versed in astrology, especially since they used the stars for navigation.

The basic conviction of ancient astrologists was that deities who controlled lives and events on earth populated the heavenly bodies. Jonah must have told the sailors that the Presences were especially present in the temple at Jerusalem. Otherwise, the sailors would think it impossible to run from astral deities.

If Jonah did not tell the sailors the Presences were in the temple, the sailors would have figured it impossible to avoid any god, unless the god's star rose and set with the seasons. If that were the case, Jonah would have had to travel north or south to a latitude where the star never clears the horizon. Jonah's destination, however, was Tarshish (Spain) (Jon 01:03), which is roughly west of Palestine. There is, however, no indication in the book of Jonah that the sailors thought Jonah's itinerary was ill conceived. So Jonah must have mentioned the Presences in the temple.

The Trinity as [All] the Gods (haElohim)
When the storm brewed, the ship's captain told Jonah:
> Get up and call on your Gods [*Elohim*]! Maybe [All] the Gods [*haElohim*] will take notice [singular verb] of us, and we will not perish" (Jon 01:06).

That the captain used a singular verb with *haElohim* may indicate that the captain knew Jonah's "own god" to be the Trinity (*haElohim*). How the captain knew the Trinity to be "[All] the Gods" (*haElohim*) is Jonah had told the sailors that he was running from the Presences of *Yahveh*. Jonah must have then collectively referred to *Yahveh* the Father and his Presences as "[All] the Gods."

Jonah's terminology would have been normal Trinitarian theology, since, in the OT, the Trinity often is called "[All] the Gods [*haElohim*]." This was discussed in the chapter on Hebrew collective nouns. Of course, if the captain had any familiarity with the Hebrew religion, he would have often heard the Hebrews using plural nouns and singular verbs in reference to *Yahveh*. Moreover, the pagans had their pseudo-trinities.

The Trinity is called "[All] the Gods" four times in the book of Jonah (Jon 01: 06; 03:09, 10; 04:07). Another indicator of the persons of the Trinity, the dual name "*Yahveh Elohim*," is found in Jon 04:06. The paired names *Yahveh Elohim* are discussed in the chapter on Hebrew collective nouns.

The Trinity in Zechariah

The Son

The *Malek Yahveh* is called *Yahveh* (Zec 03:01-02). The *Malek Yahveh* spoke as only *Yahveh* could (Zec 02:08-11; 03:02-04). The personified "Word of *Yahveh*" is *Yahveh* the Son. The phrase "this is the word of *Yahveh*" (Zec 04:06), however, is not personified, and so here the "word" does not refer to the Son.

The personified "Word [the Son] of *Yahveh* [the Father]" (Zec 07:08) spoke of the Spirit and the Father as separate persons (Zec 07:12-13). The *Malek Yahveh* is shown to be distinct from *Yahveh* the Father by the *Malek Yahveh*'s saying that *Yahveh* the Father "sent me" (Zec 02:08-09, 11; 04:09; 06:15).

The *Malek Yahveh* has a spirit that extends throughout the earth. Zechariah mentioned that the "Interpreting" *Malek*'s spirit extends to a north country (Zec 06: 08). Combining these insights with facts about previous encounters with the *Malek Yahveh* indicates that the *Malek Yahveh* in Zechariah is the Word of *Yahveh*, who is *Yahveh* the Son.[120]

The Spirit

The "Interpreting" *Malek* who talked to Zechariah is identified as *Yahveh* (Zec 01:20). The "Interpreting" *Malek* is shown to be a separate person from the *Malek Yahveh* (Zec 01:09-13; 02:03-04; 03:01 and elsewhere). The "Interpreting" *Malek* is mentioned in Zec 01:09, 13-14, 19; 02:03; 04:01, 04-05; 05:05, 10; and 06:04-08.

Based on the fact that the "Interpreting" *Malek* is not the *Malek Yahveh*, and based on the other facts given by Zechariah, the "Interpreting" *Malek* in Zechariah is *Yahveh* the Spirit.

The Father

In Zechariah, *Yahveh* of hosts refers to a person distinct from the Word of *Yahveh* (Zec 07:08) and the Spirit (Zec 07:12-13). By process of elimination, one can say the "*Yahveh* of hosts" mentioned in Zechariah is *Yahveh* the Father.

Chapter 8

The NT Use of OT Yahveh Texts

Background

The greater part of this chapter concerns whether *Yeshua* primarily spoke Greek or Aramaic. The language issue has some bearing on whether *Yeshua* identified himself as:

- *Yahveh* the Son by applying OT *Yahveh* texts to himself (see Isa 35:02-05; 40:03, 08, 09; Dan 07:14 and other instances in the NT Use of OT *Yahveh* Texts appendix),
- The divine Son of Man of the Dan 07 vision (as is discussed in the Song of Moses chapter),
- The "I AM" (as is discussed in the "I AM" and the Song of Moses chapters), and
- The subject of the *Shema* along with the Father (as is discussed in the *Shema* chapter).

The evidence will show that *Yeshua* spoke both Aramaic and Greek. Since *Yeshua* preached in Hellenized areas and his followers and audience tended to be Hellenized, *Yeshua* likely spoke as much Greek as Aramaic while in Galilee.

Aramaic was prevalent in Judea, but inscriptions and other literary evidence show that Greek was common, too. This suggests that *Yeshua* may have spoken more Aramaic than Greek in Judea, but there too his audience tended to be more Hellenized than Judeans taken as a whole.

These above estimates, of course, are predicated on the assumption that *Yeshua* drew an audience representative of the population centers he visited. In all likelihood, however, *Yeshua* appealed more to Hellenized Jews and gentiles. This helps explain why the NT is written in Greek, and why Pilate had the sign posted on the crucifix in three languages: Aramaic, Greek and Latin.

Wherever *Yeshua* went, he could count on the majority knowing Greek, at least as a second language. *Yeshua*, however, visited areas where he could not assume the crowds knew Aramaic. Except in special circumstances that will be discussed,

Yeshua spoke Greek when the crowd mostly spoke Greek, and Aramaic when the crowd mostly spoke Aramaic.

Yeshua and the Father spoke for the benefit of their hearers, whether Jew or Gentile (Joh 12:30). So apparently *Yeshua* spoke Greek to Greeks, even when the Greeks happened to be in Aramaic-speaking Judea (Joh 07:35; 12:20-30). Only later, after the Jews had rejected the gospel, did God speak to Jews through foreign tongues (Isa 28:11; 1Co 14:21).

The evidence will show that *Yeshua* and the NT writers knew both Aramaic and Greek, and were familiar with the OT in both languages. This meant that *Yeshua* and the NT writers consciously applied OT "I AM" statements and *Yahveh* texts to *Yeshua*. Since the NT writers were familiar with the OT in two or three languages, no meaning was inadvertently added or lost in translation from the OT to the NT.

The Impact of Whether the Bible Personages Immediately Recognized Allusions or Quotations

The disciples kept the OT in mind during *Yeshua*'s ministry (Joh 01:45: 02:17; Mar 09:11). The disciples did not catch every subtle allusion to the OT, but they did dutifully teach and record what they heard. For example, when the owners asked why the disciples were untying their donkey, the disciples did not say, "This is to fulfill what was written in Zechariah..." (Mat 21:04-05). The disciples said what they were instructed to say, "The Lord needs it" (Zec 09:09; Mar 11:04-06; Luk 19:32-34).

In the estimation of *Yeshua*, it made little difference whether the disciples and other NT characters recognized a quote or allusion as such (Joh 02:17). He knew they would eventually recognize his quotations and allusions because he would make that happen.

Yeshua informed the Emmaus disciples that their training and OT knowledge were sufficient to understand the OT, but their attitude needed adjustment (Luk 24: 25-32). *Yeshua* also said "the Counselor, the Holy Spirit, whom the Father will send in my name, he will teach you all things, and will remind you of all that I said to you" (Joh 14:26). Apparently, the Spirit did come because the inspired NT writers proceeded to reference the OT hundreds of times.

The NT reader can also make valid associations and conclusions not already spelled out in the OT or NT. This is similar to how prophecies are valid even though the prophecies may have been unintelligible to the prophet (Dan 08:27). Most prophecies, in fact, were meant to be understood only by later generations, and the Bible does not interpret most of its prophecies.

Future generations have more information and can "connect all the dots" (1Pe 01:10-12; Dan 12:04). Later generations are situated in a better position to determine how literal or figurative a prophecy was by looking at its fulfillment (1Ki 21:23; 2Ki 09:36). As the saying goes, "Hindsight is 20/20."

The NT Writers Distinguished the Persons of the Trinity in the OT

The NT writers applied OT *Yahveh* texts to the Trinity and to individual members of the Trinity. For examples, see the NT use of OT *Yahveh* Texts appendix. The NT writers were aware that certain OT *Yahveh* texts were only applicable to one person of the Trinity. That this is the case suggests that the NT writers were able to discern the persons of the Trinity in the OT.

Yeshua's Quotations of, and Allusions to, *Yahveh*'s "I AM" Statements and the *Shema*

Background

Though erudite theological books on the OT elucidate plenty of Trinitarian proofs, many people fixate on *Yahveh*'s use of the pronoun "us" in Gen 01:26, 03:22, 11:07 and Isa 06:08. These people usually think that:

- The OT only "hints" of the existence of the Trinity, and
- Theologians barely eke the doctrine of the Trinity out of the OT (1Co 03:02; Heb 05:12-13).

Theological liberals often hold the opinion that the OT was either unitarian or was adapted from polytheistic texts. Naturally, they miss or gloss over the forest of OT Trinitarian proofs. Liberals also miss or misread the many OT indicators that the *Malek Yahveh* was divine, and that the coming Messiah would be divine. Of course, a divine *Malek Yahveh* and Messiah would be an unexpected development if one viewed the OT to be unitarian.

Liberals who hold that the OT is unitarian often conclude that Paul and the early Church were mythmakers. Paul supposedly transformed three Bible characters into the Trinity:

- The itinerate preacher, *Yeshua*, into the Messiah,
- The Messiah into the son of God,
- The son of God into the Son of God,
- The Son of God into God the Son,
- *Yahveh* into God the Father, and
- The spirit of *Yahveh* into God the Spirit.

There just, however, was not enough time between the Crucifixion and Paul's death for mythmaking of this magnitude. Furthermore, this view does not explain why the OT has so much material that lends itself to a Trinitarian interpretation.

What is more likely the case is that the NT accurately reported the fact that *Yeshua* identified himself as God the Son, just as the Jews said *Yeshua* did (Joh 05:18; 10:33). *Yeshua* was killed by the Jews because he identified himself as the "I AM" (Exo 03) and as the Son of Man (Dan 07). The Jews also did not like how *Yeshua* seemed to identify the Father and himself as subjects of the *Shema*.

The above scenario is more likely than any spin a liberal has tried to put on the NT and early Church history. Previously, liberals said that *Yeshua* was killed because he was a messianic "freedom fighter." That is because liberals wanted to support socialistic and communistic guerrilla leaders. Then liberals tried to say *Yeshua* was a traveling rabbi. Then someone realized that there would be no reason to kill a traveling rabbi.

Lately, liberals have been saying that *Yeshua* was a victim of a dispute about:
- Ceremonial washings at the temple (Joh 03:25), and
- Whether it was proper for priests to exclude the blind, lame and lepers from the temple (Mat 21:14; Luk 17:14).

This interpretive shift seems to match the shift in liberal politics and church fundraising efforts. Liberals church congregations are graying, and there is a need to raise money for elevators and wheelchair access ramps.

Liberals know that "god-man" myths take a long while to develop and propagate. Since the NT was written only decades after the crucifixion, liberals would rather not believe that the NT calls *Yeshua* "God" at all. Liberals say that the NT writers' application of OT *Yahveh* texts to *Yeshua* was not meant to say that *Yeshua* was *Yahveh* the Son incarnate. Liberals also say it is only a fluke that the "I AM," *Shema*, and "Son of Man" statements applied to *Yeshua* appear to be allusions to, or quotations of, the LXX and MT.

How liberals attempt to discount the idea that the "I AM," *Shema*, and "Son of Man" statements are allusions to, or quotations of, the OT is by saying:
- The NT is Greek,
- The OT is Hebrew, and
- *Yeshua* only spoke Aramaic.

If *Yeshua* spoke Aramaic, liberals think this would distance *Yeshua*'s "I AM" and *Shema* statements from those found in the Greek LXX and the Hebrew OT.

The liberal argument is thwarted, however, when one realizes that the popular Targums were written in Aramaic. Also, if *Yeshua* spoke Aramaic, this would strengthen the tie between *Yeshua*'s many Son of Man statements and the Dan 07 Son of Man vision. Dan 02:04b—07 is written in Aramaic, while the rest of Daniel is written in Hebrew.

Perhaps it is counterintuitive, but if *Yeshua* spoke in Aramaic, the tie between the Greek LXX and Hebrew Scriptures would still be strong. The reason is that translators would be extra careful to choose their words well so as not to give any false impressions. For instance, if *Yeshua* were not God, the NT writers would have made disclaimers when writing about *Yeshua*'s "I AM" and Son of Man statements.

Whatever view one takes, logic suggests that *Yeshua* really did apply OT "I AM," "Son of Man," and *Shema* statements to himself. Besides, whatever language *Yeshua* used, this fact is clear: the Jews undoubtedly understood *Yeshua* to be claiming to be God the Son. *Yeshua* never told the Jews that there was a misunderstanding. He only complained of their stubborn disbelief (Joh 05:18; 10:33).

Whether *Yeshua* Spoke Predominantly Aramaic or Greek

Background

The conservative scholar Alfred Edersheim wrote:
> [*Yeshua*] spoke Hebrew, and used and quoted the Scriptures in the original...although, no doubt, He understood Greek, possibly also Latin.[121]

Edersheim further wrote about the language situation in first century Palestine:
> If Greek was the language of the court and [military] camp, and indeed [Greek] must have been understood and spoken by most in the land [Palestine]...[122]

The mantra espoused by liberals such as those in the "Jesus Seminar" has been: the NT contains very few words actually spoken by *Yeshua*. Liberal analysis of the literary evidence had determined that Aramaic was the dominant, if not the exclusive language of the Jews in Palestine. Liberals taught that the Greek NT was, at best, a translation of *Yeshua*'s words, and, at worst, a total fraud.

Lockstepping liberals did not question these assertions, even though Josephus, an eyewitness of first century Palestine spoke of the prevalence of Greek. Now, however, the cherished idea that Palestine was wholly Aramaic and Hebrew speaking has been discarded due to archeological evidence. The evidence will be discussed shortly.

The reader will recall from the Hebrew collective nouns chapter that other cherished ideas have fallen by the wayside in the last century. These include the ideas that classical Judaism was aniconic, devoid of figural art, and free of astrology.

Interpolating Anachronistic Ideas into the Past

It is unlikely that *Yeshua* would have been monolingual in the multilingual environment of the first century Palestine. Palestine then was a part of the multilingual Roman Empire. The ancients became conversant or fluent in other languages more readily than moderns today. The reason is that the vocabulary of many ancient languages amounted to merely several thousand words each.

The vocabularies of many modern languages total seventy-five thousand words. English runs into more than ten times that, according to the Oxford English Dictionary! By contrast, the Torah contains 7,704 words.[123] What makes for speedy vocabulary growth is moveable type printers (circa 1455 AD), cheap wood pulp paper (1800's AD), and affordable personal computers connected to the Web (1993 AD).

To complicate matters, some modern languages are not spelled phonetically. Some languages have so many exceptional spellings that teachers are tempted to give up teaching a plethora of spelling rules. The task of teaching spelling has fallen to word processing software where the users learn by trial and error. In ancient times, however, spelling often did not matter since words were spelled phonetically, or spelling was not standardized, or a language was not even written down due to the lack of an alphabet.

That vocabulary and spelling were not major obstacles to learning ancient languages meant people could more readily become conversant or fluent in:

- A second or third language,
- A hybrid language (*lingua franca* or *koine*), or
- A language with a reduced vocabulary (creole or pidgin).

The Language Situation in First Century Judea

Joseph Ben Matthias (later Josephus Flavius) was a Jewish priest, Pharisee, general and historian. Josephus lived from 37/38 AD to 100 AD. He wrote, between the years 75 and 79 AD, *The History of the Jewish War*. This book is a history of the Jewish Revolt (66-70 AD) and the siege of Masada (72–73 AD). Josephus finished writing *The Antiquities of the Jews* in 93 AD. This is a history of the Jewish people from the Creation to 66 AD.

Josephus grew up in an aristocratic, priestly family in Jerusalem. Josephus' native language was Aramaic. Undoubtedly, Josephus was taught Greek because many of the priests were Hellenists. The Greek influence in Judea grew nearly unbounded from the days of Alexander the Great (circa 330 BC).

By 165 BC, during the reign of Antiochus (Epiphanes) IV, Hellenism had made enough inroads into Judaism to become a major cause of the Maccabean revolt. During the Maccabean period and subsequent Roman period, the influence of Greek never abated. Greek was ubiquitous in Palestine even after the seventh century Muslim conquests.

That Greek had made inroads into Judea since 330 BC explains why prior to 70 AD, many religionists in Judea read the Greek LXX. This is evidenced by the presence of Greek scrolls and fragments among the Dead Sea scrolls. These Greek fragments were one or two hundred years old by the time they were left for posterity in 70 AD![124] Greek LXX fragments were even found at Masada, the Jewish fortress besieged by the Romans from 72-73 AD. Though Edersheim wrote long before these archeological discoveries, he was on target about the LXX being…

> …the people's Bible, not merely among the Hellenists, but in Galilee, and even in Judea.[125]

Josephus, a former priest, needed to know Greek for commerce, and to talk to the Romans and the Greek-speaking Jews of the diaspora. The Roman aristocrats spoke Greek, so knowing Greek helped Josephus as a negotiator in Rome from 64 to 66 AD. Edersheim wrote about another Jewish official:

> Yet even the Jewish patriarch, Gamaliel II, who may have sat with Saul of Tarsus at the feet of his grandfather, was said to have busied himself with Greek, as he certainly held liberal views on many points connected with Grecianism. To be sure, tradition justified him on the ground that his position brought him into contact with the ruling powers…[126]

Josephus wrote *The History of the Jewish War* in Aramaic, a version now lost to history. The Greek translation, which was prepared under Josephus' personal supervision by fluent Greek speakers, survives. Josephus wrote his later works in Greek rather than Aramaic. Linguists have concluded that Josephus' later works show that he had a good grasp of Greek, but he used some clumsy idioms. This is what one would expect if Greek were Josephus' second language.

Greek was the native language of many people in first century Palestine. Josephus, however, likely wrote of the language situation specific to Jerusalem and Judea. Josephus wrote that there was no incentive for Judeans to learn Greek perfectly as a mark of educational distinction, because even servants commonly knew Greek! It seems what Josephus was hinting at was that Greek was used for commerce and government functions. Scholars attempting to write great literary works naturally thought it best to write works in their native language.

What was considered an accomplishment was to learn Hebrew and Aramaic, and then to become familiar with the Jewish law! This explains why the crowd at the temple became quiet when Paul started to speak in Aramaic. Perhaps the crowd thought Paul, who hailed from the Greek colony of Tarsus, would only know Greek. They were surprised when Paul started speaking the language of the learned Jew (Act 21:40; 22:02).

That Aramaic was the language of the learned is why Paul bothered to mention that *Yeshua* spoke some Aramaic (Act 26:14). Paul mentioned that *Yeshua* spoke Aramaic while making his defense before King Agrippa, who was "well acquainted with all the Jewish customs and controversies" (Act 26:03). This would show that *Yeshua* had been familiar with rabbinic writings and the law as King Agrippa was. Otherwise, King Agrippa might think Christianity centered on an unlearned, Greek-speaking Galilean (Luk 23:05-07).

Josephus wrote about the Greek-speaking situation in Judea:

> I have also taken a great deal of pains to obtain the learning of the Greeks, and understand the elements of the Greek language, although I have so long accustomed myself to speak our own tongue that I cannot pronounce Greek with sufficient exactness; for our nation does not encourage those that learn the languages of many nations, and so adorn their discourses with the smoothness of their periods; because they look upon this sort of accomplishment as common, not only to all sorts of freemen, but to as many of the servants as please to learn them. But they give him the testimony of being a wise man who is fully acquainted with our laws, and is able to interpret their meaning; on which account, as there have been many who have done their endeavors with great patience to obtain this learning, there have yet hardly been so many as two or three that have succeeded therein who were immediately well rewarded for their pains.[127]

Greek was more prevalent in Palestine north of Judea and Jerusalem, but Pieter W. Van Der Horst wrote that even:

One of the most surprising facts about these funerary inscriptions is that most of them are in Greek—approximately 70 percent; about 12 percent are in Latin; and only 18 percent are in Hebrew or Aramaic. These figures are even more instructive if we break them down between Palestine and the diaspora. Naturally in Palestine we would expect more Hebrew and Aramaic and less Greek. This is true, but not to any great extent. Even in Palestine approximately two-thirds of these inscriptions are in Greek. Apparently for a great part of the Jewish population the daily language was Greek, even in Palestine. This is impressive testimony to the impact of Hellenistic culture on Jews in their mother country, to say nothing of the diaspora. In Jerusalem itself about forty percent of the Jewish inscriptions from the first century period (before 70 AD) are in Greek. We may assume that most Jewish Jerusalemites who saw the inscriptions *in situ* [Latin for "on site"] were able to read them....This is not to say Hebrew and Aramaic ever died out completely as languages for the Jews. Especially in the eastern diaspora, Jews continued to speak a Semitic language. But in the first five centuries of the Common Era, exactly the period when rabbinic literature was being written in Hebrew and Aramaic, a majority of the Jews in Palestine and the western diaspora spoke Greek.[128]

The recently discovered ossuary purported to be that of "James, son of Joseph, brother of *Yeshua*" is inscribed in Aramaic.[129] James was martyred in Jerusalem in 63 AD, so Jerusalem was likely where the ossuary was inscribed. This ossuary inscription would be part of the sixty percent of Jerusalem inscriptions written in a language other than Greek.

So it would seem that the idea that "*Yeshua* only spoke Aramaic" is just liberal nonsense that is needed to make liberal argumentation work. The idea that *Yeshua* was monolingual is not grounded on the literary and archeological data.

Biblical Data on the Language Situation in Judea

The Jews were exposed to Aramaic mainly in the synagogues, while Greek was increasingly prevalent everywhere else. This helps explain why Paul's speaking in Aramaic silenced the throng at the temple (Act 22:02). The crowd may have quieted down out of habit because they heard Aramaic mainly in the synagogue. As Josephus said above, the populace respected most those who took the time to learn Jewish law well. This pursuit required an advanced knowledge of Aramaic.

Another incident that suggests not all Judeans were conversant in Aramaic was *Yeshua*'s appearance to Paul on the road to Damascus. *Yeshua* said in Aramaic, "Saul, Saul, why do you persecute me?" (Act 09:04; 26:14). Paul should have known who the person was right away since Paul was persecuting Christians.

Previously, Paul even heard Stephen say *Yeshua* was standing in glory at the right hand of the Father (Act 07:55-56, 58). Paul did not immediately recognize *Yeshua*, likely because Paul figured *Yeshua* was a Greek-speaking Galilean (Joh 07: 35, 41, 52), while the man in the vision spoke Aramaic (Act 26:14-15a).

Notably, Paul's companions heard the voice, but they did not "understand" the voice (Act 09:07; 22:09). This suggests that Paul's companions were not conversant in Aramaic. Of course, this might be the very reason why *Yeshua* spoke in Aramaic since he wanted to have a private conversation with Paul.

Paul's companions may have been Greek-speaking diaspora Jews who attended the Synagogue of the Freedmen in Jerusalem (Act 06:09). Whatever the case, the account seems to show that not every resident in Judea spoke Aramaic. Of course, it was for this very reason that Pilate posted his sign on the cross in three languages: Aramaic, Greek and Latin.

That not everyone in Palestine, including Paul's peers, spoke Aramaic sheds light on some of Paul's statements. Paul said he was "a Jew to the Jews" (1Co 09: 20), and "a Hebrew of Hebrews" (Phi 03:05). Paul said he surpassed his peers in all things Jewish (Gal 01:13-14).

Paul may have meant he was a Pharisee while most of his peers were not (Act 23:06; Phi 03:05). Paul may also have meant that he knew both Hebrew and Aramaic better than his peers. As Josephus said, the populace respected those most who took the time to learn Jewish law well. This pursuit, of course, required an advanced knowledge of Aramaic.

The First Century Language Situation in Galilee of the Gentiles

Before 70 AD, Galilee was not known for being especially Jewish. After the First Jewish Revolt and the destruction of Herod's Temple by the Romans (70 AD), Galilee became a center of Jewish learning. Rabbi Yohanan ben Zakkai, a leading Jewish rabbi, formed a center for Jewish learning at Yavneh (Jabnah or Jamnia) by Tiberias on the Sea of Galilee.

The Romans crushed the final Jewish rebellion (132-135 AD) led by the false messianic figure Simeon Bar Kokhba (or Bar Koziba). Jewish scholars then moved from the Sea of Galilee to Usha near modern Haifa. Haifa is located straight west of the Sea of Galilee in a nook of Israel's Mediterranean seacoast. So Galilee became a center of Jewish learning after 70 AD, but was a Jewish hinterland previously. This fact may have led to some anachronistic thinking about the Jewishness of Galilee.

In the seventh century BC, Galilee was called "the Galilee of the Gentiles" (Isa 09:01-02). This still was a fitting name in *Yeshua*'s time (Mat 04:15-16). There were many reasons that the majority of Galileans were gentile:
- The Israelites failed to drive the Canaanites out of Galilee (Jdg 01:30-36),
- The southern border of Galilee was seventy miles distant from Jerusalem. This meant that Galilee was far away from where the bulk of the Jewish population resided. Moreover, gentile territories bounded Galilee on all sides,
- The Assyrian king Tiglathpileser III (Pul) expelled some Jews and deported others out of Galilee in 734 or 732 BC (2Ki 15:19, 29),
- In 165 BC, Simon Maccabeus evacuated many Jewish Galileans to safety in Judea (1Ma 05:23), and

- Samaria served somewhat as a barrier that hindered Jews from spreading into Galilee. The Assyrian king, Sargon II, deported many Jews out of Samaria. The Jews that remained intermarried with gentiles that Sargon II settled in Samaria.

The Ptolemaic and Seleucid Empires alternately ruled Galilee from 324 to 166 BC. Hellenistic rulers proselytized their subjects to adopt Greek culture and language. That gentiles populated Galilee meant Galilee was more receptive to Hellenization than Judea. During this period many Greeks immigrated, and twenty-nine Greek cities sprung up in Palestine. Hellenized cities include Hippus, Julius, Gadara, Scythopolis, Caesarea and Caesarea Philippi. Hellenistic towns near Nazareth included Sepphoris and Tiberias.

That gentiles were the majority population in Galilee meant the process of Hellenization went fairly smoothly. Scrupulous Jews in Judea, however, had qualms over Hellenization, as the Intertestamental literature points out. Though the Jewish Maccabees (164 BC-63 AD) ruled Galilee for a time, they could not reverse or even stem the tide of Hellenization. Hellenization continued in Galilee until Galilee became impoverished and depopulated after the Arab conquest (636 AD). Galilee never did recover until modern times.

Joseph, Mary and *Yeshua* were Galileans who resided in Nazareth most of their lives (Luk 01:04; Mat 02:22-23). The small town of Nazareth may have been entirely Jewish, but Nazareth was near Hellenistic towns. This suggests that *Yeshua*, like most other Galileans, was at least conversant with, if not fluent, in Greek. *Yeshua*'s upbringing in the Jewish town of Nazareth allowed him to learn Aramaic well. This meant that at age twelve he could converse well with the temple teachers for whom Greek was a second language (Luk 02:46-47).

Moreover, even if *Yeshua* would have been more comfortable preaching in Aramaic, this does not necessarily mean he used Aramaic much in his ministry. *Yeshua* may have felt the need to use the language of the people in Galilee and Syrian Phoenicia, among whom he lived out most of his ministry years. *Yeshua* would have been like most missionaries down to the present who speak in one language to their congregation, and in their native language to their colleagues.

So *Yeshua* likely preached in Greek, the language of commerce and the arts, rather than in Hebrew and Aramaic, the traditional languages of his religion. That *Yeshua*'s ministry was conducted in a language foreign to Judeans would be a partial fulfillment of Isaiah's prophecy (Isa 28:11; 1Co 14:21). Later, many nations would evangelize Israel using foreign tongues.

Whether *Yeshua* Spoke Predominantly Greek or Aramaic

Was *Yeshua* a Hellenized Jew or an Aramaic-speaking Jew? (Act 06:01). Hellenized Jews were found all over the eastern Mediterranean, even in Jerusalem synagogues (Act 06:09; Act 09:28-29). Greek-speaking Jewish Christians were also found in Jerusalem (Mat 27:32; Act 02:10; 09:29; 11:19-20; 21:37).

Many Greek-speaking Christians were driven out of Jerusalem by persecutions and revolts (Mat 24:16; Mar 13:14; Luk 21:21). Many Greek-speaking Christians voluntarily left Jerusalem between 67 and 70 AD. They took Mat 24:15-20 to be a warning of Jerusalem's impending doom, and decided to take refuge in the Greco-Roman city named Pella. Pella was named after the Macedonian birthplace of Alexander the Great. So it would seem that if Hellenized Jews resided in Jerusalem and Pella, surely many Galilean Jews were Hellenized.

Some Hellenized Jews knew Hebrew and Aramaic. Paul knew Greek since his formative years were spent in a former Greek colony, Tarsus. Paul, however, became familiar with the Hebrew Scriptures and Aramaic (Act 21:40; 22:02; 26: 14). Being a Hellenized Jew did not necessarily detract from his Jewishness. Even non-Hellenized Jews spoke Aramaic and languages besides Hebrew (Act 02:08-11).

Paul would have brooked no suggestion that his being Hellenized meant he was any less Jewish than his contemporaries. Paul thought of himself as being Jewish (Rom 02:29), "a Jew to the Jews" (1Co 09:20), and "a Hebrew of Hebrews" (Phi 03:05). Moreover, Paul said that while he was in Jerusalem, he surpassed his peers in all things Jewish (Gal 01:13-14). Paul did not need to sacrifice one culture for the other. For Paul, being a Hellenized Jew was a cultural "both-and" situation, not an "either-or" dilemma.

Yeshua's Parents

Matthew related that Joseph, Mary and *Yeshua* stayed in Egypt awhile (Mat 02: 13-15). The Jewish community in Egypt had translated the Hebrew and Aramaic Scriptures into the Greek LXX. The LXX and its precursor translations had been used in Alexandrian synagogues since the second century BC, or even earlier.

That Mary and Joseph fled to the Greek-speaking Jewish diaspora in Egypt suggests that they spoke Greek well. If they did not speak Greek, they might have instead fled to Aramaic-speaking Jewish communities in Mesopotamia. Surely, as natives of Galilee, Mary and Joseph would have been familiar with the LXX (Luk 01:26; 02:04, 39). The least that one could safely conclude is that Mary and Joseph's stopover in Egypt increased their exposure to Greek.

Yeshua in the Nazareth Synagogue

Some assert that *Yeshua* actually read a Hebrew Isaiah manuscript, and read from an Aramaic commentary in the Nazareth synagogue (Luk 04:16-30). This is based on the shaky assumption that what was the norm in Judea was the norm in Galilee. The norm in Judea was that a reader would read the Hebrew Scriptures, and then a "translator" (*turgeman* or *meturgeman*) would comment on the text in Aramaic, or read an Aramaic Targum.[130]

The language situations in Galilee and Judea could have been entirely different. Just because Aramaic was spoken in Judean synagogues does not prove that *Yeshua* spoke Aramaic in Galilean synagogues.[131] Besides, reading from Targum commentaries would have been a rather safe occupation. *Yeshua's* comments, however, almost got him thrown off a cliff. Certainly his comments did not come from an Aramaic Targum (Luk 04:21-30)!

Yeshua made disparaging remarks about those rabbinic teachings based on the errors and nonsense propagated through the Targums (Mat 15:05; 22:29; 23:16; Luk 11:46; Joh 12:34). Moreover, the LXX and MT are quoted in the NT to the near exclusion of the Targums. The people recognized that *Yeshua* had new teachings (Mar 01:27). This all suggests that *Yeshua* did not read from Targums during his ministry.

The norms current in Judea say only so much about the norms in Galilee of the Gentiles. Galilee was seventy miles away from Judea, which was several days' walk in ancient times. Galilee and Judea were distant enough to have differing accents, likely in both the Greek and Aramaic languages (Mat 26:73). Besides, the norm of reading Aramaic Targums in Judea speaks more about how Babylon was a center of Jewish learning than it does about the language situation in Judea.

In Isaiah's day (8th century BC), the people spoke Hebrew but not Aramaic. Otherwise, it would have been pointless to ask the Assyrian commander to speak in Aramaic rather than in Hebrew if the people understood both (2Ki 18:26, 28; 2Ch 32:18; Isa 36:11, 13).

After the exile (6th century BC), many Judean men intermarried with foreigners. Half of their children knew the language of Ashdod, Ammon and Moab, but not "the language of Judah," meaning Hebrew (Neh 13:24). So even after various Aramaic-speaking empires exercised their influence in the region for centuries, small states maintained their own languages. So it seems we can dispense with the notion that empires imposed their languages on the conquered peoples to the near extinction of the native languages.

That most of the OT is written in Hebrew shows that the Judeans continued to speak Hebrew right up to the Intertestamental period. Interestingly, the only Aramaic portions of the OT consist mainly of correspondence written by gentiles, and chapters that concern gentiles (Dan 02:04—07:28; Ezr 04:08—06:18; 07:12-26). Also, it seems many Intertestamental books were originally written in Greek, and the Greek copies are the only remnants to survive.

Until the Intertestamental period, Hebrew was able to compete with Aramaic in Judea, especially since they are sister languages. Hebrew, however, went into steep decline when Greek was introduced. Most people would have been bilingual, given both the circumstances in ancient times and also human limitations.

The norm of reading Aramaic Targums in Judea started after the return from exile (6th century BC). Aramaic did not supplant Hebrew, however. Then Greek arrived in Palestine with Alexander the Great (332 BC). As Hebrew trailed off, Aramaic and Greek filled the language vacuum. This seems to explain why forty percent of the inscriptions in Jerusalem were Greek while most of the rest were Aramaic.

The norm of reading mostly Aramaic in the synagogues of Judea during *Yeshua*'s time resulted from Hebrew's slow decline. By contrast, in Galilee of the Gentiles there were fewer Hebrew speakers even before the exile. Then the Greek settlers came speaking only Greek. So the language norms in Judea during *Yeshua*'s day speak even less about conditions in Galilee than one might imagine. Moreover, archaeologists tell us that Aramaic was not as deeply entrenched in Judea and Galilee as was commonly assumed.

Besides, the norms in Judea could not simply be imposed elsewhere since the norms presuppose certain conditions. For the norm in Judea to be the norm elsewhere required that the synagogue have:

- A *geniza* (storeroom) stocked with expensive scrolls of the Hebrew Scriptures as well as Aramaic Targums, instead of the less expensive Greek equivalents, and
- A person on hand with the required expertise to read Hebrew and Aramaic.

Most synagogues outside of Judea and Mesopotamia did not have an audience that understood Aramaic. In these places it likely was deemed impractical to incorporate Aramaic into the worship services.

The Greek LXX was much easier to procure than Hebrew Scriptures due to:

- Supply and demand efficiencies,
- More slave copyists knew Greek than Hebrew, and
- "From the extreme labor and care bestowed on them, Hebrew manuscripts of the Bible were enormously dear."[132]

So the majority of eastern Mediterranean synagogues used the LXX. As Edersheim wrote:

> Accordingly, manuscripts in Greek or Latin, although often incorrect, must have been easily attainable, and this would have considerable influence of making the Greek version of the Old Testament the 'people's Bible.'[133]

The LXX was most likely read even in Jerusalem synagogues such as in the Synagogue of the Freedmen. This synagogue drew members from Cyrene, Alexandria, Cilicia and Asia where Hebrew and Aramaic were considered foreign languages (Act 06:09). As was noted previously, Paul's companions seem not to have known Aramaic (Act 09:07; 22:09)!

Luke has *Yeshua* reading the LXX word for word (Isa 61:01-02; Luk 04:18-19). So all things considered, the LXX surely was a text that *Yeshua* read from his childhood at Nazareth. Moreover, *Yeshua* certainly used the LXX extensively in his Galilean ministry, if not also in his Judean ministry.

Yeshua Was Unschooled

Many nineteenth and twentieth century liberals read that *Yeshua* had not "studied" (Joh 07:15), and that *Yeshua*'s disciples were "unschooled" (Act 04:13). Having been misled that the language of Galilee was almost exclusively Aramaic, these liberals assumed that anyone schooled in Galilee must only have known how to write Aramaic (Joh 08:06).

This assumption in turn led many 19th and 20th century liberals to other assumptions. For instance, liberals wrote that *Yeshua*'s disciples were not capable of writing the good Attic (in other words, "Athenian") Koine Greek found in the Gospels. So some liberals taught that the Gospels and the NT originals were written in Aramaic. Other liberals wrote that the NT was conceived and written by both the Apostle Paul and apocryphal writers using pseudonyms.

This prejudice against home-schooling and synagogue-schooling is unwarranted. Even today, home-schooled children often excel beyond their peers at educational institutions. Children in Galilee likely were bilingual or even polyglot because of the necessities of Galilean commercial and cultural life. The diverse society served as a language laboratory that reinforced language lessons learned at home.

Nearly every Jewish boy went to synagogue-school. So somebody who was "not studied" and "unschooled" had schooling—just not at a theological seminary. Paul, by contrast, was "studied" and "schooled." He learned from the Rabbi Gamaliel, the grandson of Rabbi Hillel, who started a religious seminary of sorts in Jerusalem (Act 05:34; 22:03; 26:24).

Yeshua's attending seminary would have been a superfluous activity since he had already "amazed" the learned doctors at the temple at age twelve (Luk 02:42-47). Besides, the farther the ancient Jewish teachers progressed beyond the basics, the more error crept in.

When the people said that *Yeshua* and the disciples were unschooled, they were merely noting that *Yeshua* was unmatched in wisdom and authoritativeness (Mat 13:54; Mar 06:02; Joh 06:45; 08:28). Similarly, the Sanhedrin wondered how the disciples had honed their oratorical skills without attending seminary (Act 04:13).

The Form of the Gospels

Some scholars assert that *Yeshua* spoke primarily, if not exclusively, in Aramaic. This assertion is made despite the fact that:
- There are only a few scattered quotations of *Yeshua* speaking Aramaic, while the vast majority of *Yeshua*'s words were recorded in Greek,
- The majority of OT quotations found in the NT, including those of *Yeshua*, follow the Greek LXX rather than the MT recension,
- No Church father unequivocally mentioned the existence of any Aramaic collection of *Yeshua*'s sayings or an Aramaic gospel, and none has been unearthed,
- Archeologists have discovered that Greek was quite prevalent in first century Palestine, just as the first century Jewish historian Josephus said it was (*Antiquities of the Jews*, Book 20:11:01), and
- The only incidents where the NT reader is sure that *Yeshua* spoke Aramaic are those times that:
  o The general public apparently did not understand what *Yeshua* said in Aramaic, and

o *Yeshua* purposely downplayed a miracle to avoid unwanted publicity, especially so the civil and religious authorities would not feel they had to jail or
kill *Yeshua* just yet.

The above-listed facts suggest that the general public understood Greek. So
when *Yeshua* knew that only those persons familiar with the OT could possibly
know about his role as Messiah, he chose to speak in Aramaic.

This strategy made sense because, on average, Aramaic speakers knew the OT
better than those who only spoke Greek. *Yeshua* wanted to avoid situations where
people would declare him their "bread king" (Joh 06:15), or would offer sacrifices
to him as though he were Zeus, and to his disciples as though they were Olympian
gods (Acts 14:12).

Most agree that all the NT books, except perhaps Matthew, were first penned
in Greek. The early Church father Papias wrote that Matthew's gospel was
written "in Hebrew." Some have taken "in Hebrew" to mean "in Aramaic,"
but not even a fragment of an Aramaic proto-Matthew has been found.

There is no independent confirmation by another Church father or historian
that Matthew's gospel was originally written in Aramaic. Matthew was a tax
collector, so it would seem he would need to know Greek to talk to the Romans
(Mat 09:09; 10:03).

Not surprisingly, scholars consider Papias' assertion a dubious tradition. Others
hold the opinion that Papias' words "in Hebrew" should be understood as "in the
Jewish style" or "using Hebraisms." In any event, Matthew still quoted from the
Greek LXX far more than from the Hebrew. This indicates that:
- Matthew's audience was Greek-speaking,
- *Yeshua*'s preferred OT text was the LXX, and
- *Yeshua*'s audience was mainly Greek speaking (Joh 07:35).

Interestingly, Matthew explained simple Hebrew and Aramaic terms in his
gospel (Mat 01:23; 27:33, 46). These explanations suggest that Matthew wrote his
gospel in Greek for Hellenized Jews and Greeks rather than for Aramaic speakers.
That Matthew quoted from the LXX as well as from the Hebrew or Aramaic shows
that Matthew was fluent in two or three languages. One can easily assume that
Yeshua was fluent in as many languages as Matthew was.

Perhaps looking at the big picture would help. How would one expect the
gospels to read if *Yeshua* spoke chiefly Greek and primarily quoted the Greek
LXX? How might the gospels read if both Aramaic and Greek were well known in
Palestine? Bilingual people often produce bilingual books.

Bilingual books usually are written in one language, but have a smattering of
a second language. Likewise, most quotations would naturally be sourced from
books written in one language, and a smattering would be sourced from books
written in a second language. That is exactly what we have in the gospels. The
gospels are Greek with a smattering of Aramaic, and similarly the quotations
mainly come from the Greek LXX.

In the NT there are scattered Aramaic place names and phrases transliterated
into Greek, sometimes accompanied by an explanation (Mat 27:46; Mar 05:41; 07:

34; Joh 01:38, 41). Also, there are alternate, non-transliterated Greek names and place names (Joh 19:13, 17; 20:24; 21:02).

Naturally, Aramaic and Hebraic thought and culture are reflected in both the NT storyline and in occasional Hebraisms. The good Attic *Koine* Greek and the absence of clumsy, wooden translations suggest that the NT was originally written in Greek and not Aramaic.

The Aramaic Words and Phrases in the NT

That Aramaic was fading in importance in Palestine explains why NT Jewish Greek speakers occasionally used Aramaic words as cognates. Most NT instances of *rabbi* and *abba* are indeclinable, which suggests they were loan words. There are two NT instances of *rabboni* used as an Aramaic word rather than as a borrowed word. Interestingly, both occurrences (Mar 10:51; Joh 20:16) were spoken in Judea near Jerusalem (Mar 10:01 and 11:01).

The Apostle John wrote that Mary addressed *Yeshua* with the Aramaic title *Rabboni*. This seems to show Mary's surprise and disbelief at *Yeshua*'s resurrection (Joh 20:16).[134] Mary had thought she was talking to an Aramaic-speaking gardener. Mary failed to switch from Aramaic to Greek when she found out she was addressing the Greek-speaking Galilean. John's Greek-speaking gospel readers would have caught how surprised Mary must have been to address *Yeshua* in Aramaic rather than Greek.

In areas of Palestine populated by Greeks, naturally Greek was spoken more and Aramaic less. Lest Ness points out:

It was almost unknown for a Greek to learn a 'barbarian' language.[135]

This fact explains why *Yeshua* used Aramaic in these areas the several times he did not want publicity. This is similar to how *Yeshua* spoke Aramaic to Paul on the road to Damascus. Evidently, *Yeshua* wanted a private conversation with Paul. Paul said his companions heard but did not understand *Yeshua*'s voice (Act 09:07; 22:09). The situation was the same in the Decapolis. Mark wrote:

Yeshua took a man aside from the crowd...*Yeshua* looked up to heaven and with a deep sigh said to him, *Ephphatha!* meaning, 'Be opened!'...
Yeshua commanded them not to tell anyone. The more he commanded, however, the more they kept talking about the miracle (Mar 07:33-36).

Yeshua's purpose in speaking Aramaic while performing a miracle served the same purpose as taking the man aside, out of view of the market. The Decapolis crowd was generally Greek speaking, so speaking Aramaic helped to keep the miracle under wraps. Unwanted publicity had caused *Yeshua* to move out of areas before (Mar 01:45; Luk 05:16; Joh 04:01-03).

Yeshua was sent mainly to the Jews who often happened to know Greek and Aramaic (Mat 15:24-28). *Yeshua* was not sent to the Greeks who often happened to know Greek and Latin (Joh 19:20). Keeping publicity down meant that though the Jewish leaders might investigate (Joh 09:08-35), they would not conclude that they had to kill *Yeshua* just yet (Joh 07:25-26; 11:47-57). The same could be said for the civil authorities (Luk 13:31).

Greeks unfamiliar with the OT would not put *Yeshua*'s miracles in the proper context. *Yeshua* knew that the Greeks in the Decapolis naturally spoke more Greek than Aramaic. So the situation at the market was similar to how *Yeshua* quoted Psa 022:01 in Aramaic from the cross (Mat 27:46). The Greek speakers who heard *Yeshua* call from the cross mistakenly thought he called out for Elijah, or for something to drink (Mat 27:47-49).

The disciples understood *Yeshua*'s Aramaic, and eventually they came to understand the OT. The NT writers wrote about the Decapolis miracles in the Greek NT. It is interesting to think that some of the Greek speakers who witnessed the miracle in the Decapolis may have later read the account in a Greek Gospel. Then they would have known a Gospel writer's translation of what *Yeshua* spoke in Aramaic. They also would have read a properly contextualized account of the miracle they had seen earlier (Luk 24:25-27).

Yeshua crossed the Sea of Galilee from the Decapolis and went to Capernaum. *Yeshua* then went to the synagogue ruler's house and raised Jairus' daughter from the dead. *Yeshua* attempted to minimize the miracle both by telling the mourners to disperse, and by saying that the daughter had only been sleeping (Mat 09:24; Mar 05:39). *Yeshua* then put the crowd outside Jairus' home so they would not be able to blab the details of the miracle all over the countryside (Mat 09:25; Mar 05:40).

Only Peter, James and John and the girl's parents were present inside the home (Mar 05:37; Luk 08:51), but *Yeshua* spoke in Aramaic anyway. Undoubtedly, people were eavesdropping outside the house. Most houses at that time were open and airy to take advantage of Palestine's temperate climate. *Yeshua* said, *Talitha koum!* which meant, "Little girl, I say to you, get up!" (Mar 05:41).

Just as at the Decapolis, *Yeshua* gave strict orders that no one speak about the miracle at Jairus' house (Mar 05:43). It is notable that the same three disciples who witnessed the resurrection of Jairus' daughter were at the Transfiguration. There, too, they were ordered not to talk about the Transfiguration until after *Yeshua* rose from the dead (Mat 17:01, 09; Mar 09:02, 09).

Apparently, *Yeshua* spoke Aramaic among the Greek-speaking Galileans to keep the miracle somewhat hushed up. This would be consistent with his use of Aramaic while performing a miracle in the Decapolis to keep the miracle secret. This shows that the Galilean Jews tended to speak Greek rather than Aramaic, just as the Decapolis gentiles tended to speak Greek rather than Aramaic.

That Aramaic was used in the Judean synagogues, while the Judean populace tended to speak Greek outside the synagogues, explains why:
- The crowd was able to converse with Pilate though Pilate undoubtedly spoke Greek (Mat 27:17, 24; Mar 15:08, 11, 15; Luk 23:04), and
- Pilate posted a sign on the crucifix in Aramaic, Greek and Latin (Joh 19:20).

There is another indication that much of the Judean populace spoke the same language as the Roman soldiers, that being Greek. A Roman centurion said that *Yeshua* was the Son of God (Mat 27:54; Mar 15:39). He had gained this information from passersby who hurled insults (Mat 27:40, 43). Pilate's trilingual sign did not mention the title Son of God, but merely said, "*Yeshua* of Nazareth, the King of the Jews."

Many of the passersby undoubtedly knew Aramaic, but apparently they chose to cast their insults in Greek. They knew *Yeshua* was Galilean, so they figured his native language was Greek. This can be ascertained from the fact that one person who mentioned "Son of God" quoted Psa 002:08:

> He trusts in God. Let God rescue him now if he wants him, for he said,
> 'I am the Son of God' (Mat 27:43).

Yet, when *Yeshua* quoted the same Psalm in Aramaic (Psa 022:001; Mat 27:46), the people around the cross did not understand what he said. This shows that the "Son of God" insults (Mat 27:40, 43) must have been spoken in Greek rather than Aramaic.

That many in the crowd did not know Aramaic explains why *Yeshua* cried out from the cross in Aramaic, "*Eloi, Eloi, lama sabachthani?*" (Mat 27:46; Mar 15: 34; Psa 022:01 [LXX 021:01]). *Yeshua* wanted to make sure his quote of Psa 022 [LXX 021] was understood in its scriptural context. Aramaic speakers tended to know the Psalms better.

Yeshua did not want the Roman soldier to hear him say in Greek, "My God, my God, why have you forsaken me?" Without knowledge of Psa 022, the Greek-speaking Roman centurion would have misunderstood the quotation. Then he would have discounted the idea that *Yeshua* had a divine origin (Mat 27:54; Mar 15:39; Act 21:31).

Those who knew the Psalms the best in Judea tended to be Aramaic speakers. They would have known that Psa 022 starts out with the speaker downtrodden by his enemies, but ends up on a happy note. The early Church figured it all out and deemed Psa 022 to be messianic.

By the way, the fact that *Yeshua* recited Psa 022 in Aramaic is no reason to accept the MT Hebrew rendering of Psa 022 rather than the Greek LXX. Rabbis have long pointed out that the MT does not describe a crucifixion since the MT supplies the nonsensical phrase "like a lion my hands and my feet" rather than "they pierced my hands and feet."

Since the MT recension converts "they pierced" into "like a lion," the reader must supply another verb to make sense of the nonsensical phrase "like a lion my hands and my feet." Interestingly, the reader does not need to supply the verb in other "like a lion" passages (e.g., Psa 007:02; 010:09; 017:12; Isa 38:13).

The "they pierced" reading of Psa 022:16 (*BHS* 022:17; LXX 021:17) is most likely the correct reading since:

- The Hebrew of the DSS (*Nahal Hever* (XHev/Se4, f.11, line 4),[136] as well as the Syriac, LXX and other translations, have the verb "pierced,"
- The *BHS* critical apparatus says that other Hebrew manuscripts have "they pierced,"[137] and
- Isa 53:05 and Zec 12:10 also say the Messiah would be pierced (Joh 19:37; 20: 25).

People who did not know Aramaic thought *Yeshua* said, "He is calling Elijah." The Greek word for Elijah is *Elias*, so the Greek speakers figured *Eli* or *Eloi* must be Aramaic for Elijah (Mat 27:46-47, 49; Mar 15:35-36).

Another Greek speaker assumed that *Yeshua* was complaining about the sun and wanted his thirst quenched (Mat 27:48). The Greek speaker arrived at this conclusion because he thought that *Yeshua*, instead of saying, "*Elias*" (Elijah), said "*helios*" (the sun). During the crucifixion the land was dark from the sixth to the ninth hour (Mat 27:45). The sun may have just appeared when *Yeshua*'s said, "*Eloi, Eloi…*," during the ninth hour (Mat 27:46).

Some of the Greek-speaking Roman soldiers may have concluded that *Yeshua* called out to their favorite god, *Helios* (the sun). Later the centurion and guards around the cross said, "Surely he was the Son of God (*theos*)!" (Mat 27:54; Mar 15:39). Unlike the thieves on the cross, the soldiers were not Jewish, so they drew their conclusions from the earthquake and the abnormal darkness rather than the Torah.

So when the soldiers said *Yeshua* was the Son of God (*theos*), they probably had a son of *Helios* (*Apollo*) in mind. This was similar to how Barnabas was mistaken for *Zeus*, and Paul was mistaken for *Hermes* at a later date (Acts 14:12).

The similarity between the Aramaic for "God" (*Eli* or *Eloi*), "Elijah" (*Elias*) and "the sun" (*helios*) continued to play a role in Christian times. J. S. Trimingham wrote how astral shrines were converted to Christian use:

> The cult of the prophet Elias [Elijah] is known to have replaced the cult
> of the Sun in Hellenistic places and the similarity between the names *Elias*
> and *Helios* [Greek sun god popular in Late Antiquity] is adduced.[138]

The crucifixion account shows that *Yeshua* spoke Aramaic on the cross for the same reasons he spoke Aramaic:
- In the Decapolis,
- At the quickening of Jairus' daughter, and
- On the road to Damascus.

In certain peculiar situations, speaking Aramaic was *Yeshua*'s way of reaching out only to those who were most inclined to be spiritually minded (Mat 07:06; Gal 06:01).

Yeshua's Aramaic Phrases

The NT records that *Yeshua* spoke a few Aramaic phrases, but this does not mean that *Yeshua* generally spoke Aramaic. The same logical leap would prove that the Apostle John spoke Aramaic in his ministry among the Greeks. John mentions Aramaic place names such as Bethesda (Joh 05:02), Gabbatha (Joh 19: 13), Golgotha (Joh 19:17), Abaddon (Rev 09:11) and Armageddon (Rev 16:16).

John certainly wrote his gospel and epistles in Greek to Greeks and to Hellenized Jews. Tradition says that John wrote Revelation on Patmos, one of the Dodecanese Islands southeast of Greece in the Aegean Sea. The Apostle John was a fluent Greek speaker—as John's gospel and the book of Revelation show. That John was a fluent Greek speaker suggests that *Yeshua* was, too.

If the use of a few Aramaic phrases indicates that *Yeshua* mainly spoke Aramaic, the same leap of logic could prove the absurd—that John and Paul spoke Aramaic during his ministry to the gentiles. Paul included a few Aramaic phrases in letters to the Corinthians, Romans and Galatians ("*Marana Tha*" (1Co 16:22); *Abba* (Rom 08:15; Gal 04:06)). Paul is noted for having conversations in Aramaic once on his way to Damascus and once at the temple (Act 21:40; 22:02; 26:14).

Paul's native language was Greek. Paul grew up in Tarsus, a former Greek colony on the south coast of Asia Minor (modern Turkey) (Act 21:37-39). Paul knew Aramaic (Act 21:40; 22:02; 26:14) because he was an exceptional student of things Jewish (Gal 01:13-14). Paul also studied at Jerusalem under exceptional teachers (Act 22:03). If Paul learned Aramaic in Asia Minor, it would have been as a foreign language since the seacoast cities spoke Greek. The Asia Minor interior spoke Anatolian dialects (Act 14:11).

Paul appended the Aramaic phrase "*Marana Tha*" to the Greek word *anathema*. The resultant phrase "*Anathema, Marana Tha*" has the look and feel of an anagram and palindrome, though it is neither. The phrase means, "...a curse be on him. Come, O Lord!" (1Co 05:05). Apparently, these Aramaic phrases were part of the liturgy that the Greeks knew.

This borrowing is similar to how native English speakers may know a smattering of Greek ("*Kurie Eleison*") and Hebrew (*Hallelujah*).[139] Similarly, Paul appended the Greek article and noun "*ho Pater*," meaning, "the Father," to the Aramaic noun *Abba*, meaning, "Father" (Rom 08:15; Gal 04:06). The Greeks knew this phrase because *Yeshua* said, "*Abba Pater*" (Mar 14:36). That *Yeshua* mixed Greek and Aramaic in his speech suggests he was bilingual.

Yeshua Talked to Greek Speakers

Yeshua held several conversations with persons whom one would suspect knew Greek, but not much, if any, Aramaic. The reason for this is, as Lest Ness points out:

It was almost unknown for a Greek to learn a 'barbarian' language.[140]

It also is reasonable to suppose that Latin speakers such as Pilate, once having learned Greek, would not feel the need to learn Aramaic. Besides, a rule of thumb is there are many more monolingual people than bilingual people, and more bilingual persons than polyglots.

Yeshua talked to a Roman centurion (Mat 08:05, 11; compare Act 21:37), and to a Greek woman at Tyre who was a native of Syrian Phoenicia (Mar 07:26). Greek was certainly the common language between *Yeshua* and Pilate (Joh 19:20-22; Act 02:07-08, 10). Pilate, being an aristocrat, would have known Greek, and Pilate had many Greek-speaking subjects of Jewish and gentile extraction.

Galilean Greek (Luk 23:05-06) must not have been as distinctive as Galilean Aramaic (Mat 26:73; Mar 14:70). Peter may have spoken Aramaic to the Jews in

Jerusalem, but he was recognized for having a Galilean accent. This suggests that Aramaic was the second language in Galilee. *Yeshua* surely spoke Greek to Pilate, but Pilate had to be told that *Yeshua* was a Galilean. This suggests that *Yeshua* was a fluent Greek speaker, and that Greek was the indigenous language of Galilee of the Gentiles.

That Galileans spoke Greek may be why the Judeans were prejudiced against the idea of there being a Galilean prophet (Joh 07:41, 52). As Edersheim wrote:

> A Jewish Messiah who would urge his claim upon Israel in Greek, seems almost a contradiction in terms.[141]

That is apparently what the Jewish leaders mistakenly thought, too, as though being bilingual or trilingual were a handicap!

Edersheim's argument, however, seems based on the false assumption that *Yeshua* was monolingual, and that he either knew Greek or Aramaic, but not both. *Yeshua* used Aramaic, Greek and Hebrew as appropriate. No one should reject the Messiah on account of his use of Greek during his earthly ministry.

What helped *Yeshua* and others speak Greek fluently without a strong, distinctive accent is that Attic Koine Greek was standardized on Athenian Greek already in Alexander's time. Moreover, Aristophanes of Byzantium created a system of accent and breathing marks that helped standardize the pronunciation of Attic Koine Greek starting around 200 BC.

Later, Peter spoke to Cornelius of the Italian Regiment as well as to Cornelius' friends and family (Act 10:01). Cornelius did not learn Aramaic in Italy, but he likely learned Greek there. Learning the Greek language and culture was common in ancient Italy.

The Romans were helped in their quest to learn Greek by the fact that ancient Latin and Greek are related Indo-European languages. Proximity helped Romans learn Greek, since the Greek mainland was not far from Italy. Moreover, in B.C. times the Greeks had colonized the southern end of Italy and other nearby areas. So the account of Cornelius is further proof that *Yeshua* must have spoken Greek since his disciples both spoke and wrote Greek well.

Yeshua Taught in Greek-speaking Areas

The Greeks had settled many areas in Palestine. The Hellenized cities of Sepphoris and Tiberias were near Nazareth. Since *Yeshua* visited Hellenistic cities during his ministry years, it would be consistent for *Yeshua* to have done so also during his pre-ministry years.

The disciples seemed to have had no scruples about buying food at Samaritan towns (Joh 04:08). In fact, the disciples were shocked that the Samaritans once refused them food. The refusal occurred only because *Yeshua* and his disciples were traveling to Jerusalem for a feast (Luk 09:53).

It seems the rift between the Jews and Samaritans was kept alive mainly over the dispute about whether the temple belonged at Mount Gerizim or Jerusalem (Joh 04:20-21). It is well known that many Jews avoided Samaria on their way between

Judea and Galilee when possible (Joh 04:04). The Samaritans were not happy about Galilean Jews bypassing Mount Gerizim to attend feasts at Jerusalem (Luk 09:53).

The Samaritans thought that only the Pentateuch was canonical. Mount Gerizim (Deu 11:29; 27:12; Jos 08:33; Jdg 09:07) figures more prominently in the Pentateuch than does Jerusalem (Gen 14:18). So this may have been a reason why the Samaritans figured Gerizim ought to be the site of the temple rather than Jerusalem.

Several of *Yeshua*'s disciples grew up fishing on the Sea of Galilee. Surely, their customers included the inhabitants of the Hellenized cities of Tiberias and Gadara. Tiberias was situated on the Sea of Galilee, which is also named the Sea of Tiberias and Lake Kineret. This lake is mentioned several times in the gospels (Mat 04:18; 15:29; Mar 01:16; 07:31; Joh 06:01, 23; 21:01).

Gadara was a few miles southeast of the Sea of Galilee, in the region called the Gadarenes (Mat 08:28; Mar 05:01; Luk 08:26). Gadara belonged to the Decapolis (Mat 04:25; Mar 05:20; 07:31), a confederacy of ten Roman-controlled cities in northeast Palestine originally settled by Greeks. The confederacy was formed after 63 BC and was dominated by Damascus.

The Greek cynic philosopher Menippus and other Greek thinkers lived in Gadara. Some liberals have proposed that *Yeshua* was a wandering Stoic–Cynic preacher who called on men to repent and to be virtuous. To propose that *Yeshua* was a Greek thinker must mean these liberals thought *Yeshua* spoke Greek.

The Greeks must have noticed that *Yeshua* preached in the Greek-speaking areas of Palestine. That must be why some Greeks came to see *Yeshua* at the temple (Joh 12:20-22). Interestingly, right before the Greeks came to see *Yeshua*, the Pharisees complained that the whole world was following *Yeshua* (Joh 12:19). It would seem odd for Greeks to search *Yeshua* out at the temple if *Yeshua* did not speak Greek!

The Jewish authorities in Jerusalem also noted that *Yeshua* taught Greeks and Greek-speaking Jews in Palestine. That is why the Jewish authorities at the temple figured *Yeshua* might go teach the Greeks as well as the diaspora, Greek-speaking Jews around the Mediterranean (Joh 07:35, 41, 52; also see Act 21:28). The Jewish authorities' words were:

> Where does this man intend to go that we will be unable to find him?
> Will he go where our people live scattered among the Greeks, and teach
> the Greeks? (Joh 07:35).

That the Jewish authorities thought *Yeshua* would teach Greek speakers is significant. If *Yeshua*'s disciples mainly spoke Aramaic, the Jewish authorities would have supposed *Yeshua* would go among the Aramaic-speaking diaspora Jews in Mesopotamia (Act 02:09). That the Jewish authorities figured *Yeshua* had a better chance of eluding their grasp among the Greek-speaking diaspora suggests that *Yeshua* was fluent in Greek.

Besides, the Jewish authorities may have heard that *Yeshua* was once taken to the Greek-speaking diaspora in Egypt to elude Herod's forces (Mat 02:13-15).

Even after his return from Egypt, Joseph was warned in a dream to leave Aramaic-speaking Judea for Greek-speaking Galilee (Mat 02:21-22). So the Jewish authorities likely figured out that, to avoid arrest (Mat 21:46; Mar 12:12; 14:01; Luk 20:19), *Yeshua* avoided Judea and traveled in Greek-speaking Galilee and Syrian Phoenicia (Mat 15:21; Joh 04:03).

The factor that suggested to the Jewish authorities that *Yeshua* would go to the Greek-speaking diaspora must have been his use of Greek. It was not as though the Jews had greater access to the Fertile Crescent than to the Mediterranean. The NT shows that the Jewish leadership could send letters and cause evangelists trouble around the Mediterranean as surely as they could chase down people in the Fertile Crescent (Mat 23:15; Act 09:02; 21:28; 22:05; 28:21-23).

Yeshua likely spoke Greek to his arresters. They were a Roman cohort, officers of the temple guards, and officials of the chief priests and Pharisees (Luk 22:52; Joh 18:03). Jerusalem was an international city where several languages were spoken, and the Jews and Romans who arrested *Yeshua* were likely more sophisticated than most.

Apparently, only officers of the temple guards, but not the temple guards themselves, were sent. The guards were not trusted since they had failed to arrest *Yeshua* once before due to *Yeshua*'s persuasive words (Joh 07:32, 45-47). The commander of the cohort was a tribune (*chiliarchos*). Tribunes were usually in charge of Roman troops (Joh 18:12; Act 21:33; 22:24, 27, 28, 29; 23:10, 19, 22; Act 24:22).

The cohort is called a *speira* (Joh 18:03, 12), a Greek word derived from the Latin word meaning, "cohort." *Speira* is found seven times in the NT, and each time *speira* refers to a Roman cohort (Mat 27:27; Mar 15:16; Joh 18:03, 12; Act 10:01; 21:31; 27:01).

Unfortunately, the word *speira* is often translated as "soldiers" in Joh 18:03 and 18:12. So the reader is given no clue that a Roman cohort assisted with *Yeshua*'s arrest. That Romans were involved with *Yeshua*'s arrest would not be a unique occurrence in the NT. Romans arrested Paul and handed him over to the Sanhedrin (Act 21:31-41, 22:24-30).

Yeshua likely spoke Greek to the *speira* that arrested him, since Paul spoke Greek to the commander of the *speira* that arrested him (Act 21:31, 37). Likely the same cohort arrested both *Yeshua* and Paul. This cohort was stationed next to the temple at fortress Antonia. Of course, the cohort likely had different personnel since the arrest of *Yeshua* and Paul occurred decades apart.

Yeshua likely spoke Greek to his arresters since Greek was the only language that the entire arresting party understood. Surely the "officers" and "officials" and Roman soldiers all knew Greek. So *Yeshua*'s "I AM" statements that caused the soldiers to fall to their knees were quotations of the name "I AM" as given in the LXX (Joh 18:05-08). The "I AM" and the Song of Moses chapters discuss the "I AM" statements in Joh 18 further.

Whether the Disciples Were Hellenized or Hebraic Jews

Background

Whether the disciples were Hellenized Jews or Hebraic Jews speaks volumes about the leader who chose them, especially since they chose to stay with him (Joh 06:67-71).

The Evidence in Names

A person's name tends to indicate the culture into which the person was born. A roll call of the disciples reveals that:
- Two disciples had Aramaic nicknames (Cephas and Thomas), but were also known by the Greek equivalents (Peter and Didymus),
- Two disciples had Greek names (Andrew and Philip),
- Two disciples were known by the Grecized (Hellenized) Hebrew name "James," which comes from the name "Jacob," and
- One disciple, Simon, was known by a Greek title *Zelotes*, meaning, "Zealot."

So six of the eleven disciples from Galilee were known by Greek or Grecized names, and a seventh was known by a Greek title.

Names help to determine the degree of Hellenization in first century Galilee. Consider how some Greeks at the temple wanted to see *Yeshua* (Joh 12:20-22). These Greeks first approached Philip, who in turn approached Andrew. Then both Philip and Andrew approached *Yeshua* with the Greeks' request to see him. So it seems significant that the only two disciples with Greek given names were involved when the Greeks wanted to see *Yeshua*.

The names seem to indicate that the disciples were more or less Hellenized Jews. This is what one would expect since all the disciples but Judas were from the Galilee of the Gentiles (Isa 09:01; Mat 04:15). This explains why *Yeshua* had to tell his disciples to go to the predominantly Aramaic-speaking Judeans first before going to the Greek-speaking gentiles (Mat 10:05; Luk 24:47; Act 01:08). The eleven Galilean disciples would have found it easier to evangelize Greek speakers, and the only disciple from Judea (Judas) was no more.

Yeshua's Aramaic title *Messias* is mentioned only twice in the NT (Joh 01:41; 04:25). *Messias* is the Aramaic equivalent of the Hebrew *Meshiach* (Messiah), meaning, "Anointed." *Yeshua*, however, was commonly called by the Greek equivalent of the Aramaic *Messias*, namely, *Christos* (Mat 01:16; 27:17, 22; Joh 01:41; 04:25). *Yeshua's* popular title *Christos* was used 546 times in the NT instead of the Aramaic form *Messias*.

If *Yeshua* did not speak Greek, one would expect that more titles and more words would be transliterated rather than translated in the NT. These facts suggest that *Yeshua's* followers were thoroughly Hellenized, and that *Yeshua* himself was a Hellenized Jew. This may be one reason why Pilate had the sign over the cross written in Aramaic, Greek and Latin (Joh 19:20). The Latin, of course, was meant for the Romans from all parts of the empire.

Yeshua's ministry was mostly carried on in Hellenized areas. Thus, one could say that *Yeshua* was more commonly known by the Greek equivalent of his name, *Iesous* (pronounced "yay-zoos" or "yay-soos") (Mat 01:16; 22:17, 22; Joh 09:11).

The Aramaic name *Yeshua* was derived from the Hebrew for Joshua. Greek-speaking LXX users referred to the OT Joshua as *Iesous* at least two hundred years before *Yeshua*'s time. The form *Iesous* is used 218 times in 199 LXX verses. Translations that preceded the LXX probably introduced the Greek form *Iesous* even earlier.

Hellenized children must have been commonly named *Iesous*. The NT mentions only a representative sample of Hellenized Jewish names, but the name *Iesous* happens to appear twice (Act 13:06; Col 04:11). That *Yeshua* had many Hellenized followers, and that he was commonly known by the Greek equivalent of the name Joshua, suggests that *Yeshua* was a Hellenized Jew.

The disciples' Greek or Grecized names tend to indicate their cultural background, and even what language the people they evangelized spoke. Take, for example, Saul. Saul was born to Jewish parents who lived in the Greek-speaking colony of Tarsus (Act 09:11, 30; 11:25; 21:39; 22:03). Since Saul was a Roman citizen, Paul may have been Saul's Latin name.[142]

Between Act 07:58 and Act 13:07, Paul was known only as Saul. From Act 13:07 on, however, Saul went by the name of Paul—at least among those who primarily spoke Greek or Latin (Act 22:07, 13-14). The shift from Saul to Paul occurs when Saul was instrumental in the conversion of the Roman proconsul of the isle of Cyprus, Sergius Paulus.

Sergius is Latin meaning, "earth born," and *Paulus* is Latin meaning, "small." That Paul primarily evangelized gentiles from this point on explains the transition from Saul to Paul. The conversion of Sergius Paulus (Act 13) was a significant ministry move for Paul. Previously, Paul had debated with "Grecian Jews, but they tried to kill him" (Act 09:29).

It must have been the Grecian Jews (Act 06:01) scattered from Jerusalem who first evangelized the Greeks in significant numbers (Act 11:18-20). Interestingly, the persecution that scattered the Grecian Jews from Jerusalem began with Stephen's martyrdom. Ironically, it was Paul who guarded the coats of those who stoned Stephen (Act 07:58). Paul preached mainly in synagogues to the Jews, but in Act 13 Paul began his ministry among the gentiles in earnest. This was the ministry for which he was set apart (Act 09:15; 13:02; Rom 11:13; Gal 02:07-08; 1Ti 02:07).

The ministry shift from Jews to gentile caused John Mark to leave Paul and Barnabas and return to Jerusalem (Act 12:12, 25; 13:13; 15:37-41). John Mark was comfortable evangelizing Jews. Paul even mentioned that John Mark was helpful in the synagogues (Act 13:05).

Interestingly, John Mark abandoned Paul in Perga in Pamphylia, the last stop before Paul and Barnabas headed into the interior of Asia Minor. In the interior there were fewer Jews, and the native language was Anatolian rather than Greek (Act 14:12).

The ministry shift in Act 13 is indicated by a quote of Isa 49:06 after the conversion of some Greek-speaking gentiles:

> For this is what the Lord has commanded us: 'I have made you a light for the Gentiles, that you may bring salvation to the ends of the earth' (Act 13:47).

Paul's turning to the gentiles each time the Jews rejected him (Act 09:29; 13:46) was a fulfillment of Isaiah's prophecy. This is paralleled in *Yeshua*'s ministry. *Yeshua* attempted to conduct his earliest ministry in Judea (Joh 01:43; 04:01-03). When John was put in prison, *Yeshua* withdrew to Capernaum in the Galilee of the Gentiles (Mat 04:12-13). Matthew then quoted Isaiah's prophecy that said a light came to the gentiles who lived in darkness (Isa 09:01-02; Mat 04:14-16).

Interestingly, we find that a Roman centurion had the synagogue in Capernaum built (Luk 07:01-06). Since the Roman centurion surely knew Greek, one can assume the synagogue used the Greek LXX for readings.

Later, *Yeshua* again retreated to the Galilee of the Gentiles when the Pharisees plotted to take his life (Mat 12:14-15). Matthew then quotes Isa 42:01-04 that speaks of the Messiah preaching to the gentiles (Mat 12:17-21). So from the time of Isaiah to the time Christ, Galilee was considered the land of gentiles (Isa 09:01). During the Passion Week, *Yeshua* said:

> Is it not written: 'My house will be called a house of prayer for all nations?' But you have made it into a den of robbers (Mar 11:17).

So these facts seem to indicate that *Yeshua*'s ministry was conducted mainly among Greek-speaking Jews and gentiles (Mat 15:26-27).

Beyond the Evidence of Names

Some of *Yeshua*'s disciples were formerly followers of John the Baptist (Joh 01:37-42; Act 01:21-26). John ministered in at least two locations. One place was "Bethany beyond the Jordan" across from Jerusalem, and another was at the Samaritan-Galilean border at Aenon by Salim.

Aenon is often located near the Jordan about fifteen miles south of the Sea of Galilee. Andrew and John were one-time disciples of John (Joh 01:35-40). The Aenon location helps explain why some of *Yeshua*'s disciples were from the heavily Hellenized Galilee of the Gentiles (Isa 09:01; Mat 04:15). Judas, however, was from southern Judea.

John spoke to Roman soldiers, almost certainly in Greek (Luk 03:14; Act 21:37). John's baptism made its way to Greek-speaking areas such as Alexandria and Asia Minor (Act 18:24-25; 19:03-04). So it seems appropriate that Luke's quote of Isaiah applied to John the Baptist follows the Greek LXX. The phrase "all flesh shall see the salvation of God" is especially apropos since it refers to both Jew and gentile (Isa 40:03-05; Luk 03:04-06).

John baptized near the heavily Hellenized Galilee of the Gentiles and ministered to Hellenized Jews and even to Roman soldiers. This suggests that John the Baptist and his disciples were Hellenized Jews. That some of John's disciples became *Yeshua*'s disciples suggests that *Yeshua* was a Hellenized Jew, too.

If *Yeshua* primarily spoke Aramaic, one would expect that:
- Most of his disciples and followers would speak Aramaic,
- Grecian Jews and Greeks would have only trickled into the Church while the gospel ignited the Fertile Crescent (Act 06:01; 11:20),
- All the gospels would have been written in Aramaic originally, and there would be plenty of extant copies even today, and
- There would also have been several epistles to the Aramaic Jews in Mesopotamia, an Aramaic apocalyptic book similar to Revelation, and more Aramaic apocryphal and pseudepigraphal books.

Compared to the volume of early Church Greek literature, next to nothing was written in Aramaic. Instead, the NT books and early Church literature were written in fluent Attic Koine Greek. Christian writings in Aramaic only came at a later date except in far-off Mesopotamia, as J. S. Trimingham wrote:

> …within a few years of Jesus' death-rising…owing to the strong hold that Hellenist humanism had gained in Syria, the Gospel expression was almost exclusively through the medium of Greek, though without being able to do more than submerge the Aramean substratum which was finding more direct expression in Mesopotamia.[143]

Trimingham noted the language situation in Palestinian churches in the fourth century:

> The worship of the Christians was conducted through Greek, but the fact that the services, especially the gospel lections and discourses, were translated orally into Aramaic, shows that the majority of the people were Aramaeans.[144]

Notice that Trimingham only says the majority race was Aramean. The fact that the service was conducted in Greek suggests that the majority of Arameans in the fourth century knew Greek. Here are some details that Trimingham provides to back up his statement:

> Eusebius [circa 264–340 AD] reports that Procopius, a native of Aelia [*Aelia Capitolina*: a Roman name for Jerusalem], used to translate for the congregation of Scythopolis (Beisan in Palestine II). Egeria (circa 385 AD) writes, 'In this province [Palestine] there are some people who know both Greek and Syriac, but others know only one or the other. The bishop may know Syriac, but never uses it. He always speaks in Greek, and has a presbyter beside him who translates the Greek into Syriac, so that everyone can understand what he means. Similarly, the lessons read in church have to be read in Greek, but there is always someone in attendance to translate into Syriac so that [all] the people can understand.'[145]

Matthew, Mark, John, James, Peter, Jude, and perhaps even Luke and the author of Hebrews, heard *Yeshua* speak at some point. They apparently knew

Greek very well, judging from the books rightly attributed to them. If *Yeshua* were challenged by Greek and needed an interpreter, one would expect this to be noted somewhere in the NT.

No interpreter is mentioned even when *Yeshua* visited predominantly Greek-speaking areas of Palestine. *Yeshua* apparently had no difficulty talking to people who may have known only Greek and some Latin, such as the Greek woman from Syrian Phoenicia, the Roman soldiers, and Pontius Pilate.

Paul also talked to *Yeshua* several times (Act 09:04-06; 23:11; 2Co 12:02). The conversation may have been in Greek, Paul's native tongue, except for the time that Paul was on his way to Damascus (Act 26:14). During this incident, Aramaic was spoken to keep the conversation confidential between Paul and *Yeshua*.

After introducing himself in Greek to the Roman commander (Act 21:37), Paul addressed the crowd in Aramaic and recounted how *Yeshua* met him on the road to Damascus (Act 22:02). Another time Paul told the account in Greek, but mentioned that *Yeshua* had spoken in Aramaic (Act 26:14). Those who heard a re-counting might have been surprised on two counts—that the:

- Greek-speaking Galilean, *Yeshua*, spoke Aramaic, too, and
- The apostle who taught Greeks and brought Greeks to Jerusalem (Act 22:28-29) spoke Aramaic besides (Act 21:40; 22:02; 26:14).

The crowd (Act 22:21-22) and Festus (Act 26:23-24) both interrupted Paul at the same point in the account. They could stand to hear no more once Paul said *Yeshua* told him to bring the gospel to the gentiles. Festus said, "Your great learning is driving you insane" (Act 26:24). Evidently, it was just too incredible that *Yeshua* and now Paul could evangelize *effectively* in two languages (emphasis on "effectively").

There was no interlude after the ascension when the apostles had an opportunity to learn Greek fluently from scratch. Early on the Church had to deal with per-ceived conflicts between Grecian Jews and Hebraic Jews (Act 06:01-15). In fact, *Yeshua* had already attracted Greeks during his ministry at the temple (Joh 12:20-21). Also, there must have been Greek speakers in Galilee and in Syria Phoenicia who became Christian early on due to *Yeshua*'s ministry there. This all suggests that the disciples knew Greek fluently from childhood.

Similarly, outreach to foreign Greek-speaking gentiles came very early. For in-stance, Philip spoke to the Ethiopian eunuch. The language used was likely Greek, since Philip surely did not know Coptic or another Ethiopian language. After bap-tizing the eunuch, Philip preached in the Greek-speaking coastal towns including Caesarea (Act 08:27-40).

Another instance of the evangelization of Greek speakers occurred when Peter talked to Cornelius of the Italian Regiment, as well as to his family and friends (Act 10:01). Cornelius surely knew Greek as other Roman commanders did (Act 21:37), and there is almost no chance that Cornelius learned Aramaic in Italy. So anyway, it is significant that after Pentecost, with a few exceptions, the rest of the NT records contacts with Greek speakers.

The Post-Ascension, Pre-Pentecost Evidence

Another incident that shows the disciples were Hellenized Galileans is Act 02. The diaspora Jews were surprised that the tongues-speakers from Galilee (Act 02: 07) could speak the languages of many nations—including Judea (Act 02:09). This shows that the majority of Galileans were perceived as being Greek speakers, while the majority of Judeans were perceived as being Aramaic speakers.

That the Judeans tended to speak Aramaic while the Galileans tended to speak Greek explains the necessity of Peter's explanation to his followers, who at the time were mostly Galilean:

Everyone in Jerusalem heard about this, so they [the Judeans in Jerusalem] called that field **in their own [Aramaic] language** *Akeldama*, that is, 'Field of Blood' (Act 01:19).

The Greek words translated "in their own language" are "*idios dialektos*." It is true that bilingual Galileans, who spoke both Greek and Aramaic, had a different Aramaic accent than that found in Judea (Mat 26:73). The fact that Peter had to give a definition of the word *Akeldama* shows that Peter was referring to different languages, not to distinct dialects or accents. This is also consistent with how the Greek phrase "*idios dialektos*" is used in the rest of the LXX or NT. All three occurrences refer to distinct languages rather than dialects or accents (Act 01:19; 02: 06, 08).

Some translations put parentheses around Act 01:18-19. This is an attempt to construe the "in their own language" verses as Luke's aside to Theophilus (Luk 01:03; Act 01:01). The note would indicate that *Akeldama* was an Aramaic word transliterated into Greek.

The *NIV* is one of the modern translations that treats Act 01:18-19 as though it were Luke's rather than Peter's comment. So that the passage still makes sense in context, the *NIV* inserts the words "said Peter" after the comment (Act 01:20). However, if Luke meant Act 01:18-19 as a comment, it seems he would have inserted the word "said Peter" himself. Somehow Luke would have indicated that he was making a parenthetical comment.

Modern translators enclose Act 01:18-19 in parentheses based on misinformation. Modern exegetes and translators were taught in school long ago that both Galilean and Judeans considered Aramaic to be their native language. So it just would not do to have Peter, a Galilean, saying that Aramaic was "their own language" when Aramaic was Peter's language, too. By contrast, the King James Bible translators apparently had no problem with Act 01:18-19 being part of Peter's speech. The *KJV* translators must have thought the Galileans spoke Greek while the Judeans spoke Aramaic.

Recently, archeologists have changed their story and say that Greek was prevalent everywhere in first century Palestine. Exegetes and translators, however, have yet to catch up to the new evidence and findings. So Peter, the Greek-speaking Galilean, likely referred to Aramaic as "their own language," because Judeans tended to speak Aramaic while Galileans tended to speak Greek. Thus,

Act 01:18-19 should be interpreted as an integral part of Peter's speech, and not just a comment by the narrator, Luke.

The Evidence from the Act 02 Pentecost

At Pentecost, the Jews of the diaspora were only interested in how the Galileans (Act 02:07) could miraculously speak in "other languages" (Greek: "*heterais glwssais*") (Act 02:04). So a nation omitted from the Act 02 list of nations would be one that spoke the same language that the Galileans tended to speak. The dominant languages of the nations listed in the Act 02 were Anatolian, Arabic, Aramaic, Coptic, Demotic Egyptian, Doric Greek, and Latin.

The glaring omission from the Act 02 list of nations is the nation where Attic Koine Greek originated: Greece and its environs. The Jews must have perceived that both the first century Galileans and the Greeks tended to speak the same language—Attic Koine Greek. Greece is not found in the Act 02 list of nations for the same reason that Galilee is not in the list—it would not have been miraculous for Galileans to speak their own language!

By contrast, Judea did make the Act 02 list of nations because the diaspora Jews perceived that the first century Judeans tended to speak Aramaic while Galileans tended to speak Greek.

Whether the Pentecost Tongues-speakers Were All Galilean

The details of Act 02 serve to buttress the above interpretation of Act 02 against possible objections. For example, someone might propose that the tongues-speakers were not all Galileans. Then no conclusions could be drawn from what nations were included or excluded from the Act 02 list.

Note that the diaspora Jews indicate that all the tongues-speakers were Galilean (Act 02:07). Besides, if the tongues-speakers were not all from Galilee, than the miracle of Pentecost would not be as awesome as was described by the diaspora Jews (Act 02:08, 11-12).

There may have been twelve or one hundred twenty tongues-speakers (Act 01: 15, 26). Approximately seven major languages are represented in the Act 02 list of a dozen or so nations and provinces. This suggests that only the twelve disciples were speaking in tongues. The diaspora Jews said:

> We hear them declaring the wonders of God in our own tongues! (Act 02:11).

This seems to indicate that only about seven languages were represented. If there were more languages than seven, it would have been a cacophony. Then no one would have been able to say they understood anything (Act 02:11).

The fact that they all had been in one house when the tongues of flame rested on their heads suggests that there were just twelve tongues-speakers. If there were just twelve, the Jews would have been able to determine their nationality easily. Their Galilean accent and perhaps their clothing were clues (Mat 26:73).

The diaspora Jews' statement that the tongues-speakers were Galilean was confirmed by no less than angels. Shavuot (Pentecost, Whitsunday) occurred seven weeks after the resurrection. *Yeshua*'s ascension occurred forty days after the resurrection (Act 01:03). This meant that Pentecost occurred only ten days after the angels called the ascension watchers "men of Galilee" (Act 01:11). The ascension watchers were the same Galileans who spoke in tongues on Pentecost. This analysis further suggests that there were only twelve tongues-speakers.

The tongues-speakers likely were all Galilean for various reasons:
- *Yeshua*'s disciples and followers tended to be Galilean because of the language barrier. While many Galileans and Judeans were bilingual, still, the Galilean's language of choice was Greek while the Judean's language of choice was Aramaic,
- Judean supporters of *Yeshua* likely were disillusioned when *Yeshua*'s only Judean disciple committed suicide after betraying *Yeshua* (Act 01:18-19),
- The disciples kept a low profile out of fear of Judean Jews (Joh 20:19). This meant Judeans would not as readily be included in their close-knit group, and
- Logistics caused Judean followers to drift away because the disciples had traveled to Galilee and then back to Jerusalem shortly before Pentecost (Mat 28:07, 16; Mar 16:07).

Analysis of the Languages of the Nations Listed in Act 02

Language purists might criticize the analysis of what languages were spoken in the nations listed in Act 02. Further analysis, however, should leave this inference intact: the Galileans and nearby Hellenists such as the Greeks in the Decapolis tended to speak an Attic Koine Greek that somewhat approximated the Greek spoken in Greece by commoners.

The analysis is simplified in that the diaspora Jews only referred to languages they spoke personally. They said:

> We hear them declaring the wonders of God in our own tongues! (Act 02:11).

The diaspora Jews were not referring to minor dialects. They were referring to the languages of commerce and government that they, but not Galileans, spoke.

The diaspora Jews from the Mideast countries of Parthia, Media, Elam, Mesopotamia and Judea likely were referring to Aramaic. The Arab Jews likely were referring to the proto-Arabic spoke in Nabataea. The Jews and gentile converts from Rome referred to Latin.

The Jews from Asia Minor (modern Turkey) came from the provinces of Asia, Cappadocia, Pamphylia, Phrygia and Pontus. They were likely referring to the Anatolian language, the native language of interior Asia Minor. The Jews who lived in the interior of Asia Minor were able to speak the language of the indigenous population. That is why in Lystra, in the interior of Asia Minor, the Jews were able to win over the gentile crowd from Paul and Barnabas. Paul and Barnabas did not speak Lycaonian, an Anatolian dialect (Act 14:11).

The reason Paul did not know Anatolian is that Paul grew up in a southern coastal city of Asia Minor. Tarsus used to be a Greek colony, and Greek was likely the dominant language there. Paul did not have a chance to learn Anatolian before he was sent off for schooling in Jerusalem.

Greek is why most of Paul's missionary journeys were spent along the coasts of the Mediterranean. On the coasts that Paul visited, he could count on Attic Greek being either the primary or secondary language of commerce and government. For instance, it would be hard for the Jewish Christians Aquila and Priscilla not to know Attic Greek while doing business in Rome (Act 18:02; Rom 16:03), Corinth (Act 18:02), Syria (Act 18:18) and Ephesus (Act 18:19, 26; 1Co 16:08, 19).

The Jews in the major cities of Egypt spoke Attic Koine Greek. There the OT was translated into the Attic Koine Greek LXX. Attic Koine Greek was the language of commerce and government in the Hellenized lands conquered by Alexander the Great (356-323 BC), and these lands included Galilee and Egypt. Richard Cavendish wrote:

> After the conquest of Egypt by Alexander the Great in 331 BC the country was ruled by Greeks for 300 years, and during this period the cult of Isis became completely Hellenized. When the Romans took over the government in 30 BC they relied on the support of the Greek middle class in Egypt and the language of administration remained Greek.[146]

So at Pentecost, the Jews from Egypt would not think it miraculous that the Galileans spoke Attic Koine Greek, especially since the LXX helped standardize the Greek spoken and written by the Galilean Jewry. This would be similar to how Martin Luther's Bible translation helped to standardize German.

The reader might wonder whether Attic Koine Greek resembled the Greek spoken on the Greek peninsula. The Greek language developed on and off the Greece mainland together. Evidently, there was enough sea and overland travel and trade, and shared literature and government (empires), that Attic Koine Greek remained fairly uniform for centuries over a wide geographical area.

Not until the fifth century AD was there a split. The influential Atticist school convinced writers to return to writing in classical Attic Greek, which became known as Byzantine Greek. The continuing development of spoken Attic Koine Greek from the fifth to the fifteenth centuries AD caused an ever-widening divergence between Attic Koine and Byzantine Greek.

Attic Koine Greek was standardized by a system of accent and breathing marks introduced around 200 BC, reputedly by Aristophanes of Byzantium. Attic Koine Greek may have been the only language to have diacritical marks until the Masoretes pointed the Hebrew MT recension from the sixth to tenth centuries AD. Only in modern times did dictionaries provide pronunciation keys that serve the same purpose.

That Attic Koine was standardized had its benefits. At least during the NT period, Attic Koine Greek speakers in Greece and around the Mediterranean found their speech and writing mutually comprehensible. This explains why Paul was able to evangelize many places in Greek. Also, Paul was able to walk around

Athens reading inscriptions, quoting Greek poets, and converse with the philosophers at the Areopagus (Act 17).

The language situation in the interior of Greece, however, is a separate matter from the coasts where Attic Greek was the norm. Athens was a sea power, and rarely controlled the interior mainland of Greece. Aristophanes' pronunciation system and other means of standardization did not exist when different dialects became established in the Grecian interior.

The dialects resulted from geographical isolation and Dorian immigrations. So early Greek colonists spread Doric, Aeolic, Ionic-Attic, and Arcado-Cypriot Greek around the Mediterranean in the centuries preceding the conquests of Alexander the Great, who spread Attic Greek.

Attic Koine Greek and the other Greek dialects were on different developmental paths even before leaving the mainland. So after several more centuries of development, the linguistic rift between Attic Koine Greek and other Greek dialects bordered on mutual unintelligibility. Doric Greek was spoken in Libya, Crete, and elsewhere, and Arcado-Cypriot was spoken in Cyprus.

During Pentecost, there were Jews in Jerusalem from Libya's chief city, Cyrene, as well as from the island of Crete. Doric-speaking Greeks had colonized these and other places long before Alexander's conquests, so the Jews from these places were familiar with Doric Greek. Doric Greek was a dialect many miles and several centuries removed from Attic Koine Greek. It took some effort for Koine Greek speakers to communicate with the Doric Greek speakers of Crete, Libya and elsewhere.[147]

The same situation pertained to Jews from Cyprus, since the language situation with Arcado-Cypriot Greek was similar to that of Doric Greek. This explains why, even though Jews spoke a Greek dialect in Libya and Crete, these places made the Act 02 list of nations (Act 02:10-11). That Galileans spoke dialects of Greek incomprehensible to Attic Koine Greek speakers seemed miraculous.

Since the majority of Egyptians did not speak Greek, Jews in Egypt who traveled outside the Hellenized cities needed to know either Coptic[148] or Demotic Egyptian. This is analogous to how Paul grew up in Tarsus and spoke Greek fluently. The Anatolian dialects spoken in the interior of Asia Minor, however, were incomprehensible to Greek speakers on the coasts (Act 14:11).

That most Egyptians did not know Greek is reflected in a curious incident in Jerusalem. A Roman commander was surprised that Paul spoke Greek. Rioters misled the commander by claiming that Paul was the notorious outlaw fugitive, "The Egyptian" (Act 21:37-38).[149] This shows why Egypt made the Act 02 list of nations—most Egyptians did not know Greek. The Egyptian Jews were surprised, not that Galileans could speak Attic Greek, but that the tongues-speakers spoke Coptic or Demotic Egyptian.

The Implications of Whether *Yeshua* Spoke Primarily in Greek or Predominantly in Aramaic

This chapter has shown that *Yeshua* spoke Greek. This chapter also makes the case that *Yeshua* spoke primarily in Greek. Some critics, of course, will hold tenaciously to the misconception that *Yeshua* nearly always spoke Aramaic. This likely has to do with the theological liberals' desire to deny that *Yeshua* ever identified himself as:

- The "I AM," as is discussed in the "I AM" and the Song of Moses chapters, and as
- The subject of the *Shema* along with the Father, as is discussed in the *Shema* chapter.

This sort of denial seems plausible to those who do not see the Trinity in the OT. Moreover, it helps deniers if they can also miss or misconstrue the many passages that speak of, or suggest, the deity of the Messiah. These passages are discussed in the Trinitarian proofs appendix.

For the sake of argument, however, let us assume there are no Trinitarian proofs in the OT. Also, let us assume that there are no texts that suggest, or speak clearly of, the Messiah's deity. Still, it is a furtive ploy for critics to say that *Yeshua* spoke Aramaic just so no one can tell whether:

- *Yeshua* said he was "I AM," or
- *Yeshua* applied OT *Yahveh* texts to himself.

The reason the denial is futile is that material written in one language is often quoted in another language, and the quote is still recognizable as a quote. We need not even go outside the Bible for examples:

- The very sign that hung on *Yeshua*'s cross translated Pilate's original Latin words into Greek and Aramaic (Joh 19:20),
- The LXX is, more or less, one long quote of the OT Hebrew, and
- The NT Greek contains numerous recognizable quotations of OT Hebrew.

At least some of *Yeshua*'s audience and the disciples were bilingual or even polyglot, as was argued earlier in this chapter. These persons would have recognized a quote or an allusion, no matter whether *Yeshua* was speaking in Greek, Aramaic or Hebrew. Thus, it makes no difference whether *Yeshua* quoted or alluded to *Yahveh*'s OT "I AM" statements using Greek (*egw eimi*), Aramaic, or Hebrew (*Anee hu*).

The NT writers recorded *Yeshua*'s quotation of *Yahveh*'s OT "I AM" statements as they are found in the LXX (Deu 32:39, Isa 43:10, and the like). The NT writers also have *Yeshua* applying *Yahveh* texts to himself (as is discussed in the appendix on OT *Yahveh* quotations). The NT audience and NT writers knew the LXX well. There is no chance that they inadvertently made *Yeshua* sound as though he were applying "I AM" and *Yahveh* texts to himself. So in the case of the "I AM" quotations, whether *Yeshua* spoke in Greek, Aramaic or Hebrew makes no difference.

The NT writers also knew that a phrase is not always seen as a quote or allusion just on the basis of wording. The context should be taken into consideration. So the NT writers carefully gave the context for each "I AM" statement. For example, it would be farfetched to think every "I AM" in the Bible is a quote of *Yahveh*'s "I AM" statements (Joh 09:09). However, when:

- The *BHS* Hebrew of Exo 03:14 has *Yahveh* saying *ehyeh* ("I AM") three times,
- *Yeshua* was almost stoned (Joh 08:59) for saying, "I AM" (*egw eimi*) three times (Joh 08:24, 28, 58), and
- "I AM" (*egw eimi*) is mentioned three times in a few verses and a detachment of soldiers fell to their knees upon *Yeshua*'s mention of "I AM" (Joh 18:05-08),

then apparently at least some of *Yeshua*'s "I AM" statements should be considered quotations of *Yahveh*'s OT "I AM" statements (Exo 03:14, Isa 41:04, and the like).

In conclusion, this chapter shows that the Galileans and Judeans were familiar with both Greek and Aramaic. Many even knew Hebrew. So there is no chance that *Yeshua*'s many apparent "I AM" statements, and other overt quotations of OT *Yahveh* texts, are unintentional. There is no chance that some meaning was added in translation, either intentionally or unintentionally. It cannot be plausibly asserted that *Yeshua*'s "I AM" statements are anything but quotations or allusions to OT *Yahveh* texts.

Chapter 9

The "I AM" Statements

Background

The chapter on Proto-Sinaitic Trinitarianism mentions that Moses asked the name of the *Malek Yahveh* (Exo 03:13). Previously, the patriarchs knew only the Father as *Yahveh*, while the Son was known as the *Malek Yahveh, El Shaddai, Elohim* (God) and the like (Exo 06:03).

In response to Moses' request for a name, *Yahveh* the Son told Moses that his Name was *Yahveh* (Exo 03:15). The Son also declared himself to be "I AM," a surrogate Name for *Yahveh* found in the OT and NT (Exo 03:14). *Yahveh* the Son's words about being "I AM" read:

I AM who I AM [The Hebrew is *"ehyeh asher ehyeh"*].[150] This is what you are to say to the Israelites: I AM [The Hebrew is *ehyeh*] has sent me to you (Exo 03:14).

Note that the Hebrew word *ehyeh* is used as a signifier of deity whether *ehyeh* is the subject of the predicate, or is in the predicate. So apparently the "I AM" signifier of deity can be found in more than one grammatical construction.

Some, however, have claimed that the "I AM" signifier of deity is only found in "predicateless absolutes" such as in Joh 08:58. This view contradicts Exo 03:14, the very verse where the "I AM" Name was first revealed. Here, "I AM" does not stand alone, but has the predicates:

I AM who I AM...I AM has sent me to you (Exo 03:14).

The Hebrew of Exo 03:14 has *Yahveh* saying, "I AM" (*ehyeh*), three times. Interestingly, the Greek translators did not translate the second and third *ehyeh* with the same words used to translate the first "I AM." *"Egw eimi"* translates the first "I AM" (*ehyeh*), while *"ho wn"* is used in the LXX to translate the second and third instances of "I AM."

"Egw eimi" is the nominative pronoun (I) plus the present indicative of the verb "to be" (am). *"Ho wn"* is the definite article plus the present active participle of the verb "to be." The participle can here be interpreted with existential connotations such as "the Being One," or "He Who Exists," but a more literal rendering is "Who is."

The Greek LXX has *Yahveh* the Son saying:

I AM [*egw eimi*] WHO IS [*ho wn*].[151] This is what you are to say to the Israelites: 'WHO IS [*ho wn*] has sent me to you' (LXX Exo 03:14).

The LXX translates the Hebrew subject of the predicate *ehyeh* into Greek as "*egw eimi*." The Hebrew predicate "*asher ehyeh*" is translated into Greek as "*ho wn*" (WHO IS). The third instance of the Hebrew "*ehyeh*" is the subject of the sentence: "I AM [*ehyeh*] has sent me to you." This *ehyeh* is translated into Greek as "*ho wn*" (WHO IS).

In the second sentence "I AM [*ehyeh*] has sent me to you," one might think that the LXX translators would have used the "*egw eimi*" rather than "*ho wn*." This would have been consistent with the first phrase, which has "*egw eimi*" as the subject of the predicate: "I AM [*egw eimi*] WHO IS [*ho wn*]." This tends to show that the LXX translators thought of "*egw eimi*" and "*ho wn*" as equivalents, and that both were surrogate names for *Yahveh* meaning, "I AM." Additional facts that show the equivalency are:

- The underlying Hebrew translated into Greek as "*egw eimi*" and "*ho wn*" is nearly the same ("I AM" versus "Who I AM"), and
- No matter the language of translation, Exo 03:14 has been interpreted to indicate a Name with existential connotations, "I AM who I AM." Exo 03:14 has not been interpreted as God being complacently resigned about his personality, "I am who I am."

That Jews in the early centuries AD used "WHO IS" [*ho wn*] as a name for God is evident in the writing of Philo (circa 20 BC–circa AD 40). Philo commented on "I shall become known to thee from there" (LXX Exo 25:22) thus:

The purest and most prophetic mind [Moses] receives knowledge and understanding of the Existent One (*ho on* [*ho wn*]) not from the Existent One himself...but from his primary and guardian Powers (QE II 67).[152]

Goodenough also notes that on Jewish amulets that the angel representing the sun was sometimes called by the theophoric name the "Existing One" (*ho wn*).[153]

The NT Use of "I AM" ("*egw eimi*") and "WHO IS" (*Ho Wn*)

The NT writers followed the lead of the LXX translators and the Spirit. They applied the "I AM" ("*egw eimi*") and "WHO IS" (*ho wn*) from Exo 03:14 and other OT passages to *Yeshua* often. This is especially shown in Revelation where:

- The five "*ho wn*" passages in Revelation (Rev 01:04, 08; 04:08; 11:17; 16:05) have relative clauses similar to the wording "I AM WHO IS" found in LXX Exo 03:14, and
- Rev 01:08 has both surrogate names for *Yahveh* mentioned in LXX Exo 03:14: "*egw eimi*" and "*ho wn*."

This indicates that *Yeshua* was *Yahveh* the Son who said:

I AM [*egw eimi*] WHO IS [*ho wn*]...WHO IS [*ho wn*]...(LXX Exo 03:14).

The eight times that the NT writers applied the "*ho wn*" of Exo 03:14 to *Yeshua*, and the one time *Yeshua* applied the "*ho wn*" of Exo 03:14 to himself (Rev 01:08), are:

1) God the One and Only, 'WHO IS [*ho wn*]' at the Father's side, has made him known (Joh 01:18),
2) No one has seen the Father except the one 'WHO IS [*ho wn*]' from God (Joh 06:46),
3) Theirs are the patriarchs, and from them is traced the human ancestry of Christ, 'WHO IS [*ho wn*]' God over all, forever praised! Amen (Rom 09:05),
4) The God and Father of the Lord *Yeshua*, 'WHO IS [*ho wn*]' to be praised forever (2Co 11:31),
5) Grace and peace to you from him 'WHO IS [*ho wn*],' and who was, and who is to come (Rev 01:04),
6) "'I AM [*egw eimi*]' the Alpha and the Omega,' says the Lord God, "WHO IS [*ho wn*],' and who was, and who is to come, the Almighty" (Rev 01:08),
7) "Holy, holy, holy is the Lord God Almighty, who was, and 'WHO IS [*ho wn*],' and who is to come" (Rev 04:08),
8) "Lord God Almighty, the One 'WHO IS [*ho wn*]' and who was (Rev 11:17), because you have taken your great power and have begun to reign," and
9) "…you 'WHO IS [*ho wn*]' and who were, the Holy One" (Rev 16:05).

That *Yeshua* is the subject of the "*ho wn*" can be ascertained from the context. That *Yeshua* is the subject of "*ho wn*" in the:

- First four passages is clear to see, unless grammatical gymnastics are employed to deny the obvious (Joh 01:18; 06:46; Rom 09:05; 2Co 11:31),
- Fifth, sixth and seventh passages can be determined by noting that John said *Yeshua* is "to come" on the Last Day (Rev 01:04, 08; 04:08),
- Eighth passage can be established by noting that John said *Yeshua* has "begun to reign" after his ascension (Rev 11:17), and in the
- Ninth passage can be recognized from analysis of the details. Rev 15:08 mentions that only God was in the temple and no one else could enter the temple until the seven plagues were finished (Rev 16:01-21). Rev 15:03 mentions the Song of the Lamb. A loud voice from the temple warns that he will return like a thief in the night (Rev 16:15; compare with Mat 24:44 and 1Th 05:02). The voice from the temple also said, "It is done" (Rev 16:17; compare with Joh 19:30). The mention of the lamb, the thief and the words from the cross suggest that the Son is the person of God speaking from the temple. So he is also the person of God in the temple called "*ho wn*" (Rev 16:05).

What the "I AM" Phrase Means

Until now scholars have made their best guess as to what the phrase, "I AM who I AM," means. Reference has been made to several fields of study, including comparative religion studies, etymology, grammar, philosophy, metaphysics, and cosmology. Then each tortured interpretation has been run through the ideological gantlet of the historical-critical and historical-grammatical camps. In the end though, the lack of compelling arguments meant each reader chose the version that sounded best based on his or her conservative or liberal leanings.

Yahveh, the "I AM," is not like humans (Psa 050:21). So the best way to figure out what "I AM" means is to study the context of each occurrence of "I AM" (*ehyeh*). This reveals that *Yahveh*'s predominant use of the word *ehyeh* is to say, "'I AM' with you [or him]."[154] This phrase has also been interpreted in the future tense as, "I will be with you." This meaning fits the context of Exo 03:14, since *Yahveh* said that he would be with Moses when he went to Egypt (Exo 03:12).

The NT writers' use of "*ho wn*" gives an additional perspective on the intended meaning of "I AM" in Exo 03:14. "*Ho wn*" and "*egw eimi*" are found in a variety of contexts in the NT. It is worth noting, however, that the main thrust of the NT is that *Yeshua* is "Immanuel," "God with us" (Mat 01:23). *Yeshua* also said he would be with Christians until the end of the world. This is similar to the meaning behind "I AM" in Exo 03:14. The book of Revelation, where several "*ho wn*" statements are found, extends the "I will be with you" thought to heaven itself:

> I heard a loud voice from the throne saying, 'Now the dwelling of God is with men, and he will live with them. They will be his people, and God himself will be with them and be their God' (Rev 21:03).

The Stats on "*Ho Wn*" ("WHO IS") and "*egw eimi*" ("I AM")

There are three instances of "*ho wn*" (WHO IS) in two LXX verses, and thirteen instances of "*ho wn*" in the Greek NT. Only five of the sixteen instances of "*ho wn*" are applied to people besides *Yeshua* (LXX 1Ki 16:22; Joh 03:31; 08:47; 12:17; 18:37). There are 30,926 verses in the LXX (including the Apocryphal books), and 7,957 verses in the NT. It is statistically significant that there are only sixteen instances of "*ho wn*," and eleven are applied to *Yeshua*.

One gets the impression that "*ho wn*" (who is) could have appeared more often in Scripture. Also, "*ho wn*" could have been applied to a more representative sample of the persons mentioned in Scripture. Instead, "*ho wn*" is used reservedly. Perhaps this is because the LXX translators and the Greek NT writers figured that "*ho wn*" (WHO IS) is the equivalent of "I AM." Interestingly, the same could be said, to a lesser extent, of the phrase "*egw eimi*" ("I am" or "I AM").

Liberals criticize some conservatives for translating "*egw eimi*" as "I AM" too often in the NT. Liberals hesitate to translate as "I AM" the "*egw eimi*" in the predicateless absolute of Joh 08:58: "Before Abraham was, 'I AM.'" The reason is that the less convinced one is of the deity of Christ, the less favorably one is disposed toward applying "I AM" statements to *Yeshua*. The issue is not so much over grammar, but one of belief versus unbelief.

The case can be made that "*ho wn*" ("WHO IS") is the equivalent of "I AM" in eleven out of sixteen occurrences in the LXX and Greek NT. Twice "*ho wn*" is used with "*egw eimi*" to prove divinity (LXX Exo 03:14; Rev 01:08). The complementary and parallel uses of "*egw eimi*" and "*ho wn*" suggest that the phrase "*egw eimi*" really does mean "I AM" in more than just one or two passages: Exo 03:14 and Joh 08:58.

The Predicated, Non-Absolute "I AM" ("*egw eimi*") Statements

It was shown above that the signifier of deity, "I AM," can be the subject of a predicate (LXX Exo 03:14). This means *Yeshua*'s famous seven predicated "I AM" ("*egw eimi*") statements in John can be translated as "I AM..." Instead of saying, "I AM who I AM," *Yeshua* said, "I AM the true vine. *Yeshua*'s famous seven "I AM" statements from the Gospel of John are:
1) "'I AM [*egw eimi*]' the bread of life" (Joh 06:35),
2) "'I AM [*egw eimi*]' the light of the world" (Joh 08:12),
3) "'I AM [*egw eimi*]' the sheep gate" (Joh 10:07),
4) "'I AM [*egw eimi*]' the good Shepherd" (Joh 10:11),
5) "'I AM [*egw eimi*]' the resurrection and the life" (Joh 11:25),
6) "'I AM [*egw eimi*]' the way, the truth and the life" (Joh 14:06), and
7) "'I AM [*egw eimi*]' the true vine" (Joh 15:01).

These statements indicate that if one believes *Yeshua* is "I AM" and *Yahveh* the Son, then *Yeshua* will provide for his eternal life (Joh 06:27, 41, 51, 58). This point is made clear in the discussion between *Yeshua*, Thomas and Philip (Joh 14:08-21) regarding *Yeshua*'s statement: "'I AM' the way, the truth and the life" (Joh 14:06).

The "I AM" Statements in the MT

Yahveh created surrogate names and signature phrases by appending a predicate to "I AM." Two examples are:
1) The Hebrew phrase "*ehyeh asher ehyeh*" means "I AM [*ehyeh*] who [*asher*] I AM [*ehyeh*]" (Exo 03:14), and
1) The Hebrew phrase "*anee hu*"[155] means "'I AM [*anee*]' he [*hu*]" with or without an appended predicate such as "...who am speaking" (Isa 52:06).

MT passages that have "I AM" with a predicate include:
1) "I AM [*ehyeh*] who I AM [*ehyeh*]...I AM [*ehyeh*] has sent me to you..." (Exo 03:14),
2) "See now that I myself AM he! [*anee anee hu*]"[156] (Deu 32:39),
3) "I, *Yahveh*—[am with] the first and [I am] with the lasts [plural]—'I AM' he [*anee hu*]" (Isa 41:04),
4) "Understand that 'I AM' he [*anee hu*]" (Isa 43:10),
5) "From ancient days 'I AM' he [*anee hu*]" (Isa 43:13),
6) "Even to your old age and gray hairs, 'I AM' he [*anee hu*], and I am he who will sustain you" (Isa 46:04),
7) "'I AM' he [*anee hu*], I am the first..." (Isa 48:12), and
8) "People will know my Name...they will know that 'I AM' he [*anee hu*] who foretold it" (Isa 52:06).

Quoting the surrogate names and signature phrases created by the above predicates allowed *Yeshua* to identify himself as *Yahveh*. These quotations imply that:
▪ He was a person of *Yahveh* who spoke some of the OT *Yahveh* texts that he is quoting or alluding to, and

- He can speak just as *Yahveh* the Father or *Yahveh* the Spirit did since he is *Yahveh* the Son and "I AM."

How the NT writers applied OT "I AM" formulas such as Isa 52:06 to *Yeshua* will be discussed later in the chapter. The NT applications of "I AM" to *Yeshua* are discussed in the Song of Moses chapter, and are noted in the NT Use of OT *Yahveh* Texts appendix.

The "I AM" Statements in the LXX

The LXX translators knew that Moses (Deu 32:39) and Isaiah used surrogate names for *Yahveh:*
- The Hebrew word *anee* ("I AM"), and
- The Hebrew phrase *"anee hu"* ("'I AM' he").

The LXX translators used the Greek words *"egw eimi"* ("I AM") to translate the Hebrew *anee* ["I AM"]. The LXX translators sometimes did not translate the *hu* [he] in the phrase *"anee hu"* (Deut. 32:39; Isa. 41:4; Isa. 43:10; Isa. 43:13; Isa. 46:4; Isa. 48:12; Isa. 52:6). It is as though the LXX translators thought *hu* [he] was superfluous.

The LXX translators and NT writers used the Greek words *"egw eimi"* and *"ho wn"* as surrogates of the Name, *Yahveh:*
- Without any predicate, and
- With a predicate that means substantially the same thing as the subject "I AM."

Predicates that mean substantially the same thing as the subject "I AM" include "WHO IS" [*ho wn*] (LXX Exo 03:14) and "myself" (LXX Isa 52:06). A predicate that does not give much additional information is meant to emphasize "I AM." These predicates serve as an exclamation point to indicate that the "I AM" is a special usage. Examples of such LXX passages include:

1) "I AM [*egw eimi*] WHO IS [*ho wn*]...WHO IS [*ho wn*] has sent me to you" (LXX Exo 03:14),
2) "See, see that 'I AM [*egw eimi*],' and there is no God but me" (LXX Deu 32:39),
3) "I, God, the first and to futurity, 'I AM [*egw eimi*]'" (LXX Isa 41:04),
4) "Understand that 'I AM [*egw eimi*],' before me there was no other God" (LXX Isa 43:10),
5) "'I AM [*egw eimi*],' I am he who blots out transgressions for my own sake..." (LXX Isa 43:25),
6) "'I AM [*egw eimi*],' and there is none else" (LXX Isa 45:18),
7) "'I AM [*egw eimi*],' I am the Lord speaking righteousness" (LXX Isa 45:19),
8) "Even to old age, 'I AM [*egw eimi*],' and until you grow old, 'I AM [*egw eimi*],' I bear you" (LXX Isa 46:04),
9) "'I AM [*egw eimi*],' I am your comforter" (LXX Isa 51:12),
10) "People will know my Name...that 'I AM' myself [...*hoti egw eimi autos*]" (LXX 52:06), and

11) "Then you will know that in the midst of Israel, "I AM [*egw eimi*],' and I am *Yahveh* your God" (LXX Joe 02:27).

The Agreement of the MT Recension with the LXX Translation

Seven verses with "I AM" in the MT recension and LXX are in substantial agreement (Exo 03:14; Deu 32:39; Isa 41:04; 43:10; 46:04; 48:12; and 52:06). In five LXX verses, however, the LXX clearly has *Yahveh* saying, "I AM," when the MT recension is not so clear (LXX Isa 43:25; 45:18, 19; 51:12; LXX Joe 02:27):

1) & 2) LXX Isa 43:25 and 51:12 have "*egw eimi, egw eimi*" ("'I AM,' I am"), which translates the Hebrew "*anokee anokee hu*" ("I myself AM he...",
3) LXX Isa 45:18 has "*egw eimi*" ('I AM')," which translates the phrase "*anee Yahveh*" ("I am *Yahveh*"),
4) LXX Isa 45:19 has "*egw eimi egw eimi Kurios*" ("'I AM,' I am the Lord"), which phrase translates the word "*anee Yahveh*" ("I am *Yahveh*"), and
5) LXX Joe 02:27 has "*egw eimi*," which translates the Hebrew word *anee* ("I am"). In this verse, the Hebrew word order suggests, "I AM," more than do the words themselves. The Hebrew "I" (*anee*) ends one phrase and begins another, with only an "and" (prefixed conjunctive *vav*) in between.

In a sixth verse, the MT recension verse has *Yahveh* saying, "I AM," clearly (Isa 43:13), but the LXX does not. In a seventh verse, the LXX has "I AM," twice, but the MT recension only has "I AM" once (Isa 46:04).

Some of the discrepancies between the MT recension and LXX may have been caused by textual transmission errors. Perhaps a study of the Dead Sea Scrolls focusing on the "I AM" statements would shed more light on the subject. The discrepancies may have been caused by translators who were not aware that *Yahveh* occasionally said, "I AM," rather than just "I am."

Some discrepancies between the MT recension and LXX actually help the argument that *Yahveh* sometimes meant "I AM" when he said, "*anee*." An example is where the LXX translators used "*egw eimi*" ("I AM") to translate the phrase "*anee Yahveh*" ("I am *Yahveh*") (Isa 45:18).

The "I AM" Statements in the Greek NT

Yeshua's NT "I AM" statements show that he can speak as *Yahveh* did in the OT. This fact was already shown in the OT when *Yahveh* the Son (who later became *Yeshua*) spoke 'I AM' statements such as in Exo 03:14 and:

I, *Yahveh* [the Son], am the first and am with the lasts—'I AM' (Isa 41:04).

The Hebrew for "lasts" in Isa 41:04 is plural. The "lasts" here are the Father and the Spirit. The "lasts" are the "us" and "we" mentioned elsewhere in Isaiah (as is discussed in Isa 06:08 and Isa 41:22-23, 26 in the MT plural appendix).

In the NT *Yeshua* said, "I AM," either with or without a predicate (Joh 04:26):

1) "'I AM [*egw eimi*],' said *Yeshua*" (Mar 14:62),
2) "You say [it] because 'I AM [*egw eimi*]'" (Luk 22:70),

3) "See that 'I AM' myself [...*hoti egw eimi autos*]" (Luk 24:39),
4) "*Yeshua* said to her, "'I AM [*egw eimi*]' who am speaking to you'" (Joh 04:26),
5) "*Yeshua* said to them, "I AM [*egw eimi*];' do not be afraid" (Joh 06:20),
6) "If you do not believe that "I AM [*egw eimi*],' you will indeed die in your sins'" (Joh 08:24),
7) "When you have lifted up the Son of Man, then you will know that 'I AM [*egw eimi*]'" (Joh 08:28),
8) "Before Abraham was born, 'I AM [*egw eimi*]'" (Joh 08:58),[157]
9) "I am telling you now before it happens, so that when it does happen, you will believe that 'I AM [*egw eimi*]'" (Joh 13:19), and
10) "'I AM [*egw eimi*]," *Yeshua* said. As soon as *Yeshua* said, "I AM [*egw eimi*]," they drew back and fell to the ground...'I told you that 'I AM [*egw eimi*]," *Yeshua* answered..." (Joh 18:05-06, 08).

Would *Yeshua* Quote *Yahveh*'s "I AM" statements from the LXX Rather Than the Hebrew or Aramaic?

Liberals often are biased against the LXX for the reason that a translation cannot be as accurate as the original. A problem with this thinking is that there are no Hebrew originals extant. The MT recension is derived from copies that are centuries removed from the originals. The Aramaic Targum translations with running commentary have no more overall merit than does the LXX.

It is worth noting that from the second century BC through the first century AD, believers felt no compelling need for a better Greek translation. The attempt to replace the time-honored LXX came only after the LXX had become the *de facto* official translation for Christians. Starting in 126 or 128 AD, the Jews attempted to replace the LXX with Aquila's Greek translation.

The people thought that *Yeshua* and the apostles taught with authority, unlike the rabbis and scribes (Mat 13:54; Luk 02:47; Joh 07:15; Act 04:13). The rabbis and scribes relied on Aramaic commentaries (Mat 07:29; 2Ti 03:07). It would seem that if talking with authority derived in part from quoting Aramaic or Hebrew sources, the NT quotations would not follow the LXX. Nevertheless, the majority of *Yeshua* and the apostles' OT quotations follow the LXX.

Part of the reason that the people thought *Yeshua* and the disciples preached with authority is the people knew the LXX well. Hebrew and Aramaic manuscripts were expensive and hard to procure compared to the LXX. As Josephus said, it was an accomplishment to learn the law (*Antiquities of the Jews*, Book 20:11:01).

The Aramaic-speaking Babylonian Jews wrote the law and commentaries to which Josephus referred. Since the people were not as versed in these Aramaic commentaries as they were in the LXX, the Pharisees thought:

This mob that knows nothing of the law—there is a curse on them (Joh 07:49).

The split between the Jewish leaders and the people resulted from the leaders' reliance on Targum commentaries, astrology, apocryphal literature and Greek philosophy, all of which diverged from what scripture taught.

Apparently, even the Father was pleased to speak in Greek to glorify his Name (Joh 12:20-30). Some Greeks who wanted to see *Yeshua* approached the disciple with a Greek name, Philip. He and another disciple with a Greek name, Andrew, went to see *Yeshua*, who was commonly known by his Greek name, *Iesous*, and Greek title, *Christos*. With the Greeks in his audience, *Yeshua* said:

Now is the time for judgment on the world. Now the prince of this world will be driven out. When I am lifted up from the earth, I will draw all men to myself (Joh 12:32).

The reason *Yeshua* made this statement was to show the time was fast approaching when *Yeshua* would be crucified, and then the evangelization of the Greeks would commence in earnest (Act 11:20; 17:04).

The Jews at the temple had previously wondered aloud whether the Galilean would teach both the Greeks and Greek-speaking Jews (Joh 07:35, 41, 52). Also, *Yeshua* had just spoken of the evangelization of the world. Surely, *Yeshua* would not now start speaking Aramaic to the Greeks who just came to see him!

To show that the Father's Name would be glorified also among the Greeks, *Yeshua* said, "Father, glorify your Name!" A loud voice came from heaven saying, "I have glorified it, and will glorify it again!" *Yeshua* told the Greeks and his Greek-speaking disciples, "This voice was for your benefit, not mine" (Joh 12:30). This suggests that the voice from heaven must have spoken in Greek.

The Greek speakers in the crowd understood the voice and said that an angel had talked to *Yeshua* (Joh 12:29). The Greeks probably figured that an angel quoted the Father, as was the case after the near-sacrifice of Isaac (Gen 22:15-18). The non-Greek speakers thought that the Father's Greek words, "*edoxasa kai palin doxaso*," sounded like the clap and rumble of thunder echoing in the Kidron Valley next to the temple.

The Father said from heaven:

I have glorified it [his Name], and will glorify it [his Name] again (Joh 12:28).

How the Father's Name is glorified is through the work of the Son (Isa 49:03-07; Joh 09:03; 11:04, 40-44; 13:30-32; Eph 02:07; 03:10-11, 21). How the Father had glorified his Name was by having the Son publicly proclaim their Name, "I AM" (Joh 08:24, 28, 58).

How the Father will glorify his Name "again" (Joh 12:28) is by having the Son proclaim their Name "I AM" repeatedly (Mar 14:62; Luk 22:70; Joh 13:19 and 18:05-06, 08). The Father's Name "I AM" will also be glorified when the Son commands the disciples to baptize all nations in the Name ("Name" is singular) of the Father, Son and Spirit (Mat 28:19). Baptizing the Greek nation is ultimately what *Yeshua* had in view when he asked the Father to glorify his Name among the Greeks in the temple.

Why the voice from heaven had to speak in Greek for the Greeks' sake (Joh 12: 28) is that previously in the temple area, *Yeshua* said, "I AM" ("*egw eimi*") three times (Joh 08:24, 28, 58), the same number of times *Yahveh* said, "I AM" (*ehyeh*) in Exo 03:14:

God said to Moses, 'I AM [*ehyeh*] who I AM [*ehyeh*].' And he said, 'Say this to the people of Israel, 'I AM [*ehyeh*] has sent me to you" (Exo 03:14).

Then the Jews tried to stone *Yeshua* right on the temple grounds. So in a bid not to harden their hearts any further, *Yeshua* said that he was not about to provide any more special signs to meet the demand of Jewish unbelievers.

Yeshua said that Jewish unbelievers would only get to see the signs meant for all nations to see such as:

When you have lifted up the Son of Man [crucified him], then you will know that 'I AM' (Joh 08:28).[158]

Ministering among the Greeks, whether in Palestine or in the temple, allowed Jewish bystanders to see the signs meant for the gentiles.

Many unbelieving Jews from Judea were not conversant in Greek, so they thought the Father's thunderous voice was merely thunder (Joh 12:29). This underscores how the voice was meant for the sake of the visiting Greeks rather than for the unbelieving Jews. Joh 08 also showed why the sign had to be from the Father rather than from *Yeshua*. *Yeshua* said:

If I glorify myself, my glory means nothing. My Father, whom you claim as your God, is the one who glorifies me (Joh 08:54).

The Father spoke at the temple (Joh 12:28) to verify that previously *Yeshua* had indeed glorified the Father's Name while in the temple area. Earlier *Yeshua* said, "I AM" in the temple area (Joh 08:24, 28, 58), and the Jews tried to stone him (Joh 08:59).

That the Father apparently spoke in Greek suggests that *Yeshua*'s "I AM" statements in Joh 08 were also spoken in Greek. Also suggestive of this fact is what occurred the day before *Yeshua* spoke the "I AM" statements of Joh 08 in the temple courts. The Jews at the temple noted that *Yeshua* was a Galilean who would be comfortable teaching Greeks and Greek-speaking Jews (Joh 07:35, 41, 52).

That the Father spoke in Greek to verify that *Yeshua* had glorified their Name meant that *Yeshua* also did not have any qualms about quoting the LXX. *Yeshua* used the Greek LXX to identify the Father and himself as the subject of the *Shema*. The *Shema* was discussed in the chapter on the *Shema*.

Yeshua's quoting the Greek LXX would be another fulfillment of the prophecy that God would speak in foreign tongues to unbelieving Jews (Isa 28:11; 1Co 14:21). Jews who believed were predominantly from Galilee where Greek was spoken. Jews such as Judas who disbelieved were predominantly from Judea, where Aramaic was the predominant language.

Yeshua's "I AM" Statements of Joh 08

Yeshua said:

If you do not believe that 'I AM [*egw eimi*],' you will indeed die in your sins (Joh 08:24)…When you have lifted up the Son of Man, then you will know that 'I AM [*egw eimi*]' (Joh 08:28)…Before Abraham was born, 'I AM [*egw eimi*]' (Joh 08:58).

Yeshua's "I AM" Statements of Joh 08:24, 28

Yeshua warned listeners that they must believe that he was "I AM," or they would remain in their sins (Joh 08:24). By this, *Yeshua* indicated that he is *Yahveh* the Son. The Father also said:

'I AM' [the LXX reads *"egw eimi"*], I am he who blots out your transgressions for my own sake, and remembers your sins no more (LXX Isa 43:25).

If a person does not believe that *Yeshua* is "I AM," then he will not forgive the person his or her sins. The "I AM" only forgives sins for their own Name's sake.

Long before *Yeshua*'s ministry the Son had the authority to forgive sins for his own Name's sake. During the Exodus, the Father warned that the people should listen and do everything that the *Malek Yahveh* commanded. The *Malek* had the Name, *Yahveh*, "in him" and so he had the divine right to refuse to forgive sins (Exo 23:21-22). The Father's warning was a negative way of saying that the *Malek Yahveh* could also forgive sins. Joshua also spoke in this manner about the *Malek Yahveh*, as is discussed at Jos 24:19 in the Trinitarian proofs appendix.

The early NT Church understood *Yeshua* to be *Yahveh* the Son and the *Malek Yahveh* with *Yahveh*'s Name "in him" (Exo 23:21). Many mentions are made in the NT of "the Name of *Yeshua*."[159] In Act 05:40-41 the Name of *Yeshua* is called "the Name" (see also 3Jo 01:07). *Yeshua* means, "*Yahveh* saves" (Mat 01:21; 1Ti 01:15), so the name *Yahveh* is "in" the name *Yeshua* as well as "in" *Yeshua*.

The *Malek Yahveh* can choose to forgive or not to forgive. This holds various implications. For instance, churches may exercise "the ministry of the keys" (Mat 16:19), because *Yeshua* holds the keys of heaven (Rev 01:18; 03:07) and is in the midst of the Church. Even if an individual church has two or three members, *Yeshua* is "in the midst of them" (Mat 18:20). So even a small church can exercise the authority of the Ministry of the Keys (Mat 18:18-20; 1Co 05:04).

The ministry of the keys is the authority to forgive or retain the sins of the unrepentant, public sinners through excommunication. This refers to treating un-repentant sinners as unbelievers merely by withholding Communion—the Lord's Supper. Excommunication is not shunning, since *Yeshua* evangelized tax collectors and pagans (Mat 18:17). Shunning involves revoking the church membership of persons who make a practice of sinning in public (1Co 05:05-13; 2Th 03:14-15).

It should be noted that shunning is not a Biblical term, nor is shunning as practiced by some sects a Biblical practice. Even the excommunicated were to be treated "as a pagan and a tax-gatherer" (Mat 18:17). Yet how did *Yeshua* treat the pagans and tax-gatherers? He recognized them as being outside of the church and in need of the Gospel, and to that end used various means of evangelization, including teaching, healing their sick, attending their banquets and calling them to repentance. So Christians should not shun people, but they should make it plain to them and everyone else that they are outside rather than inside the Christian church.

Yeshua also gave the Ministry of the Keys to individual Christian churches. *Yeshua* said:

I tell you [plural] the truth, whatever you [plural] bind on earth will be bound in heaven, and whatever you [plural] loose on earth will be loosed in heaven (Mat 18:18).

Churches should refuse Communion (Eucharist) to those unrepentant over gross public sins committed against church members or the Church (false doctrine) (Mat 18:15, 21). The refusal of Communion would be imposed only after repeated interventions and attempts at reconciliation have failed (Mat 16:19; 18:15-22; 1Co 05:04-05).

Yeshua also gave the Ministry of the Keys to the Church as a whole (Mat 16:19; 2Jo 01:10). This was done so that the Church's message would not be corrupted by teachers who say, for example, that *Yeshua* was a mere prophet (Mat 16:13-20).

There are other implications of *Yeshua*'s being both *Yahveh* the Son and the *Malek* with the Father's Name in him. For instance, *Yeshua* was able to command the disciples to baptize the nations in the (singular) Name of the Father, Son and Spirit (Mat 28:19). So if anyone refuses *Yeshua*'s command to be baptized, *Yeshua* as the *Malek* with the Father's Name in him may refuse to forgive his rebellion (Exo 23:21). Indeed, Mark points out that to believe means to accept baptism, while to adamantly refuse baptism means the person never really believed in the first place (Mar 16:16; Luk 07:29-30).

Yeshua's "I AM" Statements of Joh 08:58

Yahveh the Son retained the Name, *Yahveh*, when he became incarnate. *Yeshua* said, "Unless you believe that 'I AM,' you will die in your sins" (Joh 08:24). To make sure that the Jews knew *Yeshua* was saying that he was "I AM" in Joh 08:24 and 28, he said, "Before Abraham was, 'I AM'" (Joh 08:58).

The Messiah's eternal existence before Abraham is mentioned in many passages (Mic 05:02 (*BHS* 05:01); Gen 01:01, 26; 02:04; Isa 09:06; Joh 01:01,15; 08:58; 17: 05, 24; Heb 01:11; 1Jo 01:01). It should be noted that in Isa 09:06, what is often translated as "Everlasting Father" (*KJV, NIV, RSV*) is a Hebraism that literally translates as "Father of Eternity" (*YLT*). "Father" can mean "author" or "source" in Hebrew. The intended meaning is that *Yahveh* is outside of time, and is the creator of time and eternity.

Joh 08:58 is similar to Exo 06:03. In Exo 06:03, *Yahveh* the Son wanted Moses to know that he had the Name, *Yahveh*, even during patriarchal times. In Joh 08: 58, *Yeshua* pointed out that he was *Yahveh* and "I AM" (Exo 03:14) even before Abraham's time.

That *Yeshua* had the Name, *Yahveh*, during patriarchal times (Exo 06:03) and even before patriarchal times (Joh 08:58) is quite reasonable. It does not matter that the patriarchs were unaware that the Son was named *Yahveh*. Similarly, Pharaoh, Samuel and the Israelites "did not know *Yahveh*" (Exo 05:02; 1Sa 03:07; Jer 31:34; Heb 08:11), yet *Yahveh* was stilled named *Yahveh*!

Yeshua's "I AM" Statements Yet to be Discussed

Yeshua's "I AM" statements that will be discussed in the Song of Moses chapter include those he said to:

- The woman at the well (Joh 04:26),
- The disciples while walking on the Sea of Galilee (Joh 06:20),
- The Jews in the temple courts (Joh 08:24, 28, 58),
- The disciples during the Last Supper (Joh 13:19),
- Thomas and the disciples (Joh 14:06),
- The soldiers in the Garden of Gethsemane (Joh 18:05-06, 08), and
- The High Priest during *Yeshua*'s so-called trial (Mar 14:62; Luk 22:70).

Chapter 10

The Song of Moses (Deu 32)

Introduction

The Apostle John wrote that the Song of Moses (Deu 31:22, 30; 32:44) and the Song of the Lamb were sung in heaven (Rev 15:03). Thus, the Song of Moses pertains to both OT and NT study. The Song of Moses is part history and part prophecy, and concerns the period between the time of Jacob and the end of the world.

The Song of Moses shows God's strategy for saving Jews and gentiles. The Father's strategy is to try to save errant Israel by every means, including that of sending his only Son. The Son is far superior to Moses, and is sent to save the gentiles as well as the Jews. The gentiles' relationship with God the Father and Son should make Israel jealous enough to come back into the fold.

This chapter dwells on the Song of Moses strategy, and also on how the Son is superior to Moses. Topics include the Son's being "I AM," the divine Son of Man (Dan 07), and the Son of God.

Yahveh **the Son Received Israel as an Inheritance**

Moses wrote in his Song of Moses:
> When the Most High [Hebrew is *Elyon*] gave the nations their inheritance, when he [the Father] separated the children of men, he set the bounds of the peoples according to the number of the sons of God [angels],[160] *Yahveh*'s [the Son's] portion is his people, and Jacob [Israel] is the lot of his [the Son's] inheritance (Deu 32:08-09).

The Song of Moses explains Israel's relationship to the Trinity. Israel is referred to as *Yahveh* the Son's inheritance or heritage. By contrast, Israel is referred to as the Most High's (*Elyon*) "treasured possession." This is because "the whole earth is mine [the Father's]" (Exo 19:05).

Naturally, Israel is not called the inheritance or heritage of the Father. The Most High can only possess since there is no one who could ever pass on an inheritance to the Father. Similarly, the Father can swear by none higher than himself (Heb 06: 13).

The Most High apportioned land to all the nations (Act 17:26), and then put angels (the "sons of God") in charge of those nations. Angels did protect Israel (Gen 28:12; 32:01-02; Dan 12:01), but a mere angel never ruled Israel. The Father and Son are the "makers" of Israel, as is discussed at Psa 149:02 and Isa 54:05 in the MT plurals appendix.

As soon as Jacob's family became the nation (Gen 32:07, 10) of Israel (Gen 32:28; 33:20; 34:07; 35:10), the Son received Israel in trust. The idea of a promised inheritance is common throughout the Bible, including in the NT (Mat 25:34; Act 07:05; Col 03:24; Heb 11:08; 12:16; 1Pe 01:04). Israel became the Son's promised inheritance when the Father, *Elyon*, told Jacob to sacrifice to the Son, *El Shaddai* (Gen 35:01). To convert Israel from being promised inheritance to an actual inheritance, the Son only needed to bring Israel out of Egypt and into the Promised Land.[161]

The Father said that *El Shaddai* was "the God who appeared" in Jacob's dream at Bethel in Gen 28 (Gen 35:01). The narrator said that the Father and Son, "they appeared" (plural verb) together in Gen 28 (Gen 35:07). Previous to Gen 35, the patriarchs only called on, and sacrificed to, *Yahveh* the Father (Gen 04:26). The patriarchs only sacrificed to the Son when directed to, as when Abraham sacrificed to the Son, the *Malek Yahveh* of Gen 22:11-13. Another instance is when the Father told Jacob to sacrifice to the Son, *El Shaddai*:

> ...then God [the Father] told Jacob, 'Arise, go up to Bethel, and live
> there. Make an altar there to God [the Son] who appeared to you when
> you fled from the face of Esau your brother' (Gen 35:01).

Jacob had his clan get rid of their foreign gods. Then Jacob built an altar at Bethel where "[All] the Gods, they had appeared to him" (Gen 35:07). Here Jacob referred to the epiphany of Gen 28. Jacob sacrificed to *El Shaddai* the Son, just as *Elyon* the Father had instructed (Gen 35:01). Then *El Shaddai* the Son appeared to Jacob (Gen 35:11-12).

After Jacob worshipped the Son (Gen 35), the name of the Father, *Yahveh*, is rarely heard or spoken by the patriarchs. As was discussed in the proto-Sinaitic Trinitarianism chapter, the patriarchs only knew the Father as *Yahveh* and *Elyon*. The patriarchs did not know the Son as *Yahveh*, but the patriarchs did know the Son as *El Shaddai* and *Elohim* (Exo 03—06).

The last mention in Genesis of the Father's title, "Most High" (*Elyon*), is made during conversations between Abraham and Melchizedek, and Abraham and the king of Sodom (Gen 14:18-22). Balaam is the next person to mention the title *Elyon* (Num 24:16). Balaam was Semitic, but not an Israelite, so Balaam only knew the Father as *Yahveh*. Balaam only knew pre-patriarchal Yahvism since he was not privy to the theological developments that took place during the patriarchal period.

No Israelite after Abraham mentioned the Father's title *Elyon* until Moses' day. Moses only mentioned the epithet *Elyon* once, and that was during the last days of his ministry (Deu 32:08-09). Here Moses noted that *Yahveh* the Son was Israel's national God since the Son had inherited Israel from the Father, *Elyon*, who rules all nations. The fact that, in the Pentateuch, the title Most High is mentioned only in conversations with gentiles (Melchizedek, king of Sodom, Balaam) shows that the title Most High pertains to the Father ruling over all nations.

The Name, *Yahveh,* is said or heard by Bible personages 51 times in Genesis chapters 04—32, but only once in Genesis chapters 33—50 (Gen 49:18).[162] Even the post-Sinaitic Yahvist narrator, Moses, does not mention the Name, *Yahveh,* much after Gen 32.

From the start of Genesis through chapter 32, the Name, *Yahveh,* appears a total of 128 times in 116 verses. By contrast, from chapter 33 to the end of Genesis (Gen 50), the Name, *Yahveh,* appears only twelve times in eight verses. This shows that the patriarchs had accepted the Son (*Elohim* and *El Shaddai*) as their proxy national God, just as the Father had instructed Jacob (Gen 35:01).

The Son received Israel as an inheritance (Deu 32:08-09) after Moses learned the Son's name was *Yahveh* (Exo 03—06). Exo 03—06 coincided with the Son's bringing Israel out of Egypt. Thus Israel was taken out of trust and was made the Son's full inheritance.

After Exo 03—06, the Son was known by every title by which *Yahveh* the Father was known, except the Most High (*Elyon*). Only later, according to the vision of Dan 07, did the Son inherit all the nations. Then the Father and Son were known as the Most Highs, as is discussed at Dan 07:18, 22, 25b, 27 in the MT plurals appendix.

Dan 07 described an event similar to what the Song of Moses describes. In Deu 32:08-09, *Elyon* promised "Jacob," meaning Israel, as an inheritance to the Son. The nation Israel eventually came to know the Son as *Yahveh* (Exo 03—06). In Deu 32, the Son was promised Israel as an inheritance, but in Dan 07, the Son was promised the nations as an inheritance. In the NT the Son often is spoken as being the heir of all creation—to include the nations (Mat 21:38; 28:18; Joh 16:15; 17: 02; Rom 08:17; Heb 01:02).

In a prophetic sense, the Son began to rule with the Father over all the nations already in OT times (Dan 07). In the prophetic sense, the Father and Son came to be called the Most Highs. Jeremiah and the Evangelist John wrote that the Father and Son have one throne in one sanctuary, as is discussed in the MT plurals appendix (Jer 17:12; Rev 22:01, 03-04). The NT often says that *Yeshua* has power over all things.[163]

After Moses met the Son at Mount Sinai, *Yahveh* the Son also came to be known as "*Adonai* ["my Lord"] *Yahveh.*" Genesis only records how the Father was known as "*Adonai Yahveh*" (Gen 15:02, 08). After the Son received Israel as his inheritance, the *Malek Yahveh* was also known as "*Adonai Yahveh*" (Exo 23:17; 34: 23; Deu 09:26; Eze 20:05; 36:07; 44:12).

That the "*Adonai Yahveh*" in Exo 23:17 and 34:23 was the Son was discussed in the chapter on the Presences of *Elyon.* That the "*Adonai Yahveh*" mentioned in Deu 09:26 is the Son can be ascertained from the fact that Moses said that Israel was this person of *Yahveh*'s inheritance. The Father does not inherit from anyone, so in Deu 09:26 the person of *Yahveh* is the Son.

To summarize this section, from Gen 01 to 31, the Son was known to be a member of the Trinity. The Son was known as *Elohim* and *El Shaddai*. The Son also "moonlighted" as a messenger, the *Malek Yahveh*, sent by the Father. Then, from Gen 32 to Exo 02, the Son became the proxy national God for Israel, his promised inheritance.

The *Malek Yahveh* made no appearances from Gen 32 until Exo 03:02. That is because the Son was busy being Israel's national God. After delegating authority over Israel to the Son, the Father continued with his rule over the gentiles. From Gen 32 to the Exodus, there was no point in the Son acting as the *Malek Yahveh*. The Son made the decisions concerning Israel, so there was no need for the Son to be a messenger between the Father and Israel.

During Exo 03 to 06, the Son came into his inheritance, Israel. Upon Moses asking his name, the Son was known as *Yahveh*. Dan 07 depicts how the Son after the ascension (Act 01:09) would become Most High along with the Father (Phi 02:09). Then the Son and Father will rule over the Church (Psa 110:02) and all nations as the Most Highs (Dan 07).

Yahveh the Son Later Stood to Receive the Nations as His Inheritance from *Elyon*

Moses wrote in his Song of Moses:
They have moved me to jealousy with that which is not God; they have provoked me to anger with their vanities; I will move them to jealousy with those who are not a people; I will provoke them to anger with a foolish nation (Deu 32:21).

Yahveh made commitments and covenants to both the patriarchs and to Israel that he would be the God of Israel. *Yahveh* kept his end of the bargain, but the Israelites often would not accept him as their God (2Ch 29:06; Isa 01:04; Jer 02: 27; 08:05; 32:33; Dan 09:11).

Yahveh's several recourses are mentioned in the Song of Moses and elsewhere. *Yahveh*'s options included temporary banishment of sinners from the Promised Land, or *Yahveh*'s temporary abandonment of the Promised Land.

Yahveh's response options were limited somewhat, because a recourse taken too far might backfire and not produce the intended result. Timeliness of the rebuke is critical, because people indulging in "pagan revelry" suffer the consequences of risky behaviors (Exo 32:06; 1Co 10:07). They also tend to only remember the "good times" they had serving pagan gods (Jer 44:19; compare Jer 07:18).

Certain recourses might not backfire completely, but still yield unintended consequences. For instance, Israel's suffering too many disastrous "acts of God" would just be numbing (Jer 08:14-15; Mal 03:13-15). The chastisement might serve to harden hearts (1Sa 06:06; Isa 63:17; Mat 11:23-24; 12:31-32). For example, Pharaoh came to think that he could withstand anything that *Yahveh* would throw at him until his bitter end (Exo 14:05). *Yahveh* stated that he would not destroy the Israelites lest the gentiles misunderstand (Exo 32:10-12; 33:03, 05), as *Yahveh* said:

I dreaded the taunt of the enemy, lest [Israel's] adversaries misunderstand and say, 'We have triumphed; *Yahveh* has not done all this' (Deu 32:27). *Yahveh* was always conscientious about what the nations thought (Deu 04:06; Psa 126:02; Isa 51:04; Eze 36:23; 39:27). *Yahveh* wanted the nations to know that his eternal, spiritual kingdom never failed (Dan 04:03, 34; 06:26; Psa 125:01-02; Isa 54:17; Mat 16:18; Joh 10:27-30; Heb 12:28). That way they would eventually crowd, rather than trickle, into the Church (Isa 52:14-15; 56:07; Mar 11:17).

Yahveh could not rely on Israel to inform the gentiles that Israel's troubles were caused by its abandonment of *Yahveh*. It is the nature of unbelief that unbelievers cannot admit that it was their disbelief that led to *Yahveh* abandoning them (Jer 22:08-09). In fact, most unbelieving Israelites would only have the passing thought that *Yahveh* had abandoned them (Deu 31:17). Others would become so paganized as to not care about *Yahveh* at all (Jer 44:15-19):

For they are a nation void of counsel,
There is no understanding in them.
Oh that they were wise, that they understood this,
That they would consider their latter end!
How could one chase a thousand,
Two put ten thousand to flight,
Except their Rock had sold them,
Except *Yahveh* had delivered them up? (Deu 32:28-30).

Moses knew that some unbelieving Israelites would not think *Yahveh* had abandoned them. These particular Israelites would deny that they had stopped worshipping *Yahveh* in Spirit and in truth. Moses was familiar with how Korah and his followers thought they were worshipping *Yahveh* in truth and purity to their bitter end (Num 16:01-50). Moses also remembered that after the Korah episode, the surviving Israelites still thought Korah and his followers were righteous. The Pentateuch records:

The next day the whole Israelite community grumbled against Moses
and Aaron, and said, 'You have killed *Yahveh*'s people' (Num 16:41).

Yahveh also knew that Israel would not recognize that they "come near to me [*Yahveh*] with their mouth and honor me with their lips, but their hearts are far from me" (Isa 29:13). *Yahveh* knew that they would not admit:

Their worship of me is made up only of rules taught by men (Isa 29:13;
Col 02:08).

When tragedy struck or times became hard, *Yahveh* knew that Israel would not resort to criticizing their own unbelieving selves. Instead, they would have some uncomplimentary things to say about how *Yahveh* failed them in the past or present. They would speak of *Yahveh* as though he were *Baal*:

Either he is musing, or he is busy, or he is traveling, or perhaps he is
sleeping and must be awakened (1Ki 18:27).

If unbelieving Israel did not mock *Yahveh*, then it would sentimentally plead *Yahveh*'s cause as though God were in the docket (Jdg 06:31). They would say that *Yahveh* was too weak to keep bad things from happening to good people (2Ch 32:15). So God is tried *in absentia*, and is essentially stripped of his deity by his supposed supporters. With these theologians for advocates and friends, *Yahveh* has no need for prosecutors and enemies!

Unbelieving Israel would wax philosophic and in keeping with 2Ki 01:16, they would say there was no God in Israel. They say *Yahveh* was mythical and never existed anyway. Then they would allude to Isa 46:01 and say Yahvism ought to be revised or reinterpreted because this "ism" has burdened Israel too long. They would refer to 1Ki 18:17 and say Yahvists have only brought trouble to Israel.

Unbelieving Israel would also tend to rationalize its troubles away and say that their relationship with *Yahveh* was fine. They still have their wealth and health, and that "all is well that ends well." They would flatter themselves on how they successfully they endured another round of extreme testing—as though it were the national sport (Gen 22:12; Job 13:15-16).

Yahveh figured the only way out of this predicament would be to convert the nations (Deu 32:21, 43). Then the nations would read Moses' songs (Dan 09:11-13) about which *Yahveh* said:

> Now write down this song and teach it to the Israelites, and have them
> sing the song so that it may become my witness against them (Deu 31:19;
> see also Deu 31:21, 26; Isa 08:02; 30:08).

Yahveh knew that gentiles who were informed by the Song of Moses would know exactly what motivates *Yahveh* to trouble Israel (2Ki 14:27; 13:23; Isa 45:04). *Yahveh* means to save Israel in a roundabout way, since a direct relationship proves counterproductive (1Ki 18:17-18; Jer 02:19).

Informed gentiles would know why Israel always finds itself in a tough neighborhood.[164] Informed gentiles would not jump to unfounded conclusions such as:

> Our hand has triumphed, and *Yahveh* has not done all this (Deu 32:27;
> see also Exo 32:12; Num 14:15-16; Psa 115:02; 140:08, and the like).

Yahveh knew that only converted gentiles would know the Jewish rejection of *Yeshua* was what really precipitated the loss of their homeland. The lack of a homeland was the event that meant Jews would often be in the wrong place at the wrong time. Minorities and displaced persons usually suffer the most when twisted, evil men appear on the world scene with an axe to grind (Est 03:06).

In the diaspora, Jews were always dependent on the tolerance of rulers and populaces who tended towards intolerance. In short, just as the Jews elicited the worst behavior imaginable out of Pilate, they were about to go on a road trip to make "Pilates" out of many gentile rulers.

One can only imagine how many evils recorded in history would not have occurred if the Jews had accepted the Gospel and kept their homeland. However, it was minorities like the Jews who pioneered in the field of religious rights. They paid the price so the rest of us can experience at least a semblance of religious toleration and freedom of conscience.

It is ironic though that the Jews' worldwide campaign for religious tolerance began with an act of religious intolerance—*Yeshua*'s trial. Moreover, it is ironic that still, even in modern times, Christians and Messianic Jews are restricted in their evangelism efforts among Jews in Israel—even though many or most Jews are secular!

Yahveh executed his Song of Moses strategy for converting the gentiles to make Israel jealous. *Yahveh* developed a saving rapport with Jewish and gentile Christians. The Father unites all Christians and angels in song by exhorting everyone to praise *Yahveh* the Son, as is discussed at LXX Deu 32:43 in the Trinitarian proofs appendix.

That the faith-based nation is united in song and in brotherly love (Joh 13:35) has the effect of making many in the race-based nation of Israel jealous. As *Yahveh* said:

They [the Israelites] have moved me to jealousy with that which is not God; they have provoked me to anger with their vanities: I will move them to jealousy with those [Christians] who are not a people [yet]; I will provoke them to anger with a [currently] foolish nation [pagan gentiles] (Deu 32:21).

So some persons in the race-based nation act on their jealousy and say, "If you cannot beat them, you might as well join them." Then these Messianic Christians sing along with the faith-based nation in worship of *Yahveh* the Son (Rom 11:25-26).

The NT writers relate that the "people" and the "nation" mentioned in the Song of Moses (Deu 32:21) are the faith-based nation of Christianity (Rom 09:24-26, 30; 10:19-21; 11:30; 1Pe 02:10). The nations were won over starting with the ministry of the apostles.

After *Yeshua*'s resurrection *Yahveh* the Father told *Yeshua*: Arise, God, judge the earth, for all of the nations are your inheritance (Psa 082:06-08).

This passage is discussed in the chapter on the *Shema*, as well as in the Trinitarian proofs appendix.

In the NT, the jealousy factor mentioned in the Song of Moses comes into play between Jews and Christians.[165] For instance, Paul alluded to the Song of Moses when he wrote:

By their fall, salvation has come to the gentiles to make Israel jealous...
I make much of my ministry in the hope that somehow I will provoke my own people to jealousy so as to save some of them (Rom 11:11, 13-14).

Since *Yahveh* the Son has claimed his inheritance, the gentiles are no longer looking in from the outside.[166] The gentile insiders tend to arouse the envy of Jews shut out of their relationship with *Yahveh*. Jewish outsiders are inclined to sense their lack of relationship with *Yahveh*, especially when gentiles ask the outsiders pointedly, "Where is your God?" (Psa 042:03, 10; 079:10; 115:02; Joe 02:17).

According to the Song of Moses plan, Israel notices that *Yeshua* is making Christians into a nation "high above all nations that he made, in praise, name, and honor" (Deu 26:19; 28:01). Formerly, the Israelites had the Name, *Yahveh,* named over them exclusively (Num 06:24-27; 2Ch 07:14; Isa 43:07; Isa 63:19).

Now, Jewish and gentile Christians call on God and have God's name called over them (Num 06:24-27; Isa 65:01; Amo 09:12; Mat 28:19; Act 15:17-18). Moreover, even a rebuilt Jewish temple would lack the divine presence (Mat 23:38; Luk 13:35). God dwelling on earth is in Christians (Joh 04:23; 1Co 03:16-17; 06: 19).

Israel can no longer feel justifiable pride that they are not involved in gross idolatry as the ignorant gentiles (Deu 32:21; Eze 16:56-57; Act 17:30; Mat 21:43). The vast majority of gentiles has either become Christian, or has moved on from idols to some philosophic form of unbelief.

God can hand temporal and spiritual kingdoms over to the lowliest of men (Dan 04:17). Now the sidelined and benched nation of Israel envies how *Yeshua* is in the process of making even animists and idol worshipers into Christians who are...

...an elect people, a royal priesthood, a holy nation, a people for God's own possession, that you may show forth the excellencies of him who called you out of darkness into his marvelous light (1Pe 02:09).

The Divine Son of Man Whom Daniel Saw (Dan 07)

The Son of Man vision (Dan 07:13-28) gives more detail on how *Yahveh* would make Israel jealous, as was prophesied in the Song of Moses (Deu 32:21). Daniel saw a vision of the future and wrote:

I saw visions in the night, and, behold, there came with the clouds of the sky one like a son of man, and he came even to the ancient of days, and they brought him [the Son] near before him [the Father]. There was given him [the Son] dominion, and glory, and a kingdom that all the peoples, nations, and languages should serve him [the Son]: his dominion is an everlasting dominion, which shall not pass away, and his kingdom that shall not be destroyed (Dan 07:13-14).

That the inherited nations worshipped the Son of Man (Dan 07:13-14) shows that the Dan 07 Son of Man vision is a prophetic parallel to Deu 32:08-09. In Deu 32:08-09, the Son inherits Israel from the Father, *Elyon*, and then the nations and angels are commanded to worship the Son (LXX Deu 32:43).

Dan 07 also is a prophetic parallel to the Psalms 002, 045 and 110 where the Father gives the nations as an inheritance to the Messiah. The Father and Son then rule the nations together. The Trinitarian proofs appendix discusses these Psalms and LXX Deu 32:43 further.

In the OT, except for the Dan 07 prophecy, the Father is the Most High. The Hebrew for Most High is *Elyon*, and the Aramaic is *Ilayah* (Dan 03:26; 04:02, 17, 24, 25, 32, 34; 05:18, 21; and 07:25a). After the Son of Man vision, however, the Father and Son together are called the Most Highs. The Aramaic plural is *Ilyonin* (Dan 07:18, 22, 25b, 27). Most translations disregard the fact that the Aramaic plural *Ilyonin* means "Most Highs." They translate the plurals in the singular as "Most High."

The Father and Son are called the Most Highs upon the Son's inheriting the nations. As was already noted, the Father was known as Most High by virtue of his owning and ruling the nations of the world. In fact, Melchizedek even says that the Most High is "the possessor of heaven and earth" (Gen 14:19, 22) Now that the Son has inherited and rules the nations, the Father and Son are called the Most Highs.

Paul said that *Yeshua*:

> ...who, being in very nature God, did not consider equality with God something to be grasped (*KJV* Phi 02:06).

Paul had in mind how *Yeshua* did not rush his becoming equal with the Father in terms of his owning and ruling all the nations. *Yeshua* followed the script and went on to inherit all the nations after his ascension.

When Paul wrote Phi 02:06, he likely was thinking about how *Yeshua* did not grasp at Satan's offer to hand over all the nations to *Yeshua* immediately (Mat 04:08-11; Joh 17:02; Phi 02:07-11). In a twinkling of an eye, *Yeshua* could have taken what was his from Satan, but instead *Yeshua* patiently waited to inherit the nations according to plan (Dan 07).

Yeshua alluded to the Dan 07 plan in his parable of the nobleman. The nobleman character was *Yeshua*'s allusion to himself. The nobleman went to a far country (heaven) to receive a kingdom (the earth) and then return (the post-resurrection appearances) (Luk 19:12-27). On a separate occasion *Yeshua* also alluded to the Dan 07 plan. *Yeshua* said that upon his return to the Father, the disciples would be able to do greater things than even *Yeshua* had done (Joh 14:12, 28).

Yeshua's mention of the Dan 07 Son of Man receiving his kingdom explains why:

- *Yeshua* told Pilate his kingdom was "from another place" (Joh 18:36), and
- The disciples often thought the advent of the messianic kingdom was imminent (Mat 20:21-28; Luk 19:11-27; Act 01:06).[167]

After his resurrection but before the ascension, the Son inherited all the nations from the Father in accordance with the Dan 07 Son of Man Vision. Thus, the Father and Son became the Most Highs (Dan 07:18, 22, 25b, 27).

Yeshua let the disciples know that Dan 07 had been fulfilled during one of his post-resurrection appearances when he spoke at the Great Commission:

> All authority in heaven and on earth has been given to me (Mat 28:18).

At the same time *Yeshua* said he would be present with believers as the Church conquered *Yeshua*'s inheritance (Mat 28:19-20).

Yeshua had predicted his post-resurrection appearances as the conquering Son of Man (Mat 28:18-20) when he said that:

- Some of his listeners would be alive when he inaugurated the Church Age:

> I tell you the truth, some who are standing here will not taste death before they see the Son of Man coming in his kingdom (Mat 16:28; see also Mar 09:01; Luk 09:27), and

- He would not drink of the fruit of the wine until "it finds fulfillment in the kingdom of God" (Mat 26:29; Mar 14:25; Luk 22:16, 18). Not only did *Yeshua* become one of the two Most Highs upon his ascension, but he was also ordained into the kingly priesthood of Melchizedek (Psa 110:04; Heb 05:06). The

ancient Yahvist priest-king of Jerusalem came out to meet Abraham with bread
and wine (Gen 14:18). Likewise, *Yeshua* appeared on the first day of the week
(Mat 28:01, 09-10; Luk 24:21, 33-35; Joh 20:19, 26) and broke bread and drank
wine with the disciples (Act 10:41). Thus, wine "found its fulfillment" (its
highest use) when it became customary to meet and have the Lord's Supper on
the first day of the week (Act 20:07; 1Co 16:02; Rev 01:10).

The writer of Hebrews quoted Psa 008:04-06 to say that the Son of Man had inherited the world in accordance with Dan 07. The writer of Hebrews also said the
effort to conquer his inheritance through evangelism had commenced:

For he [the Father] did not subject the world to come, of which we
speak, to angels. But one has somewhere testified, saying:

What is man that you think of him? Or the Son of Man [Dan 07:
13] that you ["the Ancient of Days" (Dan 07:09, 13, 22)] care for him?
You made him [the Son of Man] a little lower than the angels; you
crowned him [*Yeshua*] with glory and honor. You have put all things
in subjection under his feet. For in that he [the Father] subjected all
things to him [the Son], he [the Father] left nothing that is not subject to
him [the Son]. But now we do not see all things subjected to him as of
yet.[168] But we see him who has been made a little lower than the angels,
Yeshua, because of the suffering of death, crowned with glory and honor
(Heb 02:05-09a).

Paul alluded to how the Son of Man received the title Most High after his resurrection. Paul said:

God also highly exalted him, and gave to him the name that is above
every name.

In other words, the Son received the title "Most High" (Phi 02:09).

The OT (Psa 002:07; 016:11; 068:18 [*BHS* 068:19]; 089:27; 110:01; Isa 52:13)
and NT speak about the exaltation of Christ to the position of Most High with the
Father (Act 07:55; 1Co 15:24-28; Eph 01:20-23; Phi 02:09-11; Col 01:18-20; Heb
01:03-09; 1Pe 03:22; and Rev 11:17). Note that Paul quotes Psa 068:18 [*BHS* 068:
19] when referring to Christ in Eph 04:07-10. John the Evangelist wrote of the exaltation, too, when he noted that the Father and the Lamb, meaning *Yeshua*, have a
single throne (Rev 22:01, 03).

Peter, likewise, understood that *Yeshua* had become Most High along with the
Father as predicted by the Dan 07 Son of Man vision. Peter applied an OT *Yahveh*
text to *Yeshua* to say that *Yeshua* was "Lord over all" (Psa 103:19; Act 10:36).
Peter wrote that *Yeshua* was "exalted to the right hand of God," and that *Yeshua*
had poured out the Spirit (Act 02:33). The Son's promise to send the Spirit at
Pentecost is recorded in both the NT (Joh 15:26) and OT (in Act 02:16-21 Peter
quoted what the Son spoke in Joe 02:28-32). That the Son could pour out the Spirit
suggests *Yeshua*'s divinity.

Daniel found the prophetic developments of Dan 07 troubling, and kept the
matter to himself (Dan 07:15, 28). Perhaps Daniel realized the Bible's expression

of Trinitarianism was getting brighter all the time, but many Jews were drifting toward unitarianism. Perhaps Daniel kept the matter to himself because many thought Yahvism should be a race-based religion (Mar 11:17), despite the prophecies that Yahvism would bless the nations (Gen 18:18; 22:18; 26:04; 49:10; Psa 072:08-11; Isa 02:02; 11:10, 12-13; 42:01).

Previously, Yahvism had been faith-based. After the Flood, Noah's immediate descendants were Yahvists. After awhile, the vast majority became polytheists, as archaeology shows. However, through patriarchal times and up to the time of the Exodus, Yahvists were found in scattered locales (Gen 14:18; Num 22:18, 38). Eventually, Yahvism became known as Judaism since the gentile branch of Yahvists became extinct. Also, there was no broad–based consensus on any major doctrine by which the group could be known, such as:

- Baptism of repentance—the leaders were against it (Luk 07:29-30),
- Trinitarianism—the leaders taught unitarianism despite the Trinitarianism found in the OT, and despite the prophecies of a divine Messiah,
- The resurrection—the leaders could not agree whether or not there would be a resurrection (Mar 12:27; Act 23:06-08),
- The Messiah—there was too much disinformation and too many contradictory theories about the Messiah (Joh 07:27). The focus on the Messiah (Joh 09:22; 12:42; 16:02), however, became the mainstay of Christians (Act 11:26),
- The temple—it was supposed to be a "house of prayer for all nations" (Isa 56:07), but gentiles could be killed if they approached the temple as near as the Jews did (Mar 11:17; Act 21:28), and
- The Name—*Yahveh* fell into general disuse because the Name was considered "ineffable."

How could anyone call Judaism "Yahvism" when laws were crafted to make the utterance of the Name, *Yahveh,* a stoning offense? These laws were enforced though David said all should glorify *Yahveh*'s name rather than a race of people (Psa 115:01). The Name, *Yahveh,* became ineffable even though the Name, *Yahveh,* was the real reason Israel existed (Jos 07:09; 1Sa 12:22; Psa 079:09: Jer 14:07; Eze 20:14).

The Christian Church was created to be the new Yahvists (Isa 65:15). Christians glorify the Name *Yeshua* (Act 05:40-41), and *Yeshua* just happens to mean, "*Yahveh* saves" (Mat 01:21; 1Ti 01:15).

A Reason Why the Messiah Identified Himself as the Son of Man, Son of God, and as "I AM"

The Father said he would try all his options, such as first sending his prophets to warn, and then sending enemies to chastise. At last the Father would send his Son to Israel as the Messiah, as Amos states:

'I [the Father] overthrew some of you as God [the Son] overthrew
Sodom and Gomorrah. You were like a burning stick snatched from

the fire, yet you have not returned to me,' declares *Yahveh* [the Father]. 'Therefore this is what I will do to you, Israel, and because I will do this to you, prepare to meet your God [the Son], O Israel.' He [the Son] who forms the mountains, creates the wind, and reveals his thoughts to man, he who turns dawn to darkness, and treads the high places of the earth— *Yahveh* God Almighty is his [the Son's] name (Amo 04:11-13 is discussed further in the Trinitarian proofs appendix).

Amos shows that the Father was determined to extend the same opportunities to Israel as he extended to Sodom. Sodom had been sinning against *Yahveh* for some time (Gen 13:13). Before Sodom was destroyed by fiery brimstone (Gen 18—19), Lot was an example to them of righteous living (Luk 17:28-29; 2Pe 02:07). *Yahveh* also caused Sodom to be defeated by a coalition of kings (Gen 14:01-16). The Father then sent the Son and Spirit to Sodom, not only as a sort of ultimatum, but to save Lot and his daughters (Gen 18—19).

So after the prophets warned and the enemy armies invaded, the Father sent his Son and Spirit to Israel (Mat 03:16; Joh 14:26; 15:26). Their coming was even prophesied in passages such as Isa 48:16, a passage discussed further in the Trinitarian proofs appendix. The Son and Spirit delivered the last warning to Israel, just as they (as the two visitors) had done at Sodom. The Son and Spirit also saved the elect by warning them of the impending doom of Jerusalem (Mat 24:02) and the Last Day.

To fulfill Amo 04:11-13, *Yeshua* needed to show that he was God the Son delivering the Father's final ultimatum to unbelievers while rescuing believers. *Yeshua* showed his God credentials by his miracles (Joh 02:23; 10:25, 38; 12:37; 14:11), and by his saying that he was the Son of Man, the Son of God, and the "I AM." *Yeshua* delivered the last warning and said that the direst predictions of the Song of Moses were about to be fulfilled (Deu 32:21). The kingdom of God was about to be taken from the Israelites and delivered to gentiles (Luk 19:44-46).

Yeshua even alluded to the Father's statement "prepare to meet your God, O Israel" (Amo 04:12). *Yeshua* said Jerusalem would be destroyed because they failed to "recognize the time of your [Jerusalem's] inspection" (Luk 19:44). The *NIV* has "you did not recognize the time of God's coming to you" (Luk 19:44).

Yeshua also preserved the elect by warning them of Jerusalem's impending doom (Mat 24:15-22; Mar 13:14-20; Luk 21:20-24). Many Christians heeded these warnings ahead of the Roman reoccupation, left Jerusalem, and took refuge at Pella between 67 and 70 AD.

The Son of Man to "I AM" Strategy

The NT records the title Son of Man seventy-eight times, and securely threads NT doctrine into the OT. Mentioning the OT titles Son of Man (Dan 07:13) or Son of God (*KJV* Dan 03:25) made the Jewish religious authorities uneasy. This is shown in the account of Stephen's stoning:

'Look,' he [Stephen] said, 'I see heaven open and the Son of Man standing at the right hand of God.' At this they covered their ears and, yelling at the top of their voices, they all rushed at him, dragged him out of the city and began to stone him (Act 07:56-58).

Stephen definitely was alluding to the Dan 07 Son of Man vision where the Son approached the Ancient of Days (Dan 07:13; Act 07:56-58).

The Jewish religious authorities disliked the mention of the OT Son of Man and Son of God figures, who prefigure Christ. The Jews recognized that Trinitarian theology accommodates these OT figures better than does unitarianism. The Pentateuch mentions fewer seemingly divine figures, so the Jews respect the Pentateuch more than the rest of the OT.

The Jews recognized the implicit challenge that the Son of God figure posed to their unitarian misinterpretation of the OT. Thus, a law was fashioned specifically targeting anyone who would claim to be the Son of God (Joh 19:07). If the Son of God claim had not been considered so theologically threatening, one would think that the catchall blasphemy law would have sufficed.

The seventy-eight NT mentions of the Son of Man show that *Yeshua* wanted to make himself known as the divine Son of Man (Dan 07). *Yeshua*'s strategy was that the people would think of him as the Dan 07 "Son of Man." Then, with a little prompting, people would realize that the Dan 07 Son of Man was both the divine "Son of God" and the "I AM."

That the Dan 07 Son of Man was also the Son of God apparently was an easily drawn conclusion, as is shown from *Yeshua*'s trial. Here is a court excerpt:

[*Yeshua* said,] 'But from now on, the Son of Man will be seated at the right hand of the mighty God.' They all asked, 'Are you then the Son of God?' He replied, 'You are right in saying 'I AM'' (Luk 22:69-70).

At first, however, the people did not make the connection between *Yeshua*'s "Son of Man" statements and the Dan 07 vision. *Yeshua* healed a man so the crowd would "know that the Son of Man has authority on earth to forgive sins." The crowd only marveled that "God had given such authority to men" (Mat 09:06, 08). This observation mentioning "men" indicates that the crowd initially thought the title "Son of Man" only indicated humanity.

Some persons did make an immediate connection between *Yeshua*'s Son of Man statements and the Dan 07 Son of Man. They also knew that the Dan 07 Son of Man was uncreated and divine, and worthy of worship. These people had read or heard about how all nations worshipped the Son of Man (Dan 07:13-14). Take, for example, the reaction of the blind man whom *Yeshua* gave sight. He at first thought that *Yeshua* was a mere prophet (Joh 09:17):

Yeshua asked the man, 'Do you believe in the Son of Man?' The man replied, 'Who is he, sir? Tell me so that I may believe in him.' *Yeshua* responded, 'You have now seen him; in fact, he is the one speaking with you.' Then the man said, 'Lord, I believe,' and he worshiped him (Joh 09:35-38).

Christ's words were especially poignant and timely since the Pharisees had told the blind man earlier, "Give glory to God, for we know this man is a sinner" (Joh

09:24). Even so, the blind man worshipped the Son of Man who he knew to be God (Joh 09:38). Notice that *Yeshua* did not stop the man as Paul and Barnabas stopped the Lycaonians from worshipping them (Act 14:12-15).

Most people had to be informed that the divine Son of Man (Dan 07) was the "I AM" and the Son of God. *Yeshua* said it was necessary that people believe that he is the "I AM":

If you do not believe that 'I AM,' you will indeed die in your sins (Joh 08:24).

Immediately, the people asked, "Who are you?" (Joh 08:25). *Yeshua* answered:

When you have lifted up the Son of Man, then you will know that 'I AM' (Joh 08:28).

Yeshua made three "I AM" statements in Joh 08 (Joh 08:24, 28, 58). To make sure the people knew he was claiming to be "I AM," *Yeshua* said, "Before Abraham was, 'I AM'" (Joh 08:58). The Jews showed that they understood that *Yeshua* was claiming to be the "I AM" by picking up stones to stone *Yeshua* (Joh 08:59).

Notice that *Yeshua* did not try to stop them by saying that they had simply misunderstood what he was saying. At other times *Yeshua* took steps to correct his disciples when they mistook him for a ghost (Mat 14:26; Mar 06:49; Luk 24:37-39). Surely *Yeshua* would have corrected his audience if he had wrongly given the impression that he was God.

Judas and the "I AM" Statements of *Yeshua*

Yeshua moved his disciples from believing that he was just the Son of Man to believing that he was the "I AM." Some OT and NT background information is required before the discussion proceeds.

Yahveh the Son said that when his prophecies came true, the blasphemers would know that his name was *Yahveh*. They would also know that it was he who had prophesied (see 1Pe 01:11; also see Isa 42:09 and Isa 52:05-06). This would happen "in that day" (Isa 52:06) when the Good News (Gospel) came to Zion (Isa 52:07), in other words, during the NT period (Isa 61:01; Mat 04:23, Rom 10:15).

Isa 52:05 reflects how unitarianism was already taking hold in Isaiah's day. Isa 52:05 records *Yahveh* the Son prophesying that he, as *Yeshua*, would rebuff the unitarians. He would do this by teaching that he was a person of the Trinity and "I AM" (Isa 52:06). There are ample instances of *Yeshua*'s saying that he is the "I AM," as is discussed in the "I AM" chapter.

An example of the ongoing fulfillment of the prophecy of Isa 52:06 is illustrated in the account of the Samaritan woman at the well. *Yeshua* told the woman, "You Samaritans worship what you do not know" (Joh 04:22). *Yeshua* was alluding to his complaint that many did not know him (Isa 52:06). *Yeshua* then said, "a time is coming and has now come" (Joh 04:23). This is an allusion to his phrase "in that day" when the Good News would come to Zion (Isa 52:06).

Yeshua then informed the Samaritan woman that he was "'I AM,' who am speaking" (Joh 04:26). This is nearly the same phrase as is found in Isaiah, "'I

AM' myself who am speaking" (LXX Isa 52:06b). The Greek of Joh 04:26 is *"egw eimi, ho lalwn."* This is nearly the same as the Greek of LXX Isa 52:06b: *"egw eimi autos ho lalwn."* Notably, these "I AM" statements are similar to *Yahveh* the Son's "I AM" statement of LXX Isa 45:19:

'I AM [*egw eimi*]', I am the Lord speaking righteousness.

Isa 52:06 will be discussed further later in this chapter in connection with the disciple Thomas.

Surely, *Yeshua* told his disciples of his conversation with the woman at the well (Joh 04:27). The disciple John even wrote the account (Joh 04:01-43). Joh 04:26 is the first recorded "I AM" statement that the disciples heard *Yeshua* say. The second recorded incident when the disciples heard *Yeshua* say, "I AM," occurred when *Yeshua* walked on water. *Yeshua* said, "'I AM [*egw eimi*]'; fear not" (Joh 06:20).

Yahveh said, "I AM," and "Fear not!" many times in Isaiah (Isa 07:04; 08:12; 35:04; 40:09; 41:10, 13, 14; 43:01, 05; 44:02; 51:07; 54:04). The Greek phrase translated "Fear not!" in Joh 06:20 is *"may phobeisthe."* This exact phrase is found four times in the LXX of Isaiah (LXX Isa 13:02; 35:04; 40:09; 51:07).[169]

Toward the end of Joh 06, one reads that *Yeshua's* disciples grumbled about *Yeshua's* doctrine. John wrote that *Yeshua* knew Judas disbelieved. Apparently, *Yeshua's* "I AM" statements were causing Judas some indigestion (Joh 06:61, 64, 70-71). Later, Judas and the disciples were present at the temple when they saw how the Jews wanted to stone *Yeshua* (Joh 08:59). The Jews wanted to stone *Yeshua* for his thrice saying, "I AM" (Joh 08:24, 28, 58).

At the Last Supper, Judas heard *Yeshua* say:

I am telling you now before it happens, so that when it [the betrayal] does happen, you will believe that 'I AM' (Joh 13:19).

Joh 13:19 may be a parallel to Isa 52:06, but *Yeshua* was definitely alluding to Isa 43:10 where *Yahveh* the Father said:

You are my witness [to the timing of the prophecy and its fulfillment] so you may believe that 'I AM' (Isa 43:10).

The words common to both Isa 52:06 and Joh 13:19 are:

hina [that] *pisteusete* [you may believe]...*hoti* [that] *egw eimi* ["I AM"].

So at the Last Supper, *Yeshua* alluded to the Father's "I AM" statement in Isa 43:10. This was *Yeshua's* prophecy that the disciples would positively know him both as "I AM" and as *Yahveh* the Son at the betrayal.

After *Yeshua* said, "I AM" (Joh 13:19), Judas' unbelief became even more palpable to *Yeshua* (Mat 17:20; Mar 06:05-06). Judas, of course, did not believe that *Yeshua* was "I AM" (Mar 02:08; Luk 06:08). *Yeshua* was troubled in spirit and testified:

I tell you the truth—one of you will betray me (Joh 13:21).

Yeshua chose his wording carefully so that, one by one, the eleven disciples would deny that they had plans to betray *Yeshua*. The words often translated,

"Surely, not I," are literally, "Surely I am not [*egw eimi meti*] [the betrayer]" (Mat 26:22). Mark's gospel has the same phrase, but the *eimi* ("am") is only implied (Mar 14:19). This lacuna is common in Greek writing, so it would seem that Mark has the disciples saying the same phrase. Mark's version reads:

Surely I am not [*egw (eimi* is implied) *meti*] [the betrayer].

By *Yeshua*'s design, Judas heard the words "*egw eimi*" (literally, "I am") eleven times before Judas also said, "Surely, not I [*egw eimi*], Lord" (Mat 26:25). In this way, *Yeshua* allowed Judas to express with a double-entendre his rationale for the betrayal: Judas did not believe that *Yeshua* was the "I AM [*egw eimi*]" as *Yeshua* claimed to be. Judas was telling *Yeshua* that he was one with the stone throwers of Joh 08 and 10.

Judas' statement could not, of course, go unanswered. While Judas was still present at the Last Supper, *Yeshua* tied an "I AM" statement (Joh 13:19) to the vision of the Son of Man that Daniel saw (Dan 07). *Yeshua* said:

The Son of Man will go just as it is written about him, but woe to that man who betrays the Son of Man! (Mat 26:24; Mar 14:21; Luk 22:22).

Then, after Judas left, *Yeshua* said:

Now is the Son of Man glorified and God is glorified in him (Joh 13:31).

Later, in the garden *Yeshua* twice said, "I AM" (Joh 18:05-06, 08). *Yeshua* also tied these "I AM" statements to the Dan 07 Son of Man vision by saying, "Judas, are you betraying the Son of Man with a kiss?" (Luk 22:48). *Yeshua*'s question also connected the "Son of Man" and "I AM" statements at his betrayal to a Psalm:

Kiss the Son, lest he be angry and you be destroyed in your way, for his wrath can flare up in a moment. Blessed are all who take refuge in him (Psa 002:012).

Judas was present at *Yeshua*'s arrest when the soldiers drew back and fell to the ground upon hearing *Yeshua* say, "I AM." Then *Yeshua* said, "I told you that 'I AM'" (Joh 18:05-06, 08). The soldiers were encumbered with armor, chain mail and weapons, so they undoubtedly came to a kneeling position to get back on their feet. So one could say they knelt at the name "I AM" (Joh 18:05-06, 08). This is similar to how everyone on the Last Day will kneel at the Name of *Yahveh* (Isa 45:23) and *Yeshua*, which means "*Yahveh* saves" (Phi 02:10).

The events of Joh 18 at the arrest surely came across to Judas as though *Yeshua* were telling him, "I told you so—I told you that I was 'I AM.'" Judas and the disciples then came to know *Yeshua* as the Dan 07 Son of Man and as "I AM." So what *Yeshua* had prophesied earlier that evening occurred:

I am telling you now before it happens, so that when it [the betrayal] does happen, you will believe that 'I AM' (Joh 13:19).

The soldiers falling down at *Yeshua*'s words, "I AM," surely reminded Judas of *Yeshua*'s previous "I AM" statements. Judas may also have thought of how:

▪ People fell at the presence of the *Malek Yahveh* (Num 22:31; Jdg 13:20; 1Ch 21:16),
▪ It was prophesied that unbelievers would be snared and fall because of the Word of *Yahveh* (Isa 28:13), and they would quake at the Name of *Yahveh* (Isa 64:02),

- The *Malek Yahveh* (Exo 03:02) said that he was the "I AM" (Exo 03:14), and
- How the Father said the *Malek Yahveh* had his name in him (Exo 23:21).

After Judas saw the soldiers fall down at *Yeshua*'s words, "I AM," Judas realized that *Yeshua* really was the "I AM." Judas reversed his judgment about *Yeshua* and confessed to the priests, "I have sinned, for I have betrayed innocent blood."

Thomas Also Came to Know *Yeshua* as the "I AM"

Thomas told *Yeshua*:

Lord, we do not know where you are going, so how can we know the way? *Yeshua* answered, 'I AM' the way and the truth and the life. No one comes to the Father except through me (Joh 14:05-06).

After his resurrection, *Yeshua* told a group of women followers that none should touch him until he had returned from seeing the Father (Joh 20:17). Thomas wanted to touch *Yeshua*, and was commanded to by *Yeshua*. This would verify that *Yeshua* had returned from bodily seeing the Father as he said he would (Joh 20: 17). It would also prove that he had received "the sure mercies of David" from the Father (Isa 55:03; Act 13:34).

His return would prove to Thomas' satisfaction that *Yeshua* really was telling the truth when he said, "'I AM' the way to the Father" (Joh 14:06). *Yeshua* truly then would then be the Son of the Father who both ascends to and descends from heaven (Pro 30:04).

Thomas had other reasons for doubting *Yeshua*'s resurrection. Thomas' Greek name was Didymus. Both Thomas and Didymus mean "twin." If someone is called "twin" in two languages, it likely is a nickname. People from two entirely different cultures called Thomas a twin—and why? Obviously, because Thomas was a twin, perhaps even an identical twin. The Eastern Orthodox Church has never lost sight of this fact, and their non-Greek translations call Thomas not *Didymus*, but "the twin."

Being a twin, Thomas was acutely aware of the possibility that *Yeshua* had a twin, and wanted proof that no double took the place of Christ. So Thomas wanted to meet *Yeshua* personally, and even touch his wounds to ensure that a twin or double was not acting the part of a resurrected Christ.

Thomas may have also wanted to ensure that *Yeshua* was not a ghost. The disciples had momentarily thought that *Yeshua* was a ghost when he walked on the water (Mat 14:26; Mar 06:49). Besides, *Yeshua* was not the only person that resurrected on Easter Sunday, as Matthew wrote:

The tombs broke open and the bodies of many holy people who had died were raised to life. They came out of the tombs, and after *Yeshua*'s resurrection they went into the holy city and appeared to many people (Mat 27:52-53).

Also, *Yeshua* raised Lazarus not long before *Yeshua* died (Joh 11:17; 12:17). So a lot of spooky events occurred between the crucifixion and the ascension. That is why during a post-resurrection appearance the ten disciples were not convinced that *Yeshua* was flesh and blood until he ate some food (Luk 24:36-43).

Whether *Yeshua* was a ghost or not was a real issue since *Yeshua*'s soul had been separate from his body for three days. Thomas knew that the Romans had guarded *Yeshua*'s body while it lay in the grave for three days (Acts 2:23-32). Thomas also knew that *Yeshua* said his soul would be in paradise along with the thief's soul the very day of their crucifixion (Luk 23:43).

Between the crucifixion and resurrection, *Yeshua* was at the right hand of the Father (Act 02:25). He did, however, make an excursion to a metaphysical hell to preach about his upcoming victory (1Pe 03:19). So even those who were "under the earth," so to speak, bowed at the name *Yeshua*, which means "*Yahveh* saves" (Phi 02:10).

Three days after the crucifixion, *Yeshua*'s soul returned to his body. He then returned to see the Father after making some post-resurrection appearances. The second time *Yeshua* saw the Father after his crucifixion, he saw the Father bodily (Joh 20:17).

To address Thomas' doubts, *Yeshua* told Thomas:

Look at my hands and my feet [and see] 'that I AM myself [*hoti egw eimi autos*].' Touch me and see; a ghost does not have flesh and bones, as you see I have (Luk 24:39).

"*Hoti egw eimi autos*" is a quote of the Greek phrase spoken by *Yahveh* the Son in LXX Isa 52:06. As was mentioned above, *Yeshua* once before alluded to Isa 52:06 when he talked to the Samaritan woman. Thomas, now knowing that the implications of *Yeshua*'s many "I AM" statements were true, said, "My Lord and my God!" (Joh 20:28).

The Son of Man, to Son of God, to "I AM" Strategy

Yeshua was called the Son of God often.[170] *Yeshua*, however, did not *publicly* refer to himself as the Son of God because of a blasphemy law against saying just that. The punishment for breaking this blasphemy law was death (Joh 19:07). So it is not surprising that *Yeshua*'s enemies often referred to him as the Son of God. *Yeshua*'s enemies were trying to get him to divulge whether he was the Son of God in order to endanger his life (Mat 26:63-65).

Since no one under Jewish law was legally allowed to refer to himself as the Son of God, *Yeshua* referred to himself mainly as the Son of Man. The Son of God and Son of Man were equated in several passages that will be discussed later in this chapter.

The descriptions of the fiery Son of God (*KJV* Dan 03:25; Rev 02:18) and fiery Son of Man are similar (Dan 07:13; Eze 01:26-28). *Yeshua* appeared as lightning at the Transfiguration (Luk 09:29), and was bright during his appearance to Saul (Act 09:03). This suggests that *Yeshua* is the Son of Man and Son of God described in prophetic and apocalyptic books.

The Son of Man Theology

As far as types of Christ go, the Son of Man theology is fairly developed. Of course, the Son of Man is more than a type of Christ since he was the preincarnate Son just as the Angel of *Yahveh* was. *Yeshua* spoke of the Son of Man's pre-existence (Joh 06:62; 08:28, 58).

Yeshua used the title "Son of Man" and alluded to the Dan 07 vision of the Son of Man (Mat 24:30; 26:64; Mar 13:26; 14:62; Luk 21:27; Rev 01:13; 14:14). *Yeshua* even said that the Son of Man was the "I AM [*egw eimi*]" (Mar 14:62; Joh 08:28 are discussed in the "I AM" chapter).

Stephen mentioned that he saw the Son of Man in heaven at the right hand of the Father. Stephen knew what he was seeing from reading the Dan 07 Son of Man vision. Dan 07 describes the Son of Man approaching the Ancient of Days (Dan 07:13; Act 07:56-58). By contrast, Paul did not originally believe that *Yeshua* was the Son of Man. So when *Yeshua* called to Paul from heaven, Paul had to ask who the Lord was (Act 09:05).

Yeshua said it was written that the Son of Man must suffer much and be rejected (Mat 26:24; Mar 09:12; 14:21; Luk 18:31). *Yeshua* said the Son of Man would be raised from the dead on the third day (Mat 17:09; Luk 09:22; 24:07). This is similar to how *Yeshua* said it was written that the Christ would be raised on the third day (Luk 24:46).

The reader might ask, "Where was this written that the Son of Man and Christ would be resurrected?" The answer is it must have been written in the OT and not any apocryphal book since *Yeshua* said:

This is what I told you while I was still with you: Everything must be fulfilled that is written about me in the Law of Moses, the Prophets and the Psalms (Luk 24:44).

Exactly where in the OT it is written that the Son of Man would die will be discussed in a moment, but first consider this: the major OT types of Christ suffer, presumably die, and are raised to life.

The resurrection of these OT types of Christ was a given fact since heavenly figures were presumed to be immortal. *Yeshua* said that even the mortal Abraham was alive in heaven because *Yahveh* is not the God of those who survive only in blessed memory (Mat 22:32; Mar 12:27; Luk 20:38; 23:43).

Yeshua pointed out how the OT does not say "I WAS the God of Jacob," but "'I AM' the God of Jacob." This illustrates how *Yeshua* considered even a single word of Scripture such as "is" to be foundational in establishing beliefs as important as concerning the afterlife.

The belief in the immortality of the soul goes back to Adam. He named his wife Eve, meaning, "living," because she would be the mother of all the living (Gen 03: 20). Moreover, Enoch walked with God and then was taken away (Gen 05:24). Surely Enoch went to heaven like Elijah (2Ki 02:11).

A tree that has been chopped down, yet has shoots that spring forth from the stump, symbolizes death and resurrection (Job 14:08-15; 19:27; Dan 04:15, 23, 26). Two of the major types of Christ were described as a rejuvenated stump:

- The nation Israel, due to the Babylonian Exile and the Return from Exile (Isa 06:13; 49:03),
  and
- The Messiah's royal line extending from Judah to Christ (Isa 11:01).

Jacob had predicted the reason that the royal line was described as a stump. He said the scepter would depart from Judah for a short while before the Messiah arose from David's stock (Gen 49:10-11). That is why the Messiah is called a Branch (Isa 04:02, 11:01; 53:02; Jer 23:05; 33:15; Zec 03:08; 06:12). The scepter departed from Judah when the Herods ruled. The first Herod was an Edomite, and the second Herod was half-Edomite, half-Samaritan.

Yeshua said that the Son of Man came to serve (Mat 20:28; Mar 10:45). The Apostles said *Yeshua* was the Father's servant (Act 03:13, 26; 04:27, 30; Phi 02: 07). Considering all the data about the types of Christ, this seems to identify *Yeshua* as the Suffering Servant of *Yahveh* (Isa 42:01; 43:10; 49:06-07; 52:13; 53: 11). It was prophesied that the Servant would suffer and be disfigured (Isa 50:06; 52:14; 53:02-05). Based on the other types of Christ, one could easily presume that the Suffering Servant was to die and be resurrected.

David prefigured Christ, and David wrote various Psalms mentioning the Messiah's death and resurrection (Psa 016:10-11; 22:01, 12-21; Mat 27:46; Mar 15: 34; Act 02:31; 13:35-37). David was a shepherd and he himself served as a pattern for the Shepherd figure that was a type of Christ (Eze 34:23-24). *Yahveh* said the Shepherd, who was *Yahveh*'s associate, would be killed (Zec 13:07). *Yeshua* said that the Shepherd figure prefigured him (Mat 26:31; Mar 14:27).

David also was called the anointed one (Hebrew: *meshiach*) (1Sa 02:35; 2Ch 06:42; Psa 028:08; 089:38, 51; 132:10, 17). David prefigured "the Anointed One," which is often translated as "the Messiah" or "the Christ" (Psa 002:02; Act 04:26). Dan 09:25-26 is a prophecy that the Anointed One, the Christ, would be cut off. The Dan 09 vision came very close in time to the Dan 07 Son of Man vision. This suggests that the Son of Man is the Christ, and that the Son of Man would be cut off.

The "Son of Man" type of Christ was first introduced in Gen 03:15. Adam was told that if ate of a certain tree, he would die (Gen 02:17). Adam was given a reprieve, and was told a descendant would die in his stead:

I [God] will put enmity between you [Satan] and the woman, and between your offspring and hers; he [the Son] will crush your head, and you [Satan] will strike his heel (Gen 03:15).

Upon hearing Gen 03:15, Adam named his wife Eve, meaning, "living," because she was to become the mother of all the living (Gen 03:20; 1Ti 02:15). *Yeshua* was both the substitute for the first Adam, and his descendant, so Paul called the Son the last Adam (1Co 15:45). Luke even traces *Yeshua*'s genealogy back to Adam (Luk 03:38).

The Son of Man's title comes from the fact that he is Adam's descendant spoken of in Gen 03:15. The Hebrew word *adam* means "man," and the "Son" is a way of saying, "descendant." So the Son of Man could just as well have been called "the

Son of Adam." In fact, Ezekiel described the Son of Man as "a figure like that of a man [*adam*]" (Eze 01:26).

In Daniel and Ezekiel's visions, they see the Son of Man who would fulfill the prophecy of Gen 03:15 (Dan 07:13; Eze 01:26-28). Adam was a gentile, so it seems appropriate that Daniel and Ezekiel both saw the Son of Man visions in gentile territory near Babylon (Dan 07:01; Eze 01:03).

Dan 07 is written in Aramaic. The parts of Daniel written in Aramaic deal with gentile issues, while the parts written in Hebrew deal mainly with Jewish issues. The Dan 07 Son of Man vision definitely deals with gentile issues, since the Son of Man is prophesied to inherit all nations. "All nations" would be the gentiles, since the Son had already inherited Israel back in Exo 03—06 (Deu 32:08-09).

A snake biting the heel of the Son of Man symbolized the death of the last Adam. The imagery of Gen 03:15 was appropriate since Satan had just caused the Fall by possessing and speaking through a snake. Also, snake bites cause death but do not break any bones. This signifies the type of death that the Messiah would suffer (Num 21:08-09; Psa 022:14, 17; 034:20; 035:10; Joh 03:14; 19:34-37).

Satan possessed a snake in the Garden of Eden to tempt Adam and Eve. The words of the snake were deadly venom to Adam and Eve. Similarly, people listening to the words of demon-controlled persons would eventually kill the last Adam. Early in *Yeshua*'s ministry, people were not ready to hear certain facts. The reason was that during Intertestamental times, some OT truths simply were not taught, while other OT truths were twisted.

One truth that people could not immediately handle was that the Messiah would be the Son of God. In fact, the Jews had even enacted a law specifically against saying that one was the "Son of God" (Joh 19:07). Cognizant of this, the demons got off one last parting shot as they were driven out of the demon–possessed by saying *Yeshua* was the Son of God (Mat 08:29; Mar 03:11; Luk 04:41; 08:28). Similarly, a demon announced that the Apostle Paul was the servant of the Most High (Act 16:17), because some were not yet ready to handle this truth (Act 14: 11-15).

In the end Satan and the demons were successful. Their taunts about *Yeshua* being the Son of God (Mat 04:03, 06; 08:29; Mar 03:11; Luk 04:03, 09, 41; 08: 28) became the jeers that the Jews used (Mat 27:40, 43). The Jews asked *Yeshua* whether he was the Son of God in order to charge him with a capital offense when he answered (Mat 26:63; Luk 22:70). So one could say that ultimately it was the demon's venomous words that drove the fang-like nails into *Yeshua*'s hands and feet (Joh 20:25), and a snake-like spear into his side (Joh 19:07, 34).

The Mission of the Son of Man
The above was a review of the theology of the Son of Man in a nutshell. However, *Yeshua* still had to convince his listeners that not only was he the Son of Man, but also that he was the Son of God and "I AM." *Yeshua* therefore talked about how in the OT the Son of Man was concerned with spreading the gospel and ending spiritual rebellion.

Yeshua talked about how sinning against Christ was forgivable, but blasphemy against the Spirit was not forgivable (Mat 12:32). Interestingly, in Ezekiel the Son of Man (Eze 01:26-28) and the Spirit are mentioned together when the prophet was commissioned (Eze 02:02). Also, the Son of Man said that the Israelites had rebelled against him, so the Spirit and Ezekiel were sent to preach repentance and forgiveness (Eze 02:02-03).

Yeshua knew that once people accepted him either as the Son of Man or as the Son of God, they would find it easier to accept him as both. Then their next spiritual step would be to figure out either that "the Son of God" was "God the Son," or that the "Son of Man" was "God the Son." Finally, *Yeshua*'s followers would conclude that God the Son was "I AM," and their God and Lord.

Yeshua's followers came to know him as God and Lord (Joh 13:13-14; 20: 28). Just as *Yeshua* spoke to the crowds in parables, his public claims of divinity were purposely ambiguous (Mat 13:10-13; Joh 10:24). The Son of Man title was ambiguous in that the "son of man" title often was applied to mere humans in the OT, especially throughout Ezekiel. However, judging from the description and details, the "Son of Man" depicted in Dan 07 and Eze 01:26-28 is the divine Son of God (Dan 07:13-14).

The title "Son of God" was outlawed (Joh 19:07), even though the title was ambiguous:

- Adam was called "the son of God" (Luk 03:38),
- Humans were called "sons of God" (Gen 06:02, 04; Mat 05:09; Rom 08:14, 19; Gal 03:26), and
- Angels were called "sons of God" (Job 01:06; 02:01; 38:07).

Yeshua used the ambiguous Son of Man title so that the uninformed crowds would not be offended before the elect were led to faith (Isa 42:03; Mat 12:15-21). The Son of Man title was also ambiguous enough to keep *Yeshua* out of trouble with the authorities (Mat 26:63-65; Luk 11:53-54; 20:20-26; Joh 08:06; 10:24-39).

Yeshua referred to himself privately, not publicly, as the Son of God. A perusal of the Gospels shows that it was either third parties who made public mention of the title Son of God, or *Yeshua* spoke of the Son of God in the third person. Just as *Yeshua* refused to answer other questions (Mat 21:27; Mar 11:33; Luk 20:08), he left the question about his divinity unanswered in the public sphere. This way *Yeshua*'s opponents could not invoke the blasphemy law aimed at anyone who claimed to be the Son of God (Joh 19:07).

That *Yeshua* seldom publicly referred to himself as the Son of God explains why the High Priest needed to ask *Yeshua* whether he was the Son of God (Mat 26:63). The High Priest did not ask the question out of curiosity, but as a ruse so *Yeshua* would incriminate himself in the eyes of the unbelieving Sanhedrin (Mat 26:65-66).

The high priest used this blasphemy law just as the demons did when they called *Yeshua* "the Son of God" or "the Son of the Most High." They merely wanted to put *Yeshua*'s life in jeopardy (Mat 04:03, 06; 08:29; Mar 03:11; 05:07; Luk 04:03,

09, 41; 08:28). Similarly, the possessed prophetess at Philippi followed Paul and Silas yelling that they were servants of the Most High God (Act 16:17-18). There, too, the demon hoped to cause a fatal confrontation between the evangelists and the pagan profiteers (Act 16:19-21; 19:24-41).

Yeshua's strategy of moving people to accept one title and then a second title is apparent when *Yeshua* complimented Nathaniel on his believing that *Yeshua* was the Son of God (Joh 01:49).[171] Then *Yeshua* promised that Nathaniel would come to know *Yeshua* as the Son of Man (Joh 01:51).

Yeshua elsewhere linked the Son of Man title to the Son of God title. For example, *Yeshua* told the temple crowds (Joh 05:14) that he was the Son of Man and the Son of God who gave spiritual life to his hearers, and would resurrect and judge both saint and sinner on the last day (Joh 05:25-27). In Revelation, the Son of Man (Rev 1:13; 14:14) is also called the Son of God (Rev 02:18), among other titles.

Yeshua also linked the Son of Man title to the Son of God title when the high priest asked *Yeshua* whether he was the Son of God. *Yeshua* said, "I AM [*egw eimi*]" (Mar 14:62; Luk 22:69-70), which indicated that *Yeshua* is *Yahveh* the Son. This "I AM" statement is discussed in the "I AM" chapter. *Yeshua* also added that he was the Son of Man whom they would see coming in the clouds. This is a clear reference to the Dan 07 Son of Man vision (Mat 26:63-64).

Yeshua's moving people to believe that the Son of Man was God the Son was apparent when *Yeshua* said the Son of Man had the authority to forgive sins (Mat 09:06; Mar 02:10; Luk 05:24). *Yeshua* knew that the Jews would think, "Only God can forgive sins" (Mar 02:07; Luk 05:21). As if to say, "You are exactly right!," *Yeshua* healed the paralyzed man, thereby proving that he was both the Son of God and God the Son.

Yeshua's faith-building strategy was apparent when *Yeshua* asked the disciples, "Who do people say the Son of Man is?" Peter responded, "You are the Christ, the Son of the living God." *Yeshua* said that the Father had revealed this fact to Peter, and that on this fact *Yeshua* would build the Christian Church (Mat 16:13-19).[172]

Yeshua was the Son of God as well as the Son of Man. This meant that between the resurrection and the ascension, he would be given authority over the earth in accordance with Daniel's Son of Man vision (Dan 07:14, 27; Mat 28:18). At that point *Yeshua* had the authority to send his disciples to the ends of the earth to preach the Gospel and to build the Church (Mat 28:18; Joh 12:31; 17:02, 07, 09, 18; Act 16:09-10).

Peter's mention of the "living God" (Mat 16:13-19) is significant because in the Hebrew, the phrase "living God" is sometimes the plural "living Gods" (Deu 05:26; 1Sa 17:26, 36; Jer 10:10; 23:36). The "living Gods" OT passages are discussed in the MT plurals appendix. The plural "living Gods" suggests *Yahveh* is the Trinity.

That "living God" is mentioned in connection with the Son of Man (Mat 16:13-19) supports the interpretation that *Yeshua* was the divine Son of Man (Dan 07:13). The Son of Man was prophesied to be one of the two Most Highs (Dan 07:18, 22,

25b, 27). A connection was made between the Son of Man and the "living God" at *Yeshua*'s "trial."

The Mistrial of the Millennia

That *Yeshua* used the Son of Man title often is not lost on the NT writers (Act 07:56; Heb 02:06; Rev 01:13; 14:14). The Jewish officials, however, fixated on the Son of God title because there was a law tailored for that offense (Joh 19:07).

The blasphemy law against saying one was the Son of God was patently unbiblical—a law made by unitarians and anti-Trinitarians. There was no built-in exception for *Yahveh* the Son who would be the divine Messiah. That the Son would be the Messiah is discussed in the Trinitarian proofs appendix.

As *Yeshua* pointed out (Joh 10:34-35), even humans were called "gods." The OT referred to human judges as sons of the Most High (Psa 082:06-07), and judges were called gods (Exo 21:06; 22:08-09 [*BHS* 22:07-08]; Jos 24:01; Psa 082:01, 06). The judges' honorific title of "god" was appropriate because the OT-era law code was based on the Mosaic laws inspired by *Yahveh*. Hosea even prophesied that the Judeans would one day be called "sons of the living God" (Hos 01:10; Rom 09:26).

Due to contradictory witness accounts, the Sanhedrin could not make any charges stick. They felt they had no choice but to convict *Yeshua* on a blasphemy charge. The specifics of the blasphemy charge had to be that *Yeshua* claimed to be the Son of God rather than Son or Man or "I AM." The reason is that the pagan Pilate would not understand how calling oneself the "Son of Man" or "I AM" constituted blasphemy (Act 18:14-17).

The Jews hoped that Pilate would crucify an audacious person without Roman citizenship who claimed to be the Son of God (Act 14:12-19). They also knew that Pilate could be manipulated into imposing the death sentence if:
- A riot was about to ensue (Mat 27:24; Luk 13:01; 23:15; Act 19:35-41), and
- Pilate's relationship with Caesar were threatened (Joh 19:12-16).

Let us skip ahead for a moment to see whether the Sanhedrin's estimation of Pilate was accurate. Since Pilate was not a unitarian, he did not automatically disbelieve anyone's claim about being the Son of God. Ancients took such claims by miracle workers seriously (Act 14:11-12; 28:06). Pilate's mindset was the same as that of his centurion who was convinced by events at the crucifixion that *Yeshua* was the Son of God (Mat 27:54; Mar 15:39).

Pilate likely knew what Herod knew—that *Yeshua* was an itinerant miracle-worker (Mat 14:02; Mar 06:14; Luk 23:08). After finding out that *Yeshua* claimed to be the Son of God, Pilate asked *Yeshua* where he was from. Apparently Pilate thought *Yeshua* might answer "heaven" (Joh 19:07-12; compare Joh 18:36-37). Let us now return to discussing the trial before the Sanhedrin.

When *Yeshua* was being interrogated, he attempted to redirect the Sanhedrin to cross-examine witnesses about what he had said publicly (Joh 18:20-21). It makes perfect sense that no person should be tried on the basis of his private convictions.

In *Yeshua*'s case, however, he seems to have wanted to die for nothing less than his claims of divinity.

Yeshua knew that he would die based on the results of the Sanhedrin trial, since he was acquitted three times by Pilate (Luk 23:04; Joh 18:38; 19:04, 06). *Yeshua* wanted to place on the witness stand those Jews who tried to stone him (Joh 08:59; Joh 10:31). They wanted to stone *Yeshua* for:

- Publicly identifying himself as the "I AM" and *Yahveh* (Joh 08:24, 28, 58; 10: 30), and for
- Implying that he was equal to God (Joh 05:18; 10:33).

The priests could have had Judas testify that *Yeshua* said, "I AM," often, including that very evening (Joh 13:19; 18:05-08). Indeed, perhaps it was Judas' intention to testify in *Yeshua*'s behalf when he came to the chief priests and elders at the temple. Judas said, "I have sinned, for I have betrayed innocent blood." This is because Judas was belatedly convinced that *Yeshua* was "I AM."

Though the priests scoured the Passover feast crowds for witnesses (Mat 26:60, 65; Mar 14:63), they were not interested in due process, or in any witness who might exonerate *Yeshua*. They knew Judas would inform the Sanhedrin that everyone "drew back and fell to the ground" upon hearing the incriminating words, "I AM." So the priests turned Judas away saying, "What is that [betraying an innocent man] to us? That is your responsibility" (Mat 27:03-04). Out of fairness, it should be noted that later, a large number of priests did become Christian (Act 06:07).

During *Yeshua*'s "trial" the high priest Caiaphas said:

> I charge you under oath by the living God—tell us whether you are the
> Christ, the Son of God (Mat 26:63).

At this point, if *Yeshua* did not know all things ahead of time, he might have become exasperated. *Yeshua* had argued that the Jews ought to consider OT doctrine when evaluating anyone's "Son of God" claims.

Not considering OT doctrine led people to attempt to stone "the stone that the builders rejected" (Psa 118:22; Mat 21:42; Mar 12:10; Luk 20:17; Act 04:11; 1Pe 02:07). Interestingly, "the stone that the builders rejected" metaphor is apt since the Jews picked up stones from the construction site of the temple to stone *Yeshua* (Joh 08:46-47; 10:37-38; 18:21-23).[173]

Yeshua gave an expanded answer to the High Priest's question as to whether he was the Son of God. *Yeshua* said, "I AM [*egw eimi*]" (Luk 22:69-70), meaning that he was *Yahveh* the Son. *Yeshua* added that he was the Dan 07 Son of Man whom they would see coming in the clouds (Mat 26:63-64). By this statement *Yeshua* identified himself as the Son of Man prophesied to become one of the Most Highs along with the Father in Dan 07:13-28.

Yeshua claimed more than just the Son of God title because he did not want anyone reading about the trial to doubt his divine status. *Yeshua* did not want anyone to think that he only claimed to be a mere human, a mere angel, or anything less than God the Son, equal to the Father (Joh 05:18). To be convicted of only claiming to be the Son of God would be ambiguous, because to emphasize their exalted, God-given roles:

- Angels were called "sons of God" (Job 01:06; 02:01; 38:07) and were called small "g" "gods" (Psa 008:05; compare to Heb 02:07), and
- Human judges were called small "g" "gods" (Exo 21:06; 22:08, 09; Psa 082:01, 06) and "sons of the Most High" (Psa 082:06).

Yeshua was convicted without being afforded the opportunity to call witnesses to prove his innocence (Mat 26:64-68; Mar 14:63; Joh 18:21-23). The reason no due process was afforded *Yeshua* was the priests were unitarians who did not believe there even was a God the Son, much less one standing in front of them.

Yeshua did not object to the Sanhedrin's misconduct as, later, the Apostle Paul did rigorously during his trial (Act 23:02-05). Neither did *Yeshua* attempt a vigorous defense as did Paul during his trials (Act 23:06; 24:21). *Yeshua* knew that no scriptural argument would persuade the Sanhedrin (Luk 16:31; 22:67-68). Besides, they would reject *Yeshua*'s testimony out of hand because they demanded a minimum of two witnesses to prove anything:

> The Pharisees challenged him, 'Here you are appearing as your own witness; your testimony is not valid' (Joh 08:13; also see Joh 05:31).

Yeshua remained silent in court for the same reason that *Yeshua* told Judas to get the betrayal over with quickly (Joh 13:27). Judas would betray *Yeshua*, and the Sanhedrin would have *Yeshua* killed, no matter what. Arguing would have been futile, since the high priest tore his garments over the few comments *Yeshua* did make (Mat 26:65). On the deeper level, *Yeshua* stood silent because he stood in the place of sinners, and he wanted to die on his Father's timetable. His Passover death would atone for sins, to include the sins of the priests (Act 06:07).

Yeshua's producing a miracle to convince the Sanhedrin that he was the Son of God was not an option. Each subsequent miracle that *Yeshua* performed produced diminishing returns as far as the priests were concerned.[174] In fact, miracles were counterproductive since the priests considered each miracle or sign to be more evidence that *Yeshua* was in league with Satan (Luk 11:15-17).

Similarly, Herod wanted to be entertained with miracles (Luk 23:08-09). Herod had derived no spiritual benefit whatsoever from the accounts of *Yeshua*'s miracles. So *Yeshua* was determined not to perform any more signs for those who would disbelieve anyway. More miracles would only serve to harden hearts (1Sa 06:06; Isa 63:17; Mat 11:23-24; 12:31-32).

Yeshua determined that unbelievers would only see the signs meant for the whole world to see and hear about. *Yeshua* said that people would know that he was the Son of Man by the sign of Jonah (Mat 12:40). This involved *Yeshua*'s death, burial and resurrection (Mat 12:39-40; 16:04; Mar 08:12; Luk 11:29-30).[175] The sign of Jonah would also let people know that he was the "I AM." *Yeshua* said:

> When you have lifted up [in other words, "crucified"] the Son of Man, then you will know that 'I AM'" (Joh 08:28).

Joh 08:28 is discussed in the "I AM" chapter.

The specific events at the crucifixion to which *Yeshua* referred—the events that would convince people of his being the Son of Man and "I AM," were:

- The midday darkness (Mat 27:45, 51-54),
- The earthquake (Mat 27:51, 54), and
- The temple curtain ripped from top to bottom (Mat 27:51; Mar 15:38; Luk 23:45).

The temple veil ripping into two signified that *Yeshua*'s sacrifice for sin demolished the "dividing wall of hostility" between *Yahveh* and those "on whom his favor rests" (Luk 02:14; Eph 02:14). The temple curtain's being halved also signifies how the temple had indeed been left desolate, as *Yeshua* said it was (Mat 23:38; Luk 13:35). Cyril Glassé wrote:

...the veil of the Temple was rent in twain and the *Shekinah* went out of the Holy of Holies into the world.[176]

The *Shekinah* is not an impersonal phenomenon, but is the Son and Spirit. Glassé is also wrong about the Spirit leaving the temple when the curtain ripped. The temple was intended to be a house of prayer for all nations, but it was not (Mar 11:17). The curtain ripping in two signified that the Spirit had already left the temple and had taken up residence with all nations. Early in his ministry Christ indicated that the Spirit had already left the temple:

A time is coming when you will worship the Father neither on this mountain nor in Jerusalem...a time is coming and has now come when the true worshipers will worship the Father in spirit and truth (Joh 04:21, 23).

The "time is coming" in Joh 04:21 probably refers to when the temple curtain ripped at the crucifixion, or when the temple was destroyed (70 AD). Then the fact that the Spirit had already left the temple became known. This, however, was a long while after the actual event had occurred. Even at the start of *Yeshua*'s ministry, the Spirit was making baptized Christians his abode and temple (Mat 03:11, 16; Joh 04:20-24; 1Co 03:16; 06:19; Eph 02:22; 1Pe 02:05).

We have been discussing how people would come to know *Yeshua* as "I AM" after his crucifixion (Joh 08:28). The crucifixion was mentioned prominently at Pentecost, and later, "Christ crucified" was the main theme of Paul's missionary work (1Co 02:02). At Pentecost, many Jews came to know *Yeshua* as the "I AM" (Act 02:36-39). Pentecost was the first time that Diasporal Israel heard how the crucified Christ is the "I AM." That the message would be delivered in foreign tongues was predicted by Isaiah (Isa 28:11; 1Co 14:21).

Peter said that Joel's prophecy (Joe 02:28-32) was fulfilled at Pentecost (Act 02:16-21). Interestingly, in the verse just before the passage that Peter quoted, Joel has *Yahveh* saying:

Then you will know in the midst of Israel [that] 'I AM' [*egw eimi*] (LXX Joe 02:27).

It was noted in the chapter on the NT use of OT *Yahveh* texts that most of the Diasporal Jews used the LXX. They would have also known the context of Peter's quote, perhaps by heart.

At his trial, *Yeshua* knew he would be vindicated at the crucifixion, at Pentecost, and thereafter. So *Yeshua* made no defense during his trial before the Jewish

Sanhedrin (Mat 26:63), before Herod (Luk 23:09), and before Pilate (Joh 19:09). *Yeshua* made no defense even though Pilate prodded him (Joh 19:10), and sardonically asked, "What is truth?" (Joh 18:38; 1Co 01:22).

Yeshua's strategy of accepting his vindication at a later time worked (Mat 11:19; Luk 07:35). Many priests were convinced by the resurrection that *Yeshua* was the Son of God (Act 04:02; 06:07). Also, the NT writers, apologists and polemicists have convinced countless souls that the crucified Christ was the Son of God (Joh 20:31). Especially convincing to many is that the Father (Act 13:33; Heb 05:05) and the Spirit (Rom 01:03-04) raised *Yeshua* from the dead.

Yeshua said that those at his trial would know that he is the Son of God and the "I AM" at the Last Day. Then they would see him coming in the clouds (Joh 05:25; Mat 26:64; Mar 14:62; Rev 01:07). The phrase "coming in the clouds" is a clear reference to the Dan 07 Son of Man vision. After coming in the clouds, *Yeshua* will say to those at his trial:

> These things you have done, but I kept silent [during his trial]. You thought the 'I AM' was like you, but I will rebuke you and accuse you to your face (Psa 050:21).

The "I AM" in Psa 050:21 is the same Hebrew form *ehyeh* ("I AM") found three times in Exo 03:14.

Whether *Yeshua* Spoke Aramaic or Greek During His Mistrial

Caiaphas must have thought *Yeshua* claimed to be the "I AM" in either Aramaic or Greek. It does not seem plausible that Caiaphas would rip his expensive priestly garment over a lesser form of blasphemy (Mat 26:65; Mar 14:63).

If *Yeshua* spoke Aramaic during his trial, his "I AM" statement may have come across as a quote of *Yahveh*'s "I AM" statement in the Aramaic Targums. If *Yeshua* spoke Greek, than he would have come across as quoting the Greek LXX.

There is a good chance the trial was conducted entirely in Greek. As was noted in the chapter on the NT Use of OT *Yahveh* Texts, about forty percent of inscriptions in Jerusalem were Greek prior to 70 AD.[177] Josephus mentioned that even servants learned Greek in the first century Palestine (*Antiquities of the Jews*, Book 20:11:01).

The priests were thoroughly Hellenized even before Maccabean times (before 165 BC). The priests were conversant enough in Greek to speak to Romans, and write letters to the Greek-speaking Jews of the diaspora (Act 28:21).

If *Yeshua* told the Sanhedrin, "I AM [*egw eimi*]" in Greek rather than in Aramaic, this would explain why Paul quoted Exo 22:27b to the Sanhedrin:

> ...do not speak evil about the ruler of your people (Exo 22:27b; English 22:28b; Act 23:05b).

Paul knew the LXX version of this passage would irk the Sanhedrin, for the first part of the verse reads, "Do not blaspheme the Gods" (LXX Exo 22:27a [English 22:28a]). Here, "Gods" translates the Hebrew plural *Elohim*, and the LXX Greek plural *theoi*].[178] LXX 22:27 is discussed further in the MT plurals appendix.

Paul knew the Sanhedrin would eventually catch the meaning of his OT quote (Exo 22:28b; Act 23:05b) since they were familiar with the LXX. The Sanhedrin also knew that Paul considered both the Father and Son to be divine persons (Act 17:18; 20:28; Rom 09:05, and the like). Paul made two implicit points by quoting Moses:

1. There were plural divine persons whom the Israelites were not to revile. This meant the Sanhedrin should not have automatically dismissed *Yeshua*'s claim to be God the Son, the divine Son of Man, and "I AM." *Yeshua* was automatically condemned only because the priests had adopted a unitarian belief system. This system demanded that there be only one divine person and no Son or Spirit, and
2. There were two High Priests until the destruction of Jerusalem, yet each High Priest was to be considered the [singular] ruler (Exo 22:27b; English 22:28b; Act 23:05b). Just the same, two divine persons could be considered a singular God.

Doctrinal Points Relating to *Yeshua*'s Trial

The reason why *Yeshua* claimed to be the Son of God is that sons are of the same nature as their fathers. That *Yeshua* claimed to be "I AM" further underscores that he is of the same uncreated nature as *Yahveh* the Father. Nevertheless, *Yeshua* knew that in the minds of some, the Son of God title might leave the impression that the Son was somehow lesser than the Father. So *Yeshua* also claimed to be the Son of Man who approached *Yahveh* the Father in the clouds, as seen by Daniel in his prophetic vision (Dan 07:13-14; Mat 26:64; Mar 14:62).

Yeshua's claiming that he was the Son of Man would eventually indicate his equality with the Father, for the Dan 07 Son of Man vision would be fulfilled shortly after his resurrection. Then the Son of Man would become one of the two prophesied Most Highs (Dan 07:18, 22, 25b, 27). So one can conclude from the NT transcript of *Yeshua*'s trial that by claiming to be the Son of Man, *Yeshua* unambiguously claimed equality with the Father (Joh 05:18; 10:33).

Saying that *Yeshua* was the Dan 07 Son of Man was a touchy point. Caiaphas tore his clothing after *Yeshua* identified himself both as the Son of Man and as "I AM." Tearing clothing is a particularly Jewish gesture, expressing uncontrollable anguish and accompanied by a loud cry after something unbearable was said or done. In this case, Caiaphas considered *Yeshua*'s reply to be blasphemy (Mat 26: 65; compare Lev 24:16).

Another altercation involving Son of Man claims occurred when Stephen said that he saw "the Son of Man standing at the right hand of God" (Act 07:55-58). Though Stephen was just stating what he saw, the Jews covered their ears, yelled at the top of their voices, rushed at, and then stoned Stephen. Ironically, Stephen's speech only caused the Jews to gnash their teeth (Act 07:54). So it seems that Stephen's saying that *Yeshua* was the Son of Man was more provocative than his tongue-lashing speech to the Jews (Act 07:02-53).

Earlier, Peter identified *Yeshua* as the Son of the "living God." *Yeshua* said that the Father taught Peter this response (Mat 16:16-17). Caiaphas also linked "living God" with Son of God when he said:

I charge you under oath by the living God—tell us if you are the Christ, the Son of God (Mat 26:63).

So it would seem that Caiaphas' line of questioning was not said on his own, just as Caiaphas earlier made a prophetic statement that was not said on his own (Joh 11:50-52).

Caiaphas' oath formula mentioning the "living God" lends support to *Yeshua's* assertion that he is the "I AM." Caiaphas' oath also lends support to the fact that *Yeshua* is the Son of Man from the Dan 07 vision who is prophesied to be one of the two Most Highs (Dan 07:18, 22, 25b, 27). The reason is that the words translated as "living God" in the OT are sometimes plural in the Hebrew: "living Gods [*Elohim khayyim*]" (Deu 05:26; 1Sa 17:26, 36; Jer 10:10; 23:36).

Interestingly, two of the "living Gods" references (Deu 05:26; Jer 23:36) are associated with statements saying that:

- *Yahveh* is "near" (Deu 04:07; 05:27; Jer 23:23), and
- *Yahveh* is "[All] the Gods" (*haElohim*) (Deu 04:35, 39).

Furthermore, Deu 05:27 ties in with Deu 33:01-02 where Moses said that at the giving of the law, *Yahveh* appeared on three mountains in fire. Hagar also refers to the *Malek Yahveh* as "the living one who sees" (Gen 16:14; see also 24:62; 25:11). That the "living Gods" are "near" reminds one that *Yeshua* is *Immanuel* (God with us). That the "living Gods" are "[All] the Gods" (*haElohim*) reminds one that *Yeshua* is a member of the Trinity.

The fact that Caiaphas was one of two High Priests (Luk 03:02) lends support to the argument that *Yeshua* was one of the two Most Highs (Dan 07:18, 22, 25b, 27). Annas and Caiaphas were both High Priests at least since the start of John the Baptist's ministry (Luk 03:02),[179] and remained so for some time after *Yeshua's* death (Joh 18:13, 24; Act 04:06).

Having two high priests was not a one-time fluke.[180] There were two high priests until the Roman destruction of Jerusalem in 70 AD.[181] In the Talmud there is also a discussion of two high priests, one for temple service, and one appointed for war.[182] So it is ironic that the co-High Priest Caiaphas embraced unitarianism because they reasoned that there could not be co-High Gods.

Yahveh the Father Provokes Israel to Jealousy By Sending a Better Moses

To fulfill the Song of Moses (Deu 32), the Father (*Elyon*) sent *Yeshua* to be a better Moses to make Israel jealous. One, however, must have an honest evaluation of the first Moses before he can appreciate the greatness of the Second Moses. The Second Moses is so great as to make unbelieving Israel jealous. Moses and *Yeshua* have many points of comparison such as:

- Moses (Num 16:28) and *Yeshua* (Zec 02:09, 11; 04:09; 06:15; Joh 17:23) were the only two servants who said that believers would "know that *Yahveh* has sent me" (the emphasis is on "know"), and

- Moses and *Yeshua* were the only two servants who worked miracles by the "finger of God" (Exo 08:19; Luk 11:20).

Yeshua said that the "finger of God" was the Spirit (Mat 12:28; Luk 11:20). *Yeshua* said:

If I drive out demons by the finger of God, then the kingdom of God has come to you (Luk 11:20).

Yeshua was pointing out that only he and Moses exercised the finger of God. Therefore, he was the "prophet like Moses"—only better (Deu 18:15; Act 03:22; 07:37).

When Moses was tasked with bringing Israel out of Egypt, Moses said to God:

Who am I…that I should bring forth the children of Israel out of Egypt? (Exo 03:11).

God told Moses that it was not about who he was, but about whom he was with. *Yahveh* the Son's words were, "Surely, I will be with you" (Exo 03:12). So Moses was no different from many other heroes of the faith to whom God promised, "I am with you," and "I will be with you." Moses was only important because he was with the Son!

Yahveh many times takes all the credit for retrieving Israel out of Egypt (Exo 29:45-46). So it would seem that Moses' greatness was derived only from *Yahveh* being great. As the writer of Hebrews said, *Yeshua*

…has been counted worthy of more glory than Moses, just as the builder of the house has more honor than the house (Heb 03:03).

By contrast, the greatness of the Servant of *Yahveh*, who would be the Second Moses, was inherent in himself. He was so great that *Yahveh* the Father said:

This task is too small that you [the Son] should be my servant just to raise up the tribes of Jacob and restore the preserved of Israel. I will also give you for a light to the gentiles so that you may be my salvation to the end of the earth (Isa 49:06; Act 13:47).

Yeshua was superior to Moses, which allowed *Yeshua* to attract enthusiastic crowds of Jews and gentiles to himself. This would make the unbelieving Jews take note (Joh 11:47-48; Mat 27:18; Mar 15:10), especially since crowds tended to come to, and stay with, Moses only out of dire necessity.

God also does not allow those who are unenthusiastic about *Yeshua* to be apathetic or disinterested. God uses jealousy and envy in a roundabout way to save as many Jews and gentiles as possible (Mat 21:15; 27:18; Joh 03:26; 11:48; 12:19; Act 05:16-17; 07:09; 13:45, 50; 17:05). Jews may deny this. Though the emotion of jealousy is ugly green and is not considered socially acceptable behavior, still, hints of jealousy can be discerned about every aspect of Christianity, including the numbers game. For instance, Saul Singer wrote:

In an editorial last week, the *Wall Street Journal* noted that, 'contrary to perceived wisdom, Christianity is booming.' At around 2 billion adherents, Christianity is not only the largest world religion, but growing by leaps and bounds…As Jews, we tend to pretend that we do not have a horse

in this race...We are the progenitors of monotheism, and therefore of
Christianity and Islam, so what does it matter that we are tiny? We even
revel in the notion that we are tiny and indestructible, and subconsciously
connect the two attributes. We have trained ourselves to believe that
to be small is a good, perhaps elevated condition. Let's stop kidding
ourselves. It is one thing to make a virtue out of necessity, another out of
decline...Does it matter that we are moving from tiny to tinier? Yes, if it
means we are abandoning precisely what makes many of us proud to be
Jews...At the risk of sounding like Osama bin Laden and his dreams of
past Islamic glory, I would point out that Jews once numbered 10 percent
of the population of the Roman Empire, the modern [known] world of that
time. If the modern world today numbers 2 billion people [hypothetically
speaking], perhaps it is too ambitious to aim for 200 million Jews. But
why should not we aspire to a population of 50 or 100 million, particularly
at a time when the modern world is itself growing rapidly?[183]

During the Transfiguration, Moses and Elijah talked to *Yeshua*. Then the Father
said:

This is my Son, whom I love; with him I am well pleased. Listen to
him! (Mat 17:05; Mar 09:07; Luk 09:35).

The Father is clearly alluding to Moses' statement:

Yahveh your God will raise up for you a prophet from among you of your
brothers, and he will be like me; to him shall you listen (Deu 18:15-19).

The Transfiguration teaches that though Moses and Elijah's words are true and
are beneficial to read, the Father now commands us to listen to the Son (Gal 03:19,
23, 25; 04:01-04).

The NT writers saw *Yeshua* as the prophet like Moses, but only better (Act 03:
22-23; 07:37; Heb 01:01-02). The writer of Hebrews wrote that Christ is worthy of
more honor than Moses, just as the builder is worthy of more honor than the house
(Heb 03:03-06). The writer of Hebrews wrote:

He [Moses] regarded disgrace for the sake of Christ as of greater value
than the treasures of Egypt, because Moses was looking ahead to his
reward (Heb 11:24).

Yeshua said that Moses wrote of him (Joh 05:46). Paul wrote that one of the
persons called *Yahveh* (Num 21:25) and God (Num 21:27) with whom Moses
had dealings was Christ (1Co 10:09). This shows that Moses was a disciple of
Yahveh the Son. Also, when *Yeshua* followed Mosaic Law, *Yeshua* was really just
following his own code (Isa 09:06-07; Mat 03:15; 12:08; 17:24-27; Mar 02:28;
Luk 06:05; Joh 19:11; Rom 13:01-04).

Yahveh required the death of both Moses and *Yeshua* (Deu 32:50; Luk 22:42). If
one's idea of a Messiah did not die like Moses (Deu 34:05-07) and then live again
(Mat 17:03-05; Mar 09:04), then one's idea of a Messiah is neither "like Moses"
nor Biblical (Deu 18:15).

At the Transfiguration, Moses appeared with the cloud that soon enveloped him (Mat 17:05). *Yeshua*, however, shone as bright as the sun. Furthermore, *Yeshua* will not be hidden by a cloud like Moses at the Transfiguration, but will appear in the clouds before the inhabitants of the entire earth (Dan 07:13; Mat 24:30; Act 01: 09-11; 1Co 15:51-52; Rev 01:07; Rev 14:14).

Moses was not allowed to enter the Promised Land (Deu 01:37; 03:25-27). Moses did, however, appear in the Promised Land after his death—as though on the sly. The Jewish authorities effectively restricted most of *Yeshua*'s ministry to places outside of Judea by stirring up the Judeans (Luk 23:05). *Yeshua* could only enter Judea and attend feasts as though on the sly (Joh 07:10, 14; 11:56). Moreover, the resurrected *Yeshua* will return when no one is expecting him—as though on the sly (Mat 24:42-43; Luk 12:39-40).

Though Satan thought he had a right to Moses' body (Jud 01:09; see also 2Pe 02:11 and Zec 03:01-02), Moses' body was allowed to R.I.P.[184] in an unmarked grave (Deu 34:06). By contrast, the bodies of Enoch (Gen 05:24), Elijah (2Ki 02: 17), and *Yeshua* never saw decay (Psa 016:10; Act 02:27-31).

Moses was a leader and Aaron was a priest. *Yeshua*, however, is both a king and priest forever in the order of Melchizedek (Psa 110:04). Melchizedek, which means, "My King is Righteousness," was simultaneously a king and priest (Gen 14:18). *Yeshua* is a priest in the order of Melchizedek. *Yeshua* was not the same person as Melchizedek, since the writer of Hebrews said that *Yeshua* was "another priest like Melchizedek" (Heb 07:11, 15, 17). Since *Yeshua* is a king and priest forever, he is a better guarantor of a covenant than were Moses and Aaron (Heb 07: 22, 27-28).

In Psa 110, the Father said that the Son would rule "in the midst of your enemies" (Psa 110:02; compare Psa 106:47; Rom 08:37; 2Co 02:14-16). Moses also ruled Israel in the midst of enemies, but his career as ruler was cut short, and Israel fell away.[185] The Son will rule heaven and earth forever when the unbelievers are sifted out (Mat 13:24-43; Rev 11:15; 21:01-04). The believers will then be changed in the twinkling of an eye (1Co 15:52).

By fulfilling the law, *Yeshua* set aside the first law written on stone, and established the second law of Christ that is written on our hearts (Jer 31:33; 2Co 03:03; Heb 08:11; 10:09b, 16; Gal 06:02). Paul said that Moses' OT covenant is now the "Old Covenant" (2Co 03:14). The OT Covenant has been set aside and replaced by the "New Covenant" (Jer 31:31; Luk 22:20; 1Co 11:25; 2Co 03:06; Heb 08:08; 09:15; 12:24).

Moses sprinkled Israel with blood and water (Exo 24:08; Heb 09:19), but *Yeshua* sprinkles all nations (Isa 52:15) with his blood (Heb 12:24; 1Pe 01:02), water (Eze 36:25; Mat 28:19; 1Pe 03:21-22), and the Spirit (Act 11:16).

Moses had the Aaronic priests name the Name, *Yahveh*, over one nation three times—once for each person of the Trinity (Num 06:24-27). *Yeshua* told the disciples to baptize all nations in the name (singular) of the Father, Son and Spirit (Mat 28:19). The Father said that saving one nation was too small a task for

Yeshua (Isa 49:06; Act 13:47), but Moses was barely up to the task of saving one nation (Exo 04:13).

Moses was able to get the Father to send the Presences to the Promised Land with the Israelites (Exo 33:14-15). *Yeshua* returned to the Father to send the Spirit to the ends of the earth to be with all Christians forever (Joh 14:16-18; 16:07; Act 01:08). *Yeshua*, himself, is with us until the end of time (Joh 14:18; Mat 18:20; 28:20). Moses' spirit, however, is in heaven, while erosion has probably entirely disintegrated Moses' body (Deu 34:06).

Moses wished he could dispense the Spirit to more people (Num 11:17, 29; Deu 34:09). Elijah said that for Elisha to receive a double-portion of the Spirit was a hard thing (2Ki 02:09-10). "Double-portion" refers to the eldest son's share of the inheritance that was allotted so he could act as a familial or spiritual father. *Yeshua*, however, was given the Spirit without measure (Joh 03:34; Col 02:09). *Yeshua* baptizes with the Spirit (Joh 01:33), and dispenses the Spirit to all believers (Joh 07:37-39; 15:26; 16:07; 20:22).

Moses was a mere man, but *Yeshua* was the God-man. This point is discussed in the Trinitarian proofs appendix. As Balaam said, he saw that *El Shaddai* would be the Messiah (Num 24:04-17).

When away from the source of glory (Num 06:25), Moses' reflected glory faded (Exo 34:33-35; 2Co 03:07-13). Moses needed to cover his face with a veil so that the Israelites would not see the fading glory. The fading glory would have too strongly underscored the impermanence of the Mosaic covenant. The Mosaic covenant had to last until Christ fulfilled its requirements (Mat 05:17-18; Joh 19: 30).

Paul wrote that believers no longer need to look upon a leader with a veiled face. Christians look to the unfading source of Moses' glory, *Yahveh* the Son (2 Co 03:14-18). Paul wrote that *Yeshua* is the "image of God," and that the light of the knowledge of the glory of God shows in the face of *Yeshua* (2Co 04:04-06; see also Rev 01:16).

Yeshua was Greater Than Any Hero of the Faith

The reader can surely find more points of unequal comparison between Moses and *Yeshua*. However, just in case the reader thinks that someone other than Moses was the greatest OT hero of faith, one last point needs to be made: no matter how one ranks the heroes of the faith, *Yeshua* is always the greatest.

Yeshua is greater than John the Baptist (Joh 01:15, 30). John was said to be the greatest (mere) man ever born (Mat 11:11; Luk 07:28), but only because of the mission with which he was entrusted (Mat 11:10; Luk 07:27). *Yeshua* was greater than Jacob (Joh 04:12-14), and greater than any prophet (Joh 09:17, 35-38).

The writer of Hebrews said that a priest like *Yeshua* who has an indestructible life (Heb 07:08, 16) is greater than Melchizedek. Melchizedek must have been sinful and mortal because he had to be replaced by *Yeshua* (Heb 07:23). Since

Melchizedek was greater than Abraham (Heb 07:04, 06-08), and *Yeshua* is greater than Melchizedek, then *Yeshua* is greater than even Abraham. In fact, *Yeshua* can be considered greater than Abraham just on the basis of *Yeshua*'s preexistence as "I AM" (Joh 08:58).

Appendix A:
MT Plurals Referring to Yahveh

MT Plurals Referring to *Yahveh*

There are over a thousand instances of *Elohim* (Gods) referring to *Yahveh*. Due to the prejudgments and dictates of unitarianism, nearly all translations translate the Hebrew plurals referring to *Yahveh* in the singular. Besides the instances of *Elohim*, there are other Hebrew plurals referring to *Yahveh*.

List of Verses with MT Plurals in 38 Chapters of 18 MT books

1. Genesis:
   - Plurals: Gen 01:26; 03:22; 11:07; 20:13; 35:07
   - Unique Plurals Running Total: 05
2. Exodus:
   - Plurals: Exo 12:36; 32:04, 05, 08; 33:14-15
   - Unique Plurals Running Total: 08
3. Deuteronomy:
   - Plurals: Deu 04:07; 05:26
   - Unique Plurals Running Total: 10
4. Joshua:
   - Plurals: Jos 24:19
   - Unique Plurals Running Total: 11
5. 1 Samuel:
   - Plurals: 1Sa 04:07-08; 17:26, 36
   - Unique Plurals Running Total: 13
6. 2 Samuel:
   - Plurals: 2Sa 07:23
   - Unique Plurals Running Total: 14
7. 2 Chronicles:
   - Plurals: 2Ch 32:14, 15
   - Unique Plurals Running Total: 15
8. Job:

- Plurals: Job 35:10
- Unique Plurals Running Total: 16
9. Psalms:
  - Plurals: Psa 058:11 [BHS 057:12]; 149:02
  - Unique Plurals Running Total: 18
10. Proverbs:
  - Plurals: Pro 09:10; 30:03
  - Unique Plurals Running Total: 20
11. Ecclesiastes
  - Plurals: Ecc 12:01
  - Unique Plurals Running Total: 21
12. Song of Solomon
  - Plurals: Sol 01:11
  - Unique Plurals Running Total: 22
13. Isaiah:
  - Plurals: Isa 06:08; 24:16; 41:04, 22-23, 26; 43:09; 54:05
  - Unique Plurals Running Total: 27
14. Jeremiah:
  - Plurals: Jer 10:10; 17:01, 12; 23:36; 33:24
  - Unique Plurals Running Total: 31
15. Daniel:
  - Plurals: Dan 04:08, 09, 17, 18, 25, 26, 31, 32 [BHS 04:05, 06, 14, 22, 23, 28, 29]; 05:11, 20, 21; 07:18, 22, 25b, 26, 27
  - Unique Plurals Running Total: 34
16. Hosea:
  - Plurals: Hos 11:02, 12 [BHS 12:01]; 12:04 [BHS 12:05]
  - Unique Plurals Running Total: 36
17. Habakkuk:
  - Plurals: Hab 01:12
  - Unique Plurals Running Total: 37
18. Malachi:
  - Plurals: Mal 01:06
  - Unique Plurals Running Total: 38

A Detailed Look at the Plurals Referring to *Yahveh* Found in 38 Chapters of 18 MT Books

Plurals 01-11 (First Person Plural Pronouns):
The "we" or "us" in these verses refers to *Yahveh*: Gen 01:26; 03:22; 11:07; Isa 06:08; 24:16; 41:22-23, 26; 43:09; Sol 01:11; Hos 12:04 [BHS 12:05]; and Hab 01:12). The "we" or "us" in each of these verses is the translation of either a first person plural pronoun, or a first person plural verb.

The reader should be aware that translators think they have a "license" to adapt Trinitarian speech to the exegetical stipulations of unitarianism. For example, "my" often is translated as "his" in Isa 34:16, and pronouns such as "we" or "us" in the Hebrew or Aramaic are sometimes rendered as "he" or "they" in translation. For instance, in the *NIV* translation of Hos 12:04 [*BHS* 12:05], "us" is rendered as "him." So recourse to the original Hebrew or a literal translation like the *YLT* is necessary.

First Person Plural Pronouns in Gen 01:26

> God [plural noun] said [singular verb], 'Let us make [plural verb] man in our [plural suffix] image [singular noun], according to our [plural suffix] likeness [singular noun]...' (Gen 01:26).

A passage with a plural related to Gen 01:26 is found in the LXX, but not in the MT. The LXX has God saying:

> It is not good that the man should be alone. Let us make [plural verb] him a helper suitable for him (LXX Gen 02:18).

The MT, however, has "I will make."

The LXX translators have Satan saying:

> ...you would be as Gods, knowing [plural participle] good and evil (LXX Gen 03:05b).

In Gen 03:05 Satan meant that Adam and Eve would be like the Trinity rather than like false gods, since Adam did not know about false gods yet.

This is reflected in the Greek LXX translation of the Hebrew plural *Elohim* using the plural *theoi* (Gods). The LXX translation of "Gods" likely preserves the original Trinitarian sense of the Hebrew. The plural "Gods" in Gen 03:05 would be consistent with the plural "us" in Gen 03:22. After Adam and Eve ate of the forbidden fruit, God said that they had become "like one of us" (Gen 03:22).

Gen 01:26-28 does not specifically state that either the man or the woman was created in the image of God, but God said "man" was created in the image of God. "Man" is meant as an inclusive term for both man and woman (mankind, humankind), as is shown clearly by:

- The male and female being called "man" (Gen 05:02),
- The four times God referred to "man" as "them" (Gen 01:26-28), and
- God referring to "man" (Gen 01:26-27) using the plural "yours" (Gen 01:29).

That the Trinity made "man" in their singular image, and that "man" is an inclusive term for two persons, is a strong Trinitarian proof. This is especially the case in the context where God is referred to in the plural so often—as "Gods" (*Elohim*), as "*Yahveh Elohim*," and as "us" (Gen 01:26; 03:22; and LXX Gen 02: 18; LXX Gen 03:05b).

Also, a strong Trinitarian proof is the fact that the Trinity seems to be involved in making persons and nations: The "us" made Adam and Eve (Gen 01:26; LXX Gen 02:18). People have "creators" (Ecc 12:01) and "makers" (Job 35:10), and the nation Israel has "makers" (Psa 149:02; Isa 54:05). These MT plurals are discussed in this appendix.

First Person Plural Pronoun in Gen 03:22
Yahveh Elohim said, 'The man has now become like one of us, knowing good and evil' (Gen 03:22).

Earlier, the LXX translators have Satan saying:

...you would be as Gods [the Greek is the plural *theoi*], knowing [plural participle] good and evil (LXX Gen 03:05b).

By using plurals in LXX Gen 03:05b, and elsewhere (for example, in LXX Gen 02:18 and LXX Exo 22:27 (English 22:28)]), the LXX translators showed that the original Hebrew pointed to the individual persons of the Trinity—the "us" mentioned in Gen 01:26; 03:22, and elsewhere.

First Person Plural Pronoun in Gen 11:07
Yahveh said, 'Let us descend [plural verb] and confuse [plural verb]' (Gen 11:07).

First Person Plural Pronoun in Sol 01:11
Yahveh said, 'We [the Trinity] will make you [the Church] earrings of gold...' (Sol 01:11).

The Song of Solomon is a song about pure love. The reason the Song of Solomon is a canonical book is *Yahveh*'s love for his bride, the Church, is personified (Joh 03:29; Rev 19:07; 21:02, 09; 22:17). The "we" therefore indicates that *Yahveh* are persons.

First Person Plural Pronoun in Isa 06:08
Then I heard the voice of the Lord saying, 'Whom shall I send? And who will go for us?' (Isa 06:08).

Yahveh used the plural pronoun "us." John said that Isaiah saw and talked "about" the glory of *Yeshua* in his vision in the temple (Joh 12:41), but Isaiah actually talked to the Spirit (Act 28:25-26).

First Person Plural Verb in Isa 24:16
Yahveh told the earth to glorify *Yahveh* (Isa 24:15), and the same divine person said, "We hear" (plural verb) (Isa 24:16). Only *Yahveh* could demand and receive such praise from the entire earth (Isa 25:15). Note that Isa 24:15-16 is similar to Joh 12:28 where the Son asks the Father to glorify his name, and the Father's voice is heard from heaven as loud as thunder.

First Person Plural Pronouns in Isa 41:22-23, 26
God mentioned the plurals "us" twice and "we" once in Isa 41:22. God mentioned "we" and "we...together" in Isa 41:23. God mentioned "we" in Isa 41:26. Also in Isa 41, *Yahveh* refers to himself as "the Lasts":

I, *Yahveh* [the Son], am the first, and am with the lasts—'I AM' (Isa 41:04).

The Hebrew for "lasts" is plural. The "lasts" here are the Father and the Spirit. The "lasts" are the "us" and "we" mentioned elsewhere in Isaiah (Isa 06:08; 41:22-23, 26).

First Person Plural Pronoun in Hab 01:12

Are you [the Father] not from everlasting, *Yahveh* [the Father] my [the Son's] God [the Father], my [the Son's] Holy One [the Father]? We [the Father and Son] will not die (Hab 01:12).

The LXX of Hab 01:12 does not have the pronoun "my" between "Lord" and "God," but merely reads "Lord God, my Holy One." Similar passages are those where:

- The Son said that he is eternal (Isa 51:06, 08),
- The Messiah is prophesied to be eternal (as is discussed at Isa 09:06 [*BHS* 09:05]) in the Trinitarian proofs appendix),
and
- The Father said the Son is eternal (as is discussed at LXX Psa 102:26 in the Trinitarian proofs appendix).

Plurals 12-17 ("Holy Ones"):

God is called the Holy Ones (plural adjective *Qadoshim*) (Jos 24:19; Pro 09:10; 30:03; Dan 04:17 [*BHS* 04:14]; 05:11; Hos 11:12 [*BHS* 12:01]).

Joshua spoke of the "holy [plural adjective *Qadoshim*] Gods [*Elohim*]" (Jos 24:19). The context has *Yahveh* twice being called "[All] the Gods [*haElohim*]" (Jos 22:34; 24:01), and a "God of Gods" (Jos 22:22). Elsewhere, God is called a "God of Gods" (Deu 10:17; Psa 050:01; Dan 02:47; 11:36), and a "God of [All] the Gods [*haElohim*]" (Psa 136:02).

The context in Jos 22 shows that the Transjordan tribes were calling upon the Father and the Son to fulfill the Mosaic requirement that there be a minimum of two concurring witnesses (Deu 19:15). The Transjordan tribes said:

God of Gods, *Yahveh* [the Father]! God of Gods, *Yahveh* [the Son]! He knows (Jos 22:22).

Similarly, Nebuchadnezzar referred to the Trinity as "the Holy [Aramaic plural adjective *qaddiysh*] Gods [*Elohim*]" (Dan 04:08, 09, 18 [*BHS* 04:05, 06, 14]). Also, Belshazzar's wife referred to the Trinity as "the Holy [Aramaic plural adjective *qaddiysh*] Gods [*Elohim*]" (Dan 05:11).

"Holy Ones" in Pro 30:03

Agur called the Father and Son the "Holy Ones" (Pro 30:03). The "Holy Ones" are previously identified as *Yahveh* (Pro 09:10). The next verse, Pro 30:04, mentions a Father who ascends to heaven, and his Son. What is implied is that the Son ascends to heaven as the Father does.

So Solomon believed in *Yahveh* the Father and *Yahveh* the Son. This is especially plausible given the fact that Solomon wrote three plurals referring to *Yahveh* (Pro 30:03; Ecc 12:01; Sol 01:11), not to mention all the times Solomon called *Yahveh* "*Elohim*" (literally, "Gods"). Interestingly, *Yahveh* appeared to Solomon twice (1Ki 03:05; 09:02; 11:09). Perhaps the first appearance was the Father and the second the Son.

Ancient Hebrews may have associated Pro 30:03-04 with the Dan 07 vision where the Son rides the clouds to meet the Father. Ancient Hebrews may have also associated Pro 30:03-04 with Psa 068:04, 18, 33 [*BHS* 068:05, 19, 34] where *Yahveh* rode to heaven.

Paul quoted Psa 068:18 [*BHS* 068:19] in Eph 04:08-10 and applied the passage to *Yeshua*. Also, *Yeshua* may have alluded to Pro 30:03 when he told his disciples that they would believe once they saw "the Son of Man ascend to where he was before" (Joh 06:62).

"Holy Ones" in Dan 04:17 [BHS 04:14]

Nebuchadnezzar mentioned a single "Watcher" and "Holy One" (the Son) (Dan 04:13 [*BHS* 04:10]), who in turn mentioned plural "Watchers and Holy Ones" (Dan 04:17 [*BHS* 04:14]).

Since only a singular "Watcher" and "Holy one" announced a decision of God to Nebuchadnezzar (Dan 04:13 [*BHS* 04:10]), it cannot later be said that the decree is "announced" by plural "watchers" and "holy ones" (Dan 04:17 [*BHS* 04:14]). The verbs "to announce" and "to declare" are not in the MT recension, but translators have added these verbs so they can construe the "Watcher" and the "Watchers," and the "Holy One" and the "Holy Ones," to be mere angels.

Without the interpolated verbs, Dan 04:17 (*BHS* Dan 04:14) translates as:

> The decree of the Watchers is the command, and the saying of the Holy
> Ones is the affair.

This is consistent with the phrase "the decree of the Most High" (Dan 04:21 [*BHS* 04:18]), which also has no verb.

God, not angels, make decrees (Act 03:21; Rev 10:07). God is elsewhere called a "watcher" (Job 07:20; see also Gen 16:13) and a "watchman" (Hos 09:08), who keeps vigil (Exo 12:42) and never slumbers (Exo 12:42; Psa 121:03-04). So it would seem the following words refer to the Trinity: the singular "Watcher" (Dan 04:13 [*BHS* 04:10]) and plural "Watchers" (Dan 04:17 [*BHS* 04:14]), and the "Holy Ones [*Qadoshim*]" (Dan 04:17 [*BHS* 04:14]; see also Pro 09:10; 30:03; Hos 11:12 [*BHS* 12:01] in this appendix).

Daniel also showed that the "Watchers" and "Holy Ones" were the Trinity by referring to them as the Most High (Dan 05:18), and then saying that "they caused his glory to pass from him" when Nebuchadnezzar became too arrogant (Dan 05: 20). Other plurals used to refer to the Watchers and Holy Ones include:

- "They cause you to eat grass" (Dan 04:25, 32 [Dan 04:22, 29]; 05:21),
- "They drive you away from men" (Dan 04:25, 32 [Dan 04:22, 29]),
- "They drench you with dew" (Dan 04:25 [04:22]),
- "Whereas they said, 'Leave the stump...'" (Dan 04:26 [04:23]), and
- "They say to you..." (Dan 04:31 [04:28]).

See Dan 07 in this appendix for more discussion on the Watchers and the Holy Ones.

It should be noted that it would not be unusual for the Trinity to appear to Nebuchadnezzar, since the Trinity appeared to other kings and famous persons. *HaElohim* is a Hebrew form meaning, "[All] the Gods [*haElohim*]," and is used to refer to the Trinity. The OT mentions that these people saw "*haElohim*" (the Trinity): Enoch (Gen 05:22, 24), Noah (Gen 06:09), Abraham (Gen 17:18; 20:17; 22:03, 09), Abimelech (Gen 20:06), Jacob (Gen 27:28; 35:07; 48:15), Moses (Exo 03:06, 11, 12, 13; 18:12; 19:03, 17; 20:20, 21; 24:11), the Israelites (Exo 18:12; 19: 17; 20:20, 21; 24:11), Balaam (Num 22:10; 23:27), and Gideon (Jdg 06:36, 39).

"Holy Ones" in Hos 11:02, 12 [BHS 12:01]; Hos 12:04 [BHS 12:05]
Hosea wrote:
As they [the Trinity] called [plural verb] them [Israel], so they [the Trinity] went [plural verb] from them [Israel] (Hos 11:02).
Hos 11:02 has similarities to Jer 33:24 where *Yahveh* is called "they":
The Word [the Son] of *Yahveh* [the Father] came to Jeremiah, saying, 'Have you [Jeremiah] not noticed what this people have spoken? Specifically: 'The two kingdoms that *Yahveh* chose [Israel & Judah], he [*Yahveh*] has rejected them, and they [*Yahveh*] spurn my people [Judah] so that they are no longer a nation before them [*Yahveh*]"(Jer 33:24).
Hosea referred to the Trinity as the "Holy Ones" (*Qadoshim*) (Hos 11:12 [*BHS* 12:01]). Hosea provides yet another Trinitarian proof in this chapter. Hosea records *Yahveh* the Son saying that even if Israel appealed to the Most High (*Elyon*), even he, the Father, would not exalt Israel. So the Son referred to the Father in the third person as "he" (Hos 11:07), and then the Son referred to himself as "God" (Hos 11:09).
Hosea wrote that *Yahveh* the Son referred to the *Malek Yahveh* as *Elohim* (Hos 12:03-04a [*BHS* 12:04-05a]), and said that Jacob talked to "us" (Hos 12:04b [*BHS* 12:05b]). Not only does the repeated subject-object sentence structure indicate that the "us" is the Trinity, but God seemed to appear to Jacob when Jacob was alone. So humans are mostly ruled out as being the "us." Besides, the narrator, Moses, asserted:
[All] the Gods [*haElohim*], they appeared [plural verb] to him [Jacob]... (Gen 35:07).
Therefore, the "us" must refer to the Trinity.
The Son continued to speak and identified the two specific persons of the Trinity meant by the "us." The Son spoke this *Shema*-like statement:
Yahveh [the Father], God [the Son] of hosts, *Yahveh* is his [The Trinity's] name of renown (Hos 12:05 [*BHS* 12:06]).
By comparison, Moses' *Shema* reads:
Yahveh [the Father] [and] our God [the Son], *Yahveh* [the Spirit] [are] a united one (Deu 06:04).
In the Son's *Shema*-like statement, the Hebrew word that the *NIV* translates as "name of renown" is *zeker* (Hos 12:05 [*BHS* 12:06]). *Zeker* usually means

"memory" or "memorial," but it makes better sense to say that *Yahveh* is the Trinity's "name of renown" rather than a "memory" or "memorial." Also, *zeker* is associated with the Hebrew word for "name" (*shame*) several times (Exo 03:15; Job 18:17; Psa 009:05-06; 135:13; Pro 10:07; Isa 26:08, 13-14).

A literal translation of Hosea's words in Hos 12:03-05 [*BHS* 12:04-06] reads:

03. In the womb he [Jacob] took his [Jacob's] brother [Esau] by the heel; and in his [Jacob's] manhood he [Jacob] had power with God [in other words, the *Peniel*, translated "Face of God" (Gen 32:30-21)]. 04. Indeed, he [Jacob] had power over the *Malek* [the Son] and prevailed [Gen 32:24-32]; He [Jacob] wept, and made supplication to him [the Son]. He [Jacob] found him [the Son] at Bethel [Gen 35:09-15], and there he [Jacob] spoke with us [The Trinity], 05. even *Yahveh* [the Trinity], God [the Trinity] of hosts [angels]; *Yahveh* is his [the Trinity's] name of renown.

Plural 18 (Gen 20:13):

Abraham said:

Gods [*Elohim*], they caused [plural verb] me to wander (Gen 20:13).

Nehemiah wrote about the persons of the Trinity who called Abram out of Ur using the paired pronouns "you-he." Nehemiah wrote:

You-he are *Yahveh*...you-he are *Yahveh*, [All] the Gods [*haElohim*], who chose Abram and brought him out of Ur of the Chaldeans and named him Abraham (Neh 09:06-07).

Nehemiah's use of the definite article with *Elohim* (Neh 09:07), and Nehemiah's twice using the joined pair of pronouns "you-he" (Neh 09:06-07), indicate that plural persons of the Trinity called Abram out of Ur.

The narrator, Moses, said that "[All] the Gods [*haElohim*]" appeared to Abimelech (Gen 20:06). That Abimelech knew *Yahveh* to be persons explains why Abraham said, "God [*Elohim*], they caused me to wander" (Gen 20:13). Appropriately, Abraham prayed to "[All] the Gods" to heal Abimelech (Gen 20: 17).

HaElohim is a Hebrew form meaning, "[All] the Gods." *HaElohim* often refers to the Trinity. The OT mentions that these people saw or talked to *haElohim* (the Trinity): Enoch (Gen 05:22, 24), Noah (Gen 06:09), Abraham (Gen 17:18; 20: 17; 22:03, 09), Abimelech (Gen 20:06), Jacob (Gen 27:28; 35:07; 48:15), Moses (Exo 03:06, 11, 12, 13; 19:03), the Israelites (Exo 18:12; 19:17; 20:20, 21; 24: 11), Balaam (Num 22:10; 23:27) and Gideon (Jdg 06:36, 39). *HaElohim* is not mentioned in connection with Nebuchadnezzar, but Nebuchadnezzar did see "Watchers" and "Holy Ones" (Dan 04:17 [Dan 04:14]).

Plural 19 (Gen 35:07):

The narrator, Moses, said:
[All] the Gods [*haElohim*], they appeared [plural verb] to him
[Jacob]... (Gen 35:07).

Plural 20 (Exo 12:36):

A literal translation that does not hide the Trinitarianism is:
Yahveh gave his people favor in the sight of the Egyptians, and they
[*Yahveh*] caused them [the Egyptians] to give, and thus they [*Yahveh*]
plundered the Egyptians (Exo 12:36).

Yahveh said elsewhere that he would cause the plundering mentioned in Exo 12:
36 (Gen 15:14; Exo 03:21-22; 11:03; 12:36).

Other indicators that persons of *Yahveh* are the subject of Exo 12:36 are the
mentions of "*Yahveh Elohim*" (Exo 09:30). *Yahveh Elohim* refer to the Father and
Son, as is discussed in the chapter on Hebrew collective plurals. Also, the form
"[All] the Gods [*haElohim*]," meaning the Trinity, is mentioned often in connection
with Egypt and the Exodus (Gen 41:25, 28, 32; 45:08; Exo 01:17, 21; 02:23; 03:01,
06, 11, 12, 13; 04:20, 27; 14:19; 1Sa 04:08; 1Ch 17:21).

Nehemiah spoke of *Yahveh* in connection with the Egyptians and the Exodus
(Neh 09:09-12). In the same chapter that Nehemiah referred to *Yahveh* as "[All]
the Gods [*haElohim*]" (Neh 09:07), and as "you-he" (Neh 09:06-07), the LXX has
a plural verb referring to *Yahveh*:
These are the Gods that brought [plural verb] us up out of Egypt (LXX
Neh 09:18).

The Hebrew verb form of *sha'al* that is translated "they caused them to give"
(Exo 12:36), is a Hiphil with a suffix. The Hiphil mood gives a verb a causative
sense, and the suffix gives the object of the verb. Examples of other Hiphil verbs
with suffixes are "they caused him to drink" (1Sa 30:11), "idols caused them to
stumble (err)" (Jer 18:15; Amo 02:04), and "they [the priests] cause them [the
Israelites] to discern" (Eze 44:23).

Grammar note: The Hiphil of *sha'al* with a third person suffix appears twice
in the OT (Exo 12:36; 1Sa 01:28). In Exo 12:36 the form should be translated
"they [*Yahveh*] caused them to give." Similarly, in 1Sa 01:28 the form should
be translated "I cause him [Samuel] to give [a lifetime of service] to *Yahveh*, for
his whole life will be given to *Yahveh*." Notice how in the two verses, the object
given, jewelry (Exo 12:36) and "lifetime of service" (1Sa 01:28), is specified
nearby the Hiphil verb.

The account of Samuel's mother's vow shows how Hannah and *Yahveh* caused
Samuel to give his life to *Yahveh* (1Sa 01:01-28). Evidently, *Yahveh* was to "make
good on his word" (1Sa 01:23) by giving Hannah other children (1Sa 02:01, 05,
19-21) since Hannah had Samuel give his life to *Yahveh* (1Sa 01:01-28; 1Sa 02:
11). Other parents also caused their children to give themselves to *Yahveh* (Jdg 11:
30-40; Jer 35:01-19).

Plural 21 (Exo 32:01, 04, 05, 08, 23):

That the Israelites told Aaron to "make us *Elohim* who will go [plural verbs] before us" (Exo 32:01, 23) is curiously similar to how *Yahveh* said, "My Presences, they will go with you" (Exo 33:14-15).

During the golden calf incident, Aaron said that the Israelites would have a festival to *Yahveh* (Exo 32:05), who was "your Gods [plural noun], O Israel, who brought [plural verb] you up out of the land of Egypt" (Exo 32:04, 08). That Aaron mentioned the feast to *Yahveh*, and used the plural form *Elohim* (Gods) along with plural verbs, shows that Aaron was speaking of the persons of *Yahveh* as Gods. Aaron was not speaking of the single golden calf as gods. Besides, "[All] the Gods [*haElohim*]" previously had spoken to Aaron (Exo 04:27), Aaron had eaten with "[All] the Gods [*haElohim*]" (Exo 18:12), and Aaron had seen the Trinity on three mountains during the giving of the law (Deu 33:01-02, as was discussed in the Presences of *Elyon* chapter).

See Exo 32:01, 04, 05, 08, 23 in the Trinitarian proofs appendix for further explanation as to how Aaron managed to connect golden calf worship and worship of *Yahveh*.

Plural 22 (Exo 33:14-15):

> *Yahveh* [*Elyon* the Father] replied, 'My Presences [Hebrew plural *Panim*], they will go [plural verb] with you, and I will give you rest.' Then Moses said to him [*Elyon* the Father], 'Your Presences, if they [the Son and Spirit] do not go [plural verb] with us [to the Promised Land], do not send us up from here [Mount Sinai]' (Exo 33:14-15).

Exo 33:14-15 has similarities to Hos 11:02. Hosea wrote:

> As they [the Trinity] called [plural verb] them [Israel], so they [the Trinity] went [plural verb] from them [Israel] (Hos 11:02).

Exo 33:14-15 is discussed in the Presences of *Elyon* chapter.

Plural 23 (Deu 04:07):

"Coming near" (plural adjective) modifies both the gods of the nations and "*Yahveh*, our God." Moses said:

> What other nation is so great as to have their gods near them as *Yahveh* our *Elohim* [Gods]... (Deu 04:07).

The context of Deu 04:07 has Moses calling *Yahveh* both "[All] the Gods [*haElohim*]" (Deu 04:35, 39) and the "living Gods [*khayyim Elohim*]" (Deu 05:26).

Jeremiah supplied a parallel passage:

> Am I only [All] the Gods [*haElohim*] nearby—an affirmation of *Yahveh*, and not a Gods [*Elohim*] afar off? (Jer 23:23).

Then, in the same context, Jeremiah referred to *Yahveh* as "the living Gods [*khayyim Elohim*]" (Jer 23:36).

Apparently, Jeremiah is alluding to Moses' writings since both Moses and Jeremiah have sections that refer to *Yahveh* as "[All] the Gods [*haElohim*]" and as "the living Gods [*khayyim Elohim*]." These sections show that Jeremiah understood Deu 04:07 to have a plural adjective referring to *Yahveh*.

Plural 24 (1Sa 04:07-08):

The Philistines knew of the Trinity, since they said:
    Gods [plural noun] have come [singular verb]...who can deliver us from the hand [singular noun] of the mighty [plural adjective] [All] the Gods [*haElohim*]? They [plural pronoun] are the same [plural pronoun] [All] the Gods [*haElohim*] who struck [plural verb] the Egyptians with all kinds of plagues (1Sa 04:07-08).

When the Philistines were plagued for taking the Ark of [All] the Gods (*haElohim*) (1Sa 04:04, 13, 17, 18, 19, 21, 22; 05:01, 02, 10 (twice)), they said that "the hand [singular] of [All] the Gods [*haElohim*]" had come down heavily on their cities (1Sa 05:11).

The Philistines knew of the persons of *Yahveh* from the Abraham and Abimelech account, and from the Exodus (Gen 38:23; Num 14:14; Deu 32:31; Jos 05:01).

Plural 25 (2Sa 07:23):

David said:
    Gods [plural] went [plural] to redeem to himself a people...(2Sa 07: 23).

2Sa 07 begins with the Word of *Yahveh* (the Son) telling Nathan, "This is what *Yahveh* [the Father] says..." (2Sa 07:04-05). Other plural references to *Yahveh* that David recorded in 2Sa 07 are:

- "[All] the Gods [*haElohim*]," meaning the Trinity, is mentioned twice in this chapter (2Sa 07:02, 28),
- David called God "*Yahveh Elohim*" (2Sa 07:25),
- David sat before the Presences of *Yahveh* in the tabernacle (2Sa 07:18), and
- David used the paired pronouns "you-he" (2Sa 07:28).

The account of 2Sa 07 is repeated in 1Ch 17. This account mentions some of the same plural references to *Yahveh*: "[All] the Gods [*haElohim*]" (1Ch 17:02, 21, 26), "*Yahveh Elohim*" (1Ch 17:16, 17), the "Presences of *Yahveh*" (1Ch 17:16; compare 16:01), and the paired pronouns "you-he" (1Ch 17:26).

David's Trinitarian account in 2Sa 07 shows that David believed *Yahveh* the Father would send *Yahveh* the Son to be the God-man Messiah. David knew how the Father had sent the Son to redeem Israel from Egypt. After David heard that the Messiah would be his descendant and would rule on David's throne forever (2Sa 07:11-29), David recollected how gracious *Yahveh Elohim* (the Father and Son) were (2Sa 07:25). David notes how "*Elohim* [plural] went [plural] to redeem to himself a people" (2Sa 07:23).

Plural 26 (2Ch 32:14, 15):

Sennacherib's officers spoke in Hebrew (2Ki 18:28), and asked:
How much less shall your *Elohim* [plural noun] deliver [plural verb]
you out of my hand" (2Ch 32:15)?
The Chronicler wrote:
Sennacherib's officers spoke further against *Yahveh*, [All] the Gods
[*haElohim*] (2Ch 32:16).
Also note that *Yahveh* is called "[All] the Gods [*haElohim*]" twice in this
chapter (2Ch 32:16, 31).

Plural 27 (Job 35:10):

Elihu said:
But no one says, 'Where is Gods [plural noun], my Makers [plural
noun]...?' (Job 35:10).

Plural 28 (Psa 058:11 [*BHS* 057:12]):

"Most assuredly, Gods [plural noun], they judge [plural participle] the
earth" (Psa 058:11 [*BHS* 057:12]).

Plural 29 (Psa 149:02):

"Let Israel rejoice in his Makers [plural noun]" (Psa 149:02).

Plural 30 (Ecc 12:01):

"Remember now your creators [plural noun]" (Ecc 12:01).
Yahveh is called "[All] the Gods [*haElohim*]" three times in this chapter (Ecc
12:07, 13-14). Elsewhere, Solomon said that two persons together were better than
one alone (Ecc 04:09-12a), but that a cord of three strands was best of all (Ecc 04:
12b). The inspiration for this thought—that three persons were inseparable as a
three-stranded cord, may have been the Trinity.

Plurals 31-35 (Dan 07:18, 22, 25b, 27, and "Living Gods"):

The MT word translated "Most High" is the singular "*Elyon*," and the Aramaic
word translated "Most High" is the singular *Ilayah*. The earliest hint that two
persons are the Most Highs is when a Psalmist talked about the Most High having
"holy places":
There is a river whose streams make glad the city of God, the holy
places [plural] where the Most High dwells (Psa 046:04).

During the first year of Belshazzar's reign, Daniel saw a vision where the Son of Man would inherit all nations from the Father, and then all nations would worship the Son of Man (Dan 07:13-14). The Son of Man vision is a prophetic parallel of Deu 32:08-09 where the Son inherits Israel from the Father, *Elyon*, and then the Son is worshipped by the nations and angels (LXX Deu 32:43).

Then there are mentions of plural Most Highs (Aramaic plural *Ilyonin*) (Dan 07:18, 22, 25b, 27). A heavenly dweller said of the Most Highs:

> The judge is seated and they will cause its dominion to pass away (Dan 07:26).

This MT reading concurs with the LXX of Dan 07:05 where the Most Highs are called "they" in Greek: "they said to the second beast."

Thus, it seems that all along the Father was Most High merely by the elective decision that the Father would rule all the nations according to the plan of salvation. This is discussed in the chapter on the Song of Moses. Thus, the Father was not Most High by virtue of his having an intrinsic quality that the Son and Spirit had in less measure, or lacked altogether. Now that the Father shares the rule of all the nations, he also shares the title Most High with the Son. The full title, as Melchizedek states, is "Most High, Possessor of Heaven and Earth" (Gen 14:19, 22) Interestingly, John the Evangelist wrote that God and *Yeshua*, the Lamb, have a single throne (Rev 22:01, 03).

During the last night of Belshazzar's reign (Dan 05:30), Daniel referred back to the warning given by the Watchers and Holy Ones who said that the Most High had given Nebuchadnezzar his throne (Dan 05:18), but that "they caused his glory to pass from him" when Nebuchadnezzar became too arrogant (Dan 05:20). The "they" are the Most Highs (Dan 07:18, 22, 25b, 27), who are also called Watchers and Holy Ones (Dan 04:17 [04:14]).

Daniel's referring to a Dan 07 passage while discussing a Dan 05 passage (see paragraph above) might seem anachronistic; however, Daniel saw the vision of the Son of Man in the first year of Belshazzar's reign (Dan 07:01). Daniel saw the vision of the Ram and Goat in Belshazzar's third year (Dan 08:01). So Belshazzar ruled at least three years before the Handwriting on the Wall incident (Dan 05:30). So the vision of Dan 07 occurred before the events of Dan 05!

Though the Son had not yet received the title of Most High, the Dan 07 vision told Daniel that it was a "done deal" in a metaphysical sense. Daniel could call the Son "the Most High" just as we refer to the elect as "the saved" in a metaphysical sense, though Christians on earth are not yet in heaven. In the same future sense, John the Baptist's father, Zechariah, referred to the Messiah as "Most High" (Luk 01:76; see Isa 40:03, 05, 09 in the Trinitarian proofs appendix).

Daniel's prophecy that *Yeshua* would share the title Most High with the Father was fulfilled sometime between the resurrection and the ascension. On the day of his resurrection, *Yeshua* told the Marys that he had not yet returned to the Father (Joh 20:17). However, by the fortieth day after *Yeshua*'s death (Act 01:03), *Yeshua* said:

> All authority in heaven and on earth has been given to me (Mat 28:18).

This meant *Yeshua* was one of the Most Highs.

Paul alluded to how the Son of Man received the name Most High after his resurrection when he said, "Therefore, God also highly exalted him, and gave to him the name that is above every name," in other words the title "Most High" (Phi 02: 09; see also Psa 089:27; Eph 01:20-23; 04:10; Phi 02:09-11; Col 01:18-20; Heb 01: 04-09; 1Pe 03:22).

During *Yeshua*'s trial, the high priest said to *Yeshua*:

I charge you under oath by the living God: Tell us if you are the Christ,
the Son of God (Mat 26:63).

Yeshua responded:

'I AM...and you will see the Son of Man sitting at the right hand of the
Mighty One and coming on the clouds of heaven (Mar 14:62).

By this statement *Yeshua* identified himself as the "I AM" who would be one of the two Most Highs mentioned in Dan 07:13-28.

Under closer inspection, Caiaphas' line of questioning was not said on his own (Joh 11:50-52). Earlier, Peter had identified *Yeshua* as the Son of the "living God," and *Yeshua* said that the Father had taught Peter that response (Mat 16:16-17). Caiaphas said:

I charge you under oath by the living God: Tell us if you are the Christ, the
Son of God! (Mat 26:63).

As was the case with Peter, the High Priest charging *Yeshua* on oath by the "living God" was a statement not said on his own (Joh 11:50-52).

The words translated as "living God" in the OT are sometimes the plural words "living Gods [*Elohim khayyim*]" (Deu 05:26; 1Sa 17:26, 36; Jer 10:10; 23:36). Interestingly, two of the "living Gods" references (Deu 05:26; Jer 23:36) are associated with statements saying that *Yahveh* is "near" (Deu 04:07; 05:27; Jer 23: 23), and that *Yahveh* is "[All] the Gods [*haElohim*]" (Deu 04:35, 39). Furthermore, Deu 05:26 ties in with Deu 33:01-02 where Moses said that at the giving of the law, *Yahveh* appeared on three mountains in fire. This is discussed in the Presences of *Elyon* chapter.

Since Hagar referred to the *Malek Yahveh* as: "The living one who sees" (Gen 16:14; see also 24:62; 25:11), *Yeshua* was a person of *Yahveh* "near" humans. Thus, the High Priest's oath formula mentioning the "living God" lends support to *Yeshua*'s assertion that he was the "I AM," and that *Yeshua* was the Son of Man of the Dan 07 vision who is prophesied to be one of the two Most Highs (Dan 07:18, 22, 25b, 27). See the Song of Moses chapter for more discussion of Dan 07.

Plurals 36 (Isa 54:05):

For your Makers [plural] are your husbands [plural]. *Yahveh* of hosts [the Father] is his name: and the Holy One of Israel [the Son] is your Redeemer; the God [the Son] of the whole earth shall he [the Son] be called (Isa 54:05).

In Isa 45:18 and Ecc 11:05, *Yahveh* is referred to as the creator and maker, and is called "[All] the Gods [*haElohim*]."

Plurals 37 (Jer 17:01, 12):

"The sin of Judah is written...on the horns of your altars" (Jer 17:01). The Hebrew suffix "your" is plural, therefore, "your altars" refers to the Trinity's altars. Elsewhere it is said that *Yahveh* has plural altars (Num 03:31; 1Ki 19:10, 14). Similarly, *Yahveh* said, "A glorious throne, set on high from the beginning, is the place of our sanctuary" (Jer 17:12). The "our" is a Hebrew plural suffix referring to *Yahveh*. That the Trinity has a throne in an "our sanctuary" (Jer 17:12) agrees with John's statement that the Father and Son have one throne (Rev 22:01, 03-04).

Plurals 38 (Mal 01:06):

Yahveh said that he is "Masters." The Hebrew plural form translated "Masters" is *Adonim*, not *Adonai*. In Mal 02, there is a mention of "*Yahveh Elohim*" (Mal 02: 16).

Appendix B:

OT Texts That Suggest or Speak of the Deity of the Messiah

Legend

Texts marked with:
- An asterisk (*) are found in the Trinitarian proofs appendix, and
- A number sign (#) are found in the MT plurals referring to *Yahveh* appendix.

33 OT Texts That Suggest or Speak of the Deity of the Messiah

1) Gen 03:15 *
- Summary: Eve's seed is prophesied to defeat Satan
2) Gen 18—19 *
- Summary: The Trinity visited Abraham in the form of three men
3) Gen 32:24-30 *
- Summary: Jacob wrestled a man and sees the Face of God (Peniel)
- Cross-references: See Hos 11:02, 12 [*BHS* 12:01]; Hos 12:04 [*BHS* 12:05] #
4) Num 24:07b, 16-17 *
- Summary: Balaam saw *El Shaddai* as the future Messiah
- Cross-reference: See the section on Num 22—24 in the chapter on Proto-Sinaitic Trinitarianism
5) Deu 32:08-09, LXX Deu 32:43 *
- Summary: *Yahveh* the Son inherited Israel from *Elyon* the Father, and then the nations and angels are commanded to worship the Son
6) Jos 05:13—06:05 *
- Summary: The Son appeared as a man to Joshua
7) Jdg 06:11-27 *
- Summary: The *Malek Yahveh* appeared as a man to Gideon
8) Jdg 13:02-23 *
- Summary: The *Malek Yahveh* appeared as a man to Manoah and his wife, and called himself "Wonderful"

- Cross-reference: See Isa 09:06 [*BHS* 09:05]*
9) & 10) 2Sa 07:13-14; 1Ch 17:13-14
- Summary: One of David's descendants would be an eternal king who would also be the Son of *Yahveh* the Father
- Cross-reference: See 2Sa 07:23 #
11) Psa 002:02-12 *
- Summary: The Messiah is the Son of *Yahveh* the Father
12) Psa 045:06-07 [*BHS* 045:07-08] *
- Summary: The anointed Messiah was called God [the Son] by God [the Father]
13) Psa 068:18 [*BHS* 068:19]
- Summary: The Son ascended to heaven in victory
- Cross-reference: See Pro 30:03 #
14) Psa 082:06-08 *
- Summary: *Elyon* the Father told God the Son to go take his inheritance
15) Psa 091:01, 09 *
- Summary: *El Shaddai* would be the Messiah who would take refuge in *Elyon* the Father
- Cross-reference: See the section on Num 22—24 in the chapter on Proto-Sinaitic Trinitarianism
16) Psa 110:01, 04-05 *
- Summary: The Father spoke to David's master, the Son, who then became a priest forever
17) Pro 30:03-04 #
- Summary: The Father and Son descended and ascended to heaven
- Cross-reference: See Pro 30:03 #
18) Isa 07:14 *
- Summary: The Messiah would be thought of as "Immanuel," meaning, "God with us"
19) Isa 09:01-02, 06-07 *
- Summary: The Messiah would be called Wonderful, The Messenger of Great Counsel (LXX), Counselor, Mighty God, and the Author of Eternity
- Cross-references: See *BHS* Isa 08:23—09:01, 05-06 * and Jdg 13:02-23 *
20) Isa 40:03, 05, 09, 10 *
- Summary: *Yahveh* would send a messenger to prepare his way and say, "Here is your God!" Then the Glory of *Yahveh* would be revealed
21) Isa 48:12-16 *
- Summary: The Father sent the Son and Spirit
22) Isa 49:05-06 *
- Summary: The Messiah was given a God-sized task
23) Jer 23:05-06; 33:15-16 *
- Summary: Believers will associate the city where the Branch died (Jer 33:16) with the Messiah, who is "*Yahveh* [the Son], our righteousness" (Jer 23:05-06; 33:15).

24) Dan 07:13-27 #
- Summary: The Son of Man first appears in Daniel as the "Son of God" (*KJV* Dan 03:25), and as the Angel (of *Yahveh*) (Dan 03:28). The Son of Man is predicted to inherit the nations. He is worshipped by the nations, and then the Father and Son are called the Most Highs (Dan 07:13-27).
- Cross-reference: See Dan 07:18, 22, 25b, 27 #, Pro 30:03 #, and prophetic parallels in Psa 002 *, 045 * and 110 *. The Son of Man figure is also by Daniel's contemporary, Ezekiel (Eze 01:26-28). Also, see the discussion of the Son of Man in connection with Gen 03:15 in the Song of Moses chapter.

25) Hos 01:06-07 *
- Summary: *Yahveh* the Son saved Judah by sending *Yahveh* the Spirit

26) Hos 12:03-05 [*BHS* 12:04-06] #
- Summary: Hosea wrote that the man with whom Jacob wrestled (Gen 32:24-30) was a person of the Trinity
- Cross-reference: See Hos 11:02, 12 [*BHS* 12:01]; Hos 12:04 [*BHS* 12:05] #

27) Amo 04:11-13 *
- Summary: The Father calls the Son both "God" and "*Yahveh*, the God of hosts." The Father also said that Israel should prepare to meet their God (the Son), who is their creator

28) Mic 05:02 [*BHS* 05:01] *
- Summary: The Messiah would be born in Bethlehem, and the Messiah existed from eternity

29) Zec 02:03-13 *
- Summary: The *Malek Yahveh* called himself *Yahveh*, and twice the *Malek Yahveh* said that the Father would send him

30) Zec 11:12-13 *
- Summary: *Yahveh* said his shepherding would be valued at thirty pieces of silver. *Yahveh* said these pieces of silver would end up going to a potter after being tossed back into the temple

31) Zec 12:10 *
- Summary: *Yahveh* the Son sent the Spirit to make Israel mourn over their having pierced him

32) Zec 13:07 *
- Summary: *Yeshua* said he was the Shepherd of Zec 13:07 (Mar 14:27) who is the fellow (or "a neighbor" or "an associate") of *Yahveh*

33) Mal 03:01 *
- Summary: The Father said he would send a messenger (John the Baptist) on ahead of his Presence, the *Malek* of the Covenant. This indicates that *Yahveh* the Son became the Messiah and visited the temple (Luk 19:44).

Appendix C

Trinitarian Proofs

Categories of Trinitarian Proofs

Four major categories of Trinitarian proofs are:

1) MT Plurals Referring to *Yahveh*

Many passages contain MT plurals that refer to *Yahveh*. This fact is *prima facie* evidence for the doctrine of Trinity. Plurals referring to *Yahveh* are discussed in the chapter on Hebrew collective nouns, and are listed in the MT plurals appendix.

2) OT *Yahveh* Texts Applied to Individual Persons of the Trinity in the OT and NT

That OT *Yahveh* texts are applied to the persons of the Trinity in the NT is *prima facie* evidence for the doctrine of Trinity. OT *Yahveh* texts in the NT are discussed in the chapter on the NT Use of OT *Yahveh* Texts, the "I AM" Statements chapter, the Song of Moses (Deu 32) chapter, and the NT Use of OT *Yahveh* Texts appendix.

3) Texts That Speak of the Deity of the Messiah

Trinitarian proofs tend to support the Biblical assertion that the Messiah is a member of the Trinity. Likewise, all proofs of the deity of the Messiah tend to support the doctrine of the Trinity. Examples of texts that double as proofs for the deity of the Messiah and as proof of the doctrine of the Trinity include:
- Texts that show that the *Malek Yahveh* was a member of the Trinity and the future Messiah. In most Angel of *Yahveh* accounts, the *Malek Yahveh* is referred to as God and *Yahveh* (Gen 16; 21–22; 31–32; Exo 03; 14; 23; Num 22–24;

Jdg 02 (as is discussed at Jos 24); Jdg 06; 13; 1Ki 19; 2Ki 19; and Zec 02—03).
The *Malek Yahveh* texts are discussed in this Trinitarian proofs appendix, and
■ Texts that suggest or speak of the deity of the Messiah (see the appendix on this
   subject).

4) General Trinitarian Proofs

These are listed in this appendix (below).

General Trinitarian Proofs

Gen 01:02—Trinitarian Proof
   Now the earth was formless and empty. Darkness was on the surface
   of the deep. God's Spirit was hovering over the surface of the waters (Gen
   01:02).
Discussion: The Spirit is an agent of God and is God. The Spirit is a distinct
person of the Trinity. The Spirit can be provoked (Psa 106:33). The Spirit has
the qualities of a person that an impersonal force lacks: wisdom, understanding,
counsel and knowledge (Isa 11:02), and a mind (Rom 08:27). The Spirit gives
gifts of wisdom and knowledge (1Co 12:08). The Spirit speaks (Act 13:02) and
intercedes (Rom 08:26). The Spirit can be tested (Act 05:09) and grieved (Eph 04:
30), and can be lied to (Act 05:03-04). In Act 05:03-04 the Holy Spirit is called
God:
   Peter said, 'Ananias, why has Satan filled your heart to lie to the Holy
   Spirit?...You have not lied to men, but to God.'

Gen 01:03—Trinitarian Proof
   God said, 'Let there be light,' and there was light (Gen 01:03).
Discussion: If a tree falls in the woods and there is no one to hear it, did the
tree make a sound? If God gives a command to create and there is no one in
earshot capable of complying with the command, is it still a command? So the
fact that God can say, "Let there be..." shows that a personal agent of *Yahveh* was
present at the creation, and that the agent acted as only God can act by creating
matter out of nothing (*ex nihilo*). So the agent is God along with the Father
(compare Joh 01:01-03).

Gen 02:07-25—Trinitarian Proof
   This is the history of the generations of the heavens and of the earth
   when they were created, in the day that *Yahveh Elohim* made earth and the
   heavens (Gen 02:04).
Discussion: Gen 02:01-03 speaks of the Seventh Day, Gen 02:04-06 speaks of
the Third Day, and Gen 02:07-25 is an expanded account of Day Six of Creation
(Gen 01:24-31). In Gen 02:07-25, the Father and Son immediately carried out

what they determined to do on Day Six when they said "Let us..." (Gen 01:26).
The *"Yahveh Elohim"* mentioned twenty times in Gen 02—03 is the "us" mentioned elsewhere in Genesis (Gen 01:26, 03:24; 11:07 and LXX Gen 02:18): the Father (*Yahveh*) and the Son (*Elohim*).

Gen 03:15—Trinitarian Proof
   I will put enmity between you and the woman, and between your offspring and her offspring. He will bruise your head, and you will bruise his heel (Gen 03:15).
Discussion: The promised "offspring" or "seed" is one person (Gen 03:15; 15:18; Gal 03:16) who would defeat Satan. Someone might ask:
   Why did this 'seed' need to be the Son of God, the God-man, to destroy the works of Satan" (1Co 15:45-49; 1Jo 03:08)? Could not a creaturely angel have done the same?
A reason is that Satan seemed to have been in the top echelon of angels (Eze 28:01-19). Satan once may have been at the same level as, or higher than, Michael, who was called "one of the chief princes" (Dan 10:13). The archangel Michael hesitated to rebuke Satan, and referred the matter to God (2Pe 02:11; Jud 01:09). So it is logical that a person of the Trinity would be the one to utterly destroy Satan's works (1Jo 03:08). Besides, the ultimate destroyer of Satan would need to be perfect, but God charges angels with error (Job 04:18; 15:15-16).
Satan wanted Moses' body, perhaps for target practice (1Co 05:05; Eph 06:16; 1Ti 01:20), or to enshrine Moses' body in hell like the body of Lenin (1870-1924 AD) is enshrined in Moscow. God, however, was determined to let the worms have Moses' body (Deu 34:06). Michael recused himself from rebuking Satan and referred the matter to *Yahveh*, since *Yahveh* happened to be standing there (2Pe 02:10-11; Jud 01:08-09). The reason was that the archangel Michael might have met his match in the person of the fallen archangel Satan (Eze 28:01-19). The two duking it out alone on the spiritual battlefield might have led to a draw (Dan 10:13, 21; 12:01).
On another similar occasion, the *Malek Yahveh*, whom the narrator called *Yahveh* (the Son), referred the matter of rebuking Satan to *Yahveh* the Father. The Son, however, only referred the matter to the Father after rebuking Satan himself. The reason *Yahveh* the Son rebuked Satan was Satan had accused Joshua the Priest of sin. Accusing Joshua was impertinent because *Yahveh* the Father, who had chosen Jerusalem, had already saved Joshua as though Joshua were "a burning stick plucked out of the fire" (Zec 03:02).
Saving Joshua as through from fire did not mean that Joshua was necessarily a weak Christian (1Co 03:15), or a hero of the faith (Heb 11:32-34). What was meant was *Yahveh* the Father had already pruned Jerusalem of evildoers by various machinations during turbulent times. So *Yahveh* obviously did not save Joshua only for Joshua to be judged by Satan (Amo 03:02; 04:11).
See the discussion of Gen 03:15 in reference to the Son of Man in the Song of Moses chapter.

Gen 06:03—Trinitarian Proof
    Yahveh [the Father] said, 'My Spirit will not strive with man forever, because he also is flesh; yet will his days be one hundred twenty years' (Gen 06:03).
Discussion: The Spirit is an agent of *Yahveh* and is *Yahveh*.

Gen 16:07-13—Trinitarian Proof
Discussion: The narrator, Moses, identified the *Malek Yahveh* as *Yahveh*, and Hagar identified the *Malek Yahveh* as God (*Elohim*) (Gen 16:07).

Gen 18—19—Trinitarian Proof
Discussion: Gen 18—19 are two related accounts in Genesis, so to avoid any logical disconnects, review all the notes on Gen 18—19 below. Gen 18—19 also are discussed in the Hebrew collective nouns chapter, as well as in the Presences of *Elyon* chapter.

Gen 18:03-05—Trinitarian Proof
Discussion: Abraham addressed three men as *Adonai*, literally as "Lords...your [singular] sight [singular]" (Gen 18:03). *Adonai* literally means "Lords," but *Adonai* is often translated as "Lord," sometimes even when persons are being addressed (Gen 18:03). This is due to the overly persistent belief that plurals referring to *Yahveh* are majestic plurals rather than plural collective nouns. That "they answered Abraham" (Gen 18:05) shows that each of the three men were, in fact, Lord.
    That each Lord, rather than a Lord, replied shows that either there was no such thing as a majestic plural, or at least these heavenly visitors were unfamiliar with the majestic plural. That "they" replied and that "they" have a singular "sight" suggests that "they" were three persons, yet one God, in other words, the Trinity.
    For the sake of argument, let us assume the unitarians are correct that:
- The majestic plural existed in the OT,
- The three visitors were all angels, or God and two angels, but, in any case, not the Trinity.

If this were the case, then the two angels would have assumed Abraham addressed God using a majestic plural *Adonai*. This is especially the case since Abraham said:
    If now I have found favor in your [singular] sight [singular] (Gen 18:03).
    Similarly, Lot addressed two persons as "Lords" (*Adonai*), and "they" both answered (Gen 19:02). If the two angels were familiar with the majestic plural, one of the two angels would have assumed Lot had addressed the other angel as "lord," but instead "they" both answered (Gen 19:02).
    Gen 18—19 show that there was no such thing as the majestic plural. Trinitarian accounts such as Gen 18—19 and the three men of 1Sa 10:03 served as the basis of later theological assertions that *Yahveh* was the Trinity: a God of Gods and a Lord of Lords (Jos 22:22; Psa 050:01; Isa 26:13; Dan 02:47; 11:36; 1Ti 06:

15; Rev 17:14; 19:16), a Lord of [All] the Lords (*haAdonim*) (Deu 10:17; Psa 136:
03), and a God of [All] the Gods (*haElohim*) (Psa 136:02).

Gen 18:14—Trinitarian Proof

Is anything too hard for *Yahveh*? At the set time I will return to you,
when the season comes round, and Sarah will have a son (Gen 18:14).
Discussion: *Yahveh* spoke of *Yahveh* in the third person.

Gen 18:19—Trinitarian Proof

For I [the Son] have known him, to the end that he may command
his children and his household after him that they may keep the way of
Yahveh, to do righteousness and justice; to the end that *Yahveh* [the Father]
may bring on Abraham that which he has spoken of him (Gen 18:19).
Discussion: *Yahveh* spoke of *Yahveh* in the third person (see Eusebius, *Proof of
the Gospel*, Book V, Chapter 9).

A clear indicator that there are at least two *Yahveh*s in Gen 18—19 is that one
Yahveh said that he would go down to Sodom, and then two of the three (Gen 18:
02, 22; 19:12) men went toward Sodom. Meanwhile, Abraham remained standing
before another person called *Yahveh* (Gen 18:21-22). Later, a person called *Yahveh*
is mentioned as being in heaven and a person called *Yahveh* is mentioned as being
in Sodom (Gen 19:24).

If one accepts the logical conclusion that there are at least two *Yahveh*s in
Gen 18—19, then it also makes sense to conclude that the three men who visited
Abraham were the Trinity. This especially makes sense considering the extensive
amount of Trinitarian evidence there is in Genesis.

Gen 19:24—Trinitarian Proof

Then *Yahveh* [the Son and Spirit] rained on Sodom and on Gomorrah
sulfur and fire from *Yahveh* [the Father] out of the sky (Gen 19:24).
Discussion: Two *Yahveh*s are mentioned in Gen 19:24.

Gen 21:01-02—Trinitarian Proof

[1] *Yahveh* visited Sarah as he had said, and [2] *Yahveh* did to Sarah as
he had spoken. Sarah conceived, and bore Abraham a son in his old age, at
the set time of which [3] God had spoken to him (Gen 21:01-02).
Discussion: Three times the narrator, Moses, referred to *Yahveh*'s promises
about Isaac's birth in Gen 15—18. The Hebrew verbs in Gen 21:01-02 that are
used to say that *Yahveh* spoke three times are *amar*, and *davar* (used twice). This
suggests that three persons named *Yahveh* predicted Isaac's birth.

Gen 21:17-20—Trinitarian Proof

Discussion: The *Malek Yahveh* said that he would make Ishmael into a great
nation—something that only God is able to both promise and do.

Gen 22:01-18—Trinitarian Proof
Discussion: The *Malek Yahveh* spoke using first person speech (for example, "I," "me") when he said that Abraham feared God, because Abraham did not withhold Isaac from "me" (Gen 22:11-12). This shows that the *Malek Yahveh* is God, and that Abraham was sacrificing to the *Malek Yahveh*.

Abraham's "fear" of the *Malek Yahveh* included how Abraham knew that the Son had the power to raise Isaac from the dead (Joh 11:24; Heb 11:19). Abraham knew that the *Malek Yahveh* would resurrect Isaac, if necessary, because of the promise that the Messiah would come from Isaac's seed (Gen 17:19, 21; Heb 11:19). That is why Abraham was able to tell his servants "we will return" from Mount Moriah (Gen 22:05).

Gen 22:16—Trinitarian Proof
'I have sworn by myself,' says *Yahveh* [the Father], 'because you have done this thing, and have not withheld your son, your only son...' (Gen 22:16).
Discussion: The *Malek Yahveh*, who elsewhere is called *Yahveh* and God, is a distinct person from *Yahveh* the Father. That the *Malek Yahveh* is a distinct person is why he was able to quote *Yahveh* the Father in the third person.

Gen 26:02-05, 24—Trinitarian Proof
Discussion: *Yahveh* the Father appeared to Isaac, blessed him, and said that he would confirm the oath he swore to Abraham (Gen 26:02; see also Gen 22:16). Then *Elohim* the Son appeared to Isaac with the same blessing (Gen 26:24).

The pattern of God appearing twice in succession occurs elsewhere Genesis (for instance, Gen 06:02-08, 11-22; 12:01-03, 07; 31:03, 11-13). God appearing twice also occurred outside Genesis. An example is when *Yahveh* appeared to Moses at Midian (Exo 04:19) after meeting him at Mount Sinai (Exo 03). Both times *Yahveh* told Moses to go to Egypt (Exo 04:19). God appeared twice to Solomon (1Ki 03:05; 09:02; 11:09). This suggests two persons of the Trinity, the Father and the Son, made successive appearances.

Gen 28:12-22 (also 31:11-13; 32:24-30; 35:01-03, 07) —Trinitarian Proof
Discussion: Eusebius wrote concerning Gen 28:20-22 that Jacob spoke of two persons of the Trinity who appeared to him (Eusebius, *Proof of the Gospel*, Book V, Chapter 12). Eusebius pointed out that in Gen 35:01, God spoke of God in the third person (Eusebius, *Proof of the Gospel*, Book V, Chapter 12). In Gen 35:01, God the Father said that God the Son had appeared to Jacob at Bethel in Gen 28. This interpretation is upheld by:
- The statement of the narrator, Moses, that "[All] the Gods [*haElohim*], they appeared [plural verb] to him [Jacob]" at Bethel in Gen 28 (Gen 35:07),
- The *Malek* of [All] the Gods (*haElohim*) (Gen 31:11) said that he was God (*El*) who appeared to Jacob at Bethel (Gen 31:13). So Gen 31:11, 13 shows that the

Malek Yahveh was one of the persons of *haElohim* ("[All] the Gods") who appeared at Bethel in Gen 28 (Gen 35:07),

- After Jacob built the altar as commanded by the Father (Gen 35:01), *El Shaddai* (the Son) appeared to Jacob (Gen 35:11), and
- During the time of the Judges, Samuel told Saul about three men making what seems to have been a Trinitarian offering to [All] the Gods (*haElohim*) at Bethel (1Sa 10:03-04): three loaves of bread and three goats, yet one skin of wine. The Trinity may have posed as three men in 1Sa 10 as they did in Gen 18.

Here are some proofs that the "man" with whom Jacob wrestled was *Yahveh* the Son:

- The man with whom Jacob wrestled said that Jacob had wrestled with God (Gen 32:28), and Jacob believed the man was telling the truth (Gen 32:30). That the divine wrestler said that Jacob had wrestled with "men" (Gen 32:28) means that Jacob had wrestled with the preincarnate Messiah at the Jabbok. Jacob also wrestled with Esau (Gen 25:26; Hos 12:03) and Laban (Gen 31:42),
- Jacob said that the man with whom he wrestled was *Elohim*. Jacob said that he saw *Elohim* "face to face" (Gen 32:30). Elsewhere, *Yahveh* and the *Malek Yahveh* spoke to people "face to face" (Exo 33:11; Num 12:08; 14:14; Deu 05: 04; 34:10; Jdg 06:22),
- The God-man with whom Jacob wrestled changed Jacob's name to Israel (Gen 32:28). The wrestler gave Jacob the name Israel, and the narrator of Kings said it was *Yahveh* (the Son) who gave Jacob the name Israel (1Ki 18:31; 2Ki 17:34),
- The narrator, Moses, recounted the wrestling match and the renaming of Jacob in Gen 32. This was to indicate that this same God-man wrestler appeared to Jacob at Bethel (Gen 35:09-13). When he appeared this time, he said he was *El Shaddai* (Gen 35:11). The *Malek Yahveh* was known as *El Shaddai*, just as the *Malek Yahveh* (Exo 03:02) said in Exo 06:03 — he was known to the patriarchs as *El Shaddai* but not as *Yahveh*, and
- Hosea said that Jacob wrestled with a *Malek* (referring to Gen 32:24-25), and then he met the *Malek* again at Bethel (referring to Gen 35:09-13). Hosea declared that this *Malek* was one of the persons of the Trinity who was both God and "*Yahveh*, God of Hosts. *Yahveh* is his Name of renown!" See the discussion at Hos 11:02, 12 [*BHS* 12:01]; Hos 12:04 [*BHS* 12:05] in the MT plurals appendix.

Gen 28:20-22—Trinitarian Proof

Jacob vowed a vow, saying, 'If God will be with me, and will keep me in this way that I go, and will give me bread to eat, and clothing to put on, so that I come again to my father's house in peace, and *Yahveh* will be my God, then this stone that I have set up for a pillar, will be God's house. Of all that you will give me I will surely give the tenth to you' (Gen 28:20-22).

Discussion: Jacob mentioned God three times in his vows to God (Gen 28: 20-22; and see Gen 31:42 in this appendix). This suggests that Jacob made a vow to the three persons of *Yahveh* who appeared in Gen 28. This would be consistent without how the narrator, Moses, later said, "[All] the Gods [*haElohim*], they appeared [plural verb] to him [Jacob]" at Bethel (Gen 35:07).

It is worthy of note that Jacob spoke of God as "they" (Gen 35:07) right after the Father spoke of the Son in the third person:

> Then God [the Father] said to Jacob, 'Go up to Bethel and settle there, and build an altar there to God [the Son], who appeared to you when you were fleeing from your brother Esau' (Gen 35:01).

The Angel of God (Gen 31:11) was one of the "they," "(All) the Gods [*haElohim*]," who appeared to Jacob at Bethel (Gen 35:07). This fact can be ascertained from the statement of the Angel of [All] the Gods (*haElohim*) (Gen 31: 11, 13). The Angel said that he was the God of Bethel to whom Jacob had anointed a pillar (Gen 31:13). So Gen 31:11, 13 and Gen 35:07 taken together are evidence both of the Trinity and of the deity of the *Malek Yahveh*.

The five Trinitarian statements of Jacob are Gen 28:20-22, 31:42, 32:09, 48:15-16 and 49:24-25.

Gen 31:11-13—Trinitarian Proof

> The Angel of God said to me in the dream, 'Jacob,' and I said, 'Here I am.' He said, 'Now lift up your eyes, and behold, all the male goats which leap on the flock are streaked, speckled, and grizzled, for I have seen all that Laban does to you. I am the God of Bethel, where you anointed a pillar, where you vowed a vow to me. Now arise, get out from this land, and return to the land of your birth' (Gen 31:11-13).

Discussion: The *Malek* of [All] the Gods (*haElohim*) said that he was God (*El*) and one of the persons who appeared to Jacob at Bethel. This is discussed at Gen 28:12-22 in this appendix.

Gen 31:42—Trinitarian Proof

> Unless the God of my father, the God of Abraham, and the fear of Isaac, had been with me, surely now you would have sent me away empty. God has seen my affliction and the labor of my hands, and rebuked you last night (Gen 31:42).

Discussion: Jacob mentioned God three times in his vows to God (Gen 31:42), as he did in Gen 28:20-22. Gen 28:20-22 is discussed in this appendix. Jacob mentioned the words "*Elohim* of my father" (Gen 31:42). The "father" may refer to Abraham as "father" does in Gen 32:09, or the "father" may refer to Isaac. Either way, Gen 31:42 is still Trinitarian.

Here are two possible interpretations of Jacob's oath invocation:

* The God of my father Abraham, the God of my father Abraham, the Fear of Isaac, or
* The God of my father Isaac, the God of my father Abraham, and the Fear of Isaac.

Jacob may be differentiating the two persons of the Trinity that Abraham served, the *Malek Yahveh* (Gen 22:12) and *Elyon* the Father (Gen 14:18, 19, 20, 22). Remember that Abraham did say:

Gods [*Elohim*], they caused me to wander (Gen 20:13).

Otherwise, Jacob is differentiating the two persons of the Trinity that Isaac served, *Yahveh* the Father (Gen 25:21; 26:02) and *El Shaddai* (Gen 28:03).

The five Trinitarian statements of Jacob are Gen 28:20-22, 31:42, 32:09, 48:15-16 and 49:24-25.

Gen 32:09—Trinitarian Proof

Jacob said, 'God of my father Abraham, and God of my father Isaac, *Yahveh*, who said to me:

Return to your country, and to your relatives, and I will do you good (Gen 32:09).

Discussion: Jacob prayed to the three members of the Trinity, whom Jacob called *Elohim, Elohim,* and *Yahveh*.

The five Trinitarian statements of Jacob are Gen 28:20-22, 31:42, 32:09, 48:15-16 and 49:24-25.

Gen 32:24-30—Trinitarian Proof

Discussion: See Gen 28:12-22 in this appendix.

Gen 35:01-03, 07—Trinitarian Proof

Discussion: See Gen 28:12-22 in this appendix.

Gen 48:15-16—Trinitarian Proof

Discussion: See the section in the Hebrew collective nouns chapter that discusses how the repetition of *Elohim* indicates persons.

Gen 49:24-25—Trinitarian Proof

Discussion: Jacob mentioned the three persons of the Trinity when Jacob blessed Joseph. The logical divisions of the blessing each mention one person of the Trinity. In the *KJV* translation, these divisions just happen to be introduced by the word "by." Here is an abbreviated version of the *KJV* rendering:

...by...the Mighty One of Jacob...by the *Elohim* of your father...by the *Shaddai*.

Here is an interpretation of Gen 49:24-25 using the *KJV* translation. Jacob said...

...by the hands [the Son and Spirit] of the Mighty One [the Father] of Jacob; (from thence is the Shepherd [the Son], the Stone [the Son] of Israel), even by the *Elohim* [the Spirit] of your father...by the *Shaddai* [the Son] (Gen 49:24-25).

Jacob differentiated the two persons of the Trinity that he served when he said, "by the Mighty One of Jacob" (Gen 49:24) and "by the *Elohim* of your father"

(Gen 49:25). Here Jacob is saying, "By God the Father…by God the Spirit" (Gen 49:24-25). This interpretation is supported by:
- The many Trinitarian proofs of Genesis,
- The statement of the narrator, Moses, that "[All] the Gods [*haElohim*], they appeared [plural verb] to him [Jacob]" at Bethel (Gen 35:07), and
- The weight of Jacob's five Trinitarian statements: Gen 28:20-22, 31:42, 32:09, 48:15-16 and 49:24-25.

Exo 03:02-18—Trinitarian Proof
   The Angel of *Yahveh* appeared to him in a flame of fire out of the midst of a bush. He looked, and behold, the bush burned with fire, and the bush was not consumed (Exo 03:02).
   Moses said to God, 'Behold, when I come to the children of Israel, and tell them, 'The God of your fathers has sent me to you;' and they ask me, 'What is his name?' What should I tell them?' 14 God said to Moses, 'I AM WHO I AM,' and he said, 'You shall tell the children of Israel this: 'I AM has sent me to you" (Exo 03:13).
Discussion: In Exo 03 the narrator, Moses, referred to the *Malek Yahveh* as *Elohim* and as *Yahveh*. In Exo 03 the *Malek Yahveh* referred to himself as *Elohim*, I AM, and as *Yahveh*. The narrator placed the *Malek Yahveh* (Exo 03:02) right in the same bush as God and *Yahveh* (Exo 03:04). This meant the *Malek Yahveh* was *Yahveh* the Son. That both the Father and the *Malek Yahveh* are named *Yahveh* tends to show that the concept of the Trinity is biblical. See the chapter on Proto-Sinaitic Trinitarianism on these points.
   Yeshua said that he is "I AM" (Joh 08:24, 28, 58 and elsewhere). It seems significant that *Yahveh* said, "I AM" three times in Exo 03:14, and *Yeshua* said "I AM" three times in Joh 08. Also, *Yeshua*'s mention of saying, "I AM," is repeated three times in the narrative of his arrest (Joh 18:05, 08). This helps to identify *Yeshua* as the person of *Yahveh* who said, "I AM" in Exo 03:14. See the discussion on the "I AM" statements in the "I AM" and the Song of Moses chapters.

Exo 06:02-03—Trinitarian Proof
   God spoke to Moses, and said to him, 'I am *Yahveh*; and I appeared to Abraham, to Isaac, and to Jacob, as God of Mighty Ones; but by my Name, *Yahveh*, I was not known to them' (Exo 06:02).
Discussion: The *Malek Yahveh* (Exo 03:02) later mentioned in Exo 06:03 that the patriarchs did not know him as *Yahveh*, but they did know him as *El Shaddai*. Reading Genesis with *El Shaddai*'s statement in mind reveals that the *Malek Yahveh* was known as *El Shaddai*, and that only the narrator, Moses, knew the Son to be *Yahveh*. The patriarchs knew the Son as the *Malek Yahveh* and as *El Shaddai*, but not as *Yahveh* the Son. Only the Father was known as *Yahveh*.
   See the Proto-Sinaitic Trinitarianism chapter.

Exo 06:08—Trinitarian Proof
I will bring you into the land that I swore to give to Abraham, to Isaac, and to Jacob; and I will give it to you for a heritage: I am *Yahveh* (Exo 06:08).
Discussion: *Yahveh* the Son swore with uplifted hand, which suggests that *Yahveh* the Son was swearing with *Yahveh* the Father in heaven as a witness (Mat 23:22). The *Malek Yahveh* later said that he swore to the forefathers to bring Israel into the land of Canaan (Jdg 02:01-04).

Exo 13:21-22; 14:19-24—Trinitarian Proof
Discussion: *Yahveh* was in a pillar (Exo 13:21-22; 14:19-24). The fact that the pillar moved from the vanguard to the rearguard when necessary (Exo 14:19-24) suggests that there was only one pillar. The pillar changed appearance, which fact might mislead people to think there were separate pillars. The same pillar was a cloud by day and a fire by night (Exo 24:15-18, 24; Num 09:15-16).
That the pillar could change appearance is demonstrated by an incident that happened at night. The pillar appeared as fire on one side, but as a dark cloud on the other side (Exo 14:19-20, 24). Moses wrote:
Then the *Malek* of [All] the Gods [*haElohim*], who had been traveling in front of Israel's army, withdrew and went behind them. The pillar of cloud *also* moved from in front and stood behind them (Exo 14:19).
Various translations of Exo 14:19b include the word "also" (*LXE, RSV, NIV*). The "also" indicates that the *Malek Yahveh* (Exo 14:19a) is a separate entity from the pillar (Exo 14:19b). This would agree with how Isa 52:12 seems to speak of two divine persons: *Yahveh* (the Father) is said to be the vanguard and the God of Israel (the Son) is the rear guard.
In Exodus the Father was not the pillar itself since the Father came down and talked to Moses from within a cloud, but not "as" the cloud (Exo 24:16; 34: 05). The Father was no more the pillar itself than the *Malek Yahveh* was the burning bush from within which the Son spoke (Exo 03:02). Similarly, during the Transfiguration the Father was the voice, and neither the Father nor the Son were a cloud. The Son is described as being the spiritual rock during the Exodus (1Co 10: 04; also see 1Pe 02:08).
The Exodus pillar was *Yahveh* (Exo 13:21-22; 14:19-24). Since, however, the pillar was neither the Father nor the Son, the pillar must have been the Spirit. The chapter on the Presences of *Elyon* discusses the several times the Spirit appeared as a pillar or cloud, including Exo 34, Isa 06, and at the Transfiguration.

Exo 15:26—Trinitarian Proof
'If you will diligently listen to the voice of *Yahveh* your God, and will do that which is right in his eyes, and will pay attention to his commandments, and keep all his statutes, I will put none of the diseases on you that I have put on the Egyptians; for I am *Yahveh* who heals you' (Exo 15:26).

Discussion: *Yahveh* spoke of *"Yahveh,* your God" in the third person.

Exo 20:07, 10-12—Trinitarian Proof
You shall not take the Name of *Yahveh* your God in vain, for *Yahveh* will not hold him guiltless who takes his Name in vain (Exo 20:07).

But the seventh day is a Sabbath to *Yahveh* your God. You shall not do any work in it, you, nor your son, nor your daughter, your man-servant, nor your maid-servant, nor your cattle, nor your stranger who is within your gates; 11 for in six days *Yahveh* made heaven and earth, the sea, and all that is in them, and rested the seventh day; therefore *Yahveh* blessed the Sabbath day, and made it holy. 12 "Honor your father and your mother that your days may be long in the land that *Yahveh* your God gives you (Exo 20:10-12).

Discussion: *Yahveh* spoke of *Yahveh* in the third person. See Eusebius, *Proof of the Gospel*, Book V, Chapter 16.

Exo 22:27 LXX [English 22:28] —Trinitarian Proof
Discussion: Moses wrote, "Do not blaspheme the Gods..." (LXX Exo 22:27 [English 22:28]). The Hebrew translated "Gods" is *"Elohim,"* and the LXX Greek is *theoi* (Greek plural meaning, "Gods"). See the chapter on Hebrew collective nouns, and especially the Song of Moses chapter for more discussion of this verse.

Exo 23:20-21—Trinitarian Proof
'Behold, I send an Angel before you, to keep you by the way, and to bring you into the place that I have prepared. Be watchful because of his presence, and hearken to his voice, rebel not against him, for he bears not with your transgression, for My name [is] in his heart (Exo 23:20-21).

Discussion: The *Malek Yahveh* has *Yahveh*'s Name in him. The Father referred to "the *Malek* with his Name in him" as "God" (Exo 23:19, 25). This parallels how the Father twice called the Son "God" in the Psalms (see Psa 045:06-07 and 082: 06-08 in this appendix).

The early NT Church understood *Yeshua* to be *Yahveh* the Son and the *Malek Yahveh* with *Yahveh*'s Name "in him" (Exo 23:21). Many mentions are made in the NT of "the Name of *Yeshua*" (Act 02:38; 03:06, 16; 04:10, 18; 05:40; 08:12; 09:27; 10:48; 16:18; 19:13; 26:09; Phi 02:10). In Act 05:40-41 the Name of *Yeshua* is called "the Name" (see also 3Jo 01:07). *Yeshua* made a statement that sounds like something Israel's protector, the Angel with *Yahveh*'s name, would say:

I will remain in the world no longer, but they are still in the world, and I am coming to you. Holy Father, protect them by the power of your name—the name you gave me—so that they may be one as we are one (Joh 17:11).

Yeshua means, *"Yahveh* saves" (Mat 01:21; 1Ti 01:15). So, like the Angel with *Yahveh*'s Name "in him" (Exo 23:21), the name *Yahveh* is "in" the name *Yeshua* as well as "in" *Yeshua* (Exo 23:21). Exo 23:21 and other similar passages are mentioned in the discussion of the Aaronic Blessing (Num 06:22-27) that is found in this appendix.

Exo 32:01, 04, 05, 08, 23—Trinitarian Proof
Discussion: The Israelites told Aaron to "make us *Elohim* [gods] who will go [plural verb] before us" (Exo 32:01, 23). The Israelites were trying to replace the Angel of *Yahveh* (the Son) and the Spirit (the pillar of cloud and fire) who went before them as they marched out of Egypt (as was discussed at Exo 13:21-22; 14: 19-24 in this appendix).

The Son and Spirit were not with the Israelites, but perhaps were on Mount Sinai with Moses for forty days. It seems this was the reason the Israelites had lost faith and thought the Trinity and Moses had abandoned them (Exo 32:01, 23). That the Israelites were trying to replace the power vacuum the Son and Spirit left is confirmed by the fact that shortly after the Golden Calf incident, the Father told Moses:

My Presences [the Son and Spirit], they will go [plural verb] with you (Exo 33:14-15).

Exo 33:14-15 is similar to the words that the Israelites had spoken about the gods that they wanted Aaron to make (Exo 32:01, 23). That the Israelites were trying to replace the Son and Spirit with gods suggests that the Israelites knew the Son and Spirit to be divine persons, and members of the Trinity.

Calves would have gone ahead of the Israelites as the Son and Spirit had previously. Some ancients thought that gods hovered above representations of bulls and calves, as Bernard Goldman wrote:

We are accustomed to the motif of gods standing on the backs of animals which become their vehicles, or avatars, and come to represent the power of the divine.[186]

The calf that Aaron made was meant to replace of the Ark of the Covenant that was only in the planning stages at the time (Exo 25:15).

The Ark of the Covenant was meant to go before the Israelites (Num 10:33; Jos 04:07; Jos 06:08) with the Son and Spirit in the vanguard (Exo 23:20; 33:14-15). This interpretation of the Israelites' intentions is confirmed by the fact that shortly after the Golden Calf incident, the Father told Moses to make the Ark of the Covenant that would be carried before the Israelites (Deu 10:03). Around the same time, the Father promised that the Son and Spirit would go with Israel into the Promised Land (Exo 33:14-15).

Now, the question remains as to whether there was one calf or two. Apparently, there was one calf, perhaps split in two as each ceremony demanded. The Israelites had asked for two calves, but Aaron only made them one. The Israelites told Aaron to make plural "gods." The Israelites did not intend the plural "gods" to be understood as a majestic plural, as though they wanted Aaron to make a singular, majestic god.

The above interpretation is confirmed by the Israelites' use of the plural Hebrew verb ("they [the gods] will go"). Naturally, the Israelites wanted two calves to replace the Son and the Spirit. Also, Stephen used the plural form *theoi* (Greek meaning, "gods") in Act 07:40 when he recounted the golden calf incident.

Evidently, Aaron only half complied with the Israelite demand, and made one calf rather than two. Aaron never even called the golden calf a "god" or "gods." During the golden calf incident Aaron said that the Israelites would have a festival to *Yahveh* (Exo 32:05), who was

...your Gods [plural noun], O Israel, who brought [plural verb] you up out of the land of Egypt (Exo 32:04, 08).

Exo 32 repeatedly mentions "they said," meaning that it was the erring Israelites and not Aaron who spoke of the calf or calves as "gods" (*elohim*):

- Then they said:
  These are your gods, O Israel, who brought you up out of Egypt (Exo 32:04),
- They have bowed down to it and sacrificed to it and have said:
  These are your gods, O Israel, who brought you up out of Egypt (Exo 32:08), and
- They said to me, "Make us gods who will go before us" (Exo 32:23).

So Aaron mentioned the feast to *Yahveh* and used the plural noun *Elohim* (Gods) and plural verbs referring to *Yahveh*. This shows that Aaron spoke only of the persons of *Yahveh*, and not the golden calf, as "Gods." After all, Moses recognized that Aaron had been forced to do something against his will and better judgment (Exo 32:21; Deu 09:21).

Someone might ask, "How did the Israelites syncretize the worship of *Yahveh* with the golden calf?" Because of the crescent shape of bulls' horns, bulls were a common symbol of moon gods. Calves do not have horns, but archeologists found a copper calf at *Tell-el-Obeid* with a crescent moon on its forehead, the sign of the moon god Sin. During the Byzantine period, horses in the hubs of zodiac circles had crescents on their foreheads.

Sin and his consorts or muses were worshipped widely in the Mideast including along the Nile. The Israelites just happened to be in the Wilderness of Sin, hence the name Sinai. Similarly, Plutarch wrote that not far from Haran, a major Sin the moon god center in Syria, the hill where Crassus was assassinated was called "Sinnaca."[187] Sinasi Gunduze wrote that close to Haran was a place called, *sanamsin*, "the idol of Sin."[188]

Perhaps the Desert of Zin (meaning, "flat") also was originally named after the moon god Sin, but the form of the name may have changed over time (Num 13: 21). This seems plausible given the fact that Mount Nebo was named after the Sumerian god Nabu, and Zin and Nebo are mentioned just two verses apart (Deu 32:49, 51). Also, Sin "the moon god was regarded as the supreme lord and owner not only of the countries of Harran and Ur, but also of the vast territories described by the geographic term *Amurru*."[189]

Since the Israelites thought Moses was dead, who better to turn to than the god whose peninsula they were in—or so they thought (2Ki 17:26). The Bible seems to indicate that the syncretism between the moon god Sin worship and Yahvism involved walking through two halves of a golden calf (Jer 34:18-19).

So the calves may have served multiple purposes. The ceremony may have been patterned after both ancient custom and how *Yahveh* walked through the halved calf and other halved animals in Abram's dream (Gen 15:08-21). A stove and a lamp hovered through the carcasses to finalize a sworn covenant. The smoking stove represented the Father, and *Yahveh* the Son was represented by the flaming torch.

The Father and Son walked through the halved calf as part of an ancient Mesopotamian covenant ritual to assure Abraham that his descendants would inherit Canaan (Gen 15:08). The ceremony was done in response to Abraham's question, "O Lord *Yahveh*, how can I know that I will gain possession of it?" The idea behind the ceremony was: may the gods make me like this divided calf if I do not fulfill this oath.

In later times, the golden calf was used as a prop in the reenactment or the recounting of Gen 15:08-21. The ceremony represented Aaron's attempt to reassure the Israelites that they would inherit the Promised Land. This is another reason why the Israelites wanted the golden calves to go ahead of them into the Promises Land. They would serve as a talisman to reassure them that the land was theirs for the taking (Exo 32:01).

King Jeroboam copied Aaron's golden calf ceremony to reassure the Israelites that they would still remain in the Promised Land. Perhaps there were doubts because they did not worship *Yahveh* in Jerusalem (Joh 04:20). Jeroboam had two calves made. Each one was perhaps halved and then walked through (Jer 34:18-19). Jeroboam said:

Here are your Gods, O Israel, who brought [plural] you up out of Egypt.

One calf was set up in Bethel, and the other in Dan (1Ki 12:28-29).

Like Aaron, Jeroboam was not so much interested in introducing a false god, but he wanted the people to worship the persons of *Yahveh* at Dan and Bethel rather than in Jerusalem (1Ki 12:25-28). So Jeroboam tried to mimic the temple worship at Jerusalem (1Ki 12:28-33). Just as in the case of Aaron's calf (Exo 32:06; 1Co 10:07), the worship at Dan and Bethel immediately degenerated into crude, pagan idol worship (2Ki 10:29; 12:30; 2Ch 13:08).

The Samaritans also had rites that include a calf that, apparently, was halved. This would explain why Hosea mentioned "calves," but then refers to the calves using the singular "it":

The people who live in Samaria fear for the [literal translation] calves of Beth Aven. Its people will mourn over it, and so will its idolatrous priests, those who had rejoiced over its splendor, because it is taken from them into exile (Hos 10:05).

Num 06:22-27—Trinitarian Proof

Discussion: The Aaronic Blessing was given so that the priests could put the Name on the people by mentioning *Yahveh*'s Name three times. In the following passage, the *Panim*, meaning, "Faces" or "Presences," refer to the Son and Spirit. *Yahveh* said:

This is how you should bless the children of Israel. You shall tell them:
'*Yahveh* [the Father] bless you, and keep you;
Yahveh [the Father] make his [the Father's] Face [*Panim*, the Spirit] shine on you, and be gracious to you;
Yahveh [the Father] turn his [the Father's] Face [*Panim*, the Son] toward you, and give you peace.'
So shall they [the priests] put my [the Father's] Name [*Yahveh*] on the children of Israel; and I [the Father] will bless them (Num 06:22-27).

The Trinitarian interpretation of the Aaronic Blessing—that three persons have one singular Name, *Yahveh*, is a fact reflected in other passages such as:

- *Yahveh* the Father told Moses that the *Malek Yahveh* (the Son) has his Name in him (Exo 23:21),
- David mentioned God as the subject of three verbs:
  o May God [the Father] [1] be gracious to us and [2] bless us and [3] make his [the Father's] Faces [the Son and the Spirit] shine upon us (Psa 067:01),
- David mentioned God three times as the subject of two instances of the verb "to bless":
  o God [the Father], God [the Son], will bless us, God [the Spirit] will bless us (Psa 067:06-07),
- Daniel mentioned Lord (*Adonai*) three times, God (*Elohim*) once, and Daniel mentioned the singular Name once:
  o O Lord [the Father], listen! O Lord [the Son], forgive! O Lord [the Spirit], hear and act! For your sake, O my God [the Trinity], do not delay, because your city and your people bear your [singular] Name (Dan 09:19),
- Jeremiah mentioned the phrase the "Temple of *Yahveh*" three times (Jer 07:04), and then the temple was said to bear the Name of *Yahveh* (Jer 07:10), and
- *Yeshua* told the disciples to baptize in the singular Name of three persons, the Father, Son and Spirit (Mat 28:19). This is in keeping with how OT believers, including infants, had the Name called over them during the Aaronic Blessing (Num 06:22-27).

Today, even churches that do not baptize infants, or baptize in the name of *Yeshua* (Act 02:38; 08:16; 10:48; 19:05), rather than using the Mat 28:19 formula, often use the Aaronic Blessing as a benediction. Also, other scriptures mention, "I AM," three times (Exo 03:14; Joh 08:24, 28, 58), and these are read to the congregation. Thus the Name is named thrice over children. So Paul's words hold true concerning all believers:

For this reason I kneel before the Father, from whom his whole family in heaven and on earth derives its [singular] Name (Eph 03:14).

The above points discuss the three mentions of *Yahveh* and the singular Name in the Aaronic Blessing. For a discussion of the two mentions of "Face" (*Panim*) in the Aaronic Blessing, see the Presences of *Elyon* chapter.

Num 22—24—Trinitarian Proof
Discussion: See the section on Num 22—24 in the chapter on Proto-Sinaitic Trinitarianism.

Deu 32:08-09, LXX 32:43—Trinitarian Proof
Rejoice, ye heavens, with him, and let all the angels of God worship him; rejoice ye Gentiles, with his people, and let all the sons of God strengthen themselves in him; for he will avenge the blood of his sons, and he will render vengeance, and recompense justice to his enemies, and will reward them that hate him; and the Lord shall purge the land of his people (LXX Deu 32:43).

Discussion: A text that suggests or speaks of the deity of the Messiah should be considered a Trinitarian proof. In Deu 32:08-09, *Yahveh* the Son is depicted as inheriting Israel from the Father, who is *Elyon*, the Most High. After Israel abandons *Yahveh*, the gospel is preached to the nations to make Israel jealous (Deu 32:16, 21). Then, according to the MT Hebrew of Deu 32:43, all the nations join Israel to praise *Yahveh* the Son.

In the LXX of Deu 32:43, however, the angels and nations are to rejoice along with Israel, and all are commanded to praise the Son. Since parallel verses should be taken into consideration, a verse similar to LXX Deu 32:43 is the LXX and the Syriac versions of Psa 097:07: "…worship him, all you his angels."

A prophetic parallel to Deu 32:08-09 and LXX 32:43 is the Son of Man vision (Dan 07:13-14). Here the Son of Man inherited the nations from the Father, *Elyon*. Then the Son of Man is worshipped by the nations (Dan 07:13-14). Afterward the Son and Father are called the Most Highs (Aramaic plural *Ilyonin*) (Dan 07:18, 22, 25b, 27). Interestingly, Jeremiah and the Evangelist John wrote that the Father and Son have one throne in one sanctuary, as is discussed in the MT plurals appendix (Jer 17:12; Rev 22:01, 03-04).

The writer of Hebrews quoted the OT phrase: "Let all God's angels worship him" (LXX Deu 32:43; Heb 01:06). DSS 4QDT (the Dead Sea Scrolls in Cave 4) and the LXX both contain this last phrase, but the MT omits the phrase. The writer of Hebrews views the "him" in the LXX and the DSS versions of Deu 32:43 to be *Yahveh* the Son (Heb 01:06). This suggests that in the parallel verse, the "him" also is the Son:

…worship him, all you his angels (LXX, Syriac Psa 097:07).

The context of a verse should always be taken into consideration. Two verses after Heb 01:06, the writer of Hebrews considers the "God" in Psa 045:06-07 [*BHS* 045:07-08] to be God the Son (Heb 01:08-09). This point is discussed further at Psa 045:06-07 [*BHS* 045:07-08] in this appendix.

The fact that the Greek verbs "rejoice" and "worship" are imperatives suggests that the Father is commanding the angels, since a prophet would not command angels. Also, no mere human has a voice that could carry a command throughout the heavens and earth (Deu 04:36; Isa 06:08; 24:15-16; Heb 12:26).

Deu 33:01-02—Trinitarian Proof
This is the blessing that Moses the man of [All] the Gods [*haElohim*] pronounced on the Israelites before his death. *Yahveh* [the Father] came from Sinai, and [the Son] dawned over them from Seir; he [the Spirit] shone forth from Mount Paran. He [the Father] came with myriads of holy ones from the south, from his [the Father's] mountain slopes (Deu 33:01-02).
Discussion: [All] the Gods (*haElohim*), the Trinity, appeared on three mountains during the giving of the law. See the discussion of this text and other related texts in the Presences of *Elyon* chapter.

Deu 33:27—Trinitarian Proof
The eternal God [the Father] is [Israel's] dwelling-place, underneath are the everlasting arms [the Son and Spirit]. He [the Father] will drive out the enemy from before you, saying [to the Son and Spirit], 'Destroy! [the enemy]' (Deu 33:27).
Discussion: Moses spoke of how the Presences would accompany Israel into the Promised Land. The eternal (the Hebrew is *qedem*) Father is called the eternal (the Hebrew is *olam*) God (Gen 21:33). The Father commanded the eternal (the Hebrew is *olam*) arms, the Son and the Spirit, to destroy the Canaanite settlements so that Israel could occupy the Promised Land. So the Son and Spirit, who are the eternal (*olam*) arms, are as eternal (*olam*) as the Father is eternal (*olam*). This text is discussed further in the Presences of *Elyon* chapter.

Jos 05:13—06:05—Trinitarian Proof
Discussion: Exo 03—06 is similar to Jos 05:13—06:05. The *Malek Yahveh* told both Moses and Joshua to take off their sandals because his presence made the surroundings holy (Exo 03:05; Jos 05:15). Though the *Malek Yahveh* was *Yahveh* (Exo 03:04, 07, 14-16, 18; Jos 06:02, 08), the *Malek Yahveh* distinguished himself from *Yahveh* the Father (Exo 06:03; Jos 05:14-15). This shows that there are persons called *Yahveh*.
The narrator also wrote:
Seven priests carried seven trumpets before the Presence of *Yahveh* (Jos 06:08).
This passage refers to the commander of *Yahveh*'s armies (Jos 05:14-15) as the Presence of *Yahveh*, a person separate from *Yahveh* the Father. Clearly, Jos 06:02 is a continuation of the same conversation between Joshua and the *Malek Yahveh* started in Jos 05:13-15. The chapter division between Jos 05—06 is clearly misplaced. Otherwise, the commander of *Yahveh*'s armies appeared in Jos 05 for no reason, and had no substantive message for Joshua! So Jos 05:13—06: 05 appears to buttress the Trinitarian interpretation of the parallel section, Exo 03—06.

Jos 24:19—Trinitarian Proof
Joshua said to the people, You cannot serve *Yahveh*; for he is a holy
God; he is a jealous God; he will not forgive your disobedience nor your
sins (Jos 24:19).

Discussion: Joshua referred to *Yahveh* as "holy [plural adjective] Gods
[*Elohim*]" (Jos 24:19). If Joshua were a unitarian warning the Israelites against
having many gods, it would be counterproductive to use a majestic plural to
call *Yahveh* "holy [plural adjective] Gods [*Elohim*]." This is especially the case
considering the fact that earlier, the Transjordan tribes seem to have called upon
the Father and Son as the Mosaic minimum of two concurring witnesses. The
Transjordan tribes said:
The Mighty One, God, *Yahveh* [the Father]! The Mighty One, God,
Yahveh [the Son]! He knows (Jos 22:22).
Joshua matter-of-factly mentions there are persons of *Yahveh*. This is because
the *Malek Yahveh*, who is often identified as *Yahveh* and God, had just appeared
and said that he was no longer planning to drive out the Canaanites (Jdg 02:01-04).
That Jos 24:19 and Jdg 02:01-04 describe the same event can be ascertained when
one realizes that Jos 24:28-31 and Jdg 02:06-10 are parallel accounts.
Joshua said:
You are not able to serve *Yahveh*. He is a holy Gods; he is a jealous
God. He will not forgive your rebellion and your sins (Jos 24:19).
Joshua is merely repeating how *Yahveh* the Father had warned that the services
Yahveh the Son rendered were conditional upon the Israelites obedience to the
Malek with *Yahveh*'s Name in him (Exo 23:20-21; Jos 05:14-15).

By saying, "You are not able to serve *Yahveh*" (Jos 24:19), Joshua meant that
due to Israel's sinfulness, any of God's promises conditioned on their obedience
were temporary in nature. Joshua knew, however, that Israel's overall relationship
to God was not conditioned on obedience, but on grace. So on the spiritual plane,
God would forgive breaches until the Israelites finally terminated their relationship
with *Yahveh* altogether.

Jdg 02:01-04—Trinitarian Proof
Discussion: See Jos 24:19 in this appendix, since this verse describes the same
event as Jdg 02:01-04.

Jdg 06:11-27—Trinitarian Proof
In the account of Gideon's offering, the narrator referred to the *Malek Yahveh* as
Yahveh (Jdg 06:14, 16, 18, 23, 25, 27). *Yahveh* the Father is distinguished from the
Malek Yahveh (Jdg 06:12) and the Spirit (Jdg 06:34). The Trinity is mentioned as
being "[All] the Gods [*haElohim*]" several times (Jdg 06:20, 36, 39; 07:14). These
facts make the section Jdg 06:11-27 thoroughly Trinitarian.

The offerings of Gideon (Jdg 06:19-21) and Manoah (Jdg 13:15-20) are
discussed in the chapter on the Presences of *Elyon* in the section on the Lord's
Supper.

Jdg 13:02-23—Trinitarian Proof
Discussion: In the account of Manoah's offering, *Yahveh* the Father, the *Malek Yahveh* and the Spirit are each distinguished from the other (Jdg 13:25). Manoah identified the *Malek Yahveh* as *Elohim* (Jdg 13:22). Both the narrator (Jdg 13:19) and Manoah's wife (Jdg 13:23) refer to the *Malek Yahveh* as *Yahveh* (the Son). The Trinity is mentioned three times as being "[All] the Gods [*haElohim*]," once by Manoah, once by his wife, and once by the narrator (Jdg 13:06, 08-09). The *Malek Yahveh* calls himself "Wonderful," which is a word similar to the "Wonderful" in the prophecy of the Messiah (see Isa 09:06 in this appendix). Manoah's offering is discussed further at Jdg 06:11-27 in this appendix.

1Sa 10:03—Trinitarian Proof
Then you will go on from there until you reach the great tree of Tabor. Three men going up to [All] the Gods (*haElohim*) at Bethel will meet you there. One will be carrying three young goats, another three loaves of bread, and another a skin of wine (1Sa 10:03).
Discussion: During the time of the Judges, Samuel told Saul about three men making what seems to have been a Trinitarian offering to [All] the Gods (*haElohim*) at Bethel (1Sa 10:03-04): three loaves of bread and three goats, yet one skin of wine. The Trinity may have posed as three men in 1Sa 10 as they did in Gen 18. 1Sa 10:03 is mentioned in the discussion of Gen 18:03-05 and Gen 28:12-22 in this appendix, as well as in the Presences of *Elyon* chapter.

1Ki 18:24; 19:05-11—Trinitarian Proof
Discussion: The narrator referred to the Word of *Yahveh* (1Ki 19:09) as *Yahveh* (the Son) (1Ki 19:11). The Word of *Yahveh* was called the *Malek Yahveh* earlier in the account (1Ki 19:07):
Yahveh said [to Elijah], 'Go out and stand on the mount before the Presence of *Yahveh* (the Son), for *Yahveh* [the Father] is about to pass by' (1Ki 19:11).
That *Yahveh* spoke of *Yahveh* in the third person, saying that *Yahveh* was about to pass by, shows that there are persons named *Yahveh*. 1Ki 19 is discussed further in the Hebrew collective nouns and the Presences of *Elyon* chapters.

1Ki 22:19-24—Trinitarian Proof
Discussion: Unitarians sometimes say that 1Ki 22:19-24 shows *Yahveh* is only a single person whom angels surround. Unitarians completely miss how the prophet Micaiah referred to two persons of *Yahveh*:
Micaiah said, 'Therefore, hear you the Word [the Son] of *Yahveh* [the Father]: 'I [the Son] saw *Yahveh* [the Father] sitting on his [the Father's] throne" (1Ki 22:19).
This section is thoroughly Trinitarian since there is mention of the Father, the Word and a personal Spirit.

Job —Trinitarian Proof
Discussion: See the section on Job in the chapter on Proto-Sinaitic Trinitarianism.

Psalms —Trinitarian Proof
Discussion: See the section on Books I and II of the Psalms in the chapter on Proto-Sinaitic Trinitarianism.

Psa 002:02-12—Trinitarian Proof
The kings of the earth take a stand, and the rulers take counsel together, against *Yahveh*, and against his anointed, saying, 'Let us break their bonds apart, and cast away their cords from us.' I will tell of the decree. *Yahveh* said to me, 'You are my son. Today I have become your father. Ask of me, and I will give the nations for your inheritance, the uttermost parts of the earth for your possession. You shall break them with a rod of iron. You shall dash them in pieces like a potter's vessel.' Now therefore be wise, you kings. Be instructed, you judges of the earth. Serve *Yahveh* with fear, and rejoice with trembling. Kiss the son, lest he become angry, and you perish in the way, for his wrath will soon be kindled. Blessed are all those who take refuge in him (Psa 002:02-12).
Discussion: A text that suggests or speaks of the deity of the Messiah should be considered a Trinitarian proof. See Psa 045:06-07 [*BHS* 045:07-08] in this appendix for a discussion of Psa 002.

Psa 022:01 [LXX 021:01] —Trinitarian Proof
My God, my God, why have you forsaken me? Why are you so far from helping me, and from the words of my groaning? (Psa 022:01).
Discussion: *Yeshua* quoted Psa 022:01 from the cross, saying:
'*Eli* [the Father], *Eli* [the Spirit], *lama sabachthani?*' that is, 'My God [the Father], my God [the Spirit], why have you forsaken me?' (Mat 27:46; also compare Mar 15:34).

Psa 033:04, 06—Trinitarian Proof
For the word of *Yahveh* is right. All his work is done in faithfulness... .By the word of *Yahveh* were the heavens made, All the host of them by the breath of his mouth (Psa 033:04, 06).
Discussion: The Word (the Son) of *Yahveh* (the Father), and the breath (the Spirit) of his (the Father's) mouth made the heavens.

Psa 045:06-07 [BHS 045:07-08] —Trinitarian Proof
Your throne, God, is forever and ever. A scepter of equity is the scepter of your kingdom. You have loved righteousness, and hated wickedness. Therefore, God, your God, has anointed you with the oil of gladness above your fellows (Psa 045:06-07).

Discussion: The author of Hebrews wrote that God the Father addressed God the Son in Psa 045 (Heb 01:08-09). The section from the Psalms quoted by the writer of Hebrew reads:

Your [the Son's] throne, O God [the Son], will last forever and ever; a scepter of justice will be the scepter of your [the Son's] kingdom. You [the Son] love righteousness and hate wickedness; therefore God [the Father], your [the Son's] God [the Father], has set you [the Son] above your [the Son's] companions by anointing you [the Son] with the oil of joy (Psa 045: 06-07 [*BHS* 045:07-08]).

The NT Church knew that many of David's Psalms were messianic, and did not apply to David directly. If they applied to David at all, it was only by way of David being a type of the antitype, the Messiah. For example, Peter said that the prophecy about not being abandoned to the grave refers to the Messiah, but not to David (Psa 016:10; Act 02:27-31).

Psa 045 is a Book II Psalm that honors God (*Elohim*) the Son. Books I and II of the Psalms are discussed in the chapter on Proto-Sinaitic Trinitarianism. According to the first verse, the sons of Korah wrote Psa 045 as a royal wedding song. Psa 045 ascribes divinity to David only to celebrate how David was the type of the antitype, his God-man descendant (2Sa 07:13-14; 1Ch 17:13-14).

If Psa 045 were merely about David, the psalmist would have committed blasphemy. The Psalm would have ascribed divine actions and attributes and the name "God" (Psa 045:06-07) to a mere human king (Act 12:21-23). Surely the Levites would have torn their garments rather than read or sing such blasphemies (Mat 26:63-65; Mar 14:61-63). During NT times it was even considered blasphemy to say one was the Son of God—much less God (Joh 10:35-36; 19:07)!

Psa 002 is similar to Psa 045 in certain respects. Though the words of Psa 002 came to David through the Spirit (Act 04:25-26), Psa 002 was likely used at the temple as a coronation Psalm. The Psalm celebrates how David was the type of the antitype, his God-man descendant (2Sa 07). Psa 002 portrays the Messiah as being God's Son (Psa 002:007). Psa 002 also portrays the Messiah as being so powerful that he could only be the God-man (Psa 002:12).

Psa 110 is similar to Psa 002 and Psa 045 in certain respects. The statement, "*Yahveh* said to my Master [*Adonee*]" (Psa 110:01) may also have meant, "*Yahveh* said to my master [David]," just as Jewish rabbis assert. Still, it was applied to David only in anticipation of David's descendant, the God-man. He would one day be a priest forever (Psa 110:04) and sit on the throne of David forever (2Sa 07:13, 16; Mic 05:02 [*BHS* 05:01]).

David was not even allowed to build the temple (1Ch 22:08), much less be a priest forever in the order of Melchizedek (Psa 110:04). So everyone must have known that Psa 110 did not apply to David, but rather to David's God-man descendant (2Sa 07:23; Heb 05:06; 06:20; 07:03, 17, 21). David's death left no doubt as to whether Psa 110 applied to the Messiah, since David's bodiless soul surely is not now acting as priest in heaven forever (Act 02:29-31).

David himself believed that *Yahveh* the Father would send *Yahveh* the Son to be the God-man Messiah. This would be similar to how the Father had sent the Son to redeem Israel from Egypt. David heard from Nathan that the Messiah would be his descendant and would rule on David's throne forever (2Sa 07:11-29). Then David recollected how gracious *Yahveh* (the Father) *Elohim* (the Son) were (2Sa 07:25). David remembered especially how:

> *Elohim* [plural noun] went [plural verb] to redeem to himself a people... (2Sa 07:23).

That David was Trinitarian can also be seen from these verses discussed in MT plurals appendix:

- David twice called God the "living Gods" [*Elohim khayyim*] (1Sa 17:26, 36, as is discussed in the MT plurals appendix),
- David's statement that "Gods, they judge [plural verb] the earth" (Psa 058:11 [*BHS* 057:12] as is discussed in the MT plurals appendix), and
- *Yeshua*'s statement:

> David himself, speaking by the Holy Spirit, declared: 'The Lord [the Father] said to my Master [the Son]' (Mat 22:43; Mar 12:36-37; see Psa 110:01 and Mat 22:43 in this appendix).

Psa 067:01, 06-07—Trinitarian Proof

> May God be merciful to us, bless us, And cause his face to shine on us. Selah....The earth has yielded its increase. God, even our own God, will bless us. God will bless us. All the ends of the earth shall fear him (Psa 067:01, 06-07).

Discussion: God is the subject of three verbs in this verse:

> May God [Father] be gracious to us and bless us and make his [the Father's] Faces [*Panim*, the Son and Spirit] shine upon us (Psa 067:01).

God is also mentioned three times as the subject of two instances of the verb "to bless":

> God, our God, will bless us, God will bless us (Psa 067:06-07).

Psa 067 and similar passages are mentioned in the discussion of the Aaronic Blessing. See Num 06:22-27 in this appendix.

Psa 082:06-08—Trinitarian Proof

> I said, 'You are gods, all of you are sons of the Most High. Nevertheless you shall die like men, and fall like one of the rulers. Arise, God, judge the earth, for you inherit all of the nations' (Psa 082:06-08).

Discussion: *Yeshua* said that the judges to whom the Word (the Son) of God (the Father) came were called "gods" (Psa 082:06; Joh 10:34-35). *Yeshua* then asked:

> What about the one [the Son, the Word] whom the Father set apart as his very own and sent into the world? Why then do you accuse me of blasphemy because I said, 'I am God's Son'? (Joh 10:36).

So if "the Word" coming to human judges or rulers made them into "gods," *Yeshua* asked why "the Word" himself (Joh 01:01) could not refer to himself as "God"?

The phrase "sent into the world" (Joh 10:36a) is *Yeshua*'s allusion to the Father's statement:

Rise up, O God [the Son], judge the earth, for all the nations are your [the Son's] inheritance (Psa 082:08).

So Joh 10:35-36 is an allusion to Psa 082:06-08. *Yeshua* said he was God the Son (Psa 082:08; Joh 10:36). Psa 082:07, however, applied to all who would oppose *Yeshua*:

But you will die like mere men; you will fall like every other ruler (Psa 082:07).

Psa 082:08 must be the Father addressing the Son as "God," since God the Father cannot have the earth as an inheritance, but only as a possession. The Father, however, can give the earth to the Son as an inheritance. It should be noted that the Father's calling the Son "God" (Psa 082:08; Joh 10:36a) is not a unique occurrence. The writer of Hebrews said that the Father elsewhere called the Son "God" (Psa 045:06-07 [*BHS* 045:07-08]; Heb 01:08).

Parallels to Psa 082 include the prophecies that the Father would give Israel (Deu 32:08-09) and the nations to his Anointed Son (Dan 07:13-14). In Psa 002:07-12 the Father tells the Son to start the conquest of his inheritance. Psa 082 is discussed further in the chapter on the *Shema*.

Psa 091:01, 09—Trinitarian Proof
Discussion: Due to the demands of unitarianism, most translations of Psa 091:01, 09 follow the LXX rather than the MT recension. The literal reading of the Hebrew distinguishes *El Shaddai* (the Son as Messiah) from *Yahveh* (the Father):

He [a believer] who dwells in the secret place of the Most High [the Father] will rest in the shadow of *Shaddai* [the Son] (Psa 091:01), and

For you, *Yahveh* [the Son], are my refuge! You have made the Most High [the Father] your habitation (Psa 091:09).

Psa 091 is mentioned in the section on Num 22—24 in the chapter on Proto-Sinaitic Trinitarianism.

LXX Psa 097:07—Trinitarian Proof
Let all that worship graven images be ashamed, who boast of their idols; worship him, all ye his angels (*LXE* Psalm 97:7).
Discussion: See the discussion of Deu 32:08-09, LXX 32:43, in this appendix.

Psa 102:25 LXX; 102:26-27—Trinitarian Proof
In the beginning, O Lord [the Son], you [the Son] laid the foundation of the earth; and the heavens are the works of your [the Son's] hands (LXX Psa 102:25).

They will perish, but you [the Son] will endure. Yes, all of them will wear out like a garment. You [the Son] will change them like a cloak, and they will be changed. But you [the Son] are the same. Your [the Son's] years will have no end (Psa 102:26-27).

Discussion: The LXX version of Psa 102:25 translates as:

In the beginning you, O Lord, did lay the foundation of the earth; and the heavens are the works of your hands.

The author of Hebrews quoted Psa 102:25 LXX and Psa 102:26-27 where *Elyon*, the Father, assures the suffering Lord (*Kurios*), the Son.

The Father spoke words of comfort to *Yeshua*, who was in anguish at the end of his life. The Father said that just as he, *Yeshua*, had created the earth, so also he, *Yeshua*, would outlast the earth (Heb 01:10-12). This is similar to how the Suffering Servant is comforted that his accusers were mere mortals who "will all wear out like a garment, and the moths will eat them up" (Isa 50:09).

Similar passages where the Son is spoken of as being eternal are:

- The Son said that he is eternal (Isa 51:06, 08),
- The Messiah is prophesied to be eternal (as is discussed at Isa 09:06 [*BHS* 09: 05] in this appendix), and
- The Son tells the Father that they are eternal (as is discussed at Hab 01:12 in the MT plurals appendix).

Psa 107:20—Trinitarian Proof

He sends his word, and heals them, and delivers them from their graves (Psa 107:20).

Discussion: The Word is a personal agent of *Yahveh* and is *Yahveh*.

Psa 110:01, 04-05—Trinitarian Proof

Yahveh [the Father] says to my Master [the Son], 'Sit at my right hand, until I make your enemies your footstool for your feet'....*Yahveh* [the Father] has sworn and will not change his mind: 'You [the Son] are a priest forever in the order of Melchizedek. The Lord [the Spirit] is at your right hand. He [the Spirit] will crush kings in the day of his wrath' (Psa 110:01, 04-05).

Discussion: Psa 110 distinguished *Yahveh* the Father from the Son, who was David's Master (*Adonee*). In the NT, *Yeshua*'s interpretation of Psa 110 distinguishes the Spirit from the Father and the Son. Psa 110:01 begins, "*Yahveh* [the Father] said to my Master [*Adonee*]..." That the *Adonee* is divine is suggested by the fact that the Son will be a priest forever (Psa 110:04).

The use of *Adonai* and *Adonee* (or *adonee*) is discussed in detail in the Hebrew collective nouns chapter in the "Masters as *Adonai*" section. The chapter shows how the plural *Adonai* ("my Lord") is a plural of delegation, a collective noun variant that indicates the Father had delegated authority to the Son. The singular *Adonee* ("my Master") shows that the Son was the Father's delegate. The Hebrew collective nouns chapter, especially the *"Masters as adonai"* section, shows why the following makes perfect sense:

- The Father was not called *Adonee* ("my Master"), but only *Adonai* ("my Lord"). The *Malek Yahveh*, however, is sometimes called *Adonee* ("my Master") (Jos 05:14; Jdg 06:13; Psa 110:01; Zec 04:13). Likewise, the Spirit is sometimes called *Adonee* ("my Master") (Zec 01:09; 04:04-05; 06:04). In Psa 110:01, David spoke of the Son as *Adonee* ("my Master"), just as Joshua called the Commander of *Yahveh's* Armies, the Son, *Adonee* ("my Master") (Jos 05:14), and

- The servant Eliezer called Abraham *adonai* ("my lord") (Gen 24:09-10). The same servant, Eliezer, called Isaac *adonee* ("my master") (Gen 24:65). It seems that upon delegating authority, the father's title was elevated from *adonee* ("my master") to *adonai* ("my lord"). The Son was then called *adonee* ("my master"). So in the case of the Trinity, the Father had delegated authority to the Son, for instance, authority over Israel (Deu 32:08-09 is discussed in the Song of Moses chapter). So the Father was appropriately called *Adonai* ("my Lord"), and the Son was called *Adonee* ("my Master").

Yeshua showed that David was Trinitarian when he quoted Psa 110:01 and said:

> David himself, speaking by the Holy Spirit, declared: 'The Lord [*Kurios*] said to my Master [*Kurios*]' (Mat 22:43; Mar 12:36-37).

In the above NT quote of the OT, the same Greek word *Kurios* is used to translate two Hebrew words: *Adonai* and *Adonee*. The Greek word *Kurios* can mean "master, lord, owner, or sir." In any case, the Greek should follow the Hebrew. In the case of *Adonai*, *Kurios* should be translated as "Lord." In the case of *Adonee*, *Kurios* should be translated as "Master."

Yeshua connected the Spirit with Psa 110:01, and so does Peter:

> Exalted to the right hand of God, he [*Yeshua*] has received from the Father the promised Holy Spirit and has poured out what you now see and hear. For David did not ascend to heaven, and yet he said, 'The Lord [the Father] said to my Master [the Son]: 'Sit at my right hand until I make your enemies a footstool for your feet" (Act 02:33-35).

Yeshua and Peter can connect the Spirit to a quote of Psa 110:01, because they can ascertain that the "Lord" (*Adonai*) in Psa 110:05 refers to the Spirit:

> The Lord [the Spirit] is at your [the Son's] right hand; he [the Spirit] will crush kings on the day of his [the Spirit's] wrath (Psa 110:05).

In Psa 110:01, the Lord (the Father) had told the Master (the Son) to sit at his right hand. Thus, the Father is at the Son's left hand. Since the Father is already at the Son's left hand (Psa 110:01), the Spirit must be "the Lord" at the Son's right hand (Psa 110:05).

Psa 110:05 is a prophecy of how *Yeshua* will be raised from the dead and will return to the Father to rule over the Church (Joh 20:17). Then the Father will send out the Spirit to spiritually conquer the earth for the Son (Joh 14:26; 15:26) until all the elect are saved (Rom 11:26; 1Ti 02:04).

That the Lord (*Adonai*) in Psa 110:05 is the Spirit is verified in at least two ways:

- In the OT, the person who helps is said to be at the right hand of the person being helped (Psa 073:23; Isa 41:13). Since the Spirit helps the Son, it is the Spirit who is at the right hand of *Yeshua*. The Spirit was already at *Yeshua*'s right hand when he helped raise *Yeshua* to life (Act 02:25; Rom 08:11; 1Pe 03:18), and

- That the Lord (*Adonai*) in Psa 110:05 is the Spirit is shown by the fact that the Spirit was not poured out on the Church until after Psa 110:05 was fulfilled. *Yeshua* was then at the Father's right hand in heaven (Act 07:55-56; Heb 01:03; Eph 01:20). The Spirit at *Yeshua*'s right hand was sent out on Pentecost to conquer a spiritual kingdom for the Son (Joh 07:39; 16:07; Act 02:17-18, 33; 2Co 03:08).

Act 02:33-35 shows that Peter understood the Son would conquer the nations by sending the Spirit. The statement that the Son would rule in the midst of his enemies shows that the Spirit-built Christian Church is indicated. The Church exists in the midst of its enemies and will evangelize until the end of the age (Psa 110:02; compare Psa 106:47; Mat 10:23; 24:14; Luk 18:08; Rom 08:37; 1Co 15:24; 2Co 02:14-16).

Psa 113:01-03—Trinitarian Proof

Praise *Yah*[*veh*]! Praise, you servants of *Yahveh*, praise the Name of *Yahveh*. Blessed be the Name of *Yahveh*, from this time forth and forevermore. From the rising of the sun to the going down of the same, the Name of *Yahveh* is to be praised (Psa 113:01-03).

Discussion: The "Name of *Yahveh*" is mentioned three times.

Psa 119:89—Trinitarian Proof

Your [the Father's] Word [the Son], *Yahveh* [the Father], is eternal; and abides in the heavens (Psa 119:89).

Discussion: The Word is a personal agent of *Yahveh* and is *Yahveh*.

Psa 147:15-18—Trinitarian Proof

He sends out his commandment on earth. His word runs very swiftly. He gives snow like wool, and scatters frost like ashes. He hurls down his hail like pebbles. Who can stand before his cold? He sends out his word, and melts them. He causes his wind to blow, and the waters flow (Psa 147:15-18).

Discussion: The Word is a personal agent of *Yahveh* and is *Yahveh*.

Ecc 04:08-12—Trinitarian Proof

There was a man all alone; he had neither son nor brother...two are better than one...a cord of three strands is not quickly broken (Ecc 04:08-12).

Discussion: Solomon said two persons together were better than one forlorn person (Ecc 04:09-12a), but a cord of three strands was best of all (Ecc 04:12b). Surely, Solomon had the Trinity in mind when he said this. Just as three strands comprise one cord, three persons are one God.

Isa 01:03—Trinitarian Proof
The ox knows its owner, the donkey its masters' manger, but Israel does not know, my people do not perceive (Isa 01:03).

Discussion: Isaiah called a donkey's owner "masters" (Isa 01:03). Majestic plural proponents provide no overriding reason why the plural form "masters" should be translated in the singular. Besides, why would a donkey's owner necessarily be majestic? If Eliezer had two masters, Abraham (*adonai*) (Gen 15: 02) and Isaac (*adonee*) (Gen 24:12, 65), surely a donkey could have two masters!

The Trinitarian interpretation of Isa 01:03 is apparent when one notes that elsewhere *Yahveh* says they are "masters" (the Hebrew is *Adonim*) (Mal 01:06). That *Yahveh* is "masters" hints at the Trinitarian meaning of Isa 01:03. Isa 01: 03 has parallel constructions: owner, masters...Owner, Masters. The parallel construction shows that there are ellipses in the train of thought. Isa 01:03 should be understood as...

...The ox knows its owner (singular), the donkey its masters' (plural) manger, but Israel does not know... [...its singular Owner, in other words, God (Exo 06:07; 19:05-06)], my people do not perceive... [...their plural "Masters," in other words, the Trinity (Mal 01:06)] (Isa 01:03).

Isa 06:03—Trinitarian Proof
One cried to another, and said, Holy, holy, holy, is *Yahveh* of hosts: the whole earth is full of his glory (Isa 06:03).

Discussion: The Trisagion ("Thrice Holy") liturgical formula is said or sung by the angels, evidently antiphonally: "Holy, Holy, Holy is *Yahveh* of hosts." Isa 06: 03 has three mentions of "holy" while the Name, *Yahveh,* is mentioned once. The three and one aspect of Trisagions suggests that God is the Trinity. The first part of Isa 06 is especially Trinitarian since *Yahveh* asked, "Who will go for us?" (Isa 06: 08). Another Trisagion is discussed at Rev 04:08 in this appendix.

Isa 07:14—Trinitarian Proof
Therefore, the Lord himself will give you a sign: behold, a virgin shall conceive, and bear a son, and shall call his name Immanuel (Isa 07:14).

Discussion: Matthew wrote that Isaiah prophesied of the Messiah's being "Immanuel," meaning, "God with us" (Mat 01:23).

All the arguments against the "virgin" translation of Isa 07:14 are faulty. Some say Isa 07:14 prophecies the birth of Isaiah's second son by a prophetess (Isa 07: 03; 08:03). Isaiah's second son, however, was named "*Mahershalalhashbaz*" ("swift is booty, speedy is prey"), not Immanuel ("God with us").

Every passage in scripture must be taken in context, and it seems that the Isa 07: 14 and 09:06 prophecies are meant to be taken together. There is no way Isaiah's second son fulfilled the Isa 09:06 prophecy!

Critics argue that if Isaiah had meant "virgin," he would have used the Hebrew word *nayarah* or *betulah* rather than *almah*. *Nayarah*, however, can refer to a non-virgin (1Ki 01:02), and *betulah* is applied to a widow (Joe 01:08).

By contrast, *Almah* is never applied to a non-virgin, although Solomon does write "the way of a man with a maid [*almah*]" (Pro 30:19). This may refer to chaperoned dating and love letters, rather than sex. Moreover, the LXX has "the way of a man in his youth [*en na'uwr*]," so *almah* may not have been in the original Hebrew of Pro 30:19.

Critics also say the Greek translated "virgin" (*parthenos*) should read, "young, unmarried woman" (LXX Isa 07:14; Mat 01:23). This is based on the notion that Dinah was called a *parthenos* (Gen 34:03) after she was raped (Gen 34:02).

Where the critics err is assuming that verse order in the Bible always indicates chronological order. The author of Genesis liked to preface a synopsis statement of the narrative before giving the details of the account (Gen 01:01, 02:04a, 4b, 05:01; 06:09; 10:01; 11:10, 27; 25:12, 19; 36:01, 09; 37:02, etc.)   So the critics mistook what is essentially the title and subtitle of the account for the narrative itself.

Criminologists would agree that the rape mentioned in Gen 34:02 occurred after Gen 34:03:

> Shechem's soul was drawn to Dinah the daughter of Jacob; he loved the maiden [virgin maiden] and spoke tenderly to her (Gen 34:03).

The details suggest this was textbook "date rape," not a classic "stalker" rape case. The ruler Shechem did not commit rape on first sight, and then sweet talk with Dinah afterward. So, Dinah was a "virgin" (*parthenos*) in Gen 34:03, and *parthenos* should be translated as "virgin" in Isa 07:14, Mat 01:23, and elsewhere.

Isa 09:01-02, 06-07 [BHS 08:23—09:01, 05-06] —Trinitarian Proof
> For to us a child is born, to us a son is given; and the government shall
> be on his shoulder: and his name shall be called Wonderful, Counselor,
> Mighty God, Everlasting Father, Prince of Peace (Isa 09:06).

Discussion: Isaiah prophesied that the Messiah would be Mighty God (*El*) and Everlasting Father. "Everlasting Father" is a Hebraism that is accurately translated as "Author of Eternity" (Isa 09:06 [*BHS* 09:05]; compare Ecc 03:11; Heb 12: 02). Matthew applies Isa 09:01-02 to *Yeshua* (Mat 04:15-16). That the Son is the "Counselor" (Isa 09:06) is discussed at Isa 40:13 in this appendix.

The *Malek Yahveh* told Samson's parents that his name was "Wonderful" (*LXE, YLT* Jdg 13:18). Isaiah prophesied that the Messiah would be "Wonderful" (Isa 09:06). The words for "Wonderful" are slightly different in each verse, but the meaning can be the same: Jdg 13:18 is *pil'iy*, Strong's # 6383, while Isa 09: 06 [*BHS* 09:05] is *pele'*, Strong's # 6382. So this would indicate that the *Malek Yahveh* was the Son, and the Son became the Messiah.

The interpretation that the *Malek Yahveh* was prophesied to become the Messiah is supported by an additional fact. The LXX of Isa 09:06 has "the Angel [*Malek*] of Great Counsel," commonly translated "Messenger of Great Counsel." This seems to be a clear reference to the *Malek Yahveh*, the Angel of *Yahveh*.

The Angel of *Yahveh* was often called *Yahveh* and God in the OT, as was noted at the start of this appendix. So it is not surprising that here in Isa 09:06, the Messenger of Great Counsel is called "Mighty God" and "Author of Eternity." So the association between the *Malek Yahveh* and the Messiah suggests the Messiah is divine. This, in turn, leads one to believe that the Trinity is a biblical concept.

Isa 33:22—Trinitarian Proof

For *Yahveh* is our judge, *Yahveh* is our lawgiver, *Yahveh* is our king; he will save us (Isa 33:22).

Discussion: The Name, *Yahveh,* is repeated three times.

Isa 34:16—Trinitarian Proof

Discussion: Mention is made of *Yahveh*, my (the Son's) mouth, and the Father's Spirit. The combination of pronouns in Isa 34:16 makes sense if *Yahveh* the Son were the speaker:

Seek you [the reader] out of the book of *Yahveh*, and read: 'Not one of these shall be missing, none shall want her mate;' for my [the Son's] mouth has commanded, and his [the Father's] Spirit has gathered them (MT Isa 34:16).

The *YLT* and *KJV* follow the Hebrew and translate "my mouth." However, other translations change the pronoun to read "his mouth" (*NIV* Isa 34:16). The reason is that the translators do not recognize that the Son is the speaker of this passage. Translators here exercise their "license" to adapt Trinitarian speech to the demands of unitarianism by changing the pronoun "my" to "his."

Changing pronouns is done elsewhere in the OT, for instance, in the *NIV* translations of Hos 12:04, the Hebrew pronoun "us" is rendered as "him." This is discussed in the MT plurals appendix under Hos 12:04.

Isa 40:03, 05, 09, 10—Trinitarian Proof

The voice of one who cries, 'Prepare in the wilderness the way of *Yahveh*; make level in the desert a highway for our God' (Isa 40:03).

The glory of *Yahveh* shall be revealed, and all flesh shall see it together; for the mouth of *Yahveh* has spoken it (Isa 40:05).

You who tell good news to Zion, go up on a high mountain; you who tell good news to Jerusalem, lift up your voice with strength; lift it up, do not be afraid; say to the cities of Judah, Behold, your God! Behold, the Lord *Yahveh* will come as a mighty one, and his arm will rule for him: Behold, his reward is with him, and his recompense before him (Isa 40: 09).

Blessed be the Lord, the God of Israel, for he has visited and worked redemption for his people (Luk 01:68).

You, child, will be called a prophet of the Most High, for you will go before the Lord to make ready his ways (Luk 01:76).

Discussion: John the Baptist would prepare a path for *Yahveh* (the Son) (Isa 40:10) who is "our God" (Isa 40:03, 09; Mat 03:03; Luk 01:76b). Thus, "the glory [the Son] of *Yahveh* [the Father] will be revealed" (Isa 40:05).

Isaiah prophesied that John the Baptist's message would be equivalent to publicly saying of *Yeshua*, "Here is your God!" (Isa 40:09; Luk 01:76a). Indeed, John's public statements about the greatness of *Yeshua* were tantamount to saying that *Yeshua* is God (Mat 03:11; Luk 03:16). Perhaps John did refer to *Yeshua* as God privately to his disciples, but overt statements saying *Yeshua* was God would have been incendiary (Joh 01:41, 45).

John the Baptist's father Zechariah understood "the prophets of long ago" (Luk 01:70), such as Isaiah (Isa 40:03, 05, 09), to say, "the Lord, the God of Israel...has come" (Luk 01:68). John's father Zechariah also understood that his son John would "be called a prophet of the Most High; for you will go on before the Lord to prepare the way for him" (Luk 01:76).

Zechariah was not referring to the Targum on Isa 40:09. Targums are Aramaic paraphrases and explanatory translations of the Hebrew. The Targum for Isa 40: 09 changes the words "Behold your God!" to "The Kingdom of your God is revealed."[190]

Zechariah also referred to the Messiah as "a horn of salvation" (Luk 01:69), a phrase previously used to refer to *Yahveh* (2Sa 22:03; Psa 018:02). The Messiah elsewhere is called a "horn" (Eze 29:21). This suggests Zechariah knew the Messiah to be *Yahveh* the Son.

Isa 40:13—Trinitarian Proof
Discussion: *Yahveh* the Son asked:
Who has understood the Mind [literally, the *Ruach*, meaning the Spirit] of *Yahveh* [the Father], or as his [the Father's] Counselor [the Son] has taught him [the Father]? (Isa 40:13).

In Isa 40:13, what the Son asked was tantamount to asking, "Who can comprehend any member of the Trinity?" Later in Isaiah, the Son asks a similar rhetorical question about who was with him [the Son] and with "the lasts [the Father and Spirit]" (Isa 41:04). Isa 40:13 is similar to Isa 48:12-16 and Isa 63:07-14 in that these passages mention all three persons of the Trinity. Isa 48:12-16 and Isa 63:07-14 are discussed elsewhere in this appendix.

In Isa 40:13, the Spirit is the "Mind" of *Yahveh*. The Hebrew word *Ruach* is variously translated "mind," "wind" or "Spirit." When *Yeshua* counseled Nicodemus, *Yeshua* alluded to Isa 40:13. *Yeshua* referred to the Spirit and said, "The wind blows where it pleases" (Joh 03:08). Then, just as all three persons of the Trinity are mentioned in Isa 40:13 (as was noted just above), *Yeshua* associated himself with the Father and Spirit:

What we [Son and Spirit] have known we speak, and what we have seen we testify... For he [the Son] whom God [the Father] hath sent speaks the words of God [the Father]: for God [the Father] gives the Spirit to him [the Son as Messiah] without measure (Joh 03:11, 34).

The "we" in Joh 03:11 refers back to the Mind (the Spirit) and Counsel (the Son) of *Yahveh* in Isa 40:13. That the "we" in Joh 03:11 refers to *Yeshua* and the Spirit can be seen from Nicodemus' statement that *Yeshua* came from God (the Father), yet was also with God (the Spirit):

He [Nicodemus] came to *Yeshua* at night and said, 'Rabbi, we know you are a teacher who has come from God [the Father]. For no one could perform the miraculous signs you are doing if God [the Spirit] were not with him' (Joh 03:02).

The second time the Son alluded to Isa 40:13 was in Joh 14:16 when he called the Spirit "another Counselor." *Yeshua* said:

I will pray to the Father, and he shall give you another Counselor to be with you forever (Joh 14:16).

Yeshua identified this "another Counselor" as the Spirit (Joh 14:26).

The Greek word translated "another" is *allos*, meaning, "another of the same kind." Notably, *heteros* is the Greek word for "another of a different kind," a word never used to refer to the Trinity. So *Yeshua*'s statement saying that the Spirit was "another Counselor" (Joh 14:16, 26) was tantamount to saying that the Son was a Counselor as divine as the Spirit.

By saying the Spirit was "another counselor," *Yeshua* was saying that he was the "Counselor" of Isa 09:06 [*BHS* 09:05]. Interestingly, Isa 09:06 also relates that the Messiah would be the "Mighty God" and the "Author of Eternity." Passages related to Isa 40:13 are those where the Father said:

- The Messiah is *Yahveh* of hosts (Amo 04:11-13), and
- The Son reveals his thoughts to man as would a counselor, as is discussed at Amo 04:11-13 in this appendix.

So when *Yeshua* said the Spirit was "another Counselor" (Joh 14:16, 26), he was definitely speaking in terms of divinity.

Paul shows that he understood Isaiah to refer to three persons of the Trinity in Isa 40:13. In Rom 11:36, Paul mentions "him" three times in reference to God after quoting Isa 40:13 in Rom 11:34:

For who hath known the Mind [the Spirit] of the Lord [the Father]? or who hath been his [the Father's] Counselor [the Son]?...because of him [the Father], through him [the Son], and by means of him [the Spirit] all things exist (Rom 11:34, 36).

Even more clear are Paul's statements associating the Spirit with the thoughts and mind of God. Paul said that the Spirit communicates God's thoughts to humans. Christians understand these thoughts because we have both the Spirit and the mind of Christ (1Co 02:10-16).

Paul definitely wrote 1Co 02:10-16 with Isa 40:13 in mind, since he quoted Isa 40:13 nearby (1Co 02:16). 1Co 02:16 is the second time that Paul quoted Isa 40:

13. Paul's first quote was in Rom 11:34. Paul therefore interpreted Isa 40:13 to mean that the *Ruach* (meaning, "the Spirit" or the "Mind") of the Father is the Spirit, and that the Father's Counselor is the Son.

Isa 43:10—Trinitarian Proof

'You [the Israelites] are my witnesses,' said *Yahveh* [the Father], 'and my Servant [the Son] whom I have chosen, that you may know and believe Me, and understand that I am He. Before Me there was no God formed, nor shall there be after Me' (Isa 43:10).

Discussion: Here the Father said that the Servant is his witness that no God was ever formed before or after the Father. This means that the Son, who is the Servant of *Yahveh*, is as eternal as *Yahveh* the Father is. Logically, this bears out, too, since if the Son were not as eternal as the Father, how could the Son attest that no god was formed before the Father? The "you," meaning the Israelites, could only attest that, to their knowledge, no gods were formed during their lifetimes.

Isa 48:12-16—Trinitarian Proof

Discussion: Isa 48:16 and 61:01-02 are famous Trinitarian prophecies where *Yahveh* the Son said that the Father would send him to be the Messiah, and the Father would send the Spirit with the Messiah. That the Son and Spirit are sent together is not surprising since the Son and Spirit are sent out singly often. This is the case even when just Isaiah is considered (Isa 11:02; 34:16; 40:13; 42:01, 48:12-16; 59:20-21; 61:01-02; 63:10-14).

Several verses after Isa 61:01-02, the Servant of *Yahveh* calls himself *Yahveh*: "For I, *Yahveh*, love justice..." (Isa 61:08). *Yeshua* quoted Isa 61:01-02 in Luk 04:18-19. This fact suggests that the Messiah, *Yeshua*, is the same person as the "sent" *Yahveh* (the Son) who spoke in Isa 48:16 and Isa 61:08.

The Trinitarian interpretation of Isa 48:16 is consistent with Isa 61:01, 08, and with the rest of Isaiah in that *Yahveh* the Son is speaking. Isaiah did not break into *Yahveh*'s monologue to say that *Yahveh* had sent Isaiah and the Spirit, as some have suggested. See the chapter on the Prophet Behind the Prophets.

Isa 49:05-06—Trinitarian Proof

Now says *Yahveh* who formed me from the womb to be his Servant, to bring Jacob again to him, and that Israel be gathered to him (for I am honorable in the eyes of *Yahveh*, and my God is become my strength); yes, he says, 'It is too light a thing that you should be my Servant to raise up the tribes of Jacob, and to restore the preserved of Israel: I will also give you for a light to the Gentiles, that you may be my salvation to the end of the earth' (Isa 49:05).

Discussion: A text that suggests or speaks of the deity of the Messiah should be considered a Trinitarian proof. *Yahveh* the Father gave the Servant of *Yahveh* (the Messiah) a God-sized task of saving the nations. Moses was not even up to the job of saving Israel, and he knew it (Deu 31:27).

The difference between Christ's starting Christianity and innovators starting other religions is that Christianity actually saves people for eternity. By contrast, it takes no talent whatsoever to ensure that people on the broad road get to their final destination (Mat 07:13).

Isa 52:12—Trinitarian Proof
For you shall not go out in haste, neither shall you go by flight: for *Yahveh* will go before you; and the God of Israel will be your rearguard (Isa 52:12).
Discussion: The fact that *Yahveh* is the vanguard and the God of Israel is the rear guard suggests that there are persons of the Trinity. Isa 52:12 is mentioned in the discussion on Exo 14:19-24 in this appendix.

Isa 55:11—Trinitarian Proof
So shall my Word be that goes forth out of my mouth: it shall not return to me void, but it shall accomplish that which I please, and it shall prosper in the thing whereto I sent it (Isa 55:11).
Discussion: The Word is a personal agent of *Yahveh* and is *Yahveh*.

Isa 59:20-21—Trinitarian Proof
A Redeemer will come to Zion, and to those who turn from disobedience in Jacob, says *Yahveh*. As for me, this is my covenant with them, says *Yahveh*: my Spirit who is on you, and my words that I have put in your mouth, shall not depart out of your mouth, nor out of the mouth of your seed, nor out of the mouth of your seed's seed, says *Yahveh*, from henceforth and forever (Isa 59:20-21).
Discussion: The Redeemer, the Son (Isa 59:20a), who is divine (Isa 07:14; 09:06), is distinguished from *Yahveh* the Father by the Father's words: "As for me..." (Isa 59:21a).

Isa 61:08—Trinitarian Proof
For I, *Yahveh*, love justice, I hate robbery with iniquity; and I will give them their recompense in truth, and I will make an everlasting covenant with them (Isa 61:08).
Discussion: The Servant of *Yahveh* said that he is *Yahveh*. Isa 61:08 is mentioned in Isa 48:12-16 in this appendix.

Isa 63:07-14—Trinitarian Proof
Discussion: *Yahveh* (the Father), "the *Malek* [the Son], His [the Father's] Presence [the Son]" (Isa 63:09b), and the Spirit of God (Isa 63:10-11 and 14), are all mentioned as co-causes.

Jer 07:04, 10—Trinitarian Proof
Do not trust in deceptive words, saying, 'The temple of *Yahveh*, the temple of *Yahveh*, the temple of *Yahveh*, are these'....and come and stand before me in this house, that is called by my Name, and say, 'We are delivered; that you may do all these abominations?' (Jer 07:04, 10).

Discussion: The phrase the "Temple of *Yahveh*" is mentioned three times (Jer 07:04), and then the temple is said to bear the Name of *Yahveh* (Jer 07:10). This three and one pattern is Trinitarian.

Mentioning *Yahveh* three times and then once are "false words" (Jer 07:04) only in the sense that in Jeremiah's day, the Trinity had already abandoned Solomon's temple to destruction. So to think that Jerusalem would not be destroyed because the persons of the Trinity still inhabited the temple was a false hope.

Besides, the temple was *Yahveh*'s in name only. At some point it became a house of perjurers (Jer 07:09) and robbers (Jer 07:11). Similarly, when *Yeshua* left Herod's temple desolate (Mat 23:38; Luk 13:35), it became a den of robbers (Mat 21:13) and a house of false swearers (Mat 23:16). So the temple fell under *Yahveh*'s curse on the houses of robbers and thieves (Zec 05:04).

For more discussion on this subject, see Jer 07:11-15, 34 and Luk 13:35; 19:46 in the NT Use of OT *Yahveh* Texts appendix.

An interesting parallel to how the Name, *Yahveh*, was mentioned thrice, and then once in regard to the temple, is when Eli did not know that the Word of *Yahveh* was calling Samuel. Samuel was sleeping next to the Ark in the temple (1Sa 03:03-08). *Yahveh* called out to Samuel three times before Eli realized *Yahveh* was calling Samuel. Then *Yahveh* called Samuel again and Samuel said the Name, *Yahveh*, in the temple, according to Eli's instructions (1Sa 03:09).

Jer 16:16-21—Trinitarian Proof
Yahveh [the Father], my [the Son's] strength, and my [the Son's] stronghold, and my [the Son's] refuge in the day of affliction, to you [the Father] shall the nations come from the ends of the earth...Therefore, behold, I [the Son] will cause them to know, this once will I [the Son] cause them to know my [the Son's] hand and my [the Son's] might; and they shall know that my [the Son's] name is *Yahveh* [the Son] (Jer 16:19, 21).

Discussion: *Yahveh* [the Son] said:
Now I will send for many fishermen and they will catch them [the Jews of the diaspora] (Jer 16:16).

Then *Yahveh* [the Son] acknowledged *Yahveh* [the Father] as his [the Son's] strength and stronghold. The Son said:
Therefore, I will teach them—this time I will teach them my power and might. Then they will know that my Name is *Yahveh* (Jer 16:21).

Similarly, *Yeshua* said, "Come, follow me, and I will make you fishers of men" (Mat 04:19). This parallels Jer 16:21. *Yeshua* really did show the world he is *Yahveh*, since billions of Christians have been baptized into the Name of the Father,

Son and Spirit by *Yeshua*'s command (Mat 28:19). Also, many know him as the "I
AM" (Joh 08:58), so they know his name as he predicted they would (Jer 16:21).
    See the discussion in the "I AM" and the Song of Moses chapters, and in
Eusebius, *Proof of the Gospel*, Book V, Chapter 30.

Jer 23:05-06; 33:15-16—Trinitarian Proof
    'Behold, the days are coming,' says *Yahveh*, 'when I will raise to David
    a righteous Branch, and he shall reign as king and deal wisely, and shall
    execute justice and righteousness in the land. In his days Judah shall be
    saved, and Israel shall dwell safely; and this is his name whereby he shall
    be called: '*Yahveh*, our righteousness" (Jer 23:05-06).
    Discussion: The "Branch" is the Messiah and, by association, the scepter (Gen
49:10-11; Num 24:17; Isa 04:02, 11:01; 53:02; Jer 23:05; 33:15; Zec 03:08; 06:
12). Jeremiah said the Branch is "*Yahveh, Our Righteousness*" (Hebrew: *Yahveh-
tsidkenu*) (Jer 23:06). *Yahveh-tsidkenu* is the only OT personal name that uses the
complete Tetragrammaton. Most composite names use only one (*Y*) or two (*YH*) of
the four consonants (*YHVH*) that comprise the name *Yahveh*.
    Because the Messiah was sacrificed for our sins in Jerusalem, believers will
associate Jerusalem with the Son, who is "*Yahveh, Our Righteousness*" (Jer 33:
16). Jerusalem will also become known by the eponymy, "*Yahveh-Shammah*,"
meaning, "God Is There" (Eze 48:35). This is similar to another name for *Yeshua*,
"Immanuel," meaning, "God is with us." So it is not surprising that Jerusalem is
called "the holy city" in both the OT and NT (Neh 11:01, 18; Isa 48:02; 52:01; Dan
09:24; Mat 04:05; 27:53; Rev 11:02; 21:02, 10; 22:19).
    The connection with Jerusalem further explains the name "*Yahveh, Our
Righteousness*." *Yahveh* the Son is the priest-king replacement for Melchizedek,
a priest-king at Jerusalem (Gen 14:18; Psa 110:04; Heb 05:06, 10; 06:20; 07:01,
10, 11, 15, 17). Melchizedek means "King of Righteousness." A king who came
after Melchizedek at Jerusalem was similarly called Adoni-Zedek, meaning, "Lord
of Righteousness" (Jos 10:01). So it is consistent that both *Yahveh* the Son and his
"holy city" should be called "*Yahveh, Our Righteousness*" (Jer 23:06; 33:16).
    Epiphanies led to place name changes. Abraham called the temple mount,
Mount Moriah, meaning, "Chosen by *Yah*[*veh*]." After the *Malek Yahveh* appeared
at the near-sacrifice of Isaac, Abraham called the temple mount, *Yahvehjireh*,
meaning, "*Yahveh* will provide" (Gen 22:14).
    Similarly, Jacob called a place by the Jabbok River *Peniel* because the Son
appeared there (Gen 32:30). *Peniel* is Hebrew for "Face of God." Gideon called
a place "*Yahveh* is Peace" after the Son, the *Malek Yahveh*, appeared there (Jdg 06:
24). So because *Yeshua* was himself an epiphany, it is consistent that the "holy
city" should be called by the eponymy, "*Yahveh, Our Righteousness*" (Jer 23:06;
33:16).
    That Jerusalem has held on to its original name is in keeping with how places
were referred to by different names even after being renamed by Yahvists. For
example, Luz became Bethel, meaning, "House of God," after "[All] the Gods

[*HaElohim*], they appeared to Jacob there" (Gen 35:07). The new name for Luz, namely, Bethel, did not "take" until hundreds of years later (Gen 28:19; 35:06; 48: 03; Jos 16:02; 18:13; Jdg 01:23, 26). Even after Luz was destroyed, the survivors went off and built a new city in another area with the same name, Luz (Jdg 01:26).

Eze 02:02—Trinitarian Proof
The Spirit entered into me when he spoke to me, and set me on my feet; and I heard him who spoke to me (Eze 02:02).
Discussion: The Spirit is an agent of *Yahveh* and is *Yahveh*. See the section on Ezekiel in the chapter on Various OT Presentations of the Trinity.

Eze 08:03—Trinitarian Proof
He put forth the form of a hand, and took me by a lock of my head; and the Spirit lifted me up between earth and the sky, and brought me in the visions of God to Jerusalem, to the door of the gate of the inner [court] that looks toward the north; where was the seat of the image of jealousy, which provokes to jealousy (Eze 08:03).
Discussion: The Spirit is an agent of *Yahveh* and is *Yahveh*. See the section on Ezekiel in the chapter on Various OT Presentations of the Trinity.

Eze 40:01—47:12—Trinitarian Proof
Discussion: The narrator referred to "the man" as *Yahveh* (Eze 44:02, 05), and "the man" referred to the Glory (Eze 43:01) as *Yahveh* (Eze 44:02). "The man" is the anthropomorphized Spirit and the "Glory" is the Son. See the section on Ezekiel in the chapter on the Various OT Presentations of the Trinity.

Dan 02:22—Trinitarian Proof
...he reveals the deep and secret things; he knows what is in the darkness, and the Light dwells with him (Dan 02:22).
Discussion: Light (the Son) dwells with the Father (compare Joh 01:09; 09:12, 12:46).

Dan 07—Trinitarian Proof
Discussion: The Song of Moses chapter and the MT plurals appendix discuss Daniel's vision of the Son of Man (Dan 07). Prophetic parallels to the Son of Man vision (Psa 002, 045 and 110) are discussed in this appendix.

Dan 09:19—Trinitarian Proof
Lord, hear; Lord, forgive; Lord, listen and do; do not defer, for your own sake, my God, because your city and your people are called by your Name (Dan 09:19).
Discussion: In Dan 09:19, there are three mentions of Lord (*Adonai*), one mention of God (*Elohim*), and one mention of the (singular) Name. The Father listens, the Son forgives, and the Spirit hears and acts. The three persons who are

Lord and God do not delay because the city and people bear their (singular) Name, *Yahveh*.

Dan 09:19 and similar passages are mentioned in the discussion the Aaronic Blessing (Num 06:22-27) in this appendix.

Hos 01:06-07—Trinitarian Proof

She conceived again, and bore a daughter. [*Yahveh* the Son] said to him, 'Call her name Look-Ruhamah; for I will no more have mercy on the house of Israel, that I should in any wise pardon them. But I will have mercy on the house of Judah, and will save them by *Yahveh* their God [the Spirit], and will not save them by bow, sword, battle, horses, or by horsemen' (Hos 01:06).

Discussion: A text that suggests or speaks of the deity of the Messiah should be considered a Trinitarian proof. Hosea wrote that *Yahveh* (the Son) would save the people of Judah by *Yahveh*, their God (the Spirit). A similar text is Zec 04:06 where the Spirit quoted *Yahveh* the Father as saying that he (the Spirit), would help Zerubbabel rebuild the temple.

Hos 11:07-09—Trinitarian Proof

My [the Son's] people are determined to turn from me [the Son]. Though they call to the Most High [the Father], He [the Father] certainly will not exalt them. How can I [the Son] give you up, Ephraim? How can I [the Son] hand you over, Israel? How can I [the Son] make you like Admah? How can I [the Son] make you like Zeboiim? My [the Son's] heart is turned within me [the Son], My [the Son's] compassion is aroused. I [the Son] will not execute the fierceness of my [the Son's] anger. I [the Son] will not return to destroy Ephraim: For I [the Son] am God [the Son], and not man [This is the preincarnate Son speaking]; the Holy One [the Son] in the midst of you; and I [the Son] will not come in wrath (Hos 11:07-09).

Discussion: See the discussion of this passage in the MT plurals appendix in the section on Hos 11:02, 12 [*BHS* 12:01]; Hos 12:04 [*BHS* 12:05].

Amo 04:11-13—Trinitarian Proof

'I [the Father] have overthrown [cities] among you, as when God [the Son] overthrew Sodom and Gomorrah, and you were as a brand plucked out of the burning: yet have you not returned to me,' says *Yahveh* [the Father]. 'Therefore, thus will I [the Father] do to you, Israel; [and] because I will do this to you, prepare to meet your God [the Son], Israel. For, behold, he [the Son] who forms the mountains, and creates the wind, and declares to man what is his thought; that makes the morning darkness, and treads on the high places of the Earth *Yahveh* [the Son], the God of hosts, is his Name' (Amo 04:11-13).

Discussion: A text that suggests or speaks of the deity of the Messiah should be considered a Trinitarian proof. *Yahveh* (the Father) said that *Elohim* (the Son) overthrew Sodom. The Father's words were:

I [the Father] have overturned you as God [the Son] overturned Sodom... declares *Yahveh* [the Father] (Amo 04:11).
See the mentions of Amo 04:11-13 in the Song of Moses chapter, and see Eusebius, *The Proof of the Gospel*, Book V, Chapter 23.

Mic 05:02 [BHS 05:01] —Trinitarian Proof

But you, Bethlehem Ephrata, which are small among the thousands of Judah, out of you shall one come forth to me that is to be ruler in Israel; whose goings forth are from of old, from everlasting (Mic 05:02).
Discussion: A text that suggests or speaks of the deity of the Messiah should be considered a Trinitarian proof. Micah says the Son, who would become the Messiah, existed from eternity (Mic 05:02). The Son is as eternal as the Father and the Spirit (Psa 041:13; 090:02; 103:17; 106:48). Matthew applied Mic 05:02 to *Yeshua* (Mat 02:06). That the Son is eternal is confirmed by *Yeshua*'s statement, "Before Abraham was, 'I AM'" (Joh 08:58).

Hab 01:12—Trinitarian Proof
O *Yahveh* [the Father], are you not from everlasting? My God, my Holy One [The LXX does not have the pronoun "my," but reads "Lord God, my Holy One."], we [the Father and Son] will not die. O *Yahveh*, you have appointed them to execute judgment; O Rock, you have ordained them to punish (Hab 01:12).
Discussion: In his intercession for Israel, the Son reminded the Father that they will never die.

Zec 02:03-13—Trinitarian Proof
Discussion: The *Malek Yahveh* referred to himself as *Yahveh* throughout this section (Zec 02:05, 06 (twice), 08, 10, 12). Twice the *Malek Yahveh* said that *Yahveh* the Father would send him (Zec 02:08, 09, 11). The key to ascertaining the:
- Referent for each pronoun in this section (Zec 02:03-13), and
- The person of *Yahveh* meant by each mention of the name "*Yahveh*,"

is to note that Zechariah wrote down word for word what he (Zechariah) overheard *Yahveh* the Son (the *Malek Yahveh*) telling the Spirit to tell him (Zechariah).
That the sent "me" is *Yahveh* the Son not only can be seen from the pronoun usage, but in Zec 02:12, *Yahveh* (the Son) said he would inherit Judea and Jerusalem. The Son can inherit, but the Father cannot inherit. Also, Zec 02:03-13 is similar to Isa 48:12-16 and Isa 61:01 in that *Yahveh* the Son said that he was sent. Isa 48:12-16 and Isa 61:01 are discussed in this appendix.
See the chapter on the Various Presentations of the Trinity, and Eusebius, *The Proof of the Gospel*, Book V, Chapters 25-26.

Zec 03:01-04—Trinitarian Proof
He showed me Joshua the high priest standing before the Angel of
Yahveh, and Satan standing at his right hand to be his adversary. *Yahveh*
said to Satan, *Yahveh* rebuke you, Satan; yes, *Yahveh* that has chosen
Jerusalem rebuke you: is not this a brand plucked out of the fire? Now
Joshua was clothed with filthy garments, and was standing before the
angel. He answered and spoke to those who stood before him, saying,
Take the filthy garments from off him. To him he said, Behold, I have
caused your iniquity to pass from you, and I will clothe you with rich
clothing (Zec 03:01-04).
Discussion: The *Malek Yahveh* is called *Yahveh*. The *Malek* here forgives sins,
something only God can do (Mar 02:07; Luk 05:21).

Zec 04:06—Trinitarian Proof
Then he [the Spirit] answered and spoke to me, saying, 'This is the
word of *Yahveh* [the Father] to Zerubbabel, saying, 'Not by might, nor
by power, but by my [the Father's] Spirit [the Spirit],' says *Yahveh* [the
Father] of hosts" (Zec 04:06).
Discussion: The Spirit quoted *Yahveh* the Father's statement that the Spirit
would help rebuild the temple. A similar text is Hos 01:06-07 where *Yahveh* the
Son said he would save Israel by sending his Spirit. See the discussion of Hos 01:
06-07 in this appendix.

Zec 06:08—Trinitarian Proof
Then cried he to me, and spoke to me, saying, 'Behold, those who go toward
the north country have quieted my spirit in the north country' (Zec 06:08).
Discussion: The *Malek Yahveh*'s spirit extends throughout the earth. Zechariah
also says that the spirit of the *Malek Yahveh* extends to the north country (Zec 06:
08).

Zec 07:08-13—Trinitarian Proof
Discussion: The "Word [the Son] of *Yahveh* [the Father]" (Zec 07:08) spoke of
the Father and the Spirit as persons distinct from himself (Zec 07:12-13).

Zec 10:12—Trinitarian Proof
'I [the Father] will strengthen them in *Yahveh* [the Son]; and they will
walk up and down in his [the Son's] name,' says *Yahveh* [the Father] (Zec
10:12).
Discussion: *Yahveh* the Father said that he would strengthen Israel in *Yahveh*
the Son and in his [the Son's] name.

Zec 11:12-13—Trinitarian Proof
I said to them, 'If you think it best, give me my wages; and if not, keep
them.' So they weighed for my wages thirty pieces of silver. *Yahveh* said

to me, 'Throw it to the potter, the handsome price that I was valued at by them!' I took the thirty pieces of silver, and threw them to the potter, in the house of *Yahveh* (Zec 11:12-13).

Discussion: A text that suggests or speaks of the deity of the Messiah should be considered a Trinitarian proof. *Yahveh* the Son said that his work was valued at thirty pieces of silver. Judas was paid thirty pieces of silver to betray *Yeshua* (Mat 26:15). *Yeshua* twice said, "I AM," at his betrayal, and twice the soldiers fell back (Joh 18:05-08). This is discussed further in the "I AM" and Song of Moses chapters. Judas then realized *Yeshua* was the "I AM." So the prophecy of Zec 11:12-13 was fulfilled at *Yeshua*'s prompting, and Judas' life cut short as *Yeshua* anticipated (Psa 109:08).

Zec 12:08—Trinitarian Proof
In that day *Yahveh* [the Father] will defend the inhabitants of Jerusalem. He who is feeble among them at that day will be like David, and the house of David will be like God [the Father], like the *Malek* [the Son] *Yahveh* (Zec 12:08).

Discussion: Notice the favorable comparison or even the equation in terms of strength between the Father and the Son, the *Malek Yahveh*.

Zec 12:10—Trinitarian Proof
I [the Son] will pour on the house of David, and on the inhabitants of Jerusalem, the Spirit of grace and of supplication; and they will look to me [the Son] whom they have pierced; and they shall mourn for him [the Messiah], as one mourns for his only son, and will grieve bitterly for him [the Messiah], as one grieves for his firstborn (Zec 12:10).

Discussion: Zec 12:10 was fulfilled in Act 02:33 when Peter said that the Son poured out the Spirit at Pentecost. Luke then wrote:
When the people heard this [that the Messiah had been killed for their sins], they were cut to the heart and said to Peter and the other apostles, 'Brothers, what shall we do?' (Act 02:37).

A text that suggests or speaks of the deity of the Messiah should be considered a Trinitarian proof.

Zec 13:07—Trinitarian Proof
'Awake, sword, against my Shepherd, and against the man who is my fellow,' says *Yahveh* of hosts: 'strike the Shepherd, and the sheep shall be scattered; and I will turn my hand on the little ones' (Zec 13:07).

Discussion: A text that suggests or speaks of the deity of the Messiah should be considered a Trinitarian proof. Zec 13:07 is a prophecy about the Messiah. *Yeshua* said he is the Shepherd of Zec 13:07 (Mar 14:27). That this Shepherd is the fellow (or "neighbor" or "associate") of *Yahveh* suggests the Messiah's deity. Zec 13:07 is similar to passages such as Psa 045:06-07 [*BHS* 045:07-08], where *Yahveh* the Father called the Son, "God," and set him above the Son's companions.

As Eusebius notes, there are many passages where one person of the Trinity spoke of another in the third person, such as in Gen 35:01.

Mal 03:01—Trinitarian Proof
'Behold, I send my messenger, and he will prepare the way before me; and the Lord, whom you seek, will suddenly come to his temple; and the messenger of the covenant, whom you desire, behold, he comes!' says *Yahveh* of hosts (Mal 03:01).
Discussion: A text that suggests or speaks of the deity of the Messiah should be considered a Trinitarian proof. The Father said that he would send John the Baptist as a messenger to go before his [the Father's] Presence [the Son] (Mal 03:01). This is similar to how *Elyon* said his Presences (or "Faces"), the Son and Spirit, would go with Moses into the Promised Land. On this last point, see the discussions of Exo 33:14-15 and Mal 03:01 in Presences of *Elyon* chapter.

The NT—Trinitarian Proof
Discussion: All the New Testament books contain *prima facie* Trinitarian texts except perhaps James and Third John. Below is a representative sampling of NT Trinitarian passages.

Mat 03:16-17—Trinitarian Proof
Yeshua, when he was baptized, went up directly from the water: and behold, the heavens were opened to him. He saw the Spirit of God descending as a dove, and coming on him. Behold, a voice out of the heavens said:
'This is my beloved Son, in whom I am well pleased' (Mat 03:16-17).
Discussion: The Father is represented by a voice from heaven, the Spirit by the dove, and the Son is *Yeshua*.

Mat 17:15—Trinitarian Proof
Lord, have mercy on my son, for he is epileptic, and suffers grievously; for he often falls into the fire, and often into the water (Mat 17:15).
Discussion: A text that suggests or speaks of the deity of the Messiah should be considered a Trinitarian proof. A father asked *Yeshua*, "Lord, have mercy on my son." The English transliteration of the Greek for "Lord, have mercy" is *"Kurie Eleison."* This common liturgical phrase is found in the Greek LXX (Psa 040:05, 11; 122:03; Isa 33:02).

By itself, Mat 17:15 may not be the most compelling proof of *Yeshua*'s deity. Note, however, how often *Yeshua* is asked to have mercy, or is said to be merciful (Mat 15:22; 17:15; 20:30, 31; Mar 05:19; Luk 01:58; 1Co 07:25; 1Ti 01:02; 2Ti 01:02, 16, 18; 1Pe 01:03; Jud 01:21). This frequency suggests *Yeshua*'s deity.

Mat 22:43-45—Trinitarian Proof
He said to them, 'How then does David in the Spirit call him Lord, saying, 'The Lord said to my Master, 'Sit at my right hand, until I make your enemies a footstool for your feet?" If David called him 'Lord,' how is he his son?' (Mat 22:43-45).

Discussion: *Yeshua* said that David spoke in the Spirit and said, "The Lord [the Father] said to my Master [the Son]." Note the mention of each person of the Trinity. A parallel account is found at Mar 12:36-37.

Mat 22:43-45 is mentioned in the *Shema* and the Prophet behind the Prophets chapters, and in the NT use of OT *Yahveh* texts appendix.

Mat 28:19—Trinitarian Proof
Go and make disciples of all nations, baptizing them in the Name [singular] of the Father and of the Son and of the Holy Spirit (Mat 28:19).

Discussion: Mat 28:19 and the baptisms at Pentecost (Act 02:41) are the start of the fulfillment of Zechariah's prophecy:
It will happen in that day, that living waters [baptismal water] will go out from Jerusalem; half toward the eastern sea, and half toward the western sea; in summer and in winter will it be. *Yahveh* will be King over all the earth. In that day *Yahveh* will be one, and his name one (Zec 14:08-09; see also Joh 07:38-39; Act 02:38).

Zec 14:08-09 refers to the fact that the members of the Trinity have the same Name, *Yahveh*. When the disciples spoke of "the Name" being "*Yeshua*" (Act 05:40-41), they were conscious of the fact that *Yeshua* means "*Yahveh* saves" (Mat 01:21; 1Ti 01:15). The disciples also knew that the Father said in the LXX of Isa 42:04b that the gentiles would trust in the Name of the Servant of *Yahveh* (Mat 12:21).

Mat 28:19 and other similar passages are mentioned in the discussion the Aaronic Blessing (Num 06:22-27) in this appendix.

Luk 02:21, 25, 29, 49—Trinitarian Proof
Discussion: *Yeshua* means, "*Yahveh* saves" (Luk 01:31; 02:21). The Holy Spirit was upon Simeon (Luk 02:25). Simeon thanked the Sovereign Lord (Luk 02:29), who is *Yeshua*'s Father (Luk 02:49).

Joh 01:01—Trinitarian Proof
In the beginning was the Word, and the Word was with God, and the Word was God (Joh 01:01).

Discussion: The Word (the Son) was with God (the Father), and the Word was God (the Son).

Joh 01:01-03—Trinitarian Proof
In the beginning was the Word, and the Word was with God, and the Word was God. The same was in the beginning with God. All things were

made through him. Without him was not anything made that has been made (Joh 01:01-03).

Discussion: The Word (the Son) created everything. Interestingly, the Word said that he even created the vegetation in the Garden of Eden on the Sixth Day (compare Eze 31:01, 09).

Those who would say the Son is a creature created by the Father must interpolate the words "except himself" twice into John's statements like this:

All things were made through him [except himself]. Without him was not anything made that has been made [except himself].

So without the interpolations, it is clear that the Son is divine and not a creature.

Joh 01:15, 30—Trinitarian Proof
Discussion: John the Baptist said that *Yeshua* existed before him, even though John the Baptist was born six months before *Yeshua* (Luk 01:24, 26, 36, 56). John the Baptist was speaking in an eternal sense.

Joh 01:18—Trinitarian Proof
No one has seen God [the Father] at any time. The only begotten God [the Son], who is in the bosom of the Father, he [the Son] has declared him [the Father] (Joh 01:18).

Discussion: Abraham, Moses and other mere humans talked to the Father, but his essential essence and glory were hidden from them so they would not die (Exo 33:18-20).

Some translations read, "only begotten Son," because some copyist long ago changed Joh 01:18 to match the familiar Joh 03:16 passage. The change to "Son" is reflected only in manuscripts from one area, but the study of older manuscripts from around the Mediterranean shows that the original definitely read, "only begotten God." However, proofs of the deity of Christ as so many and powerful, that Christians need not insist on this reading.

Joh 03:02, 11, 34—Trinitarian Proof
Discussion: These passages are discussed in relation to Isa 40:13 in this appendix.

Joh 05:17—Trinitarian Proof
Yeshua said to them, 'My Father is always at his work to this very day, and I, too, am working' (Joh 05:17).

Discussion: The Jews believed that since God rested on the first Sabbath, Jews ought also rest each Sabbath day—as was directed by Moses. *Yeshua* informed the Jews that this reasoning was not applicable to him, since the Father and the Son have always been at work (Joh 05:17, 36; 14:10). The Father and the Son worked through the Sabbath, so the person of *Yahveh* who rested on the Seventh Day was the Spirit. *Yeshua* definitely thought and spoke in Trinitarian terms.

Joh 08—Trinitarian Proof
Discussion: *Yeshua* alluded to *Yahveh*'s "I AM" statements by making various "I AM" statements himself (Joh 08:24, 28, 58; 13:19; 18:05-08; see Exo 03:02, 13-14 in this appendix). *Yeshua*'s statement, "Before Abraham, 'I AM'" (Joh 08: 58), is a parallel to Mic 05:02 in that both statements show the pre-existence of the Messiah. Mic 05:02 is discussed in this appendix. Concerning the "I AM" statements, see the "I AM" and "Song of Moses" chapters, especially.

Joh 09:24, 38—Trinitarian Proof
Discussion: Though the Pharisees told the blind man:
Give glory to God, for we know this man is a sinner (Joh 09:24),
still the blind man worshipped *Yeshua* (Joh 09:38). See the Song of Moses chapter for discussion about this incident.

Joh 10:30—Trinitarian Proof
Discussion: "I and the Father are [Greek for "are": *esmen*] one" (Joh 10:30). The verb "are" is plural, so the "I" and "the Father" indicate two persons. Therefore, Oneness Theology, a.k.a., Modalism, is contradicted by this passage. Joh 10:30 is discussed at Psa 082:06-08 in this appendix, and in the chapter on the *Shema*.

Joh 14:16-17, 26—Trinitarian Proof
I will pray to the Father, and he will give you another Counselor, that he may be with you forever, the Spirit of truth, whom the world cannot receive; for it does not see him, neither knows him. You know him, for he lives with you, and will be in you. But the Counselor, the Holy Spirit, whom the Father will send in my name, will teach you all things and will remind you of everything I have said to you (Joh 14:16).
Discussion: See the discussion of these passages in Isa 40:13.

Joh 14:23-26—Trinitarian Proof
Yeshua answered him, 'If a man loves me, he will keep my word. My Father will love him, and we will come to him, and make our home with him. He who does not love me does not keep my words. The word that you hear is not mine, but the Father's who sent me. I have said these things to you, while still living with you. But the Counselor, the Holy Spirit, whom the Father will send in my Name, he will teach you all things, and bring to your memory all that I said to you' (Joh 14:23-26).
Discussion: *Yeshua* engaged in Trinitarian speech, and talked as only God the Son could talk.

Joh 15:26—Trinitarian Proof
When the Counselor has come, whom I will send to you from the Father, the Spirit of truth, who proceeds from the Father, he will testify about me (Joh 15:26).

Discussion: The Father, Son and Spirit are mentioned.

Joh 17:05, 24—Trinitarian Proof
Now, Father, glorify me with your own self with the glory that I had with you before the world existed....Father, I desire that they also whom you have given me be with me where I am, that they may see my glory, that you have given me, for you loved me before the foundation of the world (Joh 17:05, 24).
Discussion: *Yeshua* is preexistent.

Joh 20:28—Trinitarian Proof
Thomas answered him, 'My Lord and my God!' (Joh 20:28).
Discussion: The literal rendering of what Thomas said to *Yeshua* is: "the Lord of me and the God of me." Nearly the same Greek construction and wording are used in Rev 04:11 where the twenty-four heavenly elders said: "the Lord and the God of us." David said nearly the same thing in Hebrew: "My God, and my Lord" (Psa 035:23). This suggests that David, Thomas and the twenty-four elders spoke of *Yeshua* as being God.

Notice that *Yeshua* made no attempt to correct Thomas by denying he was God. If *Yeshua* were not God, then a correction certainly would have been in order (Act 14:15; Col 02:18; Rev 22:08-09). This is similar to Joh 08:59 where people knew *Yeshua* was claiming to be God, and *Yeshua* neither retracted or clarified his remarks to deny that he was God the Son.

Act 16:31, 34—Trinitarian Proof
They replied, 'Believe in the Lord *Yeshua*, and you will be saved—you and your household.' The jailer brought them into his house and set a meal before them; he was filled with joy because he had come to believe in God—he and his whole family (Act 16:31, 34).
Discussion: A text that suggests or speaks of the deity of the Messiah should be considered a Trinitarian proof. The jailor believed in the Lord *Yeshua* (Act 16:31), whom the narrator calls "God" (Act 16:34).

Act 17:18, 23—Trinitarian Proof
Some of the Epicurean and Stoic philosophers also were conversing with him. Some said, 'What does this babbler want to say?' Others said, 'He seems to be advocating foreign deities [plural],' because he preached *Yeshua* and the resurrection....'For as I passed along, and observed the objects of your worship, I found also an altar with this inscription, 'To an unknown god [singular].' What therefore you worship as unknown, this I proclaim to you' (Act 17:18, 23).
Discussion: A text that suggests or speaks of the deity of the Messiah should be considered a Trinitarian proof. The narrator Luke asserted that the Greek

philosophers thought Paul was talking about "gods" because Paul was talking about *Yeshua* and the resurrection (Greek: *anastasis*) (Act 17:18).

Evidently, the Greek philosophers thought Paul preached that *Yeshua* had a consort named Anastasia, since *anastasis* is a feminine noun. The ancients worshipped personifications such as the Seasons, Fate, and Power, as well as "Reverence, Temperance and Obedience-to-Law."[191] So Paul disabused them of this notion by proclaiming that *Yeshua* was their "unknown god [Greek: *theos* (singular)]" (Act 17:23).

Act 20:28—Trinitarian Proof
Therefore, take heed to yourselves and to all the flock, among which the Holy Spirit has made you overseers, to shepherd the Church of God [*Yeshua*] which He [*Yeshua*] purchased with His own [*Yeshua*'s own] blood (Act 20:28).
Discussion: Paul called *Yeshua* "God."

Rom 08:09-11, 16—Trinitarian Proof
You, however, are controlled not by the sinful nature but by the [Holy] Spirit, if the [Holy] Spirit of God [the Father] lives in you. And if anyone does not have the spirit of Christ, he does not belong to Christ. But if Christ['s spirit] is in you, your body is dead because of sin, yet your spirit is alive because of righteousness. And if the [Holy] Spirit of him [the Father] who raised *Yeshua* from the dead is living in you, he [the Father] who raised Christ from the dead will also give life to your mortal bodies through his [the Father's Holy] Spirit, who lives in you...The [Holy] Spirit himself testifies with our spirit that we are God's [the Father's] children (Rom 08:09-11, 16).
Discussion: Paul referred to the "spirit of Christ" living in all Christians, along with the Holy Spirit sent by the Father. That Paul meant "spirit of Christ" rather than the "Holy Spirit sent by Christ" is seen from the subsequent statement, "But if Christ is in you." Christ's sending the Holy Spirit would not, by itself, constitute Christ living in a Christian.

Rom 09:05—Trinitarian Proof
Christ came, who is over all, the eternally blessed God. Amen (Rom 09:05).
Discussion: Paul here referred to *Yeshua* as being God.

Rom 11:36—Trinitarian Proof
...because of him [the Father], through [*dia*] him [the Son], and by means of him [the Spirit] are all things (Rom 11:36).
Discussion: The typical pattern seen in the NT is: ultimate agency is attributed to the Father, intermediate agency is credited to *Yeshua*, and means is ascribed to the Holy Spirit. So according to the NT pattern, the first "him" refers to the Father,

the second "him" to the Son, and the third "him" to the Spirit. For instance, see Tit 03:04-07 in this appendix.

1Co 12:04-06—Trinitarian Proof
Discussion: Paul said that each member of the Trinity is the source of diverse gifts that are manifested in the Church. In Paul's Trinitarian summations, generally the "Spirit" refers to the Spirit, "Lord" refers to *Yeshua*, and "God" refers to the Father. For example:

- Now there are various kinds of gifts, but the same Spirit. There are various kinds of service, and the same Lord [the Son]. There are various kinds of workings, but the same God [the Father], who works all things in all (1Co 12: 04-06),
- There is one body, and one Spirit, even as you also were called in one hope of your calling; one Lord [the Son], one faith, one baptism, one God [the Father] and Father of all, who is over all, and through all, and in us all (Eph 04:04-06), and
- May the grace of the Lord *Yeshua* Christ, and the love of God [the Father], and the fellowship of the Holy Spirit be with you all (2Co 13:14).

2Co 13:14—Trinitarian Proof
Discussion: See 1Co 12:04-06 in this appendix.

Gal 01:01, 15-16—Trinitarian Proof
   Paul, an apostle (not sent from men nor through the agency of man, but through *Yeshua* Christ and God the Father, who raised Him from the dead)...But when God, who had set me apart even from my mother's womb and called me through His grace...(Gal 01:01, 15).
Discussion: Paul wrote that the Father and the Son sent him. Paul also said he was not sent "from men, nor by a [mere] man" (Gal 01:01, 15-16). So here Paul specifically excludes *Yeshua* from the category of mere men. Paul puts *Yeshua* in the same category as God.
   In a parallel passage, God said, "Who will go for us?" Isaiah answered, "Here am I. Send me!" The NT writers say that Isaiah saw and talked about the glory of *Yeshua* (Joh 12:41), but talked to the Spirit in his vision in the temple (Act 28:25-26). So the Spirit sent Isaiah for the Son and Spirit (the "us").

Eph 04:04-06—Trinitarian Proof
Discussion: See 1Co 12:04-06 in this appendix.

Phi 02:05-07—Trinitarian Proof
   Let this mind be in you, which was also in Christ *Yeshua*, who being in very nature God, did not consider equality with God something to be held dearly, but made himself nothing, taking the very nature of a Servant, being made in human likeness (Phi 02:05-07).

Discussion: *Yeshua* was by his very nature God.

Col 02:09—Trinitarian Proof
For in him all the fullness of the Godhead dwells bodily (Col 02:09).
All the fullness of God dwells in Christ. Surely *Yeshua* is the God-man.

1Ti 01:16-17—Trinitarian Proof
However, for this cause I obtained mercy, that foremost in me, *Yeshua*
Christ might display all his patience, for an example of those who would
believe in him to eternal life. Now to the King eternal, immortal, invisible,
to God who alone is wise, be honor and glory forever and ever. Amen (1Ti
01:16-17).
Discussion: In many passages in the Bible, it is hard to distinguish which
phrase refers to which member of the Trinity. The reason is that to some extent,
most phrases could apply equally to all three members of the Trinity, either
individually or collectively.

1Ti 03:16—Trinitarian Proof
And without controversy great is the mystery of godliness: He was
manifested in the flesh, justified in the Spirit, seen by angels, preached among
the gentiles, believed on in the world, received up in glory (1Ti 03:16).
Discussion: The "He" in the above passage is the Son. Some early manuscripts
have "God" instead of "He."

1Ti 06:14-16—Trinitarian Proof
...until the Lord *Yeshua* Christ's appearance, which he will manifest in his
own time, he who is the blessed and only Ruler, the King [the Son] of Kings
[Father and Spirit] and Lord [the Son] of Lords [Father and Spirit], who alone
has immortality, dwelling in unapproachable light, whom no man has seen or
can see, to whom be honor and everlasting power. Amen (1Ti 06:14-16).
Discussion: Paul called *Yeshua* the "only ruler," but then said *Yeshua* was
a King of Kings. Since Paul just said *Yeshua* was the only ruler, Paul must be
speaking of the Father and Spirit when Paul spoke of plural Kings and Lords. So
perhaps "King of Kings" is better translated "King among Kings," meaning that
Yeshua is a King among Kings, the Trinity.

Tit 02:13-14—Trinitarian Proof
...looking for the blessed hope and glorious appearing of our great God
and Savior, *Yeshua* Christ (Tit 02:13).
Discussion: Paul spoke of the Son "appearing" elsewhere (2Th 02:8; 1Ti 06:
14; 2Ti 01:10; 04:01, 08). According to the Granville-Sharp Greek grammatical
rule (defined below), Paul called *Yeshua* "the Great God and Savior" (Tit 02:13).
Paul alluded to Psa 130:07-08 in Tit 02:13. The psalmist said believers are
said to wait on *Yahveh* their redeemer. Paul said believers wait on "the Great God

and Savior" *Yeshua* who redeems them. *Yahveh* is called the "Great God" several times in the OT (Deu 10:17; Ezr 05:08; Neh 08:06; Psa 095:03; Dan 02:45). These passages are discussed in the NT Use of OT *Yahveh* Texts appendix under Psa 130: 07-08.

So by saying, "we wait," on *Yeshua* (Tit 02:13-14), Paul alluded to Psa 130:07 and so applied a *Yahveh* text to *Yeshua*. The OT calls *Yahveh* "Great God" several times, so Paul applied several *Yahveh* texts to *Yeshua* by saying he is "Great God."

Here is a definition of the Granville-Sharp rule: NT Greek sometimes uses two singular nouns joined with a *kai* (and) to represent a single entity or person. This compound structure is a hendiadys: article + noun + *kai* + noun = one unit. The nouns must be of the same gender and case, and should both be singular. The first noun must have an article while the second noun must not have an article.

Tit 03:04-07—Trinitarian Proof

But when the kindness and love [*Yeshua*] of God our Savior [the Father] appeared, he [the Father] saved us, not because of righteous things we had done, but because of his [the Father's] mercy. He [the Father] saved us through the washing of rebirth and renewal by the Holy Spirit, whom he [the Father] poured out on us generously through *Yeshua* Christ our Savior, so that, having been justified by his [*Yeshua*'s] grace, we might become heirs having the hope of eternal life (Tit 03:04-07).

Discussion: A typical Trinitarian pattern seen in the NT is: ultimate agency is attributed to the Father, intermediate agency is credited to *Yeshua*, and means is ascribed to the Holy Spirit. For instance, see Rom 11:36 in this appendix.

1Th 03:11—Trinitarian Proof

Now may [1] God and our [2] Father himself and our [3] Lord *Yeshua* clear the way [the verb is singular] for us to come to you.

Discussion: The singular verb for three divine subjects indicates the Trinity.

Heb 01:01-14; 02:05—Trinitarian Proof

Discussion: A text that suggests or speaks of the deity of the Messiah should be considered a Trinitarian proof. The writer of Hebrews says *Yahveh* the Father calls the Son, "God" (Heb 01:08). Heb 01:08 is discussed elsewhere in this appendix (Deu 32:08-09, LXX 32:43; Psa 082:06-08). The writer of Hebrews argues that *Yeshua* could not be a mere angel. "All" angels are ministering spirits who are to worship the Son, *Yeshua*. *Yeshua* is not a ministering spirit, but is ruling the world and the heavens (Heb 01:06). Elsewhere, the angels are said to serve *Yahveh* (Psa 103:20), and are commanded to worship *Yahveh* (LXX Deu 32:43; Psa 097:07). This suggests the Son is *Yahveh* the Son.

Heb 03:07-11—Trinitarian Proof

Therefore, even as the Holy Spirit said, 'Today, if you will hear his [the Father's] voice, 'Do not harden your hearts, as in the provocation, like as in the day of the trial in the wilderness, where your fathers tested me [the Father] by proving me [the Father], and saw my [the Father's] works for forty years.' Therefore I [the Spirit] was displeased with that generation, and said, 'They always err in their heart, but they did not know my [the Spirit's] ways;' as I [the Spirit] swore in my [the Spirit's] wrath, 'They will not enter into my [the Spirit's] rest' (Heb 03:07-11).

Discussion: The writer of Hebrews wrote that the Spirit spoke of *Yahveh* (the Father) in the third person. An impersonal force like electricity would not refer to others as third persons.

Heb 09:14—Trinitarian Proof

How much more will the blood of Christ, who through the eternal Spirit offered himself without blemish to God, cleanse your conscience from dead works to serve the living God? (Heb 09:14).

Discussion: *Yeshua* offered the sacrifice of himself to the Father through the agency of the Spirit. The sacrifice of a mere man would not cover the sins of many, but the willing sacrifice of the God-man would. *Yahveh* said that the righteousness of men like Noah, Daniel and Job barely sufficed to save a few people from a temporal disaster (Eze 14:14, 20). It would require the righteousness and sacrifice of a God-man to suffice for all believers for an eternity.

2Pe 01:01—Trinitarian Proof

Simon Peter, a servant and apostle of *Yeshua* Christ, to those who have obtained a like precious faith with us in the righteousness of our God and Savior, *Yeshua* Christ (2Pe 01:01).

Discussion: Peter said that he was "a bondservant and apostle of *Yeshua* Christ." Peter called *Yeshua* "our God and Savior *Yeshua* Christ." Similar passages include Tit 02:13; 2Pe 01:11; 02:20; 03:02 and 18.

1Jo 05:07-08—Trinitarian Proof

For there are three that bear record in heaven, the Father, the Word, and the Holy Ghost: and these three are one. And there are three that bear witness in earth, the Spirit, and the water, and the blood: and these three agree as one (*KJV* 1Jo 05:07-08).

Discussion: Apparently, a copyist augmented the Trinitarianism of 1Jo 05:07. The original *KJV* translators relied on the *Textus Receptus*, and did not have the benefit of later manuscript finds, so a non-revised *KJV* reads:

For there are three that bear record in heaven, the Father, the Word, and the Holy Ghost: and these three are one (1Jo 05:07).

Perhaps this was the same copyist who augmented the Trinitarianism of Rev 04:08 as passed down in the Greek Majority Text, as is discussed at Rev 04:08 in this appendix.

The inspired original perhaps literally read:
> For there are three that testify: the Spirit, the water and the blood; and the three are one [*heis*] into the one [*hen*] (1Jo 05:07-08).

This last phrase is sometimes translated as "and the three agree as one." Though 1Jo 05:07-08 is not talking about the Trinity, it seems to be modeled on a Trinitarian understanding of the *Shema* in that three entities are united as one. See the chapter on the *Shema*.

1Jo 05:20—Trinitarian Proof

> And we know that the Son of God has come and has given us an understanding, that we may know Him [the Father] who is true; and we are in Him who is true, in His Son *Yeshua* Christ. He [the Son] is the true God and eternal life (1Jo 05:20).

Discussion: Note that John elsewhere associates *Yeshua* with "eternal life" (1Jo 01:02; 05:11, 13). A text that suggests or speaks of the deity of the Messiah should be considered a Trinitarian proof.

Rev 04:08—Trinitarian Proof

> The four living creatures, having each one of them six wings, are full of eyes around about and within. They have no rest day and night, saying:
> Holy, holy, holy is the Lord God, the Almighty, who was and who is and who is to come (Rev 04:08).

Discussion: The angels sang the Trisagion ("Thrice Holy") liturgical formula. This refrain is similar to Trisagion in Isa 06:03.

Rev 05:11-14—Trinitarian Proof

Discussion: John wrote that all creatures worshipped God and the Lamb, who is *Yeshua*. Note that John did not include *Yeshua* with mere creatures, meaning that he was the God-man.

Rev 15—16—Trinitarian Proof

Discussion: Rev 15:08 mentions that only God was in the temple and no one else could enter the temple until the seven plagues were finished (Rev 16:01-21). Rev 15:03 mentions the Song of the Lamb. A loud voice from the temple warns that he will return as a thief in the night (Rev 16:15; compare with Mat 24:44 and 1Th 05:02). The voice from the temple also said, "It is done" (Rev 16:17; compare with Joh 19:30). The mention of the lamb, the thief and the words from the cross suggest that the Son is the person of God speaking from the temple. So *Yeshua* is called God (Rev 15:08).

Rev 19:09-10; 22:06-09—Trinitarian Proof

Discussion: The Apostle John heard the angel say, "These are the true words of God" (Rev 19:09). John thought that the angel had called himself God. John then bowed down to worship the angel because he mistook the angel for the *Malek Yahveh*, the Son (Rev 19:10).

Later, John heard another angel say:

> The Lord, the God of the spirits of the prophets, sent his angel to show his servants the things that must soon take place (Rev 22:06).

Once again, John thought an angel was identifying himself as the *Malek Yahveh*, the Son (Rev 22:08-09).

That this second angel that John mistakenly attempted to worship was an angel is confirmed a few verses later where the Son said, "I, *Yeshua*, have sent my angel" (Rev 22:16). This meant *Yeshua* was the "the Lord, the God of the spirits of the prophets" who had "sent his angel" (Rev 22:06).

The reason John thought the Rev 22 angel was *Yeshua* is because the Father spoke of the *Malek Yahveh* (the Angel of *Yahveh*) as "my *Malek*" (Exo 23:23; 32:34). To others, the *Malek Yahveh* was known as "his Angel" (Gen 24:07, 40; Dan 03:25, 28; 06:22). So the reason John bowed down to worship the second angel (Rev 22:08-09) was because John mistakenly thought the second angel was the Son, the Angel of *Yahveh* (Heb 01:06). John would never worship any person he knew to be a mere angel (Gal 01:08; Col 02:18).

The two angels' reactions show that John was bowing down to worship just as one would worship God in person (Rev 19:10; 22:09). The angel could have accepted John's bowing down if John were merely showing honor or obeisance, as was the custom in the ancient Near East (Gen 19:01; Num 22:31; Dan 02:46). This shows that John thought the *Malek Yahveh*, the Son, should be worshipped as God—God equal to the Father.

Rev 21:22-23—Trinitarian Proof

> I saw no temple in it, for the Lord God, the Almighty, and the Lamb, are its temple. The city has no need for the sun, neither of the moon, to shine, for the very glory of God illuminated it, and its lamp is the Lamb (Rev 21:22-23).

Discussion: The Lord God and the Lamb "is" (singular verb) a temple. The next verse also shows the compound unity in that "the glory of God [the Father] lights the city, and the Lamb [the Son] is its lamp." Notice that the Father is the light that comes from the proximity of the Son who is the lamp.

Rev 22:01,03-04—Trinitarian Proof

> He showed me a river of water of life, clear as crystal, proceeding out of the throne of God and of the Lamb...The throne of God and of the Lamb will be in it, and his servants serve him. They will see his face, and his name will be on their foreheads (Rev 22:01, 03-04).

Discussion: The Apostle John shows the compound unity of the Trinity in that God [the Father] and the Lamb [the Son] together have a (singular) throne, his (singular) servants serve him (singular), and they will see his (singular) face and have his (singular) name on their foreheads.

That the Father and Son have a singular throne agrees with *Yahveh*'s OT statement:

A glorious throne, exalted from the beginning, is the place of our sanctuary (Jer 17:12, as is mentioned in the MT plurals appendix).

Note that in Jer 17:12, a singular throne is found in "our" sanctuary.

Appendix D

A Sampling of the NT Use of OT Yahveh Texts
A sample of the Yahveh texts
applied to the Father in the NT

OT Citations: Lev 26:12; 1Ch 22:10; Isa 52:11; Eze 37:27
Extract: 2Co 06:16-18
Extract Usage: Quote
Summary: The mention of the Father in 2Co 06:18 indicates that Paul knew the Father spoke the four OT passages (Lev 26:12; 1Ch 22:10; Isa 52:11; Eze 37:27) that Paul quoted in 2Co 06:16-18.

OT Citations: Deu 32:43; Psa 018:49; 117:01
Extract: Rom 15:08-11
Extract Usage: Quote
Summary: Paul's messianic reading of MT Deu 32:43, Psa 018:49 and 117: 01 (Rom 15:08-11) means the person mentioned as being *Yahveh* and God is the Father, and the Son is the God-man who instructs Jews and gentiles to praise the Father.

OT Citation: Psa 016:08
Extract: Act 02:25-31
Extract Usage: Quote
Summary: Peter read Psa 016 messianically (Act 02:25-31) where the Father is called God (Psa 016:01), Lord (Psa 016:02) and *Yahveh* (Psa 016:02, 05, 07, 08). The Son trusted the Father to resurrect him before putrefaction (Psa 016:10).

OT Citation: Psa 031:05 [*BHS* 031:06]
Extract: Luk 23:46
Extract Usage: Quote
Summary: *Yeshua* read Psa 031 messianically, meaning that David prophetically penned the words the Messiah would speak to the Father while on the cross (Psa 031:05; Luk 23:46). The person of *Yahveh* in view in Psa 031 is the Father.

OT Citation: Isa 66:01-02a
Extract: Act 07:48-50
Extract Usage: Quote
Summary: Stephen spoke of the "Most High" (Act 07:48) before quoting Isaiah (Isa 66:01-02a; Act 07:49-50). This shows that Stephen understood that the Son was quoting the Father, who is elsewhere called *Elyon*, meaning the Most High.

OT Citation: Jer 09:24
Extracts: 1Co 01:30-31; 2Co 10:17
Extract Usage: Quote
Summary: Paul wrote:
   Because of him [the Father] you are in Christ *Yeshua*…as it is written, 'Let him who boasts boast in the Lord [the Father]' (Jer 09:24; 1Co 01:31).
Much credit for one's salvation goes to the Father (Joh 03:16).

OT Citation: Amo 09:11-12 LXX
Extract: Act 15:16-17
Extract Usage: Quote
Summary: The Father would raise David's fallen tent (LXX Amo 09:11-12; Act 15:16-17). This meant that after the scepter departed Judah (Gen 49:10), the Messiah would conquer the earth through evangelism (Mat 28:18-20).

A sample of the *Yahveh* texts applied to the Father and Son in the NT

OT Citation: Gen 01:26
Extract: Joh 01:03
Extract Usage: Allusion
Summary: God the Father said to God the Son, "Let us make…" (Gen 01:26). The Father's creating through the agency of the Son is shown clearly by John's writing that everything was made "through" and "with" the Son (Joh 01:03).

OT Citation: Gen 01:26
Extract: Heb 01:03
Extract Usage: Allusion
Summary: *Yeshua* is the exact image of *Elyon* (Heb 01:03), and this is why the Father could say "our [singular] image," rather than "your image," or "my image" or "our images" (Gen 01:26).

OT Citation: Exo 23:20-21
Extracts: Joh 08:19, 24, 58
Extract Usage: Allusion
Summary: The Father said to obey the *Malek* with his name ("I AM") in him, or else the *Malek* would not forgive their rebellion (Exo 23:20-21). *Yeshua* said one ought to believe he is "I AM," or else die in unforgiven sin (Joh 08:24).

OT Citation: Deu 06:04
Extract: Joh 10:30-33
Extract Usage: Allusion
Summary: The Jews understood *Yeshua* to mean that the Father and Son were two subjects of the *Shema*, and that *Yeshua* and the Father were equal (Joh 10:30-33) (see the *Shema* chapter and Psa 082:06-08 in the Trinitarian proofs appendix).

OT Citation: Deu 06:04-05
Extracts: Mat 22:37; Mar 12:29-30
Extract Usage: Quote
Summary: To show that the *Shema* (Deu 06:04; Mat 22:36-40) is Trinitarian, *Yeshua* said that the Spirit inspired David when David said the Father and Son were his Lord (Psa 110:01, 05; Mat 22:43-45; Mar 12:36-37; Luk 20:42, 44).

OT Citation: Deu 30:10-18
Extracts: Rom 10:05-09, 17
Extract Usage: Quote
Summary: Moses said the Word was in mouths and hearts (Deu 30:14). Paul equated the Word (Deu 30:14) and the Voice (Deu 30:02, 08, 10, 20) of the Father with the "Word of Christ" (*NIV, RSV* Rom 10:17, but the *KJV* reads "word of God").

OT Citations: Deu 32:43 LXX & DSS 4QDT; Psa 097:07 LXX & Syriac
Extract: Heb 01:06
Extract Usage: Quote
Summary: Heb 01:06 quoted the DSS and LXX of Deu 32:43, and the Syriac and LXX of Psa 097:07, where the Father tells the angels to worship the Son. The MT of Deu 32:43 has the Son instructing Hebrews and gentiles to praise the Father.

OT Citations: 2Sa 07:11-13, 27; Psa 069:09; Zec 06:12
Extract: Joh 02:16-21
Extract Usage: Allusion
Summary: *Yahveh* said *Yahveh* would extend David's dynasty and build a temple (2Sa 07:11). The Son raised his body to both extend David's line and build a temple (Joh 02:21), so *Yeshua* is the person of *Yahveh* spoken of by the Father.

OT Citation: Psa 002:01-02
Extract: Act 04:26
Extract Usage: Quote
Summary: Psa 002:12 speaks of the Messiah as a God-man (see the Trinitarian proofs appendix). *Yeshua*'s saying that rulers committed sin (Joh 19:11) justified Peter's application of Psa 002:01-02 to *Yeshua*'s mock trials (Act 04:26-08).

OT Citation: Psa 002:07
Extract: Mat 03:17
Extract Usage: Allusion
Summary: The Spirit was sent to *Yeshua* at his baptism in fulfillment of Isa 42: 01, 48:16; 61:01 and other prophecy. Then the Father alluded to Psa 002:07, 2Sa 07:14 and other texts by his saying, "This is my beloved Son" (Mat 03:17).

OT Citation: Psa 045:06-07 [*BHS* 045:07-08]
Extract: Heb 01:08-09
Extract Usage: Quote
Summary: The writer of Hebrews noted that the Father called the Son "God" (Psa 045:06-07; Heb 01:08-09). Psalms ascribing divinity may have been applied to kings only in anticipation of the God-man who would rule from David's throne.

OT Citations: Psa 069:25 [*BHS* 069:26]; 109:08
Extract: Act 01:20a
Extract Usage: Quote
Summary: Peter read Psa 069 and Psa 109 as messianic Psalms (compare Psa 069:09 and Joh 02:17). The Messiah asked that the Father ensure the position vacated by the Messiah's betrayer would be filled by another disciple (Act 01:20).

OT Citation: Psa 091:11-12
Extracts: Mat 04:06; Luk 04:10-11
Extract Usage: Quote
Summary: The Devil's temptation of *Yeshua* is consistent with the messianic reading of Psa 091, and with the Psalmist's belief that the Messiah would be *Shaddai* and *Yahveh* the Son, and that the Father was *Elyon* (Psa 091:01, 09).

OT Citations: Psa 102:[25 LXX] 26-27 [*BHS* 102:26-27]
Extract: Heb 01:10-12
Extract Usage: Quote
Summary: Heb 01 contains several quotes of the Father speaking both to the Son and about the Son. Heb 01:10 says LXX Psa 102:25-27 is the Father assuring the Son that since he (the Son) created the earth, he will outlast the earth.

OT Citations: Psa 118:22-23; Isa 28:16
Extracts: Mat 21:42; Mar 12:10-11; Luk 20:17-18; 1Pe 02:06
Extract Usage: Quote
Summary: The Father himself is a stumbling stone (Isa 08:14; Rom 09:32; 1Co 01:23; 1Pe 02:08). The Father also makes the Son a stumbling stone (Psa 118:22-23; Isa 28:16; Mat 21:33-46; Mar 12:01-12; Luk 20:09-19; Rom 09:33; 1Pe 02:06).

OT Citation: Psa 118:26
Extract: Luk 19:38-39, 44
Extract Usage: Quote
Summary: The Father said:
Israel, prepare to meet your God [the Son]...*Yahveh*, the God of hosts is his name (Amo 04:12-13).
The crowd was prepared and sang Psa 118:26 at God's visit, but the leaders wanted them rebuked (Luk 19:39).

OT Citations: Pro 09:10; 30:03; Hos 11:12 [*BHS* 12:01]
Extracts: Mar 01:24; Luk 01:35; 04:34; Joh 06:69; Rev 16:05
Extract Usage: Allusion
Summary: *Yahveh* are the Holy Ones (Jos 24:19; Pro 09:10; 30:03; Dan 04:17 [*BHS* 04:14]; 05:11; Hos 11:12 [*BHS* 12:01] (see the MT plurals appendix). The Father and Son are Holy Ones (Pro 30:03-04), and the Son is a Holy One (Rev 16:05).

OT Citation: Isa 02:10-11
Extract: 2Th 01:09-10
Extract Usage: Quote
Summary: 2Th 01:07 says that *Yeshua* will be revealed as the Father's Presence and Glory (Isa 02:10-11; 2Th 01:09-10). The Son is the Fear (Gen 31:42, 53; Isa 02:10). Isa 02 and 2Th 01 are discussed in the Presences of *Elyon* chapter.

OT Citation: Isa 07:14
Extract: Mat 01:22-23
Extract Usage: Quote
Summary: The Messiah would be "Immanuel," meaning, "God with us." That the name "Immanuel" is meant to be taken literally can be seen from prophecies that suggest or speak of the Messiah's deity (see the Trinitarian proofs appendix).

OT Citation: Isa 28:16b
Extract: Rom 10:11
Extract Usage: Quote
Summary: The Father himself is a stumbling stone (Isa 08:14; Rom 09:32; 1Co 01:23; 1Pe 02:08). The Father also makes the Son a stumbling stone (Psa 118:22-23; Isa 28:16; Mat 21:33-46; Mar 12:01-12; Luk 20:09-19; Rom 09:33; 1Pe 02:06).

OT Citation: Isa 34:04
Extracts: Mar 13:24-28; Luk 21:26-29; Rev 06:04, 08, 13-17
Extract Usage: Allusion
Summary: Isa 34:04, Mar 13:24-26, Luk 21:26-27 and Rev 06:13-14 note a fig tree. Isa 34:05-07 and Rev 06 note a sword and scroll. Both Rev 06:16-17 and the first (Isa 34:05) and third person speech in Isa 34 denote Father and Son.

OT Citation: Isa 43:10
Extract: Joh 13:19-20
Extract Usage: Quote
Summary: Words common to Isa 43:10 and Joh 13:19 are:
    hina [that] *pisteusete* [you may believe]...*hoti* [that] *egw eimi* ["I AM"].
Yeshua applied Isa 43:10 to himself to prove by his prophesying future events
that he is "I AM" and God.

OT Citation: Isa 53:01 LXX
Extracts: Joh 12:38; Rom 10:16-17
Extract Usage: Quote
Summary: The quotes of LXX Isa 53:01 in Joh 12:38 and Rom 10:16-17 say
the Messiah spoke to the Father. Greek NT manuscript finds attest that the phrase
in Rom 10:17 is "word of Christ" (*NIV, RSV*) rather than "word of God" (*KJV*).

OT Citations: Isa 53:05; 55:03, 07
Extract: Joh 20:17
Extract Usage: Allusion
Summary: *Yeshua* alluded to Isa 55:07 in Joh 20:17 to say none should touch
him until he was pardoned for others' sins (Isa 53:05), and had received "the sure
mercies of David" (Isa 55:03; Act 13:34).

OT Citations: Dan 07:13; Zec 12:10
Extracts: Mat 26:64; Rev 01:07
Extract Usage: Allusion
Summary: The vision of Dan 07 relates that the Son of Man became Most High
with the Father (see the Song of Moses chapter). Rev 01:07 alludes to Dan 07:13
and Zec 12:10 when it says that those responsible for *Yeshua*'s death would see his
return.

OT Citations: Hos 11:01; Num 24:08
Extract: Mat 02:15
Extract Usage: Quote
Summary: Hos 11:01, a verse similar to Num 24:08, is applied to *Yeshua* (Mat
02:15). Num 24:16-17 says the Messiah would be *Shaddai* (One of the Mighty
Ones) (see the section on Num 22-24 in the Proto-Sinaitic Trinitarianism chapter).

OT Citation: Joe 02:32 [*BHS* 03:05]
Extracts: Rom 10:09, 13
Extract Usage: Quote
Summary: Paul quoted (Rom 10:09,13) a *Yahveh* text (Joe 02:32) spoken by the
Son (Act 02:33). The NT and "the Elect" call *Yeshua* "Lord" often (Act 08:16; 09:
27; 15:26; 19:05, 13, 17; 21:13; 1Co 01:02; 2Co 04:05 and many like texts).

OT Citation: Zec 11:12-13
Extract: Mat 27:09-10
Extract Usage: Quote
Summary: Judas realized that *Yeshua* was "I AM" when his saying, "I AM," knocked down soldiers (Joh 18:05-08). So the prompting of the Shepherd (Zec 13:07; Mar 14:24) fulfilled Zec 11:12-13 (see the "I AM" and Song of Moses chapters).

OT Citation: Zec 13:07
Extract: Mar 14:27
Extract Usage: Quote
Summary: *Yeshua* said he was the Shepherd of Zec 13:07 (Mar 14:27). That the Shepherd is *Yahveh*'s fellow (Zec 13:07) suggests the deity of the Messiah, and this in turn is a proof for the Trinity (see the Trinitarian proofs chapter).

OT Citation: Zec 14:04-05
Extracts: Act 01:11; 1Th 03:13
Extract Usage: Allusion
Summary: The Father said the Son will return with his holy ones (Zec 14:04-05). The angels and Paul alluded to Zec 14:05 to say that the Son will return in the clouds with his holy ones—the saints and angels (Act 01:11; 1Th 03:13).

OT Citations: Mal 03:01; 04:05-06
Extracts: Mat 11:10; Mar 01:02-03; Luk 01:16-17
Extract Usage: Quote
Summary: The Father sent the Baptist ahead of his Presence, who was the *Malek* of the Covenant and the person of *Yahveh* who would come to his temple (see Mal 03:01 in the Presences of *Elyon* chapter and the Trinitarian proofs appendix).

A sample of the *Yahveh* texts applied to the Father and the Spirit in the NT

OT Citation: Psa 095:07b-11
Extracts: Heb 03:07-11, 15; 04:03-04, 07
Extract Usage: Quote
Summary: The writer of Hebrews quoted the Spirit who spoke of himself in the first person (I, me, my), and the Spirit spoke of the Father in the third person by saying:
...hear his [the Father's] voice (Psa 095:07b-11; Heb 03:07-11; 04:07).

A sample of the *Yahveh* texts applied to the Son in the NT

OT Citation: Gen 16:13-14
Extracts: Joh 04:26, 29, 39
Extract Usage: Allusion
Summary: The *Malek* who met Hagar at the well was "*Yahveh*" and "the God who sees" (Gen 16:13). *Yeshua* said, "I AM," and the woman at the well said he was one "who told me all I did" (Joh 04; see the "I AM" and Song of Moses chapters).

OT Citations: Gen 32:30; 35:11, 14
Extract: Hos 12:03-05
Extract Usage: Allusion
Summary: Hosea said that Jacob wrestled with God (Hos 12:03), and met God again at Bethel (Hos 12:04). This God (Gen 32:30), *El Shaddai* (Gen 35:11), is a member of the Trinity—the "us" of Hos 12:04 (see the MT plurals appendix).

OT Citation: Exo 03:02-07
Extract: Act 07:30-38
Extract Usage: Quote
Summary: Stephen said the *Malek* (Act 07:30, 35, 38) at the burning bush was both Lord and God (Act 07:32-33). The narrator located both the *Malek Yahveh* and *Yahveh* in the same bush (Exo 03:02, 04; see the Trinitarian proofs appendix).

OT Citation: Exo 03:14 LXX
Extracts: Rev 01:04, 08; 04:08; 11:17; 16:05
Extract Usage: Allusion
Summary: *Yahveh* said that he is "I AM WHO IS" [*egw eimi ho wn*] (LXX Exo 03:14). *Yeshua* is God, Lord, "I AM [*egw eimi*]" and "WHO IS [*ho wn*]" (Rev 01:08). See the "I AM" chapter to find more OT and NT "I AM" and "WHO IS" statements.

OT Citations: Exo 03:14 LXX; 06:03
Extracts: Joh 08:58; 18:06
Extract Usage: Allusion
Summary: *Yahveh* said, "'I AM' [Greek is "*egw eimi*"]" (LXX Exo 03:14). *Yeshua* told of his preexistence by saying, "'I AM' [*egw eimi*] before Abraham was" (Joh 08:58). See the "I AM" chapter to find more OT and NT "I AM" statements.

OT Citation: Exo 17:06
Extract: 1Co 10:04
Extract Usage: Allusion
Summary: *Yahveh* the Son was the "spiritual rock" that gave Israel living water (Exo 17:06; 1Co 10:04; see the Presences of *Elyon* chapter). Similarly, the Son offered water to Hagar (Gen 16) and living water to the Samaritan (Joh 04).

OT Citation: Num 21:05-09
Extract: 1Co 10:09
Extract Usage: Allusion
Summary: The narrator said the Israelites spoke against God (Num 21:25), and the people said they spoke against *Yahveh* (Num 21:07). Paul said the Israelites tested Christ (*KJV, YLT* 1Co 10:09), so Paul knew *Yeshua* as *Yahveh* the Son.

OT Citations: Jdg 06:21; 13:20
Extract: Joh 06:62
Extract Usage: Allusion
Summary: Proof of *Yeshua*'s metaphysical presence in bread (Joh 06) was the ascension after the crucifixion (Joh 06:62), an allusion to the *Malek Yahveh*'s ascending at Gideon and Manoah's offerings (see the Presences of *Elyon* chapter).

OT Citations: 2Sa 22:03; Psa 018:02
Extract: Luk 01:69
Extract Usage: Allusion
Summary: John the Baptist's father, Zechariah, referred to the Messiah as "a horn of salvation" (Luk 01:69), a phrase used to refer to *Yahveh* (2Sa 22:03; Psa 018:02; see Luk 01:69 in the Trinitarian proofs appendix under Isa 40:03).

OT Citation: 2Sa 24:16
Extract: Mat 26:51-53
Extract Usage: Allusion
Summary: The Son told an angel outside Jerusalem, "Enough! Withdraw your sword" (1Ch 21:15). The disciples said, "Here are two swords." *Yeshua* said, "That is enough" (Luk 22:38). Outside Jerusalem *Yeshua* told Peter put away his sword.

OT Citation: 2Ch 30:18-20
Extracts: Mat 12:06; 19:21; Mar 10:21; Luk 18:22
Extract Usage: Allusion
Summary: *Yahveh* pardoned seekers who failed to comply with purity laws (2Ch 30:18-20). *Yahveh* the Son is greater than the Sabbath and the temple, and he pardoned his seekers who broke man-made rules and the Mosaic Sabbath (Mat 12:01-08).

OT Citation: Psa 002:12
Extract: Luk 22:48
Extract Usage: Allusion
Summary: Psa 002 speaks of the Messiah as God-man (see the Trinitarian proofs appendix). *Yeshua* alluded to Psa 002:12 (Luk 22:48) at his betrayal when he said he is "I AM" (Joh 18:05-08; see the "I AM" and Song of Moses chapters).

OT Citations: Psa 014:03; 053:03 [*BHS* 053:04]
Extracts: Mat 19:17; Mar 10:18; Luk 18:19
Extract Usage: Allusion
Summary: *Yeshua* alluded to Psa 014:03 (Mat 19:17), and nearby is penned: "God is present in the company of the righteous" (Psa 014:05). *Yeshua* meant that he is Immanuel and he imputes righteousness to sinners (see the *Shema* chapter).

OT Citation: Psa 028:04
Extracts: 2Ti 04:01, 08, 14
Extract Usage: Allusion
Summary: The Lord is identified as *Yeshua* who will appear at the Last Day (2Ti 04:01, 08). If Paul meant the person called Lord to be *Yeshua* throughout this section, then Paul applied a *Yahveh* text to *Yeshua* (Psa 028:04; 2Ti 04:14).

OT Citation: Psa 034:08a [*BHS* 034:09]
Extract: 1Pe 02:03
Extract Usage: Quote
Summary: That *Yeshua* is "Lord" in 1Pe 02:04-08 suggests Peter applied Psa 034:08 to the Son (1Pe 02:03). "God" in 1Pe 02:09 is the Father who possesses but does not inherit believers (see the Song of Moses chapter on that last point).

OT Citation: Psa 039:07 [*BHS* 039:08]
Extract: Col 01:27
Extract Usage: Allusion
Summary: David said that the Lord is a believer's "hope" (Psa 039:07), and Paul said that *Yeshua* is a believer's "hope of glory" (Col 01:27).

OT Citation: Psa 050:21
Extract: Act 08:32
Extract Usage: Allusion
Summary: "I [*Yahveh*] kept silent. You thought the 'I AM' was like you, but I will rebuke you" (Psa 050:21). *Yeshua* kept silent, but said all would know him as the "I AM" and Son of Man on the Last Day (see the Song of Moses chapter).

OT Citation: Psa 062:12 [*BHS* 062:13]
Extracts: Mat 16:27; Rev 22:12
Extract Usage: Quote
Summary: David said that *Yahveh* rewards "every man according to his work" (Psa 062:12), and *Yeshua* said that he "will render to everyone according what he has done" (Mat 16:27; Rev 22:12).

OT Citation: Psa 066:16
Extract: Mar 05:19-20
Extract Usage: Allusion
Summary: *Yeshua* said, "Tell what great things the Lord has done for you" (Mar 05:19). The man took "Lord" to mean "*Yeshua*" (Mar 05:20), just as *Yeshua* intended. So *Yeshua* seems to have applied a *Yahveh* text (Psa 066:16) to himself.

OT Citation: Psa 068:18 [*BHS* 068:19]
Extract: Eph 04:07-08
Extract Usage: Quote
Summary: Paul applied a *Yahveh* text Psa 068:18 to Christ (Eph 04:07) to say that *Yeshua* was with his disciples to the end of time as they free sin's captives through evangelism (Mat 28:18-20). *Yeshua* leads these believers heavenward.

OT Citation: Psa 094:01
Extract: 1Th 04:06
Extract Usage: Allusion
Summary: The "Lord" in 1Th 04:01, 02, 15, 16, and 17 is *Yeshua*, so the "Lord" in 1Th 04:06 likely is *Yeshua*. So Paul quoted a *Yahveh* text (Psa 094:01) in reference to *Yeshua* (1Th 04:06), and vengeance belongs also to *Yahveh* the Son.

OT Citation: Psa 102:27 [*BHS* 102:28]
Extract: Heb 13:08
Extract Usage: Allusion
Summary: Psa 102:25-27 is quoted in Heb 01:10-12 in reference to the Son (see this appendix). Thus, the second quote of Psa 102:27 (Heb 13:08) shows that the author of Hebrews believed the Psalmist ascribed changelessness to the Son.

OT Citation: Psa 103:19-21
Extract: Act 10:36
Extract Usage: Allusion
Summary: Peter applied a *Yahveh* text (Psa 103:19; Act 10:36) to *Yeshua* to say he was *Yahveh* "over all," since he became Most High along with the Father in fulfillment of the Dan 07 Son of Man Vision (see the Song of Moses chapter).

OT Citation: Psa 118:06
Extracts: Heb 13:06, 08
Extract Usage: Quote
Summary: The nearby text noting *Yeshua*'s eternality (Heb 13:08) suggests the *Yahveh* text (Psa 118:06) quoted in Heb 13:06 refers to *Yeshua*. *Kurios* (Lord) is the LXX and NT translation of *Yahveh*, and the NT calls *Yeshua Kurios* often.

OT Citations: Psa 130:07-08; also Deu 10:17; Ezr 05:08; Neh 08:06; Psa 095:03; Dan 02:45
Extract: Tit 02:13-14
Extract Usage: Allusion
Summary: By saying, "we wait" on *Yeshua* (Tit 02:13-14), Paul alluded to Psa 130:07 and thus applied a *Yahveh* text to *Yeshua*. The OT calls *Yahveh* "Great God," so Paul applied several *Yahveh* texts to *Yeshua* by saying he is "Great God."

OT Citation: Pro 03:11-12
Extracts: Heb 12:02, 05-06
Extract Usage: Quote
Summary: Heb 12:02 says *Yeshua* is "the author and perfecter of our faith." A text saying *Yahveh* is a reprover (Pro 03:11-12) is quoted nearby (Heb 12:05-06) and is applied to *Yeshua* since a perfecter would naturally be a reprover.

OT Citation: Isa 06:05
Extract: Joh 12:41
Extract Usage: Allusion
Summary: Isaiah saw and spoke "about" the glory of the Son when he recorded the Isa 06 vision in the temple (Joh 12:41), but Isaiah actually talked to the Spirit (Act 28:25-26; Isa 06:08-13). Isa 06:05 applies specifically to the Son.

OT Citation: Isa 09:06 [*BHS* 09:05]
Extract: Rev 01:08
Extract Usage: Allusion
Summary: The Son is called "the Almighty" (Rev 01:08) and "Mighty God" (*El Gibbor*) (Isa 09:06). That *El Gibbor* speaks of the Messiah and *Yahveh*'s deity (Isa 10:21) is consistent with the Son's being the Author of Eternity (Isa 09:06).

OT Citation: Isa 35:02-05
Extract: Mat 11:03-06
Extract Usage: Allusion
Summary: *Yeshua* alluded to "the blind see...the deaf hear" (Isa 35:05; Mat 11:05). Isaiah said the Messiah would be God nearby:
    They shall see the glory of *Yahveh*, the excellency of our God (Isa 35:02; compare Isa 09:02; Mat 04:16).

OT Citations: Isa 40:03, 09
Extracts: Mat 03:03; Mar 01:03; Luk 03:04; Joh
Extract Usage: Quote
Summary: The "voice" is the Baptist's (Isa 40:03,06, 09; Mat 03:03; and elsewhere). John's message about the coming "*Yahveh*" and "God" (Isa 40:03, 10) was tantamount to introducing *Yeshua* by the words: "Here is your God!" (Isa 40: 09).

OT Citation: Isa 40:08
Extract: Mar 13:31
Extract Usage: Allusion
Summary: *Yeshua* alluded to a verse (Isa 40:08) of the prophecy about John the Baptist's heralding the Messiah (Isa 40:06b-11). *Yeshua* applied a *Yahveh* text (Isa 40:08) to himself to say he is "God," proving his words are eternal.

OT Citation: Isa 42:04 LXX
Extracts: Mat 12:21; Luk 24:45
Extract Usage: Quote
Summary: Matthew quoted "…in his name shall the gentiles trust" (LXX Isa 42:04; Mat 12:21). Here the Father spoke of the Servant of *Yahveh*, the Messiah. That the nations trust in Christ's name is confirmed by Christ (Luk 24:45-47).

OT Citation: Isa 45:23 LXX
Extract: Rom 14:11
Extract Usage: Quote
Summary: Paul quoted a *Yahveh* text (Isa 45:23) where *Yahveh* the Son said eventually everyone will bow down to him. That *Yeshua* is the Lord in view in Rom 14:11 can be seen from Rom 14:09, 14, so Paul applied a *Yahveh* text to *Yeshua*.

OT Citation: Isa 45:23 LXX
Extract: Phi 02:09-11
Extract Usage: Allusion
Summary: Paul alluded to a *Yahveh* text (Isa 45:23; Phi 02:09-11) to say that *Yeshua* received the title *Elyon*, and so was Most High along with the Father in fulfillment of the Dan 07 Son of Man prophecy (see the Song of Moses chapter).

OT Citation: Isa 52:06 LXX
Extract: Luk 24:39
Extract Usage: Allusion
Summary: *Yeshua* said, "that 'I AM' myself [*hoti egw eimi autos*]" (Luk 24:39). This is an exact quote of a phrase in LXX Isa 52:06 spoken by the Son. See Isa 53: 05 in this appendix about *Yeshua* being touched after the resurrection.

OT Citation: Isa 52:06 LXX
Extract: Joh 04:26
Extract Usage: Allusion
Summary: *Yahveh* the Son said:
I AM [the Hebrew is *"anee hu,"* and the LXX Greek is *"egw eimi"*] myself
who speaks (LXX Isa 52:06).
Yeshua applied this *Yahveh* text to himself by saying, "I AM [*egw eimi*], who
am speaking" (Joh 04:26).

OT Citation: Isa 52:06 LXX
Extract: Joh 13:19
Extract Usage: Allusion
Summary: Words common to Isa 52:06 and Joh 13:19 are: *"hoti* [that] *egw
eimi* ["I AM"]." *Yeshua* alluded to this *Yahveh* text to prove that by his prophesying future events, he is both "I AM" and *Yahveh* the Son who spoke in Isa 52:
06.

OT Citation: Isa 65:01
Extract: Rom 10:20
Extract Usage: Quote
Summary: Paul quoted Isa 65:01 (Rom 10:20). That Paul knew Christ spoke
Isa 65:01 can be inferred from Rom 10:17. Recent Greek manuscripts finds attest
that the last word of Rom 10:17 is "Christ" (*NIV, RSV*) rather than "God" (*KJV*).

OT Citation: Isa 66:15 LXX
Extract: 2Th 01:07b-08a
Extract Usage: Quote
Summary: Paul quoted Isaiah where the Father said the Son will return at the
end in flaming fire (LXX Isa 66:15; 2Th 01:07). Paul applied this quote to *Yeshua*
by writing, "the Lord *Yeshua* is revealed...in flaming fire" (LXX Isa 66:15).

OT Citation: Jer 17:10
Extract: Rev 02:23
Extract Usage: Quote
Summary: *Yeshua* quoted his own words, "I, *Yahveh* search the mind and try
the heart" and reward according to deeds (Jer 17:10; Rev 02:23). That the Son is
the speaker of Rev 02:23 can be ascertained from Rev 02:18 and 27.

OT Citations: Jer 23:05-06; 33:15-16
Extract: Joh 08:24
Extract Usage: Allusion
Summary: The Messiah is a branch or scepter. Believers will associate the city
where the branch died for our sins with the Son who is "I AM" and *"Yahveh* our
Righteousness" (see Jer 23:06 and 33:16 in the Trinitarian proofs appendix).

OT Citation: Eze 01:26-28
Extract: Rev 01:13-16
Extract Usage: Allusion
Summary: Ezekiel depicted a preincarnate appearance of the Son who is "the glory of *Yahveh*" (Eze 01:26-28). Daniel saw the same Son of Man (Dan 07:13-14), and John described the same Son of Man in Revelation (Rev 01:13-16).

OT Citation: Dan 07:14
Extract: Mat 28:18
Extract Usage: Allusion
Summary: Dan 07 depicted the Son of Man becoming Most High with the Father (see the Song of Moses chapter). Dan 07 was fulfilled before the ascension, allowing *Yeshua* to say he had all authority to evangelize the earth (Mat 28:18).

OT Citation: Mic 05:02 [*BHS* 05:01]
Extract: Mat 02:06
Extract Usage: Quote
Summary: Micah said the Messiah preexisted and his origin is from eternity (Mic 05:02b). Matthew applied Mic 05:02a to the Messiah (Mat 02:06). Matthew expected the reader to know Mic 05:02(a) and (b) to appreciate the full implication.

OT Citation: Zec 09:09
Extracts: Mat 21:05; Joh 12:12-16
Extract Usage: Quote
Summary: In Zec 09, *Yahveh* the Son prophesied what he would do as the coming Messiah. *Yahveh* the Son is the prophesied King Messiah who came to Jerusalem riding on a donkey (Zec 09:09; Mat 21:05; Joh 12:12-16).

A sample of the *Yahveh* texts applied to the Son and the Spirit in the NT

OT Citation: Zec 12:10
Extracts: Joh 19:37; Act 02:33b, 36-37; Rev 01:07
Extract Usage: Allusion
Summary: The Son would pour out the Spirit so many would mourn how their representative institutions killed the Son (the "me" in Zec 12:10). The Spirit came at Pentecost, many "were cut to the heart," and then repented (Act 02:33-37).

A sample of the *Yahveh* texts applied to the Spirit in the NT

OT Citations: Gen 13:13; 19:06-09
Extracts: Mat 10:14-15, 20
Extract Usage: Allusion
Summary: The disciples evangelized and performed miracles (Mat 10:08, 14-15; 11:23), but some towns rejected (*Yahveh*) the Spirit (Mat 10:20). Likewise, Sodomites sinned against *Yahveh* (the Father) (Gen 13:13), but saw no miracles.

OT Citations: Gen 18:10, 14
Extract: Gal 04:29
Extract Usage: Allusion
Summary: Isaac was born by *Yahveh*'s power (Gen 18:10, 14), which was the Spirit's power (Gal 04:29). Sarah's infertility suggests the Spirit, along with the Father and Son, willed both Isaac's conception and spiritual regeneration.

OT Citation: Exo 31:18
Extract: Luk 11:20
Extract Usage: Allusion
Summary: That Moses and *Yeshua* were the only prophets to work miracles by the finger of God (Exo 08:19; Luk 11:20), who is the Spirit (Luk 11:20; Mat 12: 28), shows that *Yeshua* was the prophet like Moses (Deu 18:15; Act 03:22; 07:37).

OT Citation: Isa 06:09-10
Extracts: Joh 12:40; Act 28:25-26
Extract Usage: Quote
Summary: Isaiah saw and spoke "about" the glory of the Son when he recorded the Isa 06 vision in the temple (Joh 12:41), but Isaiah actually talked to the Spirit (Act 28:25-26; Isa 06:08-13).

A sample of the *Yahveh* texts applied to the Trinity in the NT

OT Citation: Num 06:22-27
Extract: Mat 28:19
Extract Usage: Allusion
Summary: *Yeshua* said to baptize in the singular Name of three persons (Mat 28:19). In the Aaronic Blessing, priests put the singular Name on the people by saying *Yahveh* thrice (see Num 06:22-27 in the Trinitarian proofs appendix).

OT Citation: Psa 110:01
Extracts: Mat 22:43-46 ; Mar 12:35-37; Act 02:34
Extract Usage: Quote
Summary: The Spirit informed David that the Father and Son were his Lord (Psa 110:01; Mar 12:36). Psa 110 describes David's God-man descendant (2Sa 07), so it is nonsensical to say Psa 110 refers to David except as a type of Christ.

OT Citation: Psa 110:04
Extract: Heb 07:21
Extract Usage: Quote
Summary: *Yeshua* said the Spirit told David that the Father spoke to David's master, the Son (Psa 110:01; Mar 12:36), who is a priest forever (Psa 110:04). David was not a priest, and he was not allowed to build the temple (1Ch 22:08).

OT Citation: Psa 110:05
Extract: Act 02:33
Extract Usage: Allusion
Summary: The Spirit said the Father spoke to David's master (Psa 110:01). The Father said that the Lord (the Spirit) was at the Son's right hand, and that the Spirit would help conquer (evangelize) the earth with the Son (Psa 110:05).

OT Citation: Isa 48:16
Extracts: Mat 03:16-17; Joh 03:08, 11, 34
Extract Usage: Allusion
Summary: Isa 48:16 was fulfilled when the Father sent the Spirit without limit at *Yeshua*'s baptism (Joh 03:34). Then *Yeshua* spoke of the Spirit and himself saying:
   we speak…we testify (Joh 03:11; see Isa 40:13 in this appendix).

OT Citations: Isa 61:01, 08
Extract: Mat 03:16-17
Extract Usage: Allusion
Summary: The Spirit alighted on *Yeshua* at his baptism (Mat 03:16-17) in fulfillment of Isa 42:01; 48:16 and 61:01. *Yeshua* is the Servant of *Yahveh* who is preexistent (Isa 48:16; 61:01), and he is *Yahveh* the Son (Isa 61:08).

OT Citation: Isa 61:01-02a
Extract: Luk 04:18-19
Extract Usage: Quote
Summary: *Yeshua* quoted the Servant of *Yahveh* who mentions that the Father sent him with the Spirit (Isa 61:01-02; Luk 04:18), and who said he was *Yahveh* (Isa 61:08). The Servant and the Spirit are also the "sent" *Yahveh*s of Isa 48:16.

OT Citation: Joe 02:28-32 [*BHS* 03:01-05]
Extracts: Act 02:16-21, 33
Extract Usage: Quote
Summary: Peter said (Act 02:33) that *Yahveh* the Son spoke Joe 02:28-32, the OT quote found in Act 02:16-21. The Son said he would send the Spirit (Joe 02: 28-32; Joh 16:07), and Peter said *Yeshua* sent the Spirit (Act 02:33).

Total Number of Extracts Listed Above: 97

Endnotes

[1] *"In vetere Testamento novum latet, in novo vetus patet"* (Augustine, *Questions on the Heptateuch*, II, 73).

[2] Hodder and Stoughton, *The Illustrated Bible Dictionary*, 1980, Part 3, p. 1597.

[3] Wiley, H. Orten. *Christian Theology*, Volume II, Part III, Chapter XX, "Christology," Beacon Hill Press of Kansas City, Kansas City, Missouri, 1940.

[4] "Collective Noun," *The American Heritage Dictionary of the English Language*, Fourth Edition, Published by Houghton Mifflin Company, 2000 (see atomica.com).

[5] Gesenius, W. *Gesenius' Hebrew Grammar (GKC)* (edited by A. E. Cowley and E. Kautzsch; 2d Eng. ed., based on the 28th Ger. ed.; Clarendon, 1910), p. 462.

[6] "Athanasian Creed," *The Columbia Electronic Encyclopedia*, Columbia University Press, 1999.

[7] The word "prove" in the proverb "exceptions prove the rule" comes from the Latin *probat* by way of Elizabethan English. Etymologically speaking, "prove" means "test." The meaning of the proverb is that one understands a rule only when one considers the exceptions. Also, when there are too many exceptions, the rule must be abandoned or modified. For example, earlier English grammarians made a rule against splitting infinitives. There are, however, too many exceptions of split infinitives that sound perfectly natural, so the rule was tested and discarded by most grammarians. The rule was made on the basis of the rules of Latin and Greek grammar, which, however, do not exactly apply since they do not have the word "to" (information supplied by Professor Frederick Blume).

[8] Barker, Margaret. *The Great Angel: A Study of Israel's Second God.* Westminster/John Knox, Louisville, Kentucky, 1992, as quoted in Gieschen, Charles A. *Angelmorphic Christology: Antecedents & Early Evidence.* Brill, Boston, 1998, p. 23.

[9] Geisler, Norman L. and Abdul Saleeb. *Answering Islam: The Crescent in the Light of the Cross.* Baker Books, Grand Rapids, Michigan, USA, 1993, pp. 91-92.

[10] Warraq, Ibn. *Why I Am Not a Muslim.* Promethius Books, Amherst, New York, 1995, p. 54.

[11] Because the *Koran* has so many anachronistic mistakes, translators should have inserted *sic* [Latin: "thus"] 350 times into the text rather than the word, "Say!"

[12] Warraq. *Why I Am Not a Muslim. Op. Cit.*, pp. 54-55.

[13] Goodenough, Erwin R. *Jewish Symbols in the Greco-Roman Period*, Edited and Abridged by Jacob Neusner, Princeton University Press, 1988, p. 148.

[14] Goodenough, Erwin R. *Ibid.*, pp. 155-156.

[15] Josephus, Flavius. *Wars of the Jews*, Book V *"From The Coming Of Titus To Besiege Jerusalem, To The Great Extremity To Which The Jews Were Reduced,"* Chapter 5, *"A Description Of The Temple,"* Paragraph 4. Note: The curtain that Josephus described likely hung in the temple from some time after the crucifixion (30 AD?) to the destruction of the temple in 70 AD. The curtain hanging in the temple during the crucifixion was ripped in two, and surely was replaced (Mat 27:51; Mar 15:38; Luk 23:45).

[16] Josephus, Flavius. *Antiquities of the Jews*, Book III *"Containing The Interval Of Two Years. From The Exodus Out Of Egypt, To The Rejection Of That Generation,"* Chapter 7 *"Concerning The Garments Of The Priests, And Of The High Priest,"* Paragraph 2 and 7.

[17] Josephus. *Antiquities of the Jews*, III, vii,7 confer III, vi, 7; V, v, 5. Philo Judaeus, *Quis Rerum Divinarum Heres*, XLV, pp. 224-225.

[18] Philo, *De Vita Mosis*, II, 12. See Goldman, Bernard. *The Sacred Portal: A Primary Symbol in Ancient Judaic Art*. Wayne State University, 1966, p. 111.

[19] Ness, Lester. *Written in the Stars: Ancient Zodiac Mosaics*. Shangri-La Publications, Warren Center, Pennsylvania, USA, 1999, p. 141.

[20] Goodenough, Erwin R. *Jewish Symbols in the Greco-Roman Period, Op. Cit.*, p. 167.

[21] Goldman, Bernard. *The Sacred Portal: A Primary Symbol in Ancient Judaic Art*. Wayne State University, 1966, p. 68.

[22] Meshorer, Ya'akov. *Ancient Jewish Coinage: Volume I: Persian Period Through Hasmonaeans*. Amphora Books, New York, 1982, pp. 67-68 and plates 8-55 have cornucopias, but especially see coins Jc1-Jc7.

[23] Goitein, S. D. *Jews and Arabs: Their Contacts through the Ages*, Schocken Books, New York, 1970, pp. 7-8, as quote by Newby, Gordon Darnell. *A History of the Jews of Arabia: From Ancient Times to Their Eclipse Under Islam*. University of South Carolina Press, Columbia, South Carolina, USA, 1988, p. 107.

[24] "Hebrew language," *Encyclopædia Britannica*, Accessed November 6, 2001.

[25] Drucker, Malka. *Eliezer, Ben-Yehuda: The Father of Modern Hebrew*, Lodestar Books, E. P. Dutton, NY, 1987, pp. 63, 67.

[26] Massey, Keith Andrew, Doctoral Dissertation: "The Concord of Collective Nouns and Verbs in biblical Hebrew: A Controlled Study," University of Wisconsin-Madison, 1998, p. 28 and footnote (infolearning.com/hp/Products/Dissertations.html, Order Number: 9825726).

[27] Massey, Keith Andrew. *Ibid.*, p. 28

[28] Most instances of *haElohim* (91.5% or 335 instances of 366 total instances) occur in just twelve OT books: (Gen (23), Exo (27), Jdg (15), 1Sa (24), 2Sa (20), 1Ki (26), 2Ki (36), 1Ch (48), 2Ch (51), Ezr (12), Neh (23), Ecc (30)).

[29] 295 of the 366 total instances (found in 337 OT verses) of *haElohim* are clustered in these 83 Hebrew OT chapters: 1. Gen 05 (2); 2. Gen 06 (4); 3. Gen 20 (2); 4. Gen 22 (2); 5. Gen 41 (4); 6. Gen 48 (2); 7. Exo 01 (2); 8. Exo 03 (5); 9. Exo 04 (2); 10. Exo 18 (6); 11. Exo 19 (2); 12. Exo 20 (2); 13. Exo 22 (2); 14. Exo 24 (2); 15. Deu 04 (2); 16. Jdg 06 (3); 17. Jdg 13 (5); 18. Jdg 20 (2); 19. 1Sa 04 (9); 20. 1Sa 05 (5); 21. 1Sa 09 (3); 22. 1Sa 10 (3); 23. 1Sa 14 (3); 24. 2Sa 06 (8); 25. 2Sa 07 (2); 26. 2Sa 14 (2); 27. 2Sa 15 (4); 28. 1Ki 12 (2); 29. 1Ki 13 (14); 30. 1Ki 18 (6); 31. 2Ki 01 (4); 32. 2Ki 04 (10); 33. 2Ki 05 (5); 34. 2Ki 06 (4); 35. 2Ki 07 (4); 36. 2Ki 08 (5); 37. 2Ki 23 (2); 38. 1Ch 06 (2); 39. 1Ch 09 (4); 40. 1Ch 13 (7); 41. 1Ch 14 (4); 42. 1Ch 15 (5); 43. 1Ch 16: (4); 44. 1Ch 17 (3); 45. 1Ch 21 (4); 46. 1Ch 22 (4); 47. 1Ch 23 (2); 48. 1Ch 25 (3); 49. 1Ch 26 (2); 50. 1Ch 28 (2); 51. 2Ch 01 (2); 52. 2Ch 04 (2); 53. 2Ch 05 (2); 54. 2Ch 23 (2); 55. 2Ch 24 (6); 56. 2Ch 25 (5); 57. 2Ch 26 (3); 58. 2Ch 28 (2); 59. 2Ch 30 (3); 60. 2Ch 31 (3); 61. 2Ch 32 (2); 62. 2Ch 33 (2); 63. 2Ch 36 (3); 64. Ezr 01 (3); 65. Ezr 03 (3); 66. Ezr 10 (3); 67. Neh 08 (4); 68. Neh 10 (3); 69. Neh 11 (3); 70. Neh 12 (4); 71. Neh 13 (4); 72. Job 02 (2); 73. Ecc 02 (2); 74. Ecc 03 (4); 75. Ecc 05 (7); 76. Ecc 06 (2); 77. Ecc 07 (4); 78. Ecc 08 (3); 79. Ecc 09 (2); 80. Ecc 11 (2); 81. Ecc 12 (3); 82. Dan 01 (3); Dan 09 (2); and 83. Jon 03 (3).

[30] "Syrian and Palestinian religion," *Encyclopædia Britannica*, accessed August 12, 2002.

[31] Warraq. *Why I Am Not a Muslim. Op. Cit.*, 1995, p. 108.

[32] Hastings, James. *Encyclopaedia of Religion and Ethics*, Volume 1, Part 2 (Algonquins-Art), Clark, Edinburgh (reprinted by Elibron Classics, elibron.com), 1908, "Arabs (Ancient)," p. 661 (right column, bottom).

[33] Hastings, James. *Ibid.*, p. 664 (right column, top).

[34] Warraq. *Op. Cit.*, p. 80 (also see p. 335).

[35] Wansbrough, J. *Quranic Studies*, Oxford, 1962, p. 20, as quoted in Warraq. *Op. Cit.*, p. 74.

[36] Ishaq, Ibn. *Sirat Rasul Allah.* Translated by Alfred Guillaume under the title *The Life of Muhammad.* Pakistan Branch, Oxford University Press, Karachi, 1955, p. 622.

[37] *Op. Cit.*, p. 239.

[38] Lings, Martin. *Muhammad: His Life Based on the Earliest Sources.* Inner Traditions International, Rochester, Vermont, USA, 1983, p. 130.

[39] Lings, Martin. *Ibid.*, p. 239.

[40] Goitein, S. D. *Jews and Arabs: Their Contacts through the Ages*, Schocken Books, New York, 1970, pp. 7-8, as quote by Newby, Gordon Darnell. *A History of the Jews of Arabia: From Ancient Times to Their Eclipse Under Islam.* University of South Carolina Press, Columbia, South Carolina, USA, 1988, p. 107.

[41] Newby, Gordon Darnell. *A History of the Jews of Arabia: From Ancient Times to Their Eclipse Under Islam.* University of South Carolina Press, Columbia, South Carolina, USA, 1988, p. 22.

[42] Newby, Gordon Darnell. *Ibid.*, p. 66.

[43] The reader will remember that British and American collective noun usage was discussed at the beginning of this chapter.

[44] *Larousse Encyclopedia of Mythology.* Prometheus Press, New York, 1960, p. 321.

[45] Albright, William F. *Archaeology and the Religion of Israel*, Johns Hopkins Press, Baltimore, 1942, p. 83.

[46] *Kemosh* said in line 05 that *Kemosh* was angry at Moab and thus *Kemosh* let King Omri of Israel control Moabite territory. Amends were made between Moab and *Kemosh*, so Mesha said in line 18, "*Kemosh* drove [the king of Israel] out" of Moab territory. In other lines, Mesha said several times that *Kemosh* told him to attack various cities, and then each time Mesha gave *Kemosh* the credit for taking those territories and cities. The Moabite Stone confirms what Jephthah said about *Kemosh*'s interest in territory, and about how nations would not pass up land that was theirs for the taking.

[47] Dearman, Andrew (Editor). *Studies in the Mesha Inscription and Moab*, Scholars Press, Atlanta, Georgia 1989, p. 98.

[48] Dearman, Andrew. *Ibid.*, p. 308.

[49] "Moabite is clearly a separate language, though it is most closely related to Hebrew, with which it shares many features. Aside from the *nun* of the masculine plural, Moabite shares little else of a distinctive nature with Aramaic." The degree of similarity of the Northwestern Semitic dialectical family is shown on this spectrum: Standard Phoenician, Ammonite, Edomite, Moabite, Hebrew, (space), Deir Alla, (space) Aramaic" (Jackson, Kent P. "The Language of the Mesha Inscription," from *Studies in the Mesha Inscription and Moab*, Edited by Andrew Dearman, Scholars Press, Atlanta, Georgia 1989, pp. 100, 129-130).

[50] "Among the numerous obscure notations in the genealogies of I Chron. 1-8…is the mention of a Moabite ruler of Judean descent (1 Chron. 4:22). I Chron. 8: 8-10 speaks of one Shaharaim (presumably a descendant of Benjamin…) who '…had sons in the country of Moab…'" (Miller, J. Maxwell. "Moab and the Moabites," from *Studies in the Mesha Inscription and Moab*, Edited by Andrew Dearman, Scholars Press, Atlanta, Georgia 1989, p. 18).

[51] Byblos was an ancient city of Phoenicia north-northeast of present-day Beirut, Lebanon. *Baalat* of Byblos is mentioned in many inscriptions. See the article Jackson, Kent P, "The Literary Genre of the Mesha Inscription," from *Studies in the Mesha Inscription and Moab*, Edited by Andrew Dearman, Scholars Press, Atlanta, Georgia 1989, pp. 132, 134, 138, 140-142.

[52] "Syrian and Palestinian religion," *Encyclopædia Britannica*, accessed August 12, 2002.

[53] Perhaps Dagon's consort was a single siren, or a school of mermaids!

[54] In the case of *Ashtar*, however, things may have been a bit more complicated. Depending on the culture and time period, *Ashtar* was also known as *Astarte*, *Inanna*, *Ishtar*, *Ashtorah*, *Ashtoreth*, *Asherah* or *Asherim*. *Astarte* was the Queen of the Morning Star, goddess of war, and Queen of the Evening Star,

goddess of passionate love. When astrologers figured out that the morning star and evening star were the same planet Venus, for awhile *Astarte* was viewed as being "androgynous, being male in the morning and female in the evening" (Albright, William F. *Archaeology and the Religion of Israel, Op., Cit.*, p. 83).

55 There is a shortened form of the Name, *Yahveh*, namely, *Ya*. *Ya* is found 49 times in 45 verses, for instance, Psa 068:04 (*BHS* 068:05).

56 The 52 verses where the Name, *Yahveh*, is spoken or heard by humans in Genesis are: Gen 04:01, 26; 05:29; 09:26; 10:09; 12:08; 13:04; 14:22; 15:02, 07, 08; 16:02, 05, 11; 18:14; 19:13, 14; 21:33; 22:14, 16; 24:03, 07, 12, 27, 31, 35, 40, 42, 44, 48, 50, 51, 56; 26:22, 25, 28, 29, 27:07, 20, 27; 28:13, 16, 21; 29:32, 33, 35; 30:24, 27, 30; 31:49; 32:09; 49:18.

57 That the Son spoke for the Trinity at Mount Sinai will be discussed further in the chapter on Proto-Sinaitic Trinitarianism.

58 *Yahveh* is associated with *haElohim* in most of these 80 verses: Exo 04:27; 18:11; 19:03; Deu 04:35, 39; 07:09; 10:17; Jos 14:06; 22:34; Jdg 13:08; 16:28; 1Sa 04:04; 06:20; 2Sa 06:02, 07, 12; 07:28; 15:25; 1Ki 08:60; 13:05, 06, 21, 26; 1Ki 18:21, 24, 37, 39; 20:28; 2Ki 05:20; 07:02; 07:19; 08:08; 19:15; 23:16; 1Ch 13:06, 14; 15:02, 15, 26; 17:26; 21:15, 17; 22:01, 19; 23:28; 25:06; 28:12; 2Ch 01:03; 05:01, 14; 10:15; 11:02; 13:12; 23:03; 24:07, 20; 25:07; 26:05; 28:24; 30:12, 19; 31:14; 32:16; 33:13; 36:16, 18; Ezr 01:03, 05; 02:68; 03:08; 06:22; Neh 05:13; 08:06; 09:07; 10:30; Job 01:06; 02:01; Isa 37:16; 45:18; Jer 35:04.

59 It should be noted that the *NIV* omits the word "companions" in its translation of Jdg 20:11.

60 That the plural of "one" is best translated "a few" is similar to how the plural of *payam* (time) is best translated "twice" in the dual (plural-looking) form.

61 Note that in *NIV* Dan 11:20, the Hebrew for "a few days" is interpreted as "a few years."

62 Another place where Jacob spoke in a collective sense about individuals occurred when he spoke to Ephraim and Manasseh saying, "In you [singular "you" meaning, "in your name"] will Israel bless, saying, 'God make you as Ephraim and as Manasseh'" (Gen 48:20).

63 This section is especially important since it helps to explain a Trinitarian proof. See Psa 110:01, 04-05 in the Trinitarian proofs appendix.

64 The *Easton's Bible Dictionary* entry on "Familiar Spirit" reads: "Sorcerers or necromancers, who professed to call up the dead to answer questions, were said to have a 'familiar spirit' (Deu 18:11, 2Ki 21:06; 2Ch 33:06; Lev 19:31; 20:06; Isa 08:19; 29:04). Such a person was called by the Hebrews 'an *'ob*,' which properly means a leathern bottle; for the sorcerers were regarded as vessels containing the inspiring demon. This Hebrew word was equivalent to the *pytho* of the Greeks, and was used to denote both the person and the spirit that possessed him (Lev 20:27; 1Sa 28:08; compare Act 16:16). The word 'familiar' is from the Latin *familiaris*, meaning, "household servant," and was intended to express the idea that sorcerers had spirits as their servants ready to obey their commands."

[65] *Owb* is also mentioned elsewhere in the OT (Lev 19:31; 20:06, 27; Deu 18:11; 2Ki 21:06; 23:24; 1Ch 10:13; 2Ch 33:06; Isa 08:19; 19:03; 29:04).

[66] Zwemer, Samuel M. *The Influence of Animism on Islam: An Account of Popular Superstitions.* The Macmillan Co. New York, 1920, Chapter 6: "The Familiar Spirit or *Qarina.*" (See online version at answering-islam.org.)

[67] Legon, Jeordan. "Scholars: Oldest evidence of Jesus?" CNN (cnn.com), Monday, October 21, 2002.

[68] Ishaq, *Op. Cit.*, p. 625.

[69] "Syrian and Palestinian religion," *Encyclopædia Britannica,* accessed August 12, 2002.

[70] The 52 verses where the Name, *Yahveh,* is spoken or heard by humans in Genesis are: Gen 04:01, 26; 05:29; 09:26; 10:09; 12:08; 13:04; 14:22; 15:02, 07, 08; 16:02, 05, 11; 18:14; 19:13, 14; 21:33; 22:14, 16; 24:03, 07, 12, 27, 31, 35, 40, 42, 44, 48, 50, 51, 56; 26:22, 25, 28, 29, 27:07, 20, 27; 28:13, 16, 21; 29:32, 33, 35; 30:24, 27, 30; 31:49; 32:09; 49:18.

[71] *HaElohim* is found in Genesis and Exo 01-03 in these verses: Gen 05:22, 24; 06: 02, 04, 09, 11; 17:18; 20:06, 17; 22:03, 09; 27:28; 31:11; 35:07; 41:25, 28, 32; 42:18; 44:16; 45:8; 48:15; Exo 01:17, 21; 02:23; 03:01, 06, 11, 12, 13.

[72] The book of Job mentions the name *Shaddai* in these nineteen chapters (Job 05, 06, 08, 11, 13, 15, 21, 22, 23, 24, 27, 29, 31, 32, 33, 34, 35, 37, 40). *Yahveh* is mentioned in these six chapters (Job 01, 02, 12, 38, 40, 42). The 23 verses where *Shaddai* is mentioned are: Job 05:17; 06:04, 14; 08:03, 05; 11:07; 13:03; 15:25; 21:15, 20; 22:03, 17, 23, 25, 26; 24:01; 27:02, 10, 11, 13; 29:05; 31:02, 35; 32:08; 33:04; 37:23; and 40:2. The 21 verses where *Yahveh* is mentioned 27 times are: Job 01:06, 07, 08, 12, 21; 02:01, 02, 03, 06, 07; 12:09; 38:01; 40:01, 03, 06; 42:01, 07, 09, 10, 11 and 12.

[73] Eisegesis is a form of misinterpretation wherein one reads his or her own ideas into the text. By contrast, exegesis is a deep, thorough, detailed and painstaking analysis of a text.

[74] Geisler, Norman L. and Abdul Saleeb. *Answering Islam: The Crescent in the Light of the Cross.* Baker Books, Grand Rapids, Michigan, USA, 1993, p. 214.

[75] The "Presences of *Yahveh*" phrase is found in these verses: Gen 19:13, 27; Exo 32:11; 34:24; Deu 16:16; 31:11; 1Sa 01:22; 02:17, 18; 26:20; 2Sa 21:01; 1Ki 13:06; 2Ki 13:04; 2Ch 33:12; Job 01:12; 02:07; Jer 26:19; Dan 09:13; Zec 07: 02; 08:21, 22.

[76] See the discussion of how the Spirit is a distinct person of the Trinity at Gen 01: 02 in the Trinitarian Proofs appendix.

[77] *Koehler, Edward W. A.* A Summary of Christian Doctrine (Second Revised Edition). *Concordia Publishing House, St. Louis, Missouri, 1952, pp. 219-220.*

[78] Hawting, G. R. *The Idea of Idolatry and the Emergence of Islam: From Polemic to History.* Cambridge University Press, Cambridge, United Kingdom, 1999, pp. 36-37.

[79] Cohen, Mark R. *Under Crescent & Cross: The Jews in the Middle Ages."* Princeton University Press, New Jersey, USA, p. 156.

[80] Cohen, Mark R. *Ibid.*, p. 250, note 81.

[81] Zwemer, Samuel M. *The Moslem Christ* (First Edition). Oliphant, London, 1912, Chapter 1, as quoted in Zwemer, Samuel M. *Islam and the Cross: Selections from 'The Apostle to Islam.'* Edited by Roger S. Greenway, P&R Publishing Company, Phillipsburg, New Jersey, 2002, p. 16.

[82] Deu 05:26 is discussed in the MT plurals appendix.

[83] Gen 19:13; Exo 23:20-23; 32:34; 33:14-15; Isa 48:16; Mal 03:01; Mat 11:10; Mar 01:02; Luk 07:27; Joh 14:16-18; Act 03:19-20 (Greek 03:20).

[84] Gen 04:14, 16; 2Ki 13:23; 17:18, 20; 23:27; 24:03; Jer 07:15; 23:39; 52:03.

[85] Gen 03:23; Deu 28:64-68; 29:28; 30:04; Jer 08:03; 16:15; 23:08; 23:12; 24:09; 27:10; 27:15; 29:14; 32:37; Jon 02:04; Zec 05:03; 13:02.

[86] Act 02:38; 03:06, 16; 04:10, 18; 05:40; 08:12; 09:27; 10:48; 16:18; 19:13; 26:09; Phi 02:10.

[87] That God targets sinners with his plagues can be seen from how often sinners die from complications of their sin, and see these Bible verses: Exo 20:05; 34:07; Num 11:04, 34; 14:18; 16:38; 25:05-18; 27:03; Deu 02:14-16; 04:03-04; 05:09; Jos 22:17; Psa 021:10; 091:06-08; 106:16-18; 43; 107:39-41; Isa 48:18, 22; Eze 09:04-06; 18:04; Amo 09:10; Zep 03:11-12; Heb 11:28; and Rev 02:22-23.

Those who say that God only allows consequences to punish sin in general (Gen 03), but does not target specific sins he strongly warns against in the Bible, cause unnecessary suffering. They do not deliver the warning (Jer 23:22; Eze 33:01-09) and so dilute the deterrence effect that the consequence of sin has (Deu 13:11; 21:21). Some people try to be nice and "tolerant" at all costs, including the staggering cost of people dying prematurely, thereby ending their time of grace prematurely (Heb 09:27).

Overly meek individuals should worry less about whether they might appear judgmental, and worry more that someone will accuse them of keeping silent just so certain insufferable individuals will leave this earth prematurely without leaving any troublesome offspring. These meek individuals could worry about their being labeled "Sons of Balaam" (Num 31:16; Rev 02:14), "Sons of the Old Prophet of Bethel" (1Ki 13:11-32), and "Sons of Zedekiah the False Prophet" (1Ki 22:05-24; 2Ch 18:04-27; see also Act 08:09-24; 13:06-11; 19:13-16).

[88] The LXX translators understood the "Spirit" in Isa 57:16 to refer to the Spirit of *Yahveh*. Some translations try to make Isa 57:16 read as though the Spirit were the spirit of men. They do not want to think that the Spirit could ever be weary. The weariness, however, is not caused by a weakness in God. Weariness is a response that sinful humans need to see from their God in order to appreciate how their sin is ruining their relationship with God. Scripture shows that the Spirit of *Yahveh* indeed can exhibit weariness (Gen 06:03; 1Ki 19:12; Isa 01:14; 63:10; Neh 09:30; Act 07:51; 1Th 05:19).

[89] Gunduz, Sinasi. *The Knowledge of Life: The Origins of Early History of the Mandaeans and Their Relation to the Sabians of the Quran and to the Harranians.* Oxford University Press, Oxford, United Kingdom, 1994, p. 137.

[90] Trimingham, J. Spencer. *Christianity Among the Arabs in Pre-Islamic Times.* Longman Group Limited, London, 1979, p. 20.

[91] Hos 12:04 is discussed further in the MT plurals appendix.

[92] The chapter on the NT Use of OT *Yahveh* Texts has a discussion on whether *Yeshua* taught mainly in Greek or Aramaic, which is a peripheral but pertinent issue in the study of the *Shema.*

[93] McBirnie, Wm. Stewart. *The Search for the Twelve Apostles,* Tyndale House, Wheaton, Illinois, 1973, p. 188, quoting Newman, Dorman. The Lives and Deaths of the Holy Apostles, 1685 AD.

[94] Trimingham, J. Spencer. *Op. Cit.,* p. 20.

[95] Gunduz, Sinasi. *The Knowledge of Life: The Origins of Early History of the Mandaeans and Their Relation to the Sabians of the Quran and to the Harranians.* Oxford University Press, Oxford, United Kingdom, 1994, p. 137.

[96] The statue was approximately ninety-feet high and nine-feet wide.

[97] Nebuchadnezzar is one of the few gentiles to author parts of the Bible. Other authors who may have been gentile include the author Gen 01—11, Job and Luke.

[98] The vision where Daniel saw the Son of Man (Dan 07:13) did not happen until the first year of Belshazzar's reign (Dan 07:01). Belshazzar reigned at least three years (Dan 08:01).

[99] Blair, Sheila S. *Islamic Inscriptions.* New York University Press, New York, 1998, p. 182.

[100] Album, Stephen. *A Checklist of Islamic Coins,* Second Edition. ISBN: 0-9636024-1-1. Santa Rosa, CA, 1998, p. 5.

[101] "The value of a coin was substantially elevated over its billon value, as was commonly the case in pre-modern monetary systems, especially for silver" (Album, Stephen. A *Checklist of Islamic Coins,* Second Edition. ISBN: 0-9636024-1-1. Santa Rosa, CA, 1998, p. 10).

[102] Ya'akov, Meshorer. *Nabatean Coins.* Qedem: Monographs of the Institute of Archaeology, The Hebrew University, Jerusalem, 1975, p. 30.

[103] Gold-silver alloys are not so-called "white" gold, which is a gold-nickel-copper-zinc alloy ("Gold," *Encyclopædia Britannica,* Accessed October 9, 2001).

[104] Album, *Op. Cit.,* pp. 10-11.

[105] "Coin," Encyclopædia Britannica, Accessed November 1, 2001.

[106] "Bronze," *Encyclopædia Britannica,* Accessed October 10, 2001.

[107] Abraham H. Levey's article "Making of Coin Dies," pp. 137-141 is contained in *Studies in Memory of Paul Balog,* Edited by Dan Barag, The Israel Numismatic Society, Jerusalem, 1991, p. 139. The article was also published in "Israel Numismatic Journal," Israel Numismatic Society, Vol. 10, 1988-1989.

[108] Interestingly, the *Koran* even says Allah sent iron for the purpose of warfare: "We sent aforetime our messengers with clear signs and sent down with them the book and the balance (of right and wrong), that men might stand forth in justice. And we sent down iron in which there is material for mighty war, as well as many benefits for mankind that Allah may test who it is that will help unseen . . ." (*Koran* 057:025).

[109] Nicolle, David. *Armies of the* Caliphates, 862-1098, Men-at-Arms Series, Osprey Publishing, Oxford, 1998, p. 16.

[110] "Interior design," *Encyclopædia Britannica*, Accessed December 25, 2001.

[111] "Aluminum," *Encyclopædia Britannica*, Accessed November 12, 2001.

[112] Exo 09:35; 35:29; Lev 08:36; 10:11; 26:46; Num 04:37, 45, 49; 07:08; 15:23; 16:40; 27:23; 33:01; 36:13; Jos 14:02; 20:02; 21:02, 08; 22:09; Jdg 03:04; 2Sa 12:25; 1Ki 08:53, 56; 12:15; 14:18; 15:29; 16:07, 34; 17:16; 2Ki 09:36; 10:10; 14:25, 27; 17:13, 23; 21:10; 24:02; 1Ch 11:03; 16:07; 24:19; 2Ch 10:15; 29:25; 33:08; 34:14; 35:06, 15; Neh 08:14; 09:14, 30; 10:29; Isa 20:02; 37:24; Jer 27: 03; 29:03; 37:02; 50:01; Eze 38:17; Dan 09:10; Hos 12:10; Hag 01:01, 03; 02: 01, 10; Zec 07:07, 12; and Mal 01:01.

[113] 2Sa 12:25; 1Ki 14:18; 16:07, 12; 22:08; 2Ki 03:11; 14:25; 17:13, 23; 21:10; 2Ch 18:07; 29:25; Ezr 09:11; Neh 09:30; Jer 37:02; 50:01; Dan 09:10; Hos 12:10; Hag 01:01, 03; 02:01; Zec 07:07, 12; Mat 01:22; 02:15, 17, 23; 03:03; 04:14; 08:17; 12:17; 13:35; 21:04, 15; Luk 01:70; Act 03:18, 21; 28:25; Rom 01:02; 16:26; Heb 01:01.

[114] At the end of Rom 10:17, the *NIV* and *RSV* have "Christ," while the *KJV* has "God."

[115] 2Ki 07:01; Isa 38:04-05; Jer 02:04-05; LXX 02:31; 07:02-03; 10:01-02; 11:01-03; 17:20-21; 19:03; 21:11-12; 22:01-03; 22:29-30; 28:12-14; 29:20-21; 42:15; 44:24-26; Eze 06:03; 25:03; 34:07-11; 36:02-05; 37:04-05; Zec 01:01-04.

[116] The word sin and its permutations are mentioned 70 times in Isaiah: Isa 01:04, 18, 28; 03:09; 05:01, 18, 24; 06:07; 07:17; 09:14; 10:17; 12:05, 06; 13:09, 11; 14:07, 21; 16:10; 22:14; 23:16; 24:16; 26:21; 27:02, 09; 30:01, 13, 29; 31:07; 33:14, 24; 35:10; 36:11; 38:17, 18, 20; 40:02, 21; 42:10, 11, 24; 43:04, 24, 25, 27; 44:07, 22, 23; 46:03; 47:09, 12, 15; 48:04; 50:01, 03, 11; 53:12; 54:01; 57: 17; 58:01; 59:02, 07, 12, 20; 64:04, 05, 06, 07, 09; 65:07 and 14.

[117] "Hebrew language," *Encyclopædia Britannica*, Accessed November 6, 2001.

[118] "Provenance" is a term from the art and antique collecting world meaning: "Proof of origin authenticity or of past ownership."

[119] Latin: *"Durior lectio praeferatur ei, qua posita, oratio suaviter leniterque fluit. Durior autem est lectio elliptica, hebraizans, soloeca, a loquendi usu graecis consueto adhorrens aut verborum sono aures offendens"* (Griesbach, *The Greek New Testament*, Second Edition, Halle, 1796 AD, "The Introduction"). English translation: "The harsher reading is preferable to that which instead flows pleasantly and smoothly in style. A harsher reading is one that involves an ellipsis, reflects Hebrew idiom, is ungrammatical, repugnant to customary Greek usage, or offensive to the ears" (Alford, *Greek Testament,* London, 1849, "The Introduction" (Moody reprint).

[120] The Son and the Spirit are the subjects of several messianic prophecies in Zechariah. These are discussed in the NT Use of OT *Yahveh* Texts appendix.

[121] Edersheim, Alfred. *The Life and Times of Jesus the Messiah*, Third Edition. Hendrickson Publishers, Peabody, Massachusetts, USA, 1886, p. 252. (See the public domain versions on the Internet).

[122] Edersheim, Alfred. *Ibid.*, p. 129.

[123] Drucker, Malka. *Eliezer, Ben-Yehuda: The Father of Modern Hebrew*, Lodestar Books, E. P. Dutton, NY, 1987, p. 67.

[124] For example, 4QLXXDeut 11 is a 2nd century BC parchment roll, 4Q122 is from the 2nd century BC, 7Q1LXXEx, Exodus 28 is from 100 BC, 4Q119LXXLev\a is a parchment roll from 100 BC, 4Q120LXXLev\b is a papyrus roll from the first century BC, 4Q121LXXNum is a parchment roll from the turn of the era, 7Q2LXXEpJer is from 100 BC.

[125] Edersheim. *Op. Cit.*, p. 23.

[126] Edersheim. *Op. Cit.*, p. 22. Also, see p. 131.

[127] Josephus, Flavius. *Antiquities of the Jews*, Book 20:11:01.

[128] Van Der Horst, Pieter W. "Jewish Funerary Inscriptions—Most Are in Greek," *Biblical Archaeological Review (BAR)*, Sep-Oct 1992, pp. 48-54.

[129] Van Biema, David. "The Brother of Jesus?" *Time Magazine*, November 4, 2002, Vol. 160, No. 19, pp. 70-73.

[130] A Targum is an explanatory translation or paraphrasing of the Hebrew Scriptures.

[131] Edersheim was writing about the situation in Jerusalem when he wrote that *Yeshua* spoke Aramaic and Hebrew. This should not be taken out of context and applied to Galilee (Edersheim, Alfred. *Op. Cit.*, pp. 129-130).

[132] Edersheim, Alfred. *Op. Cit.*, p. 23.

[133] Edersheim, Alfred. *Op. Cit.*, p. 24.

[134] Someone might think that Mary never talked to *Yeshua* after his resurrection because the resurrection stories are askew or contradictory. So it should be noted that there are ways to reconcile the testimonies. Reconciling the accounts is easier if the resurrection story in Mark is held in abeyance. The most reliable early manuscripts and other ancient witnesses do not have the resurrection to ascension summation of Mar 16:09-20. Mar 16:09-20 reads like a copyists attempt to make the Gospel of Mark terminate like the other gospels. The resurrection to ascension accounts in Matthew, Luke and John are well attested by manuscript evidence. To reconcile the accounts, there is no need to divide the women into two groups led by two different Marys who see *Yeshua* at different times, as some authors have done. The three accounts (Mat 28:01-11; Luk 24: 01-12; Joh 20:01-18) merge like well-cut puzzle pieces.

At the first sign of dusk, an angel appeared causing the soldiers to faint. The angel opened the tomb entrance for *Yeshua* (Mat 28:01-04). Also, an earthquake opened the tombs of many holy persons, and they appeared to people in Jerusalem on Easter Sunday (Mat 27:52-53). One could say that *Yeshua's* raising Lazarus presaged the resurrection on Easter Sunday as well as the general resurrection on the Last Day (Joh 11:17, 12:17).

A little later on Easter Sunday morning, when the sky was gray and there was just enough light to see the footpaths, Mary Magdalene and another Mary went to the tomb. They went and told the disciples that the tomb was empty. That Mary Magdalene was with someone else can be ascertained from the "we" in

Mary's statement, "We do not know where they have put him!" (Joh 20:01-02). Then, Peter and John ran to the tomb, found it empty, and went home assuming the body had merely been moved (Joh 20:03-10). Then, still very early in the morning, Mary Magdalene went back to the tomb with other women who were carrying spices. They came back because they thought they had better inspect the tomb when there was more daylight. They thought perhaps the body had been moved. Some women were in the tomb when two angels suddenly appeared. Both angels spoke to the women (Luk 24:01-08, 23; Joh 20:12-13). One angel, however, must have been the dominant speaker since Matthew only mentions that the angel who moved the stone spoke to the women (Mat 28:02-07).

Since Mary Magdalene had already inspected the tomb, she decided to wait outside while the other women inspected the tomb, since there was not much walking space in the tomb. Mary Magdalene did, however, crouch to see in the tomb, and then she saw the two "men" (angels) who talked to her and the other women (Joh 20:11-12). Mary Magdalene then turned around and talked to *Yeshua* outside the tomb (Joh 20:13-17). Mary did not recognize *Yeshua* likely because of her tears, so Mary thought *Yeshua* was a gardener. Mary told him that "they" (the two men whom she saw in the tomb through her tears) had taken away *Yeshua*'s body away. *Yeshua* said Mary's name, and Mary called *Yeshua* "*Rabboni*." Meanwhile, the women came out of the tomb to tell the disciples what the angels said, but then saw *Yeshua* talking to Mary Magdalene. They clasped his feet and worshipped *Yeshua* (Mat 28:08-11). *Yeshua* told Mary Magdalene, "Do not [continue to] hold on to me, for I have not yet returned to the Father" (Joh 20:17). Later, Mary Magdalene and the other women together told the disciples they saw the Lord (Luk 24:09-10; Joh 20:18). Peter returned singly to the tomb for his second look, but did not see *Yeshua*. Peter went away and saw *Yeshua* somewhere else (Luk 24:12, 34). Before the Emmaus disciples reported *Yeshua*'s appearance to the eleven disciples (Luk 24:33, 35), Peter had already told the ten disciples about *Yeshua*'s appearance to him (Luk 24: 34). Then *Yeshua* appeared to the eleven disciples and the Emmaus disciples together (Luk 24:33, 36).

[135] Ness, Lester. *Written in the Stars: Ancient Zodiac Mosaics.* Shangri-La Publications, Warren Center, Pennsylvania, USA, 1999, p. 83.

[136] Flint, Peter W. *The Dead Sea Psalms Scrolls and the Book of Psalms*, Brill, 1997.

[137] The *BHS* critical apparatus says that a few manuscripts have "they pierced," but with an extra letter *aleph*, and two manuscripts have the same *Qal* form that is found in Psa 057:06 (*BHS* 057:07) and Psa 119:85. The extra letter *aleph* in "they pierced" in some Hebrew manuscripts may just be a variant form.

Dr. James D. Price, Professor of Hebrew and Old Testament, Temple Baptist Seminary, Chattanooga, Tennessee, wrote in his 15 Dec 1995 "Response To Jim Lippard's 'The Fabulous Prophecies of The Messiah'":

Hebrew words that have the same kind of middle Aleph and the same kind of re-

lationship: *bo'r, bor* (pit, cistern) from the verb *bur* (dig); *da'g, dag* (fish) from
the verb *dug* (fish for); *la't, lat* (secrecy) from the verb *lut* (be secret); *m'um,
mum* (blemish); *n'od, nod* (skin); *q'am, qam* (he arose); *ra'sh, rash* (poor)
from the verb *rush* (be poor); *sh'at* (contempt) from the verb *shut* (treat with
contempt); also in Aramaic, *da'er* (dweller) from the verb *dur* (dwell); and
qa'em (riser) from the verb *qum* (he arose). These examples are sufficient to
demonstrate that a middle *aleph* frequently occurs in words and forms derived
from middle W*aw* verbs as in this passage.

[138] Trimingham, J. Spencer. *Op. Cit.*, p. 79 (also see p. 241).

[139] *Kurie Eleison* is Greek for "Lord, have mercy" (Psa 040:05, 11; 122:03; Isa 33:
02; Mat 17:15) and *Hallelujah* is Hebrew for "Praise *Yah*[*veh*]" (Rev 19:01, 03,
04, 06).

[140] Ness, Lester. *Written in the Stars: Ancient Zodiac Mosaics.* Shangri-La
Publications, Warren Center, Pennsylvania, USA, 1999, p. 83.

[141] Edersheim. *Op. Cit.*, pp. 129-130.

[142] Deissmann, *Bible Studies*, Edinburgh, 1903, pp. 313-317, as quoted in Prat, F.
"St. Paul," *The Catholic Encyclopedia*, Volume XI, Robert Appleton Company,
1911.

[143] Trimingham, J. Spencer. *Op. Cit.*, p. 47.

[144] Trimingham, J. Spencer. *Ibid.*, p. 81.

[145] Trimingham, J. Spencer. *Ibid.*, p. 81.

[146] Cavendish, Richard (ed.). *Man, Myth & Magic: An Illustrated Encyclopedia
of the Supernatural* (vol. 11). New York: Marshall Cavendish Corp. (1970); p.
1461.

[147] There has been a lot of history between the first century and modern times, but it
is worth noting that contemporary mainland Greeks still continue to have a hard
time understanding some Cretans and Cyprians. These are those who are not
exposed to travelers from modern mainland Greece, such as those in fishing or
mountain villages.

[148] The name Copt is derived from the Greek word *Aigyptos*. The Coptic language
is the ancient language of the Pharaohs that had been written in hieroglyphs.
Coptic was written in Greek characters by the second century AD.

[149] "The Egyptian" was an infamous outlaw who eluded capture by the Romans.
The Jews who were trying to beat Paul to death no doubt told the Romans that
they were making a citizens' arrest of "The Egyptian." This ploy meant that the
assaulters would not be rounded up and whipped for disturbing the peace and
for the attempted murder of Paul, a Roman citizen.

This ploy probably worked well and likely was used often in the contentious, oc-
cupied areas of Palestine. The ploy meant that the Roman soldiers would tell
the assaulters to scatter so they could not share in the credit and reward for the
capture of "x" outlaw. Also, the ploy meant the assaulted person would be in
a peck of trouble, because he would have to prove he was not "x" outlaw in a
justice system where one was presumed to be guilty until proven innocent.

[150] The Hebrew phrase "*ehyeh asher ehyeh*" is a Qal imperfect, 1st person singular verb (*ehyeh*), plus a relative particle (adjective) (*asher*), plus another *ehyeh*.

[151] The "WHO IS" translation is consistent with the translations of "*ho wn*" in the NT, and is similar to the standard English "I AM" translation of the Hebrew.

[152] Goodenough, Erwin R. *Jewish Symbols in the Greco-Roman Period. Op. Cit.*, p. 238.

[153] Goodenough, Erwin R. *Ibid.*, p. 120.

[154] "'I AM' with you [or him]": Exo 03:12, 14; 04:12, 15; Deu 31:23; Jos 01:05; 03:07; Jdg 06:16; 2Sa 07:14; 1Ch 17:13; 28:06; Psa 050:21; Jer 11:04; 24:07; 30:22; 31:01; 32:38; Eze 11:20; 14:11; 34:24; 36:28; 37:23; Hos 01:09; 14:06; Zec 02:09; 08:08.

[155] "*Anee hu*" is a first person singular pronoun (*anee*), plus a third person masculine singular pronoun (*hu*). The reader will recall from the chapter on Hebrew collective nouns that another pair of paired pronouns, you-he (*atah-hu*) suggested persons of the Trinity.

[156] The Hebrew "*anee hu*" is a first person singular pronoun (*anee*), plus a third person masculine singular pronoun (*hu*). If *anee* is repeated, the first *anee* is a personal pronoun, and the second *anee* is an emphatic pronoun. Since the pronoun is unnecessary, being contained in the verb ending, existence of a pronoun is by itself emphatic. Reduplication is a way for a Hebrew speaker to emphasize that it is "I myself, and no other." So "*anee anee hu*" is "I myself am he."

Most often *anee* is spelled *ani*, but *anee* is a phonetic spelling. This is similar to how I phonetically spell "master" as *adonee* (not *adoni*), which also serves to distance the spelling of "master" from the spelling of "my Lord(s) [*Adonai*]."

[157] 1) Chrysostom, 2) Irenaeus, 3) Novatian, and 4) Origen were familiar with the "I AM" translation of Joh 08:58: 1) Chrysostom's "Homilies on St. John" in Philip Schaff's *The Nicene and Post Nicene Fathers*, 14:199; 2) "Irenaeus Against Heresies" in Philip Schaff's *The Nicene and Post Nicene Fathers* (14 volumes). Grand Rapids: Wm. B. Eerdman's Publishing Company, 1983), 01:478; 3) "A Treatise of Novatian Concerning the Trinity" in Roberts and Donaldson's *The Ante-Nicene Fathers*, 05:624-625; 4) "Origen Against Celsus" in Alexander Roberts and James Donaldson, *The Ante-Nicene Fathers* (10 volumes), Grand Rapids: William B. Eerdman's Publishing Company, 1981, 04:463.

[158] *Yeshua* said elsewhere that he was not about to provide unbelievers a sign that he was the Son of God, except the sign of his resurrection (Mat 12:39-40; 16: 04; Mar 08:12; Luk 11:29-30).

[159] Act 02:38; 03:06, 16; 04:10, 18; 05:40; 08:12; 09:27; 10:48; 16:18; 19:13; 26: 09; Phi 02:10

[160] The Dead Sea Scrolls read "sons of God" at the end of Deu 32:08. The LXX reads "angels of God," and the MT recension reads "sons of Israel."
The reading "sons of God" logically agrees with this parallel passage:
He made from one blood every nation of men to dwell on all the surface of the earth, having determined appointed seasons, and the bounds of their habitation,

that they should seek the Lord, if perhaps they might reach out for him and find him, though he is not far from each one of us (Act 17:26-27).

The reading "sons of God" also agrees with the doctrine of election's connection with regions where believers live:

As the gentiles heard this, they were glad, and glorified the word of God. As many as were appointed to eternal life believed. The Lord's word was spread abroad throughout all the region (Act 13:48-49; see also Gen 09:26-27).

The original may have read "sons of God." Perhaps the LXX translated "sons of God" as "angels of God" because angels are sometimes called "sons of God" (Job 01:06; 02:01; 38:07). Angels also have areas of responsibility (Dan 10:20).

The LXX ("angels of God") or DSS ("sons of God") reading is logically preferable. The MT recension reading is not likely the original reading. Why would the number of the Israelites ("sons of Israel") determine the boundaries of the nations (Deu 02:05; Jos 24:04; 2Ch 20:10; Jer 27:05-06; Dan 04:25)? It is more likely the boundaries are set up either according to the number of elect believers (Act 17:26-27) or elect angels (Dan 10:20).

[161] Gen 17:07-08; Exo 06:07; 15:17; 29:45; Lev 11:45; 22:33; 25:38; 26:12, 45; Num 15:41; Deu 04:20; 09:26, 29; 1Ki 08:51, 53; Jer 02:07.

[162] The 52 times the Name, *Yahveh*, is spoken by the patriarchs or heard by patriarchs are: Gen 04:01, 26; 05:29; 09:26; 10:09; 13:04; 14:22; 15:02, 07, 08; 16:02, 05, 11; 18:14, 19; 19:13, 14; 21:33; 22:14, 16; 24:03, 07, 12, 27, 31, 35, 40, 42, 44, 48, 50, 51, 56; 26:22, 25, 28, 29, 27:07, 20, 27; 28:13, 16, 21; 29:32, 33, 35; 30:24, 27, 30; 31:49; 32:09 and 49:18.

[163] Mat 11:27; 28:18; Luk 10:22; Joh 03:35; 05:22-27; 13:03; 17:02; Act 02:36; 1Co 15:27; Eph 01:21-22; Heb 02:08

[164] Deu 07:04; 08:19; 31:18; Jos 23:16; Jdg 02:14; 10:13-14; 2Ch 07:19-22; 15:05-06; 25:20; 30:07; 1Ki 09:09; 2Ki 22:17; Psa 106:41-43; Jer 01:16; 05:19; 22:08-09; 32:29, 32; 44:08; Amo 09:08-12.

[165] Mat 21:43-44; Joh 07:35; Act 13:45-46; 17:04-05; 18:06; 21:28-29; 22:21-22; 28:08; Rom 09:30-33, 10:19-21, 1Th 02:16, and the like.

[166] Psa 002:08; 022:27-28; 072:11; 086:09; Isa 02:02-03; 49:06; Dan 07:14; Hos 02:23; Zec 02:11; 08:23; 14:09; Mal 01:11; Rev 11:15.

[167] The messianic kingdom was never about expelling the Romans from Palestine, as liberals like to assert. *Yeshua* and his disciples, and even John the Baptist, were on friendly terms with Roman soldiers, and there is no NT mention of the disciples wanting the Romans out of Palestine. The disciples are commonly confused with the Essenes and Zealots who were interested in ousting the Romans. Interestingly, the Essenes colony at Qumran died out when, based on its apocalyptic theology, the Essenes attacked the Roman legions. *Yeshua*'s disciples, however, seemed to view the Romans as the sane alternative to corrupt government. Moreover, if a unitarian theocracy had been in charge of Judea and Galilee, Christianity would not have gotten off the ground. So the Romans were the "powers that be ordained by God" (Romans 13:1). In any case, the Romans were viewed as a people in need of evangelism.

[168] In other words, evangelism will go on until the end (Psa 110:02; compare Psa 106:47; Mat 10:23; 24:14; Luk 18:08; Rom 08:37; 1Co 15:24; 2Co 02:14-16).

[169] *Yahveh* said, "Do not fear...I am with you" (Gen 26:24; Exo 20:20; Isa 41:10; 43:05; Jer 01:08; 42:11; 46:28). This is similar to *Yeshua*'s words in Mat 28:20, Rev 01:17-18, and elsewhere.

[170] Mat 04:03, 06; 08:29; 14:33; 26:63; 27:40, 43, 54; Mar 01:01; 03:11; 15:39; Luk 01:35; 04:03, 09, 41; 22:70; Joh 01:34, 49; 05:25; 11:27; 19:7; 20:31.

[171] The Spirit had not yet been sent in greater measure (Joh 07:39; 16:13). So most people needed more convincing to be persuaded that *Yeshua* was the Son of God than did Nathaniel.

[172] *Yeshua* merely meant the "you are Peter" phrase to mimic, and thus draw attention to, Peter's previous answer, "You are the Christ, the Son of the living God." *Yeshua* was not trying to draw attention to Peter as some thought (1Jo 04:03).

[173] Herod started rebuilding the temple circa 20 BC, so it had already been under construction 46 years when *Yeshua* visited (Joh 02:20). The temple was finally completed in 62 or 64 AD, just in time for the Romans to destroy the temple in 70 AD.

Interestingly, stone throwing is still a custom at the temple site in modern times. The *Jerusalem Post* Internet Staff reported, "...in Jerusalem riot police briefly charged into the Al Aksa mosque compound and fired stun grenades after a few Muslim worshippers threw rocks that fell on Jews praying at the Western Wall below" ("IDF troops kill Palestinian teenager, riot police charge into Islamic shrine," jpost.com, October 4, 2002; also "Israeli Police Drive Protesters from Muslim Shrine," reuters.com, October 04, 2002).

[174] Joh 09:24; 12:18-19; see also Joh 06:26, 30-31; 09:24; 10:25-26; 11:46-52; 12: 37; 1Co 01:22.

[175] That *Yeshua* offered no signs or philosophical or scriptural arguments, but pointed to his public ministry and teaching (Joh 18:20-21), means that Christians are under no obligation to argue or awe people into believing (2Co 01:12). Christians may feel free to argue if they want, of course, but Christians are under no obligation to do so. Christians need only point toward *Yeshua*'s ministry and resurrection (Joh 18:20-21), and to Moses and the prophets (Luk 16:31).

Signs may seem instrumental in the conversion process, but really are supposed to be conversation starters and thought provokers (1Co 14:21). Signs validate who exactly has the right to speak for God, as in the case of Moses and Elijah. Sometimes signs and tongues have the opposite effect and turn people off to the gospel (1Co 14:23). No sign or argument can by itself remove the stumbling block of the crucifixion (1Co 01:23) that separates the elect from those who refuse to believe (1Sa 10:09; Joh 03:19-21; Act 13:46, 48).

[176] Glassé, Cyril. *The Concise Encyclopedia of Islam.* HarperSanFrancisco, 1991, p. 216, *Ka'bah.*

[177] "Jewish Funerary Inscriptions—Most Are in Greek," *Biblical Archaeological Review (BAR)*, Sep-Oct 1992, p. 48.

[178] This is similar to how Matthew quoted the first part of Mic 05:02 (Mat 02:06), but left the reader of Micah to fill in the rest of the verse: "...whose origins are from of old, from ancient times."

[179] Joseph Caiaphas was high priest from 18 to 36 AD. Archaeologists discovered his tomb which bears the Hebrew inscription "*Jehosef bar* [son of] *Caifa* [Caiaphas]." The elaborately carved stone ossuary still bore Joseph's bones when it was found in 1990 in south Jerusalem.

[180] Two persons were at the head of the "*Bet Din*" [Lesser Sanhedrin]: one, the actual president [Caiaphas] with the title *Nasi* [prince, high-priest]; the other, the second president or vice-president [Annas], who bore the title "*Ab Bet Din*" ("Father of the Court") ("Sanhedrin," *The Jewish Encyclopedia*, p. 44).

[181] "Yose Ben Joezer...and Yose Ben Johanan: All the Sages listed in this chapter from this point through Hillel and Shammai are known as the Pairs (*Duran*), and they were the heads of the Sanhedrin...one serving as *Nasi* and the other as *Ab Bet Din*. (Vitry)" (Mishnah, Avot. *The Living Talmud: The Wisdom of the Fathers and Its Classical Commentaries*; translation Judah Goldin, p. 9).

[182] Talmud—Mas. Sotah 43a; Talmud—Mas. Nazir 47b; Midrash Rabbah—The Song of Songs II:33. Note: Apparently, various biblical verses were used to rationalize having a deputy high priest (Lev 20:02; Num 31:06; Deu 20:01-03; 1Sa 14:03, 19; Isa 59:17).

[183] Singer, Paul. "Interesting Times: What good are Jews?," *The Jerusalem Post* (jpost.com), January 2, 2003.

[184] R.I.P. is the abbreviation for the Latin phrase: *Requiescat In Pacem*, which means, "Rest in Peace," or as humor would have it: "Recycled Into [the] Planet."

[185] Since Moses did not experience peace in his lifetime, the prophet "like him" (Deu 18:15) would not experience worldwide peace in his lifetime (Mat 10:34). Only after the Messiah returns the second time will there will be peace (Heb 10: 13).

[186] Goldman, Bernard. *The Sacred Portal: A Primary Symbol in Ancient Judaic Art*. Wayne State University, 1966, p. 74.

[187] Green, Tamara M. *The City of the Moon God: Religious Traditions of Harran*. E. J. Brill, New York, 1992, p. 65.

[188] Gunduz, Sinasi. *The Knowledge of Life: The Origins and Early History of the Mandaeans and Their Relation to the Sabians of the Qur'an and to the Harranians*. Oxford University Press, 1994, p. 201.

[189] Gunduz, Sinasi. *The Knowledge of Life, Ibid.*, p. 193.

[190] Edersheim, Alfred. *Op. Cit.*, Chapter XI.

[191] MacMullen, Ramsay. *Christianity & Paganism in the Fourth to Eight Centuries*. Yale University Press, New Haven, Massachusetts, 1997, p. 147.

Index

Jdg 13: 37, 39, 54, 68, 83, 133-134, 228, 265-266, 270, 287-288, 294, 297, 305, 343, 345, 357
1Sa 10: 27, 40, 59, 82, 112, 143, 272, 275, 288, 343, 355, 357
2Sa 07: 29-31, 75, 100-101, 117, 119, 146, 249, 259, 266, 290-291, 325-326, 338, 343, 353, 357
Psa 002: 77, 156, 180, 222, 228, 232, 266-267, 289-290, 292, 305, 325-326, 332, 354, 357
Psa 045: 63-64, 111, 116, 123, 156, 266-267, 280, 285, 289-290, 292, 305, 309, 326, 357
Psa 068: 75, 222, 254, 266, 333, 345, 357
Psa 082: 10, 17, 57, 63-64, 116, 122, 156, 219, 236, 238, 266, 291-292, 313, 318, 325, 357
Psa 091: 75, 266, 292, 326, 357
Psa 110: 10, 82, 124, 128, 216, 221, 245, 266, 290-291, 293-295, 304, 325, 338-339, 345, 355, 357
Pro 30: 123, 133, 229, 253-254, 266-267, 297, 327, 357
Isa 07: 13, 34, 41, 68, 80, 101, 108, 117, 125, 146, 148, 152-154, 156, 165, 219, 223, 226-227, 250, 256, 266, 296-297, 302, 327-328, 349, 357
Isa 09: 41, 88-90, 103, 151, 171, 186, 188, 210, 226, 244, 253, 266, 288, 293, 297-300, 334-335, 354, 357
Isa 40: 102-104, 144, 188, 261, 266, 297-301, 312-313, 331, 335, 339, 358
Isa 48: 84, 103, 203-204, 224, 266, 299, 301-302, 304, 307, 339, 347, 358
Isa 49: 188, 207, 243, 246, 266, 301, 358
Jer 23: 29, 40, 74, 100, 141, 145, 153, 232, 242, 258, 262, 266, 304, 336, 347, 358
Dan 07: 11-13, 68, 101, 106, 116, 125, 140, 157, 163, 165-166, 213, 215-216, 220-222, 224-226, 228, 230-235, 237, 240-242, 245, 254, 260-262, 267, 285, 292, 305, 321, 328, 333, 335, 337, 348, 354, 358
Hos 01: 30, 51, 75, 89, 92, 143, 236, 250, 255, 265, 267, 275, 306, 308, 328, 353, 358
Hos 12: 10, 30, 51, 69-70, 117, 142, 148, 152, 250-251, 253-256, 265, 267, 275, 298, 306, 327, 330, 348-349, 358
Amo 04: 148, 224, 257, 267, 300, 306-307, 327, 347, 358
Mic 05: 68, 75, 154, 210, 267, 290, 307, 313, 337, 356, 358
Zec 02: 54, 63, 67, 88, 91, 100, 161, 242, 267, 270-271, 307, 311, 346-347, 349, 353-354, 358
Zec 11: 49, 52, 153-154, 245, 267, 308-309, 329, 354, 358
Zec 12: 10, 143, 153, 180, 267, 307-309, 325, 328, 337, 358
Zec 13: 148, 153, 232, 267, 294, 309, 328-329, 346, 358
Mal 03: 92, 103-104, 216, 267, 310, 329, 347, 358
Joh 08: 10, 64, 68, 94, 99, 102, 116, 122-123, 156, 176, 183, 197, 199, 202-203, 206-211, 226-228, 231, 234, 237-239, 247, 278, 284, 292, 299, 304, 307, 313-314, 324, 330, 336, 339, 353, 358

Printed in the United States
82448LV00003B/48